Faith

Faith

LESLEY PEARSE

MICHAEL JOSEPH
an imprint of
PENGUIN BOOKS

MICHAEL JOSEPH

Published by the Penguin Group

Penguin Books Ltd, 80 Strand, London WC2R ORL, England

Penguin Group (USA) Inc., 375 Hudson Street, New York, New York 10014, USA

Penguin Group (Canada), 90 Eglinton Avenue East, Suite 700, Toronto, Ontario, Canada M4P 2Y3
(a division of Pearson Penguin Canada Inc.)

Penguin Ireland, 25 St Stephen's Green, Dublin 2, Ireland
(a division of Penguin Books Ltd)

Penguin Group (Australia), 250 Camberwell Road, Camberwell, Victoria 3124, Australia
(a division of Pearson Australia Group Pty Ltd)

Penguin Books India Pvt Ltd, 11 Community Centre, Panchsheel Park, New Delhi – 110 017, India

Penguin Group (NZ), 67 Apollo Drive, Rosedale, North Shore 0632, New Zealand
(a division of Pearson New Zealand Ltd)

Penguin Books (South Africa) (Pty) Ltd, 24 Sturdee Avenue, Rosebank, Johannesburg 2196, South Africa

Penguin Books Ltd, Registered Offices: 80 Strand, London WC2R ORL, England

www.penguin.com

Published 2007

1

Set in 13.5/16 pt Monotype Garamond
Typeset by Rowland Phototypesetting Ltd, Bury St Edmunds, Suffolk
Printed in Great Britain by Clays Ltd, St Ives plc

A CIP catalogue record for this book is available from the British Library

ISBN: 978-0-718-15281-9

To David Stoyle for his outstanding generosity in bidding in an auction of promises to be a character in *Faith*. I hope, David, that you enjoy being immortalized and that your new role as lawyer/super sleuth amuses you, Julia and your children. If I didn't make you as ravishingly handsome or brilliant as you'd have liked, I apologize, but the fictional David couldn't upstage super-hero Stuart. He had to be a thoroughly nice guy and a good sport, as you really are.

Acknowledgements

A huge thank you to Alan Hamilton at Cornton Vale prison in Stirling for giving me his time and expert knowledge about how it is for women in prison.

His work at the time of my visit was mainly focused on young offenders in countering their behaviour by challenging attitudes and conduct, giving them the opportunity to learn new skills and enhance their learning and awareness of current affairs. Part of Alan's role was in Restorative Practices, new work which in 2006 earned Cornton Vale prison the Butler Award. This, as I understand it, is to help offenders understand the short-term and long-term effects that their offences and behaviour have had on the people harmed by them. They do not just look at the victim alone, but the families of victims and offenders, witnesses, friends and peers. While this scheme is voluntary for the offenders, most do take part, and it is a worthwhile way of making amends or restoring the harm done, and an addition to their punishment.

Many of my previously held ideas about women's prisons were challenged by my visit to Cornton Vale. Aside from Alan Hamilton, whose deep commitment to the women in his care was very obvious. I was also impressed by the compassion and enthusiasm of all the staff I met there. I was left with the feeling that a good proportion of the young offenders were being given the help they need to ensure they do not re-offend.

I'd also like to thank all those good people, too numerous to name individually, in Anstruther, Cellardyke, Crail and

Edinburgh, who helped and inspired me during my stay in Scotland while I was researching the background for *Faith*.

And finally a huge and very special thank you to Gordon Erasmuson, without whom I would never have even got the idea for the book, let alone written it. Your belief in me, encouragement, those wonderful little Scottishisms you fed me, and all the laughs along the way, helped more than you'll ever know. Bless you, General Gordon.

1995

'Dried-up auld fuckwit!' Donna Ferguson said loudly and scathingly as she dolloped broccoli on to Laura Brannigan's plate.

Laura had always found that particular Scottish insult amusing yet she stifled her laughter as she knew Donna, the eighteen-year-old behind the serving counter, would see that as further evidence of her dementia. But then, as Donna weighed close on twenty stone, she probably thought any-one asking for more broccoli and less mashed potato was seriously barmy.

'I may be old and dried-up but broccoli keeps my wits sharp and my body slim,' Laura retorted. 'Maybe you should try it.'

As she turned away with her tray to find a seat in the dining room, she could sense the charge in the air which always came when her fellow prisoners thought a fight might kick off. But they would be disappointed today, as they had been on so many occasions when someone insulted Laura. It was tough enough to be fifty and serving a life sentence for a crime she hadn't committed, without looking for trouble. Besides, Laura felt sorry for Donna; she was forced to act tough to make up for looking like a beached whale.

Glancing around the dining hall at the thirty or so women, Laura thought how wrong film-makers got it when they portrayed women prisoners. There were no sexy-looking beauties here, and precious little intelligence. They came in all shapes and sizes, ranging from seventeen to over sixty, but they were unified by the same dull skin, lacklustre hair, and a look of defeat. She saw the same look staring back at her each time she was foolish enough to glance in a mirror.

'Come and sit by me, Law,' Maureen Crosby called out. 'Us auld fuckwits should stick together!'

Laura did smile then for it was uncharacteristic of Maureen to display a sense of humour. She was a rather dour Glaswegian of fifty-two who liked her own company and rarely involved herself in anything which was going on around her.

'Thanks, Maureen,' Laura said, taking her up on her offer. 'Did I commit a cardinal sin by wanting more broccoli?'

Two years earlier, when Laura first arrived on remand in Cornton Vale, Scotland's only women's prison, Maureen was one of the few inmates who made no sarcastic remarks about her age, her English accent or her insistence that the police had made a terrible mistake in charging her with murder. This could have been purely because Maureen was a similar age to her, but more likely because she'd been through too much misery in her own life to wish to inflict any on anyone else. There were scars on her cheeks made by a razor and her wrist stuck out awkwardly, the result of a break which had never healed properly. Most of her teeth were broken and she had a recurring back problem.

'You're looking very nice today. Expecting a visitor?' Laura said as she began to eat. Maureen was a big woman and usually slopped around in a black tracksuit which did nothing for her rotund shape or her sallow complexion. But today she was wearing a pair of smart grey trousers and a pale pink shirt. Her grey hair had been washed and blow-dried, and she'd even made up her face.

'Aye, my Jenny's coming,' Maureen replied, her voice lifting from its usual dejected tone.

'That's great,' Laura exclaimed. Maureen had confided in

her a few weeks earlier that when she was convicted of grievous bodily harm for driving a car at her husband, her eldest daughter had vowed she'd never see her again. 'What changed her mind?'

Maureen shrugged to imply she didn't know exactly. 'I done what you said and wrote and told her how I felt about her. Maybe it was that.'

Laura nodded. Maureen was on the point of leaving her abusive husband when she discovered he'd stolen the stash of money she'd been saving to make good her escape. That same evening he beat her up again, and early the following morning as she was driving home from her office-cleaning job, she spotted him coming out of the house of a woman who she had long suspected he was having an affair with. In a fit of rage she drove the car straight at him, breaking both his legs and causing massive internal injuries, from which he would probably never completely recover.

Jenny had taken her father's part, refusing to acknowledge the humiliation and brutality he'd put Maureen through over the years. She had even refused to allow her younger siblings to see their mother.

'I expect your husband has shown his true colours to her too,' Laura said thoughtfully. 'And your younger children will probably have told Jenny things they saw and heard him doing to you in the past. She'll have weighed it all up and realized you were at your wits' end. Girls need their mothers and I'm sure she's missed you terribly.'

'You're a good woman,' Maureen said unexpectedly. 'I didnae believe you was innocent at first, but I do now. You haven't got it in youse to kill anyone, specially an auld pal like Jackie.'

Laura smiled ruefully. Two years ago such a remark would have filled her with hope; she would have believed the lawyers, police and jury would all see her that way too. But the jury had found her guilty and her lawyer had said they had no grounds for an appeal.

She knew now that everyone involved in the case was totally convinced of her guilt, and that was the hardest thing of all to bear. 'It means a lot that you believe in me,' she sighed. 'But don't let's talk about that today. You must be so excited about your visit.'

'That I am.' Maureen beamed. 'Just to look at her pretty wee face again will be enough. She's thirty now, with a second wean on the way, and I didnae even know I had a grandson.'

'Try not to mention her father,' Laura suggested gently. 'Ask her about your grandson, her pregnancy, home and stuff like that. She'll be feeling awkward because of how she was with you, but she must want to build bridges or she wouldn't be coming.'

Maureen looked at Laura speculatively. 'Why don't you get visitors, Law?' she asked. 'A good woman like you must have had loads of pals.'

'I wasn't a good woman,' Laura said ruefully. 'I treated people badly and used them. Jackie was the only person whose opinion of me ever counted for anything and I loved her. But now I've been convicted of her murder, the few people I liked to think of as friends vanished, and there's no one left that gives a jot about me.'

When Laura got back to her cell after dinner, she lay down on her bed and closed her eyes. Her fellow prisoners had decorated their cells with pictures and photographs, but apart from a picture of a white rose which she'd cut from a glossy magazine, the walls of her cell were as bare as they were when she was first given it a year ago after she received her sentence.

Back then she'd felt too outraged to consider the idea of

making it more homely, for that would have seemed like acceptance of what had happened to her. In her darkest moments she would stare at the grille over the window and contemplate hanging herself from it. Yet suicide seemed more like an apology than a declaration of her innocence.

Leaving the cell bleak and depersonalized was a form of protest. She didn't mind its small size – she had lived in equally small rooms in the past. She could escape to a certain extent by listening to her radio and by looking at the view of hills from her window. But the constant noise in this place often made her feel she was going mad.

Banging, singing, crying, shouting, talking and raucous laughter were incessant in Bravo Block. She could shut the other women out with her door, she could even avoid the smoke and stink of their cigarettes, but the noise was there all the time, and sometimes she wanted to scream out for silence.

She could remember how much she had loved the Scottish accent when she first came to live in Scotland, but now it grated; even the gentler burr of those from places like Inverness irritated her. She thought she'd give anything to hear a London accent, a Brummie or a Geordie, but even her own voice, after twenty-three years in Scotland, had little trace of its London origins left.

She got up wearily from her bed to find her earplugs. They didn't shut out the noise, but at least they muted it. She found them on the wash basin, and as she put them in, caught a glimpse of herself in the mirror.

The sight only depressed her further, for her face reflected her weary and hopeless state of mind, and her hair had the colour and texture of dirty straw. As a child it had been mousey-brown, but for all of her adult life she had coloured it – black, red, dark brown, blonde and even pink once – so it was hard to recall its exact original colour. Yet she could remember precisely how it looked the day she'd found Jackie dead, for she'd been to the hairdresser's the previous day and had it cut short and bouncy, with blonde highlights.

It was long and straggly now, so she kept it tied back with a rubber band, but when she did brush it out, those highlights amounted to nothing more than orange tips at the ends, the rest an ugly pepper-and-salt grey.

Glamorous, chic, elegant, perfectly groomed, those were the phrases people used to describe her two years ago when she had her shop. Five feet five, a perfect size ten, she still got wolf whistles when she passed a building site, and there was hardly a night out when some man didn't try to chat her up, for she looked closer to thirty-five than in her late forties.

No man would look at her twice now. She might still be slender, but her skin was as grey as her hair, and her brown eyes, so often described as lustrous, were dull now. Even if she were to be dressed up in a smart suit, with high heels, hair cut and recoloured, and her face made up, she knew she could never look the way she once did, for it was as if a light had been switched off within her.

'Brannigan!'

Laura turned at her name being called, to see Prison Officer Beadington at the door. She was universally known as Beady, a nickname that suited her perfectly as she was short and stout with beady dark eyes. Laura pulled out her earplugs.

'A letter was handed in for you,' Beady said, holding out the sheet of paper. 'The man came here just now, wanting to visit you. The officers at the gate had to turn him away, but they told him he could write and ask you for a visiting slip.'

Laura's heart lurched as she saw the familiar handwriting.

She might not have seen it for years, but it was unmistakable.

'It's not another of those journalists, is it?' Beady asked. 'You know how the governor feels about them!'

Laura was too stunned by the letter in her hand to answer immediately. She looked blankly at Beady for a few moments as if she'd spoken in a foreign language.

'No. No, it's not,' she said when she realized she had to reply.

She had sent visiting slips to several journalists just after she was convicted, in the hope they would take up her cause. Almost all of them came, but they cared nothing for her plight; not one believed that she was innocent. All they really wanted was more dirt, about her, and the series of suicides that had taken place in this prison in recent months. They used her as a reason to write sensational articles about the prison and the governor had been very angry that she had unwittingly given them inside information.

'It's from a man I knew a long time ago,' Laura said weakly. 'It's a bit of a shock!'

''They said he was a hunk,' Beady said with a wide smile.

Laura half smiled. Beady was a decent woman; she had a hard outer shell, and she could come down on anyone like a ton of bricks if they upset her, but that was to protect her soft centre. Laura had seen her comforting girls when their man had dumped them, or their children were being taken into care. Her heart was in the right place.

'He was always a hunk,' Laura said sadly. 'And a good man too, but us women are often guilty of not recognizing a man's true worth until it's too late.'

'He came looking for you,' Beady said pointedly. 'So you get a visiting slip off to him pronto.'

Laura shut her cell door and sat down on her bunk to read the letter. 'Dear Laura,' she read.

I have only just returned to the UK from South America, and was
horrified to hear about Jackie's death. We may not have seen one
another for a very long while, but I cannot believe you would have
killed her, for I know what you meant to one another. They
wouldn't let me in to see you, they said I needed a slip. Please
send me one to my hotel, for I cannot leave Scotland again until
I've talked to you.

Stuart

A tear ran down Laura's cheek unchecked as she stared at his handwriting. Twenty years ago he used to write her notes scribbled in pencil, often embellished with funny little faces. She'd received a beautiful sympathy card too when Barney died, his deep sorrow etched into each word. This one was more formal, written on embossed headed paper from the Balmoral Hotel in Edinburgh, evidence of how far removed he was from her now.

She could picture him that summer's day in 1972 when she first met him in Castle Douglas. Tall, bare-chested, his cut-down Levi shorts threatening to slide off his slim hips. Chestnut-brown hair in need of a wash tangling on his shoulders, bare feet as brown as new conkers, and the widest, warmest smile she'd ever seen.

He was twenty-one, still an innocent boy full of exuberance and joy. She was twenty-seven, a calculating, wordly woman who should have known better than to run off to a hippy enclave with her two-year-old son. She was clutching at straws of course – anything was better than staying in London and letting people see she'd messed up.

She seduced Stuart that same night on a mattress on the floor of a place that was little more than a shed, and he woke the following morning to tell her he loved her.

Running a finger over the embossed letter heading, Laura

could imagine the sophistication of the world he lived in now: king-size beds, sumptuous bathrooms, fast cars and designer clothes. She had had many reports from Jackie over the years about how successful he was, that he was head-hunted by national companies to act as their project manager all over the world. Yet according to Jackie, he'd made that climb from the Edinburgh tenement he'd been brought up in, not by sharp practice and conniving, but with his skill, hard work and total honesty, just the way he'd always claimed he would.

How different her life might have been if she'd only believed in him!

Holding the letter to her heart, she flopped down on to her bed, sobbing.

Nineteen seventy-two was her 'summer of love', when for just a few short weeks everything was golden. No other man, before or since, had ever touched her in quite the same way, and what they had was precious and beautiful. But she had destroyed it, just as she had so often before, and after, destroyed so much that was good in her life.

2

Laura lay on her bed holding Stuart's letter, the delight she'd felt initially on receiving it pushed aside by shame. It wasn't so much that he had discovered she was in prison, but that by now he would have found out about her real family.

He had worked for Jackie for a few years, and become involved with all her family, and although that was a long time ago, they'd retained some contact with one another. He would've been upset enough to hear Jackie had died of natural causes, but once he was informed that she was murdered by Laura, he would have scoured the newspaper archives to find out more.

Every sordid detail about her was there, for the press had been like hyenas after a kill, tearing chunks off her credibility as they unearthed more and more unsavoury facts about her and her background.

She wasn't concerned about the stuff that she'd been involved in since they split up; he had probably heard about most of that on the grapevine long ago anyway. But what must he have felt when he discovered that she had not been orphaned as she told him? That she had in fact got two living parents and five brothers and sisters she'd airbrushed out of her life?

She could imagine him thinking back to things she'd told him about her fictional childhood and adolescence and asking himself why she'd never told *him* the truth, even if she chose to lie to the rest of the world.

Stuart's family background was working-class too, and he'd have been quick to admit to any skeletons in the closet.

Yet he'd been proud of his origins, and would never have resorted to glitzing it up to climb the social ladder.

There were many times in the two years they were together that she almost told him the truth. She'd known he would have understood then why she lied; indeed, he would probably have loved her even more because he'd been a compassionate man who was always on the side of the underdog. The reason she resisted the temptation was because he would have made her come clean to Jackie, and nagged her into contacting her mother. She was too much of a coward to face that.

Tears welled up in her eyes and she brushed them away impatiently. If she'd known at sixteen what future heartache she was storing up, she wouldn't have reinvented herself. But back then it was just self-preservation, not intentional deceit.

She was twelve when it really dawned on her that everything was stacked against her. It was October 1957, one of those glorious autumn days when you notice the leaves on the trees have changed to gold, red, russet and yellow, yet the sun is warm enough to fool you into thinking it is still summer.

There were no trees in Thornfield Road, Shepherds Bush, where she lived. Even the narrow strips of soil in front of the decaying three- and four-storey houses that the residents liked to call their 'front garden' held nothing but overloaded dustbins, bicycles and junk. But that day Laura had taken herself off to Ravenscroft Park nearby and had marvelled at the festival of colour there, and wished she lived in one of the nice houses surrounding the park.

She went there most Saturday afternoons, but normally she took her baby brother Freddy in his pram, along with her sisters, Meggie and Ivy, to give her mother a break. But that morning Laura had taken one look at the dark, damp and chaotic basement flat they lived in, and she'd had an overwhelming need to get out and be alone in peaceful surroundings.

She was still in the park, sitting on a bench daydreaming about having a bedroom of her own, a bathroom, and never again having to wear second-hand clothes or having other girls jeering at her in school because her clothes smelled of fried food and mildew, when she suddenly became aware it was late afternoon. The sun had turned bright orange and was sinking down behind the trees, making long shadows, and all at once she was chilly in her cotton dress.

She walked home reluctantly, aware her mother would be furious she'd stayed out all day, and as she turned the corner into Thornfield Road, she saw Janice Potts and Margaret Jones from school, sitting on the wall outside her house.

Her stomach turned over in fright because they'd been bullying her since the start of the new term in September. She knew they had come to pick a fight with her, because, like most of the girls at the grammar school in Holland Park, they lived well away from dingy Shepherds Bush, and had no reason to pass through her street.

Right since her first day at grammar school Laura had felt like an impostor because almost everyone else was posh and glossy. The other girls had tennis and ballet lessons, their fathers had cars and wore suits, and she was absolutely certain no one else had a second-hand uniform or took a bath in the public ones. It didn't help that she was so skinny and plain – every time she looked in a mirror she winced at her plaited hair which never looked sleek because it was so dull and wispy.

All through her first year there she was aware the other girls whispered about her behind her back, they hid her books and never let her join in any of their games in the playground. But since she'd moved up to the second year, it had become far worse.

On the first day back at school in September, Brenda Marsh had said she didn't want to sit next to a 'guttersnipe'. Someone else asked if she got her blazer from the rag-and-bone man. From then on it seemed as if the whole class was out to torment her. They left notes in her desk about her fusty smell. In the PE changing room girls would pick up her blouse or jumper between thumb and forefinger and wince, as though it had some disease on it. She even saw one girl polishing a chair that Laura had been sitting on with a handkerchief. Whispers, nudges and rude gestures went on all the time in class. In the playground and as she left school, girls would shout out cruel remarks and try to trip her up. Now the two ringleaders had discovered where she lived, and Laura was afraid.

'Hey, Stinky Wilmslow! Had a wash this year yet?' Janice yelled out.

It was tempting to run into a neighbour's house to ask for help, but she knew that if she did Janice and Margaret would be on to her again on Monday at school. 'Go and boil your head,' she called back defiantly and doggedly walked on towards them.

'You still got nits?' Margaret jeered as she got close to them.

That jibe stung for she'd never had nits. She washed every day too, although that didn't stop the smells from her home attaching themselves to her clothes. But there was no point in protesting, it would just give them an excuse to hurl more insults at her.

'Probably – and you'll catch them if you touch me,' Laura responded. She had a sinking feeling that the sadistic duo were going to start hitting her, and that would mean she'd have to show them that common girls like her also learned to defend themselves from the cradle.

As she reached them, Janice stuck out her foot to trip her up. Laura kept her nose in the air and pretended she hadn't seen, but quick as a flash, kicked out at Janice's other leg and made her topple over on to the pavement.

As Janice cried out in shocked surprise, Margaret jumped forward, her fingers hooked, ready to claw at Laura's face. Laura kneed her in the stomach and Margaret reeled back, clutching herself.

By anyone's reckoning it was a formidable display of superior wits, speed and guile, and both girls looked suitably stunned and afraid. Laura put her hands on her hips and looked scathingly at them. 'Have you had enough?' she asked. 'Or do you both want a good kicking so you can run crying home to your mummies?'

They turned tail and fled, their short skirts fluttering up to show their white legs and navy-blue knickers. They weren't even brave enough to call her more names from a distance.

Laura watched them go. She felt the incident ought to have made her feel powerful and triumphant, but it had quite the reverse effect. What she wanted was for them to like her, so they could spend Saturday afternoons in Woolworth's listening to the week's Top Twenty and looking at the makeup. But that was never going to happen now.

She slumped down on the wall of number 12 where she lived, suddenly, blindingly aware that it would take a great deal more than passing her eleven-plus and putting on a striped blazer to overcome the stigma of being a Wilmslow.

She'd been so proud when she got her place at the grammar school, and she thought her older brothers were just jealous when they said she wouldn't fit in there. Even when it was clear her brothers were right, ever the optimist, she had told herself she'd win everyone around in time.

But she knew now she could never do that. She'd never get invited to one of the other girls' parties, or home to tea;

no one would ever want her around them. She didn't mind that her parents had no money for the school trip to France, or for ballet lessons, but she didn't think she could stand another four or more years at school without a single friend.

Until now she had comforted herself when things looked blackest by the fact the teachers said she was clever. She had believed that one day she'd get to be something brilliant like a doctor, a scientist or a lawyer, and then all those who had looked down on her would be ashamed.

But now she could see that Janice and Margaret's prejudice against her was representative of how the whole world would see her. With a father in and out of prison, two older brothers who showed every sign of going the same way, and home a squalid hovel, she really didn't have any chance of getting on in life.

Turning her head slightly, Laura looked down into the basement flat and winced when she saw what Janice and Margaret would have seen. Filthy windows, net curtains yellow with age and full of holes, and the dustbins for the entire four-storey house which were kept right outside their front door wafting out a sickly, rotten smell. If they'd seen the squalor inside, they'd have been even more shocked. The shame of it flooded through her, making her feel sick.

Dragging her feet, she went down the concrete steps to face her mother.

'Where've you been all day?' Mrs Wilmslow yelled as soon as Laura walked in. 'I've been stuck in here with these kids fighting and the baby bawling, I ain't even had a minute to nip out to buy some fags.'

Laura stood in the doorway of the front room which also doubled as her parents' bedroom, and her spirits plummeted to rock bottom. No sunshine ever made its way in here, the couch had the stuffing coming out of the arms, and the wallpaper had been up so long that any pattern it had originally had been obliterated. The air was thick with cigarette smoke and smelled as though six-month-old Freddy had a dirty nappy. He was lying on the floor, grizzling. Ivy, the three-year-old, had jam all over her face and a bare bottom. Meggie, who was five, was playing with her doll. The room was a mess, toys, used cups and plates everywhere; even the double bed hadn't been made.

June, Laura's mother, was only thirty-two, a small, slender woman with bottle-blonde hair, a muddy complexion and a harassed expression. She still looked very pretty when she did her face and hair, but she rarely bothered with that unless she was going down the pub. She had curlers in her hair now, so she was obviously intending to go out later, but her dress had a tomato sauce stain down the front and she had holes in the elbows of her cardigan.

'Go and get your fags now then,' Laura retorted. She was tempted to point out that her mother could have taken the little ones out for a walk and got her cigarettes then, but she bit that back.

'The kids kept on asking me where you were.' Her mother's voice had turned to a disgruntled whine. 'For all I knew you could have been run over.'

'Well, I wasn't,' Laura retorted. 'You go and get your fags, I'll tidy up in here and change Freddy – he stinks.'

It was an odd thing that her mother rarely asked what Laura or her older brothers did when they went out. It was as if she didn't care other than to feel aggrieved that they hadn't been around to do something for her. Mark was fourteen now, Paul thirteen, and without any kind of discipline they were running wild.

'Peel some spuds too,' June said, lighting up her last cigarette and dropping the empty packet on the floor. 'We'll have egg and chips for tea.'

*

Laura opened the window when her mother had gone, and found the reason Ivy had no knickers on was because they were wet, and lying on the floor behind the sofa.

'You must use the potty,' she rebuked her little sister, and found her a clean pair to put on. She stacked up all the dirty plates and cups and carried them out into the kitchen, only to find the sink still piled high with the breakfast things. Groaning, she put the kettle on for some hot water, then heaved all the dishes out on to the table so she could bathe Freddy.

Mrs Crispin upstairs often said June should be ashamed of herself for being such a bad mother, that she was slovenly, lazy and a disgrace. Laura hated the woman for sticking her nose in her family's business, but she was right.

June Wilmslow *was* slovenly. She seemed unable to see dishes that needed washing, the pile of clothes in a chair that required ironing, and she would walk over things dropped on the floor rather than pick them up and put them away. As for cleaning, she would keep moaning that it needed doing, but that was as far as she got.

Laura had been taught in domestic science that a good housewife should make a weekly timetable to fit in all the work needing to be done. Several times she'd drawn one up for her mother, along with a menu for the week so she could get the shopping all in one go to save her time. But although June agreed it was a good idea, she couldn't stick to it. What she did with herself all day was something of a mystery, for when Laura got home from school, it was she who was invariably sent out to buy the groceries, or take the washing to the public baths.

Bill, her father, made matters worse. He had been in and out of prison for as long as Laura could remember. Each time he came out he would get work on building sites or something for a few weeks, but he soon went back to his old ways. Most nights he was out drinking and he slept till late the following day, making it difficult for June to get a routine going. He could be generous and jolly when he was in the money, but if there wasn't enough for him to buy a few drinks or go down the dog track, he was very grumpy and took it out on June.

In Laura's opinion, however, it was the overcrowded, dark, damp flat that had got her mother down most. She often said wearily that it didn't look any better even when it was tidy and clean, and that if only they had a garden, a bathroom and an inside lavvy she'd feel like she'd won the pools.

Laura had accompanied her to the council loads of times to try to make them give them a house. Her mother pleaded with them that it wasn't right that Mark and Paul slept in a room where water ran down the walls, or that the three girls had to sleep in the same bed, because there was no room for another one. But her pleas were ignored.

Laura had overheard a neighbour saying that it was because of Bill going in and out of prison all the time. She said they didn't want 'rough' families living on the new estates.

As if they had special food sensors on their noses, Mark and Paul arrived home just as their mother was frying the chips. They were skinny versions of their burly father, with the same dark brown hair, sharp features and cocky manner. Laura sensed they were plotting something as they looked annoyed when June told them she wanted them to stay in that evening to look after the little ones as she was going down the pub to meet Bill.

'He had a few quid when he went out to the football this afternoon,' June said. 'He'll go straight to the pub afterwards and if I don't go and join him he'll stay out until he's spent every penny he's got on him.'

Laura, Mark and Paul exchanged resigned glances. They'd all too often heard their father stumbling in dead drunk late at night, and witnessed the rows when their mother found his pockets empty in the morning. It would make no difference to the amount he spent if their mother joined him at the pub, but at least they came home drunk together, kissing and cuddling like lovebirds. That usually meant their parents were much nicer to them all the following day.

At half past seven June left the house all dressed up in her best pink dress and her hair looking really nice, but she'd no sooner left than Mark and Paul said they were going out too.

'You tell Mum and Dad and you'll be sorry,' Mark warned Laura, giving her a shilling and a Mars bar as a bribe.

Laura was quite happy to go along with this; she didn't know why her parents always insisted the boys had to babysit anyway, for they were worse than useless with the little ones and nasty to her. She warned them to be sure to get back before their parents or there'd be hell to pay, and felt glad she was to be left alone.

Freddy fell fast asleep the minute he'd had his bottle, and Ivy and Meggie were in bed by half past eight, so Laura had the luxury of being able to lie on her parents' bed to read with no one to interrupt her.

At half past ten her brothers returned, but they went straight to their room without speaking to her. Laura got into bed with her sisters soon after and was dozing off when she heard her parents come home. She knew they were tipsy because they were laughing, and her last thought before she dropped off to sleep was to hope Dad had had a win on the horses and they'd all get some kind of treat tomorrow.

A splintering sound, quickly followed by her mother's scream, woke her later. For a moment she thought it was a burglar, but when she heard her father swear and make a dash down the passage to the kitchen and the back door, she realized it had to be the police.

All at once there was angry shouting from both front and back doors. Ivy and Meggie woke up and their alarmed cries added to the tumult. Clearly her father had been caught, for there were thuds and scuffles as the police hauled him back up the passage past her bedroom door.

'What are they doing to Daddy?' Meggie asked, clinging to Laura in alarm.

'It's only his friends having a drink with him,' Laura lied.

The police often came here for her father, but they had never broken in like this before, or come at night. In fact when she was little she thought they really were her dad's friends because they just sat and talked to him. Even on the occasions when they took him away in a police car, it had never been frightening, and mostly Dad was back within a few hours, making jokes about it.

But it *was* really scary now. She could hear furniture being overturned; Mum was crying and Dad was bawling and swearing. Then she heard one of the police shout at her father to tell them where the gun was or he'd rip the flat apart.

Terrified, Laura grabbed her little sisters tightly and pulled the covers over their heads. But heavy boots tramped down the passage again, this time into her brothers' room, and judging by the sounds from there, they were ransacking it.

'I don't know where it came from,' she heard Mark shout a few minutes later. 'It ain't nothin' to do with me.'

Laura assumed that meant the police had found a gun in their room, and clutched her little sisters even tighter into her arms. Freddy was bawling his head off in the front room, her mother was shouting abuse at the police, and again and again she heard scuffling as if her father was trying to fight them.

Suddenly the light in her room snapped on. 'Come on out, girls,' a big policeman with a red face said as he pulled the covers off them. 'We need to search in here too.'

With Ivy in her arms and Meggie clinging around her waist, Laura watched helplessly as the two policemen pulled the mattress up and looked under the bed, dragging out old toys, colouring books and bits of rubbish. They knocked over Ivy's potty as they were doing it, and the pee ran all across the lino.

'What's this?' one of the policemen said, pulling out a shoe box tied up with string.

'I don't know,' Laura said truthfully, for she hadn't seen it before.

The man cut the string with a pocket knife and opened it, and to Laura's shock it was full of banknotes.

She gasped, for she'd never seen so much money in her life. A ten pound note was a rare sight to her, but this was bundles of tens and twenties, and as the box was stuffed with them, there had to be hundreds of pounds.

'Who put this here?' the red-faced man asked her.

'I don't know,' Laura said again, and suddenly she felt as though she was going to be sick. 'I didn't know it was there.'

'Don't you lie to me,' he said, coming right up to her and bending so he could look straight into her eyes. 'How old are you?'

'Twelve and three-quarters,' she replied.

'That's old enough to know what's right and wrong,' he said. 'Tell me when your dad put it here.'

'I don't know, I didn't see him put it there.' She began to cry then. 'It could have been there for weeks. That's all old stuff under there.'

The policeman ordered her back into the bed and left the room with the box in his hands, and suddenly the commotion and angry raised voices subsided. Laura couldn't hear what was being said because Freddy was crying so loudly, but she thought she heard her mother pleading with the police. Unable to bear it any longer, she got out of bed, just in time to see her father, Mark and Paul all being led out of the front door in handcuffs.

'You can't take the boys,' her mother sobbed. 'They're only kids – look how frightened they are!'

Laura had never seen the boys look afraid of anything before, but they certainly were now; their faces were like chalk, and they were trembling. But the older plain-clothes man showed no sympathy. 'In a reform school they might get straightened out,' he said to June. 'Now, get back to that baby and stop him bawling before he wakes the whole neighbourhood up.'

There were six policemen in all: three led their prisoners up the basement steps and the last three followed laden with boxes and a long object covered by a sack.

Laura could hardly believe what the police had done to the front room: furniture turned over, the mattress on the floor, drawers hanging open, cushions off the chairs. She picked Freddy up to comfort him and Meggie and Ivy came sidling in, both crying hard.

June had her old checked coat over her nightie, and her eye makeup was smeared down her cheeks. 'Bill promised me he was going straight,' she sobbed. 'Haven't I had enough grief over the years?'

'What did they say Mark and Paul had done? Why did they have a gun?' Laura asked. 'Did they go out robbing with Dad?'

'It weren't them that had the gun, that was Bill. Looks like the little buggers had been thievin' on their own,' June wailed. 'They had heaps of cigarettes in their room and never even gave me a couple of packets.'

That went some way to explain why her brothers had been so furtive when they came home earlier. But Laura was shocked that her mother was more upset that the boys hadn't shared their spoils with her than by their becoming thieves too. 'There was an awful lot of money in that box under our bed,' she said hesitantly. 'Did you know it was there?'

'Do you think we'd have had egg and chips for our tea if I'd known there was money around?' her mother wailed indignantly. 'I'll swing for that man! Fancy him not hiding it somewhere safe, and leaving the shotgun under our bed! What if the little ones had found it? The police said Bill robbed a post office. I just don't know him any more!'

Laura had heard her mother claim she didn't know Bill any more dozens of times in the past. The implication was that he'd once been very different to the man who only came home to sleep and took little interest in his family. But Laura had no recollection of him ever being any different. Even before the last three children were born, when she could remember going to the fair, to a circus or out for a day at the seaside with her mother, Mark and Paul, her father had never been with them. Sometimes she would look at the wedding photograph on the mantelpiece and try to equate that handsome, dark-haired man with the wide smile with the sullen, overweight man who bellowed at them to be quiet when he was in bed. He never ate with the family – his meals were kept hot over a saucepan of boiling water till he came home to eat them. When he spoke it was usually to bark out an order for one of them to get something for him, and on the rare occasions he stayed in for an evening it was clear by his morose manner that he didn't want to be there. In truth Laura couldn't once remember him asking how she was getting on at school, picking up Freddy or talking to Meggie and Ivy.

Laura made up her parents' bed again and Ivy and Meggie climbed into it. Freddy calmed down after a nappy change and another bottle of milk and fell back asleep. Laura wanted to get into the bed too, but she felt unable to do so while her mother was white and tense, chain-smoking as she paced up and down the room.

'They said the boys were seen tonight robbing the newsagent,' she spat out. 'I couldn't even trust the buggers to stay in with you and the little ones for one night. As if it isn't bad enough having my old man in the nick all the time, without the boys following him! How are we supposed to manage now? All I've got is a couple of quid.'

'We'll be all right, Mum,' Laura said in an effort to reassure her. 'We'll go down the Assistance office on Monday, and maybe I can get a paper round.'

Going down to the National Assistance office had been a regular feature throughout Laura's childhood because they had to go there every time her father went to prison. She often wondered why he kept on thieving when he always got caught.

'I can't take no more,' her mother sobbed. 'Six kids, a crummy flat, never a holiday or a day out at the seaside. Now I've got to go cap in hand to that lot down at the Assistance, and they never give me enough to live on. It's too much to bear.'

Over the following months Laura came to agree with her mother that it was too much for anyone to bear. Not only had Mark and Paul robbed the newsagent's, but the police had found various other goods in their room which had come from burglaries in private houses. The magistrate said they needed a sharp shock to teach them a lesson and gave them two years in borstal.

Her father, along with another man, was found guilty of

armed robbery at a post office in Uxbridge, and they both received ten-year prison sentences. It was said that the only reason they didn't get eighteen years apiece was because the gun had the firing pin missing and couldn't have been used. But as her mother pointed out at the time, ten or eighteen years made little difference to her; she was still left with four children to feed and clothe and she didn't think she could survive another winter in the damp, cold flat.

It was the bleakest time Laura had ever known. It had been bad enough at school before, but once the cases were reported in the newspapers the jeering and nastiness got a hundred times worse. Someone made a poster which said 'Stinky Wilmslow's father's a robber', and stuck it on the wall in the cloakroom.

Not one person showed a shred of sympathy for her. Her headmistress kept picking on her because she didn't have the correct uniform and didn't always do her homework. But how could she do her homework when her mother was constantly moaning about something, Freddy screaming and Ivy and Meggie begging her to play with them? There wasn't any money to buy the right uniform, she had to make do with whatever her mother found at a jumble sale, and she was often hungry because the Assistance money ran out too quickly.

Life had always been feast or famine for the Wilmslows. One day her father would come in with joints of meat, bags of fruit and even cigarettes to last her mother a month. At those times they went down to the market and bought new clothes and they could have an ice cream every time the van came by. But then there would be long periods when they lived on Spam or egg and chips, and when their shoes got holes in the soles, June cut up cardboard to put inside them. But there had never been such a prolonged, relentless time of hardship as there was now. It cost two shillings to wash and dry their clothes at the public baths, and if her mother decided it had to be done, then there was no money left for the electric meter and they had to go to bed when it was dark.

It was hunger that finally drove Laura to theft. She had never thought it was wicked to steal, only stupid because she'd grown up with her father constantly being caught and punished for it. But on an icy cold Saturday morning soon after her thirteenth birthday in January, when she knew there was nothing but bread and marge at home for their dinner, she decided she had to provide some food for the family.

Outside the butcher's shop in Goldhawk Road there was always a table with raw chickens wrapped in cellophane and boxes of eggs on it. She'd watched women pick them up before going into the shop to pay for them countless times. The blind outside the shop had a flap hanging down on the side next to the newsagent's. All she had to do was stand and read the postcards advertising items for sale long enough to make sure no one was looking, then put her hand under the flap, grab a chicken, hide it under her coat and walk away.

No one saw her, it was the easiest thing she'd ever done, and as she walked home she didn't feel ashamed or even guilty, just happy.

'You shouldn't have,' her mother said, but she was already taking off the cellophane bag and getting out a roasting tray from the cupboard. 'I don't want another of my kids snatched away from me.'

But once she'd put the chicken in to roast, she caressed Laura's face tenderly. 'You're a good kid,' she said. 'I wish I didn't have to lean on you so much, you are far too young.'

Those words of praise, and the delight on Ivy and Meggie's faces as they tucked into the roast chicken later, made Laura's mind up for her. She would become their provider.

Her teachers had always said that she was bright and quick; by the time she was six she could read anything and do quite hard sums. She sailed through the eleven-plus, and if it hadn't been for the difficulties of doing her homework, she knew she'd be top of the class. She loved doing problems in maths, and it struck her that thieving without getting caught was like a problem too – all she had to do was think it through before she acted.

She'd read somewhere that it was greed that caught most thieves out, so she resolved she would never allow herself to take anything her family didn't really need. On the way home from school and on Saturdays, she studied shops and familiarized herself with the people who worked in them, and exactly where everything was kept.

Her school raincoat was a gift to a thief. With it over her arm she could easily conceal a packet of soap powder, a toilet roll or a packet of biscuits beneath it. Every day she went home with something they needed, and the only irritation was that she couldn't get cheese, bacon or meat because such things were behind the counter.

Soon she had progressed to stealing clothes for the little ones and stockings and underwear for her mother, often taking the tube up to Kensington High Street or Oxford Street where there was a better selection of goods. She took pride in selecting good-quality items and felt very adult because she was taking care of her family.

'You mustn't do it any more,' her mother would say each time she came home with something, but she was just as quick to point out what else they needed and Laura got the message that her mother depended on her.

By the time Bill had been in prison for a year, things had improved a little. June got a job cleaning offices two evenings a week, and along with the Assistance money and the goods

Laura brought home they no longer went hungry and the little ones looked healthy and neatly dressed.

Once a month her mother went to visit Bill in Wormwood Scrubs, and though she was usually weepy when she came home, it seemed to Laura that apart from visiting days, she was far happier than she'd been for a long time. She often came out with Laura and the little ones to the park during the summer holidays, and at home she made more of an effort to clean and tidy.

'I hope you'll have the sense to find yourself a husband who has a trade,' she said one day when they had just finished spring-cleaning the kitchen. 'My mother always said Bill was a bad 'un and he'd come to a sticky end, but I didn't believe her.'

'Did he have a job in those days?' Laura asked.

'Not what you'd call a proper one, but it was during the war and lots of the men like him who'd been turned down by the Army filled in here and there. I met him in the munitions factory where I worked and thought he was God's Gift.'

Laura smiled. 'But if he was God's Gift, why did the Army turn him down?'

'Because he had flat feet. Not that it stopped him dancing and carousing, or climbing into people's houses. The Army might have made something of him if they'd taken him; as it was, the blackout gave him opportunities to get up to all sorts without being caught. He got to thinking work was a mug's game.'

'But you loved him, didn't you?' Laura asked. She was becoming very interested in love and romance, fired still further by going to the pictures once a week. Several of the girls at school had boyfriends, but Laura felt no boy would ever like her because she was so plain and skinny.

'Yeah, I loved him all right,' June replied, blowing smoke

28

rings up to the ceiling. 'Worshipped the ground he walked on. But if I'd known then what I know now, I wouldn't have married him.'

'But you can't help it if you fall in love,' Laura said, for this was the message she'd got from so many romantic films.

'Love ain't like what you see at the pictures,' June said sagely. 'It's not all pretty and sweet. It's more like a kind of madness that takes over your brain. You don't see what the bloke really is. All you can think about is him kissing you and holding you. But that don't last, let me tell you. If you're lucky, when that wears off you're left with a decent bloke who'll take care of you, but if you aren't, then you'll regret the day you ever set eyes on him.'

'But you and Dad were happy together!' Laura exclaimed indignantly. She might not actually remember Bill being very happy and joyful with his children, but he had seemed happy enough with June when they came home from the pub together.

'How could anyone be happy living like this?' June gestured at her surroundings with her cigarette. 'He never saw this as being anything more than a kind of dosshouse to fall into when he'd had a skinful of beer. He never valued me.'

Laura was shocked by that. 'Surely he does!'

'Oh, he does now he's in the nick,' June spat out. 'He tells me that he adores me and you kids, that he's sorry and it will all be different when he comes out. But words are cheap, he's said all that before, and I was stupid enough to believe him. I'll be forty-two when he comes out this time, a middle-aged woman who's spent her life in a slum, no holidays, no nice things, and precious few good memories. And he expects me to wait for him!'

It was in November, thirteen months after her father had been arrested, that Laura found out her mother wasn't waiting for Bill. June had been doing her two nights a week cleaning for months, but then she upped it to three in September. About the same time she began having her hair done at the hairdresser's, bought herself some new clothes, and put makeup on every time she went out.

Laura was glad to see her mother looking better, and it was easier to get her homework done on the nights June was working because once the little ones were in bed, she had peace and quiet.

She had begun sharing the double bed in the front room with her mother when Bill went to prison, and she was often so sound asleep she didn't wake when June came home at night. But one morning Freddy woke early and Laura found she was alone in the bed.

Just a few minutes later, as she was changing Freddy's wet nappy, her mother came in. She was wearing the same blue costume she'd gone out in the night before, and high heels, but she said she'd just popped out for some cigarettes.

Laura knew she was lying, for there were a couple of cigarettes in a packet on the table, and if her mother had slipped out to the shops she would only have pulled on old clothes and gone in her slippers.

That day at school Laura kept thinking about it, and remembered that a couple of weeks earlier she'd woken up to find her mother fully dressed making a cup of tea in the kitchen. At the time she'd believed her story that she couldn't sleep so she'd washed and dressed, but now it looked as if she'd been out all night both times. It could only mean she'd been with a man.

As soon as she got home, she asked her mother point-blank.

'What do you mean, have I been with a man?' June replied, getting up and looking at herself in the mirror over the fireplace, which was what she always did when faced with something awkward.

'I know you have, Mum,' Laura said. 'And you're married, so that's wicked.'

June whipped round, her small face sharp with spite. 'I'll tell you what's wicked,' she said. 'A daughter who can't bear to see her mother have a bit of life. Do you know what it's like to be stuck in here day after day with only you four kids? Well, I'll tell you, it's enough to drive anyone mad.'

Laura was mature enough to understand why June had been tempted by another man; she was after all well aware of her father's shortcomings. She might even have been glad for her if she hadn't been so nasty.

What hurt was that she had been lumped together with the three younger children as a burden, when she had been her mother's sole friend and helper in the past year.

She was also scared that this new man, whoever he was, might want to move in with them.

His name, Laura discovered three or four weeks later, was Vincent Parish. He was a sixty-year-old widower and he had an office in the block June cleaned in. He was, according to her mother, everything Bill Wilmslow wasn't: successful, well-bred and a gentleman.

On 3 January 1959, two days before her fourteenth birthday, Laura met Vincent for the first time. He invited them all to Lyons Corner House in the Strand, and bought them knickerbocker glories. Laura was rather impressed by his posh voice, his hand-tailored suit and gold watch, but less by his wide girth, lack of hair, and the coldness in his pale blue eyes.

'I am so glad to meet you all at last,' he said with a tight-lipped smile. 'Your mother and I have made so many plans for you all.'

Laura sensed immediately that all he really wanted was her pretty young mother, but as he couldn't have her without her children, he was pretending that he was happy to have them too.

She watched as he fawned over Ivy and Meggie, who did look sweet in blue velvet dresses bought specially for the occasion. He winced at Freddy smearing the ice cream all around his face, and went bright red when he started screaming to get out of the high chair he'd been put in. Laura didn't hold that against Vincent for she was embarrassed herself that Freddy was showing them up, but she really didn't like the way he kept smirking at her across the table.

She had a new dress too, and she was thrilled with it, for it was red wool, with a full circular skirt and a low scooped neckline trimmed with satin ribbon. Beneath it she had a net can-can petticoat, and her first pair of high heels. Her mother had even let her have her hair cut at the hairdresser's, and put it in curlers for her. But the way Vincent was looking at her made her all too aware of her breasts which had appeared out of nowhere in the past three months.

'Seeing Laura is like having a glimpse of how you must have looked as a young girl,' he said to June. 'I'm sure she'll grow into a beautiful woman too.'

Her mother glowed at the compliment, but to Laura it sounded as if he was implying her daughter was an ugly duckling. It was on the tip of her tongue to make some retort about how she could copy her mother by bleaching her hair, but she bit that back because she didn't want to spoil the day for June.

'I want you all to come and live with me,' Vincent said a little later, beaming at them all. 'I have a very nice house in Barnes, right on the river. Meggie can go to the school there, and Ivy and Freddy will follow when they are old enough.

But you, Laura, your mother and I think you should stay at your present school. It's not that far on the tube.'

'It's a beautiful house,' her mother interrupted, her face alight with excitement. 'You just wait till you see it! It's got two bathrooms, can you believe that! Ivy and Meggie will have a room together, and there's a little one for Freddy and another one just for you, Laura. Vincent is going to get you a real desk too so you can do your homework in peace.'

'What's Dad going to say about this?' Laura asked. Part of her was delighted that they'd be leaving Thornfield Road: the thought of a real bathroom and a room of her own was like a glimpse of heaven. If her mother had just talked about this to her first, before today, maybe she could have been really happy about it. But as it was, Laura felt her feelings and opinions meant nothing at all.

'I couldn't care less what he says,' her mother snapped. 'He didn't think of me and you kids when he went off holding up that post office. The chances were he was planning to run off from us with that box of money.'

'Your mother has had a very difficult time,' Vincent chimed in reprovingly. 'And you are old enough to understand that, Laura.'

Laura leapt up from her seat. 'Understand it! I've supported her through it! If it wasn't for me these three would have gone hungry and had no clothes to wear. You'll soon find out how she is! All she cares about is her fags and getting her hair bleached. She can't even clean up.'

She ran out of the Corner House then, ignoring her mother calling her back, and kept on running until she came to Regent Street, where she was too out of breath to run any further.

Leaning against a wall to catch her breath, she knew she'd

said too much and that her mother was unlikely to forgive her. What's more, she'd left her coat at the Corner House and the wind was icy. And she had no money to get on the tube, or even a key for the front door; that was in her coat pocket.

An hour later Laura arrived home. She'd got on the tube without a ticket easily enough, but when she got off at Goldhawk Road she had to spin a yarn to the ticket collector that she'd had her coat stolen, and ask if she could bring the fare along to him the next day. He let her off, but as she walked up the road shivering in her thin dress, she was really frightened about the reception she would get at home.

Meggie opened the front door to her. 'Mum's really angry with you,' she whispered, her dark eyes wide with anxiety. 'Uncle Vincent put us in a taxi to come home. He said you needed taking in hand.'

Laura gave her little sister a squeeze. Meggie was a worrier; at only seven she already had frown furrows in her little brow. She and Ivy were prettier than Laura had been; their hair was dark brown and very shiny, and their eyes were bigger. But Meggie's worrying spoiled her looks – right now she looked like a little old lady.

'I don't care if I'm in trouble,' Laura said loud enough for her mother to hear. 'And that man isn't your uncle, he's just Mum's fancy man.'

Her mother appeared in the doorway. 'How could you be so nasty?' she asked, her voice sharp with hurt. 'Why can't you be glad for me, and that you'll all live in a nice warm, comfortable home? He'll make a much better father to you all than Bill.'

'Will he?' Laura replied insolently. 'He doesn't want any of us, only you. How long will it be before he's picking on Freddy, telling Ivy off for wetting her knickers, or getting angry with Meggie because she's timid?'

'He'll grow to love you all once he's got to know you. But he'll be out at work all day so you won't see much of him except at weekends.'

In a flash Laura saw that her mother wasn't entirely convinced about Vincent. She could see it in her eyes, hear it in her voice. She loved his house, she loved what he could do for her, but she didn't love him.

'I think you're making a mistake, Mum,' Laura said. 'Once we're in his house, if anything goes wrong and he throws you out, where will you go then?'

'Nothing will go wrong unless you mess it up for us,' she replied. 'He's a good man, Laura. A kind and decent one with a bit of brass too. Don't go looking for problems.'

Laura went on into the living room and flopped down on the bed. She remembered only too well how her dad used to moan about the noise his children made, so it was obvious a man who had never had any of his own would have no real idea of what it meant to have four readymade ones suddenly swarming round his house. She thought her mother must be stupid if she hadn't thought about that.

Her mother followed her into the front room and stood there silently looking at her for a couple of minutes.

'Can't you try to like him?' she said eventually, her voice quivering as if she was going to cry.

'Can't you just be his mistress and we carry on living here?' Laura asked, thinking that was the perfect solution. 'I could babysit on the nights you want to be with him.'

'You silly mare,' her mother exclaimed. 'Don't you understand that I want to get us all out of this rat trap? You've got no chance in life living here. I know you get called names at school because of the way we live and it makes me feel really bad. You're clever, and I want you to go on to university and have all the chances I never had. This is the only way I can see you getting that.'

Laura was stunned that her mother had actually considered her future, and it made her feel ashamed of herself.

'Okay, Mum, I'll try my best to like him,' she said, feeling as though she might burst into tears. 'I'm sorry about today.'

'That doesn't matter now,' her mother said, coming over to the bed and sitting beside her. She put her hand on Laura's shoulder and squeezed it. 'I know it isn't going to be easy adjusting to a new life, especially for me. I'm not a very good housewife, am I? But I'll have to learn to be because we might never get a chance like this again.'

It was the Easter holidays before they moved to Barnes, and on the night before they were due to leave, as Laura took yet another bag of old clothes and rubbish out to the dustbins for collection, she was excited and happy.

They had all visited the new house back in February and it was all her mother had said, and more: a detached thirties house, backing on to the Thames, and the kind of elegant, spacious and sun-filled home that Laura had only ever previously glimpsed in films and glossy magazines. It had all those luxuries like a television, refrigerator, washing machine, fitted carpets and vacuum cleaner that her mother used to reel off when she imagined winning the pools. Nothing was shabby; it had huge comfy settees and armchairs, a dining room with chairs for eight people, and the kitchen had at least twenty cupboards. Laura was thrilled to find she was to have a room which looked out on to the river. There was the kind of triple-mirrored dressing table like a film star's and she even had her own small armchair and the desk Vincent had promised her.

She had spent ages in the bathroom she would share with the little ones, drinking in every detail of the shiny pale pink tiles, the heated towel rail and the lights either side of the mirror. Yet it was the things Vincent had done for the little ones which made her lose all her reservations about him. He'd redecorated the room for Ivy and Meggie with a wallpaper covered in flowers and fairies. They had new twin beds and there was a lovely doll sitting on each one. Freddy's room was tiny but Vincent had got a specially made small bed for him, and the curtains had jungle animals on them. He'd also bought him a shiny red tricycle. No one would go to such trouble if they really didn't want children living in their house.

Vincent had also said they should start out afresh and so they were only taking their best clothes and most treasured possessions with them to his house. He was going to get them everything else they needed. For the last couple of weeks they had been getting rid of things; they sold a few bits of furniture to a neighbour, and outgrown clothes, pots, pans and china went to a jumble sale. The rest of the stuff was just rubbish and they had filled over twenty sacks with it.

Laura didn't feel the least bit sad to be leaving Thornfield Road. They were going up in the world at last, and even if the girls at school didn't come round when they saw her in her new summer uniform dress after Easter, she was too happy to care.

Ten months later, as Laura sat down for her special tea for her fifteenth birthday in January and looked at the beautiful cake with icing roses, and Meggie, Ivy and Freddy's plump, healthy, smiling faces, she wished she could wholeheartedly believe, as they did, that they really were in paradise.

To be fair to Vincent, he was generous and affectionate to them all. He didn't complain when the children were noisy, and he showered them all with new clothes, toys, books and anything else they so much as hinted at wanting. As for their mother, she had blossomed; she had her hair and nails done every week, she wore the kind of clothes and shoes rich women wore, and she no longer had that weariness about her which had been so much a part of their old life.

But Laura was always aware of a kind of undercurrent, as if her mother was acting out a role which wasn't entirely to her liking. She was often nervy, particularly when Vincent was due home from the office, and he didn't help by commenting on anything which was untidy or dirty.

Laura was by nature tidy-minded, and she loved things to be clean, but she was aware that some people were not like that. June was one of them. Even the modern labour-saving appliances in Grove House couldn't transform her into a super-housewife. She failed to see fingermarks on paintwork, or an overflowing kitchen bin, and her cooking skills were very limited.

So Laura covered for her by rushing home from school and running around the house picking things up, cleaning this, tidying that, and more often than not supervising whatever her mother was preparing for the dinner she would eat with Vincent later.

It was hard for Laura to understand what her mother found so difficult about cooking; after all, she was no longer on a tight budget and all she had to do was read a recipe book and follow the instructions. But perhaps she was intimidated because Vincent was used to more sophisticated food than she had ever eaten. She certainly seemed very afraid that he would find out her failings.

Vincent, it transpired, had two adult sons from whom he was estranged. They had parted company with him after their mother died, and Laura wondered if this was because Vincent had been unkind to her.

He did have a very hard streak. Back in September, when they were expecting Mark and Paul to be released from borstal, he had said point-blank that they couldn't live at Grove House. He used the excuse that there was no room, but it was plain his real reason was that he knew sixteen- and seventeen-year-old boys were likely to be trouble. As it turned out he was right, because they were not released after all: they assaulted one of the staff and received another year. Yet if they had been released Vincent would gladly have seen them go to some kind of hostel.

Comparing life at Grove House to Thornfield Road, Laura often felt guilty that she wasn't down on her knees thanking God for Vincent. It was wonderful to see the little ones so happy and confident, and Meggie and Ivy were doing really well at their new school. She loved seeing her mother looking pretty and not having to worry about money all the time.

Sometimes Laura thought her misgivings were just self-ishness because she didn't appear to have benefited as much from the move as everyone else. Even a brand-new uniform, no smell of damp and mould lingering about her, and a new stylish haircut hadn't made the other girls at school like her any better. She wasn't bullied as such any more, just ignored, and she hadn't made any friends in Barnes because she went to a different school.

Yet her main worry, and it niggled away at her all the time, was Vincent. She always felt uneasy with him, though she found it difficult to explain why. He seemed to sit too close to her and she would catch him staring at her in a strange way. Perhaps if her father had been the sort who cuddled her and asked her to sit on his knee, she wouldn't think anything of Vincent doing it, but it gave her the creeps.

He came into her room when she was doing her home-work and leaned over her, he made comments about her developing figure, and several times he'd tried the bathroom door when she was in the bath.

She had attempted to talk about it to her mother, but June only got cross and said she should be grateful that Vincent showed her affection and wanted to be a father to her.

'You've got to light the candles now,' Meggie said, breaking into Laura's reverie. 'When you cut the cake, can I have one of the roses?'

'Of course you can,' Laura said. 'We'll all have one and leave one for Uncle Vincent for when he gets in from work.'

Meggie struck a match and lit the candles, and as they all burst into 'Happy Birthday', Laura looked round the table and smiled. Freddy was now three and a half, a chunky little boy with ruddy, plump cheeks, black hair and eyes full of mischief. Ivy was six, and her hair had turned mousey like Laura's, but she had lovely big dark brown eyes. Meggie had changed the most since moving here; she'd lost her worried look, put on some weight, grown an inch or two, and her long hair was dark and silky, making her very pretty. As for her mother, she looked lovely in a rose-pink twinset and the pearls Vincent had given her for Christmas. She didn't smoke so much now because Vincent didn't approve of it, and her complexion was clearer and brighter.

Laura blew out the candles and removed them to cut the cake. In the past a Swiss roll was all they got for a birthday tea, and she was touched that Vincent had bought this pretty one for her. She knew it must have cost a lot, and as she'd had a transistor radio too, her thoughts of him, for now, were all good ones.

Laura was in her bedroom later that evening, when Vincent put his head round the door. 'How was the cake, birthday girl?' he asked.

'It was gorgeous,' she said. She had come up to do her

homework after tea, and as Vincent was working late, she hadn't seen him until now. 'And thank you for the radio too. That was just what I wanted; now I can listen to Radio Luxembourg in the evenings.'

'I like to give my ladies what they want,' he said, coming right into the room. As always, he looked very smart in a charcoal-grey suit, white shirt and blue striped tie. He might be tubby and balding, but he had a distinguished appearance. 'Now, how about a kiss for an old man?' he asked, pulling a comic face.

She laughed and went over to him to kiss his cheek, but he put his arms around her and his mouth came down on hers, all wet and sloppy. Laura wriggled away, unsure if that was what he intended to do, or if it was an accident.

'I always wanted a daughter,' he said, sitting down on the bed. 'Now I've got three. What a lucky man I am.'

At that she felt ashamed she was so suspicious of him. 'We are lucky, too, that Mum found you,' she said a little awkwardly. 'You've been very good to us.'

'The pleasure is all mine,' he said, reaching out and taking her hand. 'And you are growing into a very pretty girl. I expect before long boys will be calling round wanting to take you out.'

'I never meet any boys,' she said, giggling with embarrassment.

'Well, maybe we have to think of a club you could join to meet some,' he said, drawing her closer to the bed. 'I think there's a youth club just along the road; I've seen young people gathering outside the church hall on a Thursday night. I could go along there and inquire for you.'

'I'd be too scared to go to a club where I didn't know anyone,' she said and sat down beside him.

'Everyone feels that way at first,' he said. 'I keep telling your mum we need to find some way of introducing you to people so you can make friends. What about joining the Girl Guides?'

'I'm too old for that now,' Laura said with a sigh. 'I really wanted to join them back in Shepherds Bush but we couldn't afford the uniform.'

'You aren't too old,' he said, releasing her hand and putting his arm around her shoulder. 'I've seen girls of sixteen and seventeen at the parades on Sundays. They go camping in the summer and on all kinds of other trips. I'm sure the women who run it appreciate having slightly older girls to help with the younger ones.'

Laura liked the idea of that. 'I suppose I could go once and see how it is. But won't the girls all be very posh?'

'No posher than you,' he said with a little chuckle. 'You go to a good school, you live in a nice house. You are on the same level, or even higher, than all of them.'

'Am I?' she asked in some surprise.

'Of course you are,' he said firmly. 'You must stop thinking you are somehow inferior. You're bright and pretty, as good as anyone else.'

He hugged her then and for once she didn't move away because it felt good to be praised by him. 'That's better,' he said. 'Everyone needs a cuddle now and then.'

Suddenly his hand moved on to her breast. Like the kiss earlier it could have been a mistake, because he withdrew his hand immediately and said it was time he went as her mother would be wondering where he was.

After he'd gone Laura felt confused. Everything Vincent had said suggested he was just being kind and fatherly – her own dad wouldn't have cared tuppence whether she had any friends or not, and he certainly had never praised her. Maybe it was because of that she was so suspicious of Vincent, and perhaps she just had a dirty mind.

In the weeks that followed her birthday her feelings about

Vincent see-sawed between being sure he just wanted to be a real father and feeling he had other motives in being nice to her. He did take her along to the Girl Guides where she received a warm welcome, and the following day he took her off to buy her a complete uniform. He was really pleased that she made a new friend the very first night, a girl called Patsy who lived just further down the road, and he said she could have Patsy round any time she liked.

But he would keep touching and hugging her. She didn't like the way he patted her bottom, or the way he came into her room to kiss her goodnight. She would argue with herself that he patted Ivy and Meggie's bottoms too, and kissed them goodnight, and if he left her out she might have felt hurt. But they were only little girls, and why were his hugs and kisses so lingering, and usually when they were alone? And why did the presents he bought her seem like some kind of bribe?

He came home from work one evening with a beautiful red coat with a hood for her. She was thrilled with it, and threw her arms around him impulsively to thank him. But late that same evening he came into her room when she was reading in bed and said something about wanting to give her lovely things because she deserved them. He kissed her on the lips again, and this time it was definitely intentional.

She couldn't tell her mother, she knew she wouldn't be believed, and she'd almost certainly be accused of making trouble. But by her doing and saying nothing he became bolder. There were several occasions when he came up behind her and cupped her breasts in his hands, and though she did push him off and tell him not to touch her, he just laughed as if he believed she didn't mean it.

One very cold afternoon in early March Laura came out of school to find Vincent waiting for her in his car. He said he'd had a business appointment close by and thought he'd pick her up afterwards and drive her home. His business was office equipment and along with supplying desks, chairs and typewriters to offices, he also had a printing firm where he made business cards and headed notepaper. Laura was rather impressed that he supplied big companies; she sometimes saw invoices he'd made out for hundreds of pounds.

As she had often boasted of this at school, it was good to see the surprised expressions on the other girls' faces as she drove off in Vincent's gleaming Jaguar. She hoped it would stop them calling her a liar. It got better still when they stopped off in Chelsea for coffee and a cream cake as she felt very sophisticated.

When they got home the house was in darkness, and there was a note from her mother on the kitchen table to say she'd taken the little ones to Oxford Street to buy them new shoes and she wouldn't be back until about seven.

'That's nice, we'll have a little more time on our own,' Vincent said cheerfully. 'I'll go and stir up the fire and we can curl up in front of it.'

Laura made a cup of tea and when she took it into the sitting room Vincent had got the fire blazing, put the table lamps on, taken his shoes and jacket off and was sitting on the settee.

'I like cold, dark afternoons,' he said. 'At least I do once I'm in by the fire. Come and sit by me.'

Laura sat beside him, holding her cold feet up to the fire as she drank her tea. She had homework to do, and she knew she ought to go and make a start on the tea, but it was so cosy there that she was reluctant to move. They chatted for a while, mostly about the Girl Guides, for she was due to be enrolled the following week. Her mother never seemed to be interested in such things, in fact she had said she couldn't see the point in being a Guide, so it was nice to be able to talk about it to Vincent.

'Patsy said camping is really great, she's been on several trips, and this summer they are going to Cudham in Kent. Mum will let me go, won't she?'

'She will if I tell her she must,' Vincent said, and slung his arm around her. 'I know she thinks Guiding is a little pointless, but that's because she never had the chance to do such things when she was young.'

After a long day at school, feeling comfortable with Vincent and in the warmth of the fire, Laura must have dozed off. But she woke with a start to find him trying to put his hand up her knickers.

It was a terrible shock. Her school skirt was right up above her waist, and to her horror he had his penis in his other hand. For a moment she froze. She had never seen a fully grown man's penis before and it was huge, with a purple glistening tip.

'What are you doing?' she exclaimed, suddenly aware her blouse was unbuttoned too.

'Just loving you,' he said. 'Don't move, let me just touch you there.'

She leapt to her feet, brushing his hands away from her, shuddering with revulsion. 'You dirty bastard,' she screamed at him. 'How could you!'

Running from the room, she took the stairs two at a time and locked herself in the bathroom. She felt sick and very afraid, and a few minutes later when she heard him coming up the stairs she yelled out for him to go away.

'I couldn't help it,' he said outside the door, his voice soft and caressing. 'You looked so beautiful and I just got carried away. I'm sorry if I frightened you, but I thought you felt that way about me too.'

'Of course I didn't, you're an old man,' she shouted back. 'Mum will go mad with you when I tell her.'

He asked her to come out of the bathroom, but she

refused. He was silent for a little while, but she knew he was still there.

'Okay, so I made a mistake,' he said eventually. 'But you did bring it on yourself, snuggling up to me. How was I to know you didn't want it?'

Laura was crying now, and she couldn't put into words how defiled she felt. All she kept saying was that she was going to tell her mother.

'You must think hard before you do that,' he said. 'For one thing, I'll just tell her that you started it and that you've been flaunting yourself at me since you moved in here.'

'She'll know that's not true,' Laura sobbed. 'You've been creepy with me from the start.'

'Is giving you and the others a good home creepy?' he asked, a chilly note in his voice. 'Is giving you good food, warm clothes and anything else you need creepy? I think not, and if your mother does believe your version of what happened, then it will all end. You'll all have to go. Back to another slum, until your mother takes up with another sucker willing to keep her.'

He went on and on insistently and Laura realized then that he was cruel enough to put her family out on the street. 'I thought you loved Mum,' she sobbed. 'But you don't, you've just used her.'

'Used her! That's rich,' he exclaimed. 'She made a play for me the moment she knew I was a widower. Listen to me, Laura, and listen good. Your mother is just a whore. She'd have dropped her knickers for any man with money, I knew that from the start, but she was good company and she gave me what I wanted. It's up to you now, tell her if you must, but you'll be the one to blame if she takes your part and I have to throw her out.'

'You're horrible,' Laura shouted back at him. 'Mum will want to go when she knows what you said.'

'You'd better think about your sisters and Freddy,' he said threateningly. 'The girls won't thank you for it, not when they have to leave that school where they are doing so well, or their pretty bedroom. And what about Freddy when he has to leave his tricycle and other toys behind? But June won't take your part anyway, a good whore knows when she's on to a good thing. She'll just hate you for upsetting the apple cart.'

Laura protested, but feebly, for the thought of Meggie and Ivy's faces when they had to leave here was too awful to contemplate.

'I'm going downstairs now,' he said. 'Go to your room and stay there. I hope that by morning you'll have decided on the smartest move, which is to keep this to yourself.'

Laura heard her mother come in later, and Meggie calling out to Vincent to show him her new shoes. Every sound that wafted up the stairs was one of a happy family, and Laura sobbed into her pillow knowing that Vincent was right, everyone would suffer if she told the truth.

Her mother didn't come up to see why she was in bed, which in itself suggested she didn't care too much about her eldest daughter. Meggie brought a glass of milk and a sandwich up later, but even she was too excited about her new shoes and a jumper Mum had bought her to show any concern as to why her sister was in bed.

It came to Laura during that long night when she couldn't sleep that there was no alternative for her but to leave the house for good. She knew it would be too much of a strain living here after what had happened, and besides, Vincent might do it again.

But that meant she would have to leave school and get a job. That would be the end of her plans for university and a career.

Hate was an emotion she'd never felt for anyone until

that night. She had never hated her father, even though he wasn't much of a one. She didn't hate the girls at school who had bullied her either. But she learned to hate Vincent in the early hours of the morning as she lay there seeing her plans and dreams shattered.

She couldn't even get her revenge on him, not without putting her family at risk. If it had just been her mother she wouldn't have cared, for it struck her that Vincent had spoken the truth about her, at least in part. But Meggie, Ivy and Freddy were little innocents; she couldn't do anything that would backfire on them.

'But I can wait to get my revenge later,' she murmured to herself. 'I'll go, disappear where you'll never find me. But I'll keep tabs on you and pay you back one way or another.'

A scream further down the block brought Laura sharply back to the present. Someone was fighting again and before long others would join in. She had no intention of going out there to see what was going on, but she got off her bed and washed her swollen eyes with cold water.

'The question is, do you want Stuart to visit you or not?' she asked her reflection in the small mirror.

Her head was telling her that the only reason he wanted to come was to gloat at her misery.

But her heart told her to send him the visiting slip anyway. If nothing else, it would be good to talk to someone who had cared deeply for Jackie. And maybe she could take the opportunity to apologize for the hurt she had caused him in the past.

3

'Visitor for Brannigan!'

Laura started in surprise as the prison officer's voice boomed out along the block. She had been longing for her name to be called, but from the moment she opened her eyes this morning, she'd felt sure Stuart wouldn't come.

She didn't stop to check herself in the mirror, for she was already disappointed that the prison hairdressing salon hadn't been able to achieve the rich, deep brown colour she'd hoped for. It had come out far too red, but at least they had cut it well, and it was now a neat bob to her shoulders.

In the absence of anything smart or pretty to wear, she'd opted for jeans and a pale blue tee-shirt. The other women had said she looked great, but then they'd never seen her without pale blotchy skin, or in the kind of elegant clothes she used to wear. Most of them had friends or relatives who could bring in new clothes from time to time, but she was stuck with the things her lawyer, Mr Goldsmith, had collected from her flat after her trial. With his wife's help he'd picked practical, comfortable clothes that would wash well, though with only four sets, they all looked shabby and frumpy now. But then Laura hadn't imagined she would ever care what she looked like again.

As she made her way in the warm sunshine from Bravo Block across the prison grounds to the visiting room, it occurred to her that if she had to be in prison, it was probably better here in Scotland than in England.

She recalled seeing pictures of Holloway Prison in

London, a grim Victorian place built like a fortress, and other women here spoke of prisons where they had been locked in their cells almost all day. At Cornton Vale there were no high walls, only metal fences, and the grounds were quite attractive, with grass, trees and even a pond with ducks. Each block had its own exercise yard, and there was a view from almost every cell, either of the hills or of the grounds. It wasn't anywhere near as crowded as Holloway either: about 250 women, Laura thought, and there was variety of work and many courses like hairdressing or art to enrol in.

Yet Cornton Vale still had a high suicide rate: there had been two since she'd been here, both young girls who were not even serving long sentences. But then she supposed that two or three years seemed an eternity at their age and perhaps they had nothing on the outside to look forward to anyway.

The visiting room had not changed since the last time she had a visitor, and that was over a year ago. The walls were still drab, the same large tables prevented close contact between visitor and inmate, and the usual display of chocolate, cake and biscuits stood by the tea urn.

What was new to her though was her ability to feel the tension in the air, to notice the anxious expressions on both prisoners' and visitors' faces as they clutched at one another's hands over the tables. A years ago she was aware of nothing but her own misery.

It was good to see a few children, some playing with toys in the corner, others haring around the room, for she understood now how important these visits were to their mothers. Yet those prisoners who were cuddling babies and toddlers brought a lump to her throat. She thought it must be devastating for a new mother to be parted from her baby, and only be able to see it once a month for a brief half-hour.

Yet even harder to bear would be the fear that the baby would bond with whoever was taking care of it now and might never feel that way about its real mother when she was released.

But such thoughts vanished as she saw Stuart come into the room. Her pulse began to race and the palms of her hands were suddenly sweaty.

He stood out amongst the other visitors, not just because he was tall, suntanned, well dressed and the picture of health, but because he looked like a man who had never before come into any contact with the underbelly of society.

It was difficult to believe that he'd once been a long-haired hippy, with bare feet, ragged jeans and Indian love beads around his neck. He looked more like a man from a Martini advertisement, hair well cut, and impeccably groomed.

Although they had parted twenty years ago back in '75, she had seen him from a distance a few times when he was back visiting in Edinburgh. On each successive occasion he'd been better dressed, with a good leather jacket, expensive shoes and a general air of increased sophistication.

Laura hadn't seen him as handsome when they first met, for he'd had the rawness of youth, his nose and mouth seemingly too large for his skinny frame and his mane of chestnut-brown hair obscuring the beauty and gentleness of his grey eyes. She had been initially attracted by his ability to make anyone he spoke to feel important and valued. He really listened, he thought about what he said in reply, and cared. That wasn't something she'd found in many other men.

But a few years later, he had filled out, his features in perfect proportion to his then muscular body, and though perhaps still not classically handsome, he was arresting. Jackie had often chuckled about how women always made a bee-line for him, saying that even the coldest, starchiest women would try to flirt with him. Laura had known exactly why, for she could recall the sight of his wide mouth curling into a heart-stopping smile, and she guessed that once ruggedness had replaced rawness, there would be an edge to him which would suggest a night with him would be unforgettable.

Her assumptions about how he had developed over the last twenty years were accurate, for every single woman in the visiting room was looking at him appraisingly.

She sensed that he had purposely dressed down for this visit: his jacket was a muted olive colour, the open-necked shirt beneath it cream, and he was wearing a pair of ordinary chinos. But seen amongst other male visitors who wore denim jackets, tee-shirts and even shell suits, many of them paunchy, tattooed and shaven-headed, he looked out of place.

He didn't recognize her immediately, not until she fluttered her hand at him.

The shock in his eyes cut her to the quick, but he moved swiftly over to her table and embraced her.

Laura withdrew from his arms quickly and sat down. 'You didn't really think I'd still be a glamour girl?' she said lightly, hiding her hurt. 'But you, Stuart! You could have stepped out the pages of *Hello!*.'

He hid his confusion by saying he'd been thrown by her new hair colour as he'd seen some press photographs of her and she'd been blonde; then he quickly changed the subject by telling her he'd brought her cigarettes, shower gel, some books and sweets. 'If you still don't smoke, I'm sure you can trade them for other things you need,' he said in a low voice. 'But tell me how you are.'

The concern in his voice brought a lump to her throat, and she steeled herself not to give way to tears.

'As well as can be expected,' she replied, not daring to

look right into his grey eyes. 'I could do with a few long walks in the sunshine, some healthy food and more stimulating company, but I dare say I'll adjust to living without that in time.'

He looked shaken and she wished she'd simply said she was fine.

'A half-hour visit isn't long enough when there's so much ground to cover,' he said, leaning closer to her across the table. 'To speed things up I've done my homework and read up on the trial. But what I want to hear is your version of what happened the day Jackie died.'

Stuart had always been very direct, but it was a bit of a shock that he expected her to launch into her story without easing her into it gently by telling her his own reaction to the news, or even why he felt he had to visit her.

'I didn't kill her,' she stated firmly. 'She was already dead when I got over to Fife. I received a distressed phone call from her that morning and as I couldn't get any real sense out of her I agreed I would go to her. Whoever killed her did it just a short while before I got there.'

Stuart nodded and opened a small notebook to consult what he'd written in it. 'Then a man called Michael Fenton arrived. In his evidence he said that he had received a call from Belle.'

He looked puzzled that Jackie's younger sister was also living in Scotland.

'Belle and Charles came up to live in Fife back in '81,' Laura explained. 'They've got a guest house in Crail, just a few miles from Brodie Farm, Jackie's place.'

'Right,' Stuart said, but he still looked confused that the two sisters both ran guest houses just a few miles from each other. 'So Jackie phoned Belle that morning and sounded distressed. Belle couldn't go over there herself so she rang Fenton to ask him to pop in instead.' He paused for a moment, looking at Laura quizzically. 'I can't imagine Belle and Charles running a guest house!'

Laura understood his surprise, for all his old memories of Belle and her husband Charles Howell must have been as sophisticated city dwellers. 'I know it seems unlikely,' she said. 'I was amazed that they could leave London too. But I suppose Belle wanted to see more of Jackie, and it seemed like a good business opportunity. Also Charles has always been a golf fanatic, and with St Andrews so close by, that must have clinched it.'

Stuart nodded. 'Okay. So Fenton found you by Jackie's body and it was he who called the police. Is that correct?'

Laura didn't answer immediately, for she was mentally reliving the events of 12 May 1993.

Few people passing Imelda's, the pretty little clothes shop with its classy window displays and cream and gold interior in Edinburgh's Morningside, realized it was in fact a second-hand clothes shop. Women brought in quality clothes they were tired of, and Laura sold them on, taking a 25 per cent commission.

It was about ten in the morning and she and Angie, her assistant, had just started a stock check, to remove all the clothes they'd had for more than two months, when Jackie rang.

Laura was irritated when Jackie begged her to come over to Fife. An eighty-mile or more round trip would take up most of the day, and she had had a lunch appointment booked with her accountant.

But Jackie sounded so desperate she felt she had to drop everything and go, leaving Angie to hold the fort and cancel her lunch appointment.

Yet by the time she'd crossed the Forth Bridge and was on the pretty coastal road to Crail in bright spring sunshine, her irritation had gone. Jackie hadn't been quite herself for some time, and she thought perhaps this would be a good opportunity to get to grips with the root cause of it. Laura thought she might even stay the night and drive back to Edinburgh the following morning.

As she drove into the enclosed cobbled yard of Brodie Farm she noticed the red and yellow tulips and forget-me-nots planted in tubs either side of each of the six old stable doors that opened out on to the yard. That seemed a good omen, for if Jackie still cared about the impression flowers made on her paying guests she was clearly holding things together.

The door to the house was wide open, and as Laura got out of her car she could hear 'Moving On Up' by M People playing on the radio. She remembered thinking that meant Jackie must've pulled herself together since making the frantic call, for she always played opera when she was feeling low. The song itself made her smile, for two years earlier when it was in the charts it had almost been Laura's anthem.

She called out as she got to the front door, but walked in when she received no reply, thinking her friend was probably upstairs. As always when she came to Jackie's home, she felt a surge of admiration at her sense of style. She raked through junk shops and auction rooms and bought furniture anyone else would consider rubbish. But she stripped or painted it, made cushions or added old tiles, and somehow it always turned out looking marvellous.

The hall of the farmhouse was typical of Jackie's taste: black and white tiles on the floor, an old-fashioned hall stand painted lime green, with a selection of colourful hats hanging on it. Even the flower arrangement was just right, a rustic basket filled with late primroses and moss.

She called again, looking up the narrow staircase straight ahead of her, and when there was still no reply, she decided

Jackie must have popped out for a moment, so she went into the kitchen on her left to wait.

But as she pushed the half-closed door open, she saw Jackie on the floor. She was wearing jeans, her white shirt was red with blood and there was a knife embedded in her chest.

Much of what happened later that day had become a blur of indistinct images. She couldn't recall the faces or names of the policemen, or even the correct sequence of events. But that first sight of her friend on the floor, the way the sunshine slanted in through the window on to her vivid red hair, the pool of blood beside her, even the grotesque way her legs were splayed out, was still as clear in her mind now as if it had been just yesterday.

She heard herself scream, and threw herself down beside Jackie, grasping the big knife to pull it out. In her naivety she thought her friend was still alive because her skin and blood felt so warm, and she caught hold of her shoulders in an attempt to rouse her.

'Laura?'

She started at Stuart's voice, and was brought back to the present and the question he'd asked her.

'That's right, it was Michael Fenton who phoned the police,' she sighed. She quickly told him how she'd found Jackie. 'I was covered in her blood and kneeling beside her when he came in. I'm absolutely certain he arrived just a few minutes after me, but I expect you know that at the trial, Angus McFee, a neighbour, gave evidence that he'd seen my car go past his place well over half an hour before he saw Fenton's car.'

Stuart nodded. 'That seemed to me to be the most damning piece of evidence against you. Could you have blacked out for a while or something?'

'It was suggested, as I'm sure you know, that I might have blacked out all memory of killing Jackie,' Laura said tartly.

'But I can assure you I remember everything which led up to me going in that door and seeing her. Every detail, even the record that was playing on the radio! And I could hardly have fainted if I was still on my knees when Fenton came in. I think that McFee was either mistaken about the time gap, or he saw the real murderer, who may well have had a white car like mine too, but didn't see me pass at all.'

'He said he was painting an upstairs window.' Stuart consulted his notebook again. 'And that he had a clear view of the lane from his ladder. I drove out there to have a look round, and it's a pretty remote spot. I only saw one car pass while I was there.'

'It was different when Jackie was alive,' Laura said defensively. 'She had people turning up all the time. Why do you think that old codger watched so eagerly?'

'Point taken.' Stuart gave a knowing grin. 'So how soon after the police arrived did they arrest you?'

'A lot of that is blurry now,' Laura said thoughtfully. 'I remember I was in a state, hysterical really, and the first two policemen who came only asked me why I'd gone out there, who Jackie was to me and what she had said when she phoned me. I can remember sitting on a bench in the yard, and suddenly being aware there were dozens of police there, yet I can't remember all the cars driving in.

'It must have been late in the afternoon before they asked me to go with them to the police station. I was shivering by then; I was only wearing a thin jacket and the heat had gone out of the sun. I asked if I could go home to change first because I had blood all over me, and it was only when they said they'd need to take my clothes for forensic tests that I suddenly realized they thought I'd killed her. Then they cautioned me.'

'How did you respond to that?'

'I was livid. I couldn't believe they could think such a

thing. When they told me I'd need an advocate – you probably know that's what they call solicitors up here? – I went mad, I said I didn't need one as I hadn't done anything.'

'You flew into one of your rages?' he inquired gently, his tone reminding her that he'd witnessed many of these in the past.

'Yes, I'm afraid I did,' she said glumly. 'Well, wouldn't you? She was my best friend, I'd known her since I was sixteen. I would never touch a hair on her head. I was in shock at what I'd seen. No one ever expects to walk in on something like that.'

Stuart nodded. 'You said at the trial you had forgiven her for Barney's death. Was that true?'

Laura closed her eyes in exasperation. 'Of course I had. It was an accident. And eleven years had passed since his death, for goodness' sake.'

'Some things you don't ever get over. The death of your child is probably the main one,' he said and reached out to take her hands in his.

It was his big, hard, brown hands holding hers that cracked the shell she had built around herself since being in this place. Stuart had loved Barney as if he were his own flesh and blood. She had watched those same practical hands washing him, dressing him and caressing him, and she owed it to him to tell him the truth about how she felt.

'I still grieve for him, Stuart,' she said brokenly. 'I also feel a huge burden of guilt that I wasn't a better mother to him. But I *had* come to terms with his death. As God is my witness, I didn't hold a grudge against Jackie for it. She loved him too, I could see that it tore her apart thinking she was responsible because she hadn't made him put his seat belt on. Yes, I had really forgiven her. What made me sad was that she couldn't forgive herself.'

'I sensed that too in a couple of letters she sent two or three years afterwards,' he agreed. 'I also thought that was maybe why her letters to me tapered off in the past few years. Perhaps putting pen to paper to someone so closely connected to Barney was too difficult? But did you think that last phone call was about that?'

'In as much that I think Barney's death was often behind her low moments, and there were plenty of those, just as there still are for me,' Laura said sadly. 'But she said nothing that morning that would suggest she was brooding on that. She just sounded crazy, like she'd hit some crisis but couldn't explain it.'

'What did she actually say to you on the phone?'

'She just asked if I could come over right away. I asked what was wrong and she said "Everything". She was crying, Stuart. She said there was so much she'd kept from me, and that she needed to talk about it. But that was about all that made any sense. I told her it would take me more than an hour to get there, and she began sobbing as if that was too long.'

'Did you feel it was an emergency as in that she was being threatened, frightened or menaced?'

'No, not at all.' Laura shook her head. 'If I'd got that idea I would have phoned the police. I thought her problem was a man. For some time I'd suspected there was someone special to her, but she wouldn't admit it or tell me anything about him. I assumed her problem was that he'd dumped her, or if he was married his wife had found out. She didn't give me even the vaguest idea that she was in danger.'

'You said at the trial that there were several men; that she was drinking too much and letting her business in London fall apart.'

'That's right. So she was.'

'But no one else seemed to agree with that.'

'Well, they wouldn't, would they?' Laura retorted. 'Married men aren't going to come forward and admit they'd been shagging her, nor would Belle want to own up that her big sister was becoming a lush. As for the business in London – well, you know what Roger is like! Their marriage might have ended, but Roger was still involved in her business. He wouldn't want to admit publicly that it wasn't in great shape.'

Stuart just sat and looked at her for a moment or two, his eyes scanning her face as if looking for evidence she was lying.

'Who do you think killed her then?' he asked eventually.

'Almost everyone she knew could have had some kind of motive,' Laura sighed. 'Gain, jealousy, spite, you name it, someone probably felt it, but I can't pin it on any one of them, because I didn't know what was troubling Jackie. She'd been less open with me in the last few years, she no longer told me every last thing she'd done or said, like she used to.'

'Why do you think that was?'

Laura made a 'don't know' gesture with her hands. 'That we'd grown up enough not to need to divulge everything to each other perhaps? Or maybe she had done something, or had someone in her life she couldn't tell me about? We were still the very closest of friends, but I was pretty much engrossed in my shop, I wasn't exactly on her case every five minutes.'

'Right. Let's get back to suspects,' Stuart said.

'Well, some of the people in her life can be ruled out because they were too far away,' Laura went on. 'But you know what a sucker she was for lame dogs, Stuart! She met all kinds of way-out people and invited them home; any one of them could have been a weirdo who wanted more than she was prepared to give. I said that in my evidence, but Belle

60

denied it was true. Anyway, Jackie might have rung someone other than me and Belle that morning, or they could just have dropped by. All I know is that I was a gift to whoever really did it. Stupid bloody Laura who didn't have the sense to back out that door and phone the police immediately!'

Stuart said nothing more for a few moments, just looked at Laura thoughtfully.

'It's exactly that which makes me believe in you,' he said eventually. 'I know how devious you can be. If you were going to do anything dodgy, you'd plan it properly. You certainly wouldn't tell people you were going to Fife if you had murder on your mind, nor cover yourself with blood and wait to be caught.'

She laughed mirthlessly. 'That's a back handed compliment, if ever I heard one!'

'I know you, Laura,' he said, half smiling. 'Really know you, warts and all. I also know the time you received that call from Jackie, and I've driven the distance between your shop and Brodie Farm several times to check how long it takes. With no hold-ups on the Forth Bridge, no traffic jams in Edinburgh, it can be done in an hour, which would have got you there at the time the neighbour claimed he saw your car.'

'You checked that out?' She frowned.

'Yes.'

'Why?'

'Because I can't believe you killed her, despite all the compelling evidence to the contrary. Of course it does seem as if I'm the only person of this opinion, but I hope to change that. For one thing it would be practically a miracle if there wasn't some sort of delay anywhere. I only managed it in an hour once, and that was late in the evening. All the other times it ranged from an hour and fifteen minutes to worst case, an hour and three-quarters.'

Laura looked into his eyes and felt that strange tugging feeling in her belly that he'd so often given her in the past. She used to say it was his voice, the deepness of it, the soft Edinburgh accent, and the self-belief. She could recall times when she'd hungered for that voice so much that she'd play an old tape recording of him speaking, then laugh at herself for being so soft. But it wasn't his voice alone, not now, it was the determination in his face, the touch of his hands on hers. And his belief in her.

'I went to see Barney's grave too, and took some flowers,' he said, his voice soft with sadness. 'Someone has been looking after it – there were masses of pansies planted on it and it looked very pretty. As Belle is still there I expect it was her.'

'Really!' Laura exclaimed, for she had expected to hear it was totally overgrown with weeds. 'That's very nice of her. She and Charles were very fond of him, but under the circumstances I didn't expect them to concern themselves with his grave.'

'A child's death touches everyone who knew them,' he said simply. 'I know how devastated I felt, even though I hadn't seen him for years. I wished I'd been in the country when it happened. I would have come to his funeral.'

'I'm glad you didn't, I don't think I could have borne that,' she said. 'Yet I did appreciate your card. I still have it amongst my things. But visiting time is nearly up and I'm sick of talking about me,' she went on, afraid of what she was feeling. 'Tell me what you've been doing. What on earth were you doing in South America?'

'Overseeing a building project,' he said with a smile. 'But I can write and tell you all that. Before I get chucked out I want you to promise me you'll give me written authority to speak to your lawyer and anyone else connected with you. I've got to try and find a way to get you out of here.'

Laura's heart leapt. No one else had expressed real belief in her, much less stated that they intended to try to help her. 'There's no way you can do it. Short of finding the real murderer and sticking lighted matches under their nails until they confess.' She smiled glumly.

'Then that's what I'll do.' He grinned, showing perfect teeth.

Strangely she felt a little sadness at his teeth, for they had been far from perfect when they'd first met. But he wasn't suave and sophisticated then either. She guessed that another woman had taken him in hand, and she wondered, but couldn't ask, if he was still with her.

'It isn't even possible to appeal unless we can bring on some completely new evidence,' she said wearily.

'I'll find some,' he said.

'How are you going to do that? The police dug into every aspect of Jackie's life, and interviewed dozens of people. Not all of that evidence was used in the trial, but for an appeal you have to have brand-new material, not the unused stuff.'

'You once said you had every faith in me!'

'I did, didn't I?' she agreed, remembering how he'd promised to find a home for her and Barney, and came up with it. 'You always were the kind of man who instilled faith in anyone.'

'Well, try it again now. I work better when someone really does have that faith.'

'How can you believe in me when you must have discovered all those lies I told you about my background?' she asked, hanging her head. She had to bring it up; she wouldn't be able to sleep tonight wondering if he knew or not.

She felt his finger on her chin and he lifted it gently so she was forced to look into his eyes. She saw he did know it all.

'I *was* hurt you didn't feel able to tell me the truth,' he said. 'But it wasn't a total surprise as I always suspected there was something you had hidden. I once broached the subject with Jackie, and she agreed with me. She said there was a sadness in you, a lack of the silly little tales we all dig out about our childhoods. But we haven't got time to talk about that now. Why don't you write it all down for me? I've often found it's the easiest way to deal with hurtful things, and I know it must have been very painful for you to hide it so well.'

Laura gulped to get rid of the lump in her throat. 'I don't deserve you being so understanding. And I'd like you to know the whole truth. The way the papers reported on it made it sound like I was a confidence trickster. I wasn't ever that. I will write it all out and send it to you.'

He took her hand and squeezed it, his way of showing his understanding. 'While you are dredging up the past, think hard about all you know of Jackie's life and the people who came into it too. The bond between you was so strong I've no doubt it was forged though some kind of adversity when you were both very young. Jackie often mentioned your flat-sharing days; I got the idea there were quite a few men in both your lives then. I want to know about them.'

'Do you think that her killer was from way back then?'

'Perhaps. It wouldn't hurt to explore the possibility.'

The bell rang and people started to move.

'Just tell me, Stuart, why are you doing this?' she asked.

He stood up and smiled, moving towards her to embrace her. His arms went round her in a bear hug, and he smelled of something akin to cinnamon. 'For first love,' he murmured against her neck. 'For Barney. For inadvertently pushing me on to the road to success. Take your pick.'

*

Back in her cell, the many questions she'd had fired at her from the other women about her visitor still ringing in her ears, Laura felt very strange. It was almost as if she'd been slipped a mild hallucinogenic drug. The light seemed brighter, the normal prison noises louder, and she was even more aware of the smell of the place: that strange mixture of cleaning fluids, cigarettes, cheap scent and stale food.

When she first arrived at Cornton Vale it was the terrible smell of body odours in the reception area that she noticed above all else. She wasn't all that fresh herself, for she'd been in police custody for some thirty-six hours, including the brief court appearance that day, with no opportunity to wash and no clean clothes to change into. But some of the women brought in that day had been sleeping rough for weeks; there were drug addicts and those who had no idea of personal hygiene anyway. She found it appalling, after all she'd been through already, that she was treated the same as these women and was forced to strip off in a tiny cubicle before being driven into a shower as if she too was lousy.

It made her feel like 'Stinky Wilmslow' again, alone, unloved and bullied.

Yet if she had retained everything she had been and known at the age of twelve, the months she spent on Romeo, the remand block, might not have been such a shock to her system. The women there were very much like those she'd grown up with in Shepherds Bush – rough, uneducated, loud and often violent. They called her Lady Muck or The Duchess, and claimed she was a snob. Hardly a day passed without someone trying to pick a fight with her.

When the police came to question her, or Patrick Goldsmith, her lawyer, visited, all she managed to convey to them was her rage and indignation that she'd been charged with murder. She couldn't find the right words to explain her grief.

Yet it was the all-consuming grief which was the very worst thing. Jackie was her dearest and closest friend, the only entirely true friend she had in the world. Even if she had been miles away when Jackie died, with no connection to her death, she would still have felt the same. She had loved Jackie for her entire adult life and they were closer than most sisters, real soulmates – even marriages and Barney's death had never managed to shake their friendship. To have her snatched away in such a brutal manner, and then to find she was accused of the crime, was just too much to bear.

Yet somehow she managed to keep her sanity. She told herself that any day the police would find the real killer and she'd be released. There were also the distractions of weekly visits from Goldsmith, Angie, her assistant in the shop, who was being a rock in keeping the place going, and a few other friends. She really believed that even if she did end up in court, once she'd told her side of the story she would be acquitted.

She remembered during the last couple of weeks before the trial how she used to plan what she'd do when she got home to her flat in Morningside Road. It was on the second floor, above an electrical shop, and only some hundred yards from her own shop.

For the first two years at Imelda's she lived in a scruffy bedsitter some distance from genteel Morningside because that was all she could afford. She spent her days encouraging rich women to bring in their obsolete beautiful clothes, and then had to persuade less comfortably off women that it was better to have a gorgeous second-hand dress or jacket than a less stylish, inferior-quality new one. But the hard ground-breaking work paid off eventually, and once she had built up a large customer base, with new clothes arriving each day, and often being sold on immediately, she felt able to find herself a decent place to live.

Of all the places she'd ever lived in, that flat at number 42 was the one which gave her the most joy. It was spacious and bright, warm and comfortable, and she'd kept the decor to simple pale blue and cream, and trawled all the second-hand shops until she found the right kind of shabby-chic furniture which had what Jackie called 'A nod to French Farmhouse'.

In her little prison daydream she imagined arriving home with an armful of scented lilies, pulling up the blinds and opening the windows wide to hear the bustle of the busy street below. Then she would run a bath, pouring in a huge quantity of scented bath oil, and lie there soaking until the smell of prison was finally gone. Later, wearing her favourite cream linen dress she'd bought in Rome, with her hair and makeup perfect, she'd go out to Marks and Spencer and buy salad, tiger prawns and a bottle of the best Italian wine. She would spend her first evening alone, looking at her clothes, paintings and ornaments while listening to music, revelling in the delight of being home again, with the freedom to do what she liked, when she liked.

She knew of course that even if she were acquitted she would probably have to sell the shop and give up the flat, for gossip about her was bound to continue. Angie had already hinted that she'd like to buy her out, and Laura thought that would probably be the best plan.

Going south again seemed a good idea, maybe to start up the same kind of shop again in Bath, Cheltenham or Cardiff. She even thought at that time that it would be good to have a complete change. She would of course want to visit Barney's grave in Crail churchyard, so she'd need to come back once or twice a year.

*

Almost from the outset of the trial Laura sensed that there was going to be no new start for her. The prosecution had dug deeply and widely into her past, and as the more unsavoury aspects of it stacked up against her, she knew she was doomed.

Even the tragedy of her son's death did not gain her any sympathy with the jury, for there were several witnesses called who testified she had been a neglectful mother. Questions were asked as to why Barney was in Jackie's car when he died, and that brought forth answers that Jackie had shown him more care and attention than his own mother did.

Laura's instability after Barney's death was laboured over. There was even a police report of her being picked up wandering the streets at night wearing only a nightdress.

Roger Davies, Jackie's estranged husband, claimed Laura had always been jealous of Jackie because she was so successful. He stated that after Barney's death she blackmailed Jackie into lending her money to start up the shop, and he inferred that Laura killed her in a fit of rage when she called the debt in.

It seemed with every witness called that the jury was hearing more evidence that she was volatile, manipulative, greedy or jealous. Laura winced herself many times as some incident she was ashamed of, but had thought was buried in the past, was resurrected and painted even blacker than it really was.

Even loyal Angie, a witness for the defence, who knew nothing of Laura's wildness when she was younger, or even about her losing her son, had her words twisted. She had worked for Laura for the past eight years, during which time Laura had led a completely blameless life, yet the skilful way the prosecution lawyer questioned Angie created quite the opposite image. By the time he had finished with her, he'd succeeded in painting a picture of an ambitious, erratic hothead, who on the morning in question had left the shop seething with anger at Jackie because she had to miss her lunch appointment.

Yet it was Belle's testimony which really sealed Laura's fate. Being the younger sister of the victim, with angelic long blonde hair and wide blue eyes which kept filling with tears, was almost enough alone to make her a compelling witness. Yet it was her obvious affection and long-held loyalty for Laura, which made her stumble over her words when forced to admit to her shortcomings, that really sold her to the jury.

Belle told the court that she had been only eight when Jackie first met Laura, who had become almost a member of their family. She stated that she had preferred Laura to her own sister because she was fun and had so much time for her. Belle's lack of spite, even though her sister was now dead, and the way she kept turning from the judge to look at Laura in the dock, as if silently apologizing for her being there, was enough for anyone to trust every word she said.

When asked if she'd ever witnessed Laura fly into a violent rage, she stalled, not wishing to admit to it. But the prosecution pointed out that it was on public record that she had been present at a party in London when Laura pushed a broken glass into another girl's face, and she had in fact been a police witness. Belle protested, quickly stating that this case had been dropped before coming to court.

Just that it had been disclosed was enough. To the jury, whether Laura was prosecuted or not, it was confirmation of her violent disposition. That the younger sister of the victim in this case was attempting to defend her only went to show that Laura was a practised manipulator.

Belle said that she believed it would have been better for her sister if she had distanced herself from Laura after

Barney died. But her voice quavered as she added, 'How could she? Laura had no one else, and Jackie felt responsible for her loss.'

When the prosecution asked Belle what her sister had said to her on the telephone that last morning, Belle began to sob.

'"I've got important things to say to Laura which she isn't going to like," she blurted out. "And I'm afraid of what she might do."'

When asked what she thought these important things might be, Belle replied that she thought Jackie was tired of being an emotional and financial crutch to her old friend.

By then Laura was completely bewildered, for if Jackie had had anything unpleasant to say to her, she would have come over to Edinburgh to say it to her face. She certainly wouldn't have put on a show of being upset to get her over to her place. But while it could be said that Jackie had been an emotional crutch for her, she had never used her as a financial one.

The defence did their best to fight back, but their cross-examination of the witnesses couldn't disprove anything they had said. They went to town on Roger, insisting that he had a long-standing grudge against Laura because she had encouraged Jackie to move to Scotland, and that he had always been jealous because his wife was so fond of Barney. Roger reluctantly admitted he did have a grudge against Laura, not for the reasons stated, but because she had always been a bad influence on his wife, and because she used her.

Even under oath, not one witness would admit that Jackie had been drinking heavily for some months before her death or that she had several lovers.

As these witnesses appeared to be honest, upright people, it was hardly surprising that the jury chose to believe Laura was as malicious as they suggested.

It was a unanimous 'guilty' verdict. The judge proclaimed Laura 'An affront to womenkind, for she had not only viciously taken another's life, but had then sort to malign her character, distressing her victim's family still further'.

When Laura was brought back to Cornton Vale to begin her life sentence she was beside herself with rage. This was so apparent that she was put on suicide watch, and both prison officers and the other prisoners gave her a wide berth for fear of what she might do to them. She paced the floor of her cell like a caged animal, cursing a legal system that had failed her.

Perhaps because that level of anger was impossible to sustain, she had eventually sunk into complete apathy. She stopped raging at anyone who came near her, barely spoke, and spent hours lying on her bunk staring mindlessly at the ceiling. It was only when it was put to her that she might very well find herself placed in the psychiatric ward if she continued this way that she began to do the work she was given, ate her meals, read books in her spare time and occasionally held brief conversations with other women on her block. But if the officers thought this was a sign she was at last accepting her sentence, they were wrong. She just didn't care about anything any more.

The letter from Stuart had partially woken her from that apathy, making her notice her bedraggled hair, her ragged nails and the texture of her skin, but not enough to feel hope, excitement or even fear.

Yet she felt all those things now, and she wasn't sure she liked it, for if all her senses and emotions were completely awakened, how would she be able to stand being in here?

'I believe you.' Those three little words meant so much to her. Yet she didn't dare allow her hopes to be raised for fear of how it would be if Stuart failed her.

'Have faith,' he'd said. Like it was so easy just to put all your trust in another person. Trust wasn't something that had ever come naturally to her.

But she did know that Stuart couldn't help her unless she helped him. If he believed that raking over her life might give them a clue as to who did kill Jackie, then that was what she must do.

Picking up a notepad and Biro, she thought back to the day she first met Jackie.

It was one of those searingly hot days when the tar on the roads begins to melt and trickle out from under the asphalt. As a small child she could remember all the children in the street searching for lollipop sticks to poke the tar, and they'd compete to see who could make the biggest tar ball by winding the stick round and round. But such hot weather usually came in July or August when the leaves on the trees were lank with dust and soot, the milk went off so fast it had to be kept in a bucket of cold water with a cloth over it, and the butcher stopped displaying meat in his shop window.

But in 1961 the hot weather came in May, when many of the trees were still leafless. Laura met Jackie on the 24th, a date engraved on her memory because it was also Jackie's seventeenth birthday.

It was the year the Russians succeeded in putting the first man into space. Just that morning Laura was working in the Home and Colonial grocery shop in Crouch End in North London, when she overheard a customer claiming that the reason it was so hot, so early in the year, was because scientists were tampering with nature by firing rockets up through the earth's atmosphere.

Fortunately it was a Wednesday and early closing. Laura had already decided she would spend the afternoon at the open-air swimming pool just along the road.

She had put her clothes in the locker and was just pinning the key to her new blue polka-dotted swimsuit, when a redheaded girl in an emerald-green costume came running through the footbath, tripped and fell, banging her head on the floor.

Laura ran over to her, concerned because she'd gone down with such a crash.

'Bugger it,' the girl said as Laura helped her up. 'I suppose I'll get a lump on my forehead now. And on my birthday too!'

She was a bit shaken up, so Laura got a wad of cotton wool from the attendant, soaked it in cold water and held it to the girl's head.

'I'm Jackie,' the girl said, wincing at the cold water. 'Do you think it will make it better or worse if I go back to sit in the sun? I only came here to sunbathe, but I couldn't resist pushing this fat bloke in the pool and his mate came chasing after me to throw me in too. I didn't want to get my hair wet because I'm having a party tonight.'

Laura couldn't help but smile, for the injured girl was attractive in every way. Her hair was the colour of new pennies, she had a sprinkling of freckles on her nose, green eyes and a perfect figure. Her breathless explanation of what she'd been up to was so warm and friendly that it was as if she already considered Laura a new friend.

'I'm Laura, and happy birthday,' she said. 'But I think you should sit down in the shade until you're sure you're okay.'

'You sound like my mother,' Jackie replied, grinning. 'Are you with anyone?'

'No, I'm on my own,' Laura said. 'It's the first time I've been here.'

'Great, that means you can stay with me and chat,' Jackie said. 'There are a few people I know out there, but no one I want to spend the afternoon with.'

Laura never told Jackie how much that friendly invitation meant to her. To have done so would have meant she'd have had to admit how desperately lonely she'd been for the past year.

She had left the house in Barnes for good in the Easter holidays the previous year, about six weeks after her trouble with Vincent. She'd planned her exit carefully, for she wanted to leave him with the nagging anxiety that she might retaliate at a later date. During those few weeks she'd systematically helped herself to money from his wallet, never enough to alert him to what she was doing, but she managed to get £35. She found her birth certificate too, and her medical card, and she also applied for a National Insurance number so that she was totally prepared to get a job.

It was torture staying in the house for those few weeks. She knew Vincent thought her silence about what he'd done meant he was safe, but that also meant he might pounce on her again if an opportunity arose. Whenever she got home and found her mother was out, she went straight back out too. She jammed a chair under the handle of her bedroom door in the evening so he couldn't walk in. But that still didn't stop him trying to waylay her as she came out of the bathroom, or sitting watching her as she washed up in the kitchen. Every hour she was in the house with him she felt menaced; she was nervy and found it hard to eat anything at all when he was around.

She had been looking in the *Evening Standard* for somewhere to live for some time, and had been to see several bedsitting rooms, but the ones she felt she could afford on low wages were all so dirty and poky that she'd begun to despair. However, on the day after Easter Monday she went to see one in Crouch Hill in Hornsey, and realized this was as good as she was ever going to get.

Nearby Crouch End was a nice place, though Finsbury Park in the other direction was not so good, and the room on the second floor was small. But it was very clean, the sink and cooker were hidden in a cupboard, and the windows overlooked gardens. The shared bathrooms were all decent enough, and as the landlord told her that all the other tenants were business people, she didn't think it would be too rough. He was concerned that she was so young, even though she'd said she was seventeen, and that was the point when she invented her big lie.

'My parents died when I was small,' she said. 'I was living with an aunt who was my guardian, but she felt I was old enough to fend for myself when she went off to live in France. I'm going to college in September, but until then I'm going to get some secretarial work.'

Maybe he felt sorry for her, for he agreed she could have the room. But he made her pay a month's rent in advance and said he'd evict her if she ever got behind with the rent, or had any parties. With that he gave her the keys and her rent book, and the room was hers.

The next problem was moving out of Barnes. She could only do it when everyone was out, but as it was the Easter holidays her mother expected her to go everywhere with her and the little ones. She had a suitcase packed and ready under her bed, and finally, on the last Friday of the holidays, she resorted to pretending to be violently sick just minutes before they were all about to go to the cinema.

There was no kiss goodbye, no concerned 'I hope you feel better soon', or even an offer to stay home and take care of her. Instead her mother said, *'This is just like you, Laura. I arrange a treat and you have to spoil it somehow.'*

Laura watched them with tears flowing down her cheeks as they walked along the road to the bus stop. Freddy was holding her mother's hand, Meggie and Ivy skipping along excitedly in front, and she knew she would never see them again while they still lived under Vincent's roof. He would malign her as soon as he was told she was gone; she could just imagine him strutting around the house reeling off all the things he had given her, and how ungrateful she'd been.

She waited half an hour before she left, just in case they came back for something. Then she wrote a brief note to say that she hated school so she was getting a job and somewhere else to live, and placed it on the hall table with her house keys.

On the bus and tube ride to Finsbury Park she thought how her mother would rage because she'd thrown away the chance of going to university for the short-term pleasure of no more studying. Laura doubted it would ever cross June's mind that she'd run away from Vincent.

She found the job in the Home and Colonial shop in Crouch End the very next day. She didn't want to work in a shop, especially not weighing up cheese and bacon with her hair under a white net. But as she walked in there to buy some groceries she saw the sign on the window that they had a vacancy and applied there and then, purely because it was so close to her room. She told herself it was just a stop-gap until something better came along.

She had thought living in fear of what Vincent might do to her was the worst thing that could ever happen to her, and that as soon as she got away everything would be fine. But that wasn't so. She was frightened, lonely and missed her mother and the little ones so badly she cried if she dared think about them.

At work she could cope, even though the other staff were mainly older married women and didn't want to bother with her. But when she got back to her room in the evening the feeling of total isolation was so bad that she would often crawl into bed and cry herself to sleep. For as long as she could remember she'd always had chores to do, the younger ones to take care of, and in later years a lot of homework. She might have felt hard done by sometimes, but now she was experiencing having nothing to do and no one to care for, there was a huge hole in the centre of her life which she had to idea how to fill.

All through the summer months, she went into parks on Sundays, in the hope she'd meet someone of her own age in a similar plight. She did see many other young girls, but they were never alone. She would watch them walking hand in hand with a boyfriend, or giggling with a friend, and wish desperately that she had someone.

At Christmas she cried nearly all day, imagining her brother and sisters' joy as they opened their presents. She didn't have a single Christmas card, let alone a present. When her sixteenth birthday came in January it was just as bad, and by then she'd come to think that this was how it would be for ever.

Then, out of the blue, along came the chance encounter with Jackie that suddenly transformed her life.

They stayed by the pool that afternoon chatting as though they'd known each other for years. It was all about records, boys, makeup and clothes, and the party Jackie was having that evening.

'You must come too,' she said, her green eyes dancing with excitement. 'Come home with me when we leave here. If you want to change for the party you can borrow something of mine.'

'I can't do that,' Laura said, astounded at the invitation.

'Yes you can,' Jackie grinned. 'I can guess what you'll do

if I don't make you come home with me. You'll go on home and then bottle out of coming later. I can't let that happen, can I?'

She was right. Laura probably would have been too scared to go to the party alone. Back in her room she would have started to doubt that the tale she'd first told her landlord about her dead parents and her guardian, which she continued to tell anyone who asked, including Jackie, would stand up to more rigorous questioning. She would also be afraid of wearing the wrong clothes or just not sounding right.

On the way to Jackie's house she ran into a record shop and bought a copy of 'Runaway' by Del Shannon that was currently in the Top Ten. Laura remembered feeling it was a bad omen and that soon she would be exposed as a fraud.

But it didn't turn out to be a bad omen, for within an hour or two Laura discovered Jackie didn't care about people's backgrounds, how they dressed, spoke or even where they lived. She got that from her parents.

Frank and Lena Thompson were artists. Frank worked as a cartoonist for the *Beano* comic, and Lena designed greetings cards, and the only word Laura knew at that time which would describe them was bohemian. Even their own children called them by their Christian names, and they appeared to have no regard for convention. Their house in Duke's Avenue in Muswell Hill was a large one, with the kind of good-quality but scruffy furniture that could only be inherited.

Frank had a full, bushy beard, and wore paint-splattered corduroy trousers and a shapeless jumper, while Lena wore a dress which looked suspiciously like a Victorian petticoat. She too had hair the colour of new pennies, but it was long and plaited and she wound the plaits round her head like a crown. Laura had never met people like them before. If she'd passed them in the street she might have taken them for a couple of extras from some weird film.

Yet from the moment Laura walked into their vast, astoundingly untidy kitchen, she wished she had been born into their family, for there was an all-pervading sense of love and warmth amidst the chaos.

Toby and Belle, Jackie's younger brother and sister, twelve and eight respectively, watched by their mother, were icing a birthday cake for Jackie. It reminded Laura of one in a cartoon, large and lopsided, with bright pink icing dripping down the sides. They had smeared and dropped icing everywhere, including their clothes and faces, yet Lena sat casually drinking a cup of tea, unconcerned by the mess.

'We're going to write "Happy Birthday Jackie" in chocolate icing,' Belle trilled out.

Maybe it was because Belle was a similar age to Ivy that Laura felt an instant affection for Jackie's little sister. She was supremely confident, with her golden hair, blue eyes, pink cheeks, dimples and the cutest little nose, but it was her willingness to accept a complete stranger as a friend that touched Laura the most.

'You'll have to wait until the pink icing dries,' she said, smiling at the child.

'We don't usually worry about such refinements in this household,' Lena said with a chuckle. 'But as you seem to know about these things, maybe you could instruct Belle.'

Jackie explained how they'd met at the swimming pool, and that she'd invited Laura back for the party.

'You're very welcome, Laura,' Lena said with the kind of smile that proved she meant what she said. 'But I hope my birthday girl explained that our parties tend to be rather mad affairs.'

*

It *was* a mad sort of party, for there appeared to be no organization about numbers of guests, or even what time it was to start. People arrived in dribs and drabs as early as five o'clock, some bringing plates or bowls of food, others with drink, all of which was plonked unceremoniously around the kitchen. There were children of Belle's and Toby's age, a great many adults, and about sixteen or so teenagers who seemed almost as eccentric as the adults.

Music blared out from the large sitting room at the front of the house. 'Runaway' was played over and over again, along with Roy Orbison, Elvis Presley and the Everly Brothers, but every now and then an adult would come in and put on Frank Sinatra or something equally old-fashioned. The younger children chased around the house, the adults moved on out into the overgrown garden for more serious drinking, while Jackie and her friends took over the kitchen.

Laura didn't bother to change out of her pink and white spotted sheath dress when she saw that Jackie intended to wear a pair of boy's jeans and a plain white cotton shirt which she tied in a knot at her waist. 'I like myself in jeans,' she said when Laura looked at her in surprise. 'You are the frilly type. I'm not.'

That evening everything Laura had hitherto imagined about what went on in middle-class homes was turned upside down. She saw adult women getting drunk and danc-ing like teenagers and grown men playing with small chil-dren. No one seemed the least concerned about mess, noise or what the younger people were getting up to, yet strangely enough it was these friends of Jackie's who seemed to be the most sensible. One girl in four-inch stiletto winklepickers and a beehive hairdo took it upon herself to wash up. And a Teddy boy in a pink drape jacket swept up a broken glass from the kitchen floor.

Yet to Laura the most wonderful thing of all was that she was totally accepted by everyone. No one asked her awkward questions about where she came from; they didn't appear to notice that she wasn't as well spoken as they were. She almost felt that she could announce her father was in prison, her mother living in sin with an old man who'd wanted to have sex with her, and that she worked in the Home and Colonial, and they wouldn't raise an eyebrow.

Laura tucked Belle into bed around ten that night when she was almost keeling over with tiredness and Lena slung her arm around her drunkenly as she came out of the child's bedroom and declared that she was 'a poppet'. Later a boy called Dave asked her to dance with him, and as he held her tightly to 'It's Now or Never' by Elvis Presley, he asked her if he could take her to the pictures the following evening.

By midnight the party had dwindled to just a dozen or so of the older people and Jackie insisted that Laura stay the night. 'You can go to work from here,' she said with a grin. 'I'll lend you a clean pair of knickers.'

It must have been after two when Laura finally got into the spare twin bed in her friend's room, and in the darkness she heard Jackie murmur sleepily, 'You know, I think you are going to be my best friend for ever.'

Looking back with an adult perspective, and a great deal more knowledge about Jackie's early years, Laura felt she understood now why she came to that conclusion, although she'd made it rather prematurely. Jackie had floated through her childhood with boundless love and encouragement and had never had a moment of feeling insecure or worthless. She'd had nothing to rage against, nothing to fight for, and while not spoiled in a material way, for her parents were not rich, she'd been given boundless freedom to mix with whoever she liked, go wherever she wanted.

Jackie saw Laura as being intrepid, worldly, practical and independent, all because she lived alone. She marvelled that Laura could cook a meal in her bedsitter, do her own washing and get herself to work on time. But the clincher was almost certainly that at only sixteen Laura was all alone in the world. Her parents were the kind who welcomed waifs and strays joyfully, and Jackie was just following suit.

From that day on, Laura almost became a member of the Thompson family. Lena often remarked how good she was with her younger children, and she liked the way Laura thought nothing of doing a pile of ironing or cleaning her kitchen for her. Frank often said she was an answer to his and Lena's prayers because she'd made Jackie more appreciative of them.

Lena did eventually ask her more about her parents' death and Aunt Mabel who had become her guardian. By then Laura had the story off pat: she said her parents died in a car accident when she was only four so she remembered very little about them, but her father had been a vet. As for her Aunt Mabel, she embellished her into a kindly but scatty spinster who had done her best as her guardian for years, but felt Laura was old enough to look after herself now. Lena tutted with disapproval, saying she thought it very irresponsible of her to clear off abroad while Laura was still so young, but that she admired Laura for her lack of bitterness and ability to cope alone.

'You'll go far,' she said, giving Laura a cuddle. 'You are bright, level-headed and practical. And if you want a stand-in mother, then you've got me.'

All through that first summer of 1961, the two girls spent at least two evenings a week together, and all day on Sundays. Jackie worked as a copy typist in the City, so she only worked Monday till Friday, and Laura hated that she had to work in the shop on Saturdays. But Jackie invariably came to meet her after work so that they could get dressed and do each other's hair together before going out.

Too young to go into pubs, they mostly hung about in coffee bars and parks and went to the rollerskating rink looking for boys. They giggled and flirted, but the relationships they formed with boys never went beyond necking in the park or going to the pictures. Jackie always said she wasn't going to go 'all the way' until she met the boy she intended to marry, and that he would have to be very rich as well as handsome because she had no intention of living in poverty, even for love.

Laura agreed that she felt the same, but she never told Jackie she had real, first-hand experience of poverty and had been put off the idea of any kind of intimacy with men because of Vincent. Sometimes she ached to spill out the truth about her background, especially how much she missed her younger siblings, but she was afraid to. As each week passed she seemed to add more embroidery to the life she'd shared with dotty Aunt Mabel, and the house they'd lived in on Holland Park. She felt she was too far down the road to do a U-turn and admit it wasn't true because Jackie might despise her for lying.

As the summer slipped by Laura had another problem beyond the lies she'd told. Her wages at the Home and Colonial were very low, and by the time she'd paid the rent on her room and bought food, there was precious little money left for clothes, bus fares or any kind of entertainment.

Jackie's parents let her keep her entire wages to spend on herself. Laura felt compelled to keep up with her, and the only way she could do it was by stealing. Even before she met Jackie she had been in the habit of helping herself to a few groceries and the odd blouse, skirt or the swimsuit she'd been wearing when she met her friend, but suddenly she found that she needed more cash.

The solution presented itself when she had gone up to Oxford Street to steal a new dress. She found a pretty blue one in Selfridges, which she just tried on in the changing room, then put her own clothes over it and walked out, but then she wished she had money for some new shoes.

While wandering around Marks and Spencer she observed a woman getting a cash refund for a garment which didn't fit. The assistant didn't ask for the woman's receipt, just opened the till and gave her the money back. There and then Laura slipped a cardigan into her bag and left the shop. An hour later she was at the other Marks and Spencer down the bottom of Oxford Street claiming a refund for it.

It was so simple and easy that she hugged herself with delight at her cleverness. She felt no guilt – after all, Marks and Spencer was a big company and they could afford it.

From then on she had a regular source of cash. She varied the branches she went to, always making certain she claimed her refunds at times when the shops were busy, and on these expeditions she invariably helped herself to items in other shops too. Having a wardrobe full of beautiful, expensive new clothes helped her to forget the image of 'Stinky Wilmslow', and gave her the confidence she needed to keep up the fictitious background she'd created for herself.

Laura shook her head despairingly as she thought back to those days. It was a miracle she was never caught, and even more surprising that Jackie was never suspicious of how she managed to live and dress so well on a shop assistant's wages. But then, Jackie was an innocent in those days; she buried her head in glossy magazines and aspired to the kind of glamorous life she saw depicted there. She saw her family as being quite poor because they had no car, didn't eat out in fancy restaurants or go abroad, and she had no idea of what a struggle life was for most ordinary people.

Yet it was Jackie who persuaded Laura she could do far better than working on the bacon counter of the Home and Colonial, and with her friend's encouragement she got a job as a junior wages clerk in Pawson and Leaf, a wholesale company by St Paul's Cathedral.

Pawson and Leaf was an old-fashioned company that supplied everything from corsets to haberdashery to the retail trade. It had a Dickensian atmosphere in its four or five dusty, gloomy floors filled with goods which had to be picked out when a customer rang in with an order. The wages department was on the top floor, with a wonderful panoramic view of London, but when Laura was sent with inquiries to any of the various departments below, she found it all quite fascinating. There was a huge steel chute, something like a helter-skelter, and once the goods had been picked out and invoiced, they were tied up and dropped down the chute to the packing department in the basement. Quite often the younger lads would slide down it during the lunch hour or at the end of the day, accompanied by shrieks and yells.

Yet it wasn't just that it was a more fun place to work, or that she earned two pounds more a week and had the whole weekend off that delighted Laura, it was the whole package of working in the City. It felt so sophisticated to catch the tube to work and never again to have to wear an overall and a net covering her hair. She was proud to say she was 'in wages', it was good working alongside people of a similar age, and she often met Jackie straight from work so they could go home together.

She had begun work at Pawson and Leaf in early December and there was already a buzz of excitement in the air about the Christmas party to be held on Christmas

Eve. Laura heard it was always a great opportunity to get off with someone you fancied, and she was told many stories about staff who had 'had it off' in the post room, a drunken telephonist who was put down the chute, and an elderly floor manager who'd had too many drinks and fell asleep and got locked in the building for the whole of the Christmas holiday.

The girls, it seemed, were in the habit of bringing in their party dresses to change into, so when Jackie suggested the night before the Christmas party that they should go to a pub she knew in Moorgate frequented by bankers and stockbrokers, Laura was all for it. That meant she'd get two opportunities to wear the stunning midnight-blue lace dress she'd recently stolen from a West End shop.

'It's time we moved on from boys,' Jackie said airily. 'We are never going to meet anyone rich in Crouch End. All the local boys want is sex and they don't even take you out anywhere. The blokes that stop in this pub for a few drinks before going home are all men of the world, they'll know how to treat us properly.'

Although the girls had had a lot of fun locally during the summer, since the weather got colder and wetter they'd been stuck for places to go in the evenings. On Saturday nights they often went dancing at The Empire in Leicester Square, but they rarely met anyone they liked enough to make a further date with. Jackie had been saying for quite some time that she thought the best men, the ones with smart suits, good jobs and cars, went to pubs. But it wasn't really done for girls to go into pubs as it sent out a signal they were there to be picked up. However, at the pub in Moorgate they could pretend they'd just left an office party and were on their way home.

Laura chuckled to herself when she recalled how she'd changed into her dress at the end of the day in the toilets at

Pawson and Leaf. Even now, when over the years she'd had many gorgeous dresses, that one was still in her top five. The diaphanous lace sheath dress had a deep scooped neck and three-quarter sleeves, but for decency's sake it had a built-in skimpy petticoat beneath it. With a mahogany rinse on her hair, which she'd put up in a beehive, sheer black stockings and four-inch stilettos, Laura could have passed for twenty-one, when in fact she was only a couple of weeks short of seventeen.

It wasn't far to go down Cheapside to Moorgate to meet Jackie but her excitement grew even stronger because several men whistled at her, even though she was clutching her coat round her tightly because it was so cold. Jackie was waiting for her at the tube station, and she got two little crowns of tinsel out of her pocket for them to wear.

Once in the pub they went straight to the toilets to take off their coats, put on more lipstick and check each other's appearance.

Jackie was wearing an emerald-green satin dress with a boat neck, her auburn hair in loose waves on her shoulders, and she looked like a film star, but when she saw what Laura was wearing she looked stunned.

'You're not just pretty, you're beautiful,' she gasped. 'That dress, your hair! I can't believe it!'

Jackie had often told her she was pretty, but Laura had never really believed it. This was partly because of being insulted at school, but also, next to her friend with her vivid colouring, poise and bounce, she had always felt drab. But she could see in the mirror that the colour of the dress seemed to make her skin glow, and the rinse made her hair shine with coppery lights. Maybe 'beautiful' was an exaggeration, but she had certainly never seen herself looking so good before.

As Jackie had predicted, The Plume of Feathers was full

of businessmen, and from the moment the girls walked out of the toilets, they got attention. They were not the only girls in the bar, there were perhaps ten or so others, but they were certainly the two most attractive ones. They didn't even have to buy a drink; the barman just waved their money away when they asked for two Babychams and gestured vaguely to one end of the bar to say it had already been taken care of.

Three drinks later they were already feeling tipsy for neither of them was used to drinking, so after a brief confab in the toilets they decided they'd better not have any more, and that Roger and Steven, the two youngest men in the bar, were the ones they should encourage.

They were both undeniably good-looking, tall and smart in their pinstriped suits, and amusing too. Steven worked on the Stock Exchange, Roger for an insurance company, and though Laura privately thought that they were out of their league with a couple of twenty-four-year-olds, she didn't dare say so because Jackie was really smitten by blond, blue-eyed Roger.

But being left with Steven was hardly like drawing the short straw. He was rather like Dirk Bogarde, with his dark hair and crinkly, smiley eyes, and the way he looked at Laura made her feel really desirable.

Later, the men took them by taxi to an Italian restaurant in Villiers Street, just off The Strand. Jackie kept pinching Laura's knee under the table, her secret signal that she was prepared to go anywhere, do anything with Roger. Perhaps it was fortunate that both men were going home to their families for Christmas the following day, and didn't appear to be anxious to stay out half the night.

'So where do you live then?' Jackie asked, tucking into spaghetti bolognese as if she hadn't eaten for a week.

'In Kensington,' Roger replied. 'We share a flat with a

couple of other chaps. It's very squalid, you'd be appalled.'

They made the girls laugh telling them how their landlady raged at them for having a kitchen full of empty beer bottles and never cleaning up, and said she'd seen pigs living in better conditions. 'We'll have to do something about it in the New Year,' Roger said with a wide grin, 'or we'll be chucked out.'

'We'll come over and help you,' Jackie volunteered, once again pinching Laura under the table. 'I don't believe it can be that bad when you two look so smart.'

'That's down to a laundry service,' Steven said. 'But it's a good thing we're going home tomorrow because I haven't got one clean pair of socks left. But what about you two? Do you still live at home?'

Laura said nothing while Jackie explained about her family and then went on to tell the men how organized and independent Laura was.

'Her room is spotless. She cooks proper meals, she hangs her clothes up in groups of colours, and she even cleans the bathroom for everyone else. I wouldn't be like that. I'm far too messy.'

'Then perhaps Laura had better come over and sort us out,' Roger said.

Laura wasn't sure she liked being portrayed as a paragon of domestic virtue. She thought it made her sound very dull. But Steven leaned across the table and lightly touched her cheek. 'I've always found that beautiful girls are the worst kind of sluts,' he said. 'I'm really glad you aren't one.'

After the meal in the Italian restaurant, the four of them had walked up to Trafalgar Square to see the Christmas tree. Roger and Jackie kept stopping to kiss, but although Steven kissed Laura quite a bit too, mostly they talked. He told her his family lived in Hastings. He even described his younger brother and sister, and explained that his father was a doctor and his mother sang in a choir. She could imagine his family – nice, well-bred, upper-middle-class people, living in a comfortable, well-cared-for house. None of that was extra-ordinary; just looking at Steven with his good manners, highly polished shoes, immaculate white shirt and well-pressed suit told her about his background.

But what was extraordinary was that he assumed she came from a similar one. Several times he'd said things like, 'But of course your family must be just the same.' She had simply smiled and nodded, mainly because she didn't feel up to launching into her usual story about her dead parents and her Aunt Mabel.

His goodnight kiss before she and Jackie got into the taxi to go home was tender and lingering. He'd held her face in his hands and said that he wished he hadn't promised to go home for so long, and that he'd ring her as soon as he got back. She knew he would too, for he'd paid the taxi driver in advance, and he'd double-checked that he had her phone number written down right.

Jackie was ecstatic as both girls waved goodbye out of the back window of the taxi. 'What a couple of dreamboats!' she squealed. 'You and I are made, Laura. No more pimply-faced louts for us. A world of glamour and sophistication awaits us.'

As the taxi sped through the streets towards Crouch End, Jackie nodded off against Laura's shoulder. But Laura was wide awake, her pulse racing and her mind whirling at the possibilities ahead in the New Year.

The taxi dropped Laura off first, Jackie rousing herself enough to say she was to ring and tell her what her works party the following day was like. Laura let herself in, switched on the light in the hall and darted up the stairs to the second floor before it turned itself off.

She'd grown quite fond of her bedsitter. In summer when

the trees in the garden below were in full leaf, she could look out on to a sea of green. The room was small and square, but it had everything she needed, and she was always rearranging the furniture to make the most of the space. At present she had the small table in front of the window and her single bed, covered in a dark green bedspread, up against the opposite wall so it looked like a sofa. With the bedside light on and the gas fire lit, it was cosy, and she'd made it more homely with a few posters and bright scatter cushions.

'I don't need to be ashamed of it,' she murmured to herself as she took her coat off and hung it up in the wardrobe.

She took one more look at herself in her dress before taking it off. Her hair was coming loose now and she had specks of mascara under her eyes, but she decided she didn't have to be ashamed of how she looked either. Steven had said he thought she was beautiful, and that was how she felt. As she carefully hung her dress up on a hanger she smiled to herself, feeling a little like Cinderella after the ball.

That Christmas, which Laura spent with the Thompson family, was the happiest she'd ever known. Not just because she was surrounded by good people and stuffed with delicious food, not even because the decorations, presents and games were far better than anything she was used to. The source of her happiness was the way Steven had treated her.

Jackie was convinced she was in love with Roger. She kept drifting off while she mooned about him, and she was counting the hours until 27 December, when she was going to see him again. She assumed that Laura felt the same about Steven, but Laura couldn't quite bring herself to admit how it really was for her.

On Boxing Day night when the girls went to bed, Jackie

could talk about nothing except Roger. 'I gave him my number at work and at home. Which do you think he'll phone me on tomorrow?'

'Here, in the evening, I expect,' Laura replied. 'But be careful what you say about me, won't you?'

Jackie sat up in her bed, looking across at her friend with a puzzled expression. 'What do you mean?'

Laura was putting some rollers in her hair. 'Well, I'd rather you didn't say too much about my parents dying and my aunt leaving. It makes me sound a bit tragic.'

'I don't think it does. It just makes people admire you more for being strong,' Jackie said a little indignantly.

Laura was embarrassed then. She went over and sat on her friend's bed, but didn't really know what to say.

She couldn't tell Jackie the truth about herself, not after so long, but she was afraid of this lie going on and on, repeated again and again for the rest of her life. 'I just want to be like anyone else,' she said eventually. 'You know what I mean. Normal.'

'Well, you certainly can't invent a family you haven't got,' Jackie said. 'You weren't think of doing that, were you?'

'No, of course not,' Laura said quickly. 'But I did want to play down what happened.'

'I won't say anything more than that you are my best friend,' Jackie replied. 'I'll leave it up to you to tell Steven as much or as little as you like. But for all we know we may never get the opportunity to tell either Roger or Steven anything. They might have girlfriends, they might not even like us.'

Laura put down her Biro and rubbed her eyes. She had only jotted down the major points of those early days with Jackie, barely a whole page. But the meeting with Steven and Roger was an important milestone in both their lives for more reasons than that they became their first lovers, and that much later Jackie would marry Roger.

Laura hadn't of course known then what was in store for either of them, but that wasn't the point when she should, and could, have come clean about her background to Jackie.

But she didn't, and so the lie was spread further and further like a tumour. It was of course benign back then, but she might have known that if she didn't cut it out it would become malignant.

It was one of the newspapers who exposed it at the start of her trial. She didn't know who told them the story of her parents being killed while she was still a child, but they obviously checked it out and found it wasn't true. It didn't take them long to discover her real father had been a criminal, or for that matter to find plenty of people who were prepared to reveal she had lied to them too.

'A life built on lies' was one of the headlines, and Laura could remember thinking that would make an appropriate epitaph for her.

4

Belle got up from her chair as the telephone rang. 'I'll just answer that,' she said, smiling at Stuart. 'It might be someone wanting to come and stay.'

Stuart was glad of a moment or two alone to consider how he should proceed with Belle. She had been very surprised when he turned up unannounced at the door of Kirkmay House in Crail. In fact she had been almost giddy with excitement until he told her he'd only just heard about her sister's death as he'd been out of the country, and that he'd come to offer his condolences. He found it rather disquieting that on opening the door to him she didn't immediately realize that was why he'd come. Had she forgotten what good friends he and Jackie had been when he worked for her?

He gazed reflectively out of the window to Marketgate beyond, thinking what a coincidence it was that Belle's house was the one he remembered from when he used to come here on holiday as a child. He and his family never stayed in this village; they rented a cottage by the harbour in Cellardyke, a smaller fishing village further back down the coast. But they would walk here sometimes, clambering over rocks along the beach, and his father always used to buy crab to take home for their tea.

Sometimes they came up the steep wynds from the harbour to the main road so his parents could have a drink in the East Neuk Hotel, and he and his brother and sister would go exploring. Once they had slipped into this very garden to pick some apples from a tree, and an old lady had chased them out brandishing a stick. They were sure she was a witch, and that the big old house was haunted; his sister used to have nightmares about it, prompted by stuff he and his brother made up about the place.

It was weird enough that Belle and Charles had uprooted themselves from London to open a guest house here, but even weirder that they'd bought the very house which was imprinted on his memory.

Crail was very quaint and pretty, perhaps the prettiest of all the villages along this stretch of the Fife coast, but it was hardly the kind of place he would expect Belle and Charles to be attracted to. Belle had always been the kind of woman who craved excitement, sophisticated entertainment, smart shops and hordes of people around her. As for Charles, he was the original city slicker, with handmade suits, fast sports cars, and an eye for the ladies. Neither of them had the kind of servile mentality to run a guest house successfully, and as far as he knew they had no great love of Scotland either, not like Jackie.

Jackie had fallen for its charms twenty years ago when she was visiting Laura in Edinburgh. It had been Stuart's idea to take the girls and Barney over the bridge to Fife to show them around, but he hadn't expected the elegant and poised Jackie to be so enthusiastic. She had raved about Fife all the way back to Edinburgh, and though he was pleased he had found something to impress Laura's very worldly friend with, he didn't realize that she really had lost her heart to the place.

She bought a tiny fisherman's cottage in Cellardyke soon afterwards and her passion for the area grew with every visit. Then she bought tumbledown Brodie Farm, a few miles inland from Crail. A great many people laughed at her grandiose plans for it, and her claims that she was going to live there permanently once the renovations were complete.

But she had done exactly as she said she would, in fact she'd told Stuart once that she felt Fife was her spiritual home and nowhere else made her feel quite so happy.

Stuart was still puzzled as to why Belle followed her sister here. He could understand her wanting to be nearer Jackie, and that Charles was lured by the golf in nearby St Andrews. But it would have made far more sense for them to buy a place in Edinburgh where they could still live as they had in London, with all this on their doorstep.

So far he and Belle had only made small talk. He'd admired her house and garden, mentioned his childhood holidays here, and she asked what he had been doing over the past few years and seemed surprised he'd never married. He had expected her to launch into a graphic account of the murder and trial, for as he remembered Belle had been a drama queen, and dramas didn't get any bigger than your sister's murder. Yet apart from saying 'I've had a terrible time,' she hadn't enlarged on it.

He wanted and needed her to talk about it, to pour it all out so he could see another perspective, but he had to be very careful, because if he let it slip that he'd studied the case, and been to see Laura, she might suspect he had a hidden agenda.

'What are you going to do now?' he asked, hoping that might make her open up. 'Are you thinking of selling up and going back to London? Or will you stay?'

Belle lit up a cigarette. 'We can't make our minds up,' she said somewhat guardedly, blowing the smoke up to the ceiling. 'I'm sure you can imagine what we've been through since Jackie's death. There have been many times when we've just wanted to run away to a place where there are no reminders. But this house and the friends we've made here are precious to us.'

Stuart nodded. He thought the last part of the reply

sounded insincere and very well rehearsed, for there was something about this beautiful but soulless drawing room which suggested few friends had ever come into it. As a young woman Belle had been a party animal, a vivacious, warm chatterbox who would tell anyone her life story at the drop of a hat. Maybe it was the murder that had changed her, for she was restrained now, and the bubbly personality had become stiff and cool.

But she was still a very beautiful woman. Her natural honey-blonde hair, wide blue eyes and the clarity of her complexion hadn't changed since they first met two decades ago in London. If he hadn't been nursing a broken heart at the time, they might well have become much more than friends for they were a similar age and got on very well.

She was as slim as a whippet in those days, her blonde hair so long she could sit on it. He used to call her Rapunzel, for she had the look of a fairytale princess awaiting a prince who would carry her off to some enchanted land. Her hair was shoulder-length now, she'd gained some weight and her blue eyes looked hard and cold, but she made up for that with her glamour. In pale blue slacks and a cream silk shirt left unbuttoned just low enough to give a glimpse of voluptuous cleavage, with long pink talons and gold jewellery, she could have stepped out of an episode of *Dynasty*.

Kirkmay House suited her image, for it was an impressive, large double-fronted Georgian house with all the grand embellishments of that period. Belle had furnished and decorated it in her own style with sumptuous cream sofas, pale pink carpets, huge gilt-framed mirrors and the kind of curtains, swags and pelmets that must have cost a king's ransom. It would all have been perfect in a similar townhouse in London or Edinburgh, but here in a fishing village it seemed rather overblown and ostentatious. He had been puzzled too when she showed him some of the guest rooms, for none of them appeared to be taken. In June she should have been at least half full.

'What's happening with Brodie Farm?' he asked.

'We don't know yet,' she said, her face tensing. 'We found the will Jackie made back in the early eighties when she split up with Roger. In that she'd left equal shares of her entire estate, Brodie Farm and the London property to Toby and myself. But Roger claims Jackie made another will, in 1988, leaving the property in London to him.'

Stuart nodded, even though he couldn't possibly imagine Jackie making one will, let alone two. She'd always claimed she intended to spend everything she had in her own lifetime. But if she had made one, he would have been very surprised if she hadn't made provision for Roger. They might have been apart for years, but they'd remained very close friends, and Roger had after all funded the first couple of properties she bought.

'He hasn't produced this more recent will yet, and I personally doubt it really exists,' Belle said waspishly. 'So while the lawyers hang fire, I'm looking after Brodie Farm, handling the lettings and keeping it all together. But I can't go on like this. It needs to be settled.'

At that point the telephone rang and Belle hurried to answer it.

'A booking for a long weekend,' she said when she came back. 'I was tempted to say we were fully booked, it's such a drag having people here.'

'A funny thing for a guest-house proprietor to say,' Stuart remarked lightly.

'You'd have to run one to find out just how tedious it can be,' she retorted. 'Most of the guests are earnest walkers who wear anoraks, and the rest are perishing Americans chasing their Scottish roots. I don't know which are the most boring.'

She ranted for some minutes about the tedium of changing bed linen, of cooking breakfasts and feeling her home was not her own. 'Jackie had the right idea, her guests were all self-catering and not in her house,' she ended up. 'But then when she left Roger she said she never wanted to share anything with anyone again.'

Stuart smiled. He remembered Jackie saying such things, but she didn't really mean them. She loved people and was never happier than when she had a houseful.

'Did they ever get divorced?' he asked.

Belle shook her head. 'No, they started proceedings once, then dropped it. Jackie could be very weak about Roger. She couldn't live with him, but she liked to hold him on a string so she could tweak it in whenever she felt like it.'

Stuart thought that remark was rather spiteful, and it was tempting to reciprocate by pointing out that if Jackie hadn't divorced Roger, he might well stand to inherit the bulk of the estate, but he thought better of that, fearing he might be shown the door.

'I know what you're thinking,' she burst out when he made no comment. 'That I shouldn't say such things, not now she's dead. But I get weary of making out she was some kind of saint. Well, she was never that, and she'd have been the first person to say so. But that evil bitch Laura took everything from me, even the right to tell the truth about my own sister.'

Stuart perked up. This was how he remembered Belle – self-centred perhaps, but passionate and with a lot to say.

'The bitch had already heaped guilt on to Jackie for Barney's death,' Belle went on, her cheeks flushing with anger. 'That was why she funded Laura's business, but it didn't stop the cow from pestering her all the time, turning up whenever she felt like it. Even after she'd killed her that wasn't enough for her, she had to destroy Jackie's reputation too by claiming she was a promiscuous lush. A life sentence isn't enough for what she's done.'

Stuart might have wanted to see some real emotion, but he was shocked by such venom. It was well documented that Belle hadn't been vindictive towards Laura during the trial, in fact she came across as not believing Laura could have done it. But he supposed that the guilty verdict and her own grief for her sister had altered her view.

'And your parents and Toby?' he asked, gently trying to draw her away from further malice. 'How are they bearing up?'

'Dad died of a heart attack soon after the murder,' Belle said. 'I blame Laura for that too; he was only seventy-five and in good health until then. Mum's in a nursing home now. As for Toby, well, he's made a fortune designing stage sets, he's become quite a celebrity because of the murder. He milked it for all he was worth. Now he's shot off to Australia without a thought for Mother and me.'

'I'm so sorry about your parents,' Stuart said truthfully. He found it odd Belle thought so badly of her brother, for as he recalled they had once been very close. 'They were very good to me when I first came to London. I feel ashamed I didn't keep in touch with them over the last ten years. But perhaps I could go and see Lena when I go back to London. I'm sure you know how much she encouraged and supported me. I loved going to the house in Muswell Hill.'

'That's gone now of course,' Belle sighed. 'But Mum is close by, and mostly she thinks she's still in Duke's Avenue. I shouldn't bother to go and see her though, she probably won't know you. She hardly knew *me* last time I visited.'

'I know it was an open and shut case against Laura,' Stuart said very cautiously. 'But I found it hard to believe she could have done such a thing. I mean, Jackie was her best friend, and what could have gone wrong to make her react so violently?'

'I might have known you wouldn't believe anything bad of her,' Belle said with a disdainful toss of her head. 'You never could see her for what she really was.'

'I think I did, Belle,' he retorted. 'She hurt me very badly, and one doesn't come through that without seeing the truth about a person. I just can't imagine her stabbing Jackie.'

'She was always mad with jealousy and spite because she could never be the hotshot she wanted to be,' Belle spat out. 'She was devious, manipulative and greedy. She cocked everything up, used people and trampled on their feelings. She watched Jackie succeeding at everything she touched, and she couldn't bear it. At the trial Laura's advocate tried to make out that she loved Jackie, and held no grudge against her for Barney's death, but that wasn't true. She brought it up every time she saw Jackie and she didn't care how miserable it made her. She who was such a terrible mother! We all did more for that poor kid than Laura ever did.'

Stuart couldn't ask why, if this was true, she hadn't said so in court. Admitting he knew what had been said there would alert her to his true motive in coming here today. But it was hard not to say what he felt, for though Belle was right about Laura in some areas, she was very wrong in others.

'Maybe. But we're all flawed, Belle. Few people's lives stand up to close scrutiny, I know mine doesn't.'

'You, who used to think you were so perfect!' she retorted with heavy sarcasm.

Stuart blushed. He knew she was referring to words they'd had years ago. She'd had something of a crush on him when he first arrived in London after splitting up with Laura. He did take her out several times, but it was a mistake on his part. Belle was lovely, but he was too bruised to embark on a sexual relationship, and although he had told her this, she wouldn't give up trying for it. It ended badly and embarrassingly, and Belle had chosen to believe he was some kind of pompous puritan.

'I was hurting then, Belle,' he said reproachfully. 'And I had the image in my head that you were like Laura's little sister. She used to talk about you a lot when we were together. Besides, I'd have been all wrong for you – beautiful Belle was a go-getter, a girl aiming for the stars, you'd have only got the gutter with me.'

He saw a little smirk playing at the corners of her mouth and was relieved she seemed pleased with his explanation.

'Have you seen your folks yet?' she asked.

'I've got no one left here now, that's why I didn't get to hear about Jackie,' Stuart said. 'Mum went out to live in Australia with my sister when my father died. My brother is in Canada. Scots always seem to go to the ends of the earth, don't they? But I intend to stay awhile, visit some old friends, maybe look for some new project to get into. Edinburgh is a happening place these days. I'm staying at the Caledonian at the moment, but I'm going to get a flat on a short lease. If you and Charles fancy coming into town sometime I'll buy you a slap-up dinner.'

He instinctively knew Belle wasn't going to tell him anything more about Jackie, but Charles might have something to say. Stuart had never liked the arrogant know-all, but if he could get him on his own and ply him with drink, who knows what he might reveal?

'By the way, where is Charles today?' he asked. 'Playing golf?'

'Who cares?' she said with a sullen shrug.

'You haven't had a tiff?' As Stuart recalled, they were always falling out.

'Not exactly. Let's say we don't always see eye to eye. This business of the will is getting us both down. We can't go off anywhere, not now I've got to keep my eye on Brodie Farm. We can't make any plans about anything, we are tied. But I'm always quite relieved when he takes off, at least then he's not under my feet.'

'Well, here's my hotel number.' Stuart quickly wrote it down on a business card, then stood up. 'If you want him out from under your feet for an evening, tell him to come and have a drink with me. I will be moving on, but they'll pass on the new number, and wherever I'm staying he'll be able to crash out there.'

'And does the same apply to me?' she said flirtatiously. 'I could do with a day of shopping, a nice meal and a handsome escort.'

'Yes, of course it does,' he said gallantly, but hoping she wouldn't take him up on it. 'That is, if Charles doesn't mind.'

'I don't much care what he minds about any more,' she said blithely. 'It was good to see you again, Stuart, do feel free to call again if you have reason to come out this way. I'll always have a bed here for you.'

That offer sounded very much like she meant sharing her bed and it made him feel uncomfortable. 'You haven't given me your mother's address,' he said as he got to the door. 'Could I have it?'

'Surely you don't want to go there,' she replied, pulling a face. 'It's full of doddery old folk dribbling and wheezing.'

'Not my favourite kind of place to visit,' Stuart agreed. 'But I feel I must go and see her for old times' sake.'

Belle took one of the cards for the guest house and scribbled the nursing-home address on the back.

'Is Roger still at the same address?' he asked. 'I thought I ought to see him too.'

'Yes, still in Kensington. Though why you'd want to look him up I can't imagine! You'll only get chapter and verse on how badly Jackie treated him.'

'He was another person who was good to me when I most needed it,' Stuart said evenly. 'Goodbye, Belle, look after yourself. The clouds will pass.'

Stuart decided against returning to Edinburgh. Instead he walked down to Crail harbour. Everything was just as he remembered, the picturesque tiny cottages huddled up against one another as protection from the harsh weather, the sense of all those men and women who had made their living from the sea for so many centuries. Crail had always been a more prosperous place than its neighbours; in fact he remembered from history lessons at school that for a time it was the wealthiest of the Royal Burghs. Marketplace, the street Belle's house was in, was where merchants sold their goods, and the Dutch influence of the design of the Tolbooth across the street from Kirkmay House was evidence of the important trade and ideas that came to Crail from across the North Sea.

Tourists were bringing new prosperity now. Many of the old cottages had been renovated for holiday lets, and he noted an art gallery, a pottery and a café that would never have been thought of when he was a boy.

But the harbour was still the same, with the crab stall, the boats and the heaps of lobster pots. He glanced up at the high grey stone wall where the old castle had been centuries ago and saw two elderly ladies sitting on a bench having a picnic. Suddenly he was reminded of sitting on that same bench with Laura and Barney some twenty-two years ago. He could see Laura in a pink sundress and Barney with a bucket and spade asking when they were going to look for crabs.

He didn't want those kind of memories, not now Barney was dead and Laura in prison. So he turned round and walked purposefully towards the coastal path to Cellardyke.

As he walked, Stuart carefully analysed everything Belle had said, and the more he thought about it the odder it seemed that she was still so bitter and angry about everything. It was after all two years since Jackie's death.

Maybe the bitterness wasn't through grief alone? It could be that things were bad with Charles, or that she felt trapped in a place she didn't really belong in. They could even have financial problems and were waiting for Jackie's estate to be settled to solve them. Worries about money were always debilitating, just as bad as broken hearts.

As he picked his way along the coastal path, looking at the sun glinting on the sea and the waves washing over the low black rocks which were a feature of this stretch of coast, he tried to turn his thoughts back to happier thoughts of Fiona, Angus and himself as children searching the rock pools for crabs and small fish. But his thoughts wouldn't go the way he wanted them to; the earlier memory of Laura and Barney on that bench had opened a door he'd rather have kept closed.

The day he first met them.

It was right at the end of July '72, a warm, sunny day on the west coast of Scotland, by Castle Douglas. A week earlier he'd finished his five-year apprenticeship as a joiner and he had to decide whether he was going to start up on his own or join another company. It seemed a good idea to have a bit of a holiday first, so he hitch-hiked over to Castle Douglas to look up some old friends who were squatting in an old house there.

It was a disappointment to find all but one of his friends had moved on to Ibiza. Only Ewan was left, and the others had been replaced by a bunch of English hippies. Ewan had always been mad as a bucket of frogs: small and stocky, with flame-red hair which he'd started growing at fifteen and had never cut since. He embraced the whole peace and love thing chapter and verse. He ate brown rice, grew his own dope, consulted the Tarot cards at least once a week and believed every way-out philosophy going. Yet give him a few whiskies and he'd revert to early programming from his father, and he would fight anyone.

The house was not the sturdy, small stone cottage Stuart had expected either, but a rambling, dilapidated old farmhouse at the end of a long rutted track. The London hippies were a welcoming bunch, though, if a little spaced out, and the weather was good, so Stuart thought he might as well stay for a while and help Ewan fix up a few things around the house.

Stuart knew that he was often referred to as a part-time hippy by those who considered themselves the real thing. He wore his hair long, he had the obligatory cheesecloth shirts and flared loons, smoked a bit of dope and listened to Cream, Traffic and Led Zeppelin. But he had always had a work ethic; he had wanted to be a joiner like his father since he was six and old enough to hold a saw. He would hitch-hike to rock concerts and drop a bit of acid now and then at the weekends, but nothing had ever got in the way of going to work and serving his time, for he believed having a trade was all-important

Yet that first week in Castle Douglas, he lay around like all the others smoking dope, listening to them talking about going to Marrakech, or overland to India, and for the first time ever he considered dropping out as they had done.

He was weary of being treated like a kid by the older men at work, of the jokes about his long hair, his girlfriends, and the kind of music he liked. He was an oddity because he didn't down eight pints of beer after work or get into fights, and there was a faint implication that this made him unmanly. But he didn't need alcohol to make himself feel good, he felt that way by doing a job well, by walking through the park, reading a book or playing his guitar. At work the other men had no real conversation and he was often frustrated and irritated by their narrow views. It would be so good to travel, to mix with people with broader outlooks and who wanted to challenge the old regimes.

The day that his life changed for ever started early. He was sleeping on an old mattress on the floor of one of the outhouses, and as there was nothing over the window, the sun came in and woke him just after five. The day before, he'd scrubbed out the room and painted it all white, and as he lay there looking around him, he thought he'd better get up on the roof and check there were no loose tiles, otherwise it would leak when it rained.

All at once he was fired up. If he could get some work near here he could save enough money to travel next winter. Josie, the girl who looked like a Red Indian squaw, had already asked him if he'd like to go to India with her group of friends.

He was still up on the roof at eleven that morning, wearing just a pair of shorts. He'd taken all the tiles off, patched up the felt beneath with some he found in a shed, and he'd nearly finished putting the tiles back when he saw a yellow Volkswagen Beetle driven by a woman coming up the track.

Knowing that none of the others were up yet, he climbed down and waited for the car to reach him.

As it came nearer he saw there was a little boy of about two kneeling up on the back seat. And the woman driving was beautiful.

Everything seemed to go into slow motion then, every detail of the scene in front of him so clear and bright. The long waving grass in the fields either side of the track, the intense blue of the sky, a row of tall fir trees down by the road, the sound of birdsong, and the heat of the sun on his bare shoulders.

The car stopped. The door opened, and she got out, but leaned on the open door.

'Is this Ewan's place?' she called out.

She had an English accent, long, shiny auburn hair, and wore a little suntop with no bra. He was struck by how brown she was, a deep golden colour that he rarely saw up in Scotland, especially on redheads. When she moved away from the car door he saw her legs. Long and slender, equally brown as her arms, and the smallest pair of denim shorts he'd ever seen.

'Yes, it's Ewan's place,' he said, hardly able to get the words out because of how she looked.

'Thank God for that,' she said and smiled. 'I was beginning to think I was lost without trace.'

The fact she had a car and a child suggested that she was several years older than him, but the warmth of her smile, and the appraising way she was looking at him, was all he cared about.

'I want a drink, Mummy,' the little boy shouted from inside the car, and she leaned back in and moved the seat so he could get out.

'May we have a drink?' she asked, coming closer to Stuart, holding the little dark-haired boy by the hand. 'This is Barney. We've been driving all night and I'm just about wiped out.'

Stuart pulled himself together then, and rushed into the house to get some water and put the kettle on for tea.

She sat on the bench outside, the boy beside her, and it was only when he handed her the water that he saw how tired she was. She could hardly keep her eyes open, and though she rallied enough with the water to explain that she was Laura Brannigan, and that she'd driven up from London because a friend had told her Ewan would put her up, it was clear she really was all in.

Barney wasn't a bit tired, for he'd been asleep most of the way. He drank two glasses of water, then asked where the toys were.

'Toys?' Stuart said stupidly.

'I told him there would be lots of other children because it's a commune,' Laura said.

'It's nae a commune,' Stuart said. 'Just a bunch of hippies and there's nae weans.'

To his surprise she laughed. 'Your accent is so lovely,' she said. 'I thought I wouldn't be able to understand anything anyone said to me. But your voice is like music.'

She told him she'd left her husband, Gregory Brannigan, because he was carrying on with another woman, and that she'd gone down to stay in Cornwall for a while. 'I couldn't find anywhere there to live,' she said, her lovely face clouding over. 'Then I met Rob, Ewan's friend, and he told me about this place. He said that he thought I could get my head together here, and that the women all helped one another with the children. I thought it sounded perfect for us.'

Stuart guessed that Rob, who was well known for his tall stories, had spun Laura this yarn in the hope that she'd be sufficiently grateful to go to bed with him. Perhaps he hadn't thought she was desperate enough to drive all this way, but it was wrong to have misled her and Stuart didn't think Ewan or any of the others would be happy about having such a young child here.

He couldn't bring himself to tell her this, not now she was so tired, so instead he asked if she'd like to have a sleep in his room and offered to look after Barney for her.

*

As Stuart walked on into Cellardyke, images from that day kept coming back to him. He knew nothing about small children then; as the youngest in his own family he'd never come into close contact with any before. But he blundered his way through that day, just letting the two-year-old tag along behind him. Fortunately Barney turned out to be the easiest kid in the world to take care of; he played with sticks, stones, anything to hand, and was delighted when Stuart drew different faces on some pebbles and told him a story with them. He was a nice-looking kid too, with his dark hair and eyes, peachy skin and a wide smiley mouth. When Stuart made him a sandwich later, he didn't complain that the bread was stale, or that there was nothing to put in it but Marmite. He just ate it, even the crusts.

But stronger still than the image of Barney was that of Laura. Several times that day he peeped round the door to see if she was awake yet. And each time he looked he was stunned by her beauty. She lay on her side, one arm curled round her head, the other stretched out behind her, a glimpse of white breasts showing above her suntop. Her shorts were so brief he got an erection at the sight of her bottom, and he covered her up with a blanket because it made him feel guilty.

There was no doubt in his mind that he fell in love with her then, for when the others got up and he told them about her arrival, he found he was worried that one of the other five men would snatch her from him.

'We cannae have a wean in the house!' Ewan said, looking troubled. 'We've got enough bother with the folks in the village as it is.'

'You can't send her packing now,' Stuart said. 'I don't think she's got anywhere else to go.'

By the time Laura woke up, Barney had charmed every-one, and as Laura had brought not only a box of groceries with her but a lump of best black Kabul, all reservations about them staying vanished.

It was a magical evening in every way, for it was warm enough to sit outside playing guitars and singing. The chilli someone cooked was good, and everyone was relaxed and happy.

Stuart couldn't remember the names, or even many of the faces, of that bunch of hippies from London any more. Yet he could remember how he sat with his back against the trunk of an old apple tree surrounded by them, Laura beside him. Every now and then she would smile at him and put a hand on his arm, and he knew he was teetering on the edge of something mind-blowing.

He asked her about her husband during the evening, but she just put her finger on his lips as if to silence him. 'Greg was the biggest mistake in my life,' she said, and he could see sadness and regret in her eyes. 'The only good thing to come out of our marriage was Barney. Don't ask me any more about it, Stuart. I just want to put it behind me.'

Barney came and sat by him as it grew dark, and gradually his head slumped down on to Stuart's legs as he fell asleep.

'I should put him to bed now,' Laura said. 'Are we to sleep in that same room tonight?'

Stuart managed to lift the child up into his arms and stand up. 'That's my room,' he said. 'But I suppose I could find somewhere else to crash.'

'You don't need to,' she said, once again touching his arm in that delicious familiar manner which made his pulse race. 'I've got a couple of lilos and sleeping bags in my car – we could share the room. I looked around earlier and every-where else is pretty rough.'

As he stood up from tucking Barney into the bed, she came right up to him, put her hands on his cheeks and looked straight into his eyes. 'You are the sweetest man,' she said softly. 'You let me sleep, you took care of Barney, and now he's got your bed. All without asking me anything.'

Then suddenly she was kissing him, her arms going round him tightly, and Stuart felt as though he was shooting off to another planet.

He shook himself out of his reverie as he finally reached Cellardyke, delighted to see it still looked much the same as when he was a child. The pub had been smartened up, with a restaurant above it, and the sweetie shop was now a hairdresser's, but there were still washing lines on the tiny beach inside the harbour. He remembered seeing vast old ladies' drawers and men's woolly combinations hanging there, much to Angus's and his amusement. Now it was pretty duvet covers and Babygros. But the old cottages tucked around the harbour were even quainter than he remembered. He recalled how excited Jackie had got when he first brought her here with Laura and Barney. She was practically jumping up and down with it. He thought she'd forget all about it once she got back to London, but she didn't. Just a few months later she bought the first cottage, got men in to renovate it, and that summer Laura and Barney came over to have a holiday here with her. He still had a snapshot of Barney sitting on the bench outside it. He tore up all the ones of Laura after they split up, but he couldn't bring himself to destroy that one.

He made for the pub and ordered a pint. It was quiet in there, only a couple of old men with their dogs in the bar, and they merely nodded at him and went back to their conversation.

As he sat back in a chair by the window, he found himself slipping back to that first night with Laura and reliving it.

She kept tickling him as he tried to blow up the lilos, and

only told him she had a pump when he was purple in the face with the exertion. If it hadn't been for the little boy sleeping in the room, he would have thrown her down on it there and then. But once he'd got one blown up, he laid the sleeping bag on it, then lifted the child on top and zipped the bag up round him.

'Do I need to blow up the other one too?' he asked, and she shook her head, smiling seductively at him.

His head told him it was wrong to make love to a woman with her small child so close, and he felt too that he ought to know more about her first, but when she began opening the buttons on his shirt and kissing his chest, all he wanted was to possess her.

He'd had about five different girlfriends before, but they paled into insignificance beside Laura. She was like a tigress the first time, clawing at him, devouring him in a way that was both thrilling and frightening. He came far too fast, and collapsed against her breasts feeling a failure, but she lifted his face up and kissed him.

'We've got all night yet,' she said.

Even now, twenty-three years and scores of other women later, that night was the one Stuart could hold up as the very best in his life. Since then he had made love all over the world, in luxurious hotels, romantic hideaways, in swimming pools, cars, fields and even trains, but nothing could ever top that night on an old stained mattress in a farm outhouse.

It had everything – wild passion, exquisite tenderness and raunchy fun – and Laura taught him more about women and sex that night than most men learn in a lifetime. When dawn came creeping through the window, they were sated, lying entwined and dripping with perspiration. For him it was love, the kind that could only come once in a lifetime.

He was ready to lay down his life for her, and he believed then that it was the same for her.

'On holiday?'

Stuart was startled by the question, and surprised to find it was asked by an attractive blonde with a couple of empty glasses in her hands.

'You were miles away,' she laughed, showing large, very white teeth. 'Perhaps I should have left you there?'

She was curvy and looked as if she'd poured herself into her jeans and slinky, low-necked top. He thought she was probably around the same age as him.

'Not at all,' he grinned. 'I was remembering coming here as a child for holidays. Maybe we played together on the beach?'

'If I'd played with you I would have remembered,' she laughed. 'I'd have stuck you in a lobster pot and waited for you to grow up.'

'I'm Stuart Macgregor,' he said holding out his hand, delighted that he'd found someone who'd not only clearly lived here all her life, but had a lively sense of humour.

'And I'm Gloria White,' she said as she shook his hand. 'I know a dozen Stuarts, but I don't think I've met you before. Where do you stay?'

'I'm from Edinburgh, but I've been working away for a long while,' he replied.

'So what's brought you back just now?' she asked.

'Hearing an old friend was dead,' Stuart said. 'Can I buy you a drink?'

'I'll have a beer, thank you,' she said. 'And would I know your friend?'

'Maybe. Jackie Davies.'

'Och, that was a terrible business.' She winced. 'I couldnae understand it. I got to know Jackie when she bought her first cottage here. We became good friends, and when Laura came over from Edinburgh we'd all have a drink together. I liked their company, always so much laughing and so much to blether about. They told me they'd been friends since they were wee girls, and I couldnae believe it when people said Laura killed Jackie.'

Stuart told her how he had been out of the country and had come over here to see Belle. 'Do you know her too?' he asked.

Gloria nodded. 'Aye, she and her husband stayed in the village when they were buying the place up at Crail. She's having a hard time of it now, they say; she'd do better to sell up and go back to London.'

'Because the guest house isn't doing so well?' Stuart asked. 'I noticed she had no one staying there.'

Gloria shrugged. 'There's still a lot of bad feeling around, folk round here don't like to be put under a spotlight, and they don't like incomers. The auld ones grumble that they push up the house prices so the young people from here can't afford them and have to leave.'

Stuart nodded in sympathy. 'That's happening everywhere now, but I suppose it's worse here when there isn't that much work about either.'

'I always say that some of them need to get off their backsides and adapt,' she said with a good-natured grin. 'Jackie wasn't born rich. She told me she made her money from property development, and if she could do it, so could others around here. What about you, Stuart? Were you born rich?'

Stuart laughed. 'Definitely not! I lived in a tenement in Edinburgh and served my time as a joiner. It was Jackie who helped me on to the first rung on the ladder. I worked for her on her properties in London.'

'Did you know Laura too?'

'Aye, to my cost,' he said and laughed lightly. 'She broke my heart, Gloria, but she was the one who made me go to London, so I learned to forgive her.'

'I liked her,' Gloria said reflectively. 'I know Jackie used to worry about her and the wee boy, and that maybe Laura was a careless mother, but it's a tough one being a single mum. I know because I'm one. You have to make a living if you want them to have the things other kids have, you need friends too or you'd go mad with loneliness, but that's bound to cut down on the time you've got to spend with your child.'

Stuart was touched by her sympathy for Laura. 'People are always very quick to judge,' he said. 'But my mother used to say we need to walk a few miles in someone's boots to know how it is for them.'

Gloria nodded in agreement. 'It was a terrible thing that wee Barney died in that accident. It changed both Laura and Jackie; neither of them was quite the same again. But whatever passed between them, I've never been quite convinced Laura killed Jackie, not in my heart. How about you?'

It was very tempting to admit where he stood, but for all he knew Gloria might be as thick as thieves with Belle and the other witnesses. 'I can't believe it of her either,' he said. 'She could be wild, treacherous sometimes, but she and Jackie had a very special friendship, and I can't imagine anything changing that. But then I've been away a long time, I can only go on what I've been told. Belle's opinion is pretty damning.'

'She's an unhappy woman,' Gloria said darkly. 'I dinnae ken what made her and Charles come up here to live, but I know she didn't want to be here, she's always trailed her resentment about like a bad smell.'

'She told me she loved it, and she had friends here!'

'What friends?' Gloria scoffed. 'She's too high and mighty

to mix with most of us. I tried to be her friend at the start, but it was like flogging a dead horse. She doesnae understand friendship, that's why she was so jealous of Laura.'

'Was she? But Laura was really fond of Belle, at least she was when I knew her.'

'Aye, Laura was fond of her, she dinnae see what was in the woman's heart. But then Laura dinnae pay attention to what folk thought of her.'

Stuart half smiled, for that last remark was very perceptive. Laura had never been one to think about the effect she might have on anyone. He was a fine example, for it never occurred to Laura that a mere lad of twenty-one would be blown away by an experienced older woman, and she couldn't comprehend his pain and anguish when she'd grown tired of him either.

'You don't think Belle did the dirty deed, do you?' he joked.

Gloria chuckled. 'And get her pretty manicured hands dirty? I dinnae think so, Stuart. Besides, her car was in the garage that day, and it's a good long trek out to Brodie Farm for a woman who never even walks to do her messages.'

'So do you favour anyone else as a suspect?'

She shook her head as if amused at the question.

'What about the many lovers?' Stuart prompted.

She raised one eyebrow and pursed her lips. 'That's all best laid to rest,' she said firmly. 'Their families have suffered enough from their foolishness already without me making more of it. And now I must get back to work.'

Stuart left the pub and walked up the hill to the main road to catch the St Andrews bus back to Crail and his car. He felt somewhat justified in his faith in Laura now that he knew Gloria liked her and didn't believe she was guilty; if nothing else, it proved he wasn't totally crazy. Her views on Belle were interesting too. She hadn't shot him down in flames either about Jackie's lovers, which to him meant they not only existed, but she knew perfectly well who they were. He would bet that they were men she'd known all her life, and that was why she wouldn't say anything more. He would have to find some other way to discover who they were.

Once back in his car, which was parked by Crail Tolbooth, he sat for a moment, suddenly daunted by just how difficult it was going to be to get at the truth of how Jackie died, two years on. Was he really up to it? He knew nothing about detection or law, and he knew precious little about how Jackie and Laura had lived in the last ten years and what went on between them.

But more than that, why should he care if Laura had been punished for a crime she hadn't committed? She hadn't given a damn about him when she played around with the man from the casino.

He could see himself on the London train, squashed between a very large woman who never stopped eating and a Glaswegian drunk who kept offering him a swig from his bottle of whisky. It was January 1975 and bitterly cold. The carriage was full of cigarette smoke which stung his eyes, but every time he closed them he saw Laura's face, and the pain in his heart was so bad he felt he could easily die from it.

All he had in the world was about £10, a bag full of carpentry tools and a few clothes. He was scared, too, that Jackie's offer to give him work might have been just hot air and he wouldn't be able to find anywhere to live. He'd only met Jackie a few times on her brief visits to Scotland, and although she had seemed to be the dynamic businesswoman Laura had always described her as, he had no real proof of it. London was unknown territory to him too, he had no other contacts to find work, and if he failed to make it there he didn't know what he was going to do.

'But you did make it there, thanks to Jackie,' he murmured to himself, shaking himself out of his reverie. 'Even if you don't owe anything to Laura, you do to Jackie. You've got to find out the truth for her sake.'

Instead of returning to Edinburgh as he'd intended, Stuart turned off on the lane that led to Brodie Farm, left his car outside the last cottages and began to walk the rest of the way. He had already driven here several times while checking the time it took from Edinburgh, but it was only by walking that he could get the real feel of the area, notice small landmarks and the other houses on the route which he'd hardly taken in while driving.

When Jackie had first bought Brodie Farm Stuart had been puzzled as to why she would buy a place inland. Fife's attraction to him was the small, quaint coastal villages. He saw the rest of the county as rather flat and bleak, with none of the majesty of the Highlands, or the scenic beauty of the rolling hills and valleys of the Borders.

But as he walked down the lane, the sun on his back, he saw what Jackie must have seen – miles and miles of gently undulating fields, lush and green now with crops, a feeling of immense space. When he turned round to look back towards Crail, the sea was as blue as the sky, and suddenly he understood why Jackie had spoken of the freedom she felt here. For a girl who had grown up in London, hemmed in by houses, surrounded by people, her ears bombarded by traffic noise, it must have been wonderful to stand at her door seeing and hearing only the sounds of nature – the wind blowing the crops, birds wheeling overhead – and watching the colour of the sea change according to the weather. Stuart remembered her saying that being exposed to all the elements made her feel strong, that being able to see for miles and miles gave her power. He had laughed at the time, assuming it was another of her wacky ideas that would be thrown aside when a new one came to her. But though she stopped trying to convince others to embrace the simple life, she remained faithful to it. And now he was here in this wide open, vast space, feeling the wind tugging at his hair, he understood what she loved about it.

Brodie Farm was visible from a long way off because it stood up on slightly higher ground, surrounded by trees. Once Stuart was closer, he climbed on to a farm gate to study it in detail. The two-storey farmhouse and its single-storey outbuildings formed an open-ended square around the yard. When Jackie bought the place there were no windows on the outside walls; in fact, when she had shown him photographs of it, to him it looked like a tumbledown, forbidding fortress. He hadn't aired his real opinion, that she was crazy to buy it, for by then he knew Jackie well enough to appreciate she had vision.

She had already drawn up tentative plans to convert each of the stables and other outhouses into guest rooms, but it was his suggestion that she put windows in the outside walls to make the rooms lighter, and give her guests the benefit of the extensive views across the countryside.

Stuart had never had the chance to see the place, not before she began the work, or during, or after, its completion. She had asked him if he'd like to manage the project, but he'd turned it down because he'd been offered work in South America, and anyway in those days he had no wish to return to Scotland, not while Laura was up there.

But it pleased him to see she had acted on his suggestion about the windows, and they, and the many trees and shrubs along the boundary of her land had softened the severity of the building. Seen now in bright sunshine, it looked so idyllic and peaceful it didn't seem possible that a horrific murder had taken place there.

Once again he wondered what had caused Jackie to freak out that morning and phone Laura. She might have been troubled for some time, but in Stuart's experience there was usually some dramatic incident which suddenly sent people over the edge.

Could someone have dropped in and threatened her? If they had hung around afterwards they might have heard her make the call to Laura, and panicked because they knew Jackie was likely to spill the beans when she arrived. But unless the neighbour who saw Laura and Michael Fenton's cars was wrong, that would mean the killer had come on foot.

Stuart got down off the gate and continued along the lane, climbed over another gate near to Brodie Farm's boundary fence and walked up the side of the field to make his way right round the property. To his surprise there was a window open upstairs in the farmhouse, and music from a radio wafted out. He was rather shocked that Belle had let the farmhouse, he had expected that she would only take bookings for the stable rooms, and leave Jackie's home untouched. But perhaps that was naive of him; if Belle hadn't got many bookings at her place, she probably needed the extra money.

Because there was someone in the house, and he didn't want them to think he was prying, he made a point of going straight on across the field at the back of the farm before completing the square route back to the lane. But as he turned, with the open farmyard on his left, he glanced in and saw a bright red convertible BMW parked there.

Instinctively he knew it was Charles's car. He hadn't been told what car Belle's husband drove, but it was the kind of flashy motor he'd always gone for. There were two other cars as well, a well-worn Landrover and a green Volvo estate, but they were parked over by the stable rooms, and they were the type of cars he would expect the kind of person who took self-catering holidays in Scotland to drive.

He memorized the car number and walked quickly back to the lane, then jotted it down in a notebook to check on later. Belle had said she handled the letting here, and she'd also said she didn't know where Charles was today. Why would she say that if he was up here doing some maintenance?

Belle had met Charles Howell just a few weeks after Stuart turned her down. He remembered Jackie didn't approve of Charles because he was thirty-nine, divorced, with two teenage children, and he was a playboy who was renowned for always having a pretty young blonde on his arm.

'I don't like the slimy bastard,' was what Jackie said, never one to mince her words. 'And I don't like the thought of Belle following in my footsteps and going for men with money.'

'You didn't marry Roger for his money, did you?' Stuart asked.

He could see Jackie now. They were in the kitchen of her house in Kensington, a room that Stuart always looked back on fondly, not just because it was the place she comforted him in when he first arrived in London, or because she fed him there so often in the months that followed, but because it reflected her personality so well. It had a passing resemblance to the 'Country Kitchen' style that was so in vogue at that time, in as much as the units were real wood and there was a central farmhouse-style table and chairs. But a whole wallful of shelves were filled with bright enamelware, fancy cheese and butter dishes, jugs, plates and bowls. She didn't care much for real antiques; she bought items for their vivid colours or because they were funny – a cow in a bath, a frog sitting on a toilet. Junk was how she described it, but grouping it en masse made it almost a work of art.

She had an 'Afro' perm at the time and it looked like a halo of strawberry-blonde candyfloss. She wore a skin-tight denim catsuit studded with various military badges and her green eyes were full of mischief.

'Let's just say that Roger's money helped me to love him,' she laughed. 'But it hasn't helped to make me pregnant. At least Roger would love it if we had a child. Charles will never want Belle to have one; all he wants is a nubile blonde in his bed.'

Stuart had thought Jackie was a little harsh on Charles then – after all, she hardly knew him – but within a few years he discovered the man was much worse than she thought.

Charles had made his mark during the sixties with a string of record shops and a couple of night clubs. By 1974 he was investing in property, which was how he came to meet Jackie and Belle. Later, Stuart worked on several of these properties, and took an immediate dislike to the man, for he was overbearing, bigoted and dishonest. He was undeniably handsome, with jet-black hair, dark blue eyes and a cleft chin that women seemed to find irresistible. Stuart remembered how he used to police the work being done on his properties, always turning up in a flashy car wearing a hand-tailored suit, and berating the men for taking too long over the job. He skimped on everything, he cared nothing for the safety of his workers, or of those who would live in the properties. On one job he got the plumber, who wasn't even properly qualified, to put in gas boilers which were sub-standard. Stuart had seen electrical work which was potentially dangerous, and plumbing that would be leaking within weeks. By the end of the seventies Charles was involved in building entire estates of housing, but Stuart had long since declined to work for him because he wasn't prepared to be a party to dangerous and unethical practices.

Jackie was right about him refusing to allow Belle to have a child. Stuart heard she got pregnant but Charles made her have an abortion. He'd heard too that there were other women in his life, so maybe that was part of the reason for Belle's bitterness as well. He thought it quite likely that Charles had one at Brodie Farm right now, and only a complete bastard would conduct an affair in the house of his murdered sister-in-law.

Once back in the lane, Stuart walked along to the house belonging to Angus McFee, the neighbour who had witnessed Laura driving to Brodie Farm on the day of the murder. He hoped he might find a cross-country route back to where he'd left his car, for he didn't want Charles to see him up there if he should come along the lane.

McFee's house was at least a quarter of a mile from Brodie Farm, and as Stuart reached it he saw that it did have a first-class view of the lane. If the man had been working on his upstairs window he could probably see almost the whole way to Crail, and several miles the other way which led to Anstruther. Yet when Stuart turned to look back at Brodie Farm, he saw it was impossible to see into the yard of the farmhouse from here. Even more importantly, he couldn't see the track up to Brodie Farm, at least not the part that went beyond the farm. He knew it did continue – he'd crossed the ruts of it while walking round the back of the property. The track was very narrow, scarcely wider than a car, and it had snaked round the far side of the farm and down the hill. He had no idea where it led to, perhaps only to other isolated cottages, but the chances were it would eventually link up with a proper road. A car could have come to the farm from that direction, and left that way too, and Mr McFee wouldn't have been able to see it from his house, not unless he was standing on his roof.

'So much for your evidence, Mr McFee,' he murmured, and wondered why the advocate defending Laura hadn't brought up the existence of the lane during the trial.

5

Laura smiled as she read Stuart's letter. He clearly thought that all letters to prisoners were vetted very carefully, and that maybe she wouldn't get the letter at all if there was any reference to the crime or people involved in the trial. He mentioned 'my jaunt around Fife' as if he was touring around on holiday. But she knew when he said he'd met a blonde barmaid called Gloria that he'd been in Cellardyke, and that the 'faded rose' in a guest house had to be Belle.

She was a little puzzled when he mentioned standing by a farm looking at the view, considering where the narrow lane might lead to, but after a few moments she suddenly realized what he was trying to tell her.

She had no idea where that lane led to, she'd never been down it, but clearly Stuart saw it as a possible way for the real killer to have got in and out of the farm without being spotted. He asked too how her writing was coming on, and that he hoped she was finding it cathartic.

She had always sniggered at that word. It made her think of losers sitting around in group therapy discussing their addictions. She had once looked it up in a dictionary in the library and found it actually meant 'purging'.

Stuart using the word made her laugh out loud. She imagined that writing down her past history would act like a dose of laxative.

Yet she had written about her childhood, and the reasons why she made up a new one for herself. Just yesterday she'd posted it to Stuart. She guiltily wondered how he would react if he knew she nearly didn't send it as it crossed her mind he could sell it to the newspapers.

She half smiled at herself, thinking that perhaps it had been cathartic after all, for she could now see that the real damage Vincent had done to her was leaving her with the inability to trust implicitly.

Yet writing about that part of her life was the easy bit; she was, after all, just a sad kid who tried to rub out the areas of her past which hurt. It was going to be far more difficult and painful to study the adult Laura, for she *had* done things which were inexcusable. But to examine Jackie's big role in her life, and the forces and reasons they both turned out as they did, she felt she must look back and write it all down. She didn't have to show it to anyone, and perhaps by being totally honest with herself, she'd find some kind of consolation.

In the New Year of '62 Roger and Steven drove over to Muswell Hill to take Laura and Jackie out for a drink at Jack Straw's Castle on Hampstead Heath. It began to snow heavily as they were on their way to the pub, so the date was cut short as the men were afraid they might not be able to get home later.

As they left they promised they would come over again at the weekend. Laura's seventeenth birthday was on the Saturday, and Frank and Lena bought her a second-hand record player, something she'd wanted ever since she moved into her bedsitter. But Roger and Steven didn't phone or turn up, which completely spoiled the day for her.

They didn't ring until the middle of the following week, just when the girls had given up hope of ever seeing them again. They invited them to a party at their flat on the Saturday evening, and Roger suggested they should stay the night because the party would go on till the early hours.

Both Laura and Jackie were so excited that they couldn't eat or sleep and they had endless discussions about what they should wear and whether the invitation to stay the night meant the men expected them to sleep with them. Jackie took the view that it was high time she lost her virginity anyway, and as Roger was such a good kisser he'd probably be a good lover too.

Laura pretended she felt the same but inwardly she was quaking with fear. The memory of Vincent's erect penis had stayed with her, and the fact that she liked Steven made no difference to her – she was quite sure that sex with any man would be disgusting.

It was bitterly cold on the day of the party and Jackie decided she was going to wear jeans and a jumper rather than a party dress. 'I doubt anyone will dress up when it's so cold,' she insisted. 'We'll just look silly and we'll be miserable if we're shivering all night.'

Jackie, with her vivid red hair and green eyes, would never be overlooked even if she dressed in a sack, but Laura felt she looked insipid unless she displayed her legs and cleavage. She intended to look sensational in her new slinky red dress with bootlace straps and peep-toe high heels, and despite Jackie's advice she went ahead and wore it.

As they came out of South Kensington tube station the icy wind tore at her hair. She'd put it up in a beehive the evening she met Steven, but that was an amateurish affair achieved only with endless backcombing and hair lacquer. She'd spent two hours in the hairdresser's this time and they'd teased fat curls into a work of art, which was now being ruined. Her thin coat was no protection from the cold and her teeth began to chatter.

Chubby Checker's 'Let's Twist Again' was blaring out as

they arrived at number 220 Cromwell Road. The street door was open and a group of men were carting crates of beer up the stairs.

The flat was on the second floor and to Laura's disappointment it wasn't the kind of elegant pied-à-terre she'd imagined, but three rather squalid rooms, and a bathroom shared with other tenants.

From the moment they walked in through the open door of the flat, Laura knew she should have followed her friend's advice as everyone else was casually dressed in warm clothes. Roger greeted them warmly and as he took Laura's coat he said she looked lovely, but she felt he only said so out of faint embarrassment.

Steven was busy setting up a bar, and shouted over that Roger would introduce them to everyone. It seemed the only drinks were red wine, beer or cider, none of which Laura liked, but even more worrying was that Steven didn't come over to her.

Roger gave both girls a glass of cider, and then, taking Jackie's hand, he led her off to meet the other guests, while Laura tagged along behind. To be fair to Roger, he didn't leave her out in his introductions, but everyone had posh voices, and the way they looked at Laura made her feel as if she was wearing no clothes at all. It didn't help that all the light bulbs had been replaced with red ones, she supposed to try to create a more intimate atmosphere, and when she glanced in a mirror she was horrified to see it made her skimpy dress looked even brighter red and gave her bare shoulders and arms a sickly pallor. Worse still, she didn't look sensational at all, only tarty, and she wished the floor would open up and swallow her.

Jackie was in her element. Not only was she dressed like everyone else, but she was well used to meeting all kinds of people at her parents' parties. Within minutes she was chatting away to people as if she'd known them all her life.

Laura quickly downed her cider and turned to a blonde girl standing by her.

'Do you live around here?' she asked.

'In the flat upstairs,' the girl replied. 'I share with them,' she added, pointing out two girls who were dancing together. 'And you?'

There was something about the crisp way the girl spoke which unnerved Laura still further. Despite her jeans and sweater, lack of makeup and hair that looked as if she'd just got out of bed, she was very pretty, with wide blue eyes, long lashes, and a plump, pouty mouth. Laura immediately felt she was competition and after Steven.

'I have a flat in North London,' she said trying to speak and sound like the other girl. 'Jackie and I met Steven and Roger in the City after an office party at Christmas.'

'Steven told me about you,' the girl said. 'But I didn't expect you to be so young.'

Feeling she'd been slighted, Laura didn't even attempt to carry on a conversation and went back to the bar to find Steven. But he was roaring with laughter at something one of a crowd of men around him was saying, so she just topped up her glass and drank it quickly.

Steven did come over to her several times during the evening, but he kept darting off to pour drinks and change records, and Laura became convinced that he wasn't really interested in her, and she'd only been invited because Roger didn't think Jackie would have come without her.

Each time she looked at them, they were kissing or dancing cheek to cheek, and it was quite obvious that Roger was totally smitten with her friend. So Laura kept topping up her glass with more cider and tried to hide her mounting panic that she wasn't wanted by anyone.

By eleven the flat was so crowded with people that she could barely see Jackie amongst the dancers, and she couldn't see Steven at all. All at once the room began to spin, and she realized she was going to be sick. When she found the bathroom occupied, she stumbled down the stairs out into the road.

After vomiting violently several times she sobered up, but chilled to the bone because she had no coat, desperate to go home but unable to unless she went back to the flat and got her coat and bag, which would mean she'd have to explain herself, she sat down on the front steps and began to cry.

A warm hand on her bare shoulder startled her. She looked up to see Steven looking down at her with real concern. 'Laura! What on earth are you doing out here?' he asked. 'You'll catch your death of cold.'

'The cigarette smoke was making my eyes sting,' she lied.

'You'll get pneumonia if you stay here,' he said, and pulling his thick sweater off over his head, he popped it over hers. 'Come in and sit on the stairs, it's warmer there,' he added, pulling her to her feet.

Once inside the hall, he took her hands between his and rubbed them. 'I don't think it's the smoke that made your eyes run. You've been crying,' he said reproachfully. 'Why, Laura? Did you feel left out because I couldn't be with you all evening?'

She felt warmer now with his jumper on, and his gentle tone made her want to admit that was exactly how she felt, that she knew she'd worn the wrong clothes, everyone was too posh for her, and she got drunk to deal with it. But he was a sophisticated man about town, he wouldn't want a silly young girl who didn't know how to handle herself at parties. She had to come up with something that would make her look more adult.

'No, of course not. I understood you had to look after all your guests,' she said. 'It was just that I had a terrible experience earlier today. It shook me up.'

He cuddled her then and asked her to tell him about it.

'A man followed me home from the shops this morning,' she lied. 'I thought he lived in one of the other flats when he came up the stairs behind me, but he didn't. He came right into my room and tried to push me down on the bed. I think he was going to rape me.'

'God! How awful!' he exclaimed in horror. 'What did you do?'

'I screamed and kicked him hard. It stopped him in his tracks, but he grabbed my handbag and ran off with it.'

She began crying again, almost believing her story. She said her wages were in the bag and a month's rent for her flat, and she was afraid the man would be lying in wait for her another day.

'Did you call the police?' Steven asked.

Laura was thrilled that he looked so horrified as that meant he really cared about her.

'No, I didn't. I wanted to but I knew if I did they'd take me down to the station to make a statement, and I'd be there for hours. It was Jackie I was worried about. She was so excited about coming to the party, I didn't want to let her down.'

'That was kind of you, but she'd have understood,' he said, wiping her eyes tenderly with his handkerchief. 'If you'd rung me I would have come right over and taken care of you. I would even have postponed the party for another night.'

'I couldn't have let you do that,' she said, sniffing back her tears. 'I wouldn't have wanted to spoil anything for anyone. I didn't even tell Jackie what had happened because she was looking forward to coming here so much. Please

132

don't tell her now, it isn't fair to burden her with this. And don't tell Roger either because he's bound to pass it on.'

Steven wanted to take her to the police right away, but Laura deftly pointed out they would only tell them to go to the police in Hornsey tomorrow and it would spoil his party.

For a spur-of-the-moment lie it was a huge success. Steven spent the rest of the evening glued to her side, while she played the brave victim, selflessly keeping her troubles to herself.

People began drifting off around two in the morning and Jackie disappeared into Roger's room with him. Finally everyone left and Steven cuddled her on the sofa.

'You sleep in my bed, I'll stay on here,' he said gallantly.

Jackie lost her virginity to Roger that night. Whether this was because she couldn't help herself, or because once in Roger's bed she couldn't back away, she didn't say. But Laura felt rather superior because Steven hadn't put her under pressure to have sex with him, not even when she asked him to share the bed with her because she was afraid to sleep alone.

That, and because the next day he gave her £20, the money she was supposed to have had stolen, fixed it in her head that being sweet, brave and chaste was the key to holding on to him.

Two days later she rang Steven after work and said she'd been to the police to report her attacker and he asked if she would like to come over to his flat. Once again she stayed the night in his bed, but wouldn't allow anything more than kissing and cuddling. Despite having made up her mind that she was going to let the tragic fictional story of her childhood die, she ended up telling it to Steven.

His sympathy was wonderful. He even apologized for being so tactless in going on about his family and praised her for being so capable and strong. 'I have to be,' she said with a shrug. 'There isn't anyone to fall back on so I have to manage living alone. But since that man followed me home I haven't felt very safe there.'

She played that card again and again in the following weeks, especially when she knew Roger was taking Jackie out and Steven was in alone. Once at his flat she would cook for him, wash and iron his clothes and clean up, and though she would've preferred it if he asked her out properly as Roger did Jackie, she felt sure he was falling in love with her.

Often as she took the tube to work she asked herself if she loved him. She could reel off plenty of reasons why she wanted to be with him – that he was handsome, had a nice car and money – yet she didn't feel any of the heart-tugging stuff that people spoke of when they were in love. He was really quite dull, very serious and career-minded, and if Jackie wasn't spending all her spare time with Roger, she wasn't even sure she'd want to be with Steven. But it made her feel good having a real boyfriend, someone she could boast about at work, and she liked staying at his flat and having him fussing round her.

She felt no guilt about stealing a couple of pounds from his wallet here and there; after all, she saved him money because he rarely took her out. She often told him lies to make herself look smarter, braver or more vulnerable. She told him once that a male friend of her Aunt Mabel had tried to force her into having sex with him when she was thirteen, and that was why she was afraid of having sex with him.

But as time went on and she saw Jackie head over heels in love with Roger, and he with her, Laura began to feel aggrieved. She missed their girls' nights in together, meeting up after work, going to the shops on a Saturday, and the family meals at Muswell Hill on a Sunday. She might still see Jackie all the time in the boys' flat, but it wasn't the same. Jackie was becoming like all the girls in Kensington – polished, poised and too wrapped up in Roger even to notice her best friend.

Sometimes when the pair of them burst into the flat, laughing and glowing with happiness, and disappeared into the bedroom together, Laura resented it so much she wanted to spoil things for them. They did all go out in a foursome occasionally, but even then it wasn't much fun as Jackie and Roger spent the evening whispering together, and shutting her and Steven out.

Steven also began to lose patience with her refusal to have sex with him. He was becoming increasingly grumpy, often saying he wanted a night in on his own, and as Laura sat in her own bedsitter, imagining him going down to the pub and finding another more willing girl, she panicked.

When Roger took Jackie home to his parents for the weekend at the end of April, Laura decided that now was the right time to give in to Steven as they'd be alone in the flat. She was very nervous when she arrived straight from work on the Friday evening, but perhaps Steven sensed she was weakening as he'd changed the sheets on the bed and tidied up.

'Why don't you have a bath while I make us something to eat?' he suggested. 'I've got you some Babycham too, and we'll have a cosy evening by the fire.'

No girl could have had a better lover than Steven for her first time. He caressed and played with her, kissed every part of her body, telling her how beautiful she was. By the time he did enter her, she wanted to do it as much as he did. It did hurt a bit, but not as much as she'd expected, and when it was over he said such wonderful, loving things that she cried.

In the morning it was even better, and they stayed in bed

nearly all day, only getting up for food and cups of tea. They had a bath together, he washed her like a child and cuddled her dry, and to her this seemed like true love.

For six or seven weeks everything was wonderful. Steven wanted her with him all the time, and they could hardly get in the door before they ripped each other's clothes off and leapt on one another. Laura could think of nothing but Steven; he was the centre of her world.

She would sit next to him in his car studying his profile, marvelling at the length of his eyelashes, his jutting cheekbones and the neatness of his dark hair. After sex she would smile at the tender expression in his eyes, snuggle into his arms and inhale his scent gleefully. She believed they would be together for all time and any day he'd ask her to marry him.

Years later she was able to look back and see that she wasn't actually head over heels in love with Steven. She was just needy and desperate to *be* loved.

She hadn't really been ready for a sexual relationship and once into it she felt she had to justify her enjoyment of it by building it up as true love. The fact that Steven didn't ask her to marry him, or even say he loved her, always used a Durex when they made love, and only ever talked about his career when she asked him about his plans for the future, made her feel used and insecure. Because of this, she became jealous of everyone in his life.

She interrogated him about his old girlfriends; every woman he so much as glanced at was a threat; even a mention of the girls in the flat upstairs or his male friends was enough to make her sulk for hours.

When he left her alone in the flat she went through all his papers and things, looking for evidence of past affairs. She found a letter from his mother in which she urged him to be cautious because Laura was so young, and she threw a saucepan at him when he came in.

'It's just that kind of infantile behaviour my mother is afraid of,' he retorted angrily. 'How dare you read my letters? And why can't you just be happy with what we've got?'

But Laura couldn't be happy until he'd told her he loved her and asked her to marry him. And to achieve that end she resorted to telling him ridiculous lies. She would say that she'd fainted on the tube, that another girl had attacked her at work, anything to get him to say they must get married so he could look after her.

But her ploys didn't work. All she saw was exasperation in his eyes, and she felt him withdrawing from her.

The last weekend in May he didn't invite her over, but she went anyway. His face fell when he opened the door to her.

'I wanted a weekend alone,' he said stiffly.

'But we always spend the weekends together,' she said, and walked on past him, putting her overnight bag down and turning to kiss him.

He put his hands on her shoulders, holding her back from him. 'I can't do this any more,' he sighed. 'It was nice while it lasted, but you are too jealous and immature for me, Laura. Go home now. It's over.'

She burst into tears, but that didn't soften him. She begged him to let her cook him a meal, and said she'd clean up his flat which looked as though a bomb had hit it.

'No,' he said firmly. 'If I want a meal I can cook it, I can clean up too when I get sick of the mess. I made a big mistake with you. I realize now I just felt sorry for you because you have no family. But I can't do it any more, you've taken over my life and I want it back.'

'But you can't end it,' she exclaimed, feeling sick with fear. 'I love you, Steven, you're the only thing in my life.'

'That's part of the problem,' he said, his face as cold as a January morning. 'I'm sick of you depending on me for everything, you drain me dry. You don't enjoy being with any of my friends, you don't share any of my interests. All you want to do is play house, and keep me a prisoner in it.'

She argued that this wasn't so, that his friends looked down on her, but he was barely listening.

'Just go,' he said irritably, 'before I say something really hurtful. I want to go down the pub and talk to people who make me laugh. I do not want to spend another night listening to you wittering on about nothing and playing Little Girl Lost.'

She felt as if she'd been kicked in the stomach, but she was sure she could change his mind if she could just think of something dramatic enough.

'You can't pack me in,' she sobbed. 'I'm having your baby.'

She expected that would at least make him stop short. She hoped it would make him cuddle her and promise he'd do the right thing by her. But instead his dark eyes narrowed in distaste.

'Liar!' he exclaimed. 'God, you've told me some whoppers in the past. But that one beats them all.'

'I'm not lying,' she retorted. 'I'm about six or seven weeks gone.'

'You can't be, I've always taken precautions,' he insisted, running his fingers through his hair distractedly. 'For God's sake, get out of here, Laura, I'm at the end of my tether with you and I can't take any more.'

There was not a shred of sympathy in his face and he looked as if he was tempted to slap her.

'Then I'll have to have an abortion,' she threw back at him. 'And if I die because of it, it will be your fault.' Grabbing her bag, she ran out of the flat and clattered down the stairs.

She knew backstreet abortions involved knitting needles,

enema tubes and such things, and she was sure this would make him come running after her. But it didn't.

She lay on her bed the whole weekend crying, unable to believe it really was over. Each time the payphone rang down in the hall, she started, convinced it would be him. But no call came. Jackie didn't phone either, and that made her feel even more desperate. All through the following week and the next weekend she could think of nothing else. She couldn't eat or sleep, her mind churning over everything she and Steven had done together.

To gain sympathy at her work she told people that she'd caught him in bed with another girl, and Sonia, another wages clerk, invited her to spend the next weekend with her so they could go out dancing.

That gave Laura another idea, and on the Friday afternoon she rang Steven's office.

A woman answered the phone and said he was in a meeting. Laura didn't believe that for one moment, sure he'd given everyone instructions to fob her off if she phoned. But if he wasn't going to speak to her, she was determined to make trouble for him, so she told the woman that she was about to go off to Brighton to have his baby aborted. 'I don't suppose he'll care,' she sobbed down the phone. 'He just used me, then tossed me aside when he got bored. I'm really scared I might die from it, but I can't bring a baby up on my own.'

She was delighted the woman sounded very shocked, and hung up quickly when she asked for a number Steven could ring Laura back on.

She had a great weekend with Sonia in Croyden. They went to the Orchid Ballroom at Purley on Saturday night, which took her mind off Steven and even made her think that maybe it wasn't so bad being free again. But the weekend was all the sweeter for imagining Steven being frantic with worry. She hoped he'd gone down to Brighton to try to find her.

About five on Sunday afternoon she returned home. As she half expected Steven to be waiting outside her house in his car, she'd taken the precaution of putting on a black blouse that made her look pale, and left her hair all bedraggled. As luck would have it she'd got her period that morning, so she told herself that if Steven insisted on taking her to the hospital the doctor would think the blood was confirmation of what she'd done. She even staggered as she got off the bus at the end of the road, and kept stopping and holding her stomach as if she was in pain.

But Steven wasn't there waiting. Jackie was.

It was a warm day, and she was sitting on the wall outside the house wearing a green and white summer dress, her auburn hair tied back with a ribbon at the nape of her neck. Clearly Steven had told her about the message she'd left, and suddenly Laura felt genuinely tearful because her friend was concerned enough to come round.

'Thank goodness you've come, I feel terrible,' Laura said, clutching at her stomach as she ran to her friend. 'I wish I hadn't done it now, I feel like I'm going to die. But I had to, Steven didn't want it.'

But Jackie didn't embrace her and there were no words of sympathy or understanding. 'Stop right there,' she snapped at her, her face stern and cold. 'I know full well you weren't pregnant, so you can't have had an abortion. You disgust me!'

'But I have,' Laura insisted. 'I'm bleeding really heavily.'

Jackie caught hold of her arm, and manhandled her in through the front door and up the stairs. It was very quiet; all the other tenants must have gone out.

Once in Laura's room, Jackie pushed Laura down on to the bed. Her face was pale with anger and her green eyes flashed dangerously. 'You're lying, Laura, you've no more had an abortion than I have. How could you make up something like that? It's the lowest of the low!'

Laura burst into tears then and carried on insisting she wasn't lying. But Jackie just closed the door and sat down on the chair, looking at her in disgust.

'Attention-seeking, that's all this is,' she raged. 'A desperate attempt to get Steven back any way you can. But it won't work. Don't you know you lost him weeks ago by being so jealous and clingy? He's had enough of you.'

Laura tried to justify herself but Jackie just told her to grow up. 'Of course he'd been with other girls before he met you. He's twenty-four, not an innocent little boy. You've snogged and petted other boys too. But never mind that. It's this fantasy pregnancy I'm angry about. Have you forgotten that you asked me for a Tampax only last month? I even had to point out that you had some blood on your skirt. How do you explain that?'

Laura had forgotten about that and she knew she was caught out.

'You don't care about me now you've got Roger,' she blurted out desperately, unwilling to admit she had lied, even when she was cornered.

'I certainly don't care about you when you behave like this,' Jackie snarled at her. 'How could you ring Steven's work and tell such thundering, malicious lies? Have you got any idea of how embarrassing that was for him? It went round the whole firm and his boss called him in to question him about it. When Steven called me at my work I was ashamed that I even knew you. I never want to see you again!'

That last statement of Jackie's before she stormed out of the door stayed with Laura for a very long time. She never saw or spoke to Steven again and it was months before she saw Jackie either. All through the remains of that summer she cried herself to sleep at night, not so much over Steven – she'd more or less reconciled herself with that being over – but because of Jackie. She missed her, she couldn't bear the thought of losing her best friend, and she was very ashamed that Jackie had had to find out what a liar she was.

Sonia became her new friend, and all through the summer and autumn Laura told herself she was far more fun than Jackie, but that wasn't true. Sonia was cold-hearted and she only wanted to go out with Laura to pick up men. Every time she found a new one, she dropped Laura. But during the time they were together Laura learned even more ways of manipulating men, better shops to steal from, and to drink brandy.

Yet however hard she tried to convince herself that she didn't miss Jackie, it never really worked. It was like a dull pain inside her, which never went away. She wanted to go up to Jackie's house in Muswell Hill and apologize, but she was too afraid of being rejected to do it.

That Christmas was miserable. Sonia had found a new boyfriend just a few weeks before and once again dropped Laura, and she had no choice but to spend the holiday alone in her room. On New Year's Eve she passed the time going though her clothes, wondering why when she had so many lovely ones, she had so little opportunity to wear them.

Then on the morning of her eighteenth birthday in January, there was a card from Jackie. She sobbed with delight as she read the message that Jackie missed her and she'd decided at New Year that their friendship had been too good to forget.

Laura phoned her soon after and Jackie said that although she would never condone what she'd done, she thought she understood Laura's reasons and would like to draw a veil over the incident.

To Laura's keen disappointment Jackie was still going out with Roger, so she couldn't expect everything to be the same as it once had been. But even seeing her friend just once a week was better than nothing, and at least the New Year of '63 looked very much brighter.

That winter was a very bad one with endless snow, making the journey to work twice as long. Having a bath was an ordeal because the bathroom was so cold, with snow underfoot it was too much trouble to go out anywhere, and quite often Laura got into bed the minute she got home because she felt so lonely and miserable.

During the spring Jackie broke up with Roger. He had been promoted at work, and his new job involved much longer hours and a lot of travelling. Jackie thought he was using work as an excuse to get some time away from her, and after a blazing row they parted.

Laura pretended to be very sympathetic, but in reality she was delighted. She came up with the idea that they both needed to get out of London for a while, and she found unlikely allies in Jackie's parents. They had liked Roger, but had always felt Jackie was too young to settle down, and it was they who suggested the girls should apply to a holiday camp for the summer season. They said that a complete change would be the making of both of them, and that Jackie would benefit from learning to take care of herself.

They couldn't get in at Butlin's because they applied too late. But they got accepted by a far smaller holiday company called Drake's, which had several sites in Devon and Dorset, as entertainers.

Both of them were very excited, even though the grand job description only meant they had to entertain children on the site during the day, and organize games with the adults during the evening. The pay was very poor, just £2 a week, plus accommodation, and meals in the site café, but the manager said they would get tips from the holidaymakers if they worked hard, and they would get a bonus of a further £2 for every week if they stayed till the end of the season.

They arrived at Drake's near Brixham in Devon in mid-May in heavy rain to find the site a desolate sea of mud. They were tempted to turn tail and run, for the place looked run down, deserted and grim. There were no chalets, only caravans, and the amenities consisted of a shop, café, children's playground, shower block and a club room, all of which badly needed a coat of fresh paint.

In their naivety they had imagined a swimming pool, pretty flower beds, fairground rides and continental-style cafés. They'd seen themselves in the glamorous role of Butlin's Redcoats, but it was immediately clear they would not be that.

The caretaker, who introduced himself as Alf, was well over fifty, with rotting teeth. As he showed them to the old and tiny caravan which was to be their home, he warned them the damp could make their clothes and shoes go mouldy.

He left them to settle in, saying he would make them a cup of tea later and show them where the games equipment was stored. He seemed to be somewhat amused that they had been taken on as entertainers, but didn't explain why.

'It's going to be awful, isn't it?' Jackie said in a shaky voice. She prodded the seat cushions which doubled as a bed, and winced because they felt damp. 'Can you imagine what sort of people would come here for a holiday?'

Laura could. People like she'd grown up with in Shepherds Bush! There wouldn't be any nice boys, just men with braces over their vests and their trousers rolled up. The children would be evil little guttersnipes, and they'd have mothers who screamed at them all day, then got very drunk at night.

She might have known there would be a catch to the job. At the interview, the general manager hadn't even asked them what sort of relevant experience they had of organizing games with large numbers of children. All he'd really said was that they would be there to make sure everyone had a good time, and to deal with any problems which might crop up.

He'd made more of an issue about the tips they'd get if they made sure the holidaymakers enjoyed themselves. The girls were so convinced they could make the holidaymakers ecstatically happy that they imagined they'd come home rich at the end of the season. They'd almost bitten his hand off for the job.

They were unpacking their clothes and trying to fit them into an inadequately small wardrobe when the sun suddenly came out.

The caravan was instantly warmer, and when they looked through the grimy windows they saw the mist had lifted and the sea was visible at the end of the campsite.

'It doesn't look so bad now,' Laura remarked. 'Let's have some music, that might cheer us up.'

She turned on the transistor radio Lena had given them, and the song playing was 'Don't Let the Sun Catch You Crying' by Gerry and the Pacemakers. They looked at each other in astonishment, and started to laugh.

It was the laughter that summer which Laura remembered better than anything else. The caravan might have been damp and cramped, the food in the café awful, and when it rained they got daubed with mud. But the girls were back together and they both felt light-hearted after all the intensity of the previous year.

The holidaymakers were in the main quite poor and rough, but they were out to enjoy themselves and they appreciated anything Laura and Jackie did for them. The girls never did think up the brilliant games to play with the children that they'd intended, it was just rounders, team games or reading them stories. But mostly the weather was good, and people went off to the beaches even when it wasn't. By the time they came over to the club room in the evening, they were more than happy to play a few games of bingo, musical chairs, or pass balloons from one pair of knees to another, as long as they had plenty to drink.

There was a band who played twice a week, and a DJ on the other nights, and the girls would encourage everyone to sing along. They also ran a talent competition each week and these were invariably hilarious, with children singing 'Mary Had a Little Lamb,' or some old drunk trying to be Jim Reeves. During the whole summer they never found anyone who had any real talent. But the holidaymakers loved it, just as they did the Pirate Nights, when they put a patch over their eye and painted a moustache on their upper lip, or the Twist competition which everyone from three to eighty took part in.

But the best fun for the girls took place late at night. There were many like-minded young people working in the area for the summer, from chambermaids to waiters and bar staff, and they soon found them, plus the more affluent men who sailed in and out of Brixham on yachts.

Mostly they gathered at a small drinking club in the town, and as neither Jackie nor Laura was keen to have a regular boyfriend again for a while, they played the field, enjoyed the attention they got and didn't take anything too seriously.

It was the best of times. The worst they did was to give

a few men false hopes, and suck up to the holidaymakers so they'd tip them when they left.

But the real value of that summer job to Laura was that it gave her the confidence she so badly lacked and opened up her mind to other possibilities. She had only been to the seaside a few times in her life, and then only to Southend and Brighton. She hadn't known that Devon was so beautiful, and the rolling hills, thatched cottages, rivers, moors and woodland enchanted her. But she had also shone a lot brighter than Jackie with the holidaymakers, for she knew how ordinary working-class people thought, and what they wanted and needed.

Suddenly she was aware of her own potential, that she was no longer 'Stinky Wilmslow', the plain, skinny girl that no one wanted. Someone at the holiday camp had dubbed her 'Lovely Laura' and the name stuck not only with everyone she met there, but in her own mind. She realized she didn't have to wait for a man to come along to fulfil her dreams; she was quite clever enough to do that herself.

Both she and Jackie felt bereft at the end of the season when they had to say goodbye to all the friends they'd made in Devon. They dreaded the prospect of the London rush hour, the tedium of a nine to five job, when for the whole summer they'd never known what would happen next, and grown used to fresh air, lots of exercise and freedom.

They talked about it endlessly as they helped out giving the caravans a final clean. They were determined they wouldn't go back to boring office work; they both wanted exciting jobs. They thought of going abroad, but as neither of them had a passport, that would take time to organize, and in any case, the bonus money they'd get when they left the holiday camp wasn't enough to get them very far.

Back in London, Laura stayed with Jackie for some weeks in Muswell Hill, and it was while working for an agency as office temps that they heard about promotional work. Girls were needed for exhibitions, trade fairs and in-store promotions, and although the hours were usually longer than in office work, the pay was better and there was a lot of variety, as they could be selling tractors one week at an agricultural show, and promoting a new perfume the next.

They saw some glossy photographs of a team of girls working at the Motor Show in Earl's Court who were all as glamorous as models, wearing evening dresses. They heard on the grapevine that these girls got offered work all over the country; they were put up in nice hotels and had a great time while being paid for it. Jackie and Laura just looked at each other and knew it was for them.

As bells rang out for the New Year of 1965, Jackie clinked her glass of champagne with Laura's. 'We've arrived,' she whispered.

They were in Scott's, a very select night club in Mayfair, the guests of Colin Trueman, a businessman they'd met back in October while working at the Toy Fair in Earl's Court. They were both in evening dresses, Laura's cream chiffon, Jackie's pale blue, and when they looked around them they felt equal and even superior to any of the other women in the club, for their dresses, hair, nails and makeup were perfect, evidence of their new-found elegance and sophistication.

Gone for them were the days of the teetering beehive. It might still reign in places like Peckham or Shepherds Bush, but the models in *Vogue* wore their hair long, loose and shiny. Jackie had an unfair advantage as hers was thick and curly and such a glorious natural colour, but Laura wasn't far behind. She had dyed hers a rich dark brown, with a thick, straight fringe which accentuated her dark brown eyes.

In a few days' time it would be her twenty-first birthday,

and when she looked in the mirror, she liked what she saw. Her skin glowed, her hair shone, and she was blessed with a perfect size 10 body and long, slender legs. Men often told her she was beautiful but it was only in the last year that she'd finally realized it was true, and that the sad little girl from Shepherds Bush was gone for ever.

She and Jackie considered themselves seasoned promotion girls now; whether they had the glamour jobs draped across a gleaming car at the Motor Show, demonstrating oven cleaner at the Ideal Home Exhibition, or merely handing out advertising leaflets on the street, they were good at it. Sometimes Jackie joked they were born for it, a pair of life's butterflies who hated being in one place for too long.

They had their own flat too, in Eardley Crescent, Earl's Court. They had started out in a double bedsitter, and luckily they were on the spot when their landlord decided to let out his own flat on the top floor. The two bedrooms were tiny, but after being cramped up in one room for so long, to the girls it was paradise to have a separate kitchen, their own bathroom and a real sitting room.

They'd furnished it with junk-shop finds, something Jackie had a nose for, painted it all white, and got masses of cord carpeting from one of the exhibitions they were working at. Laura had even managed to sweet-talk one of the exhibition men into fitting it for them.

Life was really good. They worked long hours, often away from London, but the pay and expenses were excellent and in the last year they'd made lots of new friends, gone to parties, dinners and clubs, and they'd had countless dates and a great deal of fun.

Most of the men they went out with were married, and they didn't care as long as they were prepared to show them a good time. Jackie often hankered for another Roger, someone to love and be loved by, but Laura much preferred the thrill of illicit dinners and nights away in a hotel. Married men were invariably better lovers, they gave presents, and they were easy to get rid of once she got bored. She had no intention of marrying anyone just for love; they'd have to be rich before she'd even look twice at them.

'We can do even better,' Laura replied, clinking Jackie's glass. 'Here's to one day having our own company and becoming millionaires!'

This was their private little dream, and hardly a week passed without them coming up with an idea that might make it come true. But however good their ideas were, they had no capital to get launched. One of the reasons they liked coming to parties like this one was because they might well meet someone prepared to back them.

'So what resolutions are we going to make this year?' Jackie asked.

'Maybe to save some money,' Laura suggested. 'Or perhaps we should learn to drive?'

'Good thinking, wonder girl,' Jackie giggled. 'If we had a car we could spend the summer doing outside promotions all over England. But right now my only resolution is to get drunk on champagne. Someone told me it doesn't give you a hangover.'

A few weeks later, in early February, Jackie got a couple of weeks' work in Leeds promoting a new range of nail products. As she had met a man she fancied, she decided to stay over instead of coming home for Sunday and Monday.

Laura had been on a training course for a cosmetics company, but it finished on Wednesday and she didn't have to start work with the company until the following Tuesday. She was pleased to have a few days by herself. Jackie was never very good at cleaning up or doing her washing, and she moaned when Laura tried to do it when she was there. She spent Thursday going to the laundrette, and then spring-cleaned the flat. But by Saturday she had run out of things to do, and it was too cold and wet to go out to the shops.

It was the tidiness of the flat that set her off thinking about her family. She always felt soothed when the whole flat was immaculate, the kitchen smelling fresh and clean, and the bathroom sparkling. Jackie often teased her about her love of cleanliness and order and Laura would laugh it off, but she had a real fear that if she ever allowed things to really slide, she could become the way her mother was.

Now, as she looked at the magazines tidily stacked in a rack, the fringe on the rug in front of the gas fire neatly brushed out, and the cushions on the couch just so, she wondered if her mother had finally learned to clean the house in Barnes properly. Or if Meggie had been pressed into doing everything Laura used to do.

In the six years since she left there, she'd thought about her mother and the little ones a great deal, especially on birthdays and at Christmas. In a way it was worse than losing her family through bereavement because she knew they were out there getting on with their lives, but she could have no part in it.

She wondered whether Mark and Paul went straight when they got out of borstal, how Meggie, Ivy and Freddy were doing at school, and what they all looked like six years on. There had been many times when she was tempted to go over to Barnes and hang around in the hopes she'd see them. But she never had because she knew a glimpse of them wouldn't be enough, she'd have to talk to them.

She was totally aware that daydreams of happy reunions, June throwing her arms around her and the kids all cuddling her, were just fantasy. The reality was that June would almost certainly resent her turning up again and complicating her life with Vincent, and Laura knew she couldn't handle seeing him again.

But remembering what he did to her suddenly made her realize that Meggie was fifteen now and Ivy thirteen, the ideal ages for a man with a fondness for young girls. The thought that her pretty little sisters might suffer that was horrific, and all at once she knew she had to go over to Barnes and warn June.

All Saturday night she could think of nothing else. She had always been wary of Vincent, but her sisters hadn't. So how much easier would it be to lure them into it?

By Sunday morning she no longer cared if June sent her away with a flea in her ear. She had to go, whatever the consequences, or spend the rest of her life feeling ashamed she'd hadn't attempted to protect Meggie and Ivy.

She dressed very carefully for the visit, for she wanted to convey the message that she was successful and sophisticated so that her mother would take her seriously, yet at the same time didn't want to look as if she was showing off. Finally she settled for a navy pencil skirt and white sweater and borrowed Jackie's string of chunky dark blue beads. With high heels and her hair fixed back with a velvet bow at the nape of her neck, she thought her image was just right. Her winter coat was navy too, and she brightened it up with a red scarf and matching gloves.

The bus ride seemed endless because she had butterflies in her stomach. She wished now that she'd planned this earlier so she would have had time to buy the children a present each. All she'd been able to get on a Sunday was a big box of Quality Street, and a bunch of flowers for her mother.

She stood outside the house in Barnes for some time before she plucked up the courage to push open the gate and walk through the front garden. It didn't look so big, or as grand as she remembered, just a very ordinary double-fronted red brick house, and the dark blue front door needed painting.

There was a fence on either side of the house now, with a gate on one side. When she'd lived here it was open all the way around and she could remember Freddy riding his tricycle right round the house. The cherry trees in the front had grown very big, and the leaves which had fallen in autumn were still lying on the grass. She thought that was odd, as Vincent had always been really fussy about how the garden looked. But she was pleased to see his car wasn't there – that at least should make the visit easier.

Meggie opened the door, at least Laura had to assume it was her, for she didn't actually recognize her. She was as tall as Laura, and a lot heavier, her hair up in a beehive, her eyes dark-ringed, Cleopatra style. She looked at Laura blankly.

'It's me, Laura,' she said. 'I can't believe it's you, Meggie! You're all grown up.'

'What do you want?' her sister replied in a surly fashion, half closing the door on her body as if to prevent entry.

Laura was taken aback by such hostility. She'd prepared herself for it from June and Vincent, but she hadn't for one moment thought her sisters would be anything but overjoyed to see her.

'I wanted to see you, and Ivy and Freddy,' she said, her heart sinking.

'Who is it, Meggie?' her mother shouted from the back of the house.

'It's Laura,' Meggie shouted back. She scowled at her older sister. 'She won't want to see you!'

Suddenly June was there at the door, her expression one of complete disbelief. 'You!' she said.

'Yes, it's me.' Laura felt like running away now. 'I came to see how you all are.'

'It's taken six years to remember us, has it?' June snapped.

She looked good, far younger than Laura had expected. Her hair was still blonde, but a far prettier honey-blonde, and it curled on her shoulders. She was a little plumper, but it suited her, as did the pink sweater she was wearing.

'May I come in and talk to you?' Laura asked. 'There were good reasons why I left.'

'You slunk away like a thief in the night,' June exclaimed, her voice rising to a shriek. 'You didn't write or phone. You could have been dead for all I knew.'

'Just let me explain,' Laura retorted. 'But I can't talk about it out here, so please let me in.'

'You've come back because of the money, haven't you?'

'What money?' Laura was confused now.

'The money Vincent left,' Meggie chimed in. 'Well, you won't get anything, so you might as well sling yer hook.'

The thought flashed through Laura's mind that Meggie might as well have stayed in Shepherds Bush; she looked and sounded like the tarts that hung around the market.

Laura glanced from Meggie to her mother. 'Are you trying to say Vincent's dead?' she asked.

'As if you didn't know,' June retorted.

'I didn't. How would I know? I haven't kept in touch with anyone from around here. I only came to see you and the kids. I had no idea he was dead, and I certainly don't want any of his money.'

She held out the flowers and the box of sweets. 'I'll go right now if you don't believe me, Mum. It was because of him that I left, and he was the reason I didn't feel able to get in touch. But I got to thinking that it wasn't right not to know how you are, that's all.'

June hesitated, then begrudgingly said she'd better come in, but she flounced off towards the kitchen as if this offer was only because she wasn't prepared to stand at the front door.

Laura followed and to her horror found the once beautiful kitchen was a complete shambles. The table in the middle was strewn with dirty plates, the sink held even more, and the tiled floor was so dirty it was clear it hadn't been washed for weeks.

June sat down and immediately lit up a cigarette, and the smell of it and the mess took Laura straight back to their days in Shepherds Bush. She automatically began stacking up the dirty plates and wondered how long some of them had been on the table. 'So when did he die and of what?' she asked.

'Back in November, of a heart attack,' June said curtly. 'Since then I've hardly slept, I feel lousy, and it hasn't helped that people keep coming here and wanting what's mine.'

'Who has been here?'

'Oh, his sons, his sister and his niece, not to mention the woman he was carrying on with.'

Laura had hoped against hope that Vincent wouldn't be in today, but however much she disliked and feared him she was shocked that he was dead. It was clear from the chaos that June couldn't cope, and judging by Meggie's surly attitude, she was no help. Yet although Laura felt concern, she couldn't help but feel this was like a re-run of the old days, and that once again her mother was burdening her with problems that were not of her making. Had she looked ill or very tired Laura might have felt real sympathy, but someone who could get up and do their hair and makeup could certainly wash the dishes.

She looked round and saw Meggie was standing insolently in the doorway, arms folded. 'Help me clear up, Meggie,' she said. 'And while we do it Mum can tell me everything.'

'I'm not sodding well clearing up,' Meggie snarled. 'Why should I? I give her three quid a week for my keep and Sundays is me only day off.'

'What a charitable soul you turned out to be,' Laura said sarcastically. 'If you can't or won't help around the house you should go and live in a hotel. But you won't get one of those for three quid a week.'

Meggie turned on her heel and disappeared. 'Is she always like that?' Laura asked her mother. 'She used to be so sweet and helpful.'

'She's been a cow since she was about fourteen. She seems to hate me and everyone else. She left school the minute she turned fifteen and now she seems to think it's my fault she only got to work in a baker's.'

Laura put the kettle on, and continued clearing the table. 'You'd better explain everything to me,' she said.

By the time Laura had washed and dried up, made tea and was sitting down with her mother at the table, she had learned that her parents got divorced three years ago, while her father was still in prison. 'I got pregnant again, soon after,' June said gloomily. 'I didn't want it, I was too bloody old for another baby, but Vince thought it was wonderful and married me. Well, I lost it at six months and it made me go a bit funny. Next thing I know he's going out till all hours of the night, and he's got another woman.'

Laura made sounds of sympathy for it was sad for anyone to lose a baby, even if they said they didn't want it. But she could imagine that what June meant by going a bit 'funny' was that she'd stopped looking after the home and herself. Vincent had always been fussy, and no doubt he came to regret marrying her. Laura didn't think a man in his sixties ought to be still playing around with other women, but maybe June drove him to it.

'Who was the other woman?' she asked.

'Some stuck-up cow from Chiswick. She had the cheek to come to Vince's funeral! She had no shame, she talked to all his friends and relatives like she were the bleedin' widow. Then she comes round here and tells me Vince was going to divorce me and marry her, and he would have wanted her to have the house. I ask you! The barefaced cheek of the woman!'

'She won't have a leg to stand on unless he left it to her in his will.' Laura said. 'What was in his will?'

'That's the problem, he hadn't made a new one.' June began to cry. 'The one his solicitor had was made before his first wife died. He said he was going to make a new one when we got married, but he never did it.'

'Well, you're fine then,' Laura said. 'It all goes to the wife in that case. No one can chuck you out of the house.'

'That's not what his sons say, or that cow. The sons reckon they should get it because this house was bought with their mother's money, and that bitch says she's got a letter from Vince where he said I tricked him into marrying me. He said he was going to get rid of me and my brats because I was a lazy slut. She reckons he wanted her to have everything if he snuffed it.'

'I don't think for one moment that would stand up in court,' Laura replied thoughtfully. 'Have you been to a solicitor?'

'Yes, but half the time I don't know what he's talking about. He said that in this case, the court will look into the whole family and decide who has what. Even if they favour me, Vince's kids can appeal against it and have a share. What chance do I have over them? They went to posh schools and university, they know what they are doing.'

'Then you have to get a solicitor who knows what he is doing. I could come with you and speak up for you,' Laura offered.

'You do want a slice of the pie then?' June said nastily.

'You what?' Laura exclaimed. 'I don't want even the scrapings from his toe nails. Don't you know why I left? He was always coming on to me. Part of the reason I came today was that I was afraid he'd start on Meggie or Ivy.'

June looked at her as if she'd just come down from Mars. 'Don't be bloody silly! He didn't even like you, and he treated Meggie and Ivy like they were his own flesh and blood.'

A kind of snort from behind her made Laura turn to see Meggie was back standing in the doorway, listening. 'Did he touch you, Meggie?' Laura asked.

She had the same insolent, arms-crossed stance as earlier, but her expression had changed from sulky to wary. Instinctively Laura knew that Vincent had pestered her, and maybe that was why she was acting so hostile. 'Did he, Meggie?' she asked more gently. 'You should tell us if he did. I expect he said you were never to tell Mum or he'd throw you all out. That's what he told me.'

'Don't put such ideas into her head,' June suddenly screamed out. 'How dare you come walking in here telling lies about my Vince?'

Laura was horrified June would defend Vincent even though he had betrayed her, yet not show any concern about her own daughters.

'Do you really think I'd have left here at fifteen if there was nothing wrong?' Laura shouted back angrily. 'He made it impossible for me to stay, and you were a bloody useless mother, you couldn't even see what was going on under your very nose.'

'She hasn't changed,' Meggie said dourly.

All at once Laura wished she hadn't come. June was beyond her help, for whatever Laura did for her, whether it was practical stuff like cleaning up, or giving her sensible advice, she'd just go her own way. By tomorrow there would be more dirty dishes on the table, she'd still be sitting here smoking and not acting on advice. She wouldn't stir herself to fight this other woman, or Vince's greedy sons, she was what she'd always been, lazy and stupid.

'Where are Ivy and Freddy?' she asked.

'Out somewhere,' June replied, her tone suggesting she had no idea where and cared less.

'You've got to pull yourself together, Mum,' Laura said. 'You should know where Freddy and Ivy are, what is wrong with Meggie, and you should be a real mother to all three of them and look after this place.'

June looked Laura up and down, pursing her lips. 'Looks like you've done well for yerself anyway, gotta sugar daddy?'

'No, I bloody well haven't,' Laura snapped back at her. 'I've worked and kept myself ever since I left here. And I'm going now, I can see you don't give a toss about me, and if Vincent was touching Meggie up, then at least he can't do it any more.'

'That's right, run out on us again!' June retorted.

Laura was exasperated. 'What do you want of me?' she asked. 'To be your slave like I used to be, I suppose. Maybe you want me to nip down the shops and steal a few groceries too? Well, I'm not coming round here to clean up after you, or to be insulted. If you can't talk to me properly, I won't come again. I've got a good life now, no thanks to you, and I'm not going to let you destroy it.'

'You don't know what I went through when you left,' June said, tears coming into her eyes. 'I couldn't sleep for worry, the little ones kept asking for you. And all Vince kept saying was that you thieved money off him.'

'He was right about that, I did,' Laura admitted. 'He owed it to me after what he'd put me through. Didn't you even suspect what he was doing to me?'

'She don't care about anything but herself,' Meggie piped up. 'Soon as I've got a few bob behind me I'll be off too.'

Laura felt helpless. She could see everything that she'd

once felt in Meggie's face. If she hung around until Ivy and Freddy came back no doubt she'd see and hear more that would distress her. She was a little touched by June's claim she was very upset when she left, but that was probably yet another ruse to play on her sympathy.

'What happened to Mark and Paul?' Laura asked.

'Back inside,' Meggie said. 'They was out for a couple of years, kept coming round tapping Mum up for money, and like a mug she gave it to them. Then they got caught burgling some house in Hampstead and they got a couple of years apiece.'

Just the way Meggie spoke made Laura shudder. It was clear she was hanging around now with a rough crowd and had picked up their way of speaking and acting. She had been such a sweet little kid, so eager to please, and loving too. How could all that have gone?

'How are you managing for money?' she asked June.

'I've got a widow's pension.' She shrugged. ''Course that don't go very far, and until the probate gets sorted I can't touch nothing in Vince's bank account.'

Laura took £10 out of her purse. It was all she had apart from a few coins. 'That's all I can spare right now,' she said. 'Go back to the solicitor and tell him that you've got nothing. The more information you give him, the more likely he is to see you right. I'll phone again on Thursday, and if by then you want me to go with you to see him, I will.'

'You'd better leave us your address and telephone number,' June said, without even looking up or thanking her for the money.

A stab of fear struck Laura. She knew full well that once the address was handed over, the first time June, or even Meggie, had a problem they'd be round.

'I'll phone you,' she replied. 'I work away from London

a lot so I'm rarely at home. I must go now because I've got some work to prepare for tomorrow. Will you walk down to the bus stop with me, Meggie?'

She expected a rebuff, but Meggie nodded, then went to get her coat.

'Bye, Mum.' Laura bent to kiss June and the smell of smoke lingering around her took her right back to her childhood and made her eyes prickle. 'I always cared about you,' she blurted out. 'I only left because of Vince. But pull yourself together and clear up, eh? This is a lovely house and if you get Vince's money you'll be on easy street. You're luckier than most.'

June's arm went around Laura's waist, and for a second she leaned into her chest. 'I'll try,' she murmured. 'And I'm glad to know you're safe and grown into a beauty.'

6

Stuart paid off the taxi outside the Alexandra nursing home in Muswell Hill and walked up to the front door carrying a bouquet of flowers. The elegant Victorian terrace was very similar to Duke's Avenue where Lena Thompson used to live, but three houses had been converted into the home, and the original front gardens were now paved over.

In the middle bay window he could see two white-haired old ladies nodding off in chairs, and he was saddened to think that Lena, who had always been so young at heart, vibrant and energetic, should end up here so prematurely.

'Mrs Thompson isn't very keen on coming down to the lounge,' the plump, red-faced nurse who answered the door informed him. 'Go on up to her room, it's number six on the first floor, left at the top of the stairs.'

Stuart was horrified by the stale smell of old age and sickness permeating the home, even though it was tastefully appointed and spotlessly clean. It was very close too, with no windows open, but he supposed the old folks felt chilly when they couldn't move around. He understood now why Belle had tried to put him off visiting her mother, and perhaps he shouldn't have come.

He knocked tentatively on the door of number 6, expecting a feeble voice to reply, but to his surprise the door sprang open instantly, and there stood Lena.

She didn't look much different to when he'd last seen her ten years earlier. She was more conventionally dressed in a button-through summer frock, her hair was grey and cut short and the lines on her face had deepened, but she certainly didn't look like the old biddies he'd glimpsed downstairs.

'Stuart!' she exclaimed, clapping her hands over her mouth in shock at seeing him. 'What a wonderful surprise! I thought it was that bloody old vicar who seems to think I need to put myself straight with God before I snuff it.'

Stuart laughed with relief. If she knew him instantly she clearly wasn't senile, and that irreverent remark was typical of the kind of things she always used to say.

'It's good to see you again, Lena,' he said, handing her the flowers. 'May I come in?'

'Please do, and quickly, before anyone catches me with a man in my room,' she said impishly. She sniffed the flowers appreciatively. 'How lovely. Delphiniums and lilies, my absolute favourites.'

Lena's room was large, overlooking the gardens, with its own en suite bathroom, where she quickly placed the flowers in the wash basin saying she would arrange them in a vase later. Everything looked reassuringly comfortable and homely. In fact Stuart remembered some of the furniture, pictures, lamps and ornaments from Duke's Avenue. He saw she was still painting too; the small table in front of the window held her paint box, brushes and a large sketch pad. He felt an enormous sense of relief, for this was so much better than he had expected.

'Would you like a drink?' Lena asked. 'It is after three, and a visit from you is worthy of a celebration.' She opened a small cabinet and got out a bottle of single malt whisky, a mischievous expression on her face as if she was embarking on something wicked.

Stuart said he'd have a small one, and quickly explained how he'd been overseas and hadn't heard about Jackie's death until his return. 'I'm so sorry, Lena. It must have been shattering for you, and even worse to lose Frank so soon after.'

'Yes, it was,' she nodded, her bright smile fading. 'Absolutely awful! I was hanging on by a very slender thread after Jackie was killed, but when Frank went too the thread snapped. I'd known him since I was fifteen; he wasn't just a major part of my life, but the whole of it. But I guess I'd been very lucky to have a perfect life for so long, and that my luck just ran out.'

A lump came up in Stuart's throat, for she looked the way his mother had after his father died. Wistful but resigned, and not wishing to burden anyone else with her deep sorrow.

'I wish I could find some words to comfort you,' he said and moved forward to hug her. It was only as he held her that he realized she was far thinner and perhaps shorter than she used to be; she felt more like a child of twelve or thirteen than a grown woman.

'Enough sympathy,' she said, stepping back from him and turning to pick up their drinks. 'I miss them both terribly, but I have to carry on. And I want to know where you've been and if you've made your fortune yet.'

Stuart smiled, for he knew that when he first met her he often used the expression 'When I make my fortune'. He was touched that she remembered.

'I suppose I have,' he said, and as she sat down on one chair he took the other. 'But money's a funny thing – the more you get, the more you seem to need. I haven't got enough yet to retire to the Caribbean.'

'Still as handsome as ever though,' Lena smiled. 'Are you married yet?'

Stuart shook his head. 'Never met the right girl,' he said. 'And you were spoken for.'

He talked a little about his work and then went on to say how he'd been to Scotland to see Belle.

'She didn't tell me,' Lena said indignantly. 'I dare say she'll insist she did tell me when I reproach her, and that I'd forgotten, but she didn't. She seems to think I'm senile.'

Stuart thought it odd Belle had implied that to him too. 'Maybe she had a lot on her mind,' he said. 'But tell me why you moved in here. You don't look like you need to be in a nursing home.'

'I don't, not any more, but I was doolally after Frank died. I don't remember much about it now, but apparently I wasn't eating, acting strangely and wasn't looking after myself. My doctor recommended I came here. When I began to recover, we discussed the possibility of sheltered housing because the house in Duke's Avenue was far too big for me to live in alone. But I'd got to like it here by then, I had the nurses to have a chat and a laugh with, I've got lots of friends and old neighbours around here, so it's easy for them to drop in. They offered me this nice big room – they call it the VIP suite – and said I could bring my own stuff here to make it like my own home. So here I am, bowed but not beaten.'

'But isn't it far more expensive than living in your own place?' Stuart knew she must have got a small fortune from the sale of Duke's Avenue, but as he understood it, nursing-home fees could quickly eat that up.

'I made quite a good deal with the owners,' Lena smirked. 'You see, I don't need nursing, and they like having a few able-bodied people around as it's more cost effective for them. It's a bit like living in a hotel really, except I know I won't be kicked out if my health deteriorates.'

'Does that mean you are allowed out then?'

'Of course! It isn't a prison,' she said indignantly. 'I go up to the shops, to the library, and sometimes have a night or two away with a friend. I help in the garden, go out to dinner sometimes with friends. It's a bit depressing going down to the lounge or the dining room, mind you. Most of the other residents are gaga.'

'Well, I'm very glad you aren't,' he said, wondering why on earth Belle had told him that Lena probably wouldn't know him.

'How did Belle seem to you?' she asked, as if she'd picked up on his thoughts.

'Very bitter and angry about Laura! That's perfectly understandable, but I hadn't expected it. You see, when I read up on the trial, it seemed to me that Belle didn't believe Laura had done it.'

'And now she's rabid about her?' Lena raised one eyebrow quizzically.

'Well, yes,' Stuart agreed.

'I find that odd too,' Lena said thoughtfully. 'Frank, Toby and I went up to Scotland immediately we got the terrible news. We were all distraught of course, something like that is beyond anyone's comprehension, but Belle was hysterical, she kept being sick, and over and over again she insisted that Laura couldn't have done it.

'As it turned out, with Frank dying and me being in such a state, there was no question of my going to the trial. But Toby was there, and as I understand it Belle still believed totally in Laura's innocence and expected her to be acquitted. It was only later, when she came down here to sort me out, that she appeared to have completely changed her mind.'

'The weight of the evidence, I suppose,' Stuart said cautiously. 'What was Toby's opinion of the verdict?'

Lena frowned. 'He was very confused. It didn't help when he discovered that Laura lied to us all about her family. He said that she clearly wasn't the person he believed her to be.

As I expect Belle told you, he went off working abroad soon after – he's in Australia now.'

'I'm sorry, you must miss him a great deal,' Stuart said.

'I do, but in a way I'm glad he went, he's got a far better life there, a lovely young wife now too, and a baby on the way. They are coming over next year for a month, which will be lovely.'

Stuart smiled. 'So you'll be a granny at last, that's great. But getting back to the verdict in the trial, what did you think of it?'

'I was, and still am, convinced of Laura's innocence.'

'You are!' Stuart exclaimed in surprise.

'Belle will tell you that's because I'm losing my marbles,' Lena said, leaning towards him in a conspiratorial manner. 'But I knew Laura really well, almost as well as I knew Jackie. Yes, she lied about her family, she'd done a lot of things which perhaps she shouldn't have, but I know she was not the conniving, uncaring and evil person the lawyers and newspapers made her out to be. But you know that, Stuart, you were in love with her.'

'Yes, I was, Lena.' Stuart sighed. 'It is good to hear you stick up for her. You see, I went to see her in prison, and I believe she's innocent too.'

Lena sat back in her chair and smiled. 'That's wonderful, and very big of you to put aside past hurts. But then, you always were a very balanced and fair-minded person, that's why Frank and I liked you so much. Now, tell me how Laura is.'

'Not the glamour puss she used to be,' Stuart smiled wryly. 'But she's found some resources to keep herself sane in there and indeed she wrote to me after my visit and told me the whole story of her real childhood.'

'Will you tell it to me?'

Once again a lump came up in his throat. It was astounding

to him that this slight woman in her late seventies, who had had her happy life torn apart when she lost both her elder daughter and her beloved husband, still had the capacity to care about others.

'I can read it to you,' he said, reaching into the inside pocket of his jacket.

Lena looked at the wad of paper in his hand. 'I'll just put the flowers into a vase first,' she said. 'Would you like a top-up of your drink, or a cup of tea? I can make one, I've got my own kettle here.'

'Tea would be good,' Stuart said. 'Drinking whisky in the afternoon is great if you've got nothing on later, but I've got to meet someone this evening.'

He watched as Lena bustled about finding a large vase and scissors to trim the flower stems and filling up her kettle, her movements swift and economic. He didn't think she ought to be in this place surrounded by people waiting for death. She belonged the way she always used to, the matriarch at the very centre of not just her family, but all those other friends and friends of friends who gathered at Duke's Avenue. He remembered how she would encourage people to talk as she hastily prepared a vast dish of shepherd's pie or sausages and mash, how she always seemed to know exactly who had a problem they needed to share, or an issue they were troubled with.

By rights she should have had grandchildren running around her feet. She should be cosseted now by all those she'd helped so much with her ability to listen, her lack of bias or snobbery. And she should still have Frank by her side.

Life certainly wasn't fair.

Once the flowers were arranged and placed on the table, Lena made the tea and came back to sit down opposite Stuart.

'Right, let's have it,' she said in her typically direct manner.

It took Stuart some time to read Laura's letter. There were five pages with small, neat writing on both sides of the paper, not one crossing-out or spelling mistake, and she'd told the story so vividly he could almost smell the damp and mould in the basement of Thornfield Road. As he finished he looked at Lena for her response. She was staring at her hands on her lap and a tear trickled down her cheek.

'I suspected some of it,' she said quietly. 'Her Aunt Mabel never sounded real, more like a character invented by Agatha Christie. I thought that if she had really been that way Laura would have had better diction, and more sophisticated tastes. I noted too how wary she was of men, and how quickly and efficiently she did household chores, which isn't usual for young girls from the kind of genteel background she described. But I didn't ever probe because she had such a huge need to be liked and accepted. I was probably guilty of adding more detail to her fiction too. Etiquette, tales about my relatives, the finer points of middle-classdom – I'm sure you know the kind of things I mean.'

Stuart nodded. 'She genuinely loved you and Frank though. She used to talk about you such a lot when we first met. You had clearly been a tremendous influence on her. And she didn't exaggerate any of that, for the first time I came to Duke's Avenue with Jackie, it was, and you were, exactly how she'd described.'

'We loved her,' Lena said simply. 'She was easy to love. Frank once said she was like Judy, a stray dog we took in when the children were tiny. We saw her up at Alexandra Park and stroked her, and she followed us home. We didn't want a dog, but Judy seemed to know that and made herself as inconspicuous as possible until we'd come round to her being there. Laura was the same, she would wash up, do my ironing, put Belle and Toby to bed, she tidied Jackie's room, all without us really noticing. When she came to live here for a while after she and Jackie returned from a summer job in a holiday camp, she never encroached on any of our space, she made life easier and more ordered for me and all of us.'

She paused for a moment as if gathering herself. 'How can anyone feel betrayed that she lied? She was just fifteen when she left home, and she wanted something better than she'd been born to. A weaker person would have tried to gain sympathy for herself, but instead she rubbed it all out and began again. I actually think that is courageous. Don't you?'

'Yes, when you put it like that,' Stuart said. 'But what do you think changed her from the sweet and eager-to-please stray?' he asked.

'Ambition, bad influences and more hard knocks,' Lena said. 'When she and Jackie moved on to doing promotion work, the girls they worked with and the businessmen they met gave them the idea that wealth was the thing to strive for. In a way I was proud that they became a pair of go-getters, but I was worried about their increasing cynicism and avarice.'

'The sixties kind of encouraged that attitude.' Stuart shrugged. 'I know most people only remember the peace and love bit, but it was also a time for grabbing what you wanted.'

'I thought Laura would make it all by herself, she certainly had the hunger and the determination, and she had a good business head, but instead she tried to take a short cut to it by marrying Gregory Brannigan,' Lena stated and looked at Stuart as if she expected him to contradict her.

'I hardly know anything about Greg,' Stuart replied. 'When I first met Laura she said she left him because there was another woman, and that she didn't want to talk about it. She did tell me odd things later, that he was the owner of a toy company and that she worked for him. But mostly the lack of information about him made me afraid she still had feelings for him.'

'Nothing could be further from the truth,' Lena said stoutly. 'She hated him come the end, and she was very afraid of him. I only met him a few times but I could see that he was a very forceful, controlling man. In my opinion if it hadn't been for Jackie meeting up with Roger again, I don't think Laura would have even gone out with him for very long, much less married him.'

She smiled at Stuart's puzzled expression. 'You do know that Roger was Jackie's first real boyfriend, but they'd split up years before?'

'Yes. Laura told me that.'

'Well, she and Jackie were having the time of their lives until Roger came back on the scene and broke it up by asking Jackie to marry him. He had a down on Laura for some reason and suddenly she was left right out in the cold, lonely and rudderless. Greg seized the opportunity, whisking Laura off for weekends, dinner in smart places, and the next thing she was engaged to him. Both Jackie and I warned her that he was far too controlling, but I don't think she could see beyond his house in Chelsea, the toy company and the fact that he came out of the top drawer. She married him, then Barney came along in 1970. Jackie and I thought we were wrong about Greg then – outwardly he seemed the ideal husband – but Laura was doing what she's so often done since, covering things up. In fact I believe she was going through hell with him.'

Stuart frowned, remembering that when Laura walked out on him, he had become convinced that he and Greg had a great deal in common, for they'd both been kicked in the teeth by her.

He'd asked Jackie about him once, but she'd just passed him off as a 'perve'. As that could have meant anything from a man touching up other women at parties to liking to dress up in Laura's clothes, he let the subject drop. But he had been shocked when years later, just after Barney's death, Jackie told him in a letter how she'd telephoned Greg's parents to tell them what had happened, and to get an address or telephone number for their son. She said they'd almost bitten her head off, asking why she saw fit to tell them, as Barney was nothing to them, or Greg.

Stuart had known Gregory had never paid maintenance for his son and had never attempted to contact Laura so he could see him, but he found it unbelievable that anyone could be so callous about the death of a child.

'What sort of hell did he put her through, Lena?' Stuart asked.

She grimaced. 'It's not for me to say and anyway I only know the edited version. Ask her. If she could write all that about her childhood, I'm sure it would do her good to get him off her chest too.'

'I want to try and find grounds for an appeal against her conviction,' Stuart admitted. 'You'd better keep that to yourself for now, until I'm sure I've got something to base it on. I'm meeting an old friend tonight for dinner, he's a lawyer and I hope he'll help me. Can you think of anyone else who might give me a different slant on what I already know?'

'What about her sister?' Lena suggested. 'One of the nurses here showed me a newspaper cutting once. It was already well out of date, for I hadn't been up to reading it at the time, but it was the story Laura's mother had sold to the press. Talk about Judas and the thirty pieces of silver! She really sold her daughter down the river! But there was a small piece added on, a brief interview with Laura's sister, it would be the older one, Meggie. She didn't actually deny what her mother had said, but she said something about there being two sides to every story. Obviously the paper didn't enlarge on it as they wanted Laura to look as evil as possible. Maybe if you got in touch with the paper you could find out where she lives. I think it was the *News of the World*.'

'I'll try that,' Stuart said. 'There's one thing more, Lena. Did you see anything of Laura after Barney died?'

'Of course.' Lena looked almost indignant at the implication that she might not have done. 'She came to Duke's Avenue and stayed for a while with Frank and me when she was going through the worst of it. It was me who arranged for her to go to my friends in Italy to work after that. You surely didn't think we had abandoned her then?'

'No, Lena.' Stuart reached out and patted her hand. 'It was just because of the circumstances of Barney's death, I thought Laura might have distanced herself from you.'

'She never did blame Jackie. In fact Laura said it was her fault because she had never got Barney into the habit of putting his seat belt on. They were united in grief over him. Frank and I were too – when he was born we were almost like grandparents to him. We didn't see him very often once she moved to Scotland, but she always brought him to visit us whenever she came back to London.'

'Did his death change Laura's personality?'

'She always had more sides than a fifty-pence piece,' Lena retorted. 'You of all people know that! The side uppermost at that time was what you'd expect, a woman racked with guilt. It looked for a time as if she'd lost her mind.'

'There was a great deal in the press cuttings about her being a neglectful mother,' Stuart said gently. 'Was that true, Lena?'

Lena sighed deeply. 'Let's just say I saw no evidence of it when I saw them together, but then I only saw them about

173

once a year. I know Jackie worried about Barney, so obviously something was wrong. It certainly was true that Laura went off the rails for a while, which was why Jackie had Barney with her so often. But I don't believe it was anywhere near as bad as the press would have us believe – she certainly didn't hit or starve him.'

'You say she nearly lost her mind. They made quite a bit about that too in the trial. How long was she like that for?'

'A good six months before Frank and I brought her down here to stay with us. She stayed with us for four or five months and she was very poorly. But eventually she was well enough for me to fix her up with a job in a hotel in Italy owned by friends of ours.

'When she returned at the end of that summer, she was much quieter and more thoughtful. She never did get back that bouncy, I-know-it-all side we had all come to know so well. She was gentler and far more caring. Jackie once said that she'd give anything to see her being a real bitch again, because that way she'd feel she was genuinely getting over Barney's death.'

'Really!' Stuart exclaimed. He knew Lena had always been very observant, and not one to be easily fooled.

'Yes. So if you thought Laura might have developed a violent streak, or the desire for revenge, she certainly didn't. She threw herself into getting that shop in Edinburgh. Do you know about that?'

'Not until just recently. I know very little about how Laura lived after we split up. Although I was working for Jackie for the first few years, she rarely spoke about her to me, you know how loyal she was! I was working in Germany in '81 when Barney died, and it was Roger who rang me about it. After that my contact with Jackie was erratic. I would phone her, or send postcards, usually from airports because I was moving around quite a bit. Every now and then a letter from her would eventually reach me, but she never said much about what she or anyone else was doing, they were just her usual brand of funny letters, a joy to receive, but with very little information in them. But they fizzled out altogether by '91 and as I was in South America with new friends myself, I didn't think anything of it.'

'She was very busy with Brodie Farm then,' Lena said. 'I didn't hear from her that much either, but she was very proud of how well Laura was doing in the shop. She said it was always really busy and Laura was in her element because she loved clothes and knew what was good. She worked at it tirelessly by all accounts. I saw Laura sometimes as she had a contact down here for ballgowns she used to hire out, and she'd come and stay with me.'

'So how was she?' Stuart asked, knowing Lena wouldn't be easily fooled.

'Well, to the rest of the world she might have looked like she was over it, but I saw the deep sadness in her. Of course any woman who'd lost a child would be the same.'

'And Jackie? It must have changed her too?'

'Oh yes.' Lena sighed deeply. 'She needed some kind of anaesthetic to dull the pain. Mostly she used work, often putting in a sixteen-hour day on the house and garden. But there was drink too, and occasionally men. There was someone special, mind you! I think the problem there was that he was married. Now and then she would phone me late at night when she'd been drinking and she'd cry and say she felt hopeless. But the next day she'd be fine again and she'd apologize for worrying me. I couldn't help but worry, I just wished she'd tell me the whole story so I understood. But she would laugh it off and make out everything was fine. I used to tell myself that she had Belle nearby, and Laura in Edinburgh, but I wish now that Frank and I had gone up there more often.'

Lena sat back in her chair, and Stuart could see she was growing tired. He had so much more he wanted to ask her, but not today.

'I ought to go now,' he said, getting up. 'It's been great to find you haven't changed, and if it's okay, I'll come again.'

'Please do, Stuart.' She smiled up at him. 'It has been so good to talk to you. Toby will be pleased to hear you came too. He wanted to contact you while we were waiting for the trial. He went out to Brodie Farm and looked through all Jackie's papers, but he couldn't find an address or phone number for you.'

'I've been something of a nomad,' Stuart said. 'But I'll be back here for a while now, and I'll keep in touch.'

She got up out of her chair stiffly. 'Do what you can for Laura,' she pleaded, putting one hand on his arm. 'She's lost the two people she cared about most, and I know how that feels.'

'Well, hello, David, you old bastard!' Stuart exclaimed when he walked into the bistro in Putney and found his old friend already there, sitting at a table. David was the same age as himself, but despite being a lawyer, he had the look of a sportsman: clear, tanned skin, muscular and very fit. 'You look great – receding hair makes you look even more intelligent.'

David laughed and stood up. 'Glad you've lost none of your incisive wit. Good to see you again.'

David already had a beer and he ordered one for Stuart. They told the waiter they'd order food later.

Stuart had met David Stoyle on the plane flying out to Columbia back in the eighties. Stuart was going as a joiner to a new site the oil company had acquired in Bogotá. David was one of the company lawyers. Had they not been given seats next to each other, they would probably never have met, much less become close friends, because management and the manual workforce didn't normally socialize.

David was from a rarefied white-collar world. He'd been to public school and university, and though not a snob or a stuffed shirt, he normally mixed with people from a similar background to himself. But stuck on a long flight side by side with someone of the same age, both a little apprehensive about the unknown quantity of their destination, they soon got talking.

By the time they got off the plane with thick heads from too much whisky, their friendship was sealed. They had discovered they shared the same passion for climbing and were both adventurers at heart. David loved rugby, sailing, cycling and running. Stuart loved football, playing the guitar and chess. Yet their different interests and backgrounds didn't matter, and they knew that they would be searching each other out constantly in the next few months. As Stuart said at the time, 'We're mates now.'

Back then David had a fine head of light brown curly hair which became attractively blond-streaked in the sun. He was a good-looking man with a fine physique and bright blue eyes that won him many female admirers. Over the years Stuart had taken a mischievous delight in pointing out that his friend, who had so many great advantages over lesser mortals, was actually losing his hair. But then David took equal pleasure in teasing Stuart about his skinny legs.

'So what's the real reason for insisting on meeting up with me tonight?' David asked after they'd caught up with some of their news and ordered steak. 'I know there is one or you would have invited yourself to my house. Julia thinks you want to lure me away to the Third World but are too cowardly to do your presentation in front of her.'

Stuart laughed. Julia had been David's girlfriend when they met; now they were married with two children, Abigail and William. David was always jetting off to some far-flung place with his work, and as Stuart was often there too, as project manager, Julia jokingly blamed him for making her a grass widow.

'Julia can rest assured I have no interest in luring you away anywhere,' he said. 'I just wanted you to point me in the right direction to get help for a friend.'

As concisely as he could, Stuart explained about Laura and how he hoped he could find grounds for an appeal against her conviction. 'I've already been to see her lawyer in Edinburgh, and quite frankly I think the man is a tosser. I kind of hoped you might be up for rescuing a damsel in distress.'

'Company law is quite different to criminal law, Stu,' David said, and Stuart noticed that when he frowned two little vertical lines appeared between his eyebrows. 'I might know the basics, but I'm no Perry Mason.'

'No, you've demonstrated how well-formed and sturdy your legs are on numerous occasions.' Stuart grinned as he got a mental picture of the TV detective who solved his cases in a wheelchair. 'I know it isn't your department of expertise, but you are the only lawyer I know. I don't for one moment expect you to drop everything and handle the case yourself. But you must know other lawyers who might. You see, it seems to me that because both Laura and Jackie were English, the Scottish police didn't really put themselves out to investigate fully. There's the track by the farm for a start, which could have been the escape route for the real killer. I don't think they questioned guests who'd stayed at Brodie Farm just before the event. And they definitely didn't make much effort to discover who Jackie's lovers were. I wouldn't be surprised if one of them was actually in the police. So I think Laura needs someone to act for her who has no connection with anyone in Edinburgh or Fife.'

'It's an interesting case,' David said thoughtfully. 'And I do know a couple of criminal lawyers who could probably be tempted, if we had something really strong and juicy as bait.'

Stuart noted that David said 'we'. That could have been just a manner of speaking, but then he knew David liked a challenge, and he had often remarked in the past that company law was very dry and there was precious little satisfaction to be had from it.

'Are you involved in anything much at the moment?' Stuart asked in what he hoped sounded like a casual manner.

David laughed and reached across the small table to slap Stuart on the shoulder. 'As it happens, I'm doing very little. Julia loves the Highlands and with the school hols coming up, we could rent a cottage up there somewhere. I could do a bit of climbing with you, and maybe get to see the scene of the crime and speak to the law firm that defended Laura.'

Stuart's grin spread from ear to ear. 'I knew I could count on you. Best day's work I ever did was sit next to you on that plane.'

It was after midnight when David got home, a little wobbly on his feet from too much to drink. Julia was lying on the settee in her pyjamas, reading.

'So what did the Flying Scotsman want?' she asked.

David smiled. He thought Julia looked very cute and schoolgirlish in her pyjamas, her hair tumbling over her shoulders.

'I think I've found where he left his heart,' David said. 'And we've got to spring her from prison.'

As he expected, Julia's face lit up with keen interest. Over the years they had seen Stuart with dozens of different women because he attracted them like moths to a lantern. But Julia had always said she thought he'd left his heart somewhere, for no matter how promising any new relationship looked, Stuart appeared uninterested in it becoming permanent. It drove her mad, for she really liked the man; he was kind, honest, generous and great fun. Sensitive when necessary, tough at the right times too.

Because she and David were so happy together, she wanted the same for everyone she liked. And especially Stuart because she always felt that he actually longed for permanence, to give up travelling and return to his native Scotland and have a real home.

David told her the bare bones of the story. Julia gasped, for she vaguely remembered reading about the murder at the time. 'And Laura was an ex-girlfriend?'

'His first and perhaps only love,' David replied thoughtfully. 'Of course, he isn't the kind to wear his heart on his sleeve, but there was something about the way he spoke of her that made me feel it.'

'If I'd been there I would have dug deeper,' Julia said eagerly.

'I'm sure Stuart knew that and it was part of the reason why he wanted to meet me alone,' David laughed. 'But he sent his love to you and the kids. We'll see him again pretty soon. He's staying at a hotel near Baker Street.'

'You should have asked him to come and stay with us,' she said a little indignantly.

David smiled, for he knew Julia enjoyed having guests to stay. Their home was a big Victorian house, and they'd lavished a lot of love and care on it. She often said she wished they had less busy lives so they could entertain more.

'I wonder what she's like,' she mused, snuggling up beside David.

'Older than him. But I've kind of got the idea what she used to be like. Remember when we had that holiday in Providencia?'

'How could I forget? That was where Abi got started.'
Julia grinned, thinking back to the white sand and hot sun
of the Columbian island.

David smiled at the memory too. They hadn't been married very long and Julia's parents had been very concerned
when she didn't return to England after the holiday. She got
herself a job as health and safety officer with the company
and stayed. In fact Abi, their daughter, was actually born in
Columbia.

Stuart had been with them in Providencia too. He met
Jane there, a willowy brunette with legs that went on for
ever. They seemed to be perfect for each other, and for
once Stuart looked as if he believed this romance might be
for life. But the night Jane returned to England, David had
walked along the beach with Stuart in the moonlight. He
remembered sensing his friend was sad, and he tried to
cheer him up by suggesting he could cover for him so Stuart
could shoot off home to be with Jane.

To his surprise Stuart looked almost affronted. 'I don't
really want to be with her, I was just fooled into thinking I
did for a while because she reminded me of an old flame,'
he said. 'Don't get me wrong. Jane was quite special. Fun,
easy to be with and great in bed too. But I can't take it any
further. Jane deserves to be loved for herself, not as a
substitute for someone else I still hanker after.'

'So I guess Laura was the girl Stuart hankered after,'
David explained.

'But Jane was lovely,' Julia mused. 'A perfect figure, lovely
hair and skin. She was so lively and funny too, and clearly
swept off her feet by Stuart. How tragic is that! To have
your heart broken by a man because you reminded him of
someone else.'

'I agreed I'd help,' David said hesitantly, afraid Julia would
think that was a bad idea.

'I'm glad of that,' she said, surprising him. 'Let's just hope she deserves having two such lovely men trying to spring her.'

Stuart found it surprisingly easy to track down Laura's sister. He had gone to the newspaper's archives the day after seeing Lena and David, and chatted up a young woman in the archives, posing as a childhood friend of Meggie's. She dug out the story, and finding it was written by a reporter she knew well, she said she would ring Stuart with any information after she'd spoken to him.

Stuart had not seen the newspaper interview with June Wilmslow before, and he took a photocopy of it away with him to study it. He sincerely hoped that Laura didn't know of its existence either, for her mother had portrayed herself as a woman who had been cruelly done by. Her age was stated as being sixty-eight, but in the photograph she looked far older, and it said she was living in severely reduced circumstances and suffering from emphysema. She claimed that her late husband had taken her and her children to live in his lovely home, and given them everything, but Laura never accepted him and resented that he expected she should do her share of the chores and didn't allow her out raking the streets. She said Laura had always been trouble and she finally ran away because Vincent admonished her for stealing.

She went on to say that Laura came home again when she heard Vincent was dead because she wanted a share of his money. 'She didn't care about me and her brother and sisters, or what we were going to do if Vince's sons got it all,' June was quoted as saying. 'She turned my Meggie and Ivy against me, and later, when I ended up in a couple of rooms, she couldn't care less. She married a rich man just for his money. Money was all she cared about.'

She then went on to say she wasn't surprised to hear Laura had lied to everyone about her real family, because she'd liked to make out she was better than anyone else even when she was small.

Stuart was shocked by the article. He found it hard to believe any mother would say such damning things about one of her children, even if they were true. But knowing that Sunday tabloids bent facts to create sensation, he decided to keep an open mind until he'd had it all confirmed or denied by Meggie.

He was fully prepared that the girl in the archives might come back saying that the reporter had no record of where Meggie lived, or even of June's address. Even if he did have the information it was quite likely he'd say it was unethical to pass on an address, and that Stuart could write into the newspaper and ask that they forward his letter on to Meggie.

Yet to his surprise and delight the girl came back to him the following morning and gave him an address in Catford. 'Mick said he doubted she would still be there,' she said. 'But maybe someone there will know where she's moved to.'

Stuart decided to go straight over to Catford. Meggie would probably be at work, but he could at least ask around to discover whether she was still living there, and he was sure that by looking at the house from outside he'd get an idea of what she was like as a person.

Back in the seventies he'd worked in several of Jackie's properties in Catford and neighbouring Lewisham. She used to search out and buy large dilapidated Victorian houses, gut them and convert them into self-contained flats which she then sold on. He had an image in his mind of Meggie living in a couple of rooms in one of the dreary terraces he knew abounded in that area; in fact he visualized her living in conditions only marginally better than her mother's.

Yet when he got off the train at Catford Bridge, he found

that Bargery Road was away from the area he knew, and part of a development built in Edwardian times for the respectable middle classes, with a mixture of semi-detached and terraced houses. Unlike neighbouring Lewisham, which had suffered a slide down the respectability slope through the post-war housing shortage when so many houses began to be let out for multiple occupation, this part of Catford appeared to have retained its refinement.

There were many trees in Bargery Road and the houses were attractive, with bay windows, and pointed eaves, and most had retained stained-glass door lights, tiled porches and other original features. A few were a little run down, but the majority were either substantial family homes, or flat conversions that were well maintained and looked as if they would be expensive to buy.

Stuart checked the address twice before he was sure he'd found the right house, for number 40 was one of the nicest houses in the road. Unlike many of the others where the front garden had been paved for off-street parking, this had a very pretty garden with trees, a tiny manicured lawn and beautiful flower beds. The front door was painted a glossy dark green with a highly polished brass lion's-head knocker and letterbox.

Opening the wrought-iron gate, Stuart walked up a red brick path to the front door. He noted that there were voile blinds at all the sash windows, partially pulled down to show off the bottom edge trimmed with lace.

The bell rang in the distance, and a dog barked with it, rushing to the front door.

'Get back in here, Lucy,' he heard a woman call out, and the sound of a door closing as if she'd shut the dog in.

Stuart smoothed down his jacket and prepared himself to be rebuffed. He knew by the paintwork and the general care of the house that it had been this way for several years, and therefore Meggie might have only rented a room here for a while.

The moment the door was opened he knew immediately that the woman was Laura's sister, for the similarity was striking. She was a fraction taller than Laura, perhaps five feet eight, and her hair was dark brown, cut in a sleek shoulder-length bob, but she was slender, with identical wide brown eyes and a generous, well-shaped mouth.

'You are Meggie, aren't you?' he blurted out. He had rehearsed what he was going to say if the door was answered, but seeing Meggie in front of him had thrown him completely. 'I'm Stuart Macgregor, an old friend of Laura's.'

Her expression, which had been open, suddenly tightened. 'Go away,' she said and moved to shut the door.

'Meggie, I am not a journalist,' he said quickly, assuming that was her fear. 'I have a letter in my pocket from Laura which authorizes me to speak to people on her behalf. Please let me show it to you.'

The door didn't close any further, but she was still using it as a shield.

'I'm trying to help her get an appeal,' he went on. 'I just want to talk to you to discover how you feel about her and her murder conviction. It's okay if you aren't on her side, I don't want to try and talk you round. I just want to know the truth about her.'

'Let me see the letter first,' she said, her voice cracking a little as if she was frightened.

Stuart took it out of his pocket and handed it to her.

'You'd better come in,' she said after reading it. 'I don't think I can be any help to you, I didn't know the woman who was killed, or any of Laura's friends.'

The house was as neat inside as out: pale blue carpet in the hall and on the stairs, blue striped wallpaper up to a glossy white dado rail, and above the rail another blue and white paper.

As he followed Meggie towards the kitchen at the back of the house he felt he had walked into a Laura Ashley catalogue. He caught a glimpse of the sitting room: large cream buttoned-back Chesterfields, an original fireplace with a beautiful tiled surround. Everything was soft and feminine – even the white dog that bounded out of the kitchen looked like a fluffy soft toy.

'What a pretty house,' Stuart said, bending to stroke the dog. 'And you are a very pretty pooch too! What breed are you?'

He knew instinctively there was no man living there, and in all probability few men, if any, ever came into the house as it had an ordered, almost anti-male feel about it. Yet Meggie didn't look the type to be a man hater – she might be wearing jeans and a tee-shirt, but her sandals were dainty, strappy ones, her toe nails painted pink, and she was wearing makeup. She wasn't as beautiful as Laura, her face was flatter and her nose bigger, but she had a sexy look about her. She might be in her forties but her figure was perfect, a washboard stomach and pert breasts. He had often observed that women who didn't like men usually hid their bodies under baggy, drab clothes.

'A Bichon cross poodle,' Meggie said. 'She's usually quite nervous with men, but she seems to like you. Do sit down.'

As Stuart sat down on one of the pine kitchen chairs, the dog jumped up on to his lap and tried to lick his face. Meggie smiled. 'That's a first! She never wants to get on anyone's lap but mine. But push her down if you don't like it.'

'I love dogs,' Stuart said truthfully. 'I often prefer them to people. There isn't a downside to them, is there? Not unless you count having to take them out for walks even when it's raining.'

'Lucy won't go out in the rain,' Meggie said, and came closer to him to stroke the dog's ears. 'Would you like some tea or coffee? And will you start by explaining how you found me, and what makes you want to try and help Laura?'

Stuart said he'd like some coffee and then launched into his explanation about how he used to work for Jackie and only heard about her death recently, his belief that Laura was innocent and how long he'd known her.

'You're *that* Stuart!' Meggie said incredulously. 'I didn't connect at first, but then I never knew his surname.'

'What does "that Stuart" mean?' he smiled. 'Did she tell you terrible tales about me?'

'No, quite the reverse,' Meggie said and gave him a shy smile. 'You were one of her all-time greatest regrets. I'm surprised you want to help her, she always said she did the dirty on you.'

'I got over that,' he said, and then went on to tell Meggie how he got her address. 'I got the impression from that brief quote from you in the newspaper that you didn't entirely go along with your mother's views,' he ended up.

'I certainly didn't. Mum would do or say anything for a few quid,' Meggie said, her expression one of utter distaste. 'I haven't spoken to her since she gave that interview. I tried very hard to block it because it just wasn't true, but as you saw, I didn't succeed. They didn't even report exactly what I had said, which was that if our mother had been a better one, Laura would never have reinvented herself.'

'I am at a distinct disadvantage,' Stuart explained. 'You see, it was only very recently that Laura admitted to me the truth about her childhood. Up till then I knew nothing of you, Ivy and Freddy. I realize now what a wrench it was for her to leave you, and why she felt it necessary to keep up the fiction she'd created for herself, but there are still things I don't quite understand.'

'So you believed her "fiction"?'

Stuart nodded.

Meggie chuckled. 'She managed it then. I used to tease her by saying she'd slip up one day.'

'You knew about it?' Stuart exclaimed.

'Of course I did. I didn't like it at first, it felt like she was ashamed of me too. But eventually I saw advantages for myself – we're all pretty self-centred when we're young, aren't we?'

Stuart was confused. 'Are you saying that you were in touch with Laura all along?'

'If by all along you mean right up till she was arrested for the murder, yes. But not the first few years after she left the house at Barnes. I was just a kid then, she disappeared and Mum didn't have a clue where she was. She came back not long after Vincent died. Do you know about him?'

'I know what he did to her, she wrote the whole thing down for me to read,' Stuart said. 'But I didn't know she'd had any further contact with any of you after she left the house in Barnes. I hope that on my next visit she'll tell me about the period between then and when I met her in '72. You see, Meggie, that period of Laura's life is just a blank to me. Okay, I got tiny glimpses of it through Jackie once I was working for her, like them working at the holiday camp and doing promotions together. But it was only a couple of days ago that I discovered Greg Brannigan put her through hell. Laura only ever told me that she left him because he had another woman.'

Meggie put a mug of coffee down in front of him and sat down opposite him at the table. 'She didn't tell you he tried to poison her?'

Stuart's eyes widened. 'No!'

'Oh dear,' Meggie sighed. 'There is just so much you

should know to understand her. I hardly know where to start!'

'The beginning is always a good place,' Stuart said with a grin.

Meggie half smiled. 'Easily said, but you see, I'm just as guilty as Laura of hiding unpalatable parts of my past, and much as I'd like to help her, I guess I'm afraid of opening my own can of worms.'

7

Stuart waited as Meggie appeared to be gathering herself to tell him something. Her brow was furrowed with frown lines, and it was clear to him that she wasn't in the habit of confiding in people.

'I really thought Laura could do anything, be anyone she wanted to be,' she blurted out, breaking the silence. 'Ivy and I relied on her for everything when we were little. She was far more of a mother to us than June was. But you already know how it was before June married Vince, and what he did to Laura, so I think I'd better pick up from after he died.'

'You are very like Laura,' Stuart said thoughtfully. 'Not just your looks either – you have the same intriguing quality.'

Meggie smiled. 'She was a very good teacher. But for now you've got to imagine me at fifteen – fat, slovenly, spotty and sulky.'

'That's beyond my imagination,' Stuart said gallantly.

'Bless you.' Meggie laughed lightly, showing white, very good teeth. 'Now, don't sidetrack me with any more compliments or I'll never get to tell you what happened.'

'Okay, my lips are sealed,' Stuart made a zipping gesture across his mouth.

'I was a bitch when Laura turned up that day in Barnes. I think it was because she looked everything I felt I never could be. A grown-up, gorgeous, elegant woman. Half of me wanted to hug her and tell her how much I'd missed her, but the other half was full of resentment and bitterness because she'd left me.'

'A typical teenager then?' Stuart replied.

'I suppose so. But anyway, Laura came in, found the house looking disgusting and of course began washing up and putting things to rights just as she always used to do. Mum was bleating on about how Vince's sons would take the house and I was in and out of the kitchen earwigging. When I heard Laura say Vince had interfered with her and that was why she left, I was really shocked. It had never occurred to me that was the reason. I wanted to rush back into the kitchen and tell them he'd done a whole lot more than just interfere with me, and that I felt like cheering when he died. But I didn't say a word, and when Laura left she asked me to walk to the bus stop with her.'

Meggie could see herself walking down the road with her older sister, feeling like a fat waddling duck next to a graceful swan, but she remembered that Laura took her hand, as if she was still a little girl, and that broke the dam of her emotions and she burst into tears.

Laura caught hold of her and hugged her tightly. 'I never wanted to leave you, please believe me, Meggie. I just couldn't bear Vince any more,' she whispered into her hair. 'I should have come back before to check that he wasn't doing it to you too, but I was too afraid of seeing him.'

It was such a cold, grey day, but that hug and her sister's words made Meggie feel warmer inside. Until then she had thought she would never be able to tell anyone about what Vince did to her, much less describe how he made her feel inside. But there was something about the look on Laura's face, the tone of her voice, that told Meggie she shared all those feelings. And so there, on a cold, windy street, she blurted it all out, how Vince had started on her when she was twelve, first just touching her suggestively, but always buying her presents and telling her she was his special girl.

'I knew deep down it wasn't right, but it felt good that he loved me,' she admitted reluctantly, burying her face in her sister's shoulder. 'Mum never seemed to care about me, and he did help me with my homework and made a fuss of me. But then one evening when Mum had gone out somewhere he forced himself on me. I tried to fight him off but he was too strong, and he told me that if I said a word about it to anyone he'd throw us all out.

'After that he did it to me every time Mum went out. I used to beg him not to but he would say that I liked it really. I felt like I was caught in some sticky kind of web that I could never get out of. I used to go out sometimes and stay out half the night wandering the streets, just to get away from him. I thought if I behaved really badly, at home and at school, Mum would realize what was wrong, but she didn't even notice. He was doing it to me right up until just before he died, even though we found out he had had another woman all along.'

Laura moved Meggie back from her, and her eyes were full of tears. She put her hands on her sister's cheeks and caressed them in sympathy. 'You must come home with me,' she said. 'It's too cold to talk here.'

That day was the first time Meggie had felt entirely safe for years. Laura's little flat was so warm, bright and clean, and as they sat by the fire on the sofa, talking and talking, pouring out to each other all the hurts trapped inside them, Meggie felt as if all the poison inside her was draining away.

Laura told her how she'd been bullied at school, how she'd tried to make things better at home in Shepherds Bush by stealing things they needed. She said she'd felt like some kind of freak long before Vince came on to her because no one seemed to like her. She explained how once she'd left Barnes she got the idea that if she pretended she had no family, nothing could hurt any more. So she told people her parents had been killed in a car crash.

'I know it was wrong, but I got admiration instead of people looking down their noses at me, and it felt good,' she said. 'It never occurred to me then that I was digging myself into a hole. But I can see now that's just what I've done. My flatmate Jackie doesn't know I've got any brothers and sisters, and how can I tell her the truth now? It isn't just her, it's her whole family, they've been good to me, treated me like another daughter. What would they think of me if I was to tell them I've got a pathetic slut of a mother, a father in prison and brothers and sisters?'

Meggie could see for herself what an awful predicament her sister was in. She had told lies about herself at school too, for much the same reasons. Like Laura, she wished more than anything that she was someone else.

Meggie poured out how much she hated her job at the baker's, hearing their mother go on and on about Vince, his other woman, and how they might end up destitute, yet Laura made her see that there was a light at the end of the tunnel.

'I can't have you here while Jackie's around, but there are lots of things I can do to make your life better,' she said. 'I can help you to get a better job, get you special cream to make your spots go, and help you choose clothes that make you look nice. You'll lose that weight if you feel better inside about yourself, and maybe then you could get a flat of your own, so I can come and see you there. You don't owe anything to Mum, but you do to yourself. Vince is gone now, no one is going to do those horrible things to you again, and I'll be around to help you.'

'So that's how it was, Stuart,' Meggie said when she'd finished explaining. 'We made a kind of pact. I wouldn't turn up uninvited, and if we ran into anyone she knew when we were together, she'd say I was her cousin.

'I wasn't happy about it, it felt like I was something shameful, but later I got a buzz out of our secret meetings. We used to meet on Saturdays whenever she wasn't working. We'd go shopping and have some lunch, and she used to buy me clothes and bits of makeup, and she taught me stuff about getting on in London, speaking better, even about boys. I actually think it was better for me that way than having to share her with other people. I got the very best of her, she gave me confidence, ambition and so much love.'

'How long did this go on for?' Stuart asked incredulously. He couldn't imagine how Laura had managed to keep it from Jackie when they were so close.

'Right up till she went to Scotland and met you,' Meggie said, and smiled at the surprise on his face. 'Of course it wasn't all sisterly love, sometimes I'd be really nasty to her when I felt low. But Laura was like a rock, she kept on phoning and arranging meetings regardless.'

'Did you stay living in Barnes?'

Meggie shook her head. 'Heavens no! I left even before the house was sold!'

'What happened there?'

'The court decided that Vince's sons should get his business, and the other assets were to be divided three ways between them and June. She got several thousand pounds.'

'So she didn't have to go back to live in a hovel?'

'If she'd listened to Laura's advice she could have been on easy street for the rest of her life – she had more than enough to buy a little house of her own. And her widow's pension. But being Mum, she wouldn't listen. She farted around in one rented place, then another, and frittered the money away. I already had a room of my own in Islington, and when Ivy was fifteen she came to live with me. Freddy joined the Navy as soon as he left school. We didn't exactly cut ourselves off from Mum, but we distanced ourselves. None of us could stand her constant moaning, her slutty ways. And there were always new men coming into her life, so we let her get on with it.'

'And you did very well for yourself to end up owning a lovely house like this one,' Stuart said. 'What work do you do?'

'I buy and sell properties,' she said with a degree of pride. 'I might never have met Jackie, but I guess Laura told me enough about her to inspire me. Ivy's in it with me too. She's happily married now with two sons and she lives in Bromley, but we have a little office upstairs and she comes over two days a week and deals with the paperwork and the books. I do the buying, selling and organize any renovations.'

'You've clearly got a real talent for it,' he said, looking around appreciatively at the pine kitchen units, realizing they were custom-built, not flat-packed from MFI. 'It's a wonder our paths didn't cross before. I used to work on Jackie's houses and some were around here.'

'I wasn't here then, I was in Islington. Ivy and I were renting a little terraced house when the owner died and the relatives put it up for sale. No one wanted it with sitting tenants and the price kept going down. Laura said I ought to buy it, in fact she gave me the deposit. Ivy and I did it up, then the property boom happened in '72. I sold it, and with the proceeds bought two others. And so on, and so on.'

'Clever girl,' Stuart exclaimed. He thought it was incredible that with so much stacked against her Meggie had managed to do so well. 'And there's me who has watched countless others make their pile while I helped them with my skills, but never had the sense to jump on the bandwagon myself!'

'From what Laura told me about you, you were never materialistic.'

Stuart sighed. 'Maybe if I had been we might have stayed together,' he said. 'She wanted money, smart clothes and all the trappings, that's what went wrong. I was just a head in the clouds type, satisfied with very little. But tell me about her husband. You said earlier he tried to poison her.'

Meggie got up and went over to the French door that led into the garden and opened it. 'Let's have some lunch out here,' she said. 'It's too nice to stay inside.'

Stuart joined her at the door, about to ask why she was stalling about the poison, but as he saw the garden he was distracted.

From the end of the patio area close to the house, which was full of tubs of flowers, a narrow red brick path snaked its way through a series of rose-covered arches giving only glimpses of lawn, flower beds and trees beyond. It gave the impression it was enormously long, but that was probably an optical illusion. 'Good God, Meggie, it's beautiful!' he exclaimed. 'Is it all your own work?'

She blushed and nodded. 'Yes. And if I'm going to have to tell you about Gregory Brannigan I'd like to be relaxed for it. I'll make us some sandwiches and open a bottle of wine.'

'Can I do something to help?'

'No, just go and have a look round out there. Down the bottom there's a little summer house and I could do with your expert opinion as to whether it's worth repairing or if it's gone too far for that.'

Stuart wandered down the garden, Lucy the dog following him. He stopped every now and then to admire the dramatic combinations of colour Meggie had used in her planting. Orange with purple, bright pink and dark blue, then blue with yellow. Meggie had been a surprise in so many different ways, but this was perhaps the greatest of them all.

He was still very intrigued by her. She had told him so much, yet in fact had revealed little about herself. Had she ever been married? Was there a man in her life, and why wasn't she at the trial if she cared so much for Laura? She also hadn't said she thought her sister was innocent!

The summer house was a bit ramshackle, but he could see why Meggie was reluctant to pull it down. There were creepers almost covering it, and on the little veranda part outside was a wicker chair with fat cushions. It looked as if it was a favourite place to sit as there was a book on the table beside it. He picked it up and smiled to see it was *Lorna Doone*, a book he remembered Laura had loved.

He poked at the roofing felt, prodded the wood shingles on the walls, and shook the veranda rails. Looking inside, he found only one place water was coming in through, and the floor was sound.

'Your garden does you credit, it's astounding,' he said as he returned to the kitchen to find Meggie loading a tray with sandwiches, glasses and a bottle of white wine. 'As for the summer house, that only really needs a few shingles to be nailed in, and refelting. I could do it for you if you've got some tools and could get the felt.'

'I've got tools and the felt. I got it ages ago when it began to leak at the back. But I can't let you do it.'

Stuart gave a shrug. 'Why not? You're Laura's sister and you've let me into your house and shared your past with me. I think mending your little roof is the least I can do in return.'

To his astonishment her face began to crumple. 'I'm her sister but I didn't lift a finger to help at her trial,' she sobbed. 'I didn't even go to give her some kind of support. I haven't written to her, I haven't done anything for her. All because I was afraid for myself.'

Stuart did what he always did when women cried. He went over to her and enfolded her in his arms. 'There, there,' he said, rocking with her. 'Laura would understand, she wouldn't have wanted you to be caught up in the publicity circus.'

Meggie sobbed for some minutes. Stuart continued to hold her, murmuring little platitudes about how difficult it was for people to know what to do when something so serious happens.

Her sobs gradually abated and she wriggled out of his arms and took a step backwards away from him. Her face was wet with tears but there was a hunted look in her eyes.

'I haven't told you the whole truth about me, Stuart. All this time I've been thinking I didn't need to, that it's all in the past and it's nothing to do with the present. But that isn't so. It is relevant. Both Laura and I were damaged by Vince. It made us do things other normal women would never do. We have problems with relationships, it left us with a hardness, something nasty at the core of us.'

Stuart shrugged. 'I'm sure it did, Meggie. I know when Laura told me about Vince I understood a great many things about her that had puzzled me before. But I didn't come here today to interrogate you. I only wanted a different perspective on your shared childhood.'

'I was a prostitute,' she shouted at him.

Stuart was astounded. It was the last thing he expected to hear, especially thrown at him so suddenly. He didn't know how to respond, so he said nothing.

'Have you taken it in?' she snapped at him. 'That was the reason I stayed away from the trial because I was afraid it would be exposed. I stopped Ivy from going too because she didn't know what I did. I said we were better out of it.'

'If you think I'm going to throw my hands up in horror, you are mistaken,' he said gently. 'I've already seen how bleak your childhood was, I can see from this house what you aspired to. To get from one to the other took a monumental will, and in my mind there are far worse ways you could have done it.'

'But I can't forgive myself for it,' she retorted. 'I can find excuses, that I was very young, I had no qualifications for a good job, that I had Ivy to take care of too. But I'm so ashamed that while I was lecturing Ivy about not letting boys use her, making her go to night school to learn shorthand and typing, I was flitting off every night and taking money from seedy men who couldn't get a woman any other way.'

Stuart made no comment, just waited for her to resume where she left off.

'Ivy and Laura believed I was the assistant manager in a smart West End night club.' She gave an anguished kind of giggle. 'I was often there all right, but the only thing I managed was peeling my clothes off later in a hotel room. Okay, so I stopped it as soon as I sold the first house and bought the other two, I've worked my fingers to the bone ever since, yet however long ago it was, however lovely I make this house and the garden, I feel I'm tainted and don't deserve all this.'

The depth of her shame touched Stuart and brought a lump to his throat. 'Of course you deserve it,' he insisted. 'You didn't hurt anyone by what you did. It was just supply and demand – you needed money, the men wanted sex and they could afford to pay for it. I see that as a fair exchange.'

'There was nothing fair about it to me,' she exclaimed. 'Every single man I went with was like doing it with Vince! I had to pretend to each one of them that they were the absolute best, that I really loved doing it with them. It made me sick to my stomach. I knew I could never fall in love, get married and have children. That door was closed to me. I was just a dirty whore.'

'Oh, Meggie.' Stuart went over to her and hugged her again. 'You shouldn't feel that way. I've met women who married for money alone, and to my mind that's far worse because they are living a lie. You should put all the blame on Vince, he was the one that destroyed your innocence, and your mother is to blame too because she didn't protect you.'

'But we are all responsible for ourselves,' she said against his shoulder. 'Ivy and Freddy had the same upbringing, but they didn't turn bad.'

Stuart gripped both her arms and looked right into her eyes. 'They were not abused by Vince. He was dead by the time they were in their most formative years. And they were sheltered by you. Be proud that because of you Ivy has had a happy life, you gave her that.'

She turned away from him, found a tissue in a drawer, blew her nose and dried her eyes. She was silent for a minute or two, and Stuart realized she was trying to pull herself together again.

She turned back to face him, her lips still quivering. 'Thank you, Stuart,' she said. 'I can hardly believe I've blurted all this out to a stranger. Promise me you will never tell anyone, especially not Ivy.'

'Of course I promise. I didn't come here to see you to cause trouble. You've all had more than enough of that. But tell me, did Laura know?'

'She suspected, but I always denied it. We Wilmslows are good at keeping secrets, and we can be very plausible liars. Mum knew though, she used to ask me for money with a kind of smirk on her face. I knew if I didn't give it to her she'd tell Ivy. God, I hate her! I was with her when the news first broke in the papers about Laura's trial. She was practically gleeful. For years she blamed her for how she ended up, she was like a stuck record saying the same old stuff over and over again. Yet Laura had often sent her money, presents too. Mum never even showed any sympathy when I told her Barney had died. All she said was, "Why should I care, she never invited me to her wedding."'

Stuart felt he could easily hate June Wilmslow too. To him she was the root of all the unhappiness Laura and Meggie had gone though.

They took the tray out into the garden, and after they'd drunk some wine and chatted about more trivial things, Stuart broached the question about Gregory again.

'You've got to understand first that I never actually met him,' Meggie said. 'But I saw photos of him, I went to his house when he was away, and I read between the lines of what Laura told me. He was a control freak, though back in those days we called men like him bullies. He was rich – as you probably know, he owned a toy company. Laura met him when she was demonstrating some of his toys in Harrods.'

Stuart nodded. He did know that much.

'If it hadn't been for Jackie meeting up with Roger again, and suddenly spending all her time with him, I doubt Laura would have gone out with him more than a few times. She often told me that they had nothing in common,' Meggie continued. 'But Gregory kept wining and dining her, buying her expensive presents and taking her away to nice places. Apparently he was charm itself, very suave and handsome.'

'How old was she then?'

'Twenty-three,' Meggie said. 'He was in his mid-thirties. She was absolutely gorgeous then, tiny little mini skirts, long hair, that real sixties wide-eyed look. Gregory was under pressure from his family to settle down, and I suppose he saw her as some kind of Stepford Wife, beautiful, sexy, domesticated and utterly compliant. That of course was his big mistake. Laura wanted to help him run his company, she hadn't planned on being forced to be a stay-at-home wife.'

'I was guilty of that too,' Stuart said ruefully.

'But you weren't a bully, and anyway, she had Barney to look after then,' Meggie rebuked him. 'Gregory asked Laura to marry him around the same time Jackie and Roger got engaged and it wasn't a coincidence, he knew she'd be vulnerable. He got her a diamond ring as big as the Ritz, and began planning the wedding.'

Meggie slipped back in time, remembering the day she met Laura to go to Kensington Market. The indoor market was the trendy alternative to the boutiques of Kensington Church Street and Kings Road in Chelsea. Most of the stallholders were hippies, and you could buy anything there from patchwork floor cushions to joss sticks and Afghan coats. But there were also many stalls which specialized in handmade or antique clothing, and Laura had her heart set on an original thirties dress to get married in.

She found the perfect one, a lovely cream crêpe number with intricate beadwork. Cut on the bias, it clung to her slim hips and accentuated her cleavage. With a little feather 'fascinator' pinned in her dark hair, she looked like a Hollywood star. She insisted on buying Meggie a gorgeous twenties black velvet jacket trimmed with jet beads, and afterwards they went to the roof garden at Derry and Toms department store, and had afternoon tea.

Meggie had never been there before, and she could hardly believe there could be a real Italian garden, complete with streams and even real live flamingos, on the top of a tall building. She was so excited she could hardly sit down, but

Laura seemed a bit preoccupied and Meggie asked what was on her mind.

'It's the wedding really,' Laura sighed. 'Am I doing the right thing marrying Greg?'

Meggie was only eighteen then and she'd been working as a prostitute for almost a year. While other girls of her age were having fun, camping out at rock concerts, smoking dope and dropping acid and sleeping with anyone they fancied, she had to spend every evening with men old enough to be her father. It was hell forcing herself to sparkle when she knew that a glass of watered-down champagne would lead to yet another loveless, sordid scene in a hotel room. She always told herself that at least she was at the top of her profession, that she didn't have the indignity of having to work the streets. But as she came home in the early hours of the morning in a taxi, still smelling of her clients' sweat, sometimes bearing bruises where they'd been rough with her, she often thought that she would happily settle for marriage with a rich man, even if she didn't love him, just as long as he was good to her.

'Do you like Greg?' she asked her sister.

'Of course I do,' Laura replied with some indignation.

'And you fancy him?'

'Yes, a lot as it happens.'

'Well, that's what love is, isn't it?' Meggie replied.

Laura laughed. 'Other people seem to think there's a lot more to it than that,' she said.

'Well, he's rich, good-looking too, that is if that photo you showed me is a good likeness,' Meggie went on. 'What more could anyone want?'

'I kind of thought that when I met Mr Right we'd sort of melt together, that there would be no doubts, no what-ifs,' Laura said wistfully.

'That's just the claptrap they write in books,' Meggie insisted.

'You are so cynical sometimes,' Laura said, looking hard at Meggie. 'Was it Vince that did that to you?'

'Maybe, but I observe people too. Okay, you see couples mooning over one another when they first meet, but that soon fades. I expect even Mum felt that way about Dad once, and look where it got her. You can be a whole lot happier with money than without it.'

'But Greg always seems to want me to be something I'm not,' Laura said sadly. 'Take our wedding – he will really want me in one of those crinoline, long-train numbers, a veil and all that, but that isn't me. I'm not a pure little virgin that went to church every Sunday and I'd feel a fraud dressed like one. That dress I've bought is me, I want glamour, excitement and to look sensational. He should know what he's getting.'

'Are you afraid he wants the little woman who will kow-tow to him?'

'I know he does. I dare say he's got dreams of burying me in the country with half a dozen kids around me too. But he doesn't tell me these things, I guess that's the real problem, we don't ever talk about what we both want.'

'Then maybe you should put the wedding off?' Meggie suggested. 'Tell him you can't go through with it until you have discussed everything.'

'I'm not good at explaining my feelings and anyway, they say men like women to be intriguing, to never know exactly how they will react. I mean, I might like to live in the country one day, I might want six kids. Just because at the moment I want to live in Chelsea and drive a sports car with the hood down doesn't mean I'll want it for ever. So if I pinned him down now and made him make promises, I'd be stuck with them.'

Meggie laughed. 'What you want is a man who will kow-tow to you!'

'So she kind of started off on the wrong foot,' Meggie said after she'd told Stuart the gist of her memory of that day. 'Ivy and I couldn't be at the wedding for obvious reasons, but by all accounts Greg got a bit of a shock when Laura didn't arrive at the church in a meringue. He asked her what she thought she was doing turning up looking like something out of a Busby Berkeley musical.'

'Jackie once showed me a wedding photo,' Stuart said. 'I thought Laura looked fabulous. I think my heart would have stopped if I'd been waiting in the church and she turned up looking like that. But I guess Greg was a traditionalist.'

'She told me some time later that he spent most of their honeymoon sulking, and said she'd made him look a prat,' Meggie said, pursing her lips. 'She felt really bad about it, she wanted to be a good wife to him, so I suppose she decided to bend to his will thereafter. By the time she was pregnant with Barney, she was wearing Greg's choice of clothes, cooking the kind of meals he approved of; even their house in Chelsea was furnished in his conventional taste. She couldn't have floor cushions, candles or bead curtains, the kind of hippie stuff she loved, it was all G-Plan, red curtains and shag pile. She once joked that she didn't know why it was called shag pile, because he never wanted to shag her on it.'

Stuart laughed and poured Meggie another glass of wine. 'Laura never really talked about him when we were together, but I did get the idea he was preoccupied with his business, and that she spent a great deal of time on her own. Did you and Ivy see much of her?'

'We could only visit when Greg was safely away on business, and I guess I was too young and preoccupied with my own worries and trying to keep what I was doing from her to notice much. But she did seem a bit wistful sometimes, she was always going on about how many new opportunities there were out there for women. She used to urge me to grab them while I still could.'

Meggie paused. 'Then Barney was born. Laura didn't want to give him a name like Barnabas, that was Greg's choice, just as he had to have a conventional nursery, not the wacky, jolly room full of mobiles and bright pictures that Laura envisaged. She'd had a long and difficult labour, and with the benefit of hindsight I'd say she had postnatal depression. But in those days that wasn't really recognized, and there she was stuck at home alone with a new baby, without anyone to reassure or help her.

'Greg was no help, Laura said he looked like he was in pain every time he was forced to hold his son. He got angry when he cried, he took no real interest in his development.'

Stuart frowned. His memories of Barney were so sharp and dear to him that he felt hurt that the little boy's real father hadn't felt twice as much love for him.

'Somehow she staggered through Barney's first year,' Meggie said. 'She once said she felt she was in a black hole scrabbling with her fingertips to climb out. Then just as she was beginning to get her figure back and find herself again, Greg dropped the bombshell that he was going to buy a house in the country. Laura got really scared then, she told me she felt he was going to bury her alive. I advised her, rightly or wrongly, that she should put her foot down and refuse to go.'

'Which she did?'

'Yes, and it was at that point everything went pear-shaped. It transpired later that he had a mistress and his family were fanatically opposed to divorce, so I suppose sticking his wife and baby out in the country was plan A. When Laura dug her heels in and refused to go, I guess he had to resort to plan B, killing her off.'

'Surely not!' Stuart exclaimed.

'You are sweetly naive,' Meggie retorted. 'One thing I really do know about is men, and believe me, Stuart, some of them can be utterly ruthless. Why else did he suddenly start scoring drugs and bringing them home? Laura had often taken speed when she was doing promotions, lots of the girls did. But Greg always disapproved of that. Yet all at once he was bringing it home, encouraging her back into it. I'll tell you why, so that he could then slip her something really dangerous, and if she died it would look like it was her own doing.'

She laughed mirthlessly at Stuart's expression of disbelief. 'I was there, I saw it,' she insisted.

Meggie closed her eyes for a moment, thinking back to January of 1972, trying to picture everything so she could describe it in such a way that Stuart would understand how it was not just for Laura, but her and Ivy too.

When she and Ivy had moved into the little two-up, two-down terraced house in Islington, it was little more than a slum. The floorboards were full of dry rot, the wiring was dangerous, and the bathroom was a lean-to at the back with floor-to-ceiling black mould. All the other houses around them were much the same, built cheaply for working-class people at the turn of the century, and a far cry from the big houses nearby built for the wealthy. But however seedy it was, the rent was low, so they painted over the ancient wallpaper, washed the mould off the bathroom walls, and felt they were lucky to have a whole house to themselves.

Meggie had never imagined herself owning her own house then. As a single girl of only twenty-one she would never have got a mortgage. But when she was offered the house for £1,200, a real bargain, and Laura gave her £300 for a deposit, her bank was willing to help her.

Once the house was legally hers she was determined to get tradesmen to come in and do it up. For that she needed cash, so along with her work at night from the club, she also joined a call-girl service to take some extra clients in the afternoons. All through the autumn and the start of the winter, she and Ivy holed up in one bedroom while the kitchen, bathroom and living room were renovated. Day after day they were subjected to hammering and banging, dust and mess. Sometimes there was no electricity and for a time they had no toilet either. With men trooping in and out and the stink of wet plaster and gloss paint it was misery. Sometimes they even began to think they should have accepted the £200 they were offered from the previous owners to give up their tenancy.

Yet by the end of January when at last they had got a pretty pink bathroom, a pale blue kitchen with a brand-new cooker and fridge, and gas central heating, they felt it was all worth it. Nothing had ever been as good as seeing the sage-green carpet laid in the living room, and awaiting the two big comfy sofas that would transform it into their own real home and give them the security they'd never had before.

By then Ivy was nineteen and she had got her secretarial diploma and landed a job as a secretary with a firm of accountants. She also began a night-school course in book-keeping. Fortunately she was still naive enough to believe it cost very little to get all the work done, and she happily swallowed her sister's story that she spent her afternoons at the club doing paperwork and ordering drinks for her boss.

But Meggie was all too aware that Ivy wouldn't stay naive for much longer, and if she ever did work out what her older sister did for a living, she might very well walk away from her. It was bad enough having Laura separated from them because she had to keep her family secret, but Ivy wasn't just a sister, she was Meggie's only real friend and she couldn't bear the thought of losing her.

Physically they were very alike – the same height, slim build and dark eyes, though Ivy's hair was mousey as Laura's had once been – but Ivy was unscarred, easygoing, warm-hearted and confident in her own abilities.

She didn't agonize over anything. If a boyfriend didn't ring when he said he would, she just shrugged. If someone was unkind to her at work she found a reason for it. She never complained at being alone in the house every evening; she was happy to watch television, read a book or do the washing and the ironing for both of them.

Ivy made friends easily too, yet whoever she was friends with, or whatever boyfriend she currently had, she always kept Sundays free to spend with Meggie. The only sadness in her was because of Laura. She worried that as Barney grew older Laura might be forced to keep him away from her and Meggie in case he inadvertently spoke of them to his father.

It was on one of those stay-at-home Sundays that Laura turned up unexpectedly at the door with Barney. Coinciden-tally, Ivy and Meggie had just been discussing the possibility of getting Laura to invent some new story to Greg. The one they favoured was that she and Ivy were the fictitious Aunt Mabel's nieces. Meggie thought that maybe she could write a letter to Laura saying that they hadn't known of her existence until Mabel died, and they'd traced her through the records at Somerset House.

When the doorbell rang and there was Laura, they couldn't wait to launch into their plan. But Laura was in no state to have a serious discussion about anything. The moment Meggie looked at her she knew she was high as a kite on speed. She knew the signs well as many of the girls she worked with took it to keep going, and Meggie had taken it herself occasionally.

Laura's pupils were dilated until there was virtually no iris left. She began gabbling away about nothing the moment she came in, pacing up and down the room and firing questions at her sisters, yet not listening to the reply. Even more distressing was the way she treated Barney like a performing monkey. She kept ordering him to sing nursery rhymes, then she'd peal with laughter, pick him up and throw him up in the air. Barney looked anxious and confused, and several times hid from her behind the sofa, but that made Laura mad, and she'd haul him out and command him to do something else.

Barney was eighteen months old then, a stocky little dark-haired toddler who happily went to anyone, and it horrified Meggie that Laura had been driving her car with him in it while she was in such a state.

She had lost far too much weight, her face looked gaunt, and she was so thin that Meggie could see her hipbones jutting out beneath her skin-tight jeans. As soon as she could get Laura into the kitchen away from Ivy, she asked her what she thought she was doing.

'Having fun,' Laura said. 'You should try it, you always were a worry guts even when you were little, but now you're turning into a grumpy old maid who disapproves of everything.'

'But you'll get ill,' Meggie argued. 'And you could easily have an accident in your car if you're so spaced out.'

When Laura realized she was going to get lectures rather than admiration, she soon left, but Ivy kept asking what had been wrong with her, and the day was ruined by fear of her guessing it was drugs, and wondering if Laura got home in one piece.

The following morning just after Ivy left for work, Laura telephoned, begging Meggie to come over to Chelsea because she had the most terrible pain in her stomach and couldn't lift Barney to dress or change him.

Meggie arrived there fired up to give her sister a piece of her mind, and found Laura in bed, doubled up with pain, with a grey-green tinge on her face. Barney was still in his pyjamas, his nappy stinking.

'I had this last week, only not so bad,' Laura said weakly. 'I feel like I'm going to die.'

'It's the speed,' Meggie told her none too gently. 'It serves you right. You can only abuse your body so long before it protests.'

She tried to make her drink water, but Laura was immediately sick, and because she was in such obvious pain Meggie called the doctor.

The doctor examined Laura very carefully and asked a great many questions about what she had eaten in the last twenty-four hours. He seemed very worried, and said he thought it was some kind of poisoning and that he wanted to admit her to hospital immediately.

Meggie still thought it was purely the speed, but didn't like to admit that was what Laura had taken for fear of getting her into serious trouble. She volunteered to take care of Barney as Greg was away on business.

Laura was allowed out of hospital two days later as the cramps had gone, but although she'd had various tests, the doctors hadn't been able to find a definite cause for them.

Meggie made her sister a light meal and waited until she had eaten it, but just as she was about to leave she saw Laura go to a drawer in the kitchen and take out a tiny pill bottle.

'Don't even think of taking any more of those!' Meggie shouted, rushing forward to grab them.

'I wasn't going to, I just wanted to check them,' Laura said. 'You see, I had two of these on the morning of the day I came over to your house, and I was fine then. I took another two after I got home because I was going to go out again later. It must have been them, the pains began a couple of hours afterwards and I didn't get the buzz I usually get with speed. I thought maybe some of these are something else.'

She tipped the remains of the bottle on to the work surface and together they looked at the small black capsules. But they were all the same, absolutely identical to the black bombers both of them had seen countless times.

'You've just poisoned yourself by taking too many.' Meggie felt irritated that Laura was trying to find another reason for her pain. 'Let that be a lesson to you, for goodness' sake.'

'Laura promised me she wasn't going to take them ever again,' Meggie told Stuart. 'And I think she did stick to it for a while. But then about a month later, it happened again, and that time she was dangerously ill. I didn't know about it for some time as Greg was home – he got her to hospital and took care of Barney. Laura only phoned me as she began to recover. She said she had been close to death, and the doctor had told her she had all the symptoms of strychnine poisoning. He apparently asked Greg if she'd had any contact with rat poison.'

'Surely he wasn't lacing her with that?' Stuart didn't feel he could believe that of anyone.

'I'm a hundred per cent certain that's exactly what he did,' Meggie insisted. 'I think he opened up some of the black bombers and replaced the speed with rat poison. I doubt he did them all, I think he probably did about half in the bottle, so it was a bit like playing Russian roulette. She might get three tampered ones at once, or none, but whatever happened to her he would be in the clear as he'd just say he had always disapproved of her taking speed and she was at the mercy of her supplier. You know how straight people were about drug-taking back then – who would have had any sympathy?' Meggie paused for a moment to drink some wine.

'Laura didn't even dare admit her fears to the doctor at the hospital,' she went on. 'Greg had thrown out the bottle by the time she got home, and when she confronted him he blew his top and said she was going mad. I just wished I'd taken some of them away the first time, that way we could have had proof.'

'Even then it would be impossible to prove he was responsible,' Stuart said. 'It could have been the dealer, or anyone along the chain from the manufacturer. Anyway, Laura shouldn't have been taking drugs with Barney around. And what right-minded person would carry on taking them after a scare like that? I don't believe it was Greg!'

'You would if you'd seen what came after that,' Meggie said darkly. 'He was vile to her. He stopped hiding his mistress, he stayed out at nights, refused to allow Laura any money, told lies about her all round Chelsea. He hit her lots of times too. In the end she had no choice but to leave. All she took was her car and her clothes, and she flogged the odd bits of jewellery Greg had given her and ran off with Barney. She couldn't get a place of her own without a job, and she couldn't work unless she got Barney into a nursery. So in the end she went to Scotland, which is where you came in.'

'So why didn't she tell me all this?' Stuart asked in bewilderment.

'Maybe she was scared that she'd look too needy and

frighten you off,' Meggie suggested. 'I got a letter from her soon after she met you. She said that you were wonderful, but she was afraid it would fall apart because you were so young and innocent. But you must ask her about that. I can only guess at what was going on in her mind.'

Stuart drank some more wine, silently mulling over what Meggie had told him. 'I'm going to make a start on your summer house,' he said after a few moments. 'I think better with tools in my hands.'

Meggie protested, but Stuart insisted. 'It needs doing and today is as good as any to get cracking on it. Unless of course you want me to push off?'

'No, I don't.' She smiled. 'It's nice having you here.'

Two hours later, Stuart had removed the old roofing felt and secured all the loose shingles. As he climbed up the ladder to spread the new felt over the roof timbers, he glanced back up the garden and saw that Meggie was on her knees close to the house, pulling out weeds.

She'd got him her tools and offered to help him but he'd said he could manage alone. Apart from bringing him a cup of coffee about an hour ago, she'd stayed well away. But now as he looked at her he realized he ought to have accepted her help, for even viewing her from a distance he could sense her isolation. He was pretty certain she had no real friends; she'd probably never had anyone much in her life other than Ivy and Laura.

A wave of sympathy washed over him, for she was a good person with a lively mind and she certainly wasn't lacking in personality. But he supposed her guilt about her past made it impossible for her to let anyone get close to her.

It had been a day of revelations, and he would need a great deal more time to think through them all. Yet the one thing which stood out for him above all else was that Laura had feared their relationship couldn't last because he was so young and innocent.

He hadn't of course seen himself as innocent back then. But if innocence meant not understanding that some people are damaged, that events in their past could colour the rest of their lives, then he was definitely guilty of that.

Falling hard and fast for Laura as he did, he never questioned anything she told him, and he didn't ask about her past because he was afraid she might tell him something that would make him jealous. Indeed, the very fact that she didn't want to talk about Gregory had convinced him that she'd loved her husband deeply. When she made no attempt to get a divorce, he felt insecure, for to him that looked as if she hoped to get back with the man.

Later, when they got the flat in Edinburgh and he was unable to find work, he was aggrieved when she took a job at the casino. If she'd got work in a shop or an office he wouldn't have minded so much, even though back in those days he believed it was a man's role to be sole breadwinner. But casinos to him were dens of vice and the women who worked in them were honey traps to lure the suckers in and fleece them. He believed Laura was out looking for a rich man so she could have a glamorous life – he even saw her leaving him to mind Barney as evidence she didn't really care about her son either.

But in the light of what he now knew about her marriage, perhaps his views on how she behaved back then were distorted. She might have been afraid to file for divorce because she was frightened of Greg finding out where she was. There was no doubt the money she earned at the casino helped them through a lean time, and maybe it was better for Barney that she worked at night so he didn't have to go and stay with a stranger.

As he tacked down the roofing felt he was reminded of his first year in London. He would be doing jobs like this one, but his mind was always on Laura and dwelling on the many rows they'd had in this last year together.

He could see her now, sitting at the dressing table doing her face, all dressed up in a glamorous dress and high heels, while he ranted at her preferring the company of gamblers rather than him and her son.

'Please don't go on and on about this,' he could remember her saying, her face stubborn and cold. 'I can't help it that there isn't much work in Edinburgh for you. I know you don't like the idea of me working at the casino. But one of us has got to bring some money home or we can't eat or pay the rent. So you'll just have to put up with it.'

Back then Stuart had only been able to look at the problems from one viewpoint, his own. He was in fact such a dyed-in-the-wool male chauvinist that he thought men had a God-given right to make all plans and decisions, and that a woman's role was merely one of support.

Jackie got him out of that way of thinking. She used to laugh at his old-fashioned ideas and challenge them. She once said to him, 'Hasn't it ever occurred to you that you drove Laura into another man's arms? She was doing her best for both of you, but you threw it back in her face because she hurt your ego. Wise up, man, or you'll end up with some doormat of a woman who will bore you to tears.'

Stuart smiled wryly to himself as he hammered the last tack in the roof and collected up the tools to take back to Meggie. He'd ended up without even a doormat of his own. A life spent avoiding permanent relationships because he equated them all with hurt.

He wasn't such a tough guy after all.

8

'Good to see you again, Stuart. I thought you were stuck permanently on the other side of the world.' Roger Davies beamed welcomingly as he opened the door. 'Come on in, I've got us a few beers in, it will be good to catch up again.'

As Roger led the way into the huge kitchen at the back of Pembroke Villas in Kensington, Stuart was pleased to see everything was still much the same as when Jackie was living here. He had helped with the construction of adding a conservatory to the already large room because Jackie wanted guests to be able to lounge on settees in comfort while she was cooking.

The greenery from the garden had grown considerably and draped itself over the glass roof, the sofas were shabby now, and there was more clutter than in the old days. But it had retained some of Jackie's artistic flair along with the character and sense of comfort and conviviality she had been so keen on.

Stuart had already explained to Roger on the phone that he hadn't heard of Jackie's death until his return to the UK, and that he'd been to see Belle and Lena. Roger appeared to have moved on considerably for he didn't linger on the sadness of Jackie dying, and hardly mentioned Laura's trial. He was more interested in talking about sailing, which he'd recently taken up, and said he was considering retiring early and going to live in Spain.

Just as when he visited Belle, Stuart had no intention of revealing his views on Laura, only to get yet another perspective on the events. He was also genuinely anxious to see

Roger for his own sake, as they'd always got on well in the past.

It was a bit of a shock to find him so aged. Stuart knew he had to be around fifty-seven, but he looked far older than that. The little hair that remained was white and he had a big paunch and bags under his eyes. He looked nothing like the blond, blue-eyed Adonis he'd been when Stuart met him twenty years ago.

'It's nice to be here again,' Stuart said, sitting down on one of the sofas. 'We had some good times in this kitchen.'

'I think that's why I'm so reluctant to sell,' Roger said as he got a couple of beers from the fridge. He stood still in the middle of the kitchen, looking around him. 'It certainly doesn't make a lot of sense for me to rattle around alone in a house of this size. But I've got so much stuff and it's a daunting prospect to have to sort it all out and get rid of it.'

'That's the one and only advantage of keeping on the move,' Stuart said. 'You don't get to hoard anything. But I'm beginning to think it's time I settled down somewhere. I can't roam for ever.'

They chatted and laughed for a couple of hours, about mutual friends, old times and the property market and drank a large number of beers. It was only once the pizza they'd ordered arrived that Stuart reminded himself this wasn't purely a social call.

Belle had implied Roger would have a long list of grouses, but so far he hadn't voiced any. He had only mentioned Jackie in relation to incidents and people who were part of their set in the seventies. He seemed very balanced; he was neither dismissive about his wife's value, nor too sentimental. Stuart felt he'd accepted what had happened, and was in the process of putting a new life together, for he even mentioned a new woman friend.

Once they'd finished the pizza, and were both very mellow, Stuart thought it was time to broach more thorny issues. 'Do you still keep in touch with Belle and Charles?' he asked.

'Not if I can help it,' Roger said with a chuckle. 'I never liked Charles, he was too up himself. And Belle became a whinging bitch within a few years of marriage to him.'

Stuart grinned. 'I didn't see Charles when I called on them, he was out somewhere. Can't say I was disappointed either. But fancy them running a guest house! A bit of a comedown, isn't it?'

'Charles claimed at the time that he wanted less stress and more golf,' Roger said. 'But I think it was more likely that he was short of readies. There was a rumour going around at the time he left London that he was in a spot of bother over one of his construction sites. But then there were always rumours about Charles, you'll probably remember that he was always one for sharp practice.'

'That's why I gave him a wide berth,' Stuart agreed. 'Mind you, most of the property developers back in the seventies were the same. Jackie had the right idea – every place of hers I worked on was tip-top. No cutting corners, good design, quality fittings.'

'She believed in doing up each place as if she was going to live in it. I used to argue with her about it when she first got started.' Roger smiled ruefully. 'I said she couldn't make any profit that way. But I was wrong – her integrity showed, and they sold fast. A smaller profit but a quick turnover is more valuable in the long run.'

'I wish I'd bought one of her places back then,' Stuart said. 'She offered me a small top flat in Battersea Bridge Road and as I recall it was a couple of thousand. Typical dumb Scot, I thought the mortgage would be a millstone round my neck. I saw a flat just like it offered for sale the other day and it was a hundred and fifty thousand! And that, I'm told, is a bargain!'

Roger laughed. 'Property prices are ludicrous in London now. A young couple just starting out have no chance of getting a home like this one. Jackie tried to talk Belle into buying that flat in Battersea too. It was before she married Charles. But that little bimbo thought Battersea was too downmarket for her!'

'I bet she's sick about that now,' Stuart sniggered. 'I suppose back then she thought she ought to be living across the bridge in Chelsea. She was always a bit preoccupied with status, funny really when you think how Lena and Frank were, they didn't give a toss about such things. By the way, have you got any idea why Belle implied Lena had gone senile? I found her bright as a button.'

'Well, Belle likes to divide and rule. She wouldn't have wanted you to see Lena, just as she wouldn't want you to see me or Toby if he was still around.'

'Why on earth not?'

'I dare say because of just what we are doing right now. Discussing her. She wouldn't want me telling you that she sold the house in Duke's Avenue with undue haste.'

'Did she?'

'Well, Lena *was* in a bit of a state. But wouldn't anyone be if they'd just lost both their daughter and husband?' Roger exclaimed with indignation. 'I don't think it warranted shipping her off to an old folks' home though. A bit of TLC would have put her right in my view.'

'You think Belle ought to have taken her up to Scotland to live with her?'

Roger frowned. 'I don't think Lena would have wanted that, too many reminders of Jackie. But I think Belle should have come down and stayed with her for a while. She had no ties, she could even have got someone up there to run the guest house while she was gone. But then, Belle was always spoilt and self-centred. I dare say she told you I was a first-class ratbag, that's what she usually does.'

Stuart noted that Roger sounded jovial enough, but he thought he heard an undercurrent of bitterness.

'She did say you'd got a more recent will than the one she found,' Stuart said cautiously, hoping this might make Roger reveal his true feelings.

'I bet she said I "claimed" to have one.' Roger laughed humourlessly. 'And I assure you it is no claim, it's kosher. She likes to rubbish the idea that Jackie and I remained friends, but we did.'

Stuart was dying to ask why Roger hadn't actually produced this will if he really had it, but he thought he'd better leave that for later.

'I can testify to that,' he said. 'Jackie always spoke of you in very affectionate terms to me. That must have made it so much harder for you when she was killed.'

'I would say it was the worst day in my life when I got the news,' Roger said simply, and for the first time that evening a shadow of sadness passed over his face. 'I never really liked Laura; throughout our marriage I did my best to loosen her grip on Jackie, but I never succeeded. I wish I could feel smug that I was right about her all along, but there's no satisfaction in that – all I feel is a terrible sense of loss.'

Stuart didn't know where to go from there for it was patently obvious that Roger had never had a moment's doubt that Laura was responsible.

'So how did you react when you heard who killed Jackie?' Roger asked before Stuart could think of his next question. 'I remember of course that you left Scotland because of her.'

Stuart bristled, not liking the implication in Roger's remark. 'I left Scotland because there was no work for me there,' he said.

'You don't believe she did it!' Roger made a kind of chortling sound in his throat. 'Oh, come on, Stu, she did you up like a kipper, you were broken when you came to London.'

'Maybe, but I never saw anything in Laura to suggest she could kill someone. Certainly not Jackie, they were closer than sisters.'

'Well, we've all heard how close Laura was to her sisters! She didn't even admit she had any,' Roger said spitefully, his eyes narrowing. 'Her father was a criminal, the mother sells her sordid story to the press for a few bob. The two older brothers have been in and out of nick since they were kids.'

It was only then that Stuart remembered how Roger had talked down to him when they first met. He took the view that all manual workers were beneath him, and that snobbish attitude only changed later because of Jackie's influence.

'Laura couldn't help the family she was born into,' Stuart said indignantly.

'She cast them aside and latched on to Jackie and clung there like a bloody leech.' Roger's voice had leapt up a few octaves in agitation. 'If she'd looked after her kid properly Jackie wouldn't have needed to mind him that day. And my God, Laura made the most of that unfortunate accident. She made Jackie pay in more ways than one – a holiday in Italy, setting up that shop she opened when she returned, and heaven knows what else. Then finally when Jackie can't and won't give her anything more, she kills her.'

Stuart's blood came up and his diplomacy vanished. 'What did Laura ever do to you?' he snapped. 'Were you jealous because Jackie gave her the time you thought should have gone to you? Or maybe it was because she had a child Jackie loved and you couldn't give her one of her own?'

Roger leapt out of his chair. 'Get out of here,' he said,

pointing towards the door. 'If I'd known you still held a torch for that bitch I'd never have let you in here. You know nothing about Jackie and me.'

Stuart got to his feet. 'But I do,' he said, squaring up to Roger. 'I know she wanted to adopt a child, but you wouldn't have it. And that's the real reason she left you. Not because she couldn't have her own way either, but because you wouldn't unbend enough to take on board how much a child meant to her, or even go and have a few tests.'

'Bugger off,' Roger hissed at him and waved his arms like a windmill. 'What made you an expert on marriage? You couldn't stay with anyone longer than a month if you tried.'

Stuart didn't respond to that barb. He'd had enough and he knew he was likely to deck Roger if he stayed any longer. He picked up his jacket and left.

Once back in his hotel, he pulled a miniature whisky from the mini bar and swallowed it down in one. He felt dejected and ashamed that he'd been unable to control his temper. What was he thinking of? He had gone there expecting Roger to be vicious about Laura – he knew there had never been any love lost between them. In fact he had fully expected the man to launch into a vitriolic rant as soon as he arrived.

Roger had been warm and hospitable, so why on earth didn't he play along at being his sympathetic best mate, make out he believed the absolute worst of Laura, and get some information out of him? He should have asked him what he was doing with this recent will he claimed to have, and where the rents on Jackie's properties were going.

Stuart couldn't believe he'd been so bloody stupid. He could have got Roger to tell him about Jackie's funeral, who was there, what was said. He hadn't even asked him where he was and what he was doing on the day of the murder.

Some detective he'd turned out to be! While talking to the prime suspect all he'd managed to do was put his back up, and have the door permanently slammed in his face.

It was hot but peaceful in the library, and as Laura catalogued the new books which had been brought in that morning, she felt a surge of gratitude that the governor had given her the job of librarian. It was probably because she was better educated than most of the other women, and she had a real love of books, but she also had a feeling it had been noted she'd been more amenable of late. Perhaps he thought that if he gave her a plum job she might stay that way.

She had always loved libraries. Right from childhood when she first learned to read she'd seen them as a kind of treasure trove. She could remember getting Nöel Streatfield books and plunging herself into the world of ballet. *Black Beauty*, *Lorna Doone*, *Kidnapped* and *Tom Sawyer* had also all given her further glimpses into a world far beyond grimy Shepherds Bush. She would often curl up in a corner of the library with a book, immersing herself so totally that the librarian had to tap her on the shoulder when it was closing time.

Reading had helped her through all the most difficult times in her life: long, lonely evenings when she was in the bedsitter in Crouch End, during her marriage to Gregory, and particularly after Barney was killed. Maybe it was escapism, but a book was far better than anti-depressants, and since she'd been here in Cornton Vale books had been a lifeline.

She could spend every day in the library now, and she could help and advise the women that came in, some of whom had never read a whole book in their lives before. She thought she might organize a kind of club to discuss books too. Even if she never got out of here, she believed she could find a narrow margin of happiness and serenity, as long as she kept this job.

Yet her mind was not on books completely today, but on her sisters, for just yesterday she'd received a letter from Meggie.

Seeing her spidery writing on the envelope had sent her spirits soaring, for Meggie had written only once since she was arrested, and she was clearly so freaked out then by the murder charge that Laura had asked her not to write again.

To find she was still loved, that Meggie and Ivy were well and happy, was like being given a drink of water when she was dying of thirst.

The two closely written pages were full of explanation and remorse at letting Laura down. '*I was too scared for myself to come up to Scotland for the trial*,' she said at one point in the letter, and that frank admission was all Laura needed.

She of all people knew exactly how that felt. She had become an expert at avoiding anything and anyone who might expose her carefully maintained fabrications. In truth she would have been horrified if Meggie and Ivy had appeared at the prison even before the trial. She had wanted to see them of course, but she was afraid of what they might learn about her.

It hadn't actually occurred to her that Meggie had her own demons, but then she was so wrapped up in her own misery that she didn't think to cast her mind back and consider what might have lain beneath her sister's withdrawal from her.

It was all there in the letter, a confession about her prostitution.

The saddest thing to Laura was that she had known all along, and she could have saved Meggie so much anguish by admitting it.

When Meggie told her all those years ago that she was the

assistant manager of a night club, she had been suspicious because her sister was so young. She went to the club one evening and met the real assistant manager, a man in his fifties. She also saw what else went on there. Young, pretty women calling themselves hostesses were in reality just whores looking to pick up a client. The club made their money from overpriced drinks and got a percentage from the girls' takings.

Had Meggie only just started it, Laura would have reacted differently, but by then Meggie had been doing it for six months or even more, and it wasn't as if she was doing it for herself. She took care of Ivy, got her through secretarial school, and made a real home for her, all when she was so young herself.

Laura weighed up all the pros and cons and decided to ignore it. She didn't feel she could take the moral high ground, not when she had supplemented her own income by shoplifting for years.

How else could Meggie have bought that little house in Islington? Laura was only able to give her the deposit, and the repayments would have been impossible to meet on a shop or office worker's salary. She watched as Meggie turned into a ball of fire to do that place up; it meant everything to her. And so what if the money came from selling herself? Her motive was of the very best, creating a decent home for her younger sister.

The important thing was that Meggie stopped the moment she was able to. She didn't languish feeling sorry for herself, she just got out there, sold that house and bought two more just like it. Laura could remember her knocking old plaster off walls, digging up the gardens, painting, papering, and tiling the bathrooms. She even went to night school to learn basic building work and had her nose in DIY books night after night.

Laura was proud of both her sisters for using their limited talents and their gritty determination to make something of their lives. Yet Meggie had an extra special place in her heart, as she had been a rock, a confidante, and the one person she always knew she could turn to for support.

It shamed her to think how she had hidden her sisters away for all those years, and yet they had never been angry or bitter about it. They hadn't been able to come to her wedding, parties, or visit her in hospital when she had Barney. There'd been no holidays in Scotland with her, nor had they been able to come to Barney's funeral. So many clandestine meetings, and phone conversations that were stilted because Greg, Jackie or Stuart was within earshot. She had to buy birthday cards and presents in secret, and anything they wanted to give her she had to pretend came from a mere friend.

Freddy had refused to be party to any of that. Laura had met him only once when he was home on leave from the Navy and staying with her sisters. He was seventeen then, a skinny lad with a severe haircut and a crop of acne, but a very adult manner.

'If you aren't honest enough to admit to your husband and friends that you have brothers and sisters, then I don't want to know you,' he'd said with undisguised scorn. 'I understand why you lied in the first place. I've avoided talking about our parents and Mark and Paul too. But I wouldn't pretend they don't exist.'

He had never changed his mind. He would be thirty-eight now, married, and when she last spoke to Meggie back in '93, he had three sons, and was living in Plymouth and still in the Navy. Meggie and Ivy spoke with pride of him becoming an officer and adored his boys. Laura assumed that when he heard about her conviction he was very glad that he'd never allowed her anywhere near his wife and family.

Laura didn't feel much more than a twinge of sadness about Freddy, but then he was only three at the time she left Barnes and apart from that one meeting all those years ago, she hadn't seen him since. But her sisters were different; she had so many memories of them and she had always cared what they thought of her.

Meggie had described in her letter how Stuart had tracked her down, and how good he'd been to her, letting her get things off her chest and mending her summer house too. That made Laura smile, for she remembered how when they visited his friends, he often mended things for them. Good listener as he was, he was a great believer in doing something practical too.

She wondered what Meggie had said to him about her. She was bound to have told the story about Greg poisoning her – it was something she often brought up because she wished she'd taken Laura seriously the first time and removed the remainder of those pills to get them tested. Maybe she'd told Stuart about Greg hitting her, and refusing to give her any money too. But Meggie couldn't have told him what finally made her leave the louse, because she didn't know. Laura had kept that to herself.

It was February '72 when she was admitted to hospital with poisoning for the second time. She could still remember in vivid detail the agonizing cramps, and the certainty that she was going to die. But she had recovered, and when she got home Greg was so nice to her, convincing her that not only was she mistaken in believing he had a hand in it, but that his affair was over and he wanted to start again and make their marriage a good one.

She could see him and the Chelsea house so clearly on the bitterly cold day when he brought her home from hospital. She had to lean on him for support because she was still so weak.

'I thought you'd rather lie down on the sofa in the sitting room than be upstairs alone,' he said as he helped her in. 'Look, I've brought down an eiderdown and pillows for you, so you can be cosy and watch television. Mum's going to keep Barney for a few days until you feel up to looking after him. We've all been so worried about you.'

Laura had never liked the decor or furniture in their house. Greg had bought the place a few years before she met him, and it was all his taste. It wasn't hideous, just dull. Almost everything was cream, with teak wall units fitted with lights to illuminate his various sporting trophies. His pictures were equally dull, sombre landscapes and one with a depressing old crone sitting in a doorway.

In the first few days at home when she still felt so ill, lying there looking at the room which held nothing of her personality, she came to the conclusion that it was her own fault Greg had become so controlling. Before they were married she should have asserted her opinion about his house, and made it clear that she wanted more than to be a stay-at-home wife. That way they would have started out on an equal footing.

But the unpalatable truth was that when she met Greg she was in fact a gold-digger. She only ever went out with wealthy men. If a man couldn't afford to take her to swish places and buy her expensive presents, they got nowhere with her.

When Jackie met up with Roger again and said she was going to marry him, Laura panicked. Roger didn't like her, he'd never got over what she did to his friend Steven, and she was afraid that Jackie would bow to his opinion and abandon her. So she cold-bloodedly looked for someone to marry her.

She didn't have to look very far, for Greg was her boss. Unlike most of the men in her life he wasn't married, he was very successful, he had a house in Chelsea and an expensive car, and he could give her the sort of glamorous life she wanted.

There was also the fact that he was out of the top drawer. He'd gone to a good public school and to Cambridge, and his family, who lived in Essex, were rather grand. Marrying him was a way of casting off the last of her real origins, and any children they might have would never suffer the indignities she had. For that she was prepared to overlook Greg's minor faults: that his nose was too big, his lips too thin. He was after all over six foot, slim and fit because he played a lot of squash and golf. He wore beautiful hand-tailored suits and Italian shoes and his dark hair was impeccably cut. He was also an exceptional lover, and generous, so she decided to ignore the one trait she really didn't like, that he was very stubborn and too controlling.

Much, much later, after they were married, she came to see that he'd been equally cold-blooded in choosing her as his wife. He once told her he'd watched her from a distance in Harrods while she was demonstrating some of his toys, and he said her smile, her sleek appearance and the graceful way she moved made him realize she was the perfect wife for him.

Unfortunately for Greg, he had selected her as if she were a car in a showroom, bought without a test drive. She might have looked like quality, but in fact she was bargain-basement with a great many faults, and when they were revealed Greg wanted to trade her in.

But that February day when she was weak and sad, and he was being so kind and loving, she really wanted to put all that aside, for they had Barney to think of and she was anxious for him to have the kind of happy home she'd never had.

Greg had taken Barney to his mother's because he didn't

think it was good for him to see Laura while she was so poorly, and in the subsequent days he waited on her hand and foot, only nipping out to his office for a couple of hours now and then.

She had been home a week when she asked for Barney to be brought home. She felt very much better, she was up and about and perfectly capable of making meals, vacuuming and washing up, and she saw no reason for Barney to stay away any longer as she was missing him badly.

'You need a period of convalescence before that,' Greg said, kissing her and smoothing back her hair. 'Your problems didn't start with the poison, you were overwrought for a long while before that and your body is exhausted. You won't be able to cope with an active toddler just yet. I'm going to book you into a lovely hotel in the sun, so you can recover completely before you start being a mum again.'

It was of course what Greg had done so often in the past, turning her protests around and presenting his own scheme which appeared kindly and more logical. He argued that Barney was settled and happy with his mother, and if Laura had him back before she was really up to taking care of him, she might have a relapse and that would be bad for the little boy.

She was to go off to Madeira for a month, and the very next day Greg drove her to the airport.

Reid's Hotel in Madeira was such a splendid place that it would have been impossible for anyone sent there by their husband to imagine that he hadn't done it out of love. Set up on rocks above the harbour, it was the epitome of gracious, old-fashioned luxury and style. Laura had a beautiful room overlooking the sea, and the gardens around the hotel were stunning, for the mild all-year-round climate was perfect for the exotic plants.

At first she just revelled in the luxury of it all, for there was wonderful food and first-class service. She could spend her days lying by the pool on a padded lounger with a book, or walking around the small, pretty town. She soon began to feel really well again, the shine came back into her hair, her skin became golden-brown and she put on the weight she had lost. But although there were other people to talk to, and she took the occasional trip out with them, loneliness began to creep in during the second week.

Greg phoned her every other evening at half past six, but although he would tell her things Barney had done or said, it seemed to her that his calls were unnecessarily brief, and he brushed aside any question of her coming home early.

She had been at Reid's for sixteen days, by which time she knew every member of staff's name, had watched dozens of different guests come and go, and worked her way through almost all the English books in the library, and she was growing bored. After drinking a whole bottle of wine, plus a couple of large brandies, she felt brave enough to phone her mother-in-law to chat about Barney.

Her in-laws lived in a beautiful old country house near Brentwood in Essex, and the church where she and Greg got married was next door, but Laura had never got close to his parents. She had always felt they looked down their noses at her and Mrs Brannigan was very critical of her, sniffing and making remarks like 'Well, of course I don't understand you modern girls, in my day a wife followed her husband's wishes.'

Mrs Peebles, the housekeeper, answered the phone. She said the Brannigans were in Wales staying with friends. When Laura asked if Barney was with them, Mrs Peebles seemed puzzled by the question, and although Laura was a little drunk she realized from the woman's responses that Barney wasn't with his grandparents and never had been.

Laura rang the house in Chelsea then, but there was no

reply. She phoned a neighbour and they said they hadn't seen Greg or Barney for at least two weeks. Next she rang John Merchall, Greg's closest friend, and his hesitation suggested he knew exactly where Greg was, but needed time to think up a lie. 'He said something about maybe going to a hotel for a bit of a break,' he said eventually, but couldn't or wouldn't say where.

Laura knew immediately that Greg must have a mistress, and that she had a hand in this. Few fathers, and certainly not an inept one like Greg, would choose to take a small toddler to a hotel in the middle of winter on their own. But they might very well take their child to the woman waiting in the wings to be their next wife.

Laura cursed herself for not insisting she spoke to her mother-in-law about Barney the moment she came out of hospital, and for being stupid enough to let Greg convince her that a psychotic drug dealer had laced the black bombers with strychnine, not him. She had no doubt now that he'd told, or implied to, everyone he knew that her spell in hospital was to do with drug dependency. Unfortunately even the medical staff at the hospital, if called to give their opinion, would confirm she'd been taking amphetamines as they'd found traces of the drug while doing tests on her.

To any court she would look like an unfit mother. And if he was awarded custody of Barney, Greg would get to keep his precious house and she'd be out in the cold.

She left Reid's the following morning after persuading the hotel manager to give instructions to his staff that if her husband rang, they were to say she wasn't in her room, but not to let on she'd left the hotel. She used the excuse that she was going home because she missed him and wanted to surprise him, and the man seemed touched by the romantic gesture.

Changing her flight home was no problem and as the

plane took off, all she could think of was Barney. She didn't care about possibly losing her home, it had never felt like hers anyway, and she knew she could make a new life for herself without Greg's money. But she couldn't bear to lose her baby. Nothing and no one had ever come close to making her feel the way she did about him. She loved Meggie and Ivy, she had claimed to have loved Greg and other men, but when she held Barney or even just looked at him she knew exactly what real love was. It was something so strong and pure it made her heart swell and beat faster. She was never going to let some other woman bring him up; he was hers, and if she had to, she would kill for him.

By the time she got into Heathrow airport she had her plan worked out. As image was everything to Greg she had to put him in a position where he would have to do right by her, or lose face. So she got a taxi straight to his factory in Acton.

To her relief his silver Mercedes was parked by the offices. She had always known that work was more important to Greg than love or family, and this confirmed it. She was glad too that she looked her best, suntanned, glowing and stunning in her red full-length coat, with a black mini dress beneath and long black boots.

She paid off the cab driver, left her two suitcases out in the yard and breezed into the offices.

'Mrs Brannigan, how lovely to see you!' Miss Lofts the receptionist exclaimed. 'Is Mr Brannigan expecting you?'

Miss Lofts had worked for Greg's father before him and she was dedicated to the company. She was over fifty, with grey, tightly permed hair, favouring tailored navy suits and pussy-cat bows on her blouses, and Greg said she was the last word in efficiency.

'No, I want to surprise him,' Laura said, giving the woman a flashing smile. This was one place where she knew people liked her, for they considered her as one of them: she'd been on the Tiger Toys promotion team before her marriage and made quite a few friends in the company. 'I missed him so much I came home from Madeira early.'

'It's good to seeing you looking so well,' Miss Lofts said, her smile a genuine one. 'Go on in and give him a jolt. He's only having a chat with the sales team and they'll all be pleased to see you.'

If Laura hadn't been so anxious she might have laughed because she couldn't have timed her arrival better if she'd known Greg's itinerary for the day. The sales team were men she knew really well and had had many boozy nights out with before she began going out with the boss. She ran up the stairs feeling very much more confident.

She opened his office door without knocking. 'Tah dah,' she said, making a theatrical gesture with her arms, and sidestepping the three men seated opposite Greg at his desk, she rushed across the room and hugged him. 'Hello, darling,' she said. 'I couldn't stay away from you any longer.'

His shock was palpable, but he recovered quickly. 'Laura! You look marvellous, but perhaps you'd better wait downstairs until we've finished here.'

'You don't mind me being here, boys, do you?' she said, smiling flirtatiously at them as she perched on the desk. 'I could make you all some coffee.'

Harry Michaels, Frank Crew and Sid Emery all grinned delightedly at her. They'd all chatted her up in the past, lechers all, despite being middle-aged. But they were decent, hardworking, family men at heart and they wouldn't approve of what Greg had in mind for her.

Greg gave in and let her make the coffee, and as she expected it was only minutes before Harry complimented her on how well she looked. 'I'll be better still once I've seen Barney,' she said. 'He's down at Greg's mother's. Will you ring her, Greg, and tell her I'll be right down to collect him?'

'Later, Laura,' he said. He looked rattled.

'Then I'll ring her,' she said, reaching out for his phone. 'I can't wait to see him,' she said to the men. 'It feels like I've been away for a year, not just two weeks.'

Greg put his hand out and stopped her lifting the receiver. 'I'll go and get him, Laura, you go on home and wait.'

'But that's daft,' she laughed. 'You've got work to do. It's much easier for me to go.'

'Go on, let her get her baby, Greg!' Harry said. 'You've got that meeting with the art department later. And look at Laura, she's like a cat on a hot tin roof! Mums can't wait where their kids are concerned.'

Greg looked worried now. 'I told Mother I was coming later today, so I could go through some old accounts with Dad,' he said, and Laura could almost see him racking his brain for some plausible excuse. 'She said they were intending to take Barney out to a friend's for lunch, so she won't be back till after four. Let's just stick to that, eh?'

Laura hadn't quite got what she wanted but she could see she had him cornered. He'd be afraid not to get Barney back in case she called his mother and found out he had never been there.

'If you say so,' she said glumly and went over to him and kissed his cheek. 'Mind you hurry back then, I'll cook us something special.'

Back home later, Laura quickly unpacked her suitcases, then began a systematic search of Greg's study. In his filing tray she found a receipt from a Bond Street jeweller for a necklace costing £750, dated only two days earlier, and an application form to add a child on to an adult passport. At the bottom of a cupboard where he kept files she found an envelope containing £1,000.

Two weeks ago none of these things would have seemed suspicious. She would have thought the necklace was a surprise gift for her. When he first suggested her going to Madeira, she said she wanted him and Barney to go with her, but he'd pointed out that Barney couldn't go because he wasn't on her passport, so it was possible that he thought he'd rectify this in case she wanted to take Barney away another time. As for the money, he could well have a valid reason for keeping such a large amount of cash at home.

But in the light of finding that Barney wasn't at his mother's it all looked very different. She was absolutely certain Greg had bought the necklace for this new woman, and he'd left the receipt lying around because he hadn't expected his wife back so soon. And he was intending to put Barney on his passport to take him out of the country. As for the cash, she guessed Greg was in the process of stashing money away so that when they finally ended up in the divorce courts it would look as if he had very little.

As a precaution she dug out Barney's birth certificate and hid it away in an old toiletries bag. That at least would prevent him from making a passport application.

In the early afternoon Laura got into her own car, the yellow Beetle, and drove it back to Acton. But this time, after checking Greg's car was still there, she waited further down the street where she could watch him come out. At three-thirty the silver Mercedes nosed out of the car park, and she followed him from a distance out on to the Uxbridge Road. When he turned west towards Ealing her suspicions were confirmed, for that was the wrong direction to go to his parents.

She knew that her Beetle was far too conspicuous to be tailing anyone, so she had to hold back and let several cars get in between them. She thought she'd lost him altogether when she turned a corner she'd seen him take, then found his car had disappeared. But after driving further along the road she discovered that most of the turn-offs were into cul-de-sacs where she would have been able to see his car if he'd parked in one of them. She turned around and drove back, taking the first road she'd passed which led to a quiet, tree-lined crescent of smart, semi-detached houses. Outside one of them was Greg's car.

It was almost dark now, and she sat in her car seething with impotence. She wanted to go storming over to the house, but she couldn't, for there was a chance she might be mistaken, and if Barney was in there he'd be frightened if she went in shouting and bawling. So she just sat and waited, taking in everything about the house to try to get a fix on what the owner was like. But she could see little in the gloom, just coach lamps either side of the oak front door, a red Mini parked in front of the garage, and two leafless trees in the front garden.

She had been waiting for three-quarters of an hour when Greg finally came out, carrying a large bag. A woman followed him with Barney in her arms. Laura's blood began to boil at the sight of another woman holding her child as though he were her own. A street lamp outside the house illuminated the woman enough for Laura to see she was slim, and fair-haired, dressed in a maxi-skirt and some kind of cardigan or jacket. She looked to be in her mid-thirties, a few years younger than Greg.

Greg put the bag into the boot of his car, then opened the back door and taking Barney from the woman's arms, placed him on the back seat and shut the door. Then he turned to the woman and kissed her lingeringly.

Laura started up her car and drove off. She wasn't going to tail him home – she wanted to be there first. She knew she was driving like a maniac, but she didn't care. It didn't matter to her so much that Greg had a mistress, but the way he'd taken her son to stay in her house and let her wash, change and feed him was far too much for her to take.

She had been home some fifteen minutes before Greg arrived, and during the wait she'd tried to make herself calm down, but the moment she heard his car, she rushed outside and wrenched open the back door to reach Barney even before Greg had finished parking it.

'Hold on, you've got all evening,' she dimly heard Greg say. But she grabbed Barney anyway and holding him tightly ran back inside with him.

'Mumma,' he said wonderingly, getting a handful of her hair in his little fist. 'Mumma.'

He was dressed in dark blue wool dungarees and a red and navy striped jumper, both garments she didn't recognize. His dark hair had been trimmed, making him look suddenly boyish rather than a baby. She could smell the woman's perfume on him, something vaguely familiar. She felt murderous that this new woman had dared to put her taste and smell on her son.

She hugged and kissed him but he wriggled to be free of her tight embrace. 'Get down now,' he said.

When she put him down he toddled off into the sitting room, making straight for a box of toys that was kept in there. He looked taller and chunkier than before she went away, and when he turned and smiled at her, she began to cry.

Greg's voice behind her startled her. 'He looks well, doesn't he? He's got a lot of new words too. He said chocolate on the way home, he used to only call it choc choc.'

'Does he say I want my mummy, not daddy's tart?' Laura sobbed. 'Did he ask why he was at Ealing instead of his granny's?'

Greg's face blanched. 'What are you talking about?' he

said. 'Christ almighty, Laura, you haven't been home two minutes and already you're ranting.'

Greg was a past master at turning things to look as though she was the one at fault, and he was doing it again.

'I'm not ranting, you bastard,' she said, wiping her wet eyes on her sleeve and trying to keep her voice down because she didn't want Barney to be frightened. 'Don't even try to lie and say that woman was just a childminder, or give any other excuse. I know! Barney hasn't been anywhere near your mother's and I followed you today to see where he'd been while I'd been away. Explain that if you can.'

His face closed up. She could almost see the cogs in his brain whirling round trying to come up with a plausible tale.

'I'm not going to talk about anything while Barney is around,' he said airily. 'He needs his tea, a bath and bed. Until then, will you kindly keep your trap shut.'

He wheeled round and left the house, leaving Laura shaking with rage. She knew he would go to a pub where over a drink he'd soon concoct some kind of story, and whatever she did or said he would turn it around to make himself look like a victim.

It cut her to the quick when Barney said 'I want Jan Jan,' while in the bath and it took a monumental effort to stop herself crying.

'Jan Jan's gone now,' she said, and tickled him to make him laugh, but that didn't stop her feeling as if someone had clamped a steel band around her heart.

Greg didn't come home that night. She waited and waited, but by twelve-thirty she knew he wouldn't come. She guessed he'd gone back to the woman and that the pair of them were discussing what to do next.

All the next day Laura went through the motions of going to the shops for food, taking Barney to the swings, and all the usual daily routine of being a wife and mother. But she knew with utter certainty that Greg wanted her out of his life.

He had never been a devoted father, she doubted he really wanted Barney in the new life he'd got planned with this other woman, but once again his actions would be decided by how they affected his image.

Straightforward desertion of his wife and child would not be an option to him; he would have to make himself look like the victim. No doubt he'd already told his parents and friends that she was unstable, a user of drugs and an unfit mother. Maybe he'd even said she'd gone off abroad with another man. Everyone would admire him if he took Barney and had to struggle to bring up his son alone.

Laura couldn't understand why the other woman would want to be saddled with someone else's child. But it was possible she couldn't have any of her own, or that Greg had made her believe he and Barney were a package deal.

One thing Laura realized immediately was that she couldn't just rush off somewhere now with Barney. She had very little money of her own, nowhere to take him to either. And she would need to find somewhere to live where Greg would never find them, for she knew he'd come after her just to spite her.

That meant she would have to play for time, keep on an even keel and even seem to be going along with whatever Greg came up with, while she made her own plans.

Greg came home that evening after she'd put Barney to bed. His face was stiff and cold, and Laura took some delight in behaving as if nothing had happened. He looked shocked to see the table in the dining room laid for dinner. She felt certain he'd expected her to launch into a shouting match, which would enable him to turn round and walk right out again.

'I suppose you want a divorce,' she said as she dished up

the coq au vin. 'I don't like the idea, I thought we had married for life, but if that's what you want just let's make it as amicable as possible.'

As she expected, he tried to provoke her into a row, turning everything around to make out it was her fault, claiming she had always been 'difficult', that she wasn't cut out to be the wife of a senior executive, or a mother. He brought up her refusal to live in the country, her drug-taking, and accused her of only marrying him for his money and position anyway.

She didn't rise to his bait, just nodded as if she agreed with all his complaints. 'So let's cut to the chase,' she said. 'What are you intending to do?'

He said he didn't know. She said that they should just carry on for the time being until he did.

The winter passed, spring arrived and Laura continued to try to hold her tongue as the pressure mounted between them. Greg came and went as he pleased. He gave no explanations as to what he was doing, or what he wanted, and there was no attempt at friendliness. When he spoke he was curt and dismissive; he threw his dirty clothes down on the floor, he'd demand a meal late at night, then push it away after one mouthful claiming it was disgusting.

Outside the house in nearby Kings Road Laura saw women of her own age shopping in the boutiques, flirting, laughing and having fun, while she at only twenty-seven had no one and nothing in her life other than Barney.

Jackie had sold the first house she had bought to do up and sell on, and made a vast profit, immediately ploughing it into other properties. She could talk of nothing but building and design, and how happy she was with Roger. Meggie and Ivy had put their place on the market too after hearing of Jackie's success and they were preoccupied with finding another one. Laura didn't feel able to tell them how bad things were for her, or how scared she was that Greg might eventually do something terrible to her. So when she saw them she pretended everything was fine.

Belle often popped round to see Laura. She had left her parents' home in Muswell Hill and moved into a shared flat in the Fulham Road while she was attending a drama school. Her excitement and wonder at being in central London, the clubs, shops and her many boyfriends, made Laura feel as if she was being rubbed with sandpaper, and she wondered how much longer she could put up with Greg without cracking up.

But she couldn't leave, not till she had more money, and it was becoming increasingly difficult managing to squeeze anything extra out of the housekeeping money Greg gave her each week. If she tried to economize by buying mince, he would demand steak; if she said Barney needed new shoes he would check his feet and say his current shoes still fitted. It was as if he knew what she was planning.

By the end of April he was hitting her. The first time it was just a slap when she forgot to collect his favourite shoes from the cobbler's. He raged at her and said it was her job to take care of such things, and hit her.

That time he apologized the following day, and even cuddled her and promised it would never happen again. But it did; just a week later he punched her in the stomach, and she'd barely recovered from that when he laid into her one night for spilling some fat on the kitchen floor which he'd slipped on when he came home. He was like a man possessed, dragging her up by the hair as she lay in bed, and punching her stomach as though it was a medicine ball.

From then on it was a round of violence. She didn't have to do or say anything to set him off, he would attack her for any reason, and always he yelled at her to get out of the house and never come back. But she wasn't going to go without Barney because she knew that was what he hoped for.

Yet the more he hit her, the more verbal abuse he subjected her to, the more worthless she felt. She sometimes felt that Greg was right, that she was scum, and that maybe she had no right to Barney.

It was a Friday night in early June when she finally saw that he would kill her eventually if she didn't get out.

He came home around eight stinking of drink, and asked where she'd moved his golf clubs to. The last time he played golf he'd left his bag in the kitchen, and Barney had pulled out one of the irons and smashed a vase with it. Laura had then put them for safety in the hall cupboard where they kept the coats. She was washing up and so she told Greg where he could find them. The next minute he'd got her by the hair, dragging her out of the kitchen.

'You bloody well get them,' he roared at her. 'You lazy fucking whore.'

She knew he would hit her even if she kept quiet, and the injustice and cruelty of it made her snap. 'You hit me again and I'll go down to your factory and tell them that you're a wife beater,' she yelled back at him.

For a second she thought that had stopped him in his tracks for he opened the hall cupboard door and pulled out his golf club bag. But suddenly he whirled round on her, caught her by the shoulder, and with his other hand pulled out a club and hit her with it.

It landed on her shoulder and she managed to get away from him, running out to the kitchen. But he came after her and slashed at her legs, making her fall to the floor.

He had her at his mercy then and he hit her over and over again, yelling out obscenities that were so vile it was as though he was possessed by an evil spirit. She screamed, begged him to stop and think of Barney upstairs, but it made no difference.

The pain was incredible. Each stroke felt like a burn, and she tried to curl herself up to protect herself, but she thought the blows raining down on her back would kill her.

Then as suddenly as he'd started, he stopped, dropping the club on the floor beside her. 'You've done this to me,' he spat at her. 'You've turned me into something evil, like you.'

He left then, rushing out of the house, not even stopping to pick up his golf bag. She heard his car start up and roar off down the road.

She was beyond tears, in shock with both the pain of the beating and the idea that he could hate her that much. But she knew that somehow she had to get out with Barney that night. Once he had gathered his wits he'd be back for his son.

There was no point in calling the police. They would call it 'a domestic', and say she must stay in the house with Barney and claim her rights through the courts. Greg had the money and the legal contacts. First he'd whip Barney away, then on Monday morning he'd be at his solicitor's with some story about her endangering Barney. He'd make people believe him too, he was good at that, and she'd never get her baby back.

It took all her strength to pull herself up on the cupboard doors, and then one painful step after another until she reached the stairs.

Packing a couple of cases with her and Barney's clothes was hard enough when every movement was like having a dagger going though her, but how she got them downstairs and out into her car, she really didn't know. She filled another small bag with Barney's toys, then went into Greg's study to see if she could find any money.

The moment when she found a large brown envelope in

the same place she'd found money back in February was the only time that night when she stopped hurting for a few brief seconds. She didn't think it was the same wad of money, for it was in a different envelope, but a quick glance inside told her there was even more than in the first one.

With it safely in her handbag, she went back out on to the landing and stopped before the mirror to brace herself before lifting Barney out of his cot. Her face was thankfully unmarked, but when she pulled up her shirt she saw purple weals across her chest and stomach. She couldn't manage to twist herself enough to check her back, and she guessed that was even worse.

Picking Barney up was the hardest thing of all. Every nerve ending in her back, arms and even her legs screamed for her to stop. He was heavy, and sound asleep a dead weight, but somehow she managed to get him into her arms and wrap his blanket around him.

It was a warm night, and still light though well after ten, so she half expected her neighbours to come out. After all, they must have heard her screaming earlier and seen her putting the cases into the space behind the Beetle's back seat. But the only people in the road were down the far end by Kings Road.

Barney didn't wake as she laid him down on the back seat. Wincing with pain, she eased herself into the driver's seat, started the engine and drove off.

'Gonnae stamp my book?'

Laura was startled out of her reverie by Frances from her own block, standing in front of the desk grinning at her.

'Sexy daydream?' Frances giggled.

'A real hot one,' Laura replied and smiled. Frances was a nice kid, only eighteen, a Goth and something of a hard case, but she was bright and often very funny.

'I'll let you get back to it then,' Frances replied. 'Any good?' she asked, waving her copy of *Cover Her Face* by P. D. James.

'Great,' Laura said. 'But you might find English village life a bit tame after Glasgow, even with Inspector Dalgliesh on the prowl.'

'Is there any sex in it?' Frances asked.

Laura half smiled. 'Do you want there to be?'

'There's nae point reading it unless there's some.' Frances shrugged.

Later that same day, when she was back in her cell after supper, Laura put down her pen and notepad as she found herself thinking about Stuart. She wondered where he was and what he was doing, and smiled to herself thinking how smart he was to have found Meggie. She would love to know what they talked about – Stuart had a way of making women open up. When they were together she almost told him the whole truth about Greg many times, and now she didn't know what possessed her to keep it to herself.

Was it her ego? Afraid she would look less shiny and whole? Or because she never wanted anyone to feel sorry for her?

She really didn't know. She knew now that there was no shame in admitting hurt and fear or in showing another person you could be vulnerable. But at twenty-seven she had been something of a hothead.

That night when she left Chelsea, she drove all the way to Brixham in Devon. It was astounding that she got there, considering her injuries. She remembered that she cried on and off all the way.

'Funny how people run to places they were once happy in,' she murmured to herself.

She could have gone over to Meggie and Ivy's, to Jackie too for that matter, any one of them would have comforted her, tucked her into a bed and taken care of Barney too. But it was that pride thing. She didn't want them to see her that way.

It was just on dawn when she got to Brixham and she parked her car in the harbour and watched the sky gradually lightening. She was in such pain she could barely focus her eyes, and she was dreading Barney waking because she didn't know how she was going to be able to look after him. In her rush to leave she'd forgotten his pushchair, and she doubted she'd be able to carry him.

But as the sun rose she took comfort in the symbolism of a new day. She might be badly hurt but she'd finally got away from Greg. She had to embark on a new life now, and she'd make sure it was a better one.

Later that day she found a studio flat to rent. Just one room and a bathroom but it was spacious, light and bright and close to the harbour. She stayed there right up till the end of June when the owner had a holiday booking, spending most days on the beach with Barney, or going for long walks. In the evenings when she'd put Barney to bed, she read and watched television. As each day passed her injuries hurt less, and as the bruises faded she realized she felt happier than she had for a very long time.

She sent cards to Jackie and her sisters, just saying that she'd left Greg and would be in touch when she was settled. She didn't dare give Jackie the address as she was afraid Greg might winkle it out of her. She thought it best that Meggie and Ivy didn't know it either; they might turn up to see her and she didn't want to be questioned.

Barney became toilet-trained while she was there, and she taught him to eat with a spoon and fork and drink from a proper cup. Every day he learned more new words, and delighted in putting whole sentences together. They both became brown as berries, and Laura found herself revelling in the new closeness she had with him. Greg had never liked her playing noisy or messy games with Barney when he was home; in truth his own upbringing had been so formal and regimented that he expected Laura should be the same with Barney.

Laura set off for Cornwall when she had to give up the flat in Brixham. She would have liked to stay there, but she couldn't find anywhere to live that was cheap. Although she had the money she'd taken from Greg – there had been £1,500 in the envelope – she had to be really careful with it until she could find somewhere permanent and get a job and a childminder.

It was in Looe that she met the bunch of Scottish hippies who told her about the commune in Castle Douglas. They were fun people, warm and feckless, camping out on the cliff top, drinking too much, smoking a great deal of dope, but they welcomed Barney and her and didn't ask too many questions. She stayed with them in their tent, because like Brixham, flats or rooms in Looe cost too much in the summer season.

Fate stepped in and took a hand when her friends were arrested for allegedly driving away from a petrol station without paying. She went to the police station to see them when she heard, and they told her they hadn't done it. It seemed the police were trumping up charges for any hippies coming down to Cornwall, their way of deterring them. Her friends told her she'd better move on before she was picked up too. Rob, the guy she liked best, suggested she went up to Castle Douglas.

So that was where she went. It didn't make any sense, she knew no one in Scotland, but she couldn't face going to live in a city again. All she had in her mind was the warmth and easygoing, unmaterialistic natures of those Scots, a kind of template of the kind of people she felt she might belong with.

And she found Stuart at the journey's end.

9

Laura was running through a field of long grass. She could feel the sun biting into her arms and her hair bouncing on her shoulders. At first she was frightened, as if someone were chasing her, but then she suddenly realized she was running to a figure whose face she couldn't see, and he had his arms outstretched as if to catch her.

She woke to find herself not in a sun-filled meadow, but in her cell, with the faint glow of the lights on the prison fence shining down on her. She closed her eyes and tried to get back into the dream, but it was gone.

Wide awake now and too hot, she threw off her blanket and turned her pillow over to the cool side. This was one of those moments that brought home to her exactly what losing her freedom meant. She couldn't get up and make a cup of tea, or switch on the light and read a book. She couldn't even walk out the door.

When she first got here she often had panic attacks at night when she felt she had a band around her heart, slowly squeezing till it would eventually stop pumping her blood. Sweat would pour off her and the walls seemed to close in.

But like most of the hideous things about prison, she'd eventually found a way of dealing with it. She just had to lie still, relax first her feet, then her legs, and gradually, bit by bit, make a conscious effort to work her way right up her body, relaxing it until the whole of her felt like a soft sponge. Then she could let good thoughts come to her.

The lovely dream she'd woken from was a good place to start tonight, for she understood the symbolism in it. She hadn't exactly been pursued by anyone as she drove up to Scotland all those years ago, but she had the weight of all the unhappiness with Greg still in her head, and the anxiety that she needed to make a real home again for Barney.

She had broken her journey from Cornwall in Bristol, staying the night in a bed and breakfast. The following morning she bought food for a picnic and spent the day with Barney in a park. In the early evening when he was growing tired, she'd tucked him up on the back seat of the car and started off for Scotland.

It was an arduous journey. Her Beetle wasn't fast and the headlights were dim. As it got dark she became worried that she was losing her way, and she had to stop every now and then to check her map by the light of a torch. She had never been further north than Leeds before, and then only by train, and it was a strange and nerve-racking experience to be bombing along in the dark with no idea what lay to the right or left of her or how far she was from a town or village.

She did turn off the main road when she found herself almost nodding off. She supposed she must have slept for an hour or so, for when she began driving again, the first rays of light were coming into the sky. Her spirits rose as she saw the beauty of the Lake District unfolding before her, and the fresh, warm air coming in through the window was as intoxicating as a glass of champagne.

On the last lap of the journey from Dumfries, where they had their breakfast in a transport café, on to Castle Douglas, Barney was happily singing nursery rhymes and pointing out cows, sheep and geese on farms. Although the small stone cottages, the hills covered in firs and the moorlike wide open spaces with not a house for miles seemed very stark after the lushness of the south-west of England, Laura had an odd feeling of coming home.

She was close to total exhaustion as she spotted a man on the roof of a house which was up a farm track. By then she was afraid she was never going to find the commune. When she'd asked for directions in Castle Douglas, she'd met a touch of hostility, and only vague instructions just to take the road to Dalbeattie.

Although she couldn't see the man's face as he came towards her car, because the sun was in her eyes, his long coppery-brown hair, bare chest and cut-down Levis all made her heart leap, for at least he was unlikely to be affronted when she asked where the commune was.

Her very first thought was that he was a bit simple, for he stared at her vacantly for some moments before answering her question. But when he did speak, his voice was like music and she realized he was a little stunned by her.

She ought to have been horrified by 'the hoose', as everyone called that place. A few days later she overheard a man in Castle Douglas call it 'the hoose where all those dirty hippies stay'. It was almost falling down, with weeds growing up through the roof, no electricity or hot water, and precious little furniture. Yet she felt no horror, for the sun was dazzling, there were trees and lush long grass, and someone had fixed a gaily striped awning above a rough table and benches outside.

The man who introduced himself as Stuart told her it wasn't a commune but a mere squat, without any other children there. The fact that everyone else in the place was still sleeping meant drugs and heaven knows what else, so any sensible mother would have got back in her car and driven off. But there was something about Stuart, with his kind grey eyes, strong chin and a gentlemanly quality that made her feel she could trust him with Barney while she just slept for a while.

It was in the evening that she felt herself being drawn

towards him, and even though she tried to tell herself that he was too young for her and too unworldly, she had a feeling she was in the grip of destiny and she had no choice in the matter but just to flow with it.

His feelings showed openly on his face – a good face, she thought, as she watched him covertly in the light of the campfire while he played his guitar. She'd already been told by Josie, a hard-faced Londoner with squaw-like plaits, that Stuart had made the rough table and benches from some fallen trees and had fixed the ancient range in the kitchen so they could cook on it. Josie had joked he was the ideal man to be shipwrecked with, as he'd build you a house and catch you food without any trouble. She also added that she thought he was sexy.

Laura thought he was sexy too, though not in the strutting, narcissistic way of the men she knew around Chelsea, who had honed their skills as lovers through endless loveless practice. Stuart's sexiness was of the innate kind, which extended to everything he did. As he bent over his guitar he was almost making love to it, and while eating earlier he'd shown the same passion, enjoying every mouthful.

His lean hips, the width of his shoulders and the muscles in his arms had not been achieved by weight-lifting or strenuous sport, only through his work. He was a man at peace with himself, uncomplicated, honest and joyful.

She'd observed him playing with Barney earlier, throwing him up in the air, playfighting and rolling around with him, a natural father even though he professed to have had no previous experience with small children. She found that touching, for Greg had never been comfortable or at ease with his son.

Stuart wouldn't stand out in a crowd – his complexion was unfashionably ruddy, and his teeth weren't too good. But the thoughtfulness of his grey eyes, the sensuality of his wide mouth and the straight, rather aristocratic nose, made her pulse race. If he didn't attempt to seduce her, and she doubted he would, for he seemed a little shy and in awe of her, then she intended to seduce him.

It happened seamlessly. They went into Stuart's room to put Barney to bed and suddenly they were kissing. Laura had never known that kind of instant, all-consuming passion before. In the past, when she felt she desired someone enough to go to bed with them, there was always a period before peeling off her clothes when she felt tense and apprehensive. She would take herself off to a bathroom to wash and clean her teeth, often prolonging this to put off the moment when she'd got to go back to the man. She had often semi-jokingly told Jackie that she'd like it better if she could get undressed in the dark and slip into bed without being seen, or seeing her partner.

But Stuart just blew away all her inhibitions. Her clothes came off effortlessly and without embarrassment, and just the touch of his bare chest against hers, the smell of the bonfire on their skin, those hard, manly hands caressing her was all the aphrodisiac she needed.

His chin was stubbly, they were both sweaty and in need of a shower, but that only seemed to give the lovemaking an extra edge. Greg had made love to her as if he was following a sex manual; he knew the right buttons to push, but it was predictable and lacking in fire.

The fire was so hot with Stuart that she felt she might explode. They devoured each other like ravaging beasts, yet there were moments of such sweet tenderness that she found herself crying and felt his cheeks too were wet with tears. It was incomparable with anything that had gone before; no man had ever touched her soul the way Stuart did, and she had never wanted to please anyone more.

When the first light of dawn came peeping through the

grimy window, he was kneeling between her legs, his hands on her breasts, just looking at her. Everything she felt at that moment was mirrored in his face – wonderment, exultation and love. Nothing needed to be said; they knew that tomorrow, next week and even next year they would be bound together as tightly as they were now.

She remembered then how just before she married Greg, she'd asked Meggie's opinion on how you knew if you were truly in love. She thought it had to be love she felt for Greg, but she wasn't absolutely certain. She told Meggie she'd always imagined that real love would make you melt into each other.

It did with Stuart. She loved everything about him, from his loping walk, his tangled hair, the smell of his sweat, to his voice and kisses. She wouldn't want to change a single thing.

It was a dream of a summer. It must have rained some days, but Laura didn't remember anything but blue skies, warmth and happiness. Such happiness!

She did all kinds of things she'd never done before: bathing in a stream, which Stuart called a burn, making bread in the old range, collecting wood for the fire, and making love in woods and fields. Sometimes they drove to a beach, sometimes they walked in forests, and Stuart would carry Barney on his shoulders for miles.

In the evenings they lit a bonfire and lay around it with the rest of the gang, singing, laughing and chatting. Stuart often urged her to sing as he played his guitar, but she preferred just to listen to him. Whether he was evoking the fire of flamenco, or playing heart-rending love songs, happy folk music or joyful rock and roll, to see his head bent over his instrument, his eyes dreamily half closed and his fingers like quicksilver on the strings, made her heart contract with love for him.

She realized then she'd never truly loved before. She cared far more for Stuart than she did for herself, and never wanted to be apart from him. The way he was with Barney, natural, easy and loving, seeing him not as a slightly irritating accessory of hers, but a major part of her, was so soothing. And Barney responded to him gleefully, sensing this was one man he could trust implicitly.

She found it odd that she no longer cared about material things. She wore the same old clothes day in, day out, she didn't crave restaurant meals, night clubs or trips to the cinema. They had nothing, only each other, and it was the purest, sweetest thing she had ever known.

By the end of September they were waking to chilly mist and the nights were drawing in; suddenly everyone began to talk about moving on. Some thought they'd go to Morocco, others just back to London.

'We have to be sensible,' Stuart said when Laura suggested they went to Morocco too. 'That's no place to take Barney, he might get sick there. Besides, I've got very little money left, and I must get back to work to look after you both.'

'But where will we live?' she asked.

Stuart smiled and patted her cheek the way he always did when she looked worried. 'We can't live in a squat through a Scottish winter, but I'll find us somewhere cosy in Edinburgh.'

Laura smiled to herself at all those wonderful memories; reliving them had made her relaxed and peaceful. She wondered if Stuart thought back on them in the same way, or whether what happened later had destroyed them for him.

She often told people who knew Stuart in those days that the reason they broke up was because he was too young and naive for her, and that was a small part of it. Another part was the cultural differences between them when they moved to Edinburgh.

The south had had a huge shake-up during the late sixties. Feminism, the Pill and the hippie culture had all changed the traditional family values and moral codes Laura remembered from the 1950s. No one batted an eye at unmarried mothers or couples living together before marriage any more. Women had moved into traditionally male jobs and they could rise much higher in most companies and professions. While there was still inequality in male and female wages, things were moving in the right direction and society was becoming much fairer.

Laura had assumed the same had happened in Scotland, so it was something of a shock, after the free and easy life in Castle Douglas, to find Edinburgh still had one foot in the Dark Ages and the women were still subservient to their men.

She could hardly believe that men could come home from work, eat their tea, put on the clean ironed shirt their wife had ready for them and then disappear off to the pub, night after night. It was an unwelcome echo of her own childhood, and she couldn't understand why their women didn't protest.

She found it odd, too, that the Scots she met at that time seemed to have little interest in the decor of their homes. Going into one was like stepping back into the fifties. Even people with quite good jobs had very shabby homes, and few owned their own houses.

Her very first impression of Edinburgh was one of wonder. She gazed at the majestic Castle standing proud up on a vast rock as they drove into the city and could hardly wait to explore it. She saw, too, the elegant Georgian New Town with its wide streets and leafy squares and felt this was a city she could give her heart to.

But there was no time to explore. Stuart was anxious to find work quickly and in the meantime they were to stay with his parents.

Mr and Mrs Macgregor were welcoming enough, especially to Barney, but Laura sensed an undercurrent of disapproval that their son was involved with an older married woman. Mrs Macgregor showed Laura and Barney to Stuart's old bedroom and made it quite plain that he would be sleeping on the sofa.

'I will not have carrying on in my house,' she said quietly but firmly.

Laura wished then that she'd anticipated this and found a room to rent. She felt badly about starting off on the wrong foot with this softly spoken, sweet-faced woman.

In most ways Stuart's parents were what she expected, for his honesty, dignity and good manners were clearly the result of a careful upbringing. They were in their late fifties, both with grey hair, his mother small and tubby and his father around five feet eight with a craggy face and the same strong jawline as Stuart. But Laura was surprised by the humbleness of their two-bedroom flat. Knowing Mr Macgregor was a first-class tradesman, she had imagined he earned very good money. Yet they had no washing machine, their fridge was ancient, and the kitchen, though scrupulously clean, was very old-fashioned. Even more surprisingly, Stuart told her that they moved there when he was ten, and at that time his brother and sister were still living at home. She wondered how they had all fitted in.

Laura wasn't happy staying with the Macgregors, as by day Stuart was out hunting for work, and she was left with his mother. It seemed rude to take Barney out and explore Edinburgh when she was an uninvited guest. Stuart didn't seem to want her to look for a flat for them until he'd got a job, so she had to spend the days helping his mother with her chores and going out to the local shops to buy food for dinner.

Right from a child Laura had always been the one who cleaned, cooked and tidied up, and she found Mrs Macgregor's assumption that she was undomesticated irritating. There was no variety in the meals she cooked either, meat and vegetables ruled, and she looked alarmed when Laura tentatively suggested that a pasta or rice dish might make a pleasant change.

Even more irritating was that she had no time alone with Stuart. The minute his father had eaten his dinner he went to the pub, expecting Stuart to go with him. When she asked if she could go too, Mr Macgregor looked at her in astonishment.

'Nay, lassie,' he said. ''Tis all men there.'

When Stuart got taken on to do the joinery in a school which was being modernized, they were both overjoyed. As he had a few days before he was needed, he began looking for a home for them. Again it was made quite clear by the Macgregors that this was a man's job and Laura was to keep out of it.

On the Friday before he was due to start the new job, he came home with a key. 'I've got us a hoose,' he said, grinning delightedly. 'We can move in as soon as we've found some furniture.'

It never occurred to Laura to ask him to define 'hoose', and she was soon to discover that the word meant merely 'home' to him.

He took her to Caledonian Crescent that evening, and although Laura was delighted to find it was in the central, Haymarket area of the city, her heart sank a couple of notches when she saw it was a tenement, with a central staircase and four flats on each of the four floors. Their 'hoose', number 7, was on the second floor overlooking the street.

Compared to her old home in Shepherds Bush it was gracious, and luxurious, by comparison with the squat in Castle Douglas, but the climb up the dingy stairs put her off before she'd even seen inside the flat. The poky hallway led into one gloomy room with a kitchen in a recess, one bedroom and a tiny bathroom, but the fact it was self-contained did nothing to lift her spirits. She felt ashamed she couldn't be overjoyed – Stuart might very well have found a place where they had to share the bathroom.

Yet she bit back her disappointment and suggested they painted it all white to brighten it up. With the £200 she'd still got in the bank, they could buy a second-hand bed, a little one for Barney, some cheap carpet, and maybe a settee too. They could make it nice.

By Saturday night the bedroom was painted. They had a double bed and a single one for Barney, made up with sheets and blankets Mrs Macgregor had given them. Stuart had fixed a pole across the alcove to hold their clothes in and they even had curtains at the window and a bedside light made with a Chianti bottle.

'We'll make it all grand in time,' Stuart said as he hugged her. 'I'll be making good money, we can buy a telly and a stereo before long, and till then I'll entertain you with lovemaking and my guitar.'

That was all she wanted or needed then. All through October, November and December while Stuart was work-ing, she spent her days scouring the second-hand shops for oddments they needed, copying recipes from magazines in the library to cook economical, tasty meals for them, taking Barney on exploratory walks, and working on the flat to prettify it.

She loved Edinburgh with her whole being, from the

steep cobbled wynds and the extraordinary towering ancient tenements in the Old Town, to the magnificence of the Castle and Holyrood palace. She got books on the city's history from the library and made Stuart laugh when she gleefully revelled in the darker side of it, with Burke and Hare the notorious body-snatchers, or the ghosts said to frequent the Old Town. She cried when she heard the story of Bobbie of Greyfriars churchyard, the dog who sat on his master's grave for years after his death, and she felt indignant that Mary, Queen of Scots had been treated so badly. She couldn't wait for spring so they could climb up to Arthur's Seat, or go to the beach at Portobello.

She was happy, really happy. She soon grew used to the other people who lived 'on the stair' taking an inordinate amount of interest in her, and the cooking smells which wafted up and remained trapped. She didn't mind the biting cold, going to tea with Stuart's parents almost every Sunday and living on far less housekeeping money than she had with Greg.

There was a cosiness about living with Stuart which she'd never experienced before. He took care of her in every way, from a cup of tea when he got up to go to work, to insisting she wasn't to carry heavy shopping home but to wait for him to go with her. He was always enthusiastic about the meals she cooked him, he wanted to play with Barney when he got home, and though they couldn't afford to go out much, the evenings and weekends with him were joyful times.

But happy as she was with Stuart, she found it hard to accept that most Scots males were chauvinists. She had no problem with the 'You're just a wee lassie, let me lift that for you' attitude of gentlemanly Scotsmen, for Stuart was like that too, but she hated the way so many of them showed little regard for their wives and took no part in their children's upbringing.

She got to know many women with children around the same age as Barney, but friendly and warm as these women were, it irritated her that they were resigned to an endless round of cooking, cleaning, washing and ironing and living on the tightest budget, while their man did as he pleased. They spoke longingly of wanting to go and visit relatives, to have a family holiday, or just having their husband home long enough one evening so they could discuss how the kids were doing at school. On the odd occasion when Laura expressed her view that they should take a firmer line with their men and demand the kind of equal relationship she had with Stuart, they just shrugged. 'You an' your London ways,' they'd say, as if she came from another planet.

She heard men out in the street stumbling home drunk from the pub on a Friday or Saturday night, and the violent rows that often broke out when they got in. She would listen to her friends' complaints that their television had been repossessed because their husband hadn't met the payments, or that they'd had to pawn something to pay the rent.

Laura felt a smug superiority that Stuart was not like that. He rarely went out without her, and since they'd moved into the flat he'd built bookcases, a proper wardrobe, and more cupboards for the kitchen. On the odd occasion when he did go out for a drink with a friend he always asked first if she minded. And when he did come home drunk, he was never nasty, quite the reverse – he would make love to her for hours and hours.

She was irritated, though, by the influence his parents had over him. They didn't really approve of them living together when they weren't married, they were suspicious of Laura's worldliness, and perhaps afraid she was going to tempt

Stuart away from them and the kind of sober, industrious life they wanted for him.

In January of '73, the work on the school was finished, and it didn't lead on to another job as Stuart had hoped. Right through that month and half-way through February he couldn't get another job and they had to apply for dole. It was tough living on less than half the amount of wages he'd been used to, but they managed. It was bitterly cold then, and Laura liked the cosiness of having him home with her and Barney.

She could never forget Barney's introduction to snow. Stuart had collected his old childhood sledge from his parents' home, and they bundled Barney up in warm clothes, sat him on the sledge and Stuart pulled him round to Harrington Park.

It brought tears to her eyes to watch Stuart hurtling down the slope with Barney tucked safely between his long legs. Barney yelled with glee; each time they got to the bottom he'd race right back up the hill, looking like a little gnome in his red woolly hat, matching red cheeks and wellingtons. Laura squeezed on with them too, and yelled as loudly as Barney as the sledge gathered speed and she feared they would never stop.

That day she remembered how it had been a year earlier when she was rushed off to hospital with poisoning. She'd never had blissfully happy moments sharing Barney with Greg, he never played with his son, and he wouldn't have understood that a day spent sledging was fun.

Stuart got taken on for another job at the end of February but that job only lasted two weeks, and once again they were back on the dole. That time Stuart took it hard, and paced about looking worried. He said if he'd known his five-year apprenticeship was going to lead to no work at the end of it, he'd have joined the Navy or gone to Australia.

'I didn't want you to live like this,' he said despairingly when they had no money to put in the gas meter. 'I don't feel like a man when I can't provide for you.'

She did try to reassure him it was not his fault, that joiners, bricklayers, plumbers and electricians were all having a hard time because of the recession. Every night in the newspaper there was someone voicing an opinion that the government should fire up the economy by building new houses and public buildings.

Laura found a job as a barmaid at the Maybury Casino in April, just after Barney's third birthday. It was only two nights a week, and to her it was the ideal job, for Stuart could babysit Barney, and the extra money would be good for all of them.

She knew Stuart thought a casino was the equivalent of the gateway to hell, and that he didn't like the idea of her being out at night in the company of other men, but he accepted her decision with resignation. He almost certainly expected that she would soon get tired of it, but perhaps the reason he didn't make more objections was because he knew they really did need the money.

Yet from the first night Laura loved working at the casino. There was something about the Art Deco building, the soft lighting, plush decor, sophistication and the buzz of excitement in the air that made her spirits rise as soon as she walked in the door. It was some way from the town centre so she had no problem parking her car. She loved being able to dress up in the smart clothes she hadn't worn since she left London, to be Laura again, not Barney's mother or Stuart's lady. She mixed with interesting people who stimulated her mind and she felt good about herself.

Stuart often joked that it was like having a mistress when she came out of the bedroom looking glamorous, and if he minded being left alone with Barney, he kept it to himself. Just a few weeks in to her starting at the casino, he got work again, and she'd be rushing out just as he got in, leaving him instructions about Barney, and his dinner that she'd left in the oven.

Two nights at the casino went up to three, and still Stuart didn't complain, even though she often hadn't got his dinner ready for him when he came home, and sometimes hadn't even given Barney his. Yet on balance they were far happier that summer, they had lots to talk about, they could afford to go out for the day on Sundays, and Laura was much more enthusiastic about lovemaking. But by September, when the odd extra fourth night had become a regular one, Stuart became sullen.

'Barney misses you,' he said one evening just as she was leaving. 'He doesn't settle well now, he keeps getting out of bed and asking when you are coming home.'

Laura didn't stop to think about what he'd said, she just heard the reproach in his voice and saw it as the first stage of him becoming like all his friends and their neighbours, a man who wanted his woman right under his thumb. She'd had too much of that with Greg.

'Well, smack him then,' she snapped. 'He's only trying it on. I'm stuck at home with him all day and I need more than that in my life.'

She saw Stuart's expression harden. 'So neither of us is as important as a bunch of losers drooling at you over the bar?'

'At least they see me as a woman, not just some sort of glorified housekeeper,' she snapped, and left without even saying goodbye.

Stuart was right to some extent, she did have men drooling over her. They said her English accent was sexy, and that she was beautiful enough to be a model. She felt high on the attention, and powerful too, and although she did love Stuart just as passionately as when they first met, there were times when she regretted moving in with him.

She didn't have the status of a wife, but she couldn't do exactly what she wanted to do either. There were times when she was tempted to jump in her car and drive down to London to see Jackie, Meggie and Ivy, but she couldn't, not without money of her own, or hurting Stuart's feelings. Besides, Stuart had her car during the day to get to work. The car was often a bone of contention, for since Stuart passed his driving test he always insisted on driving it when they went out together. He said he felt like a kept man if she drove, and he didn't seem to understand that by taking it over he was snatching the last remnants of her independence.

His mother was another thorny issue. She interfered on many levels, quizzing Laura about what she cooked for her son, and even what she put in his sandwiches. She always sniffed with disapproval about her working at the casino, and made pointed remarks about Stuart being left to babysit Barney.

But the worst thing was that she kept asking Laura when she was going to get a divorce. Laura couldn't tell her that she was afraid to start proceedings because Greg would find out where she was and might attempt to get custody of Barney. But by stalling Laura knew she was creating the idea in Mrs Macgregor's mind that she was just playing with Stuart, and she was never going to marry him and have his children.

Laura wanted to have a baby with Stuart, but certainly not while they lived in such a poky flat, and how could they get somewhere better unless she worked too?

*

It was during the autumn of '74 that things really began to turn sour. There had been many rows throughout the year, about the car which always seemed to need something repaired, about Stuart's mother's interference, or the cramped conditions in the flat. But mostly Stuart got shirty about her working so many evenings a week. Laura's counter-argument was pointing out that she paid for repairs on the car, bought their fridge and a vacuum cleaner with her wages, and supported him during the times he was laid off.

It was an argument that couldn't be resolved, for Stuart knew they did need the money she earned, and that she couldn't get daytime work because of Barney. They always made their rows up passionately, but the bitter words they'd flung at each other at the height of the rows weren't always forgotten, and resentment and anger simmered below the surface, ready to erupt again the next time.

Jackie was also a mild bone of contention with Stuart. He didn't want to hear about the friend in London she had such an attachment to. Whenever Laura had a letter from her and she mentioned the latest property she'd renovated and sold on, he would look wounded, as if Laura was implying he didn't do enough to improve their standard of living. He made up his mind even before he met her that she would look down on him.

In the last year Jackie had come up to Edinburgh several times to see Laura, and though Stuart was pleasantly surprised to find she wasn't the snob he imagined, he was still wary of her because she came without her husband, stayed in a plush hotel, and splashed a great deal of money around.

He gradually grew to like her, mainly because she was so enthusiastic about the places in Scotland he took her to visit. Yet despite this, whenever he and Laura had a row he would still make caustic comments about her. He was clearly a little jealous of her affection for her friend.

Jackie grew to love Scotland so much she began looking for a cottage to buy along the Fife coast. Stuart huffed and puffed about this, for few Scots owned their own homes at that time. As he saw it, if wealthy English people came marauding over the border to buy property, the locals would soon have nowhere to live.

The pretty little two-up, two-down fisherman's cottage Jackie eventually bought was in Cellardyke in Fife, right on the old harbour. She got local tradesmen in to renovate it, and in August, when it was finished, she asked Laura, Stuart and Barney to join her for a holiday there.

Stuart couldn't take time off his work, but he was happy enough for Laura to go with Barney. Jackie drove up from London with a vanload of furniture, picking Laura and Barney up as she came through Edinburgh. Together the girls arranged it all in the cottage, hung curtains, pictures and equipped the kitchen.

It was the most fun Laura had had since Castle Douglas, for it was like their early flat-sharing days. Everything made them laugh, they chatted about old times eagerly, and filled each other in on all that had happened to them both in the past few years.

It was lovely warm weather and Barney could wander in and out, making friends with the neighbours' children and watching the fishermen in their boats. The novelty of hanging out washing on lines right on the harbour, the clean salty air, and listening to the sea breaking on the shore at night, never ceased to delight Laura. She could understand completely why Jackie had fallen in love with the place.

In the afternoons they took long walks along the beach to Crail with Barney, swam and had picnics, then stayed up half the night drinking and giggling as they recalled old boyfriends, and discussed Roger and Stuart.

Late one night Jackie fell asleep on the sofa and Laura

sat looking at her, remembering how her friend had always claimed that Laura was the one who would go far because she was shrewd and smart. It had seemed that way at the time, for Laura was the one with the ideas, determination and the ability to see the bigger picture, while Jackie had been indecisive and nervous about taking risks.

Jackie had always been pretty, but at thirty she was stunning. She'd had her long copper-coloured hair cut and permed into the latest 'Afro' style, and against the sofa cushions it looked like amber spun sugar. That night she was wearing skin-tight denim dungarees with a skimpy emerald-green top beneath, and her suntanned arms were laden with Indian bangles. She looked like a rock star, not a woman of property who spent most of her time chasing up builders.

Having a go-getting husband like Roger had undoubtedly helped Jackie get her business going, but Laura knew he wasn't, as some people thought, the brains behind the business. He had encouraged her, and financed the purchase of the first house, but it was Jackie who had the ideas. She had done the homework about the areas she bought run-down property in, and it was her flair for design and eye for detail while converting them into flats which made her such large profits. Laura felt very proud of her doing so well. It also made her want to make something of herself too. And while she was with Jackie in the tiny cottage packed with her creative vibes, it seemed entirely possible.

Laura arrived back home in Edinburgh two weeks later, deeply tanned, glowing with health and brimming with optimism. But as she opened the street door in Caledonian Crescent and the musty smell and the darkness of the stairs hit her, she felt herself deflate.

Once in the flat, Barney ran eagerly into the living room

to his toys but Laura stood in the doorway feeling only dismay. When they'd moved in nearly two years ago she'd been proud that she'd made it look so stylish and comfortable on a shoestring. But now she saw the white paint was turning yellow, the maroon second-hand sofa was threadbare, and the cheap carpet stained. The big print above the gas fire, a field of red poppies, which she'd once loved so much, looked horribly dated, and as for the Regency striped curtains, she could hardly believe she'd bothered to haggle with the woman who put them up for sale on a postcard. She ought to have taken one look at them and left.

Jackie's cottage in Cellardyke had been all cream and pale blue, a pretty, spirit-lifting place. She hadn't spent a fortune on it either; the curtains were cheap gingham, all the furniture was painted second-hand stuff.

All at once resentment that she had to live this way rose up like bile. Barney had nowhere safe to play outside in the sunshine, not even a bedroom of his own, and she doubted Stuart would ever earn enough for them to buy a house.

Barney was due to start school in September, which in theory should give her the opportunity to work all day. But she knew from mothers with school-age children that it wasn't easy to find work between nine and three-thirty, and then there were the school holidays and having to take time off if the child was sick.

She was twenty-nine, yet she was still no further forward than she'd been at nineteen.

As she unpacked and put away their clothes, edging her way around the narrow space between her bed and Barney's, the resentment grew stronger and stronger because she knew this wasn't something she could talk over with Stuart. He was completely satisfied with this flat. If she pointed out how seedy everything was he'd say that most of their neighbours' places were far worse. He'd probably relate, as he often had before, that until he was five, his whole family had lived in a one-bedroom flat which was smaller than this one.

Suddenly the differences between her mentality and Stuart's seemed vast. He didn't think beyond the end of the month: as long as he had work, a hot dinner and her in his arms at night, enough money to pay the rent, and his guitar and television, he was supremely happy.

But that wasn't enough for her.

A week after Laura's holiday in Fife, Robbie Fielding made one of his surprise visits to the casino. He was a director of the company which owned the Maybury and, by repute, a hard man who would sack anyone he didn't think pulled their weight. Laura had met him several times before, but as he'd never taken her to task about anything, she didn't quake in her shoes when she saw him walk in, as most of the staff did.

'You're looking sensational tonight, Laura,' he said as he came up to the bar. 'Where'd you get the tan?'

'Only in Fife,' she replied, flattered that he'd remembered her name. 'Can I get you a drink?'

He was about forty, five feet ten, well built with slicked-back black hair and piercing dark eyes. Not handsome exactly, but arresting – he reminded her of a well-built 'Fonz' from *Happy Days*. Someone said he came from Newcastle, and he did have a faint Geordie accent. It was said he dyed his hair black, that he wore a corset to keep his belly in, and that he was a gangster.

Laura thought all this very unlikely. The very nature of the gambling world meant most men at the top of it would be a little bent, but that didn't make them gangsters. She thought his hair colour was natural, for close up she could see the odd strand of grey, and she certainly didn't believe the story about the corset. He had the swaggering walk of a man who had worked out in a gym for his entire life.

'I'll have a single malt,' he said and looked appraisingly at her. 'You dress very well. Do you buy your clothes in London?'

Laura looked down at herself in some surprise. She was wearing a very simple white sleeveless long dress that she'd found at a jumble sale and altered by taking it in to fit tightly and opening up the side seam to make a slit right up to her thigh.

She smiled at his compliment. 'Sometimes,' she said. That was true in as much as most of her clothes dated back to her days in London, and others were cast-offs from Jackie. 'But I got this dress here in Edinburgh.'

'It's very nice,' he said. 'But then you've got the legs for it.'

They chatted while he had his drink. He asked her where she'd been in Fife and she told him about her friend buying the cottage in Cellardyke. 'It was lovely for a holiday with my little boy,' she added. 'But if I didn't have Barney, and I lived in Kensington like she does, I'd want to go somewhere hot and sophisticated for my holidays.'

Their conversation ended there as the waitress came over with an order of drinks. By the time Laura had finished, Robbie Fielding had gone.

It turned out to be a very busy night as a large group of men up in Edinburgh on business came in and were drinking and gambling heavily. Laura was just taking the till drawer out to take it to the office for the money to be checked, when Robbie reappeared.

'I'd like to talk to you. Let me take that,' he said, taking the drawer from her hands. 'You get us both a drink and bring them to the office.'

Laura knew he wouldn't suggest a drink if he was about to sack her, but she was worried about how late it was. If Stuart woke and found she wasn't in bed beside him he'd give her the third degree in the morning. Yet she could hardly tell a director that she hadn't got time to have a drink with him.

Within only a few minutes of being in the office with Robbie, Laura thought he was sounding her out for another position in the company. He complimented her on her reliability, saying he'd noted she hadn't called in sick once since starting there, and asked her what line of work she had been in back in London. But then he began asking more personal questions: how old her son was, and whether her husband minded taking care of him while she worked.

She didn't really know why she told him Stuart wasn't her husband, or that he didn't really like her working at the casino, but once she'd revealed that much she found herself unable to stop. Before she knew it she'd more or less told him that she was feeling very dissatisfied with her life just now.

'Then you must take what you want,' Robbie said. 'You are an intelligent, beautiful woman and you could go far. Men are by nature anxious to keep their women down, but that doesn't mean you have to let them.'

They talked for over an hour and by the time Laura left she'd told him that she really wanted a career, but that she couldn't see how she could fit that around taking Barney to and from school.

'It *is* possible,' Robbie said. 'I have several women working for me with children of the same age. It's just a matter of organizing child care.'

Barney began school in early September and loved it from the start. While Laura was glad he didn't cry and cling to her, it made her choke up seeing him in his smart grey shorts and too large navy blazer, lining up with the other children, his face bright with expectation.

She felt lost as she walked home. She had looked forward to having time alone, no questions to answer, no requests for her to play with him, no drinks or snacks to prepare, but suddenly everything seemed empty. She didn't want to look in the shops, visit the library or go to the laundrette, and she certainly didn't want to go home to the empty flat and stare at the walls.

It was a strange, unsettled, lonely period for her that autumn. Alone all day, then just a couple of hours with Barney before Stuart came home, then off to the casino for the evening. Stuart didn't understand why she was down in the dumps, and she certainly couldn't tell him that her spirits always lifted once she was on her way to work, and fell again when she got home.

She knew she was being selfish when she wouldn't get out of bed on Sunday mornings, and left him to entertain and feed Barney. She knew she was being cruel when she made disdainful, pointed comments about Stuart's lack of ambition, or when she turned her back on him in bed and didn't even kiss him goodnight. But she couldn't help herself. The passion she used to feel for him seemed to have gone.

She ought to have realized that Robbie Fielding's interest in her wasn't just that of an employer who appreciated an employee's efforts – after all, she'd had a lot of previous experience with predatory men. But when he began calling in at the Maybury far more often, she thought that he was checking on the croupiers, or even the management. It didn't cross her mind he was coming especially to see her.

She liked the way he asked after Barney, that he complimented her on how she looked, and she enjoyed having a drink with him at the end of the evening because he was a good conversationalist. He told her entertaining stories about gamblers and some of the colourful people he'd met while working in the gambling business. He was also very interested in her past, and what had brought her to Scotland. She told him more about her marriage to Greg than she'd ever told anyone, including Stuart.

Then one evening in November, he kissed her.

She'd had several drinks earlier, and she was too tight to see it coming, but not enough to tell herself there was nothing in it.

'I want you,' he said, holding her by the shoulders and looking right into her eyes. 'I did the first moment I saw you. Not for a quick fuck on the office floor either, but for ever.'

'But I'm with Stuart,' she said, backing away from him. She'd liked his kiss, she liked him, and if she had been free she would almost certainly have been tempted to have a date or two with him, but she hadn't realized she'd given him the green light. 'And I'm happy with him.'

'Are you?' He raised one dark eyebrow. 'I think from what you've told me that's it's all played out and you both want different things.'

She protested and told him he was wrong, but he just smiled.

'You were born for better things than living in a tenement,' he said. 'I see you as the kind of woman who wants a beautiful home, foreign travel, staying at the best hotels and your son going to a good school. You could have that with me.'

'You're married,' she retorted, feeling nervous now.

'Yes, but that doesn't mean I can't give you what you want too. I can see the ambition in your eyes, and I like that. I could set you up in a business, or help you into a well-paid job. I wouldn't even ask that you leave Stuart. I know that will come in time anyway.'

She rushed off soon after that, and drove home berating herself for allowing Robbie to get close enough to suggest such things, and that she'd stayed to listen to them.

But in the days that followed she found herself constantly thinking about what he'd said. Throughout the whole first year she was with Stuart, he'd given her the kind of inner happiness that wiped out any yearnings for wealth and luxury. She would look back on her life with Greg and feel ashamed that she'd once been so shallow that she imagined a man out of the top drawer and a house in Chelsea would compensate for real love.

She did love Stuart still, but she also wanted the things Robbie had offered. Stuart would never want her to run her own business; if she suggested foreign travel to him he'd think of doing it in a camper van. Whenever she pointed out expensive shoes or fabulous dresses in the posh shops in Princes Street, he just laughed as if such things were just for show, not bought by real women.

It wasn't that Stuart was mean, she knew he'd spend his last pound on her. It was just that he hadn't got a materialistic bone in his body, and he'd never been around rich people to learn to want what they had. But she had, and it was like a hunger inside her.

In the weeks that followed Robbie's proposal, conflict raged inside her. The evening walk down the gloomy stair, out into the cold dark street, then arriving at the Maybury with its warmth, sophistication and bright lights, seemed symbolic. She would leave Stuart dressed in tattered jeans and a scruffy sweater, and find Robbie at the other end, immaculate in evening dress.

The Maybury was where she shone; her elegance, intelligence and wit were admired. Back at home in Caledonian

Crescent she was the person who cooked sausage and mash, made the beds, washed and ironed. Barney and Stuart liked her best when she was wearing jeans and a jumper, for that meant she was in for the evening, and she wished with all her heart that she could be satisfied with just that. But she couldn't.

She snapped at them, criticized them for leaving clothes on the floor or bringing mud in on their shoes. And Stuart often bit back, asking why she had to be such a cow when she only had two or three nights at home with them each week.

There was one evening when she was manicuring her nails, and Stuart offered to paint her toe nails for her. She let him purely because it was something he'd often done when they were in Castle Douglas and she hoped it might bring back the same intimacy.

His long hair fell over his face as he bent over her foot balanced on his thigh. She could just see his tongue peeping out of his mouth as he concentrated on applying the varnish, and he looked so boyish that tears came to her eyes.

She so much wanted to tell him what was on her mind. Not that Robbie had suggested she became his mistress – that would have made Stuart explode with rage – but how confused and dissatisfied she felt.

But she couldn't. However she put it, he would take it as a reproach that he had failed her. She couldn't let him think that, for it was she who hadn't managed to hold on to the belief of 'All You Need Is Love.'

It was right at the end of December, two days before New Year, when Laura agreed to meet Robbie for lunch at the Caledonian, the smartest hotel in Edinburgh. The drinks after work had become more frequent, twice in December he'd met her during the day for a coffee, and he'd bought her a silver cocktail watch for Christmas.

There were two separate tags with it. The one intended for Stuart's eyes said, '*A token of our appreciation from the directors of Maybury Casino.*' The second one, '*To beautiful Laura, with hopes you'll be mine in the New Year. Love Robbie*'.

The tags were evidence Robbie was a practised deceiver, and wished to make her one too. Yet all the same it sent delicious shivers down her spine.

She told herself that it was okay to have lunch with him, that it wouldn't lead to anything more, not like dinner. She took Barney to school, arranged with one of the other mothers to pick him up later, in case she was late back, then rushed home to have a bath and change.

When she was in Fife, Jackie had given her a beautiful cream wool mid-calf-length dress and short fitted jacket that she felt was too dressy for her. It was too warm to wear for work at the Maybury, but perfect for a lunchtime date somewhere smart, and Laura had been dying for an opportunity to wear it because she knew it really suited her.

Jack Huggins on the ground floor was tinkering with his bike as she came out of the house and he whistled appreciatively at her which made her smile.

She'd told Stuart she was meeting one of the girls from work to help her choose her wedding dress and that they would probably go somewhere in the Old Town for lunch. She was excited by the thought of Robbie flirting with her over a boozy lunch, she needed his compliments and the way he always made her laugh, and she reconciled any guilty feelings she had by telling herself that she would be home in time to make tea for Stuart and he'd be none the wiser.

Robbie was waiting for her in the reception area of the hotel. He looked entirely at one with the opulent surroundings, wearing a light grey suit and a dark blue striped tie.

'You look a million dollars,' he said as he kissed her cheek and led her into the bar for an aperitif. 'I'm feeling like a kid on his first date, butterflies in my stomach and all that.'

Over lunch, he talked about a photographic business he had a share in. 'I'm not a photographer myself,' he said, reaching out for her hand over the table. 'I'm more on the administration side. But I know enough about it to recognize that you'd make a great model.'

Many people had suggested she should do modelling, Stuart had even insisted she could be a beauty queen, though she'd never taken it seriously before. But the intensity in Robbie's eyes made her believe it could be true.

By the time Laura was on her third glass of wine she had put all thoughts of Barney and Stuart aside, and was just enjoying the thrill of being somewhere so elegant, with such an attentive man.

She wasn't so gullible that she imagined Robbie could make her a fashion model. With her thirtieth birthday only a few days away, she knew she was too old for that. And it was plain to her, though Robbie didn't actually say so, that the kind of photography he was involved in was the glamour kind, for men's magazines. She didn't approve or disapprove, it was all just a fuzzy kind of maybe, not real somehow.

It was only when he signed the restaurant bill to his room that she realized he was staying at the hotel. He suggested they went to his room for a brandy and coffee.

'I'm not trying to lure you into anything,' he said, kissing the tips of her fingers. 'It's just that I've got some magazines I'd like to show you, and we can't stay here in the dining room all afternoon.'

It was bitterly cold outside, the sky like lead, and she had no wish to rush away from this warm, seductive place just yet. She had the night off too, so she didn't even have to think of getting ready for the club either.

Robbie's room was on the third floor, and was far more luxurious than any other hotel room she'd ever been in, with a vast bed with a dark red velvety quilt, a highly polished desk, two club armchairs before the window and soft, intimate lighting. The adjoining bathroom was a marble palace, the bath easily big enough for two, with gold taps and thick fluffy towels on the heated rail.

It was already dark outside, and the view of the flood-lit Castle from the window was pure enchantment. She forgot the cool, woman-of-the-world stance she'd tried to maintain throughout lunch and squealed with pure delight.

Robbie laughed. 'It's pretty good, isn't it? I love hotels, the luxury, having someone else tidy up for you, the mini bar, the warm towels. You can be anyone you want to be, there's no reminder of home to bring you back to reality.'

Laura couldn't have put it better herself, though she might have added that they had the effect of an aphrodisiac on her. Back in the days when she and Jackie worked in promotions and were put up in hotels out of London, she'd often slept with someone she wouldn't have looked at twice back home.

That was just how it was when Robbie caught hold of her and began kissing her. She knew she shouldn't be doing it, that she should make her excuses and leave, but she'd had enough to drink to lose herself in his kisses, and before she knew it he had her on the bed.

He peeled her clothes off like a whirlwind, and that alone should have warned her that the whole act would be equally fast and unfulfilling. He barely touched her breasts, he pushed his fingers into her roughly, and that was clearly the extent of his foreplay, for he stripped off his trousers and pants, leaving his shirt and socks on, and entered her.

'Slow down,' she pleaded, trying to wriggle out from under him. But he was too heavy to move, and too intent on possessing her even to hear what she said. His face was buried in her neck, and his expensive after-shave didn't quite mask the odour of sweat. As her hands went under his shirt to hold him, she found his back was hairy, which repelled her even more.

It was by no means the first time in her life that she'd found herself regretfully in bed with a man, and as on those other occasions she knew she had no one but herself to blame. But as he banged away at her, completely oblivious to the fact she wasn't responding in any way, she could have cried because she felt cheap and sluttish.

Stuart was slender, light and lithe and he made love with exquisite sensuality and tenderness. She wondered how she was ever going to face him after this.

Robbie's grunting became louder, his shirt was soaked with sweat and his bristly chin felt as though he was rubbing her neck with sandpaper. At the point when he grunted out that he was coming she felt anger that he could take her like an animal, yet also relief that it was all but over.

'That was great,' he gasped. 'But then I knew it would be.'

It was on the tip of her tongue to say something sarcastic, perhaps to ask if he learned his technique in a farmyard. But she was too ashamed of herself for letting it happen to say anything.

His lack of sensitivity was astounding. He didn't appear to notice she'd said nothing. He lit up a cigar and lay on the bed in his sweat-soaked shirt, positively glowing with smug satisfaction.

'I'll order us some tea from room service, babe,' he called out as she disappeared into the bathroom with her clothes. 'Shame you can't stay the night. I've got plenty more where that came from.'

By the time she'd had a bath, dressed and repaired her makeup, the tea had arrived and Robbie was pouring it. He was wearing a towelling robe now, and he had his magazine spread out for her to look at.

As she had expected, the photographs were pin-ups,

'You are lovelier than any of these girls,' Robbie said. 'You could make a hundred pounds a time easily. You could do the sessions while your son is at school.'

Laura glanced at the pictures. They were at least only scantily dressed poses, not pornography, but when she'd agreed to meet him today she was hoping for the offer of a proper job, not anything risqué.

'I'll give it some thought,' she said, wanting to get home as quickly as possible. 'I'm not sure if I'd feel comfortable doing that.'

Robbie got dressed and insisted on coming downstairs with her to get her a taxi. As they walked to the lift, Laura saw a tool box by one of the other rooms further up the corridor, but she didn't think anything of it.

'Have you had a good time?' Robbie asked, putting his arm around her waist as they walked.

'It was lovely, Robbie,' she lied, reminding herself that he was after all her boss and she couldn't offend him. 'Thank you for the lunch and I'll speak to you later about the modelling.'

Suddenly a head shot out of the door where the tool box lay, the long brown hair only too familiar.

Laura froze in horror. Clearly Stuart had been called in to replace a lock or something, and he'd recognized her voice coming along the passage.

'What is it, hen?' Robbie asked.

She couldn't speak. Her bowels had turned to water, an

icy chill running down her spine. Stuart was just staring at them, his eyes as cold as a February morning.

'Fancy you being here too, Stuart,' she said, trying to cover her shock with a quickly thought-up explanation. 'This is Mr Fielding, my boss at the casino. We've been discussing a new job he's got for me.'

'Good to meet you at last, Stuart.' Robbie's hand shot out to shake Stuart's.

Stuart's lips curled back in a snarl and he looked scornfully at Robbie's hand. 'Fuck off, arsehole,' he said, then stepped back into the room he was working in and slammed the door behind him.

Laura stood outside the door for a moment, not knowing whether to plead with him or just go. Robbie took her arm and led her away.

'Just stick to what you said when he gets home,' he told her. 'He can't prove anything.'

'He doesn't need to,' she said sadly, remembering the look in Stuart's eyes. 'That he saw me here when I was supposed to be with a girlfriend is enough.'

Robbie put her into a taxi, thrust a £20 note in her hand and said he'd come to the club the following night to see her. Laura felt sick with fear. She would stick to her story and explain that she ran into Robbie while she was in the Old Town and he asked her to come back to his hotel to talk to her. But she knew Stuart would ask why she went to his room rather than stay downstairs in the lounge. What possible reason could she give for that?

She picked Barney up and held his little hand tightly as they walked back to Caledonian Crescent. She was aware he was talking to her, but she was too immersed in her own anxiety to listen.

'You aren't listening to me, Mummy!' he said indignantly,

pulling on her hand. 'I said Gregor had a hamster called Will, and I asked if I could have one too.'

'Maybe, darling.' she said. 'We'll see tomorrow.'

Six o'clock came, then seven, and still Stuart hadn't come home. She bathed Barney and put him to bed.

'Will Stuie read me a story when he comes home?' Barney asked, his big, dark eyes looking anxious because he'd picked up that she was worried.

'He won't be in till late, so I'll read to you,' she said, and sitting down beside him she read two of his favourite Mr Men books.

Stuart didn't come home at all. Laura realized by one in the morning that he must have gone to his parents.

Later, as Laura returned from taking Barney to school, she found Stuart's father waiting in his car outside the house. She ran to him, assuming he had a message for her.

'I've come to collect my lad's things,' he said as he got out of the car. His face was craggy and cold. 'He's nae coming back.'

She tried to explain to Mr Macgregor once they were inside that Stuart had misunderstood what was going on the previous day, but he just shook his head. 'My lad is nae numbskull,' he said. 'Just put his things together and I'll be away.'

Laura felt as if her heart had cracked wide open as Mr Macgregor picked up the heavy holdall with Stuart's clothes, then moved across the living room to pick up his guitar. Somehow the guitar was everything of Stuart, and once that was gone he was really gone too.

The sound of the key turning in the cell door told Laura it was time to get up, and she wiped the tears from her face with the edge of the duvet cover. She had only wanted to remember the happy times with Stuart, not bring back all that guilt and sadness.

She saw in the New Year of 1975 huddled up in her bed crying. She heard a few days later from a neighbour that Stuart had gone to London and her heart shattered.

10

Laura waved as Stuart and David Stoyle came into the prison visiting room. She noticed that all the other women suddenly looked more animated and that they glanced at her in envy, but then one handsome male visitor at Cornton Vale was remarkable, two was astounding.

When Stuart had asked in his last letter if his lawyer friend could come with him to visit, she had imagined him to be like other lawyers she'd met, small, pale-faced and with thick glasses. But David looked like a sportsman, not a lawyer – tall, muscular, with glowing tanned skin. In a faded denim shirt and chinos, he was certain to spawn a few fantasies tonight with some of the women in the visiting room.

Stuart greeted her with a hug. 'Let me introduce you to David. As I said in my letter, I persuaded him to help us.'

Laura shook David's hand. 'It's good to meet you, David, I just hope Stuart didn't twist your arm too hard.'

'He has a silver tongue when he wants something,' David replied, and his smile was attractively shy. 'He did tell you I'm not a criminal lawyer, didn't he? I can't promise I'll be any real use to you.'

Laura privately thought he'd already been of great use to her – it would be the talk of the block tonight that she'd had two hunks visiting. David might be rather upper-crust, but he had the whiff of the great outdoors about him, as Stuart did. A real man, she thought; he looked tough, adaptable and strong-willed.

'You have already proved you're not just a pretty face,

David,' Stuart grinned. 'You knew all the right buttons to push with Patrick Goldsmith.'

'You've already been to see my solicitor?' Laura asked in surprise as they sat down opposite her at the table.

'That was our first stop when I got here,' David said. 'But he's not a man with fire in his belly, is he?'

Laura sniggered. Patrick Goldsmith was the duty solicitor who came to the police station when she was first arrested. She had been told many times since that she should have got a solicitor of her own choice. But as she didn't know any other criminal lawyers, and he seemed genuinely to believe in her innocence, she saw no reason to ask for someone else.

But his anaemic appearance and manner should have been enough to set alarm bells jangling. He had a limp handshake, pale skin, thin lips and thick glasses. There was no colour in him, and certainly no fire.

'You've got him taped,' she said. 'And what was his reaction to you two poking your noses into his case?'

'Surprised you had two such formidable friends,' Stuart said with a touch of pomposity. 'He's apathetic of course, doesn't believe we can find any new evidence to qualify for an appeal, but we're banking that his guilt at not putting together a strong defence for you will make him go the extra mile this time.'

'Have you dug up anything positive yet?' Laura asked.

'Lena is prepared to make a statement that she knew Jackie had several men friends, which if nothing else would prove you weren't making that up,' Stuart said.

'How was she? Laura asked eagerly.

'Bright as a button, and I can guess what you really want to know: no, she doesn't believe you are guilty.'

'Really?' Laura's face blushed pink with pleasure. 'Of all

the people involved, she's the one whose opinion matters most to me.'

'I thought as much,' Stuart nodded. 'Oh, and I told Goldsmith about that lane by the farm. The real murderer could have got in and out that way unseen by the neighbour.'

Laura thanked him for going to see Meggie and told him that she'd had a letter from her. She had hundreds of questions she wanted to ask about her sisters and Lena, but time was short and she knew Stuart had questions too.

'Have you remembered any names of men friends Jackie might have mentioned?'

'She wasn't one for using real names,' Laura said glumly. 'You probably remember she always gave nicknames to people who were transient in her life.'

Stuart smiled. 'She used to call me "Chisel". There was a plasterer she used she nicknamed "Bucket Head". I never knew what his real name was.'

'There was someone she called "Growler",' Laura remembered. 'She was very cagey about him, she only made the odd remark that he'd been round the night before or something. That made me think he was married. I would think she called him that because he had a deep voice. I know he drank whisky too – she mentioned having to go out to get some more for him once. But there must be millions of Scotsmen with a deep voice and a love of whisky, so that's no help.'

'He could have been a policeman,' Stuart said. 'You know, PC Growler! The very nature of a cop's job makes it a lot easier for them to have affairs than other men. And keep it hushed up.'

'How could you track him down?' Laura asked.

'I could try going back to see Gloria, the barmaid in Cellardyke,' Stuart said. 'I think she knew more about Jackie than she was prepared to tell me. A second visit and a few drinks might make her open up.'

'I really liked Gloria,' Laura said, smiling as she remembered the many chats they'd had in the past. 'And she did know Jackie very well – they used to drop in on each other all the time.'

'She liked you too,' Stuart said. 'And just for the record, she's another firmly on your side.'

Laura beamed. Discovering that two people she cared about were on her side was like striking gold.

'Is there anyone that might want to stitch you up, Laura?' David asked.

'A cast of millions,' she said ruefully. 'But it isn't feasible that any of them could have done it. How could they be sure I'd turn up at the right moment?'

'On the face of it I agree that it's not likely,' Stuart said. 'But the more I've puzzled over it, the more I'm sure whoever did do it knew both of you well enough to gauge your reactions accurately. I'm certain there was an incident at Brodie Farm earlier that morning, and I think it's very probable that the person involved overheard Jackie call you. Maybe they knew that whatever game they had would be up if the pair of you put your heads together. But they must have had a real grievance against you too, or why would they wait to kill Jackie until you were due to arrive?'

'To muddy the waters?' Laura suggested.

'Possibly, but most murders are done on the spur of the moment out of panic or extreme anger. Most of us would calm down and change our minds if we had to wait. But if you had a grudge against the person who was due to arrive, you could nurse your wrath, knowing it would be killing two birds with one stone. So let's think who could be mad enough with Jackie to kill her, and hate you enough to want to see you punished for it.'

'Jackie's husband, Roger, could fit those criteria,' David pointed out. 'I'm not convinced from what you've told me about him that his separation from Jackie was as amicable as he claimed. And he had a lot to gain if Jackie died. You also said he flew off the handle about Laura.'

'But Goldsmith said he was questioned by the police, and that he was proved to be in London at the time,' Stuart said. 'Besides, the forensic report stated that the position of the stab wound indicated it was either made by a woman or a man less than five feet nine. Roger is well over six feet tall.'

'That might be correct if the attacker just struck out wildly, but not if they aimed for her heart with the intention of killing. And people do fake alibis,' David said sagely. 'You know him pretty well, Stuart – does he have the kind of friends who would lie for him?'

'I don't know about friends,' Stuart replied. 'His alibi was that he was seen on his building site on both the day of the murder and the following one. A great many men come and go on a building site in the course of a day; anyone would be hard pressed to remember exactly who was there and who wasn't. But anyone thinking his job was on the line might say he saw him there.'

'Then maybe we should find the man who gave him the alibi and question him?' David suggested.

'That could prove difficult. Builders come and go, as I said, and even if we could track him down, I doubt he'd tell us anything different,' Stuart sighed.

'Roger would cheerfully see me hang just for a parking fine.' Laura frowned. 'He's always disliked me. But I can't really believe he'd kill Jackie. Things were good between them. Jackie would have told me if there was anything wrong.'

'Would she?' Stuart questioned. 'I'm not so sure about that, Laura, not if it had anything to do with you, like helping you get your shop.'

'Maybe, but she would have told Belle. There's no love lost between her and Roger, so if she knew he'd been hassling Jackie she'd have jumped right in and told the police the minute she got the news Jackie was dead.'

Stuart looked disappointed.

'Okay, let's put Roger aside for now,' David suggested. 'Laura, you implied that there were many people who have a grudge against you. So suppose we narrow that field and you think how many of them also knew Jackie?'

'There's Stuart,' Laura said with a grin. 'But we can safely rule him out. Charles, Belle's husband, has never liked me either because I tried to talk her out of marrying him. He referred to me as the cuckoo in the nest. He did have some up-and-downers with Jackie too, the main one being that she influenced Belle in moving to Scotland.'

Stuart told them how he'd seen Charles's car at Brodie Farm. 'Could he have been having an affair with Jackie? Or could Jackie have had something on him that she threatened to tell Belle about?'

'The last is a possibility,' Laura said thoughtfully. 'There was a certain tension between them. But we can rule out Jackie having an affair with him. She wouldn't have touched him with a bargepole, she had always despised him.'

'Why did he agree to move near her then?' David asked.

'I never really got to the bottom of that.' Laura frowned. 'I was pretty preoccupied at the time, but I got the idea Charles had a few business problems and had to liquidate his assets back in London. Property up here was much cheaper, and I assumed at the time he was going to do some developing. But they hadn't been in Crail very long when Barney was killed. After that I was so out of it for a long time that I didn't take any interest in what he or Belle was doing.'

'He couldn't have killed Jackie anyway because he was

playing golf at St Andrews at the time of her death,' David pointed out. 'The police had to phone the bar there to get him to come home when they broke the news to Belle.'

'That alibi is as fuzzy as Roger's,' Stuart retorted. 'The golf course is huge, he could have come and gone several times during the day without anyone noticing. Just because he was in the bar when the police called doesn't mean he was there all day.'

'Then we'll investigate him,' David said. 'Anyone else, Laura?'

'There is Robbie Fielding,' she said tentatively, looking at Stuart to see if he remembered that name.

Stuart gave her a long, cool look. 'Casino Man?' he said.

Laura nodded, wishing she didn't have to remind him of her betrayal.

'He was once my boss, David,' she said, avoiding looking at Stuart. 'First in the casino, and later I did some modelling for him. I pulled a fast one on him and started my own company. At the time he put the word out that he was going to mark me for life.'

David was looking at her with keen interest. 'Did he know Jackie?'

'Yes, very well. He was instrumental in her getting Brodie Farm.'

'In what way?'

'I don't know exactly, but she was after it and couldn't get it. At the time I was still on friendly terms with Robbie, and I introduced them to each other. I think he must have leaned on someone, because the next thing the farm was hers at a very low price. I was a bit worried about that because I knew he was a slimy bastard and I warned Jackie that he never did anything for nothing. It is quite possible that he came back to her, calling in his debt.'

The two men exchanged glances, and Laura blushed.

Even after everything she'd been through over the years, the period between Stuart leaving her and Barney's death was the part of her life she would most like to erase. Stuart knew about the glamour modelling – Jackie had told her that he'd seen her in a magazine and shown it to her. But he probably hadn't known that it was Robbie Fielding who got her into it. Or what it led to.

'Did the police investigate him?' David asked.

Laura shook her head.

'Why not?'

'I didn't ever tell them about him because it didn't occur to me then that he could be a suspect. Things were quite bad enough for me without my having to admit the kind of work I'd done for him.'

'Is he still in Edinburgh?' David asked.

'I don't know,' Laura said. 'The last time I saw him he was driving through Morningside, but that was over three years ago. It panicked me a bit, I got the idea he could be keeping tabs on me. I asked around about him and I was told he owned a pub somewhere around the Grassmarket. But as I say, that was three years ago, he might not be there now.'

Stuart had said nothing during her interchange with David, but suddenly he leaned towards Laura across the table. 'You'd better tell us about you and him.'

Laura licked her lips nervously. 'Must I?'

Stuart nodded. 'We can't investigate him without knowing what went on between you.'

'There isn't time before the bell goes, and anyway –' She stopped, reluctant to admit that she was too ashamed to talk about it to them.

'Could you write it down?' David asked, perhaps understanding her reluctance. 'You probably need time on your own to get it all straight anyway.'

Laura shot him a grateful glance. 'Yes, that might be better,' she said. 'I blanked out so much of the past when Barney was killed.'

Stuart had a distant look in his eyes. She wondered whether that was because he was thinking back to the events in the Caledonian Hotel.

But she decided she was wrong when he suddenly suggested David should book into Belle's guest house for a couple of nights. 'I think you could gain her confidence, get her to talk about Charles and have a snoop round.'

'Will I be safe with her?' David grinned. 'You said she was something of a maneater!'

'Belle!' Laura exclaimed. 'Of course she isn't!'

Stuart chuckled. 'Sometimes those closest to people can't see them clearly,' he said. 'But you'll be all right, David, just bang on about Julia and the kids, that should put her off.'

David told Laura that his wife and children were flying up to Scotland for a holiday in Oban in a fortnight's time when school broke up for the summer, but until then he was at Stuart's disposal.

'I've rented a flat,' Stuart said. 'That's near the Grassmarket too, so we might run into Fielding.'

'We've got a lot of ground to cover to find something to base your appeal on, Laura,' David said quickly, glancing at Stuart as if afraid he was about to take the law into his own hands. 'But I'm hopeful. Just from what I know already it seems clear to me that the police didn't investigate very thoroughly, and your solicitor didn't build up much of a defence.'

Stuart took out a card and pen and wrote down his address for her. 'Write to me here about Casino Man,' he said. 'We are going to try and get permission for another visit in two weeks' time. It shouldn't be a problem, they make special arrangements for people who have to come a long way to get here. In the meantime keep your chin up, I'll ring Meggie tonight and tell her I've seen you. Is there any message that you'd like me to pass on?'

'Just that I think about her and Ivy all the time,' she said. 'And that her letter made me very happy.'

After Stuart and David had left, Laura went back to her block. She smiled as some of the other women made saucy remarks about her two male visitors, but she didn't stop to talk to anyone.

Back in her cell, she lay down on the bed. She knew she must trawl through the years between Stuart leaving and Barney's death, but she was reluctant to for she knew how painful it was going to be.

She had never had much time for people who used the excuse 'I had no choice' for doing something they knew to be wrong. In her experience there was always an alternative; it was just that mostly the honourable, honest or legal route was harder or less lucrative.

That was exactly how it was for her, and the only excuse she could offer up for that first step on a road she knew to be the wrong one was that she already felt so bad about herself, it didn't seem to matter.

Everything came crashing down around her after Stuart left. She was devastated, unable to believe that through her own stupidity she'd lost the man she loved. Barney kept crying for him and asking when he was coming home, and every day she felt as if she was sinking further and further into a black hole.

With no one to babysit Barney she had to ring the casino and say she couldn't come back to work, and while she was trapped in the flat, day after day, night after night, the memories of Stuart pressed in on her. He had filled the place with his warm presence; even when he was at work the essence of him remained, his smell, his voice, his laughter. But once his father had removed his belongings, there was a void which nothing could fill.

The cupboards and shelves he'd built so lovingly were a constant reproach, not only bringing back memories of him sawing and sanding, a pencil tucked behind his ear, but evidence of how much he wanted to create a stable home for them all.

For a while she could still smell him on the bedding, finding an odd sock or work shirt would bring on a wave of grief, and at night she would remain sleepless, the cold, empty space beside her a constant reminder of her infidelity.

Fleeing back to London seemed the answer to everything in the first few days, but when Jackie wrote to say Stuart was there, working for her, that door slammed in her face. Jackie obviously knew exactly what had happened. *'He's a good man, Laura, he deserved better than that,'* was her comment, and in the absence of any questions as to how she was managing, or even asking for her side of the story, Laura knew she could expect no sympathy or help.

After two weeks she knew that she would have to go cap in hand to the Assistance for help. She couldn't find a job which would fit in with Barney's school hours and the rent was due. She toyed with the idea of selling her car – she couldn't afford to drive it after all – but she was reluctant to do that, for if a job did turn up, then she might need it.

The Assistance was now called Social Security, but to her there was still the same stigma as when she went to them with her mother as a child. The Edinburgh office had the same nicotine-impregnated walls and ceiling, and the same stale smell she remembered from London. The officials were marginally less curt and unsympathetic, but the wait was every bit as long, and her fellow claimants made her shudder.

Many were drunks and down-and-outs, with filthy clothes, stinking to high heaven, and they lurched around the waiting room muttering and swearing. There were slovenly young girls with babies in their arms who looked malevolently at Laura's smart clothes. Chain-smoking, cocky young men talked loudly about their misfortunes, peppering their speech with swear words. The handful of people who were neatly dressed like her avoided eye contact with anyone, perhaps afraid of being contaminated.

Laura burst into tears when the man who interviewed her in a booth with a glass screen between them said she must claim maintenance from her husband. 'I daren't let him know where I am, he's violent,' she burst out, and hearing snorting laughter behind her realized the whole waiting room had heard.

She whispered the rest of her story, begged them to give her something so she could pay the rent and buy food. Finally it was agreed that someone would visit her at home the following day, and providing everything was in order, she would receive an emergency payment.

As she went to leave the office, a man called out to her, 'Hey, missus, will this help youse?'

She turned to see the question came from one of the drunks. His grinning face was bloated and purple and he had scraps of food in his thick beard. But to her shock he was holding his flaccid penis in his hand as an offering.

She fled, his raucous laughter ringing in her ears.

The money she got from the Social Security was far less than she'd expected, and the officer who came to the flat had intimidated her by saying he had the powers to insist she took steps to claim maintenance from Greg. She and Barney lived on stews made with the cheapest cuts of meat, and she couldn't afford to have the gas fire on at all during the day, even though it was bitterly cold. At weekends she would bundle Barney into warm clothes and take him for long walks along the canal or to a park. She got her Social Security money on Mondays, and quite often she had nothing left on Sunday, so when the gas or electricity ran out, she had to go to bed.

But the loneliness was even worse than the lack of money. She didn't want to have to admit to anyone that Stuart had left her, so she avoided the people on her stair, and the women at the school gates. She couldn't even bring herself to write to Meggie and Ivy to tell them she was on her own again because she was so ashamed of herself.

She had thought of the other staff at the casino as friends, yet not one of them called round to see how she was. Not even Robbie.

While she would have slammed the door in his face if he'd appeared in the first week or two, at least it would have been evidence he did really care about her. Now it looked as if he'd just used her, and all that talk of helping her get a better job was just a ploy to manipulate her.

One afternoon right at the end of February, someone knocked on the flat door. It was a freezing cold day and Laura was sitting on the settee wrapped up in a blanket. She thought it was a neighbour from the stair, as the bell down on the street door hadn't rung.

Her first thought when she opened the door and found Robbie there was horror that he should see her in jeans, with no makeup and her hair like rats' tails.

'Hello, Laura,' he said, grinning broadly.

'You took your time,' she said sarcastically. 'I'd given you up as a bad job.'

'I'd have been round weeks ago if you'd phoned me at the casino or at least left a message for me,' he said with a shrug. 'All I got told was that you'd left. No reason was given. I thought perhaps Stuart had made you give up the job, and I didn't attempt to try and find you in case it made things worse. By the time I got to hear on the grapevine that he'd gone to London, they'd removed your details from the staff register so I couldn't find out your address. Did he leave because he saw you with me?'

She nodded, tears welling up in her eyes.

'I'm so sorry,' he said, and she felt he meant it. 'Can I come in for a minute? We can't talk out here.'

'Okay,' she said listlessly. 'But I've got to go and collect Barney soon.'

'Strewth, it's cold in here,' he exclaimed as he followed her into the living room, but on seeing her embarrassment he looked crestfallen. 'Oh, Laura, things are that bad, eh? You haven't any money for the fire?'

His sympathetic tone broke down her reserve and she couldn't hold back her tears. He put his arms around her and rocked her against his shoulder. 'Tell me all about it, babe,' he said. 'I'm so sorry I made so much trouble for you.'

That day he seemed like an answer to a prayer. He fed coins into the gas and electric meters, he made her a cup of tea and let her cry it all out. Later he drove her round to the school to pick up Barney and on the way back he stopped at the shops and bought a huge bag of groceries.

'I'm going to cook a meal for you tonight,' he said. 'You can just sit down with Barney by the fire.'

She would never have thought a man from the gambling world could be so domesticated, or so kind. Along with making a first-class spaghetti bolognese he helped Barney build a car out of Lego, and then had a game of Snakes and Ladders with him.

Laura was embarrassed by how rough she looked, but

when she blurted this out, he just smiled. 'You'd look beautiful if you were in greasy overalls,' he said. 'I like to think we
were friends, and that we can be that again. Friends don't
have to dress up for one another.'

After Barney went to bed they talked. She was blunt,
admitting she'd made a serious mistake in going to bed with
him, and that she loved Stuart. She expected Robbie to look
insulted, but he patted her cheek affectionately and said he
understood.

'I stand by what I told you before,' he went on. 'I do
want you, Laura, but if all you want is a friend, that's okay
with me.'

He was practical too. He pointed out that if she continued
living on Social Security then they would have to force her
to claim maintenance from her husband. 'You'll be on a
sticky wicket then,' he said. 'If your husband applies for
custody of Barney, he just might get it if the courts think he
can give him a better life than you can.'

The prospect of that sent a cold shudder down her spine
because she knew Greg was vindictive enough to do it.

'But you deserve a better life too,' Robbie went on. 'You
can't stay stuck in this flat all day while Barney is at school,
having no fun, friends or money. It's a living death. Why
don't you do some modelling for me? You'll earn as much
in a couple of hours as you would all week in a shop or an
office, and you'll be able to move somewhere smarter, pay
a babysitter when you want to go out, run your car and buy
yourself lovely clothes.'

Laura could remember the trepidation she felt as she drove
over for the first time to the photographic studio in Livingston. She wanted the money Robbie was offering but she
was convinced the studio would be a sleazy place and the
photographer a pervert. However, as Robbie had assured

her there was no obligation to stay if she didn't like it, she felt she had to bite the bullet and check it out.

As she parked her car in the small industrial park she was relieved to see the studio looked every bit as professional as the other businesses around it. The plate-glass doors had stylish gold lettering announcing 'Commercial Photography, Weddings and Family Portraits'.

In the black and white reception area, where the walls were covered with stunning photographs of children, weddings and family groups, she was greeted by a smartly dressed middle-aged woman. She said Ed Harris, the photographer, would come and speak to her in a few minutes, and meanwhile she would show Laura around.

By the time Laura met Ed, her nerves were soothed by the cleanliness of the changing rooms and the sophistication of the two studios. In the prop room she'd seen scores of different backdrops, ranging from a flower-covered archway to a beach scene and a romantic castle. There was no evidence of sleaze anywhere.

Ed was a big, jovial man with a very direct manner. He said she was a little older than most of the models he usually shot as pin-ups, but added she had excellent bone structure, lovely hair and a very good body. He directed her to a rail of very scanty clothes and underwear, said he'd like her to try the denim shorts and a bikini top first, and that the makeup artist would come to her as soon as she was ready.

It was all much less embarrassing than she had expected. The makeup artist talked about a job she'd had recently on a major film, adding that Laura's skin was far better than the leading lady's. The receptionist brought Laura a cup of coffee and a dressing gown to put on in case she felt cold. Neither of them gave as much as a hint that they thought glamour photography was dubious.

Once she was ready, Ed told her exactly how he wanted

her to pose, and he continued to guide her as he took pictures. They were provocative poses – at one point she had to act as if she was taking off the brief shorts. He also got her to remove the bikini top and cover her breasts with her hands, but he made it easier by making her laugh and complimenting her when she got the pose or facial expression he wanted, so she felt reasonably comfortable with it all.

She was there for four hours. Ed used up dozens of rolls of film, she changed clothes five times, and at the end he handed her £50 and said he'd like her to do another session the following week.

For the first time in weeks she felt happy. She could buy Barney the new shoes he needed, and some paint to redecorate the living room. She didn't feel ashamed.

All through March, April and May as she drove herself over to Livingston once or sometimes twice a week, she was on a rosy cloud. Ed had given her some copies of photographs, and while they were saucy, she looked good, and she wouldn't have been ashamed to show them to anyone, not even her own sisters.

At that point she contacted Meggie and Ivy again and explained about Stuart. She lied to them and said she had a part-time job in a dress shop and did a bit of modelling work on a casual basis. She promised she would drive down to see them during Barney's summer holidays, and maybe they could all spend Christmas together.

She felt so positive at that time that she redecorated the flat, bought a new carpet and curtains, had a telephone installed, and no one could force her to claim maintenance from Greg now she wasn't receiving benefits. She still missed Stuart a great deal, but the pain had become more of a dull ache, and she told herself that their break-up had been inevitable because she was so much older than him.

Because she felt happier, Barney was happier too. At the weekends she could afford to take him to nice places, and she was looking forward to the summer holidays and seeing Meggie and Ivy. She wondered what they would think of her 'Afro' perm, and her new daring, way-out clothes. Robbie claimed she looked like a teenager.

Grateful as she was to Robbie for a change in fortune, he puzzled her. He could be so kind and affectionate, taking a great deal of interest in her and Barney, yet there was a part of him which was deep, cold and unfathomable.

She hadn't wanted to start up a sexual relationship with him again, but she soon found that Robbie was a master at getting what he wanted, while acting as if he was doing it for her.

He telephoned her most evenings, and sometimes came round in the early evening for a meal with her and Barney before going on to the casino. When he came to the flat he was very sensitive towards Barney, playing and chatting with him like a visiting relative, and he never even hugged or kissed her. He remained like this for about a month, until one evening she made some joking comment about how she wouldn't mind being taken out for a drink or a meal.

The following day he sent her some flowers with a note asking her to come and have lunch with him at the Caledonian Hotel. He stayed there overnight every other Friday, and in view of what had happened the last time, she wasn't keen to go. But he was employing her, and he'd also been her friend when she most needed one, so she felt unable to refuse.

The lunch led to them spending the afternoon in bed again, and from then on it became a regular fortnightly date.

She liked going out to lunch with him; he was charming and entertaining and it was good to get dressed up and eat nice food and drink good wine in a sophisticated restaurant.

Yet at the same time it irritated her that he slotted her into his life like a visit to the barber or the dentist, and that he behaved as if the sex afterwards was some kind of reward for her.

He was without a doubt the worst lover she'd ever had. He was far too fast and frantic, selfishly taking his pleasure without any thought for her. If he'd been any other man she would have pointed this out, and unless there had been a dramatic improvement she would have dumped him. But there was something about Robbie that suggested it would be very unwise to criticize him. She couldn't afford to lose such well-paid work, and she was also just a little afraid of him.

It was in June, during one of these afternoon stints, that Robbie told her he'd cancelled his contract with the Livingston studio.

Every other man Laura had slept with became softer and more affectionate after sex. It was then that they often talked about their past, their hopes for the future, or even their family. But Robbie always became brusque, almost as if he was steeling himself not to reveal a tender side. He often sat up in bed and opened his briefcase to read reports or totted up rows of figures, and it was at that point that she always had a shower and went home.

But the day he dropped the bombshell about the studio he had been cuddling her, and it was she who sat bolt upright in alarm.

'What about me?' she asked.

He lay back on the pillows and lifted one hand to run a finger down her naked breast. 'Don't worry, babe,' he smiled. 'You can work at the studio in Glasgow.'

He looked almost handsome that day for there had been a heatwave a few days before and his face was suntanned, making his teeth whiter.

'You'll probably like it better as you'll have the company of other girls there. They are a nice bunch, been at it for years. It's a different set-up there, but if you go over on Monday you can just watch and learn from the other girls before you start properly later in the week.'

'In what way is it different?' she asked.

'You'll find that out on Monday. Like I told you when you started at Livingston, if you don't like it, you are under no obligation to stay.'

Laura immediately felt uneasy because of his take-it-or-leave-it attitude. It was very reminiscent of the way he'd asked her to lunch, then just expected her to go to bed with him. She'd often felt that if she'd refused, that would have been the end of everything.

It was raining hard on the morning she arrived at the Glasgow studio on the outskirts of town. Her heart sank when she saw it was an old warehouse, and even before she went in she sensed it would have none of the refinements she had grown used to.

Her heart sank even further when she saw there was no reception area with beautiful glossy photographs to reassure her, and that the changing room was just a curtained-off area with a few wooden forms like she remembered from the gymnasium at school. But even more telling was that the studio area was divided up into a series of rooms, the walls flimsy plywood, and almost all of them were decorated and furnished as bedrooms.

One of the three models who were sitting around wearing dressing gowns came over to her, and introduced herself as Katy.

'Robbie asked me to look after you,' she said. 'You haven't done this before I suppose?'

Katy was a statuesque mixed-race woman, with a strong

Liverpool accent. She was at least five feet ten, her crinkly dark hair was cropped very short and she had beautiful sharply defined cheekbones.

'I've been doing glamour shots,' Laura said nervously. 'But this is going to be porn, isn't it?'

It was only a stab in the dark, she wasn't sure, and she couldn't really believe Robbie was so uncaring that he'd throw her into that.

'Only soft porn.' Katy shrugged. 'Fanny shots and stuff.'

Laura's stomach lurched.

Her alarm must have showed for Katy laughed. 'If you don't like the idea you'd better get going now. But don't think Robbie will pay you for more glamour stuff, he don't make anything out of that. This is where the money is.'

It was tempting to turn and run out, but however horrible the idea of pornographic photography was, Laura needed to know more about Robbie and these other girls.

So she sat down and had a cup of tea with Katy and the two other models. The photographer had arrived late and was still setting up the lighting. The women were friendly, and Laura soon discovered they were in much the same boat as her. All three of them had children and no husband.

Julie was a small, curvaceous blonde. 'None of us could be fashion models,' she said bluntly. 'We're too old and too fat. But we've all got pretty faces and the kind of bodies men want to look at. Okay, so showing off your fanny ain't something you really want to do, but it's a darn sight better than trying to get by on the Social or doing office cleaning.'

'We have a laugh too,' Katy said, her dark eyes twinkling with laughter at Laura's horrified expression. 'We're all in it together, and we're real mates. You stay and watch what goes on, and if you don't think you can do it, go and sign on at the Social again, because you ain't going to be offered anything else.'

Anne, the third girl, a pretty, buxom redhead, was even blunter. 'So Robbie's fucking you,' she said. 'We all went down that road, thinking we was special to him. This is the end of that road, it don't go nowhere else.'

Laura instinctively knew the three girls were telling her the truth. But shocking as that was, it wasn't as bad as finding out what a fool she'd been to imagine Robbie cared for her.

She ought to have read all the signs. He'd wormed his way into her life, discovering everything about her, while giving nothing of himself away. There had never been any tenderness in his lovemaking, in truth he'd treated her like a tart. The nightly phone calls, the visits to her home were both just ways to break down her defences and make her put her trust in him.

Yet however sick she felt at being conned by him, she wasn't going to let these other women know.

The sick feeling grew ever stronger as the photo shoot began. The photographer, a middle-aged man called Don, had none of the charm and diplomacy she'd grown used to with Ed in Livingston. He was curt and crude, using the most vile language, without even a trace of humour to lighten the proceedings.

The first series of pictures he took were of Katy, wearing only a white suspender belt and stockings, and he had her lying on the bed masturbating.

'Hold yer fanny lips open more,' he barked at her. 'This ain't for a parish magazine. And look like you're getting off on it, for fuck's sake. Lick yer lips and act like you're horny.'

Laura could hardly bear to look. She was blushing with embarrassment, and she didn't know how Katy could manage to look so relaxed and even happy to do it.

Next he got Julie, who was wearing a black leather G-string and a peephole bra, on the bed with Katy to simulate lesbian acts. Laura cringed as Julie had to stick out her tongue at Katy's vagina as she was photographed from the rear, kneeling, bottom up in the air.

'Just think of it as a giggle,' Anne whispered to her as Don instructed Katy to sit up and Julie to kneel beside her, pull aside her G-string and masturbate against one of Katy's nipples. 'None of it's real, it's just an act. We go down the pub later and laugh about it. The good things about Don are that he's quick and he knows what he wants. He don't try and come on to any of us either, Katy reckons he ain't got a cock.'

In the two hours Laura watched, she saw virtually every permutation of what a woman could do sexually, alone, with a partner, or all three together. At times she found it hideous, other times erotic, yet as Julie had said, it was amusing too. She heard the women's whispered jokes to one another, she felt their affection for one another, and admiration at their ability to act so well compensated for her embarrassment.

Finally it was over. Don packed away his camera, stowed his rolls of film in a bag and unplugged the lighting.

'Think you can do it?' he called out to Laura.

'I don't know,' she said, feeling that she could easily throttle Robbie.

'If you aren't here on Friday morning sharp on ten-thirty I'll use someone else. If you come, you'll be working with Katy. Get yerself a black basque and fishnet stockings, I've got an idea for a touch of dominatrix to break you in gently. I'll bring the whip.'

Once dressed, with much of their heavy makeup removed, Katy, Julie and Anne all looked refreshingly ordinary, no different from any of the mothers Laura chatted to at the school gates.

They went to a pub nearby, and over a drink and sandwiches they asked Laura if she intended to come on Friday.

'If I don't, what will happen?' she asked.

'Robbie will drop you,' Katy said with a shrug. 'Don't kid yourself he cares, he don't care about no one but hisself. You ain't in love with him, are you?'

'No, certainly not.' Laura laughed and told them how she met him and that she'd lost Stuart because of him.

All three women nodded in sympathy. 'He done the same to all of us,' Katy said. 'I was a fashion model, but I got pregnant and that put paid to that. I was working as a stripper when I met Robbie, he did the same with me as you, got me to do the glamour stuff, then once I'd got a new flat, got used to having money, he said it was this or nothin'. Julie was a croupier at the Glasgow casino, she got sacked because she was suspected of fiddling. Robbie jumped in then. The same thing happened to her too.'

'You mean he actually looks for women who are down on their luck?' Laura exclaimed.

Anne smirked. 'You got it in one! My old man left me and the three kids and the bailiffs came to repossess stuff that was on the never-never. One of the bailiffs felt sorry enough for me to give me Robbie's number, he said he might give me a job. So I rang him, he took me out to lunch, gave me a load of old flannel, and bingo, I ended up doing this. So he don't just find women himself, he's got other blokes looking for them too.'

'And you all slept with him?' Laura asked hesitantly.

Katy's face softened. 'Yeah, 'fraid so. He made all of us believe he could give us a new start. It's funny if you think about it, the King of Porn being such a dead loss in the sack. You could get more satisfaction eating a Mars Bar.'

Laura giggled.

Anne reached out and patted her hand. 'We know how

you feel, love, we've been there! But the good news is he does pay well. We get seventy-five pounds for every session. Where else can you earn that and be home in time to give the kids their tea?'

Laura brightened up – that was much more than she expected. 'But where do these pictures end up?' she asked.

'Not in *Woman's Own*, that's for sure,' Julie laughed. 'I doubt if they even stay in Britain, if they do it would only be in under-the-counter mags.'

'Do you have to do stuff with men too?' Laura asked.

'Well of course.' Katy laughed as if she thought that a silly question. 'But that ain't any worse, some of 'em are quite nice, they usually feel worse than we do, at least us girls don't have to worry about getting it up!'

All three women laughed uproariously at this, but Laura blanched. 'Does that mean we have to actually do it with them?' she asked in a small voice.

'Not properly,' Julie said, glancing at her two friends and sniggering. 'It's kind of posed, like you saw today. There's nothing very exciting about a picture of two people at it, is there? It's the groping, the imagining what it feels like entering some delectable bird that turns men on.'

Laura's stomach was churning with anxiety now and it must have showed in her face, for Katy put her hand over hers and squeezed it. 'You really didn't know until today, did you? Are you chickening out?'

'I don't know,' Laura replied. 'I need the money, but I don't know if I'll actually be able to do it when the time comes. Were you like this?'

'We all were,' Katy replied. 'The day I started I was shaking like I had St Vitus' Dance. Then Don made it worse still by telling me I had to put some makeup over my stretch marks! I was so self-conscious I wanted to curl up in a corner and die. But the girls gave me a pep talk, got me to snort a line of coke, and suddenly I was okay about it. We always do coke before now, it makes it a doddle. We'll bring some for you on Friday if you like.'

On the drive back to Edinburgh, Laura tried to think only of what making £75 in two hours would do for her. If she managed to stick it out for a few months she'd have enough money to move anywhere she fancied. She could go and live in Devon or Cornwall, or find a place near Meggie and Ivy.

But attractive as the money was, it didn't make the work any more palatable. The thought of touching another's woman's breasts or vagina was totally abhorrent, and letting a man she'd didn't even fancy maul her was even worse. If she was told to give him a blow job she thought she'd be sick.

But then she didn't really fancy Robbie, did she? Could pretending to be in the throes of an orgasm for the camera be any worse than being trapped under a heavy, hairy, sweaty man who cared for no one but himself?

She thought then about Meggie going on the game, and reminded herself how her sister had used her earnings from that to move on to better things. She could do that too. She could start her own business, maybe a promotions agency, and Barney would get to live in a nice house, she could buy him a bike, take him on lovely holidays.

The end would justify the means.

'Close one nostril and snort up the line in the other,' Julie said, as she held out a rolled-up bank note to Laura and two lines of cocaine on a hand mirror. 'When you've done that, change nostrils and do the other one.'

Laura had only tried coke once before, but that was seven years ago and she'd been so drunk at the time she couldn't remember what sort of effect it had. But if the other girls used it and found it worked for them, then it probably would for her too.

She exhaled, then slid the banknote up her nostril and sniffed up one line. It stung her nose and made her eyes run, but she resisted the desire to sneeze and quickly did the same again in the other nostril.

'Good girl,' Julie said. 'Now sniff it right back, it makes the back of your throat feel a bit weird, but that soon passes.'

It wasn't just her throat which felt weird, everything did. She could see herself in the mirror on the wall, a person she barely recognized as Laura Brannigan, dressed in a black basque, fishnet stockings and high-heeled boots. Katy had put on her makeup for her, her eyes were dark and smoky, her lips very red, and with her dark brown 'Afro' hair, she was transformed into the kind of woman she'd only ever glimpsed before in her sexual fantasies.

'Okay now?' Julie asked.

Laura nodded, and was surprised to find she was. If she could sit here with these other girls, her breasts almost out of the basque, and nothing covering her vital parts, and not feel embarrassed, then she could do the rest.

Her debut was to be with Katy, who was wearing something which was meant to resemble a toga. It was white, and clasped on one brown shoulder with a brooch, but it was so flimsy and short that her black pubic hair was visible, as were her dark brown nipples which stood up like thimbles because she was cold.

Julie picked up an aerosol. 'Close your eyes,' she ordered and quickly sprayed something over Laura's face, neck, shoulders, breasts and her belly and thighs. 'It glistens like sweat,' she said by way of an explanation. 'So you look hot and sexy!'

'You *do* look sexy,' Katy said appraisingly. 'Great tits and arse!'

Don called them then and Laura felt like a gladiator entering the ring.

The room they were to use was rigged out like a torture chamber, only all the chains and handcuffs hanging up were black plastic. Even before Don began instructing them about what he wanted, Laura could see it for herself. Katy was the victim, and she the abuser. The first few shots were easy enough to do – Katy was to cower away from her, while Laura looked menacing with the whip in her hand. The coke was working and she felt excited and uninhibited. At one point, unasked, she even put one foot up on the bench where Katy was sprawled, a display of dominance and giving the camera a first-class view of her pubic area.

'Well done, Laura,' Don muttered in the darkness beyond the lights. 'You've got it!'

She guessed as they moved on to other poses that Don had settled on this setting for her first time because it didn't involve her having to touch Katy intimately. Katy was her slave, there to pleasure her. This idea aroused Laura a little, just as her costume had, and she found she was acting it out almost unconsciously, to the point when Don directed Katy to kneel before her open legs and simulate licking at her vagina, she looked down at her very red, pointed tongue and for a second or two wished it was for real.

'That's it, girls,' Don called out, breaking the mood. 'Very good, both of you. Laura, you are a natural.'

Julie and Anne blew her kisses as they went out for their shoot. Julie was dressed as a nurse, in a ridiculously short striped uniform and black stockings. Anne was presumably the patient in a skimpy dress and very high heels.

'Wasn't so bad, was it?' Katy said as they got dressed in their own clothes. 'Don was right, you are a natural. I got the idea you even enjoyed it.'

*

Laura got up from the bed and paced up and down her cell like a caged animal. Remembering that first shoot was bad enough, but she certainly didn't want to recall all the far worse ones that came afterwards. Where did all her modesty and dignity go? Why was money so important to her?

11

As Laura looked back at the second half of 1975, and '76 and '77, she found much of it was blank to her. That, she supposed, was because she spent so much of it out of her head on coke, speed or alcohol. There weren't that many entirely straight days, and those there were she almost wished she couldn't remember because they were invariably days of reckoning.

How odd it was that while she could vividly recall people taking her to task for her behaviour, it never had the effect of sobering her up for long.

The shock and horror she felt that first day in the Glasgow studio fizzled out pretty quickly. The other 'models' as they liked to call themselves, whether male or female, were all in it for the same reason. Money.

The very first time she worked with a man had been scary and embarrassing. She'd assumed that he had to be some kind of oversexed pervert, but he disarmed her by telling her that he got an erection whenever he took his clothes off, and that it had nothing to do with seeing her or any female body. He went on to say that he never dared go into a communal changing room after sport for that reason.

Maybe he was unique, but all the men were seasoned performers: as one casually put it one day, 'I always rise to the occasion.' They were in the main quite sleazy, many of rather low intellect, and not one of them would she ever want to go on a date with. Yet mostly they were kind and polite, and some were very funny. As long as they could both distance themselves from what they were doing and remember it was only acting, not the real thing, then it wasn't so bad.

With each successive session it became easier and easier, eventually getting to the point where she saw it all as a bit of a laugh. In fact she got so blasé, and so good at it, that the other girls nicknamed her 'The Blue Queen'.

Yet it was clear to her now that whilst losing the ability to be shocked, she also lost all her values and principles. Money was the only thing that counted to her; dignity and self-respect flew out the window.

During the summer holiday of '75 Laura had driven down to London with Barney to stay with Meggie and Ivy. It made Laura proud to see how well Meggie was doing with her houses. She didn't have the capital to think big like Jackie. She just bought one place at a time, renovated it, sold it on quickly and then bought another. But she was making an excellent living. She was equally proud of Ivy too, for she had qualified as a bookkeeper, and ran the office in a building supplies office.

They were thrilled to have their big sister and nephew staying with them, and they took a break from their work and had days out in Brighton and Hastings and went to London Zoo, the Tower of London and on a boat trip up the Thames.

Neither of her sisters asked Laura any probing questions about how she was managing. She supposed her good clothes and general confidence spoke for themselves, and of course they'd grown up believing she was a winner.

Jackie wasn't quite such a pushover. When Laura met her to take Barney for a day out to Southend, she grilled Laura remorselessly, not just about what she was doing for a living, but who she was staying with in London. As Barney had mentioned Meggie and Ivy several times, Laura passed them off as two friends she'd made at the casino, who had now moved to London. It felt like the very worst kind of betrayal of her generous, hard-working sisters, for in her heart Laura wanted to boast about how clever and resourceful they were.

She told Jackie the same story she'd told Meggie and Ivy, that she worked part-time in a dress shop, but she did admit that the modelling she did on the side was the glamour kind. Yet that was only because she felt that her friend might possibly see her pictures in one of the pin-up magazines as men on building sites were likely to leave them lying around.

To be fair to Jackie she was amused by this, certainly not horrified. But then she was in a very mellow mood because Barney was with them. He was five now, and a real boy, boisterous, funny and full of enthusiasm for everything from football to creepy-crawlies. But he was loving and demonstrative, still happy to be cuddled by anyone, and as he was so well and happy Jackie had no reason to be concerned about him.

Jackie hardly mentioned Stuart, apart from to say he was her best worker, and she didn't divulge if he was seeing anyone, whether he ever spoke about Laura, or even where he lived. But then, she didn't ask whether Laura had anyone special in her life either, and Laura got the idea that was because she'd rather not know, out of loyalty to Stuart.

By Christmas of that year Laura had moved out of Caledonian Crescent and into a spacious two-bedroom flat in Albany Street. The house was built in Georgian times, just like the old tenement, but that was the only similarity. Albany Street was one of the wide, gracious streets in the New Town, the houses built for wealthy people who had the whole house, with servants in the attic rooms and their horses in the mews at the back. Laura's first-floor flat had a beautiful marble fireplace, elaborate plaster cornices, high ceilings and shiny walnut doors. The carpets and curtains came with the lease, but there was no furniture, and the day she and Barney moved in they danced around the empty flat laughing and singing at the joy of having so much space.

Yet on Christmas Day she did have a really bad stab of guilt at what she had to do to be able to meet the high rent, furnish the flat, and shower Barney with presents. It came when she was helping him set up his new electric train set on his bedroom floor.

It was the afternoon, already getting dark, and Barney had insisted on putting on the new pyjamas Jackie had sent him. They were dark blue and fleecy lined, with a picture of Bert and Ernie from *Sesame Street* across the chest.

'This train is the best present ever, Mummy,' he said, crawling round the track to her to give her a hug. 'I wish Stuie was here to play with it too. Does he know we've moved? If he doesn't he won't know where to find us when he comes back.'

Up till then she'd been so happy. They had a big Christmas tree in the lounge, all decked out in red and gold decorations and lights, and the heady smell of pine was everywhere. She'd hung Barney's stocking on the mantelpiece, and although they had the luxury of central heating, she'd even lit a real fire before he woke to make everything extra special and cosy. They hadn't got much furniture yet, but that hadn't mattered; their beds, a settee and the television were enough for now.

But Barney's innocent remark cut her to the quick. He hadn't mentioned Stuart for weeks and she thought he'd forgotten all about him.

She hugged him tightly so he wouldn't see the tears welling up in her eyes. Last Christmas Stuart had played with him most of the day, and all the neighbours on the stair had come in for a drink or two and the flat had been noisy and crowded. This year Barney had twice as many presents, and although there had been no visitors, and no one but her to share his excitement as he opened his stocking, she had thought that was enough to make a five-year-old completely happy and he wouldn't remember how it had been the previous year.

'Stuie's working for Auntie Jackie in London now,' she said, the lump in her throat making it hard to speak. 'Maybe you'll see him again when you're big enough to go and stay with her. I don't think he'll ever come back to Edinburgh.'

Barney looked up at her, his big dark eyes sad and thoughtful. 'I should have asked Father Christmas to make him come back. That would have been an even better present than the train set. He could have done it, couldn't he?'

'I don't think so, Barney,' she said softly. 'Even all the elves that work for Father Christmas couldn't make Stuie love Mummy enough to come and visit.'

'Could Auntie Jackie make him come back?'

'No, Barney. Besides, she needs him to fix up her houses. But when you can write really well, you can write a letter to Stuie yourself. I'll put it in with my letter to Auntie Jackie.'

Jackie had sent a Christmas parcel to them at their old address in Caledonian Crescent. Luckily it arrived the day before they moved out. There was a big box of Lego for Barney, along with the pyjamas, and there had been a letter for Laura enclosed in the parcel.

I expect Barney will think pyjamas are a boring present, but I saw them while in the States and I thought they'd keep him cosy through the winter. I know things must be tougher for you than you let on in the summer, so I'm enclosing a cheque rather than sending a present for you. I worry about you, especially as I hardly ever hear from you. I expect that is because you don't want to admit how bad things are in case I tell Stuart. But I promise I'd never divulge anything you tell me, and you must promise me that you will come to me if you ever need help. You will always be my dearest friend, no matter what. Spend at least part of the money on something nice for yourself, and my wish for the New Year for you is that you find happiness again. Hug Barney for me. I couldn't believe how grown up he'd become, and it made me feel quite tearful to think he's beginning to read and do sums. I so much want to see him again soon. Please write or phone, I miss you both so much.

My love, Jackie

The cheque was for £500, and it made Laura feel ashamed that her old friend imagined they were sitting in a cold, miserable flat with no Christmas cheer, and no prospects either. She hadn't rung Jackie or written to her since the holiday in London during the summer.

She knew she must write back now and thank her for the money, but she was worried that Jackie might tell Stuart she'd moved, and if she mentioned where the new flat was, he'd be suspicious about how she could afford to live in such a smart area.

Soon after Christmas, she did write, but once again she lied to her friend. She used the excuse of working full-time at the dress shop as why she hadn't been in touch, and said a friend helped her out by collecting Barney from school. Thanking her for the cheque, she said it couldn't have come at a better time as she'd been offered a new flat with a bedroom for Barney but until the cheque came, she couldn't raise the deposit for it. Now, thanks to her friend's generosity, they had moved in, and she hoped Jackie would come and see her next time she came up to Scotland. She added truthfully that it had been a very difficult year, but she thought that things were finally improving.

She wished she hadn't been forced to tell Jackie more lies, but if she was to admit the whole truth about how she was living, Jackie would be afraid for Barney and she might even think he'd be better off with his father.

For a short while after Christmas Laura did seriously study the Situations Vacant column in the newspaper with the intention of getting a job so she could stop the photographic work. But although she thought perhaps she could become a company rep, or go back to promotions work, any jobs offered didn't pay enough.

Sometimes when she was alone in the early evening with Barney, helping him with his reading and sums, she'd look down at his earnest little face, see all that beautiful innocence, and feel very ashamed of the life she led when she was away from him.

Yet she could always justify it.

He was loved, well fed and clothed, she was there every day to collect him from school, and every weekend was spent with him alone. She didn't ever have men friends around the flat. In fact she hadn't got any, for apart from not going anywhere to meet a man she'd like to go out with, she saw enough of male bodies at work to put her off the idea. Robbie had lost interest in her now he had her where he wanted her. She only saw him occasionally if he came to the studio. All in all, she believed Barney wasn't affected in any way by how she made the money to keep them both.

But by the spring of '76 when Barney turned six, he was affected. It began by her being occasionally late to collect him from school. Once or twice it was because she was held up in traffic, but more often it was because she'd gone for a drink with Katy or one of the other girls after a session, and she'd been having such a good time she forgot about her son.

After she'd been severely reprimanded by his teacher, and warned that it wasn't to happen again, Laura paid Fiona, the mother of one of her son's classmates, to take him home with her if she didn't arrive in time. Fiona had three small children and her husband was away in Birmingham working, and sometimes didn't send any money home for them, so she was glad of the money Laura paid her.

But as spring turned to summer, what began as an occasional hour or two after school gradually stepped up to almost every time she worked in Glasgow.

Laura had told Fiona that she did modelling for a catalogue company. Fiona believed this implicitly, for she was a real 'wee wifie'; short, plump and plain, with no knowledge about anything beyond the perimeters of her home and family. To her, tall, slender Laura from London, who always dressed in the height of fashion and had her own car, was as exotic as a film star. If Laura told her she was late because they'd done a fashion shoot in Dumfries or even the Highlands she got excited about it and said one more child in the house made no difference at all to her.

One Friday at the start of July, Laura arrived at the studio in the morning to find she and Katy were to work with Craig and Pete that day. Pete, a big hunky blond guy from Manchester, was a good sort, a little thick, but good-natured. Craig, however, a redheaded Glaswegian, she found completely repellent. He was short and very muscular, but he had flaky skin, bad breath and he always smelled sweaty.

His only attribute was his large penis, and he would strut around naked, even when they were having a coffee break, as if waving it in front of the girls' faces would make them fancy him.

Laura had never actually had to do a photo session with him before, but she knew from the other girls that like many of the men who had large penises, Craig sometimes couldn't get it up. And as Don the photographer used to say, 'A man with a flaccid cock in pornography is about as useless as a chocolate fireguard.'

Dressed in just a suspender belt and black stockings and stilettos, Laura did some shots with Pete, and then Katy was called in to join in for a three-in-the-bed scene. It was all very easy, because Pete had the unusual knack of being able to pose with a hard-on and maul them both around as if he was about to really ravage them, yet not make them feel threatened at all. Don was being his usual inventive self, once again coming up with variations on the basic theme of two girls and one man. At one point Laura got the giggles, something that often happened, and Pete smacked her bottom playfully, which was applauded by Don.

Then Craig was called in.

'Katy, I want you doggie fashion, arse towards me,' Don said in his usual straight-to-the-point manner. 'Pete, you sit on the edge of the bed with Laura astride you, real close to Katy, like you're getting turned on even more by Katy about to get it. Craig, get that dong up and hold Katy's arse open so we can see where it's supposed to go.'

Craig strutted towards Katy, jerking away at his penis. He got a semi lob-on, but the harder he worked at it, the weaker it became.

'Fer fuck's sake, Craig,' Don yelled at him. 'Katy's arse would make a blind man see!'

Laura had to bury her face in Pete's shoulder to suppress her laughter, and she heard a little snort from Katy which told her she was in the same predicament.

After a few more minutes, with Craig getting redder and redder in the face, and still no erection, Don grew impatient. 'Katy, help the poor sod,' he ordered. 'Or we'll be here all day.'

Katy did as she was asked, because like Laura she was anxious for the session to be over so they could go home. Laura slid off Pete's lap on to the bed, and tried to avert her eyes diplomatically. But she couldn't resist peeping, and when she saw Katy's pained expression, and that huge flaccid penis that looked like a pork steak flapping around in her hand, she just couldn't control her laughter.

Pete was shaking, clearly fighting against laughing out loud too, but he reached out and touched Laura's hand as if warning her to do likewise. But all at once Craig flew at her, and punched her in the face so she fell back on the bed.

'You evil bitch,' he yelled at her, his Glaswegian accent so thick she could barely understand what he was saying. 'Who the fuck do you think you are?'

'You bastard,' Katy yelled, jumping to claw Craig's face with her nails. 'She didn't mean any harm.'

Pete intervened, trying to get Katy off Craig, who in turn was trying to get to Laura to hit her again. Laura glanced around for Don, expecting him to put a stop to it, but to her further shock he was clicking away, clearly thinking a fight scene with naked people might be interesting and saleable.

Craig continued to scream obscenities as Pete dragged him struggling out of the room.

'Guess that's it for the day,' Don said with an air of disappointment. 'You'd better get some cold water on your face, Laura; you'll have a shiner tomorrow.'

They heard Don ordering Craig to leave the building as Katy bathed Laura's face in the toilet.

'Do you think he'll lie in wait for me?' Laura asked, afraid now, for her face was throbbing and fiery.

'Don will have told him you're too valuable to Robbie to mess with,' Katy reassured her. 'But we'll get Pete to come and have a drink with us. Just in case.'

Laura fully intended to have just one drink and then go home. Her face hurt and she felt weepy. But Pete and Katy both wanted her to stay, and by the time she'd had a couple of drinks they were all laughing about Craig and discussing whether Don would ever use him again.

Before Laura knew it, the pub was closing for the afternoon and she was too drunk to drive, but still wanted more.

When she came to the next morning and found herself on Katy's settee, she couldn't remember anything more than that they had gone on to a drinking club in central Glasgow. She knew it was a rough place, the carpet sticky with spilled drink, but they were playing soul music from the sixties and she and Katy danced. After that it was all a blank.

Katy's flat was squalid. It was on the third floor of a high-rise block built in the sixties. The four rooms were all small, her children were cramped up in bunk beds and they could barely get into bed for the toys and clothes strewn everywhere. The living room was larger, but with no order, and a vast three-piece suite which had seen better days meant there was no room to move. The carpet was worn and stained; Katy never cleaned the windows, and makeup, used plates and overloaded ashtrays filled every available surface. Amazingly Katy was always well groomed. How she managed it living in such conditions Laura didn't know.

It was another hot day, as it had been since the start of June, but whereas the house in Albany Street was built of thick stone and remained cool in the summer, Katy's flat was not well insulated, and with such large windows it was already like an inferno.

Laura's head was throbbing and her mouth felt like the bottom of a bird cage, but Cheryl, Katy's daughter, came in to the room with a cup of coffee and some painkillers.

'You didn't come in till two,' she said, passing over the coffee. 'Mum was really sick, but you just fell on the settee and passed out.'

Cheryl was only thirteen, a pretty girl with her mother's sharp cheekbones and dusky skin, and when Laura realized that she'd been left alone with the two younger children for so long, it reminded her about Barney and that she'd given Fiona no warning she might not be coming home.

Pausing only to splash some water on her face in the kitchen and gulp down the coffee and painkillers, she rushed out, leaving Cheryl to say goodbye to Katy for her.

Fiona lived just two streets away from her old home in Caledonian Crescent, and Laura drove straight there without going home first to change or put some makeup over her bruised cheek.

A big burly man in a checked work shirt came to the door, and just the way he glowered at her was enough to tell her this was Roy, Fiona's husband, and he hadn't been pleased to come home and find another child in his house.

Laura tried the charm offensive, apologized profusely for not coming to collect Barney, but said she was on an assignment and hadn't been able to get home.

'What sort of mother are you?' he snarled at her. 'You leave your wean with a stranger all night! I had to take him to the hospital.'

Laura was horrified, asking what had happened and where Fiona was. She came forward then, fluttering her hands in anxiety. It was clear she hadn't told her husband she'd been taking care of Barney for some time and that she got paid for it, and Laura realized she was afraid it was going to come out now and get her into bother.

'He fell off a wall while out playing,' she said. 'He's fine now, just a couple of wee stitches in his knee. But Roy had to wait a very long time at the hospital with him. I had to stay here with the others.'

'I am so sorry,' was all Laura could say. 'But you aren't on the phone, and there was no way I could get a message to you. Can I see Barney now?'

'Ach, yer lucky I dinnae call the poliss to you,' Roy said

angrily. 'Look at the state of youse. Fee says you're a model, but you look and smell like a jakey!'

At that point Barney came to the door and rushed into her arms. 'Why didn't you come home?' he cried. 'I was hurt and I had stitches at the hospital.'

That incident did pull her up sharply. Laura was upset that Roy had said she looked and smelt like a wino, and by the inference that she was neglecting Barney. She promised herself she would never leave him again with anyone overnight.

His cut knee soon mended, but he didn't forget. Clearly he'd heard things said between Roy and Fiona that had given him the idea that he was unwanted and neglected.

Laura made sure she was on time to collect him from school every day until the end of the term when the holidays started, and because she couldn't work with him off school she planned to make a real effort to take him out somewhere every day. Then Jackie phoned and asked if Laura would like to stay at her cottage in Cellardyke and said she would join her there when she could get away from London.

The hot weather of 1976 continued. They said it was the hottest summer since records began, and Laura and Barney spent all day, every day, on the beach. But lovely as it was there, Laura felt bored a great deal of the time. A six-year-old boy was more interested in playing with other children than being with his mother. He swam, looked for crabs in rock pools, collected shells and played cricket, and there wasn't much else for her to do but read.

Jackie arrived from London looking a million dollars in a pale green silk dress, her hair styled like Farrah Fawcett Majors in *Charlie's Angels*. The bangles on her wrist were real gold and she was driving a new red convertible car. She laughed when Laura hugged her and said she must be making a fortune. When she took a case of champagne out of the boot, instead of the cheap wine they used to drink, that seemed confirmation.

Jackie had always been great with Barney, she was patient and loving and as interested in his development as if she were a blood aunt. But after a couple of days, Laura found herself becoming irritated that Jackie seemed far more enthusiastic about being with Barney than with her. The moment she got up in the morning she began planning the day around him. Even though he was more than happy to play with his friends, she joined in games of cricket or crab-hunting with them, leaving Laura sitting alone on the beach. She didn't want to go into the pub and leave him to play with the other kids, and when she took him up to bed in the evenings she would stay reading to him for well over an hour.

That was what started a row, a week after she arrived.

Laura had been drinking steadily since about six in the evening. They'd had a bottle of wine with dinner, and then Jackie disappeared off upstairs with Barney to bathe him and put him to bed, so Laura opened another bottle of wine and had finished it all by the time Jackie came downstairs again.

'You are so lucky, Laura,' she said breathlessly as she sat down on the settee. 'He's so bright, so handsome and so loving. I wish he was mine.'

'Then take him,' Laura retorted. 'I'll swap him for your car.'

It was a flippant remark, but her voice probably had a hard edge to it because she was drunk and fed up.

'Don't you realize what a treasure he is?' Jackie asked sharply.

'I realize I can't go anywhere, do anything because of him. It's easy for you to moon over him when you've only got him around you for a week or so, you only see the good part,' Laura snapped back.

'So where do you want to go, what do you want to do?' Jackie asked tartly.

'To be wined and dined, to stay in luxury hotels and wear fabulous clothes. I want fun and men adoring me. I want to be as rich as you are.'

'That is so shallow, Laura,' Jackie exclaimed. 'Stuart said that was how you'd become, but I didn't believe him. Yet it's true, all you've talked about since I got here is money, clothes and your hair and nails. What's happened to you?'

'You can talk,' Laura threw back. 'Sitting there with half a pound of gold on your wrists, an Ozzie Clark dress and that sports car outside! You've got everything – a wealthy husband, a business worth a fortune, even this place too for when you feel like slumming it.'

'But I haven't got a child,' Jackie said, revealing that was what she really wanted. 'And if I had to choose between all the material things and a baby, I'd choose a baby any day, even if I had to live in a council flat.'

'Oh yeah,' Laura mocked. 'Like you know anything about life in a council flat. You were born with the proverbial silver spoon. It's the easiest thing in the world to get a baby, and the hardest thing of all to bring them up, especially when you've got no money.'

'What happened between you and that man from the casino to make you change so much?' Jackie asked, her eyes glittering with unshed tears. 'Okay, so we both used to dream of being stinking rich, we used men and did things that perhaps we shouldn't have. But you loved Stuart, you were good together; what made you throw all that away?'

Laura had known that sooner or later Jackie would question her about that. She tried to think of a good excuse, but there wasn't one.

'I didn't want to throw it all away. I never intended to do anything with Robbie but he took me to lunch and one thing led to another. It was a big mistake.' Laura's voice began to rise in agitation. 'I thought he was going to help me get a really good job, but it was all hot air.'

'Was it him who got you to do the pin-up pictures?'

Laura was very drunk, but at Jackie's question she suddenly felt sober and afraid. 'Yes, it was if you must know. And what's wrong with it?'

'Nothing if they are all like the one Stuart showed me. But are they, Laura? That was an old magazine he showed me. Have you progressed to something more hardcore now?'

'Of course I haven't,' Laura said indignantly, but she was scared that Jackie might know that wasn't true. Robbie had always said the pornographic pictures were sold abroad, but he might have been lying. 'Why would you think that?'

'Well, it was a bit of a shock to both of us. You looked very sexy and lovely, but pin-ups are a bit old-hat now, and let's face it, Laura, page three girls are usually about eighteen, not over thirty.'

The last thing Laura wanted was to be reminded she was too old for real modelling. She also hated the idea that Jackie and Stuart had been looking at the picture together and discussing what it might lead to. 'Pardon me if I used the only assets I had to make some money,' she said with heavy sarcasm. 'You could go running home to Mummy and Daddy if you were left in the lurch with a four-year-old. I wasn't that lucky.'

'When are you going to realize that having Barney is the luckiest thing in the world?' Jackie asked.

'Bollocks!' Laura shouted at her. 'You make it sound like motherhood is some kind of privilege. It isn't, it's like having a ball and chain around your ankle.'

'Then I'd give everything I've got to have a ball and chain,' Jackie said.

*

That evening all Laura had really been aware of was that Jackie was suspicious about her modelling. Laura was on the defensive and what she'd said about motherhood wasn't how she really felt, just a spur of the moment counter-attack.

But the next morning when she woke and remembered what was said, she suddenly realized Jackie was trying to tell her she was afraid she'd never have a child.

It had never occurred to her before that Jackie and Roger wanted children. She'd always seen them as the couple with everything and imagined that a child would be too much of a tie in their busy lives. But when she thought of how Jackie was with Barney, she realized she was in fact hungry for one of her own.

When she got downstairs Jackie was sitting at the kitchen table with a cup of tea. She had already got Barney up and given him his breakfast, and now he was out by the harbour playing tag with the other kids. 'I'll make another pot of tea,' she said to Laura. 'And maybe you'd like some aspirin too.'

'I'll do it,' Laura said, feeling ashamed of herself. 'I'm sorry if I was nasty last night. I was a bit depressed.'

'I'm sorry too if you thought I was being judgmental about the pin-up picture,' Jackie said. 'I was just worried you were mixing with dodgy people.'

They agreed to put that tiff behind them, and over a fresh pot of tea they discussed what they would do that day. Jackie had just heard about Brodie Farm being put up for sale and thought they could go up there together and have a look around.

'Before we do that, I want to know why you are afraid you can't have a baby,' Laura said. 'Have you had any tests?'

'Dozens,' Jackie shrugged. 'And they all say there is nothing wrong with me.'

'What about Roger?'

Jackie's face clouded over. 'He won't go for any. He gets really indignant at the suggestion it might be him. To be honest, it's putting our marriage under a lot of strain. If he doesn't care enough about why I want to get checked out, I don't want to make love. If we don't make love I've got no chance of getting preggy either. Got any suggestions?'

'Lie back and think of England?' Laura said, raising one eyebrow.

Jackie laughed. 'Or maybe I should get myself a new stud.'

They saw Brodie Farm that day, and despite it being a ruin, Jackie instantly fell in love with it. Laura could see its potential, but she had a sneaky suspicion that its real attraction was that it would be a huge project which Jackie could use as an excuse to stay away from Roger. For the rest of the week she could talk of nothing else, and on several occasions she disappeared, only to come back an hour later saying she'd been up there again. Perhaps it was this pre-occupation on her part that made her ask Laura at the end of the week about her job in the dress shop.

'They can't be very pleased that you need the whole of the school holidays off,' she said. 'And you must need the money?'

'Well no, they weren't pleased,' Laura said. 'But they had to lump it, I couldn't take Barney with me. And yes, I could do with the money.'

'Well, why don't you go back to work then, and leave Barney with me? I've got to stay on through till September to oversee the renovations on that other cottage I bought. And I want to find out more about Brodie Farm. I could bring him back to you the day before he has to return to school.'

Laura felt a surge of excitement at the idea of going back to the city alone. 'Are you sure?' she asked. She could ring

Don and see if she could get some extra sessions, and she could go out at night with Katy and the other girls.

'Laura, I'd love to look after Barney.' Jackie smiled. 'Goodness knows when I'll get to see him again! To me it would be bliss.'

Laura had ten days on her own, and she filled every moment of them. Sessions at the studio each day, and out partying in Glasgow by night. She only went home to Edinburgh once to get some more clothes, the rest of the time she slept on one of the other girls' settees. Not that she slept much, for she was doing coke in the mornings, and took some speed at night to keep going. She hadn't had so much fun in years, dancing, drinking and flirting with any man who looked as if he had a few bob.

She made a point of phoning Jackie every evening at six to check on Barney, but once that was done she could relax and think about the night ahead.

It was people she met that week that set her off on a new road. Up till then she didn't have any real friends; she knew women from Barney's school and the old neighbours in Caledonian Crescent, but they were people she only had the occasional chat with, they weren't mates. Even Katy and the other girls from the studio had held themselves apart to begin with. To them she was 'posh' because she came from London and lived in Edinburgh. People in Glasgow tended to think anyone from Edinburgh was stuck up.

Yet when they saw she liked Glasgow, that she didn't look down on them for living in tenements or council flats, and could party just like them, all the barriers came down. They saw her as one of them.

Laura smiled wryly as she remembered how good it felt to be accepted back then. The irony of it didn't escape her. All her adult life she had struggled to erase her true background and climb the social ladder. But there she was at thirty-one, mixing with and loving people who lived and behaved much like the people back in Shepherds Bush. She'd come full circle, except it was a much darker circle, for instead of the women doing office cleaning or working in factories, they were in the sex industry. And the men in Glasgow didn't work on building sites and go to the pub in their working clothes, they wore sharp suits, drove smart cars, and their work was dealing in drugs, pimping and extortion.

But of course she didn't see that at the time. All she saw was that these were people who lived life to the full, they were generous and fun. She put down their living in bad housing as part of that curiously Scottish trait of not caring too much about their surroundings. The men went out with wads of money in their pockets, and they spent it carelessly. She felt excited by the hint of underlying aggression, she loved their humour and their warmth. In a way it was like going home.

'You look so tired,' Jackie exclaimed when she brought Barney back on the Sunday before he was to start school.

Laura hadn't been home more than a couple of hours, just enough time to have a bath and change her clothes.

'I've been working extra hours, what with the Edinburgh Festival on,' she lied. 'And I did some bar work too at night. But you two look marvellous!'

Barney had run in to greet her shouting at the top of his voice, climbing up her like a little monkey. He was deeply tanned, and Jackie had had his hair cut short ready for school. In a white tee-shirt and little blue shorts he looked good enough to eat.

'Auntie Jackie let me sit in the front seat and we had the hood down,' he said excitedly. 'I've got a new pencil box and a real leather satchel. And I can read lots of new words too.'

'It's been such a joy being with him,' Jackie said, looking sad that it was now to end. 'I wish I could persuade you to come back to live in London, so I could see more of you both.'

Laura knew Jackie was sincere, and part of her loved her for saying it, but the other part felt irritated. 'If I came back to London I couldn't afford to live in Kensington, like you,' she said. 'I'd be in one room in Hackney or somewhere grim.'

'It's high time you went to a solicitor and got a divorce and a settlement from Greg. You could buy your own place then.'

'I don't want anything from that bastard,' Laura snapped. 'I can keep myself and Edinburgh is my home now. I like it here.'

'I love Scotland too,' Jackie said wistfully. She didn't appear to have noticed her friend's sharp tone 'If you won't come to London, then perhaps I'll come here to live permanently. I really don't want to go back.'

'Stay with us, Auntie Jackie,' Barney piped up. 'You can sleep in my bed and I'll go in with Mummy.'

Jackie looked at Laura, apparently waiting for Laura to endorse Barney's idea. But Laura said nothing; she wanted to be alone, she was strung out and she intended to take a Mogadon the moment Barney was in bed and catch up on all the sleep she'd missed in the past week.

'I'd like that, sweetheart.' Jackie bent to kiss him. 'But I've got things to do in London and Uncle Roger's waiting for me. I'd better fetch your things out of the car and get going.'

'But you haven't even seen my bedroom!' Barney said indignantly. 'Don't go yet!'

Laura pulled herself together enough to help Jackie get his things from the car. He appeared to have twice as much as he'd taken to Fife. 'I'd ask you to stay for lunch,' she said as they brought the stuff in. 'But I haven't got much in, what with working all hours.'

Jackie looked around the flat, and even put Barney's clothes away for him. She'd bought him quite a few new shirts and trousers, and even his old things were washed and ironed. If Laura hadn't felt so strung out she would have hugged and thanked her.

'You look poorly,' Jackie said, coming over to her and taking her face in her two hands. 'I wish I hadn't suggested you went back to work now, you've overdone it. I'll ring you tomorrow night to see how you are.'

Years later Jackie told her that she thought she was on the verge of a breakdown that day, and that she worried about her all the way home. She said if she'd only insisted on staying that night she thought she would have realized that Laura had been taking drugs, and she would've taken steps to stop her. She added that if she'd done that maybe everything would have turned out differently.

'Perhaps she was right,' Laura mused aloud.

12

'Twenty years ago this pub was famous for its nightly punch-ups,' Stuart said cheerfully as he and David approached The Bear, which Robbie Fielding was reputed to own.

'I hope it's not still like that now,' David grinned. 'I can feel you getting psyched up to punch the lights out of Fielding, but let's leave everyone else alone! I don't fancy spending the night in a police cell.'

David had spent the last two days trawling through both used and unused evidence from the original investigation. Stuart had spent the time seeing people who had some connection with Laura both here in Edinburgh and in Glasgow.

David was now up to speed with the whole case, but Stuart hadn't turned up anything relevant, which was why they were now going to see Robbie Fielding.

They paused in the doorway of the pub, both a little surprised it was so quiet. There were no more than fifteen people in there, and all of them were young student types, not the kind of rough crowd they'd expected.

'It was a spit and sawdust kind of boozer before,' Stuart said somewhat regretfully.

David felt relieved. It was one of those trendy designer places which were so common in London, everything from cobbler's lasts and old tools to stone bottles arranged artfully along high shelves, scrubbed pine tables and stripped floorboards. But it didn't have an air of success about it; it looked tired and dusty, and at eight on a Saturday night, a city centre bar should have been much busier.

They ordered a couple of pints from a pretty blonde barmaid and stayed at the bar to drink them.

'After twenty years and only seeing him once, are you going to recognize him?' David asked in a low voice, glancing at two lone older men right at the end of the bar.

'I think so,' Stuart said, remembering that the man's face had haunted him for months after he left Edinburgh. 'Besides, if he's the kind of man I think he is, when he comes in he'll be swaggering around letting everyone know he owns the place.'

'How are we going to play it?' David asked.

Stuart grinned. 'Buggered if I know,' he said. 'I'm hoping it will just come to me when I see him.'

Two days earlier Stuart had received a letter from Laura in which she had told him about her relationship with Fielding. While it was pleasing to know it was never a love affair, the frank account of the kind of work the man got her into was disturbing. Yet it did explain the gossip that reached Stuart in London. He'd always assumed it was like Chinese whispers, that because she'd been seen in a couple of pin-up magazines everyone who passed on the story embellished it a little more until she became a drugged-up porn queen. But now he knew the gossip was based on truth, he understood why Jackie had often seemed extremely anxious about her friend.

While over in Glasgow he had managed to find Katy, the woman Laura had worked with for Fielding. She looked about sixty, worn down, confused and none too clean, clearly the result of a lifetime of heavy drinking and drugs. The smell that wafted out of her front door when she opened it had almost sent him scurrying away, but he had to bite the bullet and go in to talk to her.

He had never seen anything like her flat. It was so filthy and cluttered he could hardly bear to sit down, and things were made even more poignant when she showed him some photographs of her and Laura taken together in a club in Glasgow. Katy had been beautiful then, with her sharp cheekbones, smooth pale chocolate skin and shapely body. It seemed impossible that she had turned into this lumpy, bleary-eyed old woman in less than fifteen years.

She was so confused that she claimed to have seen Laura a few days earlier. So when she said Robbie Fielding had The Bear in Edinburgh, Stuart thought she'd imagined that too. It was only later that day back in the city, when he ran into a couple of old friends from way back when he was doing his apprenticeship, that he discovered Katy was right. His friends told him there had been some opposition to Fielding being granted a licence because he was rumoured to have been heavily involved in pornography and drugs. They said it was generally thought he got it in the end by greasing palms, but his days as a hard man were over now for he was in his sixties.

Stuart was no puritan – he'd looked at plenty of porn magazines in his time, and he knew all the girls in them were someone's sister or girlfriend. But Laura's letter, and seeing what had become of Katy, had shaken him. It was difficult for him to accept Laura had debased herself in that way. He understood that she didn't knowingly step on to that path, that it was more of a gradual slide on to it, and once there, earning so much money, she couldn't turn back.

Yet even more frightening was the knowledge that if Barney hadn't been killed at the age of eleven, and brought Laura's 'career' to a sudden halt, she might be as raddled, confused and prematurely old as Katy was now.

But setting aside the rights and wrongs of how Laura

lived at that time, he found it very odd that none of it had come up during her trial. It was said that she used drugs, and the glamour modelling had been discovered – one tabloid had even printed a photograph of her scantily dressed. Yet there had been no mention of pornography. Stuart would have expected that at least one of the sleazy characters she'd mixed with during that time would have rushed off to the papers in the hopes of making a few quid.

The most likely reason why none of it leaked out had to be that Fielding made certain it didn't. But why? According to Laura there was no love lost between them; she said he'd once threatened to mark her for life. So it stood to reason he was afraid for himself. That could be simply because his business interests wouldn't stand up to police scrutiny, but it could also be that he didn't want his dealings with Jackie made known.

Laura, however, didn't appear to suspect Fielding of any involvement in Jackie's murder. It seemed to Stuart that she'd only written at length about her relationship with the man because he was instrumental in getting her into the lifestyle that ultimately led to Barney's death. Even so, she put no blame on to Fielding for it, only on herself.

'*I had to snort coke to get through what I did, and then I had to have more to be able to live with myself,*' she wrote with touching honesty. '*I forgot about Barney's needs, I was dumping him on people, even leaving him alone for long periods. Jackie knew this and that's why she had him with her so often. If only he hadn't been with her that day.*'

Stuart didn't want to tell David about any of this part of Laura's life for fear that he would judge her too harshly. David had never been in a position where his high moral values were tested, and therefore he hadn't much under-standing of those who did transgress. But for David to understand why Stuart suspected Fielding he had to know the background between the man and Laura, so Stuart had been compelled to tell him some of it. David had made no comment, just raised an eyebrow and sighed in a way that suggested he wondered what more would come out of the woodwork that night.

They had just started on their second pints when Robbie Fielding came in.

Stuart had retained the memory of a big, muscular man with well-proportioned features and black, slicked-back hair, so it was something of a surprise to him that he recognized the wizened, white-haired, elderly man who had just walked in as Laura's seducer.

Yet there was enough in Fielding's expensive made-to-measure suit, the way his eyes scanned the entire bar, and a certain arrogance, to know it was him, even before he greeted the barmaid and Stuart heard his Geordie accent.

It was laughable really that he'd nursed hatred for this man for so many years, building him up in his mind to be rakishly good-looking and capable of going ten rounds with Mohammed Ali. In fact he was no taller than five eight, weighing perhaps thirteen stone. A beer paunch lolled over his belt, more loose flesh hung over his collar, and he wore thick glasses.

Stuart nudged David and smirked.

David glanced across at Fielding, then quickly looked away. 'You must be joking,' he said quietly. 'He looks as if he's off to a pensioners' party.'

Fielding walked the entire length of the bar which ran right down the left-hand side of the place, and made for a specific chair with its back to the far wall. It was high-backed, of plain wood, with arms and a cushion on the seat. The barmaid poured him a glass of Scotch and took it over to him. They had a few words together, then she went back behind the bar.

It was plain this was Fielding's customary routine. He now had an uninterrupted view of the whole bar, and he could watch the staff for any irregularities.

'I'm going to the bog and then I'll stop to talk to him as I come back,' Stuart said. 'If I manage to engage him in conversation, you come down after a couple of minutes. I'll do the just-back-from-South-America bit to see my home-town, and buy him a drink.'

'Be careful,' David frowned.

Stuart grinned. 'I can't see him doing me much damage, can you?'

Stuart walked up the bar, paused momentarily by Fielding as if he was trying to place a face he knew, then went on to the toilets. As he came back, he stopped again by the old man. 'I've just got who you are,' he said with a wide grin. 'You stole my girl twenty years ago.'

Fielding looked askance. 'I did?'

'Caledonian Hotel. Just before the New Year of '75. I was mending one of the door locks and you came along the corridor with her. I could see what had been going on so I cleared off to London. I ought to shake your hand and thank you.'

Fielding frowned. Whether this was because he was trying to remember, or afraid to say anything that would incriminate him, Stuart couldn't tell.

'Laura Brannigan!' Stuart said. 'She was a barmaid at the Maybury Casino.'

Fielding was visibly shaken. He looked round the bar as if to see whether there was anyone there he could call on if trouble started. 'There was nothing between us, she just worked for me,' he said defensively.

'Stuart Macgregor,' Stuart said, holding out his hand. 'She

talked about you a lot in the time she worked at the casino. And I never forget a face, especially under circumstances like that.'

'You've got it all wrong.'

'No sweat,' Stuart interrupted him. 'It was a long time ago and entirely unimportant now, I just recognized you and felt I had to speak. I've only been back in town a couple of weeks and I keep running into people from the past. It's weird, you think you've forgotten everything, then up someone pops and it all comes back. How are you doing? Still at the casino?'

Fielding shook the proffered hand but in a nervous, limp manner as if he didn't know what else to do. 'No, I left years ago. I own this place now.'

'Never!' Stuart exclaimed. 'I used to drink here when I was a joiner's apprentice. Can I get you something?'

Fielding hesitated.

'Go on, have one, there's no hard feelings,' Stuart said. 'Best thing that ever happened to me as it turned out. I went off to South America and had a ball.'

Fielding smiled weakly.

'Any idea what became of Laura?' Stuart asked. 'Did she go back south?'

'You haven't heard then?'

Stuart wanted to laugh at the man's expression. He still looked nervous, yet his dark eyes were gleaming as if he relished being able to pass on some information that would cut Stuart down to size.

'Heard what?'

'She's in prison, doing a life sentence for murder.'

Stuart looked suitably staggered. 'You're joking!' he exclaimed.

'I wouldn't joke about something like that,' Fielding said indignantly. 'Ask anyone. Her trial was last year.'

'Bloody hell!' Stuart said, shaking his head as if in disbelief. 'Well, you'd better have a drink now, and you can tell me all about it. Scotch, isn't it?'

When David joined Stuart and Fielding some five minutes later, he was dumbfounded by his friend's ability to play the part of a slightly slow-witted exile from Scotland who just wanted to catch up on what had happened in the city in his long absence. If David hadn't known better, he would have thought Stuart had never harboured any ill feelings towards this man.

'Guess what!' he exclaimed, looking up at David with a boyishly excited grin. 'An old girlfriend of mine is in prison for murder! Come and sit down with us, I've got to hear all about this.'

Stuart introduced David to Fielding and the older man launched into his story. Stuart played a blinder; he had exactly the right kind of awed and respectful manner to make anyone want to hold his attention.

'Not Jackie Davies?' Stuart exclaimed as Fielding mentioned the victim's name. 'But I knew her! She was Laura's oldest mate.'

David listened as Stuart incredulously talked about when and how he'd first met Jackie, the way anyone would if they'd just heard that person had been murdered.

Fielding gave a fairly accurate account of the crime, but he added nothing more than had been in the newspapers.

'But why would Laura kill her?' Stuart asked. 'They were best mates.'

'Laura's boy was killed in a car accident when Jackie was driving.'

'Barney?' Stuart gasped. 'He's dead?'

Fielding nodded. 'A terrible accident,' he said. 'It was back in the early eighties. A hit-and-run driver went straight into Jackie's sports car and it turned over. The boy was thrown out, killed instantly. Jackie had only minor injuries.'

'Oh no,' Stuart said, and tears welled up spontaneously in his eyes.

David had realized even from the little Stuart had told him about Laura's son that he had had deep feeling for him, and this was proof of the depth of them. Suddenly David felt a real pang of sorrow himself, imagining what it would be like if he lost his Abi or William in such a way.

'And there I was hoping I might run into Barney,' Stuart said sadly. 'I cared for him like he was mine. Only today I was thinking he'd be twenty-something now.'

Fielding sighed deeply, and David saw he was affected too. 'He was only eleven and a great kid,' Robbie said, his voice much softer, looking directly at Stuart with understanding. 'I was well pissed off with Laura at the time he died, but I wouldn't wish such a thing on my worst enemy.'

'So did she kill the other woman out of revenge?' David chimed in. He felt uncomfortable dwelling on the death of a child and wanted them to move on.

'It looked that way,' Fielding said. 'It never seemed right that she waited so long to do it though; it was eleven years later when she killed Jackie. Mind you, she was always a screwball, too much booze and drugs. I heard she went right off the rails after the boy died. But Jackie wouldn't hear anything bad of her – strange, that!'

'You knew Jackie too?' Stuart looked very surprised.

Fielding nodded. 'Yeah, I did some business with her. She wouldn't have got that place out in Fife but for me.'

'You must've been the minder she spoke about when I was working for her,' Stuart exclaimed, looking for all the world as if he admired the man. 'I can remember her showing me some plans for a farm in Fife, she said she'd run into some problems, but she had someone up here who had promised to sort it for her. I think that was in '76 or '77. So was that you?'

Fielding seemed to puff up with self-importance. 'Aye, it would be. I had something of a reputation back then for being the kind no one messed with. Laura was still working for me at the time, and she introduced me to Jackie.'

'Was it strong-arm stuff that was required?'

David noticed that Fielding did that extraordinary shirt cuff-tugging movement that he'd often observed hard men went in for. 'Just a question of showing the wankers who were trying to block the sale who was boss,' he said airily.

'They were after the place too then?' Stuart asked.

David had a job not to laugh. Stuart was such a straight-forward man that it had to be infuriating to him that Fielding wouldn't just come out and say what the problem was.

'Aye, that's right, but they wanted her out of the running, so they could get it cheaper,' he said. 'They'd already tried all the usual stuff of putting the frighteners on her. Well, I gave them some of their own medicine.'

'Who were they then? Local people?' Stuart asked.

'You're a nosy bastard,' Fielding said sharply.

'Sorry, mate,' Stuart grinned. 'It's only because at the time I kind of had a feeling she was having a hard time with someone up here, and I thought I was Jack the Lad then and wanted to give anyone a kicking that was bugging her. But you'd know all about that. Most of us guys were half in love with her. I'm sure you were too.'

'I wouldn't have minded giving her one,' Fielding said and laughed uproariously.

To David that was the most telling remark the man had made so far. Fielding clearly had no romance in his soul, only lust. But such men usually claimed to have made a conquest even when they hadn't, and as such he suspected Fielding had actually held Jackie in high esteem.

They had another round of drinks, then another, and there were moments when David felt sure Stuart would forget why they had come in here and reveal his true interest in Fielding. But he didn't. He skilfully wove questions about Jackie and Laura into general conversation about Edinburgh and its characters, and there was no doubt Fielding was warming to him for at one point he apologized to Stuart for his part in the break-up with Laura. 'If I'd ever met you I wouldn't have made a play for her,' he said.

'All's fair in love and war,' Stuart laughed. 'I went off to London with a right hump, but that's the way it is when you're young. I got over it and like I said before, I ought to thank you, for without that I might have stayed here and carried on working for peanuts.'

'You were well out of it. Laura was one hell of a treacherous bitch,' Fielding blurted out. 'She tried to ruin my business.'

David felt that was the only time that evening that Fielding had said something without thinking about it first. It was probably the whisky, for he looked stricken the moment the words were out.

'She did? What kind of business would that be?' Stuart jumped in.

Fielding hesitated. His hand waved involuntarily as if he was trying to search for a plausible alternative to the truth. 'Employment. I ran an agency for models, promotion girls and the like.' He smiled then, as though he was pleased with what he'd come up with.

'I once saw a picture of Laura in a men's magazine,' Stuart said. 'Page three stuff. Was it you got her that?'

'Aye. She was too old really, but I wanted to help her out. She was skint, and I was always a soft touch for single mothers. Worst day's work I ever did though – she poached my girls and set up on her own.'

'She didn't! The ungrateful little minx,' Stuart exclaimed.

David had to bite back a chuckle for Stuart sounded as though he was entirely on Fielding's side. 'Did you get back at her for it?' he asked.

'I didn't have to,' Fielding growled. 'Whatever she and her pal made went up their noses or down their throats, and they were small fry anyway. I called all the shots in Glasgow at that time and I knew they wouldn't get very far.'

'Laura worked in promotions in London before I met her,' Stuart said, seemingly innocently. 'I heard she was pretty good and knew the business well.'

Fielding looked at him sharply. 'You knew her before she got into drugs, laddie. You wouldn't like what she became.' He got up stiffly from his seat. 'It's time I checked my tills, nice talking to you both. Be lucky.'

'What do you reckon?' David asked as they walked back up the Grassmarket to the flat they'd rented. They were both disappointed that they hadn't managed to get anything out of Fielding that suggested he had a motive to kill Jackie, or indeed any information about his personal and business life. The abrupt way he had cut them off suggested he was suspicious of their interest in him too.

'Fielding's a weasel,' Stuart spat out. 'But somehow I don't think he had a hand in her death.'

'Why?'

'He would never have owned up he knew Jackie if he had. He might be old but he's no fool. Besides, it struck me that he had liked and admired her, as much as a slime-ball like that is capable of such emotions.'

'So what do we do now?'

'You go over to Fife tomorrow, book into Kirkmay House and see what you can get out of Belle and Charles. I'll go and see Angela, the woman that took over Laura's shop. I'll join you in Fife so we can compare notes. I want to have another chat with the barmaid in Cellardyke and see if she knows who Growler is. I'll meet you in the Smugglers Inn, on the harbour in Anstruther, at lunchtime on Tuesday. Is that okay?'

'Fine,' David replied. 'But how did it feel facing Fielding again after all these years?'

'Bit of an anti-climax, really,' Stuart said thoughtfully. 'He's just an old man still playing at being a hard nut. Shame he didn't say anything to wind me up, I could have reinstated the nightly brawls there used to be in that pub. He deserves a punch in the nose for dragging Laura into all that.'

David said nothing for a little while. He was thinking over everything he knew about Laura and what had been added to it tonight.

'What if she did really do it, Stuart?' he said eventually.

'She didn't,' Stuart replied.

'But how can you be so sure? Lies, porn, drugs and child neglect. Why not murder too?'

Stuart turned to him and caught him by the lapels of his jacket. For a second David thought he was going to head-butt him, something he'd seen him do to other men in the past.

'I know her,' he growled. 'I lived with her for over two years and I saw right down to her soul. She could lie and cheat, she wanted stuff I couldn't give her then, but she had no violence in her. I can still see right down to her soul, past all the crap life has thrown at her since we parted. And I tell you she didn't do it.'

'Okay, Stu.' David took a step back from his friend. 'I'm just worried you're getting in over your head. You aren't the same man that left Edinburgh twenty years ago, and I doubt she's the same woman either. If only we could have got Fielding to talk more about her ruining his business!'

'She didn't,' Stuart said. 'She started a brand-new one. He's just pig-sick cos he hadn't jumped in there before her.'

David realized then that Stuart hadn't told him everything in Laura's letter. 'So what was the business then?'

'Blue movies. And she made a lot of money.'

Laura couldn't settle to read that evening. She was twitching with anxiety, wondering what Stuart and David were doing and who they were talking to. Remembering the past was bad enough, but when she'd come to write it down, it looked even worse. She hadn't been able to get further than telling Stuart she'd gone into making blue movies. But perhaps it was a mistake to leave why, and how, to his imagination. If he had tracked Robbie down and persuaded him to talk, he would almost certainly distort the truth.

From the day she was stupid enough to spend the afternoon with Robbie in his hotel room, her feelings had fluctuated between gratitude to him for giving her a chance to earn good money when she most needed it, to the belief he was a rat of the highest order when she saw that he had always earmarked her for pornography. But once she had established herself as a veteran in the business, her opinion of him became ambivalent. On the rare occasions he came into the Glasgow studio she would chat to him; sometimes they even had a friendly drink together after a session.

But in May 1977 his wife left him to go and live in France, taking their children with her, and over a drink he confided in her.

Laura was not surprised. She knew he had been a lousy husband and an absentee father, and no doubt his wife was sick and tired of always coming second to his business interests.

What was surprising was that Robbie was devastated. As

he blurted it all out to her tears welled up in his eyes and he said he didn't think he could live without her.

Laura had plenty of reasons to be glad he'd got his come-uppance, not least that he was now experiencing the same kind of pain she'd felt when Stuart left her, but despite everything she couldn't take any pleasure in his misfortune. She felt genuinely sorry for him.

Throughout that summer she saw a great deal of him as she nursed him through his crisis. In his vulnerable and bruised state she found him to be a far nicer, gentler man than she'd thought. They had many a heart-to-heart over drinks or dinner, and he often came over to Edinburgh at weekends and took her and Barney out for the day. A seven-year-old boy needed male company and even though Laura didn't think Robbie was an ideal father figure, he was good with Barney. He played football with him, took him on scary rides at fun fairs, and added a little balance to his otherwise female-dominated life. It was during that period that she took Robbie over to Fife to meet Jackie.

Looking back, she supposed she wanted Jackie's approval. She felt her friend was suspicious about how she made her living, and Robbie could be utterly charming when he chose to be. She hoped he would put Jackie's mind at rest that both she and Barney were fine, and perhaps too she wanted to show Robbie that she did have some friends who weren't low life.

Jackie had developed a hard edge since she got into property; she wasn't above a little conniving or jiggery-pokery to get what she wanted. Although Laura hadn't been aware that day that Jackie saw Robbie as a useful ally, she clearly did, for she took his phone number and it transpired much later that she'd got him to act on her behalf in the purchase of Brodie Farm because she'd been having some problems getting it. Exactly what he did for her Laura never knew, nor did she have any idea how long they were in contact with each other afterwards. All Laura knew that day in Fife was that Jackie seemed to like Robbie, and that made Laura feel better about herself.

She and Robbie never became lovers again, but she did come to consider him a real friend, which made his subsequent actions far less understandable.

By the following summer their meetings had dwindled to less than one a month and Laura assumed Robbie had found a new lady. On the odd occasion he came to the studio, she was glad that he seemed perkier. He had also changed his style from always wearing sharp suits and dated slicked-back hair to casual, younger clothes and a fashionable blow-dry. She teased him about it once and he laughingly said that they all had to move with the times. That day he thanked her for her past kindness and understanding and said he would always value her friendship.

One day in January '78, Laura arrived at the studio as usual at ten, to find Katy and Pete, the blond hunk from Manchester, waiting outside in the cold. Katy was wearing an old embroidered Afghan coat and jeans, with a woolly hat pulled down over her ears, but she looked frozen. Pete, in a donkey jacket, didn't appear to be suffering, just perplexed because normally the studio was open at nine.

After an hour's wait, all of them huddling in Laura's car, a large van arrived and some workmen got out and opened up the studio doors. Pete went to inquire what was going on and he was told they'd been given instructions to clear the building as it was going to be used as a warehouse again.

It was immediately obvious that Robbie had known of this for some time, and they realized he must have given up or sold his magazine business, otherwise he would have found another studio to use. All three of them were furious.

Robbie knew they had rent to pay and children to provide for, yet he hadn't even had the decency to telephone one of them to apologize. As the photographer hadn't turned up, that suggested he was in on it too.

For Laura it felt like a stab in the back. She'd given Robbie so much of her time when he most needed a friend, listened to his angry tirades about his wife, comforted him when he said he was afraid he would never see his children again. Time and time again she'd dropped everything for him, she'd cooked him meals, washed and ironed his clothes, and Barney had formed a real attachment to him. She had believed Robbie was really fond of both of them, yet it seemed he had once again only used her for his own ends.

Pete went off disconsolately and Laura went back with Katy to her flat to discuss what they should do. They knew if they went cap in hand to the Social they wouldn't get any money for several weeks because they couldn't explain how they had been living up till now.

Katy was a good dancer, so she could go back to stripping if necessary. She had also been saying for some time that she thought she was getting too old for a business which was gradually becoming more demanding and explicit. She paid a very low rent for her flat, as well, so she didn't feel quite as dejected as Laura, only angry that they'd been let down so suddenly.

But for Laura it was a real calamity. She knew that a job in a shop or an office wouldn't even cover her rent, and unlike Katy who had a mother close by to keep an eye on her children if she had to work at night, she had no one to help her out with Barney.

They talked and talked around the subject. Katy even suggested that if push came to shove Laura could move to Glasgow where rents were lower and maybe take in a lodger who would babysit in the evenings so she could get work in a night club.

Laura asked her if she knew anyone else that produced pornographic magazines, for she was loath to give up her flat and work for far less money.

'No, I don't. Blue movies are the hot thing now anyway,' Katy said gloomily. 'And we aren't up to starring in one of those. They want nubile sixteen-year-olds.'

'So maybe we should make one,' Laura retorted. 'There isn't much we don't know about porn between us.'

It was like a flash of lightning brightening up the shabby room. They looked at each other and both grinned. 'Could we do it?' Katy asked breathlessly.

'I don't see why not. If we could find a photographer who has his heart set on becoming a film-maker, a couple of girls and the right man, we could start our own company.'

It seemed a preposterous idea, well out of their league, but at the same time it appeared startlingly right. For Laura, too, the thought of getting some revenge on Robbie was sweet. He would be pig-sick if they beat him at his own game.

'There's Tod,' Katy said excitedly. Tod had often been used as a stand-in for the regular photographer, and he'd told them he much preferred making films, though the only paid work he'd ever had in filming was doing a couple of short documentaries. Both girls liked him too; he was young and funny and he made things much less embarrassing for everyone.

'I could write the script and market the first film,' Laura said. 'Let's face it, you don't need much of a script anyway.'

Katy giggled. 'I'm pretty certain I could get a couple of girls, and Pete would be glad to be in it,' she said. 'But what would we do for a studio, and how would we distribute the film? Do you know anything about that?'

'We could make the first film in my flat in Edinburgh,' Laura suggested. 'That won't cost us anything. As for the distribution, I can find out about that.'

'But we haven't got any money to pay anyone.' Katy's face fell. 'We'll never get it off the ground.'

'I'll borrow some,' Laura said, thinking of Jackie. 'Look, I spent most of my early life in promotional work, this isn't that different. We can do it.'

They did do it too. Laura borrowed £1,000 from Jackie, telling her she wanted it to start up an agency for promotional work, running it from her home. She did of course get the inevitable lecture about keeping proper books and getting receipts for everything, but Jackie appeared really happy that Laura was doing what she called 'pulling her life together'.

Pete came in on it, bringing with him a petite redhead called Tansin, who had the biggest breasts any of them had ever seen, and Katy found Jazz, a pretty black prostitute who didn't want to work at nights because she had a child.

Tod joined them, bringing with him a wealth of knowledge about filming, and his charm. Laura had always secretly fancied him; he had an elfin look, with tiny sharp features, spiky hair and rather large ears, but the best thing about him was that he was very articulate and quick-witted, as well as being fun to be around.

He sent Laura to charm Sid Lyons, a night-club owner who was always interested in diversifying. Sid was in his late fifties, a great bull of a man with a hooked nose and a reputation for being as hard as nails. But he must have taken to her, for he promised that if the first video they made was up to scratch, he knew people who would distribute it. He wanted a half share of the profits, but he seemed sure that they would both make a fortune. Laura didn't believe he would have entertained her plan for a moment if he hadn't thought it would succeed.

'The script and stage directions she wrote were laughably amateurish. Pete was to be a man interviewing young women for a job as his maid. Tansin arrives and he asks that she try on her uniform, which of course is a short black dress and a frilly apron. But the dress is too small to cover her breasts, so he calls in his current maid, Jazz, to help.

Pete was surprisingly good at acting, but then he said he was only playing out a first-class fantasy of being a rich man employing maids and having his way with them. Tansin was quite vacuous, but her breasts and her pert bottom were virtually stars in their own right, so her wooden dialogue didn't really matter. Jazz played her role as the more experienced maid instructing the newest recruit in pleasing their master with great enthusiasm and sauciness.

It was a bitterly cold day in March when they began filming, but with the curtains tightly drawn, the fire blazing and all the extra lights Tod had brought with him, it was baking hot in the lounge. They had all snorted some coke, and loosened up so much they often had to break off because someone got a fit of the giggles at the wrong moment. Laura and Katy came up with more and more lewd ideas once they'd got into the swing of things, and at three o'clock when they had to stop because Barney would be coming home from school, no one was anxious to go home.

Filming was finished the following afternoon. It took Tod two days to edit it, and another week for him to get a friend to convert the cine film on to a video tape. Laura had to drive over to Glasgow on the Friday night to watch it with Katy, then take it down to Sid. She left Barney that night with Helen, a sixteen-year-old babysitter whose phone number she'd got from a postcard in a shop window. Helen was prepared to stay the night if Laura wasn't home by midnight.

It was far more shocking looking at the video than it had

been watching it being filmed. Laura was well used to seeing pornographic photographs, but they were just poses, this was real sex. She squirmed at the bit when Pete supposedly ejaculated on Jazz's face, even though she was the one who mixed up a bit of wallpaper paste for the scene and knew perfectly well it wasn't the real thing. And at the end of the film, after Pete had said goodbye to the two girls, then turned back to the settee to pick up a pair of flimsy red knickers and sniff them, her stomach churned. That was the settee she sat on with her eight-year-old son, and she felt ashamed that all that had gone on in the flat while he'd been at school.

'It's great, far better than I expected,' Katy chortled. 'Eat your heart out, Robbie, we're going to be in the money.'

Laura didn't stay with Sid in his office at the back of his club as he watched it, she couldn't. She went into the bar and ordered a double vodka which she gulped down quickly. She didn't dare think what she'd do if Sid didn't like it.

But Sid did like it. He had thousands of copies made and sold them on to various outlets in all the major cities. After taking out all the expenses, and repaying the £1,000 loan from Jackie, Laura and Katy got just over £900 each.

While they were jubilant that it had been such a success, the money had taken a long time to come in, and they'd eaten up what little savings they had. They'd both been forced to get bar work while they waited. Now they had to get stuck into making another film and turn it around more quickly.

Maybe if Barney had been a little more clingy or difficult, Laura might have stopped just long enough to consider him. But he was the easiest, most sunny-natured eight-year-old she'd ever met. He didn't mind coming home from school and letting himself into an empty flat. He'd happily make himself a sandwich and go out to play until she turned up. During the evenings she was on the phone all the time, and sometimes when she put it down she'd find he'd not only gone to bed all by himself, but washed up their supper things and tidied the kitchen too.

She and Katy made ten films that first year and a great deal of money, but it was never as easy again as it had been with the first one. They couldn't keep using the same people, and finding new talent was time-consuming and difficult. The girls had to be under thirty and attractive, and only someone really down on their luck would entertain the idea of starring in a blue movie. So they had to trawl through strip clubs, bingo halls, even resorting to hanging around Social Security offices to look for someone suitable to approach. But most of the girls they found chickened out the moment they saw the camera, and often they had to offer these girls money to stop them from talking.

Nor could they keep using Laura's flat. It was expensive to rent a studio and they had to have props and backdrops to make it look professional. Occasionally they took a hotel room for a couple of days, but this was fraught with the danger the hotel manager might suspect they weren't using it for a sales conference as they'd claimed. They made three films right out in the country in the Borders during the summer, but though isolated places seemed like a good idea while dreaming up a torrid camping story at home, in practice there were cow pats, flies, midges and the cold to contend with. Even reliable, ever-hard Pete, as they jokingly called him, sometimes couldn't rise to the occasion in a high wind or a sudden shower.

One of the most successful films they ever made was shot at Brodie Farm. Jackie was in London, and Laura had offered to go over to Fife to check how the building work was progressing. As soon as she saw the concrete mixers, scaffolding and piles of bricks she knew it would make a great backdrop for a story-line of a builder seducing the lady of the house and her friend. Jackie had furnished two rooms for herself in the farmhouse, so Laura took everyone out there when the real builders had gone home for the weekend, and by Sunday afternoon they had the film in the can. Jackie would have had fifty fits if she'd known.

Looking back on that period right up till the spring of '81 was like trying to remember the plots of films or television programmes she'd watched in the past. She could recall certain scenes vividly, even see the actors' and actresses' faces clearly, but it was just a montage of slices of action.

A blonde girl called Monica, gagged and tied to a brass bed, was one memorable one. Laura remembered so well how she and the rest of the team stood transfixed at the realistic way she struggled and bucked as the rape scene was filmed. Yet it was more realism than they needed when she wet herself, and it transpired that she'd been trying to tell them for some time that she needed to be untied.

There was Gary too, a real find, for he was hung like the proverbial horse and could keep it up. While mounting a voluptuous redhead called Irene on a kitchen table he had a bad accident. One of the legs of the table collapsed, and the pair of them slithered to the floor, knocking over a camera tripod, which in turn hit a jagged-edged tin bucket and flipped it up, and it landed on Gary's back, ripping a six-inch gash.

These were funny incidents that even the hapless victims laughed about afterwards, but there were also sordid ones, disgusting ones, and worrying ones too. It was a helter-skelter of panic, ruthlessness, fright, irritation and hysteria, with only brief moments of elation when everything went to plan. As for the actors and actresses, they were as diverse as the problems and blunders. Men like Dave who got on with it with good humour and consideration for everyone else involved were rare. Some were plain stupid, unable to follow the simplest instructions, others acted like prima donnas, constantly questioning and complaining. Some had about as much personality as a slug, others too much, wanting to be both director and star. There were the vain, the cruel, the greedy and the crude, some who had no idea about personal hygiene and others who kept everyone waiting while they primped and preened.

Yet all the diverse emotions Laura felt, along with the memories, problems and triumphs, were numbed by the coke she relied on to get her through each day, and the brandy she drank at night in order to sleep. She didn't want to think too hard about what she was doing, to herself or to others, and certainly not to what was happening to Barney.

In the early days she had mostly been back home by five-thirty or six, so Barney wasn't alone for long after school, but as it became harder to stick to office hours, she hired people to be there for him. Some were good, but others were indifferent or bad. Yet at the time she scarcely recognized the difference. The good ones were mainly students, happy to feed him, help him with his homework and tuck him into bed. But the bad ones were people she barely knew, just acquaintances only interested in the money she paid, not Barney. They ignored him, chatted on her phone while he sat waiting patiently for a meal which never came. Sometimes they never even turned up and he waited alone in the flat for hours.

Laura wished she could comfort herself with the knowledge she made it up to Barney in other ways, but she couldn't. She didn't see what was going on because she was too stoned and too busy thinking about making money.

He was such a good kid he rarely complained. He grew used to having to help himself to whatever food was in the fridge, to having to go to school in a dirty shirt because there were no clean ones. He even learned to cover up her negligence.

But though he managed to fool his teacher, neighbours and his friends' mothers that he was fine and happy and that his mother was always around, he didn't manage to hoodwink Jackie. She had finely tuned antennae where he was concerned, and even over the phone she could sense when something wasn't right. She would often make a surprise visit on her way through Edinburgh to Fife, and luckily Laura was usually there, or at least someone reasonably competent was looking after Barney. But these visits, however brief, worried Laura, for Jackie asked so many questions, made pointed remarks about the state of the flat and about Barney, and she sensed Jackie knew she was hiding something.

It was almost inevitable that Jackie would eventually find out what Laura was doing. She was too bright and intuitive to be fobbed off for long. Unfortunately she found out in the worst possible way, arriving early one evening in November '79 to find nine-year-old Barney alone in the flat.

Laura had spent all day filming in a seedy flat in Glasgow that they'd rented for a week. There had been countless problems with lights, props and the actors, and they finally finished filming around seven. But she didn't go straight home, even though she knew Barney was alone; she had to have a drink first.

She was tipsy when she got home about half past ten, and perhaps that was why she didn't notice Jackie's car parked in the street. But she did notice the smell of cleaning fluid as she walked into the flat, and her first thought was that Barney must have attempted to wash the kitchen floor to please her.

As she walked into the lounge Jackie jumped up from the settee, shocking Laura to the core.

'Where have you been?' she asked in a cold, angry voice. 'How could you leave Barney alone for so long?'

If Laura had been given some warning she might have come up with some good excuse. But her mind went blank. 'I got caught up with a client,' she said wildly. 'And the traffic was bad.'

'Why didn't you phone Barney to tell him?' Jackie asked. 'And I can smell the drink on your breath from here, so you might as well admit you've been in a pub.'

Laura couldn't remember much of what she said to that, some lame excuse she supposed, yet she could remember clearly how Jackie looked that night in an emerald-green mohair sweater and jeans tucked into long suede high-heeled boots that matched the sweater perfectly. With a table lamp behind her, her hair looked like a coppery halo, but her expression was anything but angelic; she looked angry enough to attack Laura.

'This flat was a pigsty when I got here, with no food anywhere,' Jackie raged. 'Barney was sitting here eating dry cornflakes, embarrassed that I'd caught you out. How often do you leave him alone like this?'

'I don't,' Laura insisted, but she was sobering up fast and she could see that Jackie had cleaned the room, and had probably been through the entire flat.

'Don't lie to me! Fortunately Barney doesn't seem to take after you, he's a hopeless liar. And before we go any further I've poked around in your room and I know now what kind of "agency" you are really running. Are you selling the blue movies or making them?'

She didn't wait for a reply, instead went into a rant about

the filthy kitchen floor, the unwashed dishes, the lack of clean clothes for Barney and his sheets which clearly hadn't been changed in weeks.

'If you lived alone I wouldn't care if you lived like a pig,' she said. 'It would have surprised me, seeing as you were once so fussy about cleanliness, but I wouldn't care. But drugs and porn! When you've got a nine-year-old?' She pointed out that she'd found some coke along with the videos in the bedroom. 'And don't try and tell me those videos are just borrowed from a friend, I know they are part of your business. What if Barney was to put one of them in the video machine? Or try the coke you left lying about so casually? Don't you care about him?'

'Of course I do,' Laura insisted, and knowing there was no point in trying to wriggle out of it all, she tried to explain that making films was all she could do to make enough money to keep herself and Barney.

Jackie waved her hands to silence her. 'There is absolutely nothing you can say to justify it,' she raged. 'It is wrong and you know it. Obviously you've got so far into all this filth that you've forgotten your duty as a mother, which is to keep Barney from harm. You don't deserve to have that beautiful child, leaving him all alone without a proper meal in a flat full of stuff that could corrupt his mind or actually kill him. What would you have done if you'd got back here tonight and found him dead from trying that stuff?'

Laura began crying and tried to gain her friend's sympathy by making out she couldn't help herself. But Jackie would have none of that; she was furious that Laura had lied to her about what she wanted a loan for.

'And you lied when you said you were working in a dress shop,' she spat out. 'I suspected all along that you were up to something seedy too, because you couldn't possibly afford this flat on a shop assistant's wages. But I never thought you could be debasing yourself in something as vile as this! Why? You knew that I would have helped you out if you'd needed money.'

'Why should I have to ask you for money?' Laura threw back at her. 'You aren't my keeper. I've got the right to start up any business I like. I don't need your charity or your opinion. And you had no right to come here uninvited and snoop around.'

'Has it occurred to you that if you are caught making these films you might go to prison and you'd certainly have Barney taken from you?' Jackie said heatedly. 'Can you imagine what that would do to him? For God's sake, Laura, pull yourself together and stop this right now. It's wrong and you know it.'

That night after Jackie had given up ranting, when they'd both cried and Laura had seen how clean the flat was, the cupboards stocked with food that Jackie had bought, she really did intend to stop making the films.

She looked at Barney in the morning and saw that he'd shot up in height without her noticing. He now reached her shoulder and was clearly going to be tall like his father. The stockiness of his early years was gone too, and he was skinny now. He had a look of Greg, but without the big nose, and his dark eyes had a wisdom in them beyond his nine years.

She realized too that she hadn't stopped to think about what subjects he was best at in school, and she'd never asked him if he had any idea what he wanted to be when he grew up. She hadn't even been to school parent/teacher meetings to hear about his progress or problems. If she didn't become a better mother he might go the way her older brothers had, raking the streets and getting into crime.

But for all her good intentions, it wasn't that easy just to stop what she was doing. Katy and Tod depended on her, and Sid wanted more films, offering her a bigger percentage of the profits. She did find a reliable woman to come in and act as a housekeeper and childminder each day after school. She took all the films, photographs and other incriminating evidence of her work out of the flat and rented a small office in Glasgow. She also made sure there was never any coke in the flat, and that she spent all weekend with Barney. But she didn't stop making the films, and the more money she made, the more she wanted.

Jackie was no fool, she knew Laura hadn't given up making films, but on her next surprise visit when she found everything in order in Albany Street, and nothing dangerous or corrupting there, she seemed resigned to it. 'I hate knowing you are involved in something like this,' she said, shaking her head despairingly. 'What is Barney going to think of you when he's old enough to understand what you do?'

'I won't be doing it then,' Laura said airily. 'As soon as I've got enough money I'll move into some legal business.'

'Then at least let Barney come over to Fife with me during his school holidays,' Jackie said. 'He needs other kids to play with, fresh air and normality. And I want you to go to a solicitor and draw up a legal document so that if anything should happen to you, I get custody of him.'

Laura had mixed feelings about Jackie's request. While she was happy to agree to Barney staying with her in the school holidays, and she could see the sense in having some contingency plan in the unlikely event of anything bad happening to her, she resented being policed. It seemed to her that Jackie had stopped being her friend and become her social worker. She didn't confide in Laura any more, not about the trouble she was having conceiving a child of her own, or about her marriage. It was obvious from the amount of time she was spending in Fife that she had left Roger for good, but she didn't admit it. And if she wouldn't talk about her problems, Laura felt unable to talk about hers.

Robbie had moved into making blue movies too; it turned out that was why he'd closed down the old studio. He was not amused when Laura beat him at his own game. He'd telephoned her several times threatening to mark her for life because she'd poached people he wanted to work for him, and he'd called on Katy at home for the same end. Laura also suspected he was having her followed, and there was the distinct possibility he would grass her up to the police so they would raid her flat.

She knew Jackie wouldn't be sympathetic about any of that, but she would have liked to confide in her about her torrid affair with Tod the photographer.

It had started out as a bit of fun, hot, steamy sex with no strings. But however much Laura had thought that was all she wanted, it turned out it wasn't. Tod was married, so their affair had to be conducted mainly during the day, and six months down the line Laura was feeling bruised and used.

She scrutinized herself in the mirror and saw an extremely attractive woman who looked ten years younger than her real age of thirty-four, despite drinking too much, doing drugs and not eating well. Her figure was perfect, her hair shone, and everyone she met remarked how stylish and elegant she was.

She had everything she ever wanted – money, beautiful clothes, a nice home and a new car – yet she felt desperately alone. She didn't understand how that could be, not when she was surrounded by people all day. It was that Stinky Wilmslow scenario all over again. She felt that no one really liked her for herself, only for what she could do for them.

More and more often she found herself thinking back to what she'd had with Stuart, the closeness, that all-enveloping love that made the world beautiful. Sex with Tod was very much like in the films they made, erotic perhaps, but never the magic carpet ride she'd known with Stuart. Afterwards, as Tod hastily put on his clothes and rushed off home, she felt so cheap. They never had time for a cup of tea together, a walk in the park or just a loving cuddle. Sometimes when she felt really low she thought he only made love to her to make sure she kept him on as cameraman. Even Katy, whom she had always thought of as a real friend, seemed only interested in the money they made together.

Laura and Barney spent Christmas of '79 alone in Albany Street, but they saw the New Year in at Brodie Farm with Jackie. Roger was there too, and Frank and Lena had come up from London with Belle and Charles. The stables were still in the process of being converted into guest rooms, and with only two completely finished, it was a little crowded in the farmhouse, but that made it seem even cosier for everyone pitched in with cooking and tidying up. It was so good to see Lena, Frank and Belle again, like the old days at Muswell Hill. They played board games for Barney's benefit, took long walks and ate huge meals, and at Jackie's insistence Laura stayed on in Fife until after her thirty-fifth birthday in early January.

It was the first time in a very long while that Laura felt at peace. She was touched that Jackie never once said anything that might alert the others that she wasn't running a promotions agency. Even Roger, who she knew had never liked her, had been pleasant. She was able to be herself, to enjoy seeing Barney so happy, and to laugh and chatter with the family as if she were a real member of it too.

Her memories of Barney during that period were some of the sharpest she had, so clear and vivid still they could have been just yesterday. Lena and Frank had bought him one of those leather flying hats with flaps that came down over his ears, and he wore it all the time. But he pretended to be Deputy Dog, the gormless character from the Disney cartoon, and mimicked his voice. At one point when all the adults were drinking he picked up a bottle of whisky and pretended to take a swig of it. 'Darn fine moonshine,' he said, staggering around as if he was drunk and making everyone laugh.

She remembered thinking that he would be ten in the spring, and how fleeting childhood was. Jackie and Belle were always saying what a little charmer he was, that he took such an interest in people, and cared about them. She realized then that he was the only thing in her life she could be really proud of.

Jackie came into her bedroom the night before she was due to leave to get Barney ready for school the following day. He was asleep in the other twin bed, and Jackie sat on Laura's the way they used to do when they shared a flat.

'It's New Year and a time for new beginnings,' she said, reaching out and smoothing Laura's hair back from her face. 'Roger and I are going to have one last attempt at saving our marriage, so I won't be coming up here so much this year. Will you promise me you'll behave yourself?'

There was so much affection and anxiety in her voice that a lump came up in Laura's throat. 'Of course I will,' she replied. 'Don't worry about me, I'm a big girl now.'

'You could come back to London,' Jackie suggested. 'I could let you have one of my flats. You'd soon get a good job there and we could all help out with Barney. Mum and Belle both adore him.'

'I belong here now,' Laura said, though she wasn't sure that was strictly true. She did love Scotland, especially away from the cities, and she often daydreamed of living by a loch in the Highlands, or on a river miles from anywhere.

But it was only a daydream, there was no work in such places and maybe she was too much of a city girl to live anywhere else.

'I feel I belong here too,' Jackie said sadly. 'Once I get all the guest rooms finished I'm going to try to get Roger to agree we live here all the time. But if he won't agree, and I doubt that he will, how about you running everything up here for me? When Barney's eleven he could go to that really good school in St Andrews. As long as I still had my room here to come up for holidays, you and Barney could have the rest of the house to yourselves.'

Laura had a sudden pang of conscience that she'd made one of her films here. Back then she hadn't really seen why Jackie had been so set on buying the farm. But in the last few days she had come to understand. There was a feeling of utter peace here, you could stand outside the farmhouse and see for miles around, and the magnificence of such a huge landscape made her problems seem insignificant. Jackie had made the farmhouse so pretty and homely that no doubt the guest rooms in the stables would be equally lovely. Laura felt she could be the happiest woman in the world living here.

'I'd like that,' she said, and took Jackie's hand and squeezed it. 'I would look after it too. I'd treat your guests like royalty.'

'Well, let's keep that plan in our minds,' Jackie said with a smile. 'I'll be back at Easter, and we'll talk about it again when I come to get Barney. Who knows, I might even be pregnant by then!'

She made that last remark with such longing that Laura sat up straight in bed and reached out to hug her friend. 'I hope so too. You'd make a wonderful mother. And if you are, I give you my word of honour I'll give up what I'm doing for good.'

'Would you?' Jackie asked, her voice muffled in Laura's shoulder.

'Yes, of course I will. Aunts have to be above reproach, just like you are to Barney.'

Jackie disengaged herself from Laura. 'In that case I'll make sure Roger and I are at it like rabbits,' she laughed. 'I won't lie there and think of England, but imagine you going straight.'

As David filled in his home address in the visitors' book at Kirkmay House, he glanced sideways into the drawing room off the hall and noted the opulent furnishings.

'What brings you to Fife, Mr Stoyle?' Belle asked from just behind him.

David straightened up and turned to the attractive blonde. 'I've got some business in St Andrews and I expect it will take a couple of days to wind up. May I let you know tomorrow if I'll need to stay longer than two nights?'

Belle Howell was every bit as glamorous as Stuart had said. Her pale blue silk dress rustled seductively as she moved, diamonds twinkled in her ears, and she wore a heady, musky perfume. But her smile didn't meet her beautiful blue eyes, and he'd got the distinct impression when he rang earlier and asked if she had a room free that she was reluctant to have any guests. It was only when he said he was alone that she agreed she had a room free.

'That will be fine,' she said. 'Do you play golf?'

'Not very well,' he admitted. 'Do you?'

She grimaced. 'Certainly not. I think it's the most tedious game in creation, and those outfits women golfers wear! But I'll warn you now, my husband is a golf fiend, and he's inclined to try to browbeat our guests into a game with him.'

David smiled. 'He wouldn't want to play with me. I'm actually useless at it, and I agree with you, it is tedious.'

'So what sports do you like?' she asked as she led him up the stairs to show him his room.

'Sailing and climbing,' he replied. 'I also like talking to beautiful women.'

David wasn't in the habit of saying such things, but he sensed that Belle was the type who was more likely to open up with flattery.

'You won't find many of those in Crail, Mr Stoyle,' she said, turning, and her smile was a flirtatious one.

'But I've found one right here in a guest house,' he said, feeling himself blush. 'And do call me David.'

'I'm Belle,' she said, as she opened a door at the front of the house. 'And this is your room.'

'A very pretty name, and it suits you,' he said as he glanced around the room. He thought Julia would wince at the flower-strewn flouncy curtains, the quilt and the frill round the dressing table which all matched. 'What a lovely room,' he added because he was sure she expected it to be praised.

'I pride myself on giving my guests the same comfort they have at home,' she said rather pompously. 'You'll find tea- and coffee-making facilities inside the wardrobe. If there's anything else you need, just ask.'

After Belle had gone back downstairs, David looked out of the window on to Crail's leafy Marketgate. It was a grey, rather cold day, not the best weather to explore somewhere new, but he had already roamed through the narrow winding lanes down to the harbour and thought it was the prettiest little town he'd seen so far in Scotland. Its great age – the very oldest part down by the harbour was built in the twelfth century and even the relatively modern Marketgate was laid out in 1600 – gave it enormous character and a diverse variety of buildings. He could understand exactly why Jackie, Belle and Charles had been attracted to it, for it had none of the dour, grey Calvinistic quality he'd noted in other villages. Many of the cottages were painted in soft pastel colours and there were tubs of flowers beside almost every front door. The bigger houses with front gardens looked as if they were competing for a best-kept garden competition, and a glimpse inside open front doors revealed antique grandfather clocks and Persian rugs, proving that it had remained a prosperous town. He hadn't spotted a single dilapidated house, but then he supposed developers jumped in quickly when any such place came on the market.

Yet however lovely Crail was, Belle didn't look as if she belonged here. Maybe his opinion of her had been coloured by what Stuart had told him about her, but he couldn't imagine her having anything in common with the tweedy kind of Scotswomen he'd seen as he explored. Or the coachloads of pensioners who stopped here for afternoon tea before continuing their whistle-stop tour of Scotland.

Around Putney, where he lived, glamorous women like Belle were commonplace. They lunched with friends in the chic restaurants, frequented the many beauty parlours, hairdressers and expensive dress shops. He supposed she had hoped to attract similarly-minded guests by making Kirkmay House so elegant, but in David's opinion, beautiful though it was, it had a chilly and soulless atmosphere.

Three hours later, at half past six, David returned to Kirkmay House. Belle came bustling out into the hall to greet him. 'Have you had a good walk?' she asked, and he could smell alcohol on her breath.

'Lovely, thank you,' David said, amused that she'd noted he hadn't taken his car, even though he'd parked it out on Marketgate, not in the drive. 'I'd already been down by the harbour, so I explored that road that goes inland, away from the sea.'

'There's nothing out there but fields,' she said, looking surprised.

'I like wide open spaces,' he said. 'I always envy people

who live in remote houses. I saw one out there that I really loved. It was called Brodie Farm – do you know it?'

Her face tightened. 'It's my sister's place,' she said.

'Really!' David exclaimed, determined not to be put off by her frosty expression. 'What a lucky woman – it's beautiful. Does she do bed and breakfast too? It looked to me as if the stables had been converted for that. My wife and children would love to stay there. I went up and knocked on the door to ask, but there was no one there.'

'There wouldn't be. My sister is dead,' Belle replied; her voice had an edge of cold steel. 'I'm taking care of it.'

'I'm so sorry. How tactless of me,' David said quickly. 'I have an unholy knack of putting my foot in it. Please forgive me.'

She just looked at him. He half expected her to ask him to leave. But she shrugged. 'There's nothing to forgive,' she said. 'You weren't to know. Would you like a glass of wine? I've just opened a bottle.'

David gulped hard. He'd thought he'd blown it. 'That's very kind of you. But I don't want to hold you up if you are preparing your dinner.'

She smirked. 'I don't cook when my husband is playing golf. I've wasted too many dinners in the past when he hasn't turned up. And I'd be glad of your company.'

David remembered Stuart had claimed she was a maneater and wondered if it was wise to take her up on her offer while her husband was out. But it was a heaven-sent opportunity to get to know her better, and it might be the only one he'd get.

He was still in Belle's kitchen at eight, for she'd no sooner downed another glass of wine than she began to pour out the story of her sister's murder. David found it fascinating – not the story of course, he knew that as well as she did –

375

but the way she portrayed it. There was very little about the actual crime, or indeed her devastation at losing her sister in such a terrible way, but a great deal about her court appearance as a witness, and how the murder had blighted her life.

It was almost as if she thought of herself as the true victim. Her life had been torn apart, the neighbours gossiped about her, and her business had suffered too. She also seemed very angry at being expected to look after Brodie Farm as well.

David wondered if she'd always been this self-centred, or if she was actually suffering from depression.

Fortunately he wasn't called on to make any comment. Belle seemed satisfied with the odd exclamation of horror and nods of sympathy.

By the time she was on her third glass of wine she vented her spleen on Laura. 'I thought of her as a sister, I did so much for her over the years, and yet she repaid me like that,' she said, growing red in the face with anger.

Her tirade went on and on: how Laura had fooled Jackie into believing she was her true friend and that she had given her money which she spent on drugs.

'You probably won't believe this, no one would credit anyone could be this heartless, but after her little boy was killed in a road accident she skipped off to Italy for a long holiday. I think he was better off dead than being brought up by a mother like that.'

David certainly didn't think Laura was whiter than white. There had been times since he joined up with Stuart when he'd doubted her innocence. But he knew for certain that she hadn't gone to Italy until a year after Barney's death, and it wasn't for a holiday, only to work. While he knew grief did strange things to people, he hadn't expected such malice.

He wondered if Belle told all her guests about her sister's death. He thought it would be very offputting for holiday-makers, for her intensity was enough to frighten anyone. He knew that if he and Julia had turned up here without knowing about it in advance, they'd probably have backed out the door double quick.

He found himself watching her rather than just listening. She lit up cigarette after cigarette, and she drummed her long pink fingernails on the table. Then she'd get up and pace the room, straighten china on the dresser. He didn't think he'd ever seen anyone quite so strung out and full of nervous energy.

Stuart had commented that he thought that two years after the event she should have at least begun to get over it, and David agreed totally. It was as if it had become an obsession. He was, to his knowledge, the only guest in the house, yet Crail had been buzzing with tourists that after-noon. Why weren't some of them staying here? Was it that potential guests asked around before booking a room and were put off by unfavourable reports? Or was it that she turned people away if she didn't like the look of them? He wished he'd thought to ask around about the guest house during the afternoon, it might have been enlightening.

He had only one glass of wine, refusing more when she attempted to top up his glass, yet that didn't slow down her drinking. She finished off the bottle, then opened a second one, and at that point she was turning her spite on to Roger, Jackie's husband. David really didn't want to listen to the litany of grievances she had with him, they were all about rents he was collecting on Jackie's properties, and as David understood it, the man was entitled to do this anyway. David had had enough; he wanted to go to his room and watch television in peace.

*

But mindful that Stuart would be disappointed in him if he didn't come back with some new information, he decided he must hang on a little longer.

'What made you move up to Scotland?' he asked, the moment she stopped to draw breath before another onslaught. 'Did you become disenchanted with London?'

'Not really,' she said. 'We came up here a few times to stay with my sister, and we saw how cheap property prices were. It was so tempting – in London a house this size would always be out of reach. I guess you could say it seemed like a good idea at the time.'

'I sense you regret it,' David said.

'I regretted it before we'd even repainted the front door,' she said bitterly, once again refilling her empty glass. 'It was a big mistake, but we had burned our bridges and there was no way back.'

'But Crail is lovely, I'd give my eye teeth to live here,' David said. 'And you must have made dozens of new friends?'

'You can't make friends here, it's a closed circle,' she said with disdain. 'Not that I really want to be part of that dull, flower-arranging Kirk set, they act like they think they are all superior to us English people.'

That wasn't how David had found people here. Everyone he'd spoken to had been very warm and friendly.

'And your husband? How does he feel about it?'

'As long as he's got someone to have a round of golf with and someone beside him propping up the bar, he's happy,' she said sharply.

The sound of the front door opening made David turn in his seat.

'Speak of the devil. Here he is, my husband Charles,' Belle said as if she had a bad taste in her mouth. 'And look at the state of him!'

David wanted to laugh, for Stuart had described Charles

as a handsome, smartly dressed playboy. This drunken man wearing loud checked golfing trousers with matching flat cap and a bright yellow sweater was swaying on his feet in the hall and looked more like a large Norman Wisdom.

'My little flower,' he exclaimed and staggered towards the kitchen with his arms outstretched. 'The champion returns!'

David got up from his seat to make his escape. Much as he had wanted to meet Charles, he didn't think he would get anything useful from him while he was so drunk.

'Don't go,' Belle said, then, turning to her husband, she frowned at him. 'We have a guest, Charles. David Stoyle. Now, behave yourself.'

'Pleased to meet you, Mr Boil,' Charles slurred, offering his hand.

Charles sat down at the table and began talking about golf. Belle interrupted him frequently, telling him that David didn't play and therefore had no interest in hearing about his game. Charles was too drunk to take any notice and Belle was desperately trying to drag David's attention back to herself.

It was acutely embarrassing to David to be party to the friction between the couple. Belle was in fact almost as drunk as Charles, but she took the moral high ground and berated him for driving home in such a state.

'I drive better with a few drinks in me,' he said. 'Eyes like an owl's, rapid reactions, and anyway, I came home early to be with you.'

'You don't drive better when you're drunk,' she exclaimed. 'Haven't you learned anything? It's only a matter of time before you hit someone again.'

There was a sudden electric charge in the air. Despite being drunk, Charles's eyes widened at what she'd said, Belle's face flushed pink, and she quickly leapt up to switch the kettle on to hide her confusion.

'I think we must all eat something,' she said too loudly and with desperation in her voice. 'You must be hungry, David? I could rustle up some pasta, or get a curry out of the freezer.'

There was no doubt in David's mind that Belle had blurted out something that was not only a secret, but a sore point. But he was also certain Belle wouldn't forget herself again that night, not even if he poured another gallon of wine down her throat. Furthermore, he knew that if he stayed he'd be dragged into their marriage problems. Charles was beyond talking, his chin was on his chest, and it was only a matter of time before he fell asleep.

'Not for me, thank you, Belle. But it was kind of you to offer,' he said. 'I'm bushed after driving out from Edinburgh and then the long walk this afternoon. I'm not used to this good clean air.' He made an elaborate yawn and got up. 'I'll see you both tomorrow.'

As David drove into St Andrews the following morning, his stomach rumbling with hunger because he'd refused breakfast at Kirkmay House for fear of being subjected to another of Belle's tirades, Stuart was in Morningside.

He had found Laura's old shop, Imelda's, at about nine, before it opened, and smiled at the name, guessing it was Laura's idea. The display of two very glamorous suits in the window, along with a couple of handbags, shoes and some costume jewellery, gave no hint that they were second-hand items. He peered in though the door, noting the elegant cream and gold decor, the neat rails of clothes, and the French-boudoir-style console table and chair which acted as a counter. He was impressed.

He took himself off to get a coffee, rather surprised by how much smarter Morningside had become in the last twenty years. He remembered it as a place where impoverished gentlefolk lived, the houses dignified yet a bit shabby, but it was clear it was fast becoming a very fashionable place to live. A well-stocked delicatessen, florist's and expensive lingerie shop were all testimony to the affluence of the new arrivals in Morningside. Even the butcher's and the greengrocer's looked upmarket. But he was fairly certain that it was still what his mother used to call 'a fur coat and no knickers' place, and Laura had clearly tapped into this when she decided to open her shop here.

He went back to Imelda's at half past nine and as he walked in an old-fashioned bell tinkled on the door. A willowy blonde of about forty, wearing black slacks and a white shirt, was arranging some handbags on a hat stand and turned to smile at him.

'I'm not actually open until ten, sir,' she said. 'I've got to nip out to the bank in a minute.'

'I didn't want to buy anything, I'm looking for Angie Turnbull,' he said.

'Then you've found her,' she said in a soft and cultured Edinburgh accent, which was as attractive as she was.

Her smile froze as Stuart began to explain who he was and why he'd come.

'I must stop you right there,' she said with a wave of her hands. 'I have absolutely nothing further to say on the subject. I gave what evidence I could at Laura's trial, and I cannot help further.'

Stuart knew that she and Laura had been good friends, above and beyond being employer and employee. Angie had supported Laura right through her period on remand, during and just after the trial. It was she who had packed up Laura's belongings in her flat and put them into storage, she'd continued to run this place, and Laura had given it to her because she saw no likelihood of ever getting out of prison to run it again herself.

Laura had also told him that Angie had written to her four months after she was sentenced, saying she felt unable to continue visiting her. Laura said she found this understandable.

Stuart didn't agree. To him, a friend was someone you stuck by in good and bad times.

'I don't believe Laura killed Jackie,' he said gently but firmly. 'I am going to prove it too. And when I read the transcript of her trial, I got the impression you believed in her innocence as well?'

'I did,' she said and looked flustered. 'But you see, there was so much stuff that came up in the trial that I didn't know about before. Being a witness for the defence was awful. The prosecution twisted my words and made me feel stupid and tainted somehow. It knocked me sideways, I hadn't been prepared for that.'

Stuart nodded. He'd heard from friends who had been called as witnesses in various cases that it was a stressful business.

'But it also changed your mind about her innocence?' he asked.

'Not at the time. I thought it was just a terrible mistake when she got life. But I had to come back here and carry on. I had journalists pestering me, women coming in off the street to harangue me. And all those frightful stories about her in the papers. I realized this was someone I didn't know!

'I'd promised to look after this place for Laura, but suddenly there were no customers. I didn't know what I was going to do. No money coming in, rent to find. I had nothing to live on.'

Stuart felt some sympathy for Angie then. He sensed she was genuine – the expression on her face and the tone of her voice told him that she hadn't really known which way to turn. 'I can imagine. I wish I'd known about it then, I would have given you some support.'

'That was the trouble, I didn't have any from anyone. I know it makes me sound feeble, but I got myself in an awful state.'

Stuart smiled at her. 'Well, you've obviously turned the shop round now. It looks great.'

'Thank you,' she said, blushing a little. 'I just had to get stuck into it, become single-minded. I would've gone under otherwise.'

'I know Laura would approve of what you've done,' he said. 'But surely your old feelings for her are still there? You were good friends, and I'm sure you wouldn't want her to stay in prison for something she didn't do?'

'Of course not,' she agreed. 'But I can't go through all that again. I've built back people's trust around here. And I don't know that I could ever trust Laura again; there are too many lies between us.'

Stuart knew exactly how that felt, and that other people's opinions and the poison they could drop in your ear could sway the staunchest supporter. Laura's state of mind after her conviction must have unnerved Angie too. Most people would back away in fright at that point.

'Look, I really do have to nip out to the bank,' she said, looking stressed. 'I don't want to be rude and kick you out, so if you could just hold the fort for me for ten minutes, we can resume this conversation when I get back.'

'By all means,' Stuart agreed. 'I promise I won't try any frocks on while you are gone!'

She laughed lightly and collected her handbag from a storeroom at the back of the shop. As she was leaving she turned back to him. 'If anyone brings anything in to sell, get them to leave it, with their phone number if they can't wait.'

*

For a couple of moments after she'd gone Stuart flicked through the racks of clothes, looking at the card labels on the garments, idly wondering how the system worked. There was a code number on each, along with the price, and he supposed Angie took her commission off that price when someone bought it.

He looked over at the counter, and there beside the till was a long, thin box which looked as if it might hold a card index file. Curiosity made him go over and open it. A quick glance told him that the letter before the code number on the garment referred to the surname of the person who had brought it in.

Anderson, Ruth, for instance, had brought in a whole load of stuff, each item listed on the day it was brought in, with the individual shop price beside it. Some of the items had a sold date beside them and a further note indicating when the money had been paid to the customer.

His curiosity satisfied, Stuart was about to close the file when he thought of looking up Jackie. Sure enough, she had a card under D for Davies, and there was a long list of items, all of them marked down as sold. But when he looked closer he saw that the last few items were brought in just a month before she died. Curiously the money owing to her was paid out in early July, some six weeks after her death.

He was puzzled for a moment, but then, thinking Belle might have collected the money, he flicked through to H and Howell. To his astonishment there was an even longer list of items here, going on to three different cards. The first few items brought in had the same date as the day the money had been paid out for Jackie's things. From then on there were many different dates, right up till just a couple of weeks ago. And she still had some items outstanding that hadn't been sold. One of these was a size 10 green trouser suit.

He shut the file quickly, and went over to the clothes racks. They were arranged in sizes and within seconds he'd found the suit. He might never have seen Jackie wearing it, but he knew it was hers by the vivid emerald-green that she so often chose. Furthermore, Belle was probably a size 12 or even a 14.

The doorbell rang when he was still holding the suit by the hanger. He looked round and saw it was Angie. 'No one came in,' he said to cover his guilt. 'I was just looking at the clothes. This one made me think of Jackie – she wore this colour a lot.'

'I think it could well be hers. Though her sister didn't admit it when she brought it in,' Angie replied, barely glancing at it. 'I should have sent it to a charity shop some time ago, I normally only keep things for two months, but I've hung on to that one because it's such a beautiful, expensive suit.'

Stuart was about to pursue the matter of Belle being a customer but Angie disappeared into a room at the back of the shop. When she returned she put some change into the till, then looked back at him. 'While I was at the bank I gave what you've said some thought,' she said crisply. 'I really can't help in any way. Everything I had to say in Laura's defence, I said in court. There was nothing left out. I gave as good an account of her private life, and her public one too, as it was possible to give. But it turned out that I didn't know her anywhere near as well as I thought I did. I never even knew she had a child who died.'

That surprised Stuart. 'Maybe it was too painful for her to speak about?' he suggested.

She gave him a long, cool stare. 'We were here in this shop together day after day for several years,' she said. 'I thought we were close friends, and as such I would have expected her to open up about something as shattering and recent as that. Then there were Meggie and Ivy, they rang here quite often, but she said they were friends, not her sisters. After the trial I found myself doubting almost everything she did tell me, and although I tried to stay strong about her, in the end I found that I couldn't.'

'It must've been hard for you.' Stuart could tell by her expression and her body language that even a charm offensive wasn't going to bring her round. 'I certainly didn't come here to harangue you further. I know there were compelling reasons why she resorted to subterfuge, I also know she didn't kill Jackie Davies; my only difficulty is finding the proof.'

'She is a lucky girl having you on her side.' Angie's face softened. 'I really do hope you find that proof. But I must get on now, I've a great deal of sorting out to do.'

'Does Belle Howell often come in here with clothes?' he asked.

Again she gave him a stern look. 'I really can't discuss my customers with you,' she said.

'I didn't expect you to,' he retorted. 'It just struck me as odd that she would come such a long way to the shop which has such strong connections with her sister's alleged killer.'

Angie shrugged. 'I was surprised the first time she came in, and a bit uncomfortable about it too. But some women don't like to sell their clothes too close to home.'

'Did she talk about Laura and the trial?'

Angie blushed and dropped her eyes. 'Yes, but that was to be expected. She was grieving for her sister and I knew her.'

Stuart sensed she wasn't going to open up about what Belle had said to her, so he gave her a card with his Edinburgh address and phone number and asked her to contact him if anything occurred to her later that might be useful to him.

*

'I thought Belle might have eaten you alive,' Stuart joked as David came into the Smugglers Inn on the harbour in Anstruther at twelve noon the following day. 'How's it been?'

'Let's just say that two days was far too long,' David sighed. 'I've never been so glad to leave a place.'

Stuart thought he looked tired and stressed. 'That bad, eh? Will a pint ease the pain of it?'

David smiled. 'It'll help. By day it was okay, but the two evenings! They both drink like fish and there was this atmosphere of imminent crisis all the time.'

Stuart got David a pint and he drank it like a man dying of thirst.

'Did a crisis arise?'

'No.' David laughed. 'But I can tell you there's a lot of muddy water flowing about between them, so much barely suppressed hostility and bitterness. I felt I had to keep my back to the wall at all times. No wonder they don't get any return visitors. I got chatting to the woman in the tea shop today, and when she knew I'd been staying there she said people have booked in there intending to stay for a week and they've left after one night.'

'But did you find anything useful?'

'Maybe. First we'll have to check on Charles's driving record, and if he's ever been charged with dangerous driving.'

David explained what had been said. 'Belle's actual words were, '*It's only a matter of time before you hit someone again.*' Without the '*again*' tacked on it's just a reproach. With it, it means he's definitely hit someone. They wouldn't have reacted the way they did either, if it was just a minor prang.'

Stuart frowned. 'He'd have lost his licence if he was drunk at the time.'

'Quite. That's if he was caught.'

'You think he might have hit and run?'

David shrugged. 'He's the kind of weasel who would save his own skin. And Belle's the kind that would cover it up for him if she thought it was going to affect her.'

'Just a minute!' Stuart's eyes were wide with horror. 'You aren't thinking he was the driver who killed Barney?'

'It struck me that it was possible, I mean, they can't get that many hit-and-run accidents out there.' David shrugged. 'They'd only recently bought Kirkmay House when the accident happened. Belle said she regretted buying it before they'd even repainted the front door. Suppose Jackie knew it was Charles, but didn't tell the police out of sisterly loyalty to Belle?'

'I can't see Jackie concealing that. She loved Barney,' Stuart said thoughtfully. 'She would have wanted the guilty person punished, even if it was her brother-in-law.'

'Maybe she would, but by doing so, she would also bring trouble down on her sister's head,' David said. 'That's Hobson's Choice.'

Stuart looked pensive. 'But if Charles did do it, and got away with it, surely he would have upped sticks and moved away? I wouldn't hang around in a place after something like that. Would you?'

'No, but then neither of us would have run off from an accident. Nor would we continue to drink and drive like he's doing,' David said. 'You said he's always been a slime-ball, so maybe Jackie thought she could make him toe the line and become a decent person by holding this over him?'

Stuart rubbed his chin reflectively. 'Are you trying to say that eleven years of guilt, and the pressure of being stuck in a place he didn't want to be, might make Charles mad enough to kill her?'

David chuckled nervously. 'I don't know that I'd go as far as to say that. But last night I lay awake for hours thinking about it, and it seemed possible. And there could be more to it. Charles might have had another woman and Jackie found out and threatened to tell Belle. Or maybe Jackie could see, as I saw, how unhappy they were together, and told Charles to do the right thing and push off and leave her sister in peace. Either way Charles wouldn't have liked that, not losing that big house and his income. I spoke to him for some time yesterday and I've never met a man with a more inflated ego.'

'He was always like that. I couldn't stand the man.' Stuart grimaced. 'But before we get carried away, we'll have to find out more about the police investigation into the hit-and-run. They would have discovered the colour and probably the make of car, and they would have left no stone unturned in tracking it down because a child died. How could Charles have slipped through their net? His car would have been damaged, and if he'd been drinking most of that day, some-one would have spoken up about it.'

'If he had a very supportive wife, he might have been able to manage it,' David suggested. 'But enough of that for now. How did your investigations go?'

'I'm meeting Gloria the barmaid at four this afternoon. I went into the pub in Cellardyke last night and we had a brief chat, but it was too busy to have a real talk. As for Angie, let's just say she's not batting for Laura any more.'

David ordered them another two pints. 'Really? Why's that?'

Stuart explained what had passed between them. 'I was left with the impression that she's a thoroughly honest, decent woman, but she's lost her faith in Laura.'

'So it was a waste of time then?'

'Not exactly.' Stuart grinned. 'For one thing I was impressed by the shop – that is evidence to me that Laura was entirely stable and hard-working prior to Jackie's death.

Also, when Angie had to pop out to the bank, I rifled through her index file of customers.'

David frowned. 'Why would you be interested in her customers?'

Stuart explained how the system worked and that he'd discovered Jackie was a customer. 'Well, she would've been, she was Laura's friend,' David retorted.

'Of course. But it isn't quite so understandable that Belle collected money owing to Jackie after her death, and then continued to be a customer right up to the present. You tell me why someone would go all the way from Fife across Edinburgh to flog her togs at the shop owned by her sister's killer, when there's another dress agency in St Andrews, just down the road.'

David sucked in his cheeks. 'Old habits dying hard? Maybe she felt it wasn't Laura's shop any more, just Angie's. But it is a bit peculiar, especially as Belle is so rabid about Laura. You'd think she'd avoid any reminders.'

'Even more peculiar is that I think she's been selling Jackie's clothes, not her own. Wouldn't most sisters hang on to everything for a long while?'

David frowned. 'How weird!'

'I would understand it better if she'd bundled up everything she wanted to get rid of and then took it all over in one go, but there were dozens of dates listed, with only three or four items each time, which suggests she liked to keep going there often. Why?'

'Maybe she thought Angie would refuse to take the clothes if she realized they were Jackie's?' David suggested. 'Or maybe they only take clothes according to the season. But I suspect you think she kept going there to sway Angela around to her way of thinking that Laura was pure evil.'

'That's the most likely reason I've come up with,' Stuart agreed. 'And it shows Belle had a lack of confidence in the conviction, doesn't it? Like she was afraid the case might be opened again with an appeal. Speaking of which, did you check out that track behind Brodie Farm?'

'Yes, it's very rough, but drivable. It goes on to another lane eventually, so the killer could have escaped that way. I also rifled through the visitors' book at Kirkmay,' David said. 'There was just one couple staying there the night before the murder; they'd been staying there for four days. A Mr and Mrs Langdon from Surrey. I don't remember seeing a statement from them when I looked through the evidence file at Goldsmith's.'

Stuart's eyes lit up.

'Don't get carried away,' David said dourly. 'That was probably because they'd left Kirkmay House well before the event.'

'But they might have overheard a row, or noticed the time Charles left that morning. Did you get their address?' Stuart asked.

David nodded.

'Then will you phone them and have a chat with them this evening? It's a long shot, I doubt they'll even remember anything after all this time, but it's worth a try.'

Stuart and David went for lunch at a café on the harbour that had the reputation for making the finest fish and chips in Scotland, and they chatted more about Belle and Charles.

The sun came out about three and Stuart walked with David to where his car was parked, and after saying he'd see him later that evening back in the flat in Edinburgh, Stuart went and sat on a bench on the harbour to wait for Gloria.

He had a great deal to think about, and while Charles had jumped to first place as prime suspect, Stuart was very aware that he needed time to assimilate all the various bits of information he'd gathered, and to analyse it carefully.

The sun had brought out a rash of people, and he idly watched them as they bought ice cream, shed their cardigans and jackets, and wandered aimlessly along the harbour. He wondered how many of them were already discussing how they would love to come and live here. The thought made him smile, for if they knew what it was like in winter with the raw east wind blowing in from the sea and almost cutting you in half, they would probably forget their plan.

Jackie had been different. She'd fallen in love with Fife on her first visit and that had been a bitterly cold, grey day as he remembered. She always said she found the wind bracing, that it blew all the debris she collected up in London out of her head. She loved the lack of sophistication in the fishing towns, she said people's lives here were meaningful and honest. But what was it that made Belle and Charles move up here? They certainly weren't the kind to embrace Jackie's views. And he didn't believe Belle's explanation to David that it was because property was so much cheaper. Who would take themselves off some four hundred miles to live in a bigger house that none of their old friends would ever see?

He didn't believe either that they'd fallen into the trap of imagining that running a guest house was a little gold mine, as so many people had. They just weren't that naive. Perhaps Roger was right when he said Charles was in trouble in London.

He needed to get at the truth about why they came here, and even more importantly why they stayed when they so clearly didn't like it. But how? Would Lena know?

Somehow he didn't think she'd tell him even if she did know. She'd lost one daughter and she wasn't likely to dish any dirt about the other one.

*

'Hello, Stuart.'

The greeting startled him and he turned to see Gloria standing behind his bench. 'I've brought someone to meet you,' she said, looking a little anxious and turning towards a man of about sixty just behind her. 'This is Ted Baxter, a friend of Jackie's. He's a wee bit reluctant, so please be gentle with him.'

Stuart leapt up, guessing that the man must have been one of Jackie's lovers, even if he was rather old. 'Stuart Macgregor,' he said, holding out his hand to the man. 'I do hope Gloria hasn't implied that I'm some kind of bloodhound. It's good to meet you.'

Baxter's handshake was firm and his smile was warm. 'Jackie told me about you years ago,' he said. 'She said you were the best joiner she ever had, and that you were a man who could be trusted.'

Stuart was touched and flattered by the man's statement, but the sound of his voice struck an immediate cord. It was a very deep voice, practically a growl, and his heart leapt because he was sure this was the man Jackie called 'Growler'.

He wore a well-worn tweed jacket with leather patches on the elbows, and cheap twill trousers, and he was greying and thin on top, slender and only about five feet eight. It seemed inconceivable that Jackie would have had a fling with anyone so old and ordinary. The only remarkable things about him were his voice and his slightly prominent duck-egg-blue eyes.

'You must have got to know Jackie very well for her to have bored you with tales about her early days in the property business,' Stuart said lightly.

'I did,' Ted said simply, and a look of pain crossed his face. 'I miss her so much that sometimes I feel I can't go on. Gloria knows this and that was why she persuaded me to come and meet you. She told me it would make me feel better.'

'Ted would rather talk to you alone, Stuart,' Gloria said. Her anxiety was such that her voice quivered. 'I have already told him what you're about. He needs assurance that anything he tells you is in strict confidence.'

'You have that assurance,' Stuart said, looking Ted straight in the eye. 'All I want to do is find enough new evidence so Laura can appeal against her sentence, for I know it wasn't her who killed Jackie. Now, shall we go somewhere where we can talk?'

Gloria took them to her cottage which was in the narrow street which ran from Anstruther to Cellardyke. The cottage was tiny, rather dark, and the wrong side of the road for a sea view, but it was a real home, not too tidy, lots of photographs of her family on the walls, comfortable chairs and a smell of something good cooking in the oven.

She made them a pot of tea, put it down on the coffee table and then said she was going out. 'Make yourselves at home. I'll be back about half past five.'

'I'm a surveyor,' Ted said awkwardly as the door closed behind Gloria. 'As you probably know, the first cottage Jackie bought up here was just along the road. That's how I met her – she called me to survey it. Later, whenever she wanted to buy another place, or was just considering one, she always called me.'

'I remember her telling me she'd found someone good,' Stuart said. He didn't actually remember any such thing, but he could see how nervous Ted was and wanted to put him at his ease.

Ted gave a watery smile. 'We became good friends, and as I knew the best tradesmen around here I used to give her a bit of advice, call in and check on work in progress, that sort of thing.'

'So you must have known her almost as long as me,' Stuart said. 'She got the idea about buying a place here the first time she visited Laura and me in Edinburgh and I brought her out this way to show it off.'

Ted nodded. 'Nineteen years. I just wish I could go back to the beginning again and do everything differently.'

Stuart raised an eyebrow questioningly.

'Well, as you probably realize, I'm married.' Ted blushed furiously. 'It was never a happy marriage, and I should have left my wife the moment I knew I was falling in love with Jackie, and taken the chance that she felt the same way about me. But I didn't think a beautiful and highly intelligent woman like her could possibly want me. Besides, she was married too, and some ten years younger than me.'

There was something very touching about this frank admission and Stuart thought he could understand why Jackie had liked Ted.

'Were you lovers all that time?' Stuart asked gently.

'Dear me no, that came years later.' Ted looked quite shocked at the suggestion. 'I called her Mrs Davies and she called me Mr Baxter for a whole year before we even began using Christian names. We'd chat over cups of tea, and I learned about her family, her husband, about Laura and Barney and you too, Stuart. She was so vivacious, so full of ideas, and funny too. Of course all the tradesmen who did jobs for her liked her – she was unique and very special.'

'Yes, she was,' Stuart agreed. 'I never met anyone who worked for her that wasn't a little bit in love with her. Me included.'

'I was a bit jealous of you, if truth be told,' Ted admitted ruefully. 'You see, she used to talk about you a lot, especially after you left Edinburgh and went down to work for her in London. She was worried about you because Laura had broken your heart, but she also liked you a great deal. I thought it was only a matter of time before you were ousting that husband of hers.'

'There was nothing like that between us,' Stuart said.

'I knew that later, but when a man wants a woman every other male is a threat.' Ted smiled wryly. 'Anyway, in '77, Peggie, my wife, had a riding accident which left her paralysed from the waist down. Jackie still wasn't living here all the time then of course, only coming up for holidays. I remember calling in on her one evening after visiting Peggie in hospital. I was very down because I didn't know how I was going to cope when she came home and became dependent on me for everything.'

'I expect Jackie got the whole story out of you,' Stuart said. 'She was always good at that.'

'That's exactly what happened,' Ted replied. 'I blurted out the whole thing – that we'd never had a good marriage and that she was so bitter and angry about the accident that I knew it was going to be hell from now on.'

'What advice did Jackie give you?'

'To buy a plot of land and build a bungalow suitable for a disabled person in a wheelchair. She thought that Peggie would accept her disability in a new home specially designed for her. She even offered to help me by getting in touch with people who specialized in aids for the disabled and understood what was needed. She suggested I could get a carer in during the day while I had to work which would relieve the pressure on me. That kind of sealed my friendship with Jackie because she was the only person I could admit to how scared and frantic I felt. I certainly couldn't admit it to my son or daughter, not even to the doctor.'

'Did you act on her advice?'

'Yes, I did. I bought a plot of land by the golf course in St Andrews, found the best architect in Fife, and really got stuck into it. Jackie came out a few times while it was being built; she was very encouraging and supportive.'

'Tell me, Ted, did she have a nickname for you?' Stuart asked.

Ted smiled. 'Yes, a ridiculous one. She called me "Growler". Why d'you ask that?'

'She mentioned that name to Laura. I just wanted to check it was you.'

'I never actually met Laura,' Ted said thoughtfully. 'I feel I have because Jackie talked about her so often, but then I didn't really know any of her other friends either. I know Belle and Charles Howell of course, I did the survey on Kirkmay House for them, but once Jackie and I began our affair we had to be so careful that I never called at the farm if she had anyone else there with her.'

'So when did it start?' Stuart asked, relieved that the man was finally getting to the point.

'In 1980, a year before Barney was killed. I often saw the wee boy when he was staying with her. She loved him like he was her own. I called round one afternoon and she was crying because she was worried that Laura was neglecting him. I gave her a cuddle and it just flared up.'

Ted closed his eyes for a moment. He often relived the events of that afternoon for it was the most astounding, wonderful and thrilling day of his whole life.

The front door of the farmhouse was open because it was a warm, sunny day in May. He called out to Jackie and she called back to ask him to come in. She was on her knees cleaning out a kitchen cupboard, and when she looked round he saw she was crying.

He instinctively knew the cause of it was Barney, for she often became choked up when she spoke of him. But this was the first time he'd actually seen her cry about anything.

When Peggie cried her face became red and puffy, her

mouth wobbled and she looked ugly. But Jackie looked beautiful. She was wearing a faded denim dress with studs down the front, her legs were bare, and her hair was tied up in a ponytail, making her look closer to her early twenties than her real age of thirty-seven. Her complexion was flushed but only delicately so, and the tears were trickling down her cheeks like dew drops.

He went over to her and lifted her up, embracing her tightly. 'Don't cry, you'll see him again soon,' was all he said.

He didn't actually mean to kiss her lips, he wasn't bold enough for that. But suddenly her mouth was on his and she was kissing him. It must have been ten or twelve years since he'd last experienced a real kiss, so long ago that he'd forgotten how arousing kissing was. It was like drowning, he could feel himself sinking and sinking into it, and never wanting it to end.

Stuart's chuckle brought him out of his reverie. 'It was that good, was it?' he said. 'You went off down the time tunnel then.'

Ted smiled sheepishly. 'You can have no idea how it was for me,' he said. 'All those years I'd thought the love was just on my side. But it wasn't, she felt the same way.'

'It must have been tough for you. I mean, having a disabled wife,' Stuart said.

Ted looked hard at the younger man at first, thinking that remark was veiled sarcasm, but he saw only sympathy and understanding.

'Sometimes I felt as if I was being crucified,' Ted said glumly. 'I had turned myself inside out to make things right for Peggie – the bungalow was beautiful, the garden had been landscaped – but although she'd been home from the hospital for getting on for three years, she was making no attempt to help herself. She had in truth become a monster, Stuart, nothing pleased her, she acted like she hated me.

'Then suddenly I get a glimpse of heaven, but a glimpse is all I am ever going to have. I couldn't be with Jackie for more than a couple of hours here and there, I had to go home and take care of Peggie. Can you imagine washing a woman, helping her to the toilet, cooking her meals and cleaning the house when all the time she is sullen and bitter? She acted like the accident was my fault, nothing I could do or say would please her. And she's still that way. I can understand why people kill, I'll admit now there have been times when I have been sorely tempted.'

Tears began to flow down Ted's face, and Stuart leaned forward and squeezed the man's arm in sympathy. 'I might not have been through that myself, man,' he said softly. 'But I can imagine.'

Ted mopped his face with a handkerchief and tried to pull himself together. 'When Barney was killed I thought our love affair would die too. Jackie took it so hard, and I couldn't be there all the time to comfort her.'

'Did she ever say anything about the accident to you?' Stuart asked.

'Only that the other car came round the bend in the middle of the road straight towards her and she heard Barney scream. She said the next thing she remembered was a fireman talking to her, explaining how he had to cut away part of the car to get her out. Miraculously she wasn't that badly hurt. I saw her car later that day and it was so badly crushed you wouldn't have thought anyone could have survived the crash, but all she had was a broken arm, and some very nasty cuts and bruises.'

'Did she recognize the driver of the other car?'

'She said she didn't.'

'Did you believe her?'

Ted hesitated. 'No, to be honest I didn't. I don't know why, after all it was in summer when there are lots of strangers around. I just got the idea in the back of my mind that she was hiding something, but I couldn't keep probing, she was too upset about the wee boy.'

'Were the police thorough in their investigation?'

Ted nodded. 'They called everywhere, a virtual house-to-house search. Every garage owner was questioned, they called in at every pub and hotel. But if the other car wasn't too badly damaged it could have got half-way to the Forth Bridge before the ambulance even arrived; another couple of hours and it could well have been in England.'

'Is it at all possible that the driver could have been Charles Howell?' Stuart knew he shouldn't ask such direct questions but he had to.

Ted looked horrified. 'No, it can't have been. Whatever makes you think such a thing?'

'Just something someone said,' Stuart replied.

'Well, they had no business to be saying such things,' Ted said indignantly. 'Besides, he was down in London at the time.'

'How do you know that? Stuart asked.

'Because Jackie told me. Belle went in to visit her in the hospital the evening it happened. She said Charles couldn't come with her because he was in London. He flew back the following day, stayed a few days until Jackie was discharged from hospital, then went back to London to collect his car. I remember it clearly because Belle stayed at the farm with Jackie to look after her, and that meant I couldn't go there.'

'He left his car in London, did he?'

'Yes, well, it was an emergency, Belle needed him and driving it back would have taken too long.'

From what Stuart remembered of Charles he was hardly the type to rush home just because Belle needed him. 'Isn't it possible he was having his car repaired?'

Ted looked shocked. 'Surely not!'

'I sincerely hope I'm wrong,' Stuart said. 'I've never liked Charles, but I don't want to think he was responsible for killing Barney. But tell me, Ted, how was Jackie with Charles after that accident?'

'I don't think I was ever with them both together,' Ted said, frowning as if he was trying to remember. 'Jackie had never really liked him. What she actually said was that he was "an insincere, lying, womanizing bastard".' Ted half smiled. 'Jackie didn't mince her words about people.'

Stuart laughed. 'It was one of the things I liked best about her,' he said. 'But can you remember her making any remarks about him after Barney's death?'

'She did say once that she'd make sure he never got a penny of her money when she died,' Ted said. 'I asked how she was going to do that when he was married to Belle.'

'And what was her answer?'

Ted smiled. 'She laughed and said something about Belle being almost as greedy as Charles and if she offered Belle money to leave him, she'd take it. But I didn't take any of that seriously. Jackie often made off-the-cuff remarks. Besides, Charles was a good ten years older than Jackie. I thought he'd pop his clogs long before she did.'

'Would you say that Jackie disliked him more after Barney's death?'

'Not that I noticed. She spoke about him in much the same way she always had – witheringly! Nothing to give me the idea he might be responsible, and I'm sure that is what you are getting at. But that first year was hideous: Jackie was grieving for the boy, full of guilt that he'd died while in her care, and worried about Laura too. I felt powerless to help, I couldn't even stay overnight to hold and comfort her. So I wasn't taking note of things she said about Charles or Belle.'

'Did she think Laura blamed her?'

'She did in the first year. And she couldn't understand why Laura didn't attack her for it, verbally or physically. But from what I understood Laura held herself responsible, no one else. You must understand that I never met Laura, so my opinion is only based on gut reaction to what I was told. But after she went off to work in Italy, Jackie often showed me cards and letters from her, and believe me, there was no blame, no nasty little digs or sarcasm in them. I'd say Laura felt her boy's death was her punishment for the kind of life she'd been living.'

Stuart nodded. That was exactly the impression he'd formed too from Laura, and it was good to hear the same from a man who had no reason to want to defend her.

'Did Jackie tell you about Laura's life, or did you only find out during the trial?'

'A bit of both,' Ted said. 'Jackie was a loyal friend, she wasn't one for dishing dirt. But in the two years prior to Barney's death she had confided in me about the pornography and the drugs. She didn't want to, but I asked a great many questions about why she had Barney there so often, and why she often seemed so worried sometimes. She had to talk to someone. And once our affair began we hoped that one day we could be together for ever.'

'Why then didn't she call you on the day she died?' Stuart asked.

'That is a question I've asked myself a million times,' Ted said with a sigh. 'I've also asked myself just as many times why I didn't sense something bad was happening to her and go over there. I didn't hear about it till the evening when it was on the news. They only said that a woman had been killed in an isolated house near Crail, nothing much else, but even before they showed a picture of the house I kind of knew it was Jackie. But to go back to your question about why she didn't phone me – she never phoned me at home. She knew the number, I always said she must keep it by her in case of an emergency, but she never used it. I usually phoned her from a public box because Peggie has ears like radar.'

'I take it Peggie was your reason for not going to the police too?' Stuart said with a touch of sarcasm.

Ted blushed. 'Yes, she was,' he said, hanging his head. 'But not the way you are thinking. Let me explain how it was at the time.'

12 May was a beautiful day. Ted had been working out in the garden all afternoon. Peggie was indoors sitting by the patio doors doing a jigsaw on a large tray across her wheelchair.

Around five it became chilly, and he went in to prepare the evening meal. He put his head round the sitting-room door to ask Peggie if she'd like a cup of tea, and how she was getting on with the jigsaw. She ignored both questions so he went back into the kitchen.

Once the meal was ready and the table laid in the dining part of the kitchen, he turned on the television there, and went back into the sitting room to get Peggie.

'Turn the sound up,' she snapped at him as he wheeled her up to the table.

It was one of those moments that he had had so often in the last few years, when he fervently wished the riding accident had killed her. She hadn't been the easiest of women to live with even before that. She was domineering, insensitive and self-centred and if she didn't get her way she sulked for days on end. But she had been an asset to him in his business, the perfect hostess, a great cook, and it was she who was responsible for bringing so many clients to his firm of surveyors. She'd been a good mother too; both Robert and Joan had done very well at school and gone on to university. It was only when they left home for good, moving down to London to better-paid work than they could get in Scotland, that Ted realized he and Peggie had nothing left in common. She lived for riding, while he liked reading, painting and gardening.

The accident changed everything. Peggie had always cared about her appearance; she was an attractive, slender woman with long brown hair, and she wore her clothes with style. But once she knew she would never walk again she lost all interest in the way she looked. She resented that Ted had sold their beautiful old house in South Street, right in the centre of St Andrews, even though it was obvious she could never live there, and she said she hated the bungalow.

Robert and Joan had nothing but praise for it. They remarked on how the sun came in all day and they thought the view of the golf course beyond the garden was wonderful, for the old house had only had a small garden and no view at all.

But all Peggie did was complain. Ted understood her frustration at not being able to walk, but she didn't even try to do things for herself. There was a constant whinge of 'That must be done', or 'How many more times must I point out you haven't done so and so yet?' When he had to go out to do a survey, she was on to him the moment he got back. If he went into his study to write a report, she interrupted him. There was no reason why she couldn't make a cup of tea herself, iron a few clothes sitting down, or even cook simple meals, for everything in the kitchen had been designed for a person in a wheelchair, but she refused point-blank, as if she were totally incapacitated.

Her weight had ballooned up to fourteen stone since returning home from hospital, and most days she didn't even bother to brush her hair. She would stay in her nightdress if

Ted didn't insist he helped her dress. None of the carers he took on to help lasted long, for she was as nasty to them as she was to him. Even Robert's and Joan's visits home were getting less frequent. Peggie did always improve when they were there, but she morally blackmailed them, making them feel guilty they lived and worked so far away.

Ted turned up the sound on the television just as the local news began.

'A woman was found dead this afternoon in a house near Crail in Fife,' the pretty blonde newscaster said, and even before a shot of Brodie Farm came on the screen, he knew it was Jackie and it was all he could do not to scream out his shock and pain.

He supposed there must have been some more information about Jackie and that the police had arrested someone because he remembered Peggie questioning him.

'Isn't that the woman you've surveyed properties for?' she asked. 'I always thought there was something fishy about a Londoner wanting to come and live there. And she was the woman driving the car when a boy was killed! She had it coming to her. I bet she made her money from drugs.'

'Shut your mouth, you stupid cow, you know nothing about her!' Ted yelled at her, then jumping up from the table he ran into the bathroom where he was violently sick.

Over the next couple of days, as he waited for the whole story of what had happened to filter down to him, he was so distraught that he contemplated taking his car out into a remote place and killing himself with the exhaust fumes. He didn't care what would become of Peggie, he didn't even care if the whole world found out about his affair with Jackie. If he couldn't have her in his life, he didn't want to live.

But reason prevailed. He knew Robert and Joan would

never understand his committing suicide and leaving their mother alone. Whilst he thought he ought to go to the police and tell them about his relationship with Jackie just in case he could help them in any way with their investigation, if Peggie found out she'd be impossible.

He had only managed to stay and care for her all these years because of the few hours of happiness he had with Jackie each week. Griefstricken and without that respite, he knew he couldn't cope with Peggie raging and ranting at him all day about Jackie on top of everything else. And that was what she would do, for if she saw a chink in anyone's armour, she liked nothing better than sliding the knife in. Ted knew he might snap and attack her, and he couldn't put himself in that position.

From what he heard at the time it was an open and shut case that Laura had killed her anyway. He had never met Laura and all he could tell the police about her relationship with Jackie was hearsay. Belle and Charles knew everything about her, so he would leave it to them to pass it on.

'So that's why,' Ted said with a shrug, when he'd finished saying his piece. 'I dare say that makes me look cowardly, but at the time I felt it was the best course for everyone. I suppose too that I was so blinded by my own grief that it never occurred to me Laura might be innocent.'

'You must have followed the trial very closely?'

'Yes, I read all the accounts in the papers and watched the news.'

'Did anyone ever say anything you knew to be untrue?'

'Yes, it was brought up, I think by Roger, Jackie's husband, that Laura owed Jackie a lot of money. I know for a fact that wasn't true. Jackie gave Laura the start-up money for the shop. It was a gift.'

'Really?' Stuart exclaimed. 'Are you absolutely sure of that?'

'Totally. I was with Jackie the night she wrote the cheque. I actually posted the letter to Laura on my way home. She told me that she'd gone with Laura to see the shop in Morningside, and that over lunch the pair of them had costed out what she would need – the lease money, legal fees, rails, decorations and some advertisements to attract women to bring their clothes in. Laura was intending to go to the bank for a loan, but Jackie was afraid they would make the repayments larger than that kind of business could stand. Her exact words were 'Bugger it, I'm going to give it to her. After all she's been through she deserves it.'

'You're sure she didn't ask for it back later?'

'Did you ever know Jackie to go back on a deal?'

'No, I didn't,' Stuart smiled. 'But tell me, Ted, how did you feel about Laura claiming Jackie had several lovers and drank too much?'

Ted didn't answer for a while; he just sat there looking down at his hands. 'I was hurt,' he said eventually. 'But I couldn't blame her for it as she was speaking the truth, Stuart! I might have been the man she loved, but there were other casual flings from time to time, and yes, she drank a lot too. But I blame myself for that, you see Peggie was becoming ever more demanding, I couldn't be with Jackie much and she was lonely. I think she began to stop believing that one day I'd be free to be with her.'

'Do you know any of these men?'

'There were two local ones, I don't know them, only what I've heard about them. The others were just fly-by-nights, men who came as guests and then left.'

'And the local ones?' Stuart felt as if he was torturing the man, and wished he didn't have to.

'Both married with children. They weren't affairs as such, just brief interludes. I can't give you their names, Jackie never told me. I don't believe they could be suspects. Jackie would never have made trouble for them, she admitted to me it was just sex.'

'You are a remarkably honest man,' Stuart said admiringly. 'So what made you agree to talk to me today?'

'Gloria always knew about Jackie and me. She knew Laura too and didn't ever believe she was guilty. She also felt guilty that she didn't go to the police and tell them what she knew. That was mainly out of loyalty to me because we've been friends for many years. But she knew who the other local men friends were as well, and if that got out she knew she'd be in trouble around here.' Ted paused for a few moments, frowning as if a thought was troubling him.

'Poor Gloria,' he said after a bit. 'She was in a worse position than me, she had her children's welfare and her livelihood to think of. It preyed on her mind and we often used to talk about it over a drink. But it was when you turned up and spoke to her in the pub that everything got shook up. I knew who you were the minute she said your name. I remembered everything Jackie told me about you too! It struck me that if you could believe in Laura's innocence after she'd hurt you so badly, then maybe I should have an open mind about it too. I suppose I also thought it was time that I became a real man, pinned my colours to the mast and admitted I loved Jackie!'

Stuart stayed silent for a little while. He felt somewhat aggrieved that if Ted and Gloria had been brave enough to go to the police at the time of the murder and tell them what they knew, the investigation into Jackie's murder might have been more thorough. But they had come forward now, and that took some courage.

'Would you be brave enough to give evidence if Laura does get an appeal?' Stuart asked tentatively.

'What could I say that would help her?'

'Well, there's those letters Laura wrote while she was in

Italy that you told me about. The original jury was swayed into believing Laura's motive for killing Jackie was revenge for Barney's death, and the letters could disprove that. You could also make a statement about the money for the shop being a gift.'

'There is something else that never came to light in the trial.'

'What's that?'

'Jackie was going to make a gift of Brodie Farm to Laura. I know because she had the document drawn up and I witnessed it.'

14

Stuart's mind was racing as he drove back to Edinburgh that evening. Ted was adamant that he witnessed Jackie's signature on a deed of gift, and that it was only about a month before her death.

He explained that for over a year before that, he and Jackie had been talking about him leaving Peggie and their setting up home together. They knew they couldn't possibly stay at Brodie Farm because they would be a target for malicious gossip, so they intended to move to the Borders or the Highlands.

Jackie hadn't liked the idea of selling Brodie Farm to a stranger who would never love it like she did, or appreciate all the hard work she'd put into it. She wanted to give it to Laura because she would, and she was still young and energetic enough to make a real go of it. Ted added that he also thought Jackie was concerned about Barney's grave being neglected once she was gone. Laura had always tended it when she came over to Fife, but it was a long way to come, and without Jackie there as a further incentive, she might lapse.

Stuart wasn't actually surprised that Jackie would be so astoundingly generous. He could remember her scoffing at Roger once when he was bullying her to make a will.

'*What pleasure is there in giving something away if you aren't around to see the effect it has?*' she said to him. '*I shall either spend every penny I've got, or give everything away to the people I love well before I snuff it. I want to see their gratitude and have them kissing my feet.*'

Of course, not many people could afford to give away a

valuable property like Brodie Farm, especially when they were only in their late forties and might well fall on hard times later. But Jackie could. Her other properties in London and the cottages in Cellardyke had to be worth in excess of a million and a half and she had a good income from them too.

Ted said Jackie didn't mention the deed of gift again after he'd witnessed it. He didn't know whether that meant she'd sent it on to her solicitor, changed her mind, or just shelved the idea until she and Ted were ready to up sticks and go off to the Highlands.

Stuart didn't think it was likely that Jackie had gone through with it. Knowing her as he did, the moment all the legal stuff was done she would have tied up the deeds with flamboyant ribbon and presented them to Laura herself. But he could get a solicitor to check with the Land Registry to see if she had.

Yet he couldn't see her thinking better of her plan. He never knew her do that about anything.

His guess was that she had just shelved it until she was ready to leave. She had a soft heart, and however much she wanted and intended to run off with Ted, she was probably very anxious about how his dependent, disabled wife would cope without him, and estranging Ted from his son and daughter. Stuart didn't think she'd start packing up until she knew all the arrangements for his wife's care were in place and he'd explained things to his children.

The question was, did she tell anyone other than Ted about this intended gift? And what happened to the signed and witnessed document if she didn't send it off to a solicitor?

When Stuart got home to the second-floor flat he'd rented, he smiled at the sight of David asleep on the settee in front of the television. At the time Stuart had taken the two-bedroom flat he was pleased by the starkness of it as he thought it would be easy to keep it tidy. Magnolia walls, beige carpet, the kind of cheap furniture which looked good in shop windows but could never be comfortable and would be worn out within two years.

But he and David hadn't made any effort to tidy up after themselves; shirts were hung over chairs, the table littered with books, maps and notes they'd been making. There had to be a week's supply of newspapers on the floor, and their bedrooms and the kitchen were even more untidy. But it was home for now, and Stuart was glad to be back here with his friend.

'Wake up, you lazy bastard,' he said, giving David a thump on the chest.

David rubbed his eyes. 'What is there to wake up for?' he said with a yawn.

'News,' Stuart said, and perching on the edge of the settee recounted everything he'd been told by Ted.

David's eyes were like saucers. 'Why didn't her solicitor come forward with this information? It proves there was no animosity between the two women,' he said. 'Even if Jackie eventually decided against it, ripped it up or chucked it on the fire, and so it never got legally registered with the Land Registry, her solicitor would have done all the searches and suchlike before he drew up the document. Did Ted tell you who acted for her?'

'He didn't know, but he said he thought it was someone in Edinburgh. Goldsmith could find out, I expect. We'll have to see him tomorrow – with this and Ted's other input I think we're nearly there with grounds for an appeal.'

'I've got a bit of interesting news too,' David said, getting up and stretching. 'The Langdons, the couple who stayed at Kirkmay House the night before the murder, didn't leave Crail first thing in the morning. It was about one.'

'So did they see what Charles was up to?'

'They didn't see him in the morning, only heard him talking to Belle while they were having breakfast. They left the house about nine-thirty, leaving their car in the drive because they wanted to walk along the coastal path to Anstruther. They left their car keys on the hall table in case Belle needed to move it. When they got back to collect the car, Belle seemed very distracted, so they took the keys and drove off. They were in Carlisle that evening when they heard a woman had been killed in Crail that morning, but they had no idea that it was Belle's sister until months later when they read about the trial in the papers.'

'The police didn't contact them then?'

David shook his head. 'No, they didn't. It was very remiss of them in my opinion.'

'I don't suppose you asked them what kind of car they had?' Stuart asked.

'They don't call me Super Sleuth Stoyle for nothing,' David grinned. 'It was a white Golf – I've even got the registration number – but they traded it in eighteen months ago for a newer model.'

'Bloody hell,' Stuart exclaimed. 'Laura drove a white Golf too! Charles could have gone out in the Langdons' car to Brodie Farm – that would explain why the neighbour thought Laura had arrived half an hour earlier than she really did.'

'You catch on quickly,' David said teasingly. 'If only the police had interviewed the Langdons, and got forensics to check the car, Laura might never have been arrested, let alone charged with the crime.'

'So how did you manage to sleep with that on your mind?' Stuart asked.

'I dare say I knew you were going to keep me up all night chewing the fat,' David said drily. 'So let's open a bottle of something and you can tell me more about Jackie's elderly lover.'

'I eventually realized why she fell for him,' Stuart said much later as he opened a second bottle of wine. 'Ted needed her. She never had that with Roger. Okay, Roger loved her, he got her started in property, but it wasn't that soulmate, all-encompassing kind of love. Roger was bombastic, he drove over her roughshod most of the time. He never appreciated just how much she wanted a child, he didn't even realize what a remarkable person she was. Ted did. I could feel the depth of his grief, see the hopelessness he feels now she's gone. He deserves better than that shrew of a wife.'

'Will he stay with her?' David asked.

'That remains to be seen. He told me just before I left that he intended to go straight home and tell her about Jackie. A cynic would say that was because he knows she'll find out anyway if we get the appeal. But I think he really wants to make a public declaration of his love for Jackie.'

'It's a bit late in the day for that!'

'I got the impression that he knows he should have done that years ago, and that if he had, whilst still making sure Peggie was well cared for, she'd have had more respect for him. But things can't get any worse for him than they are now, and maybe once the dust settles she'll realize what a good man he is and try to mend her ways.'

A companionable silence fell between the two men. David was reminded of the many nights they'd spent together like this in Colombia, both immersed in their own thoughts, and conversation unnecessary. David wanted to wrap this investigation up now; in his view they had more than enough evidence to prove that Laura's conviction was unsafe, and it was up to the police to open up a new investigation and find the real killer. He wanted to go sailing with Julia, Abi and William and put aside all these people whom he didn't really know, and who meant nothing to him.

But Stuart did mean something to him, and he was concerned that his friend had become so obsessed with all the characters in this investigation that he'd slipped off the rails of his own life.

'What are you going to do when this is over?' he asked.

'I don't know.' Stuart frowned. 'Get into some project I suppose, same as I've always done.'

'And Laura? Will she be part of your future?'

Stuart looked indignant. 'What sort of a question is that?'

'One you should ask yourself, mate,' David said lightly.

Laura stood at the window of her cell watching the sun go down over the hills. She ached to be out there, to stand on the top of a hill with the wind in her hair and see to infinity in complete and utter silence.

There was the usual hubbub on the wing: women shouting to one another through the windows, someone throwing a tantrum and kicking at her cell door, a drone of radios tuned to various different stations.

She and the other women often talked about what they missed most from their former lives. It wasn't always the obvious things – their children, husbands or boyfriends, that was understood – but the more trivial things like a favourite snack, walking a dog, or lying in a bubble bath.

For Laura it was always silence she missed, and that seemed so bizarre when for almost all of her life she'd lived in busy, noisy places and never even noticed it. Yet she could pinpoint the moment when she first came to value silence and to realize it had great healing properties.

It was June 1982, a year after Barney's death, and she was in Italy working in a small hotel owned by Carlo and Janet Ferratti.

Frank and Lena had got to know Carlo when he worked as a waiter in a restaurant in Muswell Hill and Lena had introduced him to Janet, one of her closest friends. They eventually got married and Carlo took Janet back to Italy where they opened their own hotel in Sorrento. But they often came back to England to see Janet's family, and Lena and Frank. It was on one of these visits in the spring that Lena asked them if they would give Laura a job for the summer.

Barney's death the year before had almost destroyed Laura. After the first couple of months of shock, self-blame and terrible grief, she wilted into a sort of zombie-like state where she didn't eat, sleep or communicate with anyone. On several occasions she was picked up by the police wandering the streets of Edinburgh in the middle of the night. She was even taken into a psychiatric ward twice because it was feared she was suicidal.

During the autumn of that year Lena and Frank drove up to Scotland to see their daughters, and prompted by Jackie they visited Laura. Lena was to say much later that she was horrified by Laura's appearance: her weight had dropped to six stone, her hair was falling out and she had several untreated boils on her neck. But she found it even more alarming that Laura was incessantly cleaning her flat, scrubbing and polishing so much that her hands were raw. Lena felt that unless she intervened, Laura would end up being sectioned.

She and Frank decided to take her back with them to London, and they contacted her landlord and told him she was vacating the flat. It was left to Charles and Belle to pack up what belongings they thought she might want in the future, and take them to their house to store for her.

Laura could remember very little of that period. She did recollect sometimes feeling mystified about how she ended up in Duke's Avenue, in Jackie's old bedroom, but it was only much later, when the medication she was given by Lena's doctor began to work, that she understood how deranged she had become.

By the following January, seven months after Barney's death, thanks to Lena's care, her health had improved, and she felt she must get a job.

There was no question of her returning to promotional or even shop work, for she couldn't have coped with talking to people, so she got an office-cleaning job. It suited her very well, for she worked alone in the early hours of the morning, and again in the evenings, and spent the rest of the day reading and sleeping. She felt a sort of strange irony that she was doing what her mother had once done, yet she didn't feel it was demeaning in any way, in fact she was glad to be doing it, for it made her feel less of a parasite.

It was in May that Lena suggested she went to work in Italy. Laura didn't want to go anywhere, but agreed because she knew Lena meant well by arranging it and she also felt that she was in danger of outstaying her welcome with her. She was terrified on the flight to Naples because she was afraid she might crack up without Lena close by to support her.

Janet met her at the airport. She was a dumpy, middle-aged woman with a sweet face and greying hair, and she had a similar down-to-earth manner to Lena. As they drove round the Bay of Naples to Sorrento, she explained that the job was simple enough, cleaning rooms, changing beds and helping Carlo in the kitchen when needed.

Vincenzo's in the Via Santo Paolo was a very old building dating back to the sixteenth century. It was a small, comfortable hotel with only twelve bedrooms, and the guests ate their breakfast down in the restaurant on the ground floor. Laura had a tiny, simply furnished room on the third floor and from the window she could just glimpse the sea over rooftops. Janet told her to go off and explore after she'd unpacked her suitcase.

Laura felt she had to go out, but she didn't want to. It was very hot and the tall old buildings either side of the narrow cobbled streets around the hotel seemed almost to press in on her. She didn't like the foreign kind of smells wafting around, or that she couldn't understand what people were saying, and the hordes of tourists, who all seemed to be going the opposite way to her, kept pushing and elbowing her.

But she forced herself to keep going, keeping her head down and not meeting anyone's eye. Then suddenly she stepped out of the shadow of the buildings to find herself at the top of a very steep lane, and unexpectedly, there below her was the sea and a pretty little harbour. She smiled involuntarily, and the cloud of greyness which had enveloped her for so long seemed to lift a little.

The work at the hotel was quite arduous. She was up serving breakfast at seven, and then cleaned the guests' bedrooms and the bathrooms. They were messy, untidy people who left their clothes on the floor, covered every surface with toiletries and dumped wet towels on their beds. But she found satisfaction in making the rooms look nice again, and she could tell that Janet was impressed by her work. She had the whole afternoon off until six, and she spent that exploring, each day walking a different way until the pretty little town became as familiar as Edinburgh.

Her favourite place was the harbour. The beach to the right of it wasn't very special, just a manmade one beneath the rocky cliffs, always crammed with sunbathers and noisy children, and she avoided that for fear of seeing boys who would remind her of Barney. But she could sit on a bench in the sunshine, well away from the beach, and watch the boats bobbing in the water, or the ferry coming back from the Isle of Capri.

But by the second or third week she found herself wanting to get away from people and craving silence. She found that just a couple of hours of complete peace in the afternoon seemed to make her calmer. One of her favourite walks was right along the Via Califano, a road going out of the town along the clifftop where there were no shops, only the odd hotel and a few sleepy little bars with terraces overlooking the sea where she could linger over a cup of coffee or a glass of wine and enjoy the view.

It was in one of those places that she came to grips with what she was doing the day Barney died.

For a whole year she had never allowed herself to think about that. Barney came into her mind all the time in vivid flashes. It was as though she had a slide show in her head, but the pictures were not in chronological order. A glimpse of him in his first school uniform would be followed by one of him sitting in his high chair, or waving his arms and legs as she changed his nappy. Then suddenly she'd see him as he was just before he was snatched from her, a tall, gangly eleven-year-old, kicking a ball around the park. His trousers were always sliding down his slim hips, his shoelaces invariably untied, and when he smiled his nose wrinkled up and his front teeth were slightly crooked, something she'd intended to get put right.

Sometimes she cursed these pictures for bringing on a fresh wave of grief; sometimes they comforted her. But she blocked out the memory of what she was doing when she heard about his death, for she was afraid that facing up to that would destroy her.

The little terrace bar was just like ones she'd so often seen in holiday brochures since then. The bar itself had green and white awning above the door, there was a shocking pink bougainvillea cascading over a whitewashed wall, and the tablecloths on the small round tables were lemon yellow. Even the black iron railings that prevented anyone falling headlong down the cliff into the sea below were festooned with scarlet hibiscus.

It was a scene so different to the greyness of Edinburgh that she had imagined it would be impossible for her mind to jump back to the city. But suddenly she found herself back there mentally, and she could not prevent herself from reliving that Saturday afternoon a year earlier.

She had met Howie, a tall, blond, muscular Australian, several times before that day, but she had put him down as an arrogant twerp who thought he was God's gift to women because he was handsome and bronzed. He had no real conversation, or even a sense of humour. Laura had once said to another woman that she thought the best use for him would be to stick him in a shop window modelling swimming trunks.

But that weekend she was on top of the world. The day before she'd paid £900 into her bank account, she had another film ready for distribution, and Barney had gone off to Jackie's until Sunday. When she woke on Saturday morning she decided she was going to have some fun.

Her hairdresser was her first port of call. He dyed her hair black and curled it into loose ringlets and it looked sensational. She had her first drink of the day while changing into skin-tight white jeans and a skimpy red and white halter top, which showed her cleavage, then made for a pub in Rose Street in the New Town.

After a couple more drinks and a line of coke in the toilets, she was ready for anything. Then she saw Howie.

As always, he had the sleeves of his pale blue denim shirt

rolled up to show off his tanned muscular arms, and he was posing at the bar with one hand curled round a pint of beer, the other in his jeans pocket. It was a look-at-me pose, I'm a real hunk, eat your hearts out, you scrawny, pale-faced Scotsmen.

The pub was crowded, mainly with men, either waiting for their women to finish shopping, or the usual losers who spent the whole of the weekend propping up a bar. Laura walked right up to Howie and grinned seductively. 'If you play your cards right you can have me tonight,' she said.

As she was wearing heels, she was almost as tall as him, and he arrogantly looked her up and down.

'Maybe I don't want you,' he said.

'Oh, I know you do,' she said, giving him a smouldering look. 'But I haven't got the patience to stand around waiting for you to make the first move.'

As several other men had overheard this exchange, and it was clear by their dropped jaws that they thought any man had to be mad, or gay, to refuse her, Howie bought her a drink.

She didn't care that his conversation was so limited. The pub was noisy anyway, the jukebox was playing 'You Drive Me Crazy' by Shakin' Stevens, and she was buzzing from the coke. He bought her a second drink, and he seemed amused and stimulated by her direct manner, but his arrogance still showed through. She had the idea she would take him home, give him the time of his life, then deflate him completely by telling him to piss off when she'd finished with him.

A couple of other Australians he knew came in, and they made it quite plain they fancied her, which made Howie move closer to her. One of the Australians put 'Jealous Guy' by Roxy Music on the jukebox and they teased Howie saying it was for him, which made her feel all-powerful.

It must have been half-three in the afternoon when they left the pub and by then Laura had had five or six drinks. They bought a bottle of wine to take back to her flat, and almost the second they were through the door Howie leapt on her, pulling off her clothes and shedding his.

It was probably the hottest, most erotic sex she'd ever had, and the fact that she hardly knew him, and didn't like him much as a person either, seemed to make it all the more exciting. He also had amazing staying power; he had her in every different position she knew, and a couple she didn't – on the floor, against a wall and on the bed. He treated her like a slut, and kept saying the crudest things, but she was so stoned she felt she was the star of a blue movie and loved it.

He had come twice, and so had she, and she was kneeling in front of him giving him a blow job when the phone rang. She let it ring, but Howie barked at her to answer it because it was putting him off.

It was Belle and she was crying. 'You've got to come over here at once,' she sobbed. 'Something terrible has happened.'

Laura's stomach lurched. Belle had only moved up to Scotland a couple of months earlier, and she'd seemed to have become aloof and cold in the couple of years since they last met. She had never phoned Laura before, and for her to do so now it had to be a real emergency. 'What is it?' she asked.

She could hear a male voice in the background, and it sounded as if he was almost wrestling with Belle to stop her saying anything more, but the only words she heard clearly were 'not over the telephone', then the phone suddenly went dead.

Stoned as Laura was, a sixth sense told her that it was something to do with Barney.

'What is it?' Howie asked, for she'd sunk down on to the floor by the phone.

'I think something has happened to Barney,' she gasped.

'Who the fuck is Barney?' Howie asked. His aggressive tone and the way he was standing above her, stark naked, suddenly made her aware of the sordid nature of the scene.

'My son,' she snapped. 'And cover yourself up.'

She rushed to find the phone book then and with trembling fingers rang Kirkmay House. The phone rang and rang, and as she waited for it to be answered, her heart was racing dangerously. She was just snatching up the bedspread to cover herself, when a man finally answered.

'Belle phoned a few minutes ago. Please tell me what's happened. It's Laura Brannigan, was it about my son?'

There was a second or two's silence as if he was considering what he should tell her. Then, 'There's been a car accident. The police called to tell Belle that her sister has been taken to hospital in Kirkcaldy,' the man said.

'But what about Barney?' she asked frantically. 'Was he with her?'

His hesitation was enough.

'He's dead, isn't he?' she cried out. 'The room was spinning round her and she was clinging to the telephone receiver as if that would stop it. 'Just tell me! I don't know who you are, but for God's sake tell me the truth.'

'I'm John and I'm just staying here,' he said. 'You shouldn't receive terrible news like this on the phone, from a stranger, but I'll have to tell you now. Yes, he's dead, Laura, and I'm so very sorry.'

She put the phone down and clutching the bedspread round her tighter sank down on to the floor. 'He's dead, Howie,' she gasped. 'My little boy is dead.'

'Strewth!' he exclaimed, and when she looked up he was buttoning his shirt, not even looking at her.

'Is that all you can say?' she asked.

She could smell a rank odour of sex and sweat, and it was

coming from both of them. They had spent all afternoon doing the most intimate things to each other, yet he didn't even move to hold and comfort her.

'You bastard!' she exclaimed.

'What?' he said, and it was at that moment she noticed his eyes were as cold and blank as a dead fish's. 'Hell, I didn't want anything heavy. It was just a bit of fun.'

'Get out of here,' she yelled at him, and seeing one of his shoes close to her she threw it at him. 'I just hope one day you get a phone call like that and find out what it feels like.'

He picked up that shoe, then the other one, and without putting them on, he turned and walked out without another word.

'*Vuole qualcosa da bere, signorina?*'

Laura was startled by the young waiter asking her if she wanted a drink – she hadn't heard him come up behind her. She hoped her sunglasses hid her tears.

'*Vino rosso, per favore,*' she said haltingly.

He came back with the glass of red wine very quickly, put it down on the table and moved off so fast it was like a re-enactment of the speed with which Howie left that day. She wondered now if the maggot even took in what had happened. Perhaps it was best that she believed he was slow-witted, rather than entirely lacking in compassion.

Yet the reality of her situation that afternoon was like finding a signpost reading, '*You have finally reached rock bottom.*'

She'd gone out looking for a man. She'd shamelessly thrown herself at him under the influence of drink and coke, and happily let him screw her all afternoon in the name of fun. She had in fact become one of the characters in her own seedy blue films, except she wasn't a nubile eighteen-year-old any more, she was a thirty-seven-year-old mother. While her only son was dying in a road accident, she was stretched out on her bed, legs in the air, letting a worthless scumbag do what he liked to her.

She cried for the whole of the drive out to Fife, tortured by the knowledge that it was the way she had allowed her life to go that had taken Barney from her. She had images of him running through her mind. The plump, smiley baby sitting up in his pushchair, his first faltering steps, sitting on his first tricycle and the funny little dance he used to do when she put some music on. She would never wake up in the morning again to see him holding out a cup of tea he'd made for her. She would never again have him run to her when she came home. She could never stroke his back for him, kiss him goodnight, listen to his laughter or dry his tears. She would never see him as a man.

She had loved him, but not enough to put him first.

The ten days up to his funeral were hazy now; only the physical pain she felt and the self-loathing remaining clear. She remembered Belle saying she couldn't stay at Kirkmay House because she was fully booked, and so she stayed in one of the guest rooms out at Brodie Farm. What she did all day was a mystery to her still. She must have had to make the funeral arrangements and go back to her flat in Edinburgh to get clothes, but she remembered none of that. The only crystal-clear image was of how Barney looked on the mortuary slab.

His face had only minor cuts and scratches. They told her that his death was caused by hitting the back of his head on rock or stone. Apart from being so pale, and his skin so cold, he looked much the way he did when he was asleep. She gently traced around his plump lips with her finger, smoothed back his dark hair from his forehead and sobbed out her heartbreak because his eyes would never open again and she'd never again see his wide smile.

She only visited Jackie once while she was in hospital, and she couldn't remember now whether that was her choice, or because Jackie refused to see her. But during that visit she knew they didn't exchange more than a few words. Jackie was lying in bed, her face as white as the pillowcase, except for a vivid scar on her forehead, and Laura sat beside her and held her hand. In Laura's mind no words were necessary. She knew Jackie loved Barney as much as she did, and that she would never have taken any risks with him in the car. But she knew now that words *were* necessary, she should have vocalized her thoughts, and maybe then they could have comforted each other.

Jackie came out of hospital two days before the funeral, her broken arm in plaster and dressings on both her legs. Belle collected her and took her home with her. She phoned Laura and said she thought it best if she didn't call round.

The day of the funeral was sunny with a stiff little breeze that made the crops in the fields around Brodie Farm dance and sway. Laura had stood watching this early in the morning, wondering how she could still appreciate the beauty of her surroundings while feeling as if her heart had been torn out. She knew Frank and Lena had arrived the night before, and wished they were staying here, and Jackie too. The fact that she was alone at Brodie Farm, except for some holidaymakers in the other guest rooms, made her feel even more alone and tainted.

During the funeral service Lena was on one side of her, Jackie on the other, both holding her hands. Looking at the coffin, that was neither mansized nor small enough for a child, was another sharp reminder that she hadn't been paying Barney enough attention to notice how tall he'd become, or even to marvel that if he had lived he would have been going to a senior school in September. She did remember during the service that when she was Barney's age it was the start of her realizing that as a Wilmslow she had no chance in life. She wondered whether if Barney hadn't been snatched from her so young, he might have looked at her later, realized what she was, and hated her for it.

She was aware of the dozens of people in the pews behind her. Some she recognized as shopkeepers in Crail and Jackie's closest neighbours and friends, but mostly they were strangers who had met Barney without her being around. She guessed they all knew she was a neglectful mother.

Tears coursed down her cheeks as they sang 'All Things Bright and Beautiful'. It had been Barney's favourite hymn, just as it had been hers as a child. He used to sing it to her in the car sometimes, and she could hear his clear, high voice inside her head.

Then finally the agony of the interment, with the birds singing, leaves fluttering in the breeze, and the grass so lush and soft around the graveyard. Even the mound of earth by the freshly dug grave was hidden from view with artificial grass and the dozens of wreaths and bunches of flowers. It was all so serene and perfect, but that made it even more obscene that a child should be buried on such a day.

Laura had made a daisy chain that morning to drop on to the coffin. Barney had loved making them and it seemed the perfect thing, far more relevant than shop-bought flowers. But although she'd wrapped it in damp tissue, it looked wilted and sad. Once again she hadn't got it right and she silently apologized to Barney as she kissed it and tossed it into the grave.

If it hadn't been for Jackie, she would have walked from the graveside and gone back to Edinburgh straight away. But suddenly Jackie's arms were round her and they stood awkwardly with her plastered arm between them, crying on each other's shoulders.

'I couldn't avoid him,' Jackie sobbed. 'He came right at me and the car rolled over and Barney was thrown out.'

Laura knew she must have cried solidly for two hours or more that afternoon in Sorrento as she examined every aspect of that terrible period, but even as she cried she knew this was the only way to exorcize her demons.

She would never forget Barney, and never forgive herself for not being a better mother, but as she walked back to the hotel she felt lighter and more hopeful. And she knew she'd taken the first step towards recovery.

Laura half smiled as she remembered the rest of her stay in Sorrento. As each day passed she got a little stronger mentally, and before long she found she could chat to guests, to Janet and Carlo, and have an occasional flirt with a waiter or barman.

She even tested herself by going to the beach and sunbathing near children, and found it didn't hurt. There were countless small boys with dark hair and eyes, and as she watch them diving off the pontoons, lithe brown bodies glistening with droplets of water, it made her heart feel warm, not sad.

On each of her days off she made a point of going somewhere. A stomach-lurching bus ride along a road hewn out of the rock face, with hairpin bends offering sheer drops to the rocks below, just inches from the bus wheels, took her to amazing Positano where the houses clung to the side of a cliff. She caught the ferry to pretty Capri where she wandered narrow alleyways and peered into tiny exotic gardens set behind rusting gates. There were the wonders of Pompeii, a bustling market in Amalfi, and twice she went into Naples, wrinkling her nose at the squalor of the slums, yet captivated by the gaiety of the place.

So many ancient churches. She visited them all, lit a candle and offered up a prayer to be forgiven and for Jackie to come to see she wasn't to blame.

Once again she reinvented herself too. Not with lies this time, but by making a conscious effort to be a nicer person. She took the trouble to talk to the older guests, ran errands for them, admired the snapshots of their grandchildren, and made them feel welcome. One evening she even babysat a fractious two-year-old so her parents could go out to dinner on their own, and she volunteered to do many jobs for Janet and Carlo to make their lives less arduous.

It felt good to be genuinely liked. She could see then that the people she'd mixed with while making her films hadn't been friends at all, they just sucked up to her because she was calling the shots. Finally she had her hair cut and bleached honey-blonde in a salon, and losing the long dark hair she'd had for so long softened her face and made her eyes brighter. She also abandoned the strong colours she'd worn most of her adult life, and bought cream, white and pastel clothes. Janet hugged her one night and said she was beautiful. Laura just hoped all her efforts had made her beautiful on the inside too.

'I suppose I hadn't completely paid back my debt,' Laura murmured to herself as the last rays of daylight vanished over the hills. 'I can't have done or I wouldn't have ended up here.'

*

'Surely someone must have thought of finding out who Jackie's solicitor was?' Stuart said irritably to Patrick Goldsmith. 'Any legal work he did for her just before her death might have been relevant to the case.'

He and David had arrived at Goldsmith's office at nine and demanded to see him the moment he came in, knowing that he'd probably be in court with one of his clients later. But Goldsmith seemed to have no sense of urgency, and showed precious little excitement at the new developments they had told him about.

'We would expect another solicitor to volunteer any information he had in a case like this, but some firms have thousands of clients, they can't be expected to remember every single one, and connect them with a murder they may or may not have even heard about,' he replied tersely. 'As I understand it, Mrs Howell produced her sister's will, and the solicitor who drew that up agreed that to his knowledge there wasn't a more recent one.'

'She made that years ago when she was in London,' Stuart said heatedly. 'Her husband, quite incidentally, claims he has a more recent one too, but that doesn't appear to have been checked out either. Now come on, Patrick! Surely she would have got a local solicitor once she moved up here? Who handled the purchase of Brodie Farm?'

'I don't know,' Goldsmith admitted ruefully.

Stuart opened his mouth to shout, 'Find out then' at him, but a warning glance from David stopped him.

'We really do need to find him,' David said calmly. 'It might transpire that Jackie changed her mind and destroyed the document. But in my experience people usually explain why that is. So this solicitor's evidence could be important to our appeal.'

'I shall look into it.' Goldsmith began shuffling papers on his desk as if their time was up. 'I'll also consult counsel about the question of the second white Golf, and Mr Baxter coming forward as a witness. I will be in touch as soon as possible.'

Stuart looked at David and rolled his eyes with impatience.

'Thank you for your time, Patrick,' David said, holding out his hand. 'But could I just remind you that for every day Laura spends in prison for a crime she didn't commit, she dies a little. Time is running out for myself and Stuart too. We must have justice, and soon.'

'Well said, David,' Stuart said as they left the solicitors and walked down Great King Street. 'I can only hope Goldsmith took it on board.'

'It isn't just down to him, it's the whole legal system.' David sighed. 'It grinds very slowly.'

'Maybe I'll try to speed things up a bit then,' Stuart retorted.

David looked sideways at his friend and saw his grim expression. 'I hope you aren't thinking of doing something harebrained,' he said.

'Not today,' Stuart said. 'I'm meeting an old mate who's in the police force. I've got him to take a look and see if Charles Howell has any convictions. You can come with me if you like.'

'No, I'll leave that to you,' David replied. 'I've got some phone calls to make. One of them will be to the prison. I'm going to try and twist the governor's arm to let us go in tomorrow to see Laura. Time really is running out for me. Julia and the kids will be here on Saturday.'

Stuart sat on a bench in Princes Street Gardens reading a newspaper until it was time to met Gregor Finlay at twelve. Princes Street was busy with shoppers and tourists and even though it was another week until the Edinburgh Festival began, he noticed there were already a great many street entertainers about, hoping to get in on the action.

The elation he'd felt yesterday had been dampened by Goldsmith. All he had now was a ball of anger lying in the pit of his stomach. He was certain that Charles had killed Jackie, and his instinct was to drive over to Fife and beat the living daylights out of him until he admitted it.

But there was something else niggling at him too: David's remark last night about whether Laura would be part of his future.

He might have had nothing on his mind but her ever since he was told she was in prison. But he hadn't really considered what would happen if and when she was released. Of course he'd imagined celebrating with her, but nothing really beyond that. Yet now he was thinking about it, he realized she would have no home to go to, no friends, and as far as he knew, no money.

That was a bit daunting. He couldn't just say, '*Well, you're free now*', and walk away, but it would put him under some pressure to take care of her.

She had been damaged emotionally when he first met her, though he hadn't realized that until recently. How much more damaged would she be now after all she'd been through? She might become a terrible liability.

Yet there was a kind of odd little yearning for her inside him. Was that just sympathy, or were the old feelings still there?

He got up from the bench and began walking briskly up to the Old Town to meet Gregor. It wouldn't do to start dwelling on what-if's.

Gregor was already in the Ensign Ewart up by the Castle. It was one of Stuart's favourite pubs, despite the fact that it was always full of tourists exclaiming on its great age, the 'cute' beams and the 'characters' who drank in it.

Gregor was probably one of the characters – his round, red shiny face, bald head and bellowing laugh weren't easily forgotten. Yet Stuart remembered him at school as being quiet, bookish and having thick fair hair.

'Am I late or were you early?' Stuart asked.

Gregor gave one of his hearty laughs. 'I'm always early when I'm meeting someone in a pub. What'll you have?'

'Just a half, I might need to drive later,' Stuart said.

They moved into the back of the bar where it was quieter, and Stuart wasted no time in asking Gregor what he'd found out about Charles.

'He's got no real record,' Gregor said, his voice lowered. 'Not for motoring offences or anything. He's been pulled a few times over the years for various things – receiving, assault, and threatening behaviour – but never charged with any of them.'

'And did you look at the hit-and-run in '81?'

'He doesn't appear to have been questioned. His wife told the local police he was in London. That was proved because he flew back the following day.'

'And left his car in London!' Stuart said pointedly. 'But did they find out what make of car caused the accident?'

'The tests were inconclusive. But it was silver, and they'd guess at it being a Mercedes. I ran a check through the DVLA and found Charles did have a silver Mercedes at that time. It went to a new owner a couple of months later.'

Stuart felt a surge of elation. 'Pretty suspicious, I'd say! So why wasn't he pulled?' he asked.

'Have you got any idea how many silver Mercedes there are?' Gregor retorted. 'It's the most popular colour. He wasn't in Fife that day anyway.'

'So he'd like us to believe!' Stuart retorted. 'Well, I think he was. He hit Jackie when he was on his way home, then beetled off out of the way.'

'Maybe,' Gregor said. 'But it couldn't be proved now anyway.'

'If it was the son of a senior police officer who was killed, you'd still be searching high and low for the panel beater that patched his car up,' Stuart snapped.

'Aye, you're right there,' Gregor admitted.

'It seems to me the police in Fife are sadly lacking,' Stuart said, and told Gregor about the Langdons and their car on the day of Jackie's murder. 'I don't think the police even bothered to consider who else might have a motive to kill her. Laura was conveniently there, the knife in her hand, and on the say-so of a nosy neighbour who said he saw her arrive half an hour earlier, they banged her up and threw away the key.'

'That's a bit harsh, Stu,' Gregor retorted. 'Of course they investigated properly.'

'Did you really believe she did it?'

'I did.' Gregor looked a little shamefaced. 'But there was a lot of talk about her after you left for London. She mixed with some heavy-duty characters, and we had scores of complaints from her neighbours about noise and people coming and going. It was thought she was dealing drugs. Then after her boy was killed she was mad as a jar of wasps. I picked her up down in the Grassmarket one night; she had no shoes on and she didn't know what year it was, let alone the time of day.'

'Who could blame her for that?' Stuart exclaimed. 'And anyway, once she recovered from that she was as straight as a die for ten years. She ran a successful business, paid her bills and kept her nose clean.'

'Us policemen only see people when they go off the rails,' Gregor admitted. 'I knew she got a shop out in Morningside, but I never ran into her.'

'And now, after all the stuff I've found out? Do you still think she's guilty?'

'I don't know,' Gregor said defiantly. 'I'd like to say

that I don't, for your sake, but I'm not entirely convinced.'

Stuart was deeply disappointed. He felt Gregor's opinion was representative of the entire force in Edinburgh. 'I've got to go now,' he said, getting to his feet. 'Thanks for delving around for me. She is innocent, Gregor. And I'll find some way of proving it.'

Stuart walked back to the flat feeling tense and angry. In his mind, if the police had done their job properly at the time of the hit-and-run, Charles would have been charged and Jackie might still be alive today. Even if Laura won her appeal, that wouldn't alter the general public's mind about her, not until the real murderer was apprehended and brought to trial. But if Gregor's attitude was anything to go by, the police wouldn't make much of an effort to do that.

As he got into the flat he heard David talking on the phone in the living room. He thought he was speaking to Julia and he felt a pang of irrational jealousy. Everything was fine for David, whatever happened to Laura: his life would remain the same; his wife, kids, job and home would all still be there waiting for him.

David put the phone down. 'Hello, Stu, didn't expect you back so soon,' he called out. 'Goldsmith just rang, he's found Jackie's solicitor. He's got an office in Portobello, wherever that might be.'

Stuart walked into the living room and he suddenly felt irritated by the mess. They'd had a takeaway curry the previous night and the dishes were still lying on the floor, along with empty bottles and dirty plates, cups and glasses.

'It's the seaside bit of the city,' he said, bending to pick up some plates and cups.

'You sound and look pissed off,' David said.

'I am, and the state of this place doesn't help,' Stuart snapped. 'But then you're used to Julia cleaning up after you.'

David just crossed his arms and looked at Stuart. 'What's eating you?' he said.

Stuart piled up the plates and took them into the kitchen. The sink was already full and he thought they must have run out of clean china by now. 'Give me the solicitor's address – I'll run down there now and cut his throat for him,' he shouted back to David. 'Maybe it needs another death to wake the fucking police up.'

David was suddenly in the kitchen doorway. 'Leave those dishes, I'll do them,' he said. 'I've had more experience of that than soothing irate Scotsmen.'

Stuart banged his fist down on the draining board. 'Don't patronize me, smart arse,' he hissed. 'Just give me the sodding name and address.'

'Okay,' David said coolly, turning and walking away. 'But if you blow it when you get there because you haven't given yourself time to calm down, don't blame me.'

He wrote down the name and address and handed it to Stuart. 'We can go to the prison tomorrow afternoon,' he said. 'Try to stay out of trouble until then.'

Stuart had always had a soft spot for Portobello. Before his world was expanded by having an annual family holiday in Fife, just across the Forth, this was where they went for a day out. The sea was always freezing, but he and Fiona and Angus always raced to be the first one in, even if their hearts did almost stop with the cold. He remembered that his mother made a kind of large towelling bag that they changed under. They never bought food in a café, his mother would take sandwiches in a bread bag, and sometimes they had an apple each too.

His dad would play cricket with them. The stumps, bat and ball were all packed in an army kit bag, along with the picnic and the swimming things. He could remember his father lugging it along over his shoulder, and he often made jokes that his entire kit when he was in the Army hadn't weighed so much.

In the last twenty years, Stuart had seen many beautiful beaches all around the world, with white soft sand, palm trees and warm turquoise sea, yet however exotic or sophisticated they were, his mind always turned back to Portobello. He would remember the hand-knitted woolly trunks he had, the joy of taking off his shoes and socks and feeling sand between his toes. Even the bus ride to get there had been seeped in adventure because from the top deck he could peer down into people's houses and gardens, and believe he was going to the ends of the earth, not just a few miles.

Stuart parked his car in a side road close to the promenade because he intended to take a walk along it after calling at the solicitors in the High Street. It was four o'clock now, and he expected they closed at five. His anger was fading, in fact he wasn't sure why he had got so irate earlier. It would serve him right if David jumped ship and went home.

Conway and Calder Solicitors were at number 156, but Stuart crossed over the road to look in an antique shop window just before he got there. He knew Julia collected old blue and white china, and he thought if they had something suitable he might take it back to David as a peace offering.

There wasn't anything blue and white, and as he turned to go back across the street, he saw a familiar figure coming out of the solicitor's office. It was none other than Robbie Fielding.

Stunned, Stuart turned back to the antique shop window so Fielding wouldn't notice him. His head told him there was no reason why the man shouldn't have the same solicitor as Jackie, in fact he could have recommended her to them. Yet in his heart he sensed sinister undertones.

Once Fielding had gone, Stuart went across the street and

into the office. A fresh-faced blonde of about twenty was at the reception desk and she smiled at him.

'Can I help you, sir?' she asked.

'I'd like to see Mr Calder, please. I'm afraid I haven't got an appointment, but Mr Goldsmith spoke to him earlier and said I would be coming. I'm Stuart Macgregor.'

'If you'd just take a seat, Mr Macgregor, I'll check if he can see you,' she said, and promptly disappeared through a door at the back of the office.

She came back and said that Calder was on the phone to a client at the moment, but if Stuart would like to wait he would see him as soon as he'd finished.

It was some fifteen minutes before a thin-faced man of about fifty, wearing a dark grey suit and gold-rimmed glasses, put his head round the door. 'Mr Macgregor? If you'd like to come this way. I'm sorry I had to keep you waiting.'

Stuart was a little surprised by the plushness of his office. All the solicitors he'd been to in the past had huge piles of papers and files littering every surface, and still more on the floor. There was no clutter here, instead a quality duck-egg-blue carpet, a mahogany desk which Stuart's experienced eye knew was a real Georgian one, not reproduction, and the leather-bound legal books in a glass-fronted cabinet looked brand-new.

'Do sit down, Mr Macgregor.' Calder indicated a dark blue leather club chair and sat down behind his desk. 'Mr Goldsmith said you had an interest in the affairs of Mrs Davies. I hadn't known until I received his call that she had died.'

Stuart's hackles rose, for that was clearly a lie. The murder had been in the nationals and local papers. During the trial it had been front-page news.

'Murdered, Mr Calder. You must be one of the few people in Edinburgh who didn't know about it.'

'I may have read about it but not connected it with one of my clients. I do have a great many and some of them I have only met once or twice.'

Stuart nodded as if that was a good enough explanation. He didn't like Calder, who had the pinched nose and lips of a mean-spirited man, but he liked him even less for implying he couldn't remember Jackie. No one ever forgot her. Her looks and personality were the kind that stayed in men's minds. 'I understand you handled the sale of Brodie Farm for her?'

'Yes, that's right, I did, though I had forgotten it entirely until Mr Goldsmith rang me. It was a long time ago now. I was just getting started in my practice then. Is there some problem with the deeds? I believe Mrs Davies kept them, rather than giving them to me for safekeeping.'

'No, there's no problem with them as far as I know. I'm sure Goldsmith informed you that he is collating new evidence for an appeal for Laura Brannigan. We've been informed by a witness that Mrs Davies had a deed of gift drawn up, in which she intended to give the farm to Brannigan.'

'Yes, that's correct.' Calder nodded. 'I tried to dissuade her. It is always foolhardy giving away property, even to members of your own family. Clearly I succeeded, for she didn't return it signed and witnessed.'

'Did she tell you why not?'

'No. But that's not unusual. And of course I don't chase clients up about such things. It is their right to change their minds.'

Stuart was dying to point out that Calder's memory appeared to be selective. He'd said he didn't remember Jackie yet he had no problem recalling she hadn't returned the signed deed. But he decided not to make any comment; after all, the man wasn't being obstructive.

'How did Mrs Davies come to you? Was she recommended by another client of yours, or what? I mean, Portobello isn't just around the corner from Fife.'

'I think it must have been a recommendation,' Calder said, not looking at Stuart. 'But I really can't remember now.'

'Would it have been Mr Robert Fielding by any chance?'

Calder hesitated. 'That name doesn't ring a bell,' he said, then picked up his pen and fiddled with it nervously.

Stuart's anger flared up again and he found it hard to restrain himself from leaning across the desk and grabbing the man by the throat. 'That's odd considering he was in your office just twenty minutes ago,' he said instead. 'And I met him a week or so ago and he claimed he helped Mrs Davies obtain Brodie Farm.'

Calder blushed. It showed clearly as his complexion was naturally very pale.

'Oh, you mean Robbie,' he exclaimed. 'I never think of him as Robert. Yes, of course he was here, but I couldn't say if it was he who recommended Mrs Davies to come to me. It was far too long ago.'

Stuart had had enough of this selective memory lark. 'Mr Calder, if you can't be straight with me, I shall have to make a complaint to the Law Society,' he said with steel in his voice. 'You are likely to be called as a witness to Laura Brannigan's affairs at her appeal, so I advise you to tell me the truth now.'

'I don't know what you mean,' the man said indignantly, but he looked alarmed. 'I have told you that I handled the sale of Brodie Farm, and about gifting it. I gave Mrs Davies proper legal advice, and clearly she acted upon it as she didn't go through with it. I can also tell you I handled other property purchases for her too, namely cottages in Cellardyke.'

'Did you draw up a will for her?'

Again the man hesitated. 'Yes,' he said somewhat reluctantly.

'When was that?'

'Well, I couldn't have told you that an hour or two ago. But I looked through her file when Mr Goldsmith rang me, to refresh my memory. It was the same day she inquired what was needed to gift the farm. In December '92. I drew it up, then a few days later she came in and signed it.'

'Who witnessed it?' Stuart asked.

'Mr Conway's secretary. Margaret Cameron.'

'And where is this will?'

'We have it here in our vault. As I said, I didn't know about her death until today. If I had I would have passed it on to her executor.'

'Who is?'

'You, Mr Macgregor.'

15

'I need a stiff drink,' Stuart said as he came back into the flat.

David looked up from some paperwork he was doing.

'You didn't thump him, did you?' he asked.

'Of course not, but I reckon Calder could do with it. I'd say he's as bent as a hairpin.'

David poured him a large Scotch, then sat down to hear what had happened. Stuart told him first what Calder had said about the deed of gift, then went on to tell him that Jackie had made a new will.

'When he said I was the executor, I nearly keeled over with shock. That was the last thing I expected. But it was a stroke of luck too, for I doubt he'd have handed it over to me, or even told me the contents, unless I was,' he said, taking the will out of his inside pocket and handing it to David. 'There was a letter for me with it explaining why she asked me. She said I was the only person she felt she could trust with it.'

David unfolded the will and began to read it. 'Bloody hell,' he exclaimed. 'She left Brodie Farm to Laura and two of the cottages in Cellardyke to Ted. Another one to Gloria.' He looked up at Stuart with a jubilant expression. 'This is brilliant, we've got the perfect reason now for calling Ted and Gloria as witnesses.'

'Read on,' Stuart said. 'The plot, as they say, thickens!'

'Roger gets some of the London property, a house in Kensington for Toby, and blimey, Stuart, you get one in Notting Hill!'

'Yeah, you could have knocked me down with a feather at that bit. But there's more astounding stuff,' Stuart said.

'Numerous other smaller bequests,' David murmured, reading out some of them, including the sum of £15,000 to Jackie's parents, which she urged them to blow on a trip around the world. 'Kirkmay House! What's that doing in here?' he exclaimed in shocked surprise. 'Kirkmay House was Jackie's, not Belle and Charles's!'

Stuart nodded. 'And she's left it to none other than Meggie and Ivy, Laura's sisters.'

'But what about Belle and Charles?' David's eyes were scanning down the page, assuming he had missed them. 'She doesn't appear to have left them anything!'

'That's right. She explains it to me in a letter.'

'I thought she didn't know about Laura's sisters?' David said. He looked so puzzled that Stuart laughed.

'You'd better read her letter,' he said, taking the envelope out of his inside pocket and handing it over. 'Read it aloud. I'm so blown away by it all that I probably haven't taken it in properly.'

David moved closer to the window to see better and cleared his throat.

'*Dearest Stuart*,' he read.

As I write this I'm quite sure you'll never read it, which makes me feel pretty silly even putting pen to paper. I always hated the idea of wills as I often told you. Roger coerced me into writing one years ago, and it made me feel like my business was the important thing about me, not me as a person. But I'm forty-eight now, and as Mum is so fond of telling me, I may just pop my clogs before I've managed to give away my little empire or spend my dosh.

I've taken the liberty of putting you down as my executor as you are the only person that is younger than me, who I know I can trust

443

implicitly. I'm sorry if it proves onerous, maybe even nasty, but your shoulders were always big enough for anything.

I've got Laura down for Brodie Farm, but I intend to give her it soon as a gift, so by the time you read this, that will be a fait accompli. She is to inherit any dosh left over too, though I intend to spend as much of it as I can! You'll also know by the time you get to read this that I've shot off to live happily ever after with Ted Baxter, who I love to pieces. But just on the off chance my life is cut short I've left him two cottages so he will be financially secure. You'll understand about Roger and the London property, I'm still fond of the old bastard, and I wouldn't have got started without him. Toby and the house in Kensington is equally understandable. What may surprise you is that I'm leaving nothing to Belle and Charles. Believe me, I didn't make this decision lightly. They've taken from me for years, and I suppose I want to show them I wasn't quite the sucker they took me for. I let them have Kirkmay House to run when they were broke, but all they did was take the piss. You wouldn't believe the bills Belle dumped on me for the furniture and soft furnishings! I think she thought she'd be having royalty staying there. Right from the start they only played at running it as a guest house, neither of them had any aptitude for work, much less running a business that requires diplomacy and a modicum of grovelling to the public.

Lately they haven't even kept to the original agreement that I was to have twenty per cent of the takings. They turn guests away, and she's out buying new clothes and drinking, while Charles lords it at the golf club. There's a lot more too, but I can't even begin to tell you about that. I have already warned them that if they don't shape up I'll throw them out, so the chances are you won't have to do anything with them anyway.

Yes, I've given you something too, because you were a loyal friend and the most trusted of my employees. It will probably come to you too late for you to find a croft up in the Highlands and get a couple of dogs. You'll probably attend my funeral on a zimmer. But I kind of hope you might have already made your dreams come true anyway.

Finally Meggie and Ivy. You don't know them, and neither do I. But they are Laura's sisters. I snooped until I found them. She hid them away for reasons only she could explain. I think I know the reason and understand it. Tell Laura that for me, and say I never thought any less of her because of it. I know that with all she went through when Barney died, she finally came to understand that riches and family background don't mean a bag of beans. What counts is the kind of person you are, and to me who knows her better than anyone, she is the tops.

By giving Meggie and Ivy Kirkmay House I hope they and Laura will draw close to one another and have the kind of loving relationship I never had with Belle.

My love and best wishes for your future,

Jackie x x

David looked up from the letter and saw tears rolling down Stuart's cheeks. He had never seen his friend cry before and wasn't sure what to say or do.

'That letter sums her up entirely.' Stuart's voice was husky with emotion. 'She was always so generous and understanding of people and she had such a great sense of humour. What I can't understand though is why such a switched-on person would entrust her will to that particular solicitor. She could normally spot a wrong'un at fifty paces!'

He told David how he'd seen Robbie Fielding leaving the solicitor's office, and that Calder tried to pretend he didn't know him. 'Where do you think Fielding fits into this?' he asked.

'I can't see that he fits in anywhere.'

'Nor me,' Stuart agreed. 'But all the same, I've got this gut reaction that he does. It's too much of a coincidence that he was there just before me. I'd bet anything Calder called him as soon as he'd put the phone down on Gold-smith. But why? What kind of jiggery-pokery could those two have been up to?'

'It must have been something to do with Laura getting Brodie Farm,' David said.

'What if Fielding was one of Jackie's lovers and he was livid when he found out she was going off with Ted and giving the farm to Laura?'

David shook his head to signify he couldn't stand any-more what-if's. 'Look, we'll be seeing Laura tomorrow. She might be able to put a different spin on this. So let's go out and get a Chinese or something. I'm starving.'

The prison visiting room was as full of people and as wreathed in cigarette smoke as on the previous occasion, but this time there were more older children, perhaps because their schools had broken up for the summer holiday. David noted how sulky or anxious many of them looked. He guessed that however much they wanted to see their mothers, the restrictions of a prison made it a distressing experience. He couldn't imagine Abi and William coping with it.

Yet he was pleased to see how much better Laura was looking since the last time he saw her. He couldn't work out what was different – she was wearing the same jeans and blue tee-shirt as before, and he didn't think she'd had her hair cut either – but something had made her look pretty and far younger than fifty. Was it Stuart visiting her? Or just that she was feeling more hopeful now?

David remained silent while Laura and Stuart chatted. He often felt he could learn more about people by just watching and listening.

Over the years Stuart had told him a great deal about Laura. In the early days when he was still hurting from their break-up he would say bitterly that all she wanted was money and expensive clothes. Then when he'd had too much to drink he'd become a bit maudlin and say how beautiful she was, what a perfect figure she had, and how much fun they'd had their first summer together in Scotland.

David had gathered all this up and formed the opinion that she was a ball-breaking, self-seeking bitch, with a touch of the siren, because Stuart couldn't seem to forget her.

But meeting her in here for the first time, a damaged, middle-aged woman in serious trouble, his constructed image of her had been erased. Now, a couple of weeks later, with a tremendous amount of information about her under his belt, some of which had come directly from her, more from other people, he had a rather confused picture.

For someone who once was a self-confessed serial liar, she had been remarkably truthful with him and Stuart. The child neglect, the pornography and drug-taking were all things which he could never take lightly, yet she had rebuilt her life honestly after Barney's death, and that took courage and determination. She had never sought to blame others, or indulged in self-pity. Overall he felt she was more sinned against than sinner.

Looking at her now talking so animatedly to Stuart, he found himself understanding why Jackie had cared so deeply about her, and Stuart still loved her. She was so vibrant, her dark eyes glowed, her smile lit up the room, and her voice, low-pitched and slightly husky, with that curious mixture of a London accent and a faint Scottish burr, was so attractive. She was an intelligent woman who had graduated at the university of hard knocks, and there was a sensuality which wafted out of her like exotic perfume.

'Are you with us?'

David almost jumped at Stuart's question. 'Of course,' he said. 'I was just thinking about something. Sorry. Where were you?'

'I take it you were off sailing with Julia?' Stuart grinned. 'I'd just told Laura about the "Growler", and I was just about to show her the star prize.'

Stuart had got the will photocopied that morning, and handed the original to Goldsmith for safe keeping. Oddly enough, suddenly this seemed to make Goldsmith far more animated and warmer. He even agreed that he felt there was something sinister about Fielding and Calder.

Stuart took the copy will out of his pocket and handed it to Laura. 'Jackie's will. Made just six months before her death. You read it while David and I get us some coffee. Would you like a cake too?'

'Umm,' she said distractedly, opening the copy will. 'Yes, please. One of the flapjacks if that's okay.'

The two men went over to the refreshments counter, dodging the many young children running about the room. But as they waited their turn to be served, they both looked back at Laura. She was engrossed, one hand up to her cheek, clearly stunned by what she was reading. 'I'd say she had absolutely no knowledge that Jackie had made that, wouldn't you?' Stuart remarked.

By the time they got back she had put the paper down and was staring into space, her face suddenly pale.

'I don't understand,' she said breathlessly. 'Why would she give me Brodie Farm? How did she find out about my sisters, and why is she giving Kirkmay House to them? I thought it belonged to Belle and Charles. And why hasn't she left them anything? Is that a mistake?'

Stuart got out Jackie's letter to him and let her read that so she would understand.

David had watched this interchange silently and was surprised that Laura showed horror, not delight. Stuart had told her when they first got there that an appeal was now in the bag, though he hadn't told her that most of the new evidence they had gathered pointed to Charles being Jackie's killer. They thought that better kept to themselves for now. So why wasn't she happy about this development which would set her up for life if she was acquitted?

A tear trickled down Laura's cheeks as she read Jackie's letter. She put it down when she'd finished and covered her face in her hands.

'What is it?' Stuart said, looking stunned by her reaction. 'We expected you to be thrilled.'

'Belle will hate me for this,' she said, her voice trembling. 'Everyone will. I didn't want anything from Jackie, just to keep all the wonderful memories of her intact.'

'She had no idea that any of us would ever read it,' Stuart reminded her. 'She thought she would live for ever. But she put down what was important to her at the time of writing. And that was that she loved you. Thank God she did, for this will and the letter prove how she felt.'

'Why didn't she tell me she knew about my sisters?'

'I dare say she thought you'd be so embarrassed that you'd never come near her again.'

'I would have loved it if she'd told me,' Laura said brokenly. 'It would have given me the chance to tell her the whole story, to get it off my chest. I can't go and live at the farm even if I am acquitted. Can you imagine what it would be like? Never mind the horror of what happened there, unless the police find the real murderer, everyone will carry on believing I killed her. I couldn't bear that.'

'We think that as soon as the appeal gets underway they will start a new murder investigation,' David said. 'We've found they were very remiss in the original one, so they'll be forced to pull out all the stops this time.'

'I kind of knew Jackie wasn't all that happy when Belle and Charles moved up to Scotland,' Laura said, dabbing at her eyes with a tissue. 'But I thought that was because she didn't think they'd fit in, not because they were broke and expected her to bail them out. I believed they were still stinking rich, Belle always implied that. And I was giving Jackie so much grief at that time too!' She broke off, looking helplessly at Stuart.

'People tend to conceal problems within their own family,' he said soothingly. 'It was no reflection on you.'

'But poor Belle,' Laura said sadly. 'She'll be devastated. As if it wasn't bad enough losing her sister, without then being made to leave her home.'

David wondered if she would manage to find any compassion for Belle if he and Stuart were proved right about the accident which killed Barney.

'I shouldn't waste any sympathy on her,' Stuart said. 'Jackie wasn't a vindictive person, she would have had good reason. I'm sure there was a lot more she hasn't told us. But I'm surprised you even care about Belle – she hasn't been very kind about you.'

'When you've been fond of someone when they were a child, you don't stop caring about them just because they didn't turn out as you expected or hoped,' Laura said reproachfully. 'I think she always felt she was living in Jackie's shadow and I'm sure she only married Charles because she felt that would put them on an equal footing. Unfortunately his greed and self-importance seem to have rubbed off on her. But if she has been nasty about me, it will only be because she's been robbed of the sister she idolized so much.'

David looked at Stuart and raised one eyebrow quizzically. He thought it astounding that Laura still had such affection and understanding for Belle.

'Let's forget the will for now and just deal with what you need to know about the appeal,' Stuart suggested. 'Goldsmith has been consulting counsel and he thought they'd get a date settled fairly soon. He'll be in to tell you about that. David has got to go off to join his wife and kids, but I'm still going to be here. I will have to find some work, but I can visit you, and I'll be cracking the whip so the lawyers don't sit on their hands and do nothing. How are you coping with the waiting?'

She smiled at Stuart. 'I'm doing fine. Reading a lot, writing too, I find it helps. And I've signed up to do a computer course. I read somewhere that by the year 2000 everyone will need to know how to use one. So I thought I'd better get prepared for if I do get acquitted.'

'There's no "if" about it, you will,' Stuart said.

She smiled weakly and David remembered he needed to ask her about Fielding. He quickly explained how Calder the solicitor hadn't wanted to admit he knew him. 'Why do you think that was, Laura?'

'I don't think anyone who likes to be seen as an upright person would want to admit to knowing Robbie,' she said with a wry smile. 'You can bet your boots he got Calder to do something crooked back when he was young and hungry. I dare say he's had the poor bloke over a barrel ever since – a bent solicitor would be very useful to him.'

The bell rang to warn them visiting time was over.

'Do you think Fielding could have leant on Calder to discover the contents of Jackie's will, and then instructed him not to inform anyone about it when she died?' David asked quickly.

'He could've done, I suppose. But why?' she said. 'What could have been in it for him?'

Everyone was leaving now, the sounds of chairs scraping on the floor and children yelling making it impossible for David to ask anything further.

Laura got up and went around the table to him and kissed him on the cheek. 'Have a lovely holiday with your family,' she said. 'I can't thank you enough for giving up so much of your time on my behalf. It was really kind of you.'

She turned to Stuart then, and David noticed she was struggling not to cry. 'What would I have done without you?' she said softly. 'But don't waste any more of your valuable time on me. You go back to work and let Goldsmith do what he gets paid for. If the appeal fails it won't be your fault.'

David had to turn away as Stuart hugged her. He could feel his friend's sorrow at leaving her here, and that his love for her hadn't diminished over the years. If anything, it appeared to have grown stronger still while he'd been fighting for her.

On Saturday, after David had finally left the flat to go and pick up Julia and the children at the airport, Stuart felt lost.

He'd already stripped the sheets off David's bed, washed up and tidied the flat. There was only the vacuuming left to do, and the weekend yawned before him with nothing to fill it.

The previous day he and David had had another meeting with Goldsmith and met the QC he wanted to defend Laura at the appeal. Goldsmith clearly had had a change of heart; he was beaming as if all his Christmases had come at once. Whether this was because he finally believed Laura deserved to be freed, or just that he saw signs he could win his case, Stuart didn't know, but it was heartening to have him acting as though he really cared.

Everything looked great, and it was down to the lawyers to tie up loose ends, prepare their arguments and sort out the witnesses they needed to call. Stuart knew there was no more he could do. As Goldsmith had so succinctly put it, 'It's the police's job to find and charge the real killer. I have spoken with the CPS and passed on all the many points you have made. It's up to them now, and you must butt out.'

Stuart knew Goldsmith was right, but it was a warm, sunny day, the streets were full of people out enjoying themselves, the airport would be crammed with others flying off to sun-drenched beaches, and Laura was in prison.

He couldn't imagine what it did to a person to be locked up for something they hadn't done. She'd had two years of it, and he'd seen by her face as they parted yesterday that she didn't really believe she would be acquitted. She wanted to. Perhaps while he and David were talking to her, telling her things they'd discovered, maybe she began to hope. But once the cell door closed on her and she was alone, or talking to all those other women in there who hadn't got a prayer of getting out, she was bound to think the worst.

Stuart walked over to the window and looked out. There was a café opposite, with tables and chairs out on the pavement. Every one of them was taken. He could see three women with bulging carrier bags all around their table. They were close in age to Laura, smart, attractive women in elegant clothes, their bare legs and arms suntanned, sunglasses pushed back on to well-cared-for hair. They were laughing, really enjoying one another's company, and he felt a pang of sorrow that Laura couldn't have a day like theirs.

As he watched, a tall, slender woman with long dark hair walked down the pavement. She was wearing red shorts, a low-cut black top and flip-flops on her feet. She looked very much like Laura did when he first met her; there was a sort of golden glow about her, oozing sensuality and a sense of mischief. Suddenly she opened her arms wide and a huge smile spread across her face. Stuart glanced down the street and saw a dark-haired boy of about eight in a football strip running towards her.

As the boy reached her, she caught hold of him and swung him round, and Stuart felt his eyes fill with tears. He had seen Laura do that so often with Barney, though he'd been so much younger then than this boy. How did Laura live with that loss?

He vacuumed the carpet, cleaned the bathroom and even made David's bed up again with clean sheets so it looked tidy. But all the while he was thinking of Laura, and suddenly he felt he had to do something to shake things up.

All this time he'd played by the rules. He'd accused no one, he hadn't pointed out their shortcomings even while they bad-mouthed Laura, except for Roger. He'd listened and nodded, been sympathetic, even stroked a few egos. So maybe an appeal was in the bag now and he'd achieved his objective, but he'd feel a darn sight more satisfied if he could just undermine Charles's security enough to get him really rattled.

It was just after twelve when he put an overnight bag in his car and drove off. He didn't for one moment think that Belle would want him as a guest once he'd told her the contents of Jackie's will, and he certainly didn't want to stay there, but then the bag was just a ruse to get him through the door. He'd also put on a cream linen shirt and chinos that several women had told him he looked handsome in. It wouldn't hurt to let Belle imagine for a few moments that he'd come with seduction on his mind.

The traffic was solid all the way out of Edinburgh, and almost at a standstill on the Forth Bridge. He expected that today would be the longest time ever to make the trip. He'd be lucky if he did it in two and a half hours.

Calder had offered to handle the bequests in the will, but Stuart had declined, not wanting him to make another penny from Jackie, and instead asked Goldsmith to appoint a suitable lawyer to do it. He knew perfectly well that he should leave the person chosen to contact each of the beneficiaries; Goldsmith certainly wouldn't approve of Stuart informing Belle and Charles that they would be getting nothing. But as Stuart hadn't actually been advised against it, he would plead ignorance.

Charles's car wasn't in the drive of Kirkmay House, and he saw Belle glance out of the drawing-room window as he drew up. She had the door open before he even reached the front step.

'What brings you over here?' she asked.

'You, Belle, what else?' he replied. 'You said if I ever needed a bed for the night!'

'Of course.' Her smile was so bright she could have been plugged into the mains. 'But you've been very naughty, you said you'd phone and take me out to dinner.'

Stuart had said no such thing, but he smiled anyway. 'Pressure of work,' he said. 'Where's the old man?'

'Golf. Where else?' she replied. 'Come in and I'll get you a drink.'

Stuart put his bag down in the hall and followed Belle into the kitchen. A half-empty bottle of vodka and an empty glass stood on the table; he wondered at what time today she'd started drinking. Yet her appearance was immaculate – full makeup, a pale pink swirly skirt and a white sleeveless top. She'd put her blonde hair up and she was even wearing high-heeled shoes.

'You look gorgeous,' Stuart said, and it was true, she did. 'Were you just about to go out?'

'No.' She laughed as she said it and poured some vodka into her glass before getting a second one out of the cupboard. 'This is just little old everyday me. If I'd known you were coming I'd have made much more of an effort.'

'Could I have a beer, please?' Stuart asked. 'I can't handle spirits this early in the day. How many guests have you got today?'

'None, well, apart from you,' she said, opening the fridge and getting out a beer. 'I had a full house all week, so I've turned everyone away today. I need a rest.'

Stuart suggested sitting in the garden as it was such a lovely afternoon.

'Will you go and get the chairs out then?' she said. 'They're in the summer house. I've got to nip upstairs.'

Stuart did as she asked, pulling out two padded sun loungers and a small table for their drinks.

She came back a few minutes later, her glass topped up, carrying an ashtray and her cigarettes. 'This is nice,' she said as she sat down, hitching up her skirt to let the sun get to her legs. 'I used to sit out here a lot, but it's a bit boring sunbathing on your own. Why don't you take your shirt off?'

That sounded an innocent enough suggestion, but Stuart was afraid if he did she'd peel her clothes off too. She did have very good legs, and she kept pulling her skirt up higher and higher.

'I'm fine,' he said. 'Now, how are things?'

'About the same really,' she said, lighting up a cigarette. 'Wishing we could get Jackie's estate sorted and make a decision about what to do with the farm. I'm worn out with running it. Charles is no help, he's never here.'

'What would you like to do if everything was squared away?'

'Well, I've got so fed up with people here questioning me all the time that I think now I'd like to move back to London.'

'What do they question you about?'

'What I'm going to do with Brodie Farm, what I'll do if that bitch Laura gets granted an appeal. You know, all those poking-their-noses-in sort of questions.'

*

It ought to have been a difficult situation, being compelled to make light-hearted conversation with Belle while waiting for Charles to come home. But in fact it was surprisingly easy as she was on good form. For the best part of two hours they chatted, and she didn't once bring up anything to do with Jackie or Laura. Stuart found himself liking her in the way he did when they first met.

Back then she'd seemed so sophisticated compared to girls in Scotland. She was at drama school at the time, and he got the idea she was destined to be a real star. She had a finger on the very pulse of London, she could talk with authority about the top groups, the best clubs, and the few times he went out with her, she seemed to make things happen around her. She was fun to be with, warm and vivacious, which had been just what he needed at that miserable time in his life.

He realized later that she was very shallow, that she would never be a good actress for she wasn't committed to it. Drama school was just part of the image she wanted to create, just as she had to have the right clothes and be seen in all the trendy night spots with people she perceived as going places. She had no originality; she was vain, lazy and avaricious. Even now her conversation centred only on celebrities, clothes and programmes she'd seen on television. Yet all the same she was full of life, amusing and very attractive. He didn't want to think he was going to have to give her devastating news before long. She may have sponged off Jackie, but he thought that was Charles's influence, just as drinking far too much was too.

He had spun out his one glass of beer, and resisted her efforts to get him to drink more. He'd come for a showdown with Charles and he needed to be sober for that.

Around five the sun went off the garden and it felt chilly.

They went back into the kitchen and Belle said she would make them something to eat.

Stuart made himself a cup of coffee, but she was still drinking vodka. Her laughter had grown louder and she kept forgetting what she was going to say, but she was still steady on her high heels, and not obviously drunk.

She had just got a curry out of the freezer, remarking that it would take forty-five minutes to cook, then suddenly she came round his side of the table, bent over, took his face in both her hands and kissed him on the lips.

It wasn't a gentle, affectionate kiss, it was a full blown, I-want-to-go-to-bed-with-you kiss. She pushed her tongue into his mouth and insinuated her breasts against his shoulder.

Stuart was alarmed that she had taken the odd flirtatious remark he'd made as proof he'd come here for this.

'No, Belle,' he said, nudging her away. 'It's not right, you are a married woman, and I came to see you and Charles.'

'Don't be coy,' she said, taking one of his hands and putting it on her breast. 'You came purposely to see me knowing Charles would be out playing golf. You want to find out what you missed all those years ago.'

Stuart snatched his hand away. 'Belle, you are drunk, and that's not what I came for. I needed to talk to you and Charles together. I've got something to tell you.'

Her seductive kitten look vanished, replaced by suspicion. 'What?'

Stuart felt angry with himself for not foreseeing Belle might react like this. He realized his plan just to sit it out with her until Charles came home was foolish and ill-conceived. The man might not arrive back for hours, if at all.

'Look, I'll go,' he said, getting up. 'I'll stay the night somewhere else and come back and see you both in the morning.'

'You'll do no such thing,' she said, her face becoming flushed. 'You'll tell me whatever it is now. That wanker of a husband of mine relies on me for everything. It's not a partnership, I'm the one that keeps everything together.'

Stuart thought that was probably true, but he could hardly tell Belle that he needed Charles there to see his reaction to the news.

'Come on, tell me,' she insisted.

'It isn't right for me to tell you alone,' he insisted. Yet as he spoke he realized that a lawyer imparting such news *would* talk directly to her; after all Jackie was her sister, Charles merely the brother-in-law. Perhaps it was best to tell her now, let her have the hysterics that would inevitably follow, and when Charles came in and she relayed it to him, Stuart could sit back and watch the fireworks. That seemed so cruel to her though, especially as for the last two hours he hadn't given her any inkling he was about to drop a bombshell.

'It's about Jackie's will,' he said nervously.

'What's that got to do with you?' she asked, putting her hands on her hips belligerently.

'I'm the executor.'

'Don't talk rubbish,' she snapped. 'It's Grant Spender, her accountant in London.'

'He might have been the executor for the will you found, but Jackie made a far more recent one. I collected it from her solicitor a couple of days ago.'

'What solicitor?'

'Mr Calder of Conway and Calder in Portobello.'

She swayed a little on her feet, and her mouth opened and shut. 'B-b-but,' she stuttered.

'But what, Belle?' Stuart asked. 'This one was duly signed and witnessed six months before she died. I take it she didn't tell you she'd made one?'

He thought she was behaving oddly, and that most people would want to rush you to tell them what was in it.

'No, she didn't,' Belle said and she reached on to the table for a cigarette and lit it. She took a long drag, then looked hard at him. 'Well, what's in it?'

'She hasn't left you anything, Belle,' he said as gently as he could. 'I'm sorry, that's why I wanted Charles to be here too.'

Belle's face seemed to crumple before his eyes, her mouth sagged and her eyes drooped. The high colour she'd had minutes before vanished and now, even with her artful makeup, she looked pale.

'Nothing?' she whispered. 'Nothing at all?'

'No, not even this house. I believe it belonged to her.'

With one hand she grabbed the back of a chair for support, with the other she drew deeply on her cigarette. Suddenly she looked old and Stuart felt very sorry for her.

He got her to sit down and made her a cup of coffee.

'Do you know why she did this?' he asked. 'Did you do something to her?'

Belle didn't answer, just carried on smoking, but he could see a muscle twitching in her cheek.

'Who did she leave it all to then?' she suddenly roared out.

Stuart backed away a little. 'Toby has the house in Kensington, Roger gets the rest of the London property, with the exception of a house she left to me.'

'Oh, you're all right then,' she said viciously. 'She leaves her killer's old boyfriend a house but nothing for her sister.'

'It was a big surprise to me,' he said.

'So who's got the farm and all the stuff up here?' she asked, picking up the vodka bottle and pouring another glass.

'Laura.'

He expected her to rage, but she just looked up at him silently with eyes as cold and hard as stone. She picked up her glass and drank the neat vodka in one long gulp. Then she suddenly hurled the glass across the room. It hit the wall by the back door, shattered and fell to the floor.

'That bitch,' she screamed out, jumping to her feet. 'She must have forced Jackie to do this. She can't have the farm, it should be mine.'

A click behind him made Stuart turn to see Charles coming through the front door. David had described how ludicrous he had looked in his golfing gear, and he was right. To Stuart he looked like a character out of an American comedy, and he could hardly credit that a man who had once boasted about his Savile Row suits would allow himself to be seen in Rupert Bear trousers and a bright yellow sweater. But then it was some fifteen years since they last met, and maybe moving to Scotland had changed the man's idea of style.

More disturbing, though, was to find that a man who had once looked something like Rock Hudson now had a heavily lined face and bags beneath his eyes.

The hall between them was some sixteen feet in length, too long a distance for Stuart to be able to smell if Charles had been drinking, but he didn't look as if he had. He was completely steady on his feet as he put his car keys on the hall table, looking at Stuart with puzzlement. 'Stuart, isn't it? What on earth are you doing here? And what's going on?' he asked. 'I heard Belle yelling.'

Belle leapt up, rushed out to Charles and began pummelling his chest with her fists. 'It's all your fault,' she yelled. 'Jackie made another will and she's left us nothing, nothing at all.'

'Calm down, for God's sake,' Charles said irritably, pushing his wife away from him. 'Hysterics never help anything.'

He came into the kitchen, sat down at the table, folded his arms and looked sharply at Stuart. 'Why have you come here? And what has Jackie's will got to do with you anyway?' he demanded to know.

All at once Stuart realized that it hadn't been a good move to come here. Belle was drunk and hysterical and Charles was sober and icy calm. Stuart began to explain, in much the same way he had to Belle, but she kept interrupting, and it was difficult to concentrate on how Charles was taking it.

He appeared to be unshaken, but then Stuart remembered he'd always been a cool customer.

'But how did you get involved enough to discover there was another will?' Charles asked, narrowing his eyes.

'Because I've been helping Laura to lodge an appeal.'

'You have been helping her?' Belle shrieked. 'When you last came here you said you wanted to offer your condolences!'

'That *is* what I came for,' Stuart said, but he kept his eyes on Charles because he guessed she'd never told him that he'd called. 'But I also didn't believe Laura killed her. Anyway, to answer your question, Charles, I spoke to someone who had witnessed a document for Jackie, and I had to check up whether she had lodged it officially or not. That took me to the lawyer who handled the purchase of Brodie Farm.'

'So you've been poking your nose in our family's business to help that scumbag?' Charles sneered.

'It is quite obvious from a letter left with the will that Jackie didn't consider her a scumbag,' Stuart retorted. 'Actually, she left me the impression that was her view of you!'

'How dare you!' Charles hissed at him.

'I dare because I can guess what you did to enrage Jackie,' Stuart said. 'It wasn't just that you'd been sponging off her for years, was it?'

'I don't know what you are suggesting, but you can get

out of this house now.' Charles rose to his feet threateningly.

'I'll go when I'm good and ready.' Stuart stood up too. 'You killed Barney, didn't you? But you were too much of a coward to stop and face what you had done. You just shot off to London to lie low.'

'That's a bloody lie,' Charles shouted and leapt towards Stuart.

Stuart caught him by the shoulders, forcing him back to arm's length. 'I know what you did,' he snarled at him. 'You killed the boy, you could easily have killed Jackie too, but all you cared about was your own skin. You disgust me. Why didn't Jackie turn you in? I bet she wanted to, but she couldn't bear the thought of Laura knowing it was a relative of hers that did it.'

'That slag didn't give a toss about the kid,' Charles flung out, trying to get away from Stuart. 'She was a junkie whore, she dumped him on Jackie all the time so she could screw more men and take more drugs. But you know all that, she chucked you out so she could find a rich man to fuck.'

Stuart's blood came up and he head-butted Charles. His legs buckled under him and as Stuart bent to yank him up again, Belle screamed.

'Are you proud of your old man?' Stuart shouted. 'He's the reason your sister turned against you. You've got nothing now, and I'm going to make certain the whole world knows why.'

Stuart was looking down at Charles, not watching Belle, when something very hard hit him on the back of the neck and he toppled forward on to the other man. He was stunned momentarily, and as he tried to get up he saw Belle was holding a white marble rolling pin in her hands and her face was contorted with rage.

'You won't be saying anything about us,' she roared at him. 'You're finished!'

She brought the heavy rolling pin down on his shoulder before he could move out of the way. He staggered under the force of the blow and Charles seized the opportunity to get to his feet. 'Enough, Belle,' he yelled. 'Let him go.'

'Let him go!' she screamed derisively. 'I haven't finished with him yet,' and she lifted the rolling pin again to hit Stuart.

He managed to dodge that blow, but still dazed from the first one, he didn't know Charles was behind him until he locked him in a half nelson.

'You always did think you were better than anyone else,' Charles hissed in his ear. 'But you won't get the better of me. You're leaving here now, and don't you ever come back.'

He began pushing Stuart towards the door into the hall. Stuart didn't struggle because however undignified it was to be forcibly thrown out, it was better than being killed, which for a moment or two he had thought was Charles's intention.

Belle brushed past as Charles forced him to the front door. 'Open it,' Charles ordered her.

Stuart felt a cold chill when he saw that Belle had a curious, almost gloating expression on her face. She wasn't attempting to open the front door, but stood with her back to it. Then he saw what she was holding by her side.

A large French cook's knife.

In fright he tried to free himself from Charles's grip just as she lunged forward, the knife held at her shoulder height. Charles released his arms and shouted for Belle to stop. Stuart tried to dodge, but she was too quick and she plunged the knife into him.

It was like a weird, slow-motion dream. He felt no real pain but the knife was sticking out of his chest and his cream shirt was turning crimson with blood. Belle had moved back from him now, and she was panting as if she'd run a mile, but her expression was not one of horror at what she'd done, only a crazed gloat.

'You're a mad fucking cow. You won't get away with this one,' he heard Charles yell at her.

Stuart felt himself growing dizzy. He thought it odd that he could feel a pain in his neck, but not his chest. He was aware of Charles pulling the knife out of his chest, and how frightened he looked, but Stuart's legs were folding under him.

He was aware he was now on the floor. He could feel the softness of the carpet and smell the wool. He could hear Belle and Charles arguing, but they seemed a long way off.

'It's through his heart. He'll die unless we call an ambulance,' Charles screamed at her, but Stuart couldn't make out what Belle's reply was, even though she was shouting. He didn't care anyway, for he was drifting off.

The next thing Stuart was aware of was being very cold. It was dark and he automatically reached out for blankets, but when his fingers met cold, dank concrete, he suddenly realized he wasn't in bed, but on the floor.

It came back to him then. Belle's face contorted with hatred as she lunged at him with a knife.

His neck was throbbing and so was his chest. He touched it lightly and felt the blood stiff on his shirt. Clearly he had passed out, and Belle and Charles had put him in their cellar.

A wave of sheer terror washed over him, but he forced himself to banish it and check how badly he was hurt. He lifted his head, which hurt, but not much worse than it did with a bad hangover. He could also move his arms and legs. Now all he had to concern himself with was the chest wound, and he'd test that by sitting up because he couldn't see it in the dark.

It hurt when he moved, and he thought he felt an increase

in blood flow from it, but he was alive, so that proved the knife had missed his heart. He could still die from loss of blood of course, and he wondered how long that would take.

But after a few moments of sitting up, it didn't appear to be flowing any faster, and although he knew his lungs were somewhere around there, he had to assume nothing vital had been punctured, so there was no need to be too alarmed.

Standing up came next, and that made him feel dizzy. He stretched out his arms and felt nothing, so he gingerly took a couple of steps sideways. His fingers encountered a rough brick wall. He shuffled up to it, put his back against it for support, and began moving along it until he felt something hard and loose beneath his feet.

It was coal. By groping with his hands in the darkness he ascertained there wasn't a great deal of it, probably the remnants from the previous winter. Slowly he made his way past the coal to the opposite wall, and back along it. He came to a wooden staircase. About six feet behind that was another wall.

Groping his way back to the staircase, he sat down on the bottom step and tried to gather himself sufficiently to decide what to do. Obviously they wanted him to die or they would have called an ambulance. Maybe they even thought he was already close to death when he passed out?

If that was the case it wouldn't do to climb the stairs and start thumping on the door, for that would alert them and he wasn't quite ready to be transported to a grave.

He couldn't see his watch face, but it felt as though it was the middle of the night. Yet he doubted it was, for it had only been six or so when Charles came in, and he couldn't have been unconscious for hours. He guessed it was no more than seven at the latest, and he wondered what Belle and Charles were doing.

He crawled up the stairs to see if he could hear anything. The exertion made him feel dizzy again, it hurt as he breathed, and his neck throbbed. The door was locked as he had expected, but the key hadn't been left on the other side, for through the keyhole he could see a tiny glimpse of the hall, and it was still daylight. He couldn't hear anything – voices, television or sounds from out in the street.

He checked his pockets. His car keys were gone, as was his wallet. A lone 10-pence piece was all they had left on him. He had nothing to try to pick the door lock with.

All at once the seriousness of his plight hit him. This wasn't some silly game, Belle and Charles weren't suddenly going to let him out, dress his wound and say they were sorry. Belle had intended to kill him, and it was blatantly obvious to him now that it was she, not Charles, who had killed Jackie. To think that just a few hours ago he was feeling sorry for her!

He cursed himself for coming out here. It was probably the most stupid and arrogant thing he'd done in his whole life. He might have believed Charles was the killer, but only a complete fool would purposely go to the home of a suspected murderer with the intention of stirring up a reaction.

At least Charles had wanted to call an ambulance. He supposed Belle must have talked him out of that.

What were they intending to do with him? Dead or alive, he was going to cause them a huge problem, and there was also his car outside to deal with.

Charles was no idiot. He would realize that this was one of the first places the police would come to once his body or car was found.

Unfortunately Stuart knew it would be some time before anyone became aware he was missing, and even longer before they called the police. David would be enjoying himself with his family, and even if he rang the flat and got no reply, he'd simply assume that Stuart had gone off to see friends, or even taken a job. As for Goldsmith, Stuart had hounded him so much recently that he'd just be glad to be left in peace to get on with his case.

Stuart slumped down at the top of the stairs in despair, very aware of the blood seeping from his wound. He guessed it would take a long time for him to bleed to death, but he knew it would gradually weaken him to the point where he wouldn't have the strength to escape if the opportunity arose.

After a few minutes he decided he must rouse himself and take stock of his situation, and he began by examining the door with his fingertips. He could feel big old-fashioned hinges on the inside of it, which if he'd had a screwdriver he could have got off in minutes. But without one that was impossible. Trying to batter the door down wasn't a good idea either; firstly, he had no room on his side to tackle it; secondly, it would bring Charles running, and thirdly, the force required would open up his wound. So that would have to be a last resort. But he could scour the cellar for something he could use as a tool.

It was only as he crawled across the floor, groping with his hands for anything useful, and reached the coal again, that it came to him that it must have been dropped in there through a hole. He'd watched coalmen delivering it to big houses as a boy and just outside the house there was always a round plate like a manhole cover, which they lifted off.

He reached up above his head with both arms, and his fingers met the cellar ceiling. But it hurt so much, with sharp pains shooting through his chest and shoulder, that he felt faint again.

The logical place to start looking for the coalhole cover was where there was the most coal, and as he crawled over it, with it digging into his knees and the dust making him sneeze, his hands found a familiar object. A shovel.

He felt a moment of exhilaration, for apart from it being a tool to hit either Belle or Charles with if they came down, he could also hack at the door with it.

Using it like a walking stick to support himself, he made a fingertip search of the ceiling with his right hand. To his delight he found the round metal hole cover, but it wouldn't budge when he tried pushing at it. Furthermore, he couldn't see even the tiniest chink of light around it either.

He was fairly certain by the dimensions of the cellar, and the position of the door that led out into the hall, that the coalhole was on the side of the house where the dining room was. Was it covered in gravel? Could a heavy plant pot be on top of it? How much noise would it make if he thumped it with the shovel handle?

Taking the 10-pence piece from his pocket, he pushed it into the rim of the hole and began scraping.

All his adult life he'd done hard physical work, humping heavy doors, roof timbers and window frames. He was used to working under cramped conditions, in extreme cold and heat, yet he'd never known anything as hard as trying to free something with a coin, and only using one hand, while standing precariously on coal in total darkness.

His shoulder and neck hurt as he scraped, he had to keep his eyes shut to prevent the dirt getting into them, and all the time he could feel his shirt becoming more sodden with blood. More alarming was the way he was wheezing, and he wondered if the knife had punctured his lung after all. But he wasn't going to start thinking about that, and carried on scraping and scraping with determination, for if he stopped to rest it would take valuable time to locate the cover again.

As he worked, he tried to think what Charles and Belle intended to do with him. If he were in their shoes, he would get a boat, take the body across the Forth and dump it close to Leith docks. There was a chance then that when it washed up somewhere, the police might think he had been stabbed in a mugging, then thrown into the sea. But to make that look plausible, his car would have to be driven back to Edinburgh and left parked close to the flat.

Maybe that was where they were now? Getting rid of his car would be the priority. Was Belle driving it and Charles following in his car to bring her back?

They might not think of a boat, because as far as Stuart was aware neither of them had ever sailed one. But perhaps Charles knew someone who would help him?

Fielding sprang into his mind. He was just the kind of maggot Charles used to surround himself with when he was playing the big shot in London. Jackie could have introduced the two men at some point, and if Fielding had Calder in his pocket, maybe he'd passed on the information about the deed of gift and the new will?

Finding out about the deed of gift would certainly have been enough to send Belle into a blind rage and driven her to attack Jackie. But the dates were all wrong. Ted said he witnessed the document before Christmas, and Jackie wasn't killed until the following May.

And Stuart was absolutely certain Belle hadn't known about the new will before he told her today. Her shock and dismay were too real.

Yet Charles was quite cool about it, so maybe he knew.

Stuart couldn't put a finger on what Fielding's role in all this was, but he was certain he did have one. Maybe he'd struck a deal with Charles that he would get Calder to suppress the new will for a percentage of what Belle would inherit in the old one?

But that still didn't explain why Belle killed Jackie when she did, or even why Calder didn't just destroy the new will.

A tiny sliver of light coming through the edge of the coalhole cover distracted Stuart from his ponderings, and in his excitement he redoubled his efforts to scrape more dirt away.

But excitement made him less cautious. He slipped on the coal and dropped his coin. He knew that he could never find it in the darkness. He slumped down dejectedly on to the coal. Sweat was pouring off him and he sensed it wasn't just because of the exertion. The loss of blood was weakening him, he could feel it seeping right down into his trousers and across the back of his shirt, and it hurt to breathe.

He looked up at the tiny crack of light and knew that even if he did manage to get the cover off, he was too weak now to be able to haul himself up through it. He was going to die here.

He lay back on the coal and closed his eyes wearily, but instead of the blankness he wanted, Laura's face jumped up. He could see her as she was when he first met her in Castle Douglas: shiny dark hair, long, suntanned legs, limpid dark eyes and a smile that rivalled the beauty of that morning. He compared that picture with the more recent one, and found that although there were a few lines around her eyes and her lips were not quite so plump, it wasn't so different. Her hair was shorter now, and more red than dark, but little else had changed. She was still beautiful to him. And he still wanted her.

'Then you must get out of here,' a small voice spoke within his head. 'Don't think about yourself, just think of Laura. She shouldn't be in prison, and you've got to get her freed. You can do that if you get out of here.'

It took a real effort to get to his feet and grab the shovel, he felt so dizzy, and pains were shooting though his chest. But he turned the shovel upside down, and grasping it firmly by the digging end, he thrust it upwards and hit the coalhole cover with the handle. The cover didn't move, but a great deal more dirt came showering down over him, and once he'd wiped his eyes he saw the chink of light had spread half-way around the cover.

He repeated it again, then again. His chest hurt so much it felt as if someone was burning him with hot coals, and blood was pumping out of the wound at an alarming rate. But he could feel movement in the cover and that was enough to keep him hammering away at it.

He guessed that if he'd had something to stand on, it would now be loose enough to push off, but he hadn't. He paused, weighing up the situation, and felt that if he could just hit it hard enough once, the cover would lift and tip back on to the ground outside.

He was in agony now, his shirt was soaked in blood, and he knew his pulse was growing weak. 'For you, Laura,' he muttered as he braced himself firmly on the coal. Grasping the shovel, he tried to shut out the pain and gather together his fast-depleting strength. 'One, two,' he counted. On three he thrust the shovel upwards with all the force he could muster.

A dull clang and the metal cover lifted. As daylight flooded in, he realized that yet another thrust was necessary to tip it completely off the hole. He braced himself yet again, every muscle in his body screaming for him to stop, but he ignored this and once again forced the shovel up. This time the cover was right off, but he fell backwards down on to the coal.

Even as he lay there panting and sweating, welcome fresh air wafting down on to his face, he knew he couldn't rest. Belle and Charles could come back at any moment, and he sensed he was only minutes away from total collapse.

With daylight streaming in, he could see how much blood he'd lost now – his shirt and trousers were completely soaked. But the next part was going to be even harder because he'd got to pull himself up by his hands, with arms which were already weak from the wound.

Embedding the shovel in the coal, he reached up for the edge of the hole, then prepared to lift one leg, ready to use the shovel as a springboard to launch his upper body far enough out of the hole to get free.

He knew it was unstable, but he reckoned if he could do it fast enough, it would work. He could only have one shot at it, for he sensed that a single leap would all but finish him.

Bracing himself, his fingers gripping the rim of the hole, he put his right foot on the handle of the shovel. 'One, two, three,' he counted, then jumped upwards.

His left shoulder jarred on the metal rim of the hole, sending shock waves down to the wound so close to it, but somehow he managed to spread his arms outside and slowly and painfully haul his body through.

The bright sunshine hurt his dust-filled eyes, his head was swimming, his legs like rubber, and the pain in his chest was excruciating. As he took the first few steps down the short drive to the gate, he felt as if he was in the middle of one of those dreams where he was being chased and trying to run but his legs were too heavy to move.

He willed himself not to faint until he reached the house next door.

'He banged on our door just as we were sitting down to dinner,' Mrs Edith Cameron told the two policemen who had arrived just seconds after the ambulance. 'I couldn't believe it. He looked like something from a horror film, all black with coal dust and soaked in blood. He could barely manage to speak, but what he did say was clear enough for me. Belle Howell stabbed him, and locked him in the cellar to die.'

Edith and her husband Henry were sedate pensioners who had lived in Crail for most of their married life. They had little to do with the Howells, and the high wall between Kirkmay House and their home meant they rarely even saw them. Edith was deeply shocked that such a thing could happen anywhere, let alone right next door to her.

'Is he going to be all right?' Henry Cameron asked as he watched the ambulance men lifting the injured man from his hall floor on to a stretcher.

'His pulse is very weak and he's lost a great deal of blood. It doesn't look good,' the ambulance man replied. 'Do you know his name?'

Henry shook his head. 'He passed out before we could ask him anything.'

The stretcher was wheeled down the garden path and lifted into the ambulance. Another minute and it was roaring off with its siren wailing.

'Now, Mr and Mrs Cameron, if you could just run through again what happened?' the older of the two policeman asked.

'You'd better come into the sitting room.' Mrs Cameron could see a bunch of people gathering on the other side of Marketgate. 'What a shock it gave us! Are you going in next door to arrest the Howells?'

16

'Hi, Patrick! Have you any idea where Stuart is?' David asked breezily when he phoned the lawyer's office.

David had rung his friend at the flat a couple of times in the last week, because he and Julia thought the kids might enjoy some time in Edinburgh seeing the sights before they went back to London, and he wanted to know if Stuart could put them up. When he got no reply, David assumed his friend had gone off somewhere for a job.

Today, with only a few more days left before they had to give up their holiday cottage in the Highlands, David thought he'd ring Goldsmith and ask if he had a contact number.

'In the hospital in Kirkcaldy,' Patrick replied.

'Hospital!' David exclaimed. 'Why, what's wrong with him?'

'Surely you heard about it on the news or read about it in the newspapers?' Patrick said, sounding puzzled. 'It got blanket coverage.'

David felt his stomach churn over. 'There's no television in the cottage we're staying at,' he said hurriedly. 'And I haven't bought a newspaper since I got here. Tell me what's happened.'

'He was stabbed and imprisoned by the Howells out in Crail,' Patrick began.

'You what!' David exclaimed. His stomach lurched again and he had to fumble for a chair to sit down on. Julia looked at him in alarm and mouthed, 'What's happened?'

She came and put her ear to the back of the phone as

Patrick explained what he knew of the events of nine days earlier and how Stuart had eventually managed to escape to the house next door where they called an ambulance for him. 'He was close to death,' Patrick said, and unusually for him his voice shook with emotion. 'Thankfully he's out of danger now, but it's been a very worrying time.'

It was a tremendous shock to David, and what he wanted was a detailed account of everything that had happened, what was said, done, the extent of Stuart's injuries and how he escaped, but frustratingly, although Patrick was clearly deeply concerned about Stuart, he was still being his usual cagey self, and seemed inclined to give him only the barest of facts, namely, that Stuart's lung had been punctured.

'Come on, Patrick,' David exclaimed in frustration. 'Why did he go there? Why did they attack him, and have the Howells been arrested?'

'I don't know what he was doing there, or how it came about,' Patrick admitted. 'But Belle and Charles were arrested later the same evening, and charged with attempted murder. When they appeared in court briefly thirty-six hours later, they were refused bail and remanded in custody pending further investigations.'

'Have you visited Stuart?' David asked, beginning to feel angry.

'I went there as soon as I heard about it, but he was in intensive care and not up to visitors. I haven't been able to get there since due to pressure of work, but I do know that he has been able to give the police enough information for them to open a new investigation into Jackie Davies's murder.'

'He's found evidence it was Charles?'

'Apparently he alleges Belle killed her.'

David left Julia and the children and drove straight down to the hospital in Kirkcaldy. The long drive, and the inevitable hold-ups because of the holiday traffic, only increased his anxiety and by the time he reached Stirling he had a thumping headache.

For as long as he'd known Stuart he'd always been something of a madcap. He would be the first to take up a challenge, always inclined to take the side of the underdog, impulsive, daring and often reckless. Perhaps that was what David liked and admired most about him, but at the same time it had often infuriated him too.

The night before Julia flew into Edinburgh, David had sensed Stuart wanted some kind of action. If he'd known that leaving him to his own devices would lead to him risking his life, he would have insisted he came up to the Highlands too. But his old friend wasn't the kind anyone could lead around by the nose. And it certainly wouldn't have occurred to him just how many people would have grieved for him if he had been killed.

It was such a relief when he walked into the ward to find Stuart sitting up in bed, grinning like a Cheshire Cat. Apart from his chest being swathed in bandages and his pale face, he looked remarkably well.

'It's a good job I didn't rely on you to rescue me,' he joked. 'Some mate you are turning up nine days too late!'

David didn't consider himself to be an emotional man, but he felt like hugging Stuart just because he was alive. He listened to the story of exactly what had transpired in Kirkmay House: the fight in the kitchen, how Belle stabbed him and how he got out of the cellar. Although he chuckled along with Stuart as if he was relating some schoolboy adventure, in fact his blood ran cold and he felt sick at the thought of what could have happened.

But he found he couldn't hide his true feelings for long. 'You harebrained imbecile!' he blurted out once he'd heard the whole story. 'What on earth possessed you to go there?'

'I just wanted to stir things up,' Stuart grinned. 'I succeeded too, didn't I?'

'Stir things up!' David shouted, forgetting that he was supposed to be a calm, mild-mannered man. 'You could easily be dead now, or so badly injured you'd never work again. The ward sister told me it was touch and go when you were brought in here. Didn't you think of those who care about you before you took such risks? You've got an elderly mother and a brother and sister, not to mention friends like me who love you!'

Stuart had the grace to look a little sheepish. 'Okay, maybe it was a tad extreme, but at least the police have arrested them both, they are looking into Jackie's murder again, and Laura will almost certainly get bail if Patrick can get an emergency hearing in court for her.' He paused, then went on, a sly grin twitching his lips, 'I never realized you loved me, Davey! Good job I didn't know that in some of the remote places we've been together!'

David had to laugh then, but that was another thing he liked about Stuart – he could find humour in anything. And the man was right. Laura's appeal in the High Court of Justiciary could now go through unchallenged, as long as the police had sufficient evidence that she hadn't committed the crime.

'It's good to see you,' Stuart said. 'I'm sorry you had to cut your holiday short and drive all this way. Do you know if they've found my car yet?'

'No, I don't. Funnily enough, I was more concerned about you than your car,' David retorted. 'But I'll find out for you. It will serve you right if Charles parked on double yellows and it's been towed away. Anyway, you won't be driving for some time.'

'You can be a bit of an old woman, you know,' Stuart

retorted. 'Now, stop worrying about me and go back to the Highlands.'

David asked him about bringing Julia and the children back to stay in the flat the following week. 'We could look after you, and we'll keep the kids out of your hair.'

'That's still full of dried blood,' Stuart grimaced, putting one hand up to touch his hair. 'I still feel as if my lungs are full of coal dust too. But it would be good to have you all around for a bit. I'm sure Julia can be trusted to wash up occasionally.'

'She can be trusted to wash your hair, feed you and tell you you're a hero.' David smiled. 'She was horrified when we found out what had happened to you.'

'Make out I'm more of a wounded soldier than I really am.' Stuart laughed. 'By the way, did you know that Belle's been taken to Cornton Vale?'

'Shit!' David whistled through his teeth. It hadn't occurred to him to ask where Belle had been taken. 'Do you think she'll come in contact with Laura?'

'Belle will be on the remand block. But knowing Laura as I do, I've no doubt she'll find a way of getting to her. I wrote to her a couple of days ago and warned her to keep away, but I don't hold out much hope of her obeying. If I'd been locked up for two years for something I hadn't done, I'd want revenge too.'

As David was visiting Stuart, Laura was busy in the library, but it wasn't revenge that was in the forefront of her mind, only a desperate need to know the truth.

She had first heard the news about Stuart being taken to hospital from Beady, a week earlier. Beady had reported excitedly that when a photograph of him was flashed on to the screen, she recognized him as Laura's visitor.

Laura's initial reaction to the information that Belle and

479

Charles had been arrested for Stuart's attempted murder was one of incredulity. She could understand them being furious that she was to inherit Brodie Farm, and her sisters to get Kirkmay House, but it made no sense that they'd taken their anger out on Stuart. She was convinced that it would turn out that it was merely a brawl between the two men which had gone too far.

When Patrick Goldsmith came to visit her the following day, and told her that Stuart had been convinced for some time that it was Charles who killed Jackie, it began to make some sense. Laura could imagine Stuart going over to Crail with the sole purpose of provoking Charles. She had just about got her head round that, when Patrick went on to say that Stuart was alleging it was Belle who had stabbed him. Furthermore, Stuart was convinced that it was she who had killed Jackie, not Charles.

But Patrick was a lawyer through and through. He used words like 'allegedly' and 'it seems likely', not once revealing his own personal opinion. Nor did he share with her any inside information gathered from the police, or even tell her the street gossip about it.

He didn't stay long with her either, leaving her with the news that the police had made a statement to the effect that they were opening a new investigation into Jackie's murder, and as such he should be able to get an emergency appeal for her on the grounds that it had been an unsafe conviction.

Laura was left totally bewildered. While it sounded very much to her as if her appeal was in the bag, and freedom was around the corner, Patrick's coolness suggested she shouldn't count on it.

That night she would have given anything to be able to phone Stuart or David for a clearer explanation and their take on the situation. Ever since she was sentenced she had watched other prisoners fighting over phone cards, spending a whole evening queuing for their turn on the phone, and never once felt the desire to ring anyone herself. Suddenly everyone was prepared to stand back and let her make as many phone calls as she liked, but apart from Meggie there was no one she could call, for she couldn't contact either of the men.

Meggie didn't know about the attack on Stuart as it hadn't reached the newspapers in England, which made it tough on Laura as she had to explain the whole thing before she could even attempt to get to the real point of her call. She never did get there, for Meggie swung between delight in speaking to her sister and anxiety about Stuart, not really taking in what Laura was trying to say. Once her phone card ran out, she was left just as bewildered and unsure about everything as she had been before.

By the next day the whole prison was buzzing with the news that the press had gone into an orgy of rehashing Jackie's murder and Laura's trial. Beady brought one news-paper in for her with a large photograph of Laura on the front page and a headline, '*Has she been wronged?*'

The press interest in Laura, and Belle's arrival on the remand block, was the talk of the prison now. Laura found it quite amusing that all those who had so often scornfully disbelieved her protests that she was innocent were now sucking up to her. But rather more worrying was the general opinion among her fellow prisoners that she should get hold of Belle and wreak her revenge.

She did want to get hold of Belle, but not to attack her. She just wanted to know the truth. It was patently obvious that Belle had stabbed Stuart, and he wouldn't have said she killed Jackie too unless he was certain of it, but Laura still couldn't quite believe it. She wouldn't until she heard it from Belle herself.

Nobody seemed to understand that, least of all Patrick

Goldsmith who had merely shrugged and said that nothing was proved yet, but it would all come out eventually at her trial.

Laura couldn't wait that long. She had been the person who found Jackie dead, she'd even pulled the knife out of her. And there had been times in the darkest moments while she'd been in this place when she'd begun to think she must have done it, but blanked it out, just as the police psychiatrist had suggested.

She had always thought of Belle as a younger sister, and as such she'd taken it in her stride when Belle was sometimes offhand with her. She did think it was unkind to banish her to stay at Brodie Farm just after Barney was killed, but she'd put that down to Belle being overwrought and not thinking straight. She had been nasty on several occasions after that too, but Laura had never had any inkling that Belle hated her. Yet she must have done if she would let her be wrongfully imprisoned for life. And that was what she wanted to know. Why she hated her.

There was no shortage of news about how Belle was faring in prison, but then even the most trivial piece of news passed along the grapevine at the speed of light. By all accounts she was fluctuating between hysteria and aggression, and treating her fellow prisoners as if they were sub-human and she was royalty. Someone said she got up one morning to find her hair was coming out in clumps. Laura had known alopecia strike other women here, but to Belle, whose appearance was everything, it must have been a cruel blow.

Laura was just putting a few returned books back on the shelves when she sensed everyone in the library stiffen. She turned to see that Belle had come in with Prison Officer

Blake, whom Laura remembered well from her time on the remand block.

Belle looked awful; her hair was like a bird's nest, and she had bald patches. She was pale and drawn, and the oversized trousers and shirt she was wearing clearly weren't her own, for they were made of the kind of polyester fabric she would never wear.

She looked aghast at finding herself face to face with Laura. Clearly she hadn't been warned that she worked in the library.

'I don't want any scenes, Brannigan,' Blake said, her tone sharp and suspicious. 'Howell just wants a book.'

Laura could hardly blame Blake for her attitude towards her – she had after all been a difficult prisoner while on remand. Yet she had a sneaky feeling that Blake had brought Belle here hoping for trouble.

'I don't do scenes any longer,' Laura said icily. She didn't like Blake – the woman had a very cruel streak, she enjoyed giving prisoners bad news and was well known for inciting trouble on her block by setting one woman against another. She walked up closer to Belle. 'Hello, Belle, what kind of book are you after?'

'I don't know,' she said, her voice little more than a whisper. 'Just something easy to read.'

'There's Danielle Steel or Catherine Cookson,' Laura said. 'The first book I read in here was *The Wheel of Fortune* by Susan Howatch. That would be appropriate for you too.'

There was a flicker of something in Belle's eyes; she'd clearly realized that was a sly dig at her. 'Anything will do,' she said.

'I would really like to talk to you,' Laura said. 'Not here in front of everyone, somewhere more private. If I ask the governor, will you agree to it?'

'Don't be ridiculous, Brannigan,' Blake roared out. 'Now, get her a couple of books pronto.'

After that chance meeting with Belle, Laura was even more unsettled and nervy. Word reached her that the police were coming almost every day to interview Belle, and she felt tortured by not knowing what was going on. She was worried about Stuart, for although he'd written from the hospital to say he was on the mend and he hoped to see her soon, the letter seemed very stilted and formal. That gave her the idea he was in a lot of pain.

Finally, on the Monday, sixteen days after Stuart had been stabbed, she was called from the library because Patrick Goldsmith had come to see her.

As she walked into the interview room, his face broke into the widest smile. 'I've got some great news for you. We've got an emergency court hearing tomorrow. I'm ninety-nine per cent sure I'll be able to get you bail until your appeal. The prosecution aren't likely to oppose it, not after the recent developments.'

Laura felt quite faint with the shock, not just of his news, but that Patrick was capable of being so jubilant. He had told her the previous week that this might be possible, but he hadn't given her any indication that things could happen this quickly.

'You mean I can just walk away from the court?' she said incredulously.

Patrick laughed. 'Yes, of course. There is one small problem though, you don't have anywhere to live, and that will be a condition of the bail. As there was no time to arrange accommodation in Edinburgh, I'm afraid I took the liberty of ringing your sister Meggie to ask her if you could stay with her in London. I hope you don't mind?'

'No, not at all,' Laura said. She had written to Meggie

since her telephone conversation with her, but as yet she had not received a reply. 'But more importantly, did she mind?'

'She's delighted, and what's more, she's flying up this evening to be with you in court tomorrow.'

Laura's eyes filled with tears of emotion. 'That's wonderful,' she said in a choked voice. 'Thank you so much, Patrick, I wouldn't have liked to ask her myself, it's a bit of an imposition, but I'll be much happier to be in London than staying here.'

'That was Stuart's feeling too,' Patrick said, and his voice had real warmth in it. 'He thought you'd be the focus of too much media attention here. He came out of hospital on Friday and I popped in to see him last night.'

'How is he?' she asked eagerly, wishing she'd known he was back home so she could have phoned him.

'Much better than he deserves to be. Weak and in some pain, but he's his old irrepressible self again. David and his wife are looking after him. I don't think he'll be in court tomorrow, he really isn't up to that, but he said he'll be thinking of you, and hopes you and Meggie can spare the time to see him before you fly back to London.'

'We'll make time,' Laura beamed, suddenly aware that this was for real, she was getting out of here, thanks to Stuart. 'He's been my guardian angel.'

'Then I'll see you in court at ten tomorrow,' Patrick said as he got up to leave. He took her hand and, in an uncharacteristic display of affection, squeezed it with both hands. 'It's the appeal I'm really waiting for. I want to see you exonerated and this awful business over once and for all. But tomorrow will be pretty good too.'

In a flash of intuition Laura suddenly understood the man better. He probably wasn't cut out to be a criminal lawyer, and over the years he'd almost certainly had to defend a great many people he found repellent. He dealt with it by detaching himself, doing the job as well as he could, but without any passion.

A cynic would say he was only unbending with her now because at last he had a winner, but she would rather think that Stuart's intervention had shown him that there was something to like about her.

She leaned forward and kissed his cheek. 'Bless you,' she murmured. 'And thank you for everything.'

Bravo Block was alight with excitement that evening, just as it always was when one of their number was going to court and their release looked likely. There was a generosity of spirit at such times, everyone offering something, be it an article of clothing, a keepsake, or just advice and good wishes.

Laura's appearance had been scrutinized by everyone. Even the girls in their late teens and early twenties who normally believed a woman of fifty was too old for anyone to care how she looked, had offered suggestions for improvements. Laura had had her hair trimmed and coloured by the hairdresser during the afternoon. It was a sleek dark brown bob again, and one of the girls had given her a manicure and painted her nails a pretty pink. Shelley, one of the young girls on the wing, had plucked her eyebrows for her too.

Getting back the outfit which had been in storage since the day she was convicted was bittersweet. The terrible memories of that day, and the sheer hopelessness she'd felt, came back with the force of a bulldozer when she was handed her clothes. But the navy-blue pinstriped suit and white shirt still fitted her perfectly, even if the power-suit shoulder pads had gone out of fashion while she'd been inside, and she began to feel excited rather than afraid. She wasn't sure she could walk in high heels again, but they felt so elegant and feminine she didn't care if they crippled her.

She had nothing other than a few toiletries and her spare sets of clothes to give away to the other women, for she hadn't ever bothered to collect stuff up like most of them did. All she was taking with her was the notebook she'd been writing her life story in, and she hoped that sometime in the future she'd have a happy postscript to add to it.

But when everyone was finally locked in their cells for the night, and she heard the women calling to one another as usual all the way down the block, she suddenly felt afraid again.

However bad it had been in here sometimes, there was a kind of safety and predictability about it. Tomorrow, when she was out in the mainstream of life again, would she be able to cope? She couldn't even imagine crossing a road, let alone driving again, or going into a pub and buying a drink. She was going to miss the other women, even though she'd made no strong friendships in prison.

Would she have anything in common with other women on the outside? What on earth would she talk about? She buried her head in books most of the time here, and when she did have a chat with someone it was mostly about their family problems. She knew more than she wanted to know about abusive relationships, out-of-control teenagers, truants, pimps, fences, alcoholism and drug-taking. It had become her world. She'd lost all sense of the Laura Brannigan who had once owned her own dress shop.

'And it is Mrs Brannigan's intention to live with her sister in Catford, London?' The judge peered over his glasses at Goldsmith below his bench.

'Yes, Your Honour,' Goldsmith replied. 'Miss Wilmslow is present in court if you would like to speak to her.'

Meggie caught Laura's eye and grinned encouragingly at her.

The sisters hadn't had any opportunity to speak to each other yet. Laura had been brought to the High Court by prison van, and was already waiting in the dock when Meggie came into the courtroom with Goldsmith. It had been over five years since they last met. They might have talked on the phone every week before Laura went to prison, and written to each other more recently, but that hadn't prepared Laura for seeing her younger sister again in the flesh.

Meggie was forty-four now, and her once long dark hair was cut into a rather severe bob. She was a little plumper too, and her navy-blue trouser suit and sensible flat shoes made her look matronly. Laura wondered if the outfit, and the lack of makeup, was intended to make her look like a very responsible person, but as Meggie had always tended to be old for her years, she suspected that this image was now her usual one.

The judge said he would like to speak to Meggie and the court usher directed her to come forward to the bench.

'Do you understand what bail conditions mean?' he asked her. 'That Mrs Brannigan must reside with you, and present herself once a week at your local police station? Bail will be set at the sum of five thousand pounds. If Mrs Brannigan does not adhere to these conditions or fails to appear at her next court hearing, you will be expected to forfeit that sum.'

'I understand, Your Honour,' Meggie replied.

'Then you may take your sister home with you now,' he said.

'Is that it then?' Laura said nervously once they'd come out of the courtroom into the vestibule. She'd been hovering on the verge of a panic attack throughout the proceedings; there were so many whispered consultations between the lawyers and she felt sure the judge was going to refuse her bail.

Goldsmith smiled at both the sisters. 'Yes. That's it, you can go. But as soon as you get to Catford make sure you present yourself at the police station and find out which day of the week they expect to see you. Don't attempt to go out of the country either. I shall keep in touch and let you know any developments. Meanwhile, enjoy your freedom, you deserve it.'

'Thank you,' Laura said. It seemed so odd that Patrick was suddenly so much warmer to her. She actually believed he cared now. She looked nervously through the door on to the street. 'Will there be press out there?'

'I'm afraid so,' he said, grimacing. 'It isn't any good trying to avoid them, they'll only follow you. If you like I could make a statement for you. You just smile for the photographs.'

There were five or six photographers and as many journalists, one of whom Laura recognized as having visited her in prison just after the trial. There was also a cameraman, presumably from the local television station. As she and Meggie got to the High Court door with Goldsmith, they pressed forward, cameras flashing and shouting out questions.

Meggie caught hold of Laura's arm tightly as she faltered. But Goldsmith took a step forward. 'Mrs Brannigan would like me to make a statement to you for her, then I ask that you respect the ordeal she has been through and allow her some privacy and peace.

'Mrs Brannigan has been granted bail pending her appeal. I have every confidence that her appeal will be successful now that the police are reinvestigating the murder of Jacqueline Davies. Mrs Brannigan has always maintained that she was innocent of the crime. It is our belief that this will soon be proved.'

'Are you staying in Edinburgh, Laura?' a female voice called out.

A man with red hair pushed his way to the front of the journalists. 'Will you be visiting Stuart Macgregor? Is it true he was stabbed because he was doing some private investigation on your behalf?' he asked.

'That's enough now,' Goldsmith said firmly, and taking Laura's arm, he drew her and Meggie through the crowd and away down the High Street.

'You'll be fine now,' he said as they reached North Bridge. He looked behind him just to check none of the press had followed them. 'But I'll come further with you if you like.'

'No, you go,' Laura said. 'We don't need an escort, and I'm sure you've got plenty of other clients that need you.'

'What's it to be first?' Meggie asked as they walked down towards the bridge. 'A big fried breakfast, a burger, or maybe some alcohol?'

Laura laughed. 'None of those. What I'd really like is a cappuccino, just to sit and drink it and watch people for a while, and of course to catch up with what you've been doing.'

'Laura, wait up!'

At the shout from behind they turned their heads to see a tall, slender woman with long blonde hair trying to run towards them, hampered not only by high heels but by a wheeled suitcase she was pulling behind her. As she got nearer Laura recognized her as Angie.

'Thank goodness I caught you,' she said breathlessly as she reached them. 'I got to the court too late, I could just see you in the distance, so I ran all the way.'

She paused to catch her breath. 'Obviously the hearing was successful or you wouldn't be out here,' she said. 'I read in the paper about Stuart being stabbed by Belle. I wanted to get in touch then, but I didn't think you'd want to know me any more. Then Stuart rang me last night and told me about the hearing today. I wanted to be there to give you some support, but I got held up in traffic.'

Laura felt a sort of inner glow to be once again listening to Angie's breathless explanation. She had always been that way, always late, always rushing, yet she never failed to look as if she'd just stepped off the pages of *Vogue*. The pale blue Chanel-style suit she was wearing had been Angie's mother's; Laura remembered helping her to alter it. That was at least five years ago, but it looked as chic now as it had then.

'It's good to see you again, Angie,' Laura said, and moved nearer to give the younger woman a hug. 'I understood how it was for you, too much poison was dripped out for anyone to believe in me. This is my sister Meggie. We were just going to get some coffee. Why don't you come with us?'

She glanced down at Angie's suitcase. 'Or are you going off somewhere?'

'Oh no.' Angie smiled. 'These are things for you. Stuart knew I'd stored your things and he asked if I could dig some of them out as you wouldn't have any clothes.'

'My clothes!' Laura exclaimed in delight. 'Wonderful! I thought I'd have to borrow some of Meggie's.'

'I'm afraid they aren't actually yours.' Angie looked a bit crestfallen. 'You see, your stuff is at my mother's, and I couldn't go there last night. So I raided the shop, and got you some new undies and things this morning. I hope you don't mind?'

Laura smiled. She didn't really care what she put on. To be out of prison was more than enough for now, and she was so touched Angie had gone to all that trouble. 'You always had good taste, so I'm sure they are lovely.'

'I'm so relieved to see you are still the same size.' Angie

looked at her appraisingly. 'Stuart said you were, but men don't always see things as we do.'

Laura picked out a coffee bar in Princes Street which was over a shoe shop. The windows were huge, giving a great view of the Castle and Old Town, plus people out shopping. She eagerly bagged a table by the window and Meggie and Angie went to get the coffee.

'Isn't it a beautiful city?' she said as they came back. She waved her hand at the view. 'You'd think I would be disenchanted with it after all the nasty things that have happened here. But I still love it.'

'I was kind of hoping you'd get to love London again so Ivy and I could spend more time with you,' Meggie said. 'But it sounds like your heart is here. Maybe after the appeal Ivy, Derek and the kids and me could come up for a holiday and find out what's so good about it.'

'You'll have your own place to stay in,' Laura said, but when she saw Meggie's puzzled expression, she realized Goldsmith hadn't yet told her about Jackie's will. She couldn't tell her now, not in front of Angie, so instead she pulled the suitcase close to her and opened it just enough to peep.

On the top was a dark red velvet jacket, and she knew without pulling it out properly that it would be fabulous.

'Oh, Angie,' she sighed. 'You can't imagine how good it will be to put on nice clothes again, thank you so much. But what do I owe you?'

'Nothing, of course.' Angie looked embarrassed. 'It's the very least I can do. You let me take over the shop, and we never sorted out a price. When you are finally acquitted we must have a talk about it and come to an agreement. I've been putting money away for you in a savings account, but it may not be enough.'

'Angie, you were there for me the whole time I was on remand,' Laura said reprovingly. 'I know it must have been tough for you to keep the shop going with all the bad press. I'm not going to come back and try to snatch it from you. I told you it was yours two years ago, and I meant it.'

'But you'll need money,' Angie insisted.

'I still have my savings.' Laura shrugged. 'And I didn't even spend all the wages I got inside. The other women spent theirs on ciggies and sweets, I hoarded mine. I'm probably the only woman ever to come out of prison richer than when I went in.'

Laura slipped off to the toilet, and when she came back Angie and Meggie were laughing about something. 'What have I missed?' she asked.

'We were just discussing how gorgeous Stuart is,' Meggie giggled. 'We think you ought to get round there right now and make him forget his aches and pains.'

'I wish I could,' Laura smiled. 'But that isn't on his agenda. He's rescued the damsel in distress, and as soon as he's well he'll be off on to some other mission.'

'Don't be daft,' Meggie said stoutly. 'He's still got the hots for you.'

'Of course he has,' Angie agreed. 'I could tell just by the way he spoke about you last night. I didn't know that he was an old flame until Meggie told me, but I can tell you, the flame hasn't gone out.'

Laura shook her head. 'I'm not what he needs. I'm all used up now and too old. What I want is a quiet life on my own, books, a dog perhaps, maybe I'll take up gardening too. I haven't got any passion left in me, it's all gone.'

Angie got into a taxi when they left the coffee bar. She had to go back to the shop in Morningside. Meggie and Laura walked back up to the Old Town to meet Stuart.

'I'm so excited about seeing him again,' Meggie admitted. 'He was so nice that day he came to see me. He's one of those rare people who is capable of putting himself in others' shoes without judging them. I ended up telling him stuff I've never told anyone else.'

'That was my biggest mistake with him,' Laura sighed. 'Not telling him everything about myself when I first met him. I spent a lot of time inside thinking over why I lied and kept on lying. I thought I had good reason at the time, but now, after all that's happened, it just seems such a waste. If I hadn't been so stubborn and afraid I could have had you and Ivy close to me.'

'Lots of sisters aren't close even when everything is completely normal in their families,' Meggie said evenly, catching hold of her sister's hand and squeezing it. 'At least we have always really loved each other, and besides, none of that matters now, we've got the rest of our lives to catch up.'

'You took your time!' Stuart said accusingly as he opened the door of his flat to them. 'I've been watching the clock, afraid that something had gone wrong and they didn't give you bail. I was just about to ring Patrick.'

'We went to have a cup of coffee with Angie,' Laura said apologetically. 'It never occurred to me you'd be waiting and worrying.'

Stuart smiled. 'You're here now, that's all that matters. I just wish I'd felt strong enough to get up to the court.'

'Is it still painful?' Laura reached out and gently touched his chest. She could feel the bandages beneath his shirt.

'It's okay unless I move too quickly. I have to put my arm back in a sling sometimes to rest it. But it's the feeling weak which bugs me. I'm not used to that. Enough of that now! Hello, Meggie, in all the excitement I'm guilty of overlooking you.'

'It's good to see you again, Stuart,' Meggie said shyly. 'But you're alone! Where are your friends?'

'Gone down to have a look at Holyrood palace,' Stuart replied. 'We didn't think it was a good thing for the kids to be here when you called, too much like Bedlam. But David and Julia are sorry not to be able to see you both. Now, how about a drink?'

Despite a very welcome gin and tonic, which ought to have relaxed her, Laura felt awkward with Stuart. She didn't know if it was because Meggie was there, because he was hurt, or just that she was overwhelmed by her new freedom, but she didn't know what to say to him.

There was just *too* much to say, she supposed. Her gratitude, remorse at hurting him in the past, how it felt to be free again, even how good the coffee in Princes Street tasted and how thrilling it was to see Edinburgh again. She wanted to ask him so many questions about what happened to him in Crail. And about his plans for the future. But although she was saying all this in her head, hardly one word was coming out of her mouth.

Meggie had no such problem. She was rattling away about another property she and Ivy had bought that they were converting into three flats.

'You are very quiet, Laura,' Stuart said after a little while. 'I hope that's not because we're boring you?'

'No, of course not,' she said quickly. 'I guess I'm just a bit stunned at being here with you both. It's a bit odd thinking I'm going to be staying in London too.'

'Would you rather have stayed here in Edinburgh?' Stuart asked.

Laura didn't know how to reply to that. Edinburgh was home, at least in her heart, and Stuart was here too. But she couldn't say that, it would make him feel awkward and hurt Meggie's feelings too.

'No, I wouldn't want to stay here. I want to be with Meggie, but I'm just a bit nervous about London, it's a long time since I was last there.'

'You'll soon adjust,' Meggie said, looking at Laura anxiously. 'Are you hungry? Maybe we should go and get something before we go out to the airport?'

Stuart got up. 'I'd clean forgotten,' he said. 'Julia made a lasagne for us. I'll go and put it in the oven to warm through.'

'I'll do that,' Meggie said. 'You sit down and talk to Laura.'

Meggie went off to the kitchen and Stuart sat down again on the settee.

'How long will it be before you can work again?' Laura asked.

'I should be fit for project managing in about two weeks,' he said. 'As long as that doesn't entail doing any manual work myself. I thought I might sign up for a computer course or something in the meantime. Once David goes back to London it's going to be very boring here on my own.'

'What if you came to London too?' Laura said. 'Maybe Meggie could do with a project manager?'

'Does that mean you'd like me to come to London? Or are you just concerned that I'll shrivel up and die of boredom up here alone?'

'Of course I'd like you to come to London,' she said, and giggled because he was looking at her so intently. 'But I suppose I'd like to see you putting your own life back together. One way or another I've kind of buggered it up again, haven't I?'

'No, you haven't. It might be true that I came back here because of you, but I don't feel you've buggered me up in any way. It was all my own idea to go over and see Belle, and even if I am a bit stuck now because of the wound, I do at least have the satisfaction of knowing it changed things enough to get you out of prison.'

'You've been wonderful, Stuart,' she said softly. 'I was trapped in a very black hole until you turned up and dropped a rope ladder down to me. I can never thank you enough for what you've done. You're such a big man, with an even bigger heart. I didn't deserve help, not from you.'

'You have a worrying tendency to always think you aren't worth anything,' he said, looking straight into her eyes. 'It isn't true of course, it never was. When I first went to work for Jackie in London I was very bitter and sad. Jackie pulled me up about it once. She said, "Never mind that she did the dirty on you. Think about what she gave you." I couldn't see what she meant at the time, but I do now.'

'What?' Laura asked. She didn't remember giving him anything other than grief.

'You opened my eyes to a wider world than Edinburgh,' he said. 'You gave me the ability to stand on my own feet, and the determination to make something of myself. But best of all you made me believe I could do anything, and that, Laura, has been the very best thing of all.'

'You would have got all those things without me,' she said.

Stuart shook his head. 'No, Laura. If I hadn't met you, I might have drifted off on the hippy trail for a while, but I'd have come back to Edinburgh and got work and stayed. No doubt I'd have married, had kids and all that stuff, and probably have been happy enough, but I wouldn't have achieved my full potential, seen the things I have seen.'

Laura shrugged. It was nice of him to credit her with improving his prospects, but she didn't believe it was down to her.

*

Laura told Meggie about Jackie's will while they were sitting waiting at the airport for their flight to be called. Not surprisingly she was overwhelmed at such generosity from a stranger, and she shed a few emotional tears.

'What on earth will Ivy and I do with a guest house?' she asked, wiping her eyes. 'We wouldn't have a clue how to run one.'

'You don't have to,' Laura said. 'You could just sell it and share the money, or get it converted into flats or something. People who work in St Andrews at the university are always after places in Crail.'

'Are you going to live at Brodie Farm?' Meggie asked.

'I couldn't bear to after what happened there,' Laura said sadly. 'I always loved the place, and Jackie knew that, and I'd like to be close to Barney too, but well, I'm sure you know.'

'Jackie must have cared an awful lot for you to give it to you, and to want us to have the other place so we could all be close,' Meggie said thoughtfully. 'But it does feel just a bit like she wanted to control us.'

'Just a bit,' Laura agreed. 'She did like to do that, and I suppose I always let her. I'm going to miss her so much now I'm out of prison. She played such a huge part in my whole adult life. I can't imagine not being able to tell her about a new job, clothes I've bought or where I'm living.'

'You've got me and Ivy for that now,' Meggie said, slipping her arm through her sister's and cuddling up against her shoulder. 'And I'll be tucking you into bed in my spare room, making you breakfast, and asking you what you want to watch on telly. That is, until Stuart comes down to London and takes over.'

Laura sniggered. 'You are seeing things that aren't there, Meggie. He didn't even hug or kiss me today.'

'His chest hurts, and anyway, he didn't get any encouragement from you. You were like an icicle.'

'I wasn't!'

'You were. You sat on the other side of the room. Even when I went into the kitchen to heat up the lasagne, you didn't move to sit beside him.'

Their flight was called, interrupting the conversation, but once they were on board and waiting for takeoff, Meggie began again.

'He still loves you, Laura. Don't let him slip away again.'

'It's kinder that I do.' Laura closed her eyes, for she was suddenly very tired. 'Like I said earlier today, I'm all used up.'

That was exactly how she felt, all used up, like an empty perfume bottle that still looked attractive on the dressing table, retained a little of its fragrance but was no use to anyone.

When she thought back to the twelve years from Barney's death to when she was arrested she could see now that she'd been like an empty shell. She looked good, she worked hard, and everyone saw her as a successful woman who had exactly the kind of life she wanted. There were men in her life, she went out to dinner and parties, and sometimes even spent weekends walking in the Trossachs. A few of the men she liked enough to go to bed with, but she never felt that vital spark which might have led to love. She remembered Alan, a sweet man who was a vet, asking in rather puzzled tones what it was she wanted, and she answered, 'Nothing'. He said that was what he suspected, and if she wanted nothing, that's what she would get. He likened her to a very high wall, and he said he had the distinct feeling that even if he managed to climb to the top of it, he'd find nothing on the other side.

He was right of course. She might have recovered from the shock of losing Barney, she no longer cried and spent long nights beating herself up about what she had been in those days. But the hole Barney left in her life remained there; work, going out, a nice flat and good clothes didn't fill it. She was empty inside, just like the perfume bottle. Alan moved on, other men came and went too. She wasn't hurt by it, mostly she was glad to be alone – that way she didn't have to feel guilty about her lack of feeling.

All she wanted now was to be with her sisters, to try to make it up to them for all the sadness and worry she'd caused them. She had indulged in a few romantic thoughts about Stuart, but this was normal for women in prison, it was just another form of escapism. She'd heard women inside talking in loving terms about men she knew to be brutes, wasters and cheats. That was just how it was, and in their heart of hearts they knew perfectly well it wouldn't work when they got out.

She was just grateful to Stuart for helping her when no one else would. She didn't have to embroider that into love.

The last days of August slipped by for Laura in a sweet, golden haze of contentment. She loved everything about Meggie's pretty, ordered house: the way the sun came into her room in the mornings, the fluffy towels in the luxurious bathroom, the light, bright kitchen, and the comfort of the big settees in the sitting room where she could watch television without the endless arguments she had grown used to in prison. But most of all she loved the garden, and she spent most of her time out there, lying in the sun, letting her mind wander at will.

Meggie spent at least two days a week out checking on her properties, dealing with repairs and overseeing building work. The rest of the week she worked in her small office upstairs, sometimes alone, sometimes with Ivy. Laura found it difficult to come to terms with the knowledge that these two smartly dressed, dynamic businesswomen were the little sisters she used to wash, change and feed when she was still only a child herself.

Laura had always seen her sisters as being very alike, and very different from her. But now she could see that she and Ivy were the two most similar and that Meggie was the odd one out. She was a fraction taller, she had a more rounded figure than Laura and Ivy, and the habit she'd had as a child of frowning a great deal had returned, making her look older than she really was. Her dark hair was naturally so, with no grey hairs at all, but she would never have resorted to dyeing it as Ivy and Laura did, regardless of the colour. All her clothes were very conservative, either plain, dark trouser suits with a crisp white shirt, or mid-calf dark print dresses. Laura felt that she didn't want to draw any attention to herself; she was happy to let anyone else have the limelight.

Ivy was now forty-two, and like Laura her hair had been every colour under the sun over the years; right now it was honey-blonde, long and wavy. She went for glamour, high heels, dangling earrings, slinky dresses or sharp Italian suits. She was the confident, talkative, fun-loving one: she enjoyed her life, loved Derek, her husband, and her sons Jack and Harry, and it showed. No one would take her for a day over thirty.

Ivy was the one who wanted to know every grisly detail of Laura's time in prison. She liked to discuss the past at length, especially the foibles of their mother, what might have happened to their older brothers, and the good times she and Meggie had had together in the house in Islington.

Meggie didn't want to discuss the past or the people who'd been part of it. She was more interested in the present and the future, how people she cared for felt now, and their plans and dreams.

Laura found the balance between her feelings for her

sisters was just right. She loved Ivy's vivacity, her sense of fun and her irreverence. But Meggie's steadiness, her keen understanding of human frailty, loyalty and compassion were like soothing cream applied to sunburnt skin.

There were many days when Laura thought how much Jackie would have enjoyed being here in the beautiful garden, with Ivy and Meggie. She would have looked at all three sisters objectively, noted their differences and their similarities, and Laura had no doubt she would have said she'd swop Belle for any one of them.

Laura found it odd she thought that. Jackie had never once said she disliked Belle; she hadn't even been particularly critical of her. Yet now Laura was here with her two sisters, she realized she'd never sensed any bond between Jackie and Belle, the way she could feel it between herself, Meggie and Ivy.

For the first couple of days in London, Laura had been too nervous to go out alone. It was freedom enough not to be locked up, to eat and drink what she liked, when she liked, and to hear no fights or arguments. But that nervousness faded after Meggie had taken her to the police station to make her bail arrangements.

Sometimes she took a train or a bus out into the countryside and walked for miles. Other times she went up to the West End to browse in the shops, and contemplated what she would do, and where she would go after her appeal.

Stuart telephoned a couple of times a week. He said that every day he felt a bit better, and that the stab wound was healing well. But he didn't say he was coming back to London, and to Laura that was evidence that his interest in her was merely that of an old friend.

Angie phoned quite often too, firstly to check if Laura liked the clothes she'd given her, and then just to chat. It was a delight to find they were able to pick up their friendship as if nothing had ever disconnected it. Laura was out of touch with fashion, and with talking to ordinary people, but each time she put the phone down after speaking to Angie she felt she was a step nearer to regaining her old spirit.

Laura loved almost all the clothes Angie had given her, though it took Ivy to convince her that she wasn't too old to wear pink pedal-pushers, or a short flippy denim skirt. But after wearing only jeans and a tee-shirt for two years, it felt marvellous to dress up again. When she got her first wolf whistle from a passing truck driver as she walked to the shops, she began to think that maybe she wasn't washed up altogether.

Half-way through September, in the early evening, she and Meggie were sitting on the patio just outside the kitchen with drinks while the dinner cooked.

'I thought we ought to ask Mother over for Sunday lunch,' Meggie said suddenly.

Laura almost choked on her wine with the shock.

'I know you don't really want to see her, but you've got to. It's all part of moving on,' Meggie continued, her mouth set and determined. 'She's a bitter, nasty old woman, and she probably deserves the lonely life she's got. But she's seventy now and she isn't in the best of health. She could pop off at any time and then you might feel bad that you'd never made it up with her.'

'I won't,' Laura said. 'I forgave her a long time ago for subjecting us to Vince, I did come to see that she was so blinded by the nice house and the money that she didn't see what he was doing to us. But I can't forgive her for not caring that Barney died, or for talking to the newspapers about me during the trial.'

Meggie sighed deeply. 'I think that was unforgivable too,

but you don't have to forgive her, just see her and talk to her. I've got this gut feeling it might make you feel better about yourself.'

'I feel perfectly good about myself, thank you,' Laura retorted.

'You don't,' Meggie insisted. 'You've got issues that have never been resolved. I know because I've got them too. We both subconsciously blame Mum for the bad things we did in the past – well, in as much that we think if we hadn't been forced out to fend for ourselves so early we might have done things differently.'

Laura had to admit she agreed with that. 'But she never gave a toss about us once we'd gone, so why should we give her the time of day now?'

'Because she's our mother,' Meggie said. 'Just think on that, Laura!'

Laura did think on it. She thought that maybe if Barney hadn't died so young, he might have rejected her later. She wondered if during the time he spent with Jackie, he sometimes wished he could stay there for ever. She wished she'd been able to apologize for neglecting him, and to tell him how much she'd loved him.

The following morning at breakfast, she told Meggie she would welcome their mother on Sunday. 'Well, welcome's pushing it a bit far,' she joked. 'But I won't greet her with a clove of garlic and a crucifix.'

'I'm glad you've come round,' Meggie said with the air of someone who had expected it. 'She tried to blackmail me once, said she'd tell Ivy about me being a prostitute.'

Laura's mouth fell open. Although Meggie had admitted what she'd been in a letter, she hadn't expected her ever to bring it up again.

'Don't look like that! I can say the word out loud if I

have to. But I only brought it up now so you'd know about Mum.'

'How did you deal with it then?' Laura asked.

'Told her everything I knew I learned from her. And recently I told Ivy the truth too, just to be on the safe side.'

'You told Ivy?'

'Yes. I didn't want to shatter her illusions, but better I did it than her hearing it from Mum.'

'How did she take it?'

'She looked thunderstruck, and for a moment I thought I'd blown it with her. But then she said it made sense of a few things which had puzzled her, mostly me being off men. After that she did the usual Ivy thing, a million questions. We drank a couple of bottles of wine and we began to laugh about it. As she said, it's ancient history.'

'You are a couple of tough cookies,' Laura said admiringly. She still had the idea she had to look out for her sisters, but almost every day of the last couple of weeks she'd had evidence that wasn't necessary.

'You take a leaf out of my book.' Meggie grinned. 'Ignore any spiteful remarks Mother dearest might make. Don't tell her about Jackie leaving us anything, and don't ask after her health or she'll bang on about her ailments all day.'

It was a shock to Laura to realize that the frail little old lady getting out of Meggie's car on Sunday was her mother. Her back was bent over, she was very thin, her hair was snow-white, and when she lifted her head Laura saw that her face was as wrinkled as a prune.

'Hello, Mum,' Laura said and helped her up on to the doorstep. She was repelled by the stale smell of drink, cigarettes and an unwashed body coming from her mother, but she tried not to back away. 'It's good to see you again.'

'Who are you?' June asked, looking puzzled.

'It's Laura, of course,' Meggie said from behind her.

'But Laura's in prison!'

Meggie smirked at Laura, and patiently explained, as they helped their mother in, that her sister was out on bail pending an appeal. 'I always told you she didn't do it,' Meggie added somewhat triumphantly. 'But never mind that now, we're going to have lunch.'

The lunch went much better than Laura expected. Meggie gave the old lady a large glass of wine and that seemed to have remarkable restorative powers, in as much that she ate a great deal, having told them before that she couldn't get food down. She didn't talk about her ailments, but that was because Meggie steered her away from the subject. She told them about a pensioners' coach trip she'd been on to Brighton, and that she often went to the cinema in the afternoons. She did repeatedly interrupt herself to ask where Ivy and her grandsons were, and Laura felt Meggie had the patience of a saint to be able to keep explaining they couldn't come because the boys were playing in a football match.

It wasn't until they had finished lunch and gone to sit down in the sitting room that June suddenly asked why Laura got bail.

Laura explained as best she could. 'It looks as if Belle, Jackie's sister, killed her,' she finished up.

'The woman who was killed came to see me once,' her mother said.

'Jackie did?' Laura said, not believing her.

'Yes, she asked me a lot of questions about you.'

'What did she look like?'

'She had red hair, and she was posh. She said she used to live in Muswell Hill. I didn't like her.'

Laura looked at Meggie for confirmation this was true, but Meggie just shrugged.

'Why didn't you like her?'

'Because she wouldn't give me any money.'

'You asked her for money?' Meggie exclaimed.

'Well, I hadn't got any, and I could see she had. She wanted to know about our family, and I said she'd have to pay for the information.'

Laura sighed deeply. 'What did she say to that then, Mother?' she asked.

'She said I'd already told her all she needed to know. What do you think she meant by that? I hadn't told her anything!'

Laura had to smile. Jackie had always been very good at grasping situations and weighing people up.

'And when was this, Mother?' Meggie asked.

'How do you expect me to remember that? All I know is that it wasn't all that long before she was killed because I recognized her face in the papers.'

When Meggie returned from taking their mother home, Laura was sitting in the kitchen drinking a glass of wine. 'I hope you turned her gas tap on before you left her,' she said.

Meggie half smiled. 'No chance, it's all electric. She really is a piece of work, isn't she? So that's how Jackie found out about us all! I suppose you're really mortified?'

'Yes and no,' Laura said thoughtfully. 'It kind of explains what Jackie meant in her letter to Stuart, when she said, "Tell Laura I understand." She was intuitive about people, Meggie, she might have hoped to learn all the ins and outs, but Mum asking her for money would have been enough for her.'

'She'd have been appalled by the way she lives too,' Meggie said sadly. 'It's really squalid. Over the years both Ivy and I have tried to improve things, but as fast as we buy her new curtains or a nice armchair, she sells them. We've given up now, just like Freddy has. So either Ivy or I go round there once a week and clear up, throw out all the bottles, put some money in the electric, and take her clean clothes. Sometimes I think we must be mad to do it, we never get any thanks.'

'You know, you turned out just fine,' Laura said, and getting up she put her arms round her sister and hugged her. 'It's a real miracle.'

Meggie disengaged herself from Laura and put her hands on either side of her sister's face. 'It isn't a miracle, Laura, it was you. I remember you giving us our breakfast, taking the washing to the laundrette, doing our hair. Always there for us. I was angry and hurt when you left without telling us. But you even came back to Barnes at just the right time. Another month or so and I'd have been a lost cause, I'd have got pregnant by some thug, ended up just like Mother, I guess. But you were like a guiding light, you led me out of that.'

'I didn't lead you very well if you went on the game!' Laura said, her eyes filling up with tears.

'I did what I had to do,' Meggie said firmly. 'I'd learned that from you. I know you used to nick food and clothes for us all when we were in Shepherds Bush, and I went on the game for the same reason, to make sure Ivy didn't go hungry. The end justifies the means. I don't regret any of it now. The only thing that makes me sad is that you've spent your whole life believing you are a bad person. You aren't!'

Laura began to cry then, and Meggie led her into the sitting room, sat her down on the settee and cuddled her as she cried.

'They call families like ours dysfunctional nowadays,' Meggie murmured against her hair. 'They have social workers running round after them, they get handouts and all kinds of help. Look at us, our dad rarely did a day's work

508

and ended up in prison, Mark and Paul are probably locked up somewhere too, and our mum is a hard-drinking slut who would sell her own grandchild if she thought she'd make a few bob. But because of you, us three younger ones got our act together and broke the mould. You should be proud of that. Your new life begins today, Laura. Stop looking backward with regret and start looking forward with optimism.'

Laura had no idea how long she cried that evening or even exactly why she was crying. All she knew was that after she stopped, she felt cleansed.

Meggie ran a bath for her, and later came and tucked her into bed as if she were a small child.

'Do you remember the story you used to tell Ivy and me?' she asked, sitting on the bed beside her sister and stroking her forehead. 'The one about the three little girls who had to do all sorts of difficult and dangerous tasks to get the magic box that held the three wishes?'

Laura shook her head, she couldn't remember it.

Meggie smiled down at her. 'Well, Ivy and I remember it very well, we often laugh about it. You used to change the tasks each time you told us it. Sometimes they had to outwit a grizzly bear, sometimes they had to swim across a river full of crocodiles, you made it more dangerous each time. But one by one they got there, and each had their wish. You always wished for a cottage in the country by a river. Ivy and I never understood why, because we wanted something to play with like a doll's pram or a bike.'

Laura smiled. She did remember the bit about the cottage and how she used to fall asleep thinking about how pretty it would be.

'Ivy was round here the evening Mr Goldsmith rang to tell me about the court hearing,' Meggie went on. 'We were talking afterwards about all you'd been through, and Ivy said she thought you were almost at the magic box, and you'd soon get your wish. Will it still be the cottage by a river, Laura? Or will it be to have Stuart back?'

17

'Come on now, Charlie boy.' Detective Inspector Ian Donaldson leaned closer to Charles across the interview table. 'Belle's told us you killed Jackie Davies. You were savage because she was going to give Brannigan the farm and turn you out of Kirkmay House. But I don't suppose you meant to kill her, whatever Belle says.'

'Belle said I killed her?' Charles exclaimed, his eyes wide with shock. 'Why, the lying bitch!'

Donaldson looked sideways at PC Price, the second officer in the room, and winked surreptitiously so Charles's lawyer wouldn't see.

When Charles and his wife were first arrested Charles had called James Rafferty, a lawyer who was a golfing partner of his. Rafferty came into the police station with another lawyer friend for Belle. The two lawyers had lengthy interviews with their clients and were present during the initial questioning by the police.

Both Belle and Charles stubbornly refused to admit anything, even though the hall carpet at Kirkmay House was splattered with Stuart Macgregor's blood, and when his car was eventually found in Edinburgh, clear imprints of both their sets of fingerprints were inside it.

Rafferty and his friend bowed out of defending them rather smartly after the first court appearance when both Belle and Charles were remanded in custody. Setting aside the fact that it was obviously a case they could never win, and that further investigations by the police were likely to result in still more serious charges, it was generally thought that Rafferty was concerned about his image. Being seen as a friend of the accused was not to his liking.

Charles's young and inexperienced replacement lawyer, Colin Urquhart, was clearly out of his depth, not just with the seriousness of the charge, but with his client. Charles had blustered and roared at him because Rafferty had departed. He wouldn't talk to Urquhart, yet kept on demanding that he get him out of prison.

Sandra Ferguson had been appointed to defend Belle now, and her task was proving equally difficult because Belle was hysterical and uncooperative.

Each time the police came to question Charles at the men's prison they found that he appeared to be shrinking, physically and mentally. Today he looked as if he hadn't slept for a week, his eyes had deep shadows beneath them, and he was gradually losing his concentration.

Urquhart too appeared to be wilting. He kept wiping perspiration from his thin pale face, and seemed intimidated by Donaldson who was old enough to be his father, a good nine inches taller, and twice his size in girth. He had made a spirited effort to guide his client through the police questioning at first, but he had gradually faded out. Maybe it was because he knew Belle had committed the crime, not Charles, and that if he let him make a statement to that end, perhaps he could go home.

Donaldson was taking full advantage of the situation. Belle had steadfastly pretended complete ignorance of the murder of her sister and there was no real hard evidence to prove she did it. She certainly hadn't claimed Charles was responsible. But she had stated that it was he who stabbed Stuart Macgregor and that against her wishes he had locked the injured man in the cellar.

But Donaldson wasn't too concerned about that crime. Forensic science and Macgregor's evidence were enough to convict Belle for it. What he wanted was to get at the truth about the murder of Jackie Davies. He was inclined to believe Macgregor's theory that the trouble between the two sisters sparked off because Charles was the hit-and-run driver who killed Barney Brannigan, but so long after the event it would be well-nigh impossible to prove.

The press were having a field day now Laura Brannigan's conviction looked unsafe, and Donaldson knew only too well that the investigation for the 1993 murder had been flawed and shoddy. But that could be brushed under the carpet if the right culprit was brought to trial quickly. And if it needed trickery to do that, he didn't care.

'No one at the golf club can verify you were definitely on the course that morning,' Donaldson said.

'I *was* at the golf club,' Charles insisted. 'You know I was there too because one of your men telephoned me there to tell me about my sister-in-law's death.'

'Yes, we know you were there in the afternoon. The usual bunch that prop up the bar confirm that, just as they could tell me exactly what time you left the clubhouse the day you stabbed Stuart Macgregor. They seem to watch one another like hawks up there, yet not one person remembered seeing you between eleven and two on the day Jackie Davies was killed.'

'I was there and I didn't stab Macgregor either,' Charles shouted back. 'That was Belle!'

'Come now, Charlie boy, Macgregor is a big man – a little woman like Belle couldn't do that much damage to him!'

'I was holding him with his arms behind his back, trying to throw him out,' Charles said heatedly. 'I asked Belle to open the front door but instead she lunged at him with the knife.'

This was of course exactly what Macgregor had said, so Donaldson knew Charles was telling the truth. 'But if you

didn't stab him, why didn't you call an ambulance for him?'
he asked.

Charles hung his head. 'I don't know. I wanted to but
Belle wouldn't have it. I suppose I panicked.'

'You panicked because you stabbed him and you knew it
would come out that you'd killed your sister-in-law too. You
drove his car back to Edinburgh, knowing he was lying in
your cellar bleeding to death. And if he hadn't escaped, you
would have disposed of his body. Any jury would pass a
guilty judgement on those facts. You, Charlie, are going to
do a long, long stretch!'

Charles opened and shut his mouth like a goldfish, he
looked desperate and terrified. Sweat was pouring off him.
'I didn't stab him, or Jackie,' he burst out. 'It was Belle who
did both.'

A tingle went down Donaldson's spine. 'Belle killed her
sister? Come on now, Charlie! How could she? Her car was
in the garage, she couldn't have walked there and back in
the time. How low can a man go to try and blame his wife
for something he did?'

Donaldson had met many men like Charles Howell in
his police career. They probably began cheating, lying and
bullying at prep school, and by the time they left their
illustrious public schools, they had the confidence and the
connections to embark on a career of trickery. Charles had
almost certainly spent his entire life ducking and diving,
cutting corners and cheating people. Now it was payback
time.

Prison had brought the man to breaking point. He was
scared to death, exhausted and no longer in control of
himself, and although Donaldson had a touch of sympathy
for him, he wasn't going to let that stop him grinding the
man down a little further.

'You drove up to Brodie Farm, you had an argument with

your sister-in-law, and as you were leaving you heard her talking on the phone to Mrs Brannigan, asking her to come over. You knew only too well that when Brannigan got there, Jackie would tell her all kinds of things you didn't want getting out. You had to prevent it at all costs. And best of all you realized that if you timed the killing right, then Laura Brannigan would be blamed.'

'No, no, no,' Charles banged on the table, his face turning a deep red with anger. 'It was Belle, not me. I swear it was. We had guests who had left their car at our place and she drove out to the farm in that. I don't think she meant to kill Jackie, but when she's in a temper she can do anything. I *am* guilty of covering up for her, but I had to, she's my wife.'

Donaldson breathed a sigh of relief. He had the admission down on tape. It would be typed up and used as evidence. 'Thank you, Charles,' he said. 'We'll take a break now.' He turned to the tape recorder and recorded the time the interview was terminated.

The following morning Donaldson and Price drove out to Cornton Vale to interview Belle. It was hot and sticky, and dark clouds indicated there was a storm on the way.

'D'you reckon she'll crack when I tell her Charlie boy grassed her up?' Donaldson grinned wolfishly at Price.

'I think it is quite likely, sir.' Price replied, keeping his eyes on the road ahead.

'I met them when they first moved up here, you know,' Donaldson said thoughtfully. 'Even then I thought there was something fishy about them. Typical Londoners, flashy and too much to say for themselves. I couldn't see why they wanted to live up here. If I was as rich as Charles implied he was, I wouldn't want to be cooking breakfast and making beds for tourists.'

'So why did they come, sir?' Price asked. 'Have the Met passed on any information yet?'

'Charles was in trouble all round it seems, people after him for money, claims that some of the places his company built were unsafe, and an insurance company were investigating him for fraud. But it's going to prove difficult to get the complete picture as most of the people he was involved with are just like him – public school rogues and as bent as a nine-bob watch.'

'Is there anything on his wife?' Price asked.

'Not apart from the speed with which she stuck her mother in a nursing home after her father died. That was right after her sister was killed, even before the trial. She got power of attorney and sold the family home. A conniving bitch if ever there was one. By all accounts the mother is a lovely woman, with all her marbles. I'm glad it wasn't me who had to go and tell her about this little lot!'

Sandra Ferguson, Belle's lawyer, was just getting out of her car as Donaldson and Price arrived at Cornton Vale. She waved and waited for them to join her so they could all go in together.

'Nice to see you again, Sandra,' Donaldson said. 'It's close today, isn't it? Think we're going to have a storm?'

He had met Sandra many times before, and he liked and respected her. She was a very plain woman in her forties, with straight mousey hair, glasses and bad skin, but she had a keen mind, a good sense of humour, and she loved the cut and thrust of her job. No lawyer in Scotland was better than she at defending women who had killed or attacked an abuser. But Donaldson guessed even she would find it hard to believe in a spoilt middle-class woman like Belle Howell.

'I hope so.' She frowned up at the sky. 'This sort of

weather always seems to bring on a rash of domestic violence.'

'So we can expect Howell to be extra-aggressive today then?' he said with a chuckle.

Sandra smiled. 'She's a difficult one, that's for sure.'

'Do you believe she's innocent?'

Sandra smile faded. 'You know better than to ask such a thing, Ian!'

'I will consider my knuckles rapped,' he said.

Donaldson had to resist the desire to smirk when Belle was brought into the interview room. She looked rougher than a down-and-out on the streets of Glasgow. She had a bruise under one eye, her blonde hair was scraped back off her face, but that didn't disguise a couple of bald patches, and her tee-shirt and tracksuit trousers were far too big for her, and an unflattering khaki colour.

Sandra showed some concern about how she got the bruise.

'How do you think, you stupid cow?' Belle responded. 'I shouldn't be in here with these animals. They stole my cigarettes and I tried to get them back.'

Sandra calmly got a packet of cigarettes out of her brief-case and handed them to Belle. 'I am not your enemy,' she said gently. 'I'm sorry to hear you've been hurt, but if you want to make life easier for yourself while you are in here, I suggest you don't go around calling people stupid cows.'

Belle just snatched up the cigarettes, tore the packet open and lit one up. She didn't thank Sandra for them or apologize for her rudeness.

'Right then, we'd better get on,' Donaldson said, putting a new tape in the machine and turning it on. He spoke into it, giving the date, time and the names of the people present.

He began by asking Belle much the same questions he'd asked her umpteen times before: what time Stuart Macgregor came to Kirkmay House on the day in question, how long they spent in the garden, what they talked about, the details of how Stuart broke the news to her about her sister's will, and her reaction to it.

'It was a shock and I was very upset,' she said. 'But then Charles came home drunk and he went mad and stabbed Stuart.'

Donaldson had already heard a great many minor variations on her story of the frightened little wife who felt compelled to assist her husband because she didn't know what else to do. But this was the first time she'd said Charles was drunk, perhaps because it had recently occurred to her that it was a good cover for any points of his version of events which didn't match hers.

'It was just after eleven at night when we arrested you and your husband on your arrival back in Crail after taking Macgregor's car to Edinburgh,' Donaldson said. 'We did blood tests on you both. You still had a high level of alcohol in yours, Belle, but Charles didn't. He had drunk no more than one pint of beer in the previous eight hours.'

Belle became irate then, shouting that Donaldson didn't know what he was talking about. Sandra tried to calm her down, but she shouted at her too.

'Belle, we have a statement from Macgregor telling us exactly what happened that evening,' Donaldson said. 'We know it was you who stabbed him, we have forensic science to back it up, and your husband's statement too. It would be far better for you to admit what you did.'

'I have told you the truth, you arsehole,' she screamed at him. 'Charles is a lying bastard!'

Her face was flushed with rage, yet Donaldson felt that it wouldn't take much more confrontation before she cracked.

'Is he lying too when he said that you stabbed your sister on 12 May 1993?'

'He said that?' Her voice was suddenly an octave lower and she looked stunned.

'He did.' Donaldson nodded. 'He said you took the car belonging to your guests which had been left in your drive, and drove out there because you were furious that she was going to give Brodie Farm to Laura.'

'I didn't, I didn't go out of the house that day,' she insisted, but the colour draining from her face proved she was afraid now. 'Why would he say that?'

'Because it is the truth and he's tired of covering up for you?' Donaldson suggested. 'He told us how you had to rush to clean the car belonging to the Langdons. It must have got very muddy on that track? And you had blood on your clothes too, didn't you? Charles got rid of those clothes for you. But we know where they are.'

Donaldson was only guessing that Charles took her clothes and disposed of them. But he reckoned that Charles had led the kind of life where he'd often had to get rid of incriminating evidence, and would know the safest way of doing it.

Sandra advised her client that she didn't have to say anything if she didn't wish to, but Belle didn't appear to take that in for she suddenly erupted with rage.

'That bastard, after all I've been through for him,' she screamed. 'He lost all our money, he forced me to go cap in hand to Jackie and move to that Godforsaken place that I hated. Me, running a guest house! Why should I be expected to clean up after people, cook them breakfast, listen to their endless complaints? Have you got any idea how demeaning that is?'

Belle glared at the two policemen. 'And what did his nibs do? He was off at the golf club all the time! I even covered

519

up for him when he killed a kid in his car and wasn't man enough to stay and face the music. But now he's told on me!'

Sandra's jaw dropped, Donaldson and Price looked at each other in shocked surprise.

Donaldson recovered first. He certainly hadn't expected that either one of the Howells would ever admit to that crime. 'That must have been terrible for you, Belle,' he said in feigned sympathy. 'Jackie was badly hurt too, wasn't she? And Barney was as good as your nephew.'

'We all loved him, he was the sweetest little boy,' Belle sobbed. 'If he hadn't been killed I could have got Jackie to give us money to go and live in Spain or somewhere, instead she punished us by making us stay in Scotland.'

'So are you saying she always knew it was Charles driving the other car?' Price butted in.

'Well, of course she did,' Belle snapped at him. 'Who wouldn't know Charles in his flash car, driving like a maniac? She was going to tell the police, but I talked her out of it. It wouldn't bring Barney back and I'd be all alone while Charles was in prison.'

'But we have it on record that he was in London at the time,' Donaldson said. 'He flew back the following day, the airline confirmed that.'

Belle gave him a withering look as if astounded he didn't realize how resourceful her husband could be when he was in trouble. 'He had been in London for almost a week before, but he was on his way home when he had the accident. He turned around and drove straight back to London, the cowardly bastard. He even had the blasted cheek to fly back and act like he was distraught at Barney's death, when all the time his car was having the dents repaired.'

Donaldson looked at Sandra, expecting her to bring the

interview to a halt for the day. But she shrugged, the cold expression on her face telling him she thought it advisable for all concerned that he went on and got a complete confession.

'So Barney's death soured your relationship with your sister?' Donaldson asked.

'She acted like we were dirt beneath her feet,' Belle said and began to cry. 'She had all the sympathy for that whore Laura, but not for us. Laura got to spend the following summer in Italy, and when she came back Jackie helped her get that crummy shop, but what did I get? Nothing, that's what! Just criticism because I didn't have many guests, or that I spoke to them too sharply. Jackie was lording it up out at her place, coining it in hand over fist with all her properties, everyone adoring her, and I'm stuck with Charles off playing golf, chatting up women and making an arse of himself. I had nothing and no one.'

Donaldson could hardly believe that anyone could be so unappreciative of all her sister had done for her, so lacking in compassion and so utterly self-centred. He wondered if she was actually mad, for surely no one sane could see others the way she did.

'How about you tell us what brought things to a head with your sister?' Sandra suggested.

Belle folded her arms and her expression was belligerent, Donaldson sighed inwardly, expecting that she would clam up now. But to his surprise she didn't.

'I went out to the farm two or three weeks before Christmas,' she began.

'Was that Christmas of '92?' Price asked, so it would be on record.

'Yes,' Belle agreed. 'I was so tired of it all, of Charles out all the time, of the guests, having no friends, everything.'

She leaned back in her chair and lit another cigarette, half closed her eyes and as she began to speak, they all realized she was reliving those events.

It was around four in the afternoon and already dark when Belle drove up the drive to Brodie Farm. But as she turned into the yard it was like suddenly entering Santa's grotto. There were Christmas lights around all the windows of the guest cottages, a holly wreath on each of the doors, and more lights on the evergreen shrubs in planters either side of the farmhouse door.

Belle gritted her teeth, irritated to be once again reminded that her older sister had the energy and enthusiasm she lacked to make things special for her guests. Yet at the same time it seemed like a good omen, for Jackie had always loved Christmas, and it was the time when she was usually at her most amenable.

It was freezing cold, and Belle turned up the collar of her mink coat as she walked to Jackie's door. She glanced through the kitchen window before knocking, and saw her sister sitting at the table wrapping up presents, surrounded by reels of coloured ribbon and rolls of paper. The kitchen looked festive with coloured lights strung along the dresser shelves, and she'd even hung some Chinese lanterns shaped like comic turkeys from the old beams.

Belle tapped on the window and Jackie waved and beckoned for her to come in.

Jackie wasn't drunk, but she'd clearly had a couple of drinks, and she had a Christmas tape of Johnny Mathis playing. She giggled and said she hoped Belle wouldn't tell anyone what she listened to, or she'd lose all credibility.

She teased Belle too for wearing a mink coat. She said she should have sold it years ago before it became politically incorrect to own one. Then she poured her sister a glass of red wine, and asked what had brought her round.

'I can't go on like this,' Belle burst out. 'I hate Scotland. I hate you despising us because Charles killed Barney, and I want out.'

Jackie stared at her as if she were speaking a foreign language. She was wearing a Fair Isle sweater and jeans tucked into long green boots. Belle thought Fair Isle sweaters were an abomination, but even she had to admit that Jackie looked lovely in it with her tousled curls showering down on to her shoulders. 'Well, go then,' she said eventually. 'Just tell me when and I'll get someone in to run Kirkmay until I can decide what to do with it.'

'You don't mind then?' Belle asked.

'Why should I?' Jackie shrugged. 'Let's face it, you aren't making a success of the place, there is no return on my investment either. Go with my blessing. I'll be glad not to have to see Charles around. Where are you planning to go? Back to London?'

'We aren't sure yet,' Belle said, feeling just a little flustered because it had been so easy. 'It depends.'

'On what? Whether you can drag Charles away from the golf club?' Jackie laughed.

'No. On how much you can give us,' Belle replied.

Jackie stood up and leaned against the Aga rail. She folded her arms, something she always did when she anticipated trouble. 'Run that past me again! I don't think I heard it quite right. You want me to pay you to leave here?'

'Well, we haven't got any money,' Belle shrugged. 'You know that.'

'Yes I do, because you spend every penny you get,' Jackie said. 'Kirkmay could make you an excellent living if you lived within your means, but I see that once again you've been to the hairdresser's, are wearing new boots, and I suspect that's a new outfit under the old coat. I reckon that little lot alone came to something like three hundred pounds.'

'I have to look nice. I've got an image to uphold.'

Jackie spluttered with derisive laughter. 'An image to uphold! Your image around here is that you are a toffee-nosed Londoner who doesn't give a toss whether anyone stays at her guest house. No one would take any notice if you were suddenly to appear in a floral pinny and a headscarf over your hair rollers. In fact I think they'd prefer that!'

They argued for some time, but Jackie remained adamant she wasn't helping out any more. She wasn't nasty, but very firm. She said if they wanted to leave that was fine, but they'd have to finance it themselves.

The phone rang and Jackie went upstairs to answer it, giving Belle the idea it was a man friend calling. As Jackie went up the stairs she called back down asking Belle to make a pot of tea.

As Belle got the teapot off the dresser, she saw the document lying there, half covered by a biscuit tin. She could see the name Laura Brannigan, and curiosity made her pull it out to see what it was about.

As she read it she felt as though she'd been kicked in the stomach, for it was a deed of gift. Jackie was giving the farm away to Laura! As she stood there in the Christmassy kitchen, she couldn't believe her sister could do this to her.

A mere friend was to get a property worth at least £150,000, but Jackie was refusing to give her a paltry few thousand when she desperately needed it.

She went to the bottom of the stairs and listened to what Jackie was saying. 'I must go,' she heard. 'Belle's downstairs on the scrounge again. But don't despair, my growling one. We'll soon be away from all the bloodsuckers, together, for ever.'

Belle had to leave then because she knew that if she stayed she might hit Jackie.

*

All over Christmas and New Year she stayed right away. She found presents from Jackie on her doorstep on Christmas Eve, but no apologetic note, no offer to reconsider. Belle didn't take a present to her because if she had she might have blurted out what she'd seen and heard.

Charles took the view that Jackie was gifting the property to Laura as a tax dodge. He didn't think there was any reason for Belle to get worked up about anything because if Jackie was going off somewhere with a man she probably intended to sell Kirkmay House, and she'd have to pay them to get out.

But Belle didn't believe Charles, and all through January and February she became more and more wound up. It was so cold, and without any guests booking to stay they had no money either, and to add insult to injury, she often saw Jackie park her car opposite her house. Sometimes Laura was with her and she would watch from her window as they walked along to the restaurant on Marketgate. Their arms would be linked, heads close together as they chatted and laughed, and it seemed to Belle they were talking and laughing about her.

Then in March Jackie came to the house to see Belle.

'This has gone on long enough, Belle,' she said. 'Let me come in, it's cold out here. I need to talk to you.'

She sat there in the kitchen dressed in a sheepskin coat and matching hat which Belle could tell cost a small fortune, and she offered her £2,000 to leave Kirkmay because she was going to sell it.

'You can take whatever furniture you need from here too,' she said. 'But you must leave the curtains and carpets as I shall be including them in the sale.'

'But that's not enough to live on,' Belle said in horror.

'It isn't intended to be,' Jackie said airily. 'You and Charles will have to get jobs like everyone else does. But it's enough for advance rent on a small flat.'

Belle protested but Jackie was adamant. 'Look, Belle, I bailed you out when you were in trouble. I got you this place, I paid for the furniture and soft furnishings and let you have a free hand. But you've never worked at it. I really thought Barney's death might sober you two up, that's the only reason I didn't shop Charles. But he's still driving his car drunk as a lord, and you, Belle, have become still greedier and lazier. That's my offer, and in my view it's a very generous one.'

'Wouldn't you have been angry if your own sister treated you that way?' Belle looked from Donaldson to Price and then to her lawyer.

Donaldson was too stunned by her selfishness to reply. A glance at both his colleagues revealed that they were equally nonplussed.

'Where could we go with only two thousand pounds?' Belle continued, not even aware they hadn't answered her question. 'Did she expect us to live in a council house?'

'So, Belle, that was in March of '93,' Donaldson said. 'What happened on 12 May, two months later?'

'I phoned Jackie that morning, she'd been getting at me constantly to leave ever since March. I wanted her to come round to my place to talk. I couldn't go to her because my car was in the garage. She was really sharp with me and said if I wanted to see her I could walk round. Well, I wasn't going to do that, it's about three miles, so as the Langdons' car was there, and the keys, I used that.

'Her nastiness about me walking was what set me off,' Belle mused.

*

She was fuming as she drove the short distance. Jackie was always saying she was lazy and that if she walked more she wouldn't have such a fat arse. But she had to see Jackie, and try again to get more money out of her. She couldn't bear to spend another summer in Scotland.

Jackie was on her knees sorting out a kitchen cupboard when she got there. She was wearing jeans and a white shirt, and the sight of her small, pert bottom annoyed Belle even more.

Jackie didn't even get up. 'If this is a plea for more dosh, save your breath,' she said, hardly bothering to take her head out of the cupboard. 'In a matter of months I'll be moving on myself, and I need what little cash I've got.'

'If you're moving on then you'll be selling this place, that's surely more than enough for anyone,' Belle said. She didn't want to admit she knew about the document giving it to Laura.

'I won't be selling it, I'm going to give it away to Laura.' Jackie stood up, then and smirked. 'I was going to do it at Christmas, but for various reasons I thought I'd wait a while longer. Now is the right time. I always did say I was either going to spend what I'd got or give it away. This is the start of it.'

'You can't give a property like this to that slag,' Belle said indignantly.

'Don't you dare call her a slag.' Jackie took a threatening step towards her. 'She is my best friend and she's never asked a thing of me, unlike you who's always whining for more. Charles killed her son, or have you forgotten that? It nearly destroyed her, and me. I can't give her Barney back, but I sure as hell can give her this place if I want to.'

'You'd help her, but not me? How can you do that to your own sister?' Belle grabbed Jackie's arm pleadingly. 'I know you hate Charles, I'll leave him if that's what you want, he's the one that caused all the problems, the one that spends the money, not me.'

'You'd sell your own mother for a few quid,' Jackie snarled at her. 'That day when I was in hospital and I said I knew it was Charles driving, you pleaded with me to keep quiet about it. You insisted you loved him, that you'd fall apart without him. Later you both promised that you would turn over a new leaf, work hard, stop drinking and acting like you were millionaires. And I stupidly believed you would. What a fool I was to believe either of you could feel remorse!'

'It was all him, not me,' Belle said wildly.

'I betrayed my best friend by not seeing her son's killer brought to justice,' Jackie roared at her. 'And you, Belle, are so bloody wrapped up in yourself that you can't see what that does to me. Get out now, out of my life for good. I shall instruct my solicitor today to draw up papers to get you evicted from my property. And I'm withdrawing the offer of two thousand. You'll get nothing.'

She caught hold of Belle and pushed her to the front door. 'And furthermore, if you try to hang on here I'll contact the police and tell them Charles was the hit-and-run driver,' she yelled after her.

Belle got back in the car and drove out of the yard and down the drive, but before she got to the road, she stopped, got out of the car and walked back. She and Jackie had had rows just as bitter as this one, and Jackie was always sorry a few minutes later.

She fully expected to look through the kitchen window and see her sobbing with her head on the table.

But she wasn't in the kitchen, though Belle could hear her voice. Realizing her sister was sitting on the stairs to use the phone, Belle tiptoed up to the partly open front door and listened.

'Just come over, Laura,' Jackie was pleading, her voice

breaking as she cried. 'I can't explain on the phone, it's too difficult. I need you.'

Belle left then. She ran back to the car and drove back home.

The moment she got indoors she poured herself a drink to steady her nerves. But they wouldn't steady. She knew what Laura would do when Jackie blurted out about who had been driving the car that killed Barney. She wouldn't wait for the police, she'd be round here in minutes to tear the place apart, and Belle with it. Logic wouldn't come into it, that it was Charles who did the killing, not his wife. All Laura would see was that she twisted Jackie's arm to keep quiet.

She had another drink, then another, and all the time she was watching the clock and imagining Laura driving out towards Fife. But as the drink went down, fear took second place to jealousy. Jackie loved Laura far more than she did her, and she was going to give her the farm.

Belle had loved Laura too, right from when she was a little girl, all through her teens to her early twenties. Laura was the one who had time for her, a real big sister, not like Jackie who dismissed her as being just a kid. She bought her lovely presents, she would spend ages curling her hair, take her to the cinema, swimming and roller skating. Even when Barney was born she was still the same. Belle could re-member going round to see her in Chelsea, and Laura always had time to listen to her news, commiserate about boyfriends who let her down, and she'd give her a hug and a few pounds and tell her that she was beautiful.

When Laura ran away from Gregory, Belle missed her very much. She'd been used to going to the Chelsea house whenever she felt lonely, and she could talk to Laura so much more easily than to Jackie, or even her mother.

After Laura settled in Scotland with Stuart, Jackie used to go up to see her. Belle wanted to go too, but she was never invited. Jackie would come back saying what a lovely man Stuart was and how happy Laura and Barney were with him, and it was obvious to Belle that Laura had forgotten all about her.

Then Laura and Stuart split up, and Stuart arrived to work for Jackie.

From the first moment Belle saw him, she wanted him. No man before or since had had that effect on her. The softness of his Scottish accent, the gentleness in his grey eyes, the width of his shoulders and that wide smile all made her tremble.

She made excuses to go to the sites where he was working, and she'd watch the way he planed or sawed wood, and imagine those big, practical hands caressing her. He used to call her Rapunzel because of her long hair, and in her night-time fantasies he was her prince.

Everything about him was perfect: the leanness of his hips, his muscular arms and thighs, his shiny, shoulder-length hair with just a hint of auburn, and those sexy full lips. He was her dream man come true.

She thought she could have him because every other man wanted her. But though he seemed to like her, he didn't want her. He was in love with Laura, and however hard she tried to make him forget her by luring him out to clubs, concerts and parties, it didn't work.

The more deeply she fell in love with him, the more her love for Laura turned to hatred. Laura didn't want him, but she had a hold on his heart, and that prevented Stuart from loving her. She didn't want to remember the humiliation she felt when she finally got Stuart into her bed, and he couldn't perform.

It began so well. She was burning up with desire as he

kissed and cuddled her; other men she'd been to bed with leapt on her with hardly any foreplay but Stuart seemed only concerned with her pleasure. It was only when she became so aroused that she straddled him that she discovered he didn't even have an erection.

'I'm sorry, babe,' he murmured. 'I just can't do it.'

She couldn't accept that. Every man she'd been with before had been rampant even before they got her into bed. She tried her best to get it up for him, but when nothing happened she began questioning him indignantly.

'It's not you,' was all he would say, with more apologies.

But she wouldn't leave it, and all at once he was wriggling away from her and reaching out for his shirt at the side of the bed.

'This was a mistake, babe,' he said wearily. 'I really like you, Belle, but I guess it's too soon to even think about another woman.'

As she watched him pulling his clothes on, she felt he had insulted her in the worst possible way. She was young and gorgeous, but he couldn't get it up because he was thinking of Laura. There was nothing on this earth Belle wanted more than Stuart, but that bitch had prevented her from getting her heart's desire.

All that came back on 12 May as she sat there drinking and watching the clock; once again Laura was blocking the way to what she wanted.

At eleven o'clock she knew Laura would now be driving over the Forth Bridge. She'd be driving fast because she was worried about Jackie, and in thirty-five to forty minutes she'd be at the farm. When she got there, Belle knew her whole world was going to come crashing around her ears.

All at once she got up and dashed out to the car, sure that by now Jackie would have calmed down enough to promise not to tell Laura about Charles. Once she agreed to that she'd surely also agree to give them some money so they could leave Scotland.

As Belle got out of the car at Brodie Farm, she could hear Jackie singing along with the radio. It was Whitney Houston's 'And I Will Always Love You', and the passion Jackie was putting into it, even if her voice was abysmal, was another reminder that she hadn't even bothered to confide in her sister about this man she was going off with.

Belle walked straight in without knocking, and Jackie wheeled round in surprise.

'I've got nothing more to say to you,' she said icily. 'You and I are finished, Belle. Go away.'

'You don't mean that,' Belle said.

'Oh, but I do. You know, Belle, every time you walk in that door or phone, I get a knot in my stomach because I know you want something. I don't think you've ever come to me because you just want to spend time with me. It's always that you've got a problem, or you need money. Well, that's it, no more. I'm going to be as selfish as you are. So bugger off.'

Out of the corner of her eye Belle saw that document again. It was on the work surface, and she guessed Jackie had got it out because she was going to show it to Laura when she arrived; perhaps they would even take it to her solicitors together.

All at once white-hot, uncontrollable rage welled up inside her. She wasn't going to let Laura have the farm. And she wasn't going to let Jackie tell her about Barney either. She had to be stopped.

'Go on, piss off, you make me sick,' Jackie said, and turned dismissively back to the sink.

The kitchen knives were all there, right at hand, gleaming stainless steel embedded in a block of wood. One second

Belle was just looking at them, the next she held a long triangular one in her hand.

'Are you still here?' Jackie said, without turning. 'I wondered what the bad smell was. Get out now, before I throw you out.'

She turned round, and she laughed when she saw the knife. 'Oh, do grow up,' she said.

Jackie had said that same thing to Belle so many times and on every occasion it had hurt. This time it was like pulling a trigger, Belle ran at her with all her force, and the knife went straight into the left side of Jackie's chest.

For a moment nothing happened. Jackie just stood there looking utterly shocked, the knife embedded in her just as it had been in the block of wood a few seconds before.

'Belle!' she said, but her voice sound disembodied and blood was coming out around the knife, staining her white shirt. 'What have you done?'

She moved towards Belle, her hands out in front of her, and Belle backed away in horror. Then, as if in slow motion, Jackie's legs seemed to crumple, and she fell backwards to the floor.

Belle couldn't move for a moment or two, all she could do was stare down at her sister in horror. She didn't know if Jackie was dead already, but she guessed from the amount of blood seeping out around the knife that it had pierced her heart and she soon would be.

'I'm sorry,' she whispered, and suddenly aware of the enormity of what she'd done, she knew she had to get out of there quickly.

She got a piece of kitchen roll, dampened it slightly and carefully wiped the knife handle, putting the paper in her pocket afterwards. She was sure she hadn't touched anything else for the door had been open on both visits. Then, picking up the deed of gift document which she needed to destroy, she ran for the car to the strains of 'Never Let Her Slip Away' on the radio.

'I didn't want to drive back on that farm track,' she told Donaldson. 'But I had to, in case I ran into Laura.'

Donaldson wiped his sweating brow with the back of his hand, for once stuck for words.

Never before in all his years of interrogating prisoners had he ever heard such a full and clear confession.

PC Price broke the silence in the room by mentioning the tape was almost at an end.

'I think we all need a break,' Sandra said.

Donaldson drew deeply on a cigarette as Price drove them back to Edinburgh. 'If only,' he sighed.

'If only what, sir?' Price asked.

'That she'd been interviewed more rigorously on the day of the murder,' Donaldson said thoughtfully. 'This, laddie, is a fine example of the folly of taking everything at face value. She was such a good-looking woman, a respectable guest house owner, and, it appeared, the loving and distraught sister. She wasn't even suspected.'

'I read in the file that after Laura Brannigan was arrested, she kept sticking up for her and saying she couldn't have done it. Why do you think that was, sir?' Price asked.

'To make herself look sweet and loving, I guess,' Donaldson replied. 'It worked too, I really fell for her tears and the bewilderment routine, and so did the jury.'

'It was lucky for Brannigan that Macgregor turned up when he did,' Price remarked. 'She must have been through hell in the last two years.'

'Aye, poor woman,' Donaldson agreed. 'I wish I could boast that I had my doubts about her guilt. But I was like everyone else; once I knew she'd been a bit wild in the past I couldn't see beyond that.'

'Do you think Belle Howell is sorry about what she's done to her?'

Donaldson gave a humourless laugh. 'She's sorry for herself, sorry she didn't clear off when her sister asked her to. Sorry too, perhaps, that her sister is dead. But I doubt she'll ever shed any tears for Laura Brannigan.'

18

Heavy rain was splattering against the windows and although it was only three in the afternoon it was so dark that Laura had been forced to turn on a table lamp to see to read. She was feeling very snug and happy. Lucy, Meggie's dog, was curled up on the settee beside her, she liked the sound of the rain on the window, and at long last she felt she had a future.

Two days earlier Patrick Goldsmith had rung to say Belle had finally confessed to Jackie's murder, and that he was pressing hard for an immediate appeal date for Laura.

It was wonderful to know that she would soon be completely exonerated, and that the two-year nightmare was over but for the formalities, yet strangely she also felt deep sadness about Belle. Meggie had burst into laughter when she admitted this; in her view there was no punishment bad enough for the woman. But Laura had known Belle for thirty-four years and loved her like a younger sister, and she couldn't switch off her feelings.

Her heart went out to Lena too. She'd lost her husband, Toby had gone off to Australia, Jackie had been murdered, and now she had to live with the knowledge that Belle was a killer. Laura had spent the whole of the first day feeling faintly sick and troubled and she certainly wasn't in the mood to celebrate.

But the previous day she had woken up to find that had passed. At last she felt ready to detach herself from the past and move forward. As so often when she wanted to mark a change of heart, or a new beginning, she took herself off to the hairdresser's.

Her hair colour was now back where she'd started. She had been through a full circle from mouse to red, on to black, dark brown, blonde and a dozen different variations and permutations along the way, and finally she was back to mouse again. Not as dreary as she remembered it as a child of course, that was only the base colour, with blonde highlights to create some definition. But what was astounding was that it had taken ten years off her real age, and she had a glow about her that she hadn't seen for years.

Last night she'd gone out to Soho for a celebration dinner with her sisters. It was just the best evening ever, they had laughed so much that the restaurant owner had given them a free bottle of wine. He said he was grateful to them for creating such a happy atmosphere in his restaurant.

The conversation had come round once again to Stuart, with both Meggie and Ivy urging her to encourage him more. Laura hadn't been able to come back with her usual excuse that she was all used up, because she realized that wasn't true any longer. She was fizzing inside, a dozen different plans for her future suggesting themselves.

But Stuart hadn't phoned for a week now, and when Laura had tried to ring him at the flat in Edinburgh the previous day, he hadn't been there. She had no doubt he would surface again before long, but in her heart she knew Meggie and Ivy were reading too much into his interest in her. She was sure he only felt friendship, nothing more. Perhaps that was just as well; after all it was a well-known fact that old loves can rarely be rekindled.

Lucy suddenly cocked her ears and began barking.

'Shush,' Laura said, stroking her. 'It's only someone walking by.'

A ring at the doorbell proved this wasn't so, and Lucy jumped off the settee in readiness. Laura frowned; she was much too comfortable to get up and she thought it was probably only a door-to-door salesman at this time of the afternoon. Her sisters had gone out to view a property and if it was them coming back they'd have let themselves in with their key.

When the bell rang again and Lucy continued to bark, Laura groaned and got up. She thought if it was Mormons or Jehovah's Witnesses intent on converting her, she'd give them a piece of her mind.

Lucy had a habit of darting out when anyone came to the door, so Laura shut her in the sitting room before opening the front door.

Two men were standing there, wet from the rain, and they had none of the usual missionary characteristics like plain dark suits or a few religious tracts in their hands.

The younger one was tall and muscular in jeans and a denim jacket. She thought he was around thirty and he had a shaved head and a ring in one ear. The other was an elderly man in a long, dark, trench-style raincoat. He looked familiar, and he was looking at her as if he expected her to know him.

'Come on now, Laura!' he said reprovingly.

'Robbie!' she gasped. Even if he had aged dramatically, his Geordie accent was just the same. 'How did you know where I was?'

'It's never hard to find someone when you've got friends in the right places,' he said, grinning at the younger man. 'So how about inviting us in?'

Laura felt a twinge of panic. Robbie Fielding was one man she never wanted to see or hear from again, and if she'd run into him out in the street she would have walked on by without speaking. She certainly didn't want him in the house for she despised him, and his companion looked like hired muscle.

He smiled at her hesitation. She remembered his teeth being good, but they were now stained brown, with several missing. 'Come on, just a cup of coffee for an old pal. You wouldn't want to leave me out here in the rain, would you?'

As far as Laura was concerned she could have cheerfully watched him drown in the Thames and not lifted a finger to help him, but she couldn't say anything along those lines for fear of him turning nasty. 'It isn't convenient right now. What do you want?' she asked.

'I was in London and I had a couple of things I wanted to talk over with you about Belle.' He moved forward and put one foot inside the door before she could gather herself. 'I also wanted to say how glad I was that you've got your appeal.'

Suddenly he was right through the door, pushing it wide open and nearly knocking her over, the other man following him. Laura's stomach lurched and she cursed herself for answering the door.

'By the way you are looking gorgeous,' he said over his shoulder as he walked straight down the hall into the kitchen. He stopped inside the kitchen, turning back to her, and waved a hand at his friend. 'And this is Andy, my right-hand man.'

'My sister will be back any minute,' she said, declining to acknowledge Andy. 'And we've got people coming for dinner, so please make this snappy.'

He took a seat at the table, the other man doing likewise, and Robbie got out his cigarettes.

Laura waved a finger at him. 'Please don't, my sister doesn't like smoking in her house.'

He put them back in his pocket and frowned. 'You aren't very welcoming!'

'Why should I be, Robbie? You are part of a past I'd rather forget.'

Only the previous evening Laura had told her sisters that she felt her recovery was mainly due to there being no reminders of her past here. Now Robbie turning up was like opening the old wound. Suddenly she was anxious and tense again, just the way she had been for much of the time when she was working for him.

He looked so old and seedy, like a stereotype of a dirty old man. He might never have been exactly handsome, but he'd had a fine physique and the kind of bearing that got him noticed. His hair was a dirty grey now and very thin, and he had a large and wobbly stomach. The trench coat he was wearing and the dark suit beneath it might be good quality, but the cheapness of his soul showed on his lined and sunken face. It made her squirm to think of all those afternoons she'd spent with him in hotel rooms.

'I think I deserve a little gratitude for stifling some of that past for you,' he said, fixing her with his dark eyes.

'With the amount of mud that was slung at me, a little more wouldn't have made any difference.' She shrugged.

'Oh, I think it would have,' he said. 'And now more than ever! How would you start out again if everyone knows what you were?'

Her stomach churned as she realized his sole purpose in coming here was to blackmail her.

'It won't work, Robbie,' she said firmly. 'For one thing, I've got no money, and for another, everyone whose opinion counts with me already knows the whole truth.'

He grinned wolfishly. 'But a few well-chosen photographs landing on the desk of a tabloid editor's desk on the day of your appeal would kind of hinder your future,' he said. 'And you've got money coming to you.'

'Piss off, Robbie,' she said angrily. 'Clear off now or I'll call the police.'

'And tell them what?' he said scornfully. 'That an old

lover has turned up? That happens a lot in your life, doesn't it? Where is golden boy now? Still nursing his wounds from sticking his nose in other people's business?'

'I think the police would be very pleased to be called to eject you from this house,' she said tartly. 'And I think they'd be keen to question you about your relationship with Mr Calder.'

'One of your biggest problems was that you always thought you were smarter than you really were,' he said scornfully. 'It seems you still have that problem. I can click my fingers and Stuart Macgregor will be dead. So don't mess with me, hen. Or you'll regret it.'

A cold shudder ran down her spine. Katy had claimed that Robbie had killed people who got in his way. Laura had always laughed at that, sure Robbie had spread the story to keep people in fear of him. But perhaps it wasn't just a myth.

'Whatever proposition you've got in mind, you'd better put it to me and then go,' she said.

'I want ten thousand pounds,' he said.

Laura gave a humourless laugh. 'You are joking of course?'

'I never joke about money and you're bright enough to know I'm more than capable of sending photographs of you to every newspaper in the country.'

'I've seen some of 'em, and they'd shake yer mum and the rest of yer family,' Andy piped up.

Laura gave him a withering glance. He sounded like he looked, a thug with no more than two brain cells. But his accent was a London one, and she had a feeling Robbie had picked him up here, not brought him down from Scotland.

'I suppose you cooked up some deal with Charles and Belle?' It was a stab in the dark as she knew there was no proof Robbie had ever met the Howells. 'I bet you were savage when they were arrested before you could make them pay up.'

He just stared at her, the fact that he made no comment suggesting she was right.

'How did you find out Belle killed Jackie?' she went on. 'Did Charles shoot his mouth off?'

Something flittered across his face, perhaps recognition that he'd underestimated her intelligence.

Laura sensed she was getting very close to the truth. 'He always was a loud-mouthed prat! But how lucky for you that you had Calder in your pocket. So what was the deal you made? You'd make sure Calder kept quiet about the new will as long as Charles and Belle gave you a chunk of what they'd inherit on the old one?'

'You always did have too much to say for yerself,' he retorted. 'I haven't come here to chew the cud with you. I want money, or I'll start sending those pictures out.'

'Send them,' she bluffed. 'I don't care, and you're an old man now, Robbie. You don't frighten me.'

'Then you are more of a fool than I took you for,' he said, his lips curling back like a savage dog's. 'I've got connections everywhere, hen. One call from me and I could wreak havoc in every corner of your life and family. If you're wise you won't play poker with me, because I've got a good hand.'

Laura put her head in the air and turned to walk to the phone in the hall. But as she put her hand on the receiver, Robbie came up behind her and knocked it out of her hand.

'I think you've forgotten what a nasty bastard I can be,' he said, pushing her up against the wall and sticking his face up close to hers. 'So I'll just have to remind you. I want what's mine by rights. I got Jackie that farm for a pittance, and she promised me she'd see me right. I don't call five hundred and a bottle of single malt seeing me right. Not when that place is worth in excess of a hundred and fifty thou.'

'That's nothing to do with me,' Laura said, trying to push him away. His breath stank and the deranged look in his eyes was frightening. 'You should have taken that up with her when she was alive.'

'It's got everything to do with you, now that place has dropped in your lap,' he spat at her. 'You influenced Jackie against me, just as you stole my girls from me.'

'You left us high and dry!' Laura exclaimed. 'We had rent to find and kids to feed. And I didn't steal anyone, the girls who worked for me had never worked for you.'

'I had it all worked out that Jackie and I would go into business,' he said, not even acknowledging what she'd just said. 'I could have got us mobile home sites, tenements in need of repair. But you dripped poison in her ear.'

Laura felt like laughing at that. 'I did no such thing, and if she turned you down it was because of what you were offering. As if she'd want mobile home sites or tenements! She was no slum landlord. Didn't you learn anything about her? She liked design, creating something beautiful, she had a soul, Robbie, she wasn't only in property for the money, it was her passion. If you couldn't see that you must be stupid.'

She didn't see the blow coming. One moment he was pushing at her shoulders, the next his fist slammed into her cheek. 'Don't you fuckin' call me stupid,' he snarled.

Laura realized as her face erupted in pain that he was not bluffing and she was in real danger. If he'd been alone maybe she could have fought him off, but with Andy ready to jump in she had no chance. She glanced round to see where he was. He was leaning against the kitchen doorpost, grinning. He looked the kind who beat women up just for fun.

'I didn't mean you were stupid,' she said to Robbie. 'You

just obviously misunderstood what Jackie was all about. Now let's go into the sitting room or the kitchen and talk about this calmly.'

'I don't want to talk. I want money,' he said, and he caught hold of her shoulders as if preparing to hit her again if she refused.

Laura's cheek was throbbing, and she didn't want to risk a second blow. 'I haven't got any,' she said. 'I won't have any either, not until probate goes through, and that could be months, because of the time I've spent inside.'

'Your sister must have some,' he said with a sly look. 'A house like this is worth a bomb. She's bound to know where to lay her hands on some readies, especially when she sees what a razor can do to a face.'

Laura was already scared, but the thought of the two men marking Meggie's face terrified her. 'Leave her out of this,' she said, pushing him away from her. 'I'll give you everything I've got in my purse, I'll even go down to the cash machine and draw out some more.'

He hit her again, this time a punch in the ribs which winded her and made her cry out in pain. Lucy began barking from the sitting room.

'A couple of hundred isn't enough for me,' he raged, 'I need ten thousand.' He turned towards Andy. 'Shut that bloody dog up,' he yelled at him.

It was the word 'need' that alerted her to the real reason behind his surprise visit. He was on the run! The police in Edinburgh must have put out a warrant for his arrest. No doubt whoever tipped him off about that would also have had access to court records, to find out her bail address.

But knowing he was wanted by the police put her in an even more vulnerable position. A desperate man didn't think logically. He wouldn't stop to consider that hurting her or Meggie would just get him a longer prison sentence, he'd do what any cornered savage animal would do – attack.

'No one, Robbie, has ten thousand pounds lying around,' she said, hardly able to get the words out for the pain in her ribs. Andy was just about to go into the sitting room and she was afraid he'd hurt Lucy. 'I don't want to see the police catch you. I've had a basinful of them myself, so get out of here while you still can. I'll give you everything I've got,' she said frantically.

Lucy came bounding out of the sitting room wagging her tail and jumping up at Laura's legs in greeting. 'Basket, Lucy,' she said weakly, hoping that for once she would obey. But she didn't, she turned to Robbie and began jumping up at him. He lifted his foot and kicked her, and squealing with fright she ran for the stairs.

Laura seized Robbie's moment of distraction to sidle towards the front door and make her escape. She got it open, then screamed as a hand on her shoulder hauled her back in. It was Andy. He grabbed her arm, twisting it up behind her back, making her scream even louder with the pain.

'Shut it,' he said in a growl as he frogmarched her back along the hall into the kitchen. Robbie came in too. He picked up her handbag, which she'd left sitting on the vegetable basket, and rifled through it. He found a £10 note in her purse and looked at it contemptuously.

'Watch her!' he ordered Andy and began to rummage through the kitchen drawers and cupboards.

Lucy was still barking. Laura thought she was at the top of the stairs, too frightened to come down, and she sincerely hoped she'd stay there because she wouldn't put it past Robbie to kick her again.

'There isn't any more money in the house,' Laura said, directing her plea at Andy because she felt he was dumber than Robbie. 'If there was any I'd give it to you. Come with me to the cashpoint – I'll get you some there.'

Andy's face brightened. Clearly it didn't occur to him that he couldn't stop her darting away from him once they were on a busy main road.

'Shall I go with her, boss?' he asked Robbie.

'Don't be fuckin' thick,' Robbie snarled.

'I could give you the card and you could go yourself,' Laura volunteered.

'Yeah, right!' Robbie said. 'As if you could be trusted to give him the right number! I didn't come down the Clyde on an orange box, you know.'

'I want you out of here, you want to go, that's all I see,' she said. 'You can't get more out than two hundred in one day anyway, and I'd gladly give you that for old times' sake.'

'Don't come all the old acid with me,' he scowled. 'You always did have more tricks than a sodding magician.'

'I'm not playing any tricks,' she pleaded. 'Don't you think I've been through enough? I was your friend when you needed one most after your wife left you. Have you forgotten that? I could have told the police you knew Jackie and you'd have been pulled in for questioning, but I didn't. I don't care what you did with Belle and Charles, or that solicitor. Go now and I won't tell anyone you've been here.'

'Liar!' he shouted back at her. 'You've always lied to me and you're still doing it.' He came at her like a bulldozer, knocking her back against the kitchen units, and grabbed hold of her neck with both hands and squeezed it. 'You sent Macgregor round to check me out, you told him that I helped Jackie. He got stuff out of Calder, and now I'm on the run. I should have had you finished off years ago, when you first double-crossed me.'

Laura couldn't breathe, she could feel her eyes popping out of her head, her legs were trapped by his, and even though she tried to lift her arms to pummel him they wouldn't seem to move.

'Come on, boss, let's go,' she heard Andy say. 'I don't want none of this, it's too fucking heavy.'

'You fucking go if you ain't got the stomach for it,' Robbie yelled back at him, still squeezing at her neck. 'You're just a bloody doughnut anyway.'

'You're on yer own then,' Andy said indignantly. 'I ain't the one wiv the Old Bill on me tail.'

Laura could see nothing but Robbie's face just a few inches from hers, and even that was blurred. But she sensed that Andy was walking away and that she was going to lose consciousness any minute. In one last concerted attempt to defend herself she forced her arms up to grab Robbie, and at the same time brought her knee up sharply into what she hoped was his crotch.

She was on target for he yelled and let go of her, and in that instant she heard the front door slam, Andy had gone. She was still gasping for breath, her eyes were stinging and still blurred, but it was suddenly quiet. Lucy had stopped barking and the only sound was Robbie's laboured breathing.

Her eyes cleared just as he began to stagger towards her, and she backed away towards the patio doors. She stumbled against something and looking down she saw it was the cast-iron cat they used to hold open the door. She snatched it up and brought it down on his shoulder with all her strength.

His eyes opened wide with surprise and he staggered back a couple of steps, but then he sort of buckled and keeled over and fell flat on his back with a thump.

Although she had wanted to stop him in his tracks, she hadn't expected it to work. She stood there looking down at him. His eyes were open but they looked vacant, and she didn't know whether to run or to check if he was still conscious.

Then the doorbell rang.

She thought it was Andy come back to get Robbie. She wanted to get to the phone and call the police, but Robbie could be tricking her and the moment she moved away from him, he might jump up and grab her again.

'Coo-ee!'

She started at the sound.

'Coo-ee! Laura! Are you there? I've got Lucy. She was out on the road!'

All at once she realized it was Mrs Hernan from next door, and she was calling through the letterbox.

Relief flooded through her. 'Call the police, Mrs Hernan!' she yelled back, moving past Robbie so the woman could hear her. 'I've been attacked! The man's still here and I've knocked him out with the doorstop, but he might come round. Please be quick.'

The letterbox slammed shut and she could hear the neighbour rushing away. But as she turned, to her horror Robbie was trying to get to his feet. She screamed and ran at him, pushing him so hard he fell down again. 'Stay there or I'll hit you again,' she shrieked at him and picked up the doorstop, brandishing it warningly.

He was just lying there, looking up at her. Whether this was because he was dazed or planning his next move she didn't know, but she knew she had to make certain he couldn't do anything more. Pulling the belt off her jeans, she bent down and rolled him over on to his stomach.

'Help me,' he said, his voice strangely feeble.

'No chance,' she said, and catching hold of his arms she pulled them together behind his back, slipped the belt like a noose around his wrists and pulled it tight.

With nothing close by to tie his feet together, and afraid he might get free if she went to find something, she sat astride his legs and held the end of the belt tightly so he couldn't move his arms.

'You're hurting my legs,' he whimpered.

'Good,' she said grimly and pressed down harder on them. 'Now you know what it feels like – you nearly strangled me.'

Her throat hurt and she could barely swallow. She could feel her face swelling and one of her back teeth was loose. But she was determined to hold him down till the police arrived.

He began to struggle and swear at her then, trying to buck beneath her to get her off him, but she held on to the belt even tighter.

'You'll pay for this,' he shouted out. 'I'll make you suffer, I've got friends who will send those pictures on to the press for me.'

'Friends!' she said contemptuously. 'You don't know the meaning of the word. I thought I was your friend, I actually saw something nice in you for a while. More fool me!'

It was agonizing waiting. Her head was spinning, her ribs ached, she just wanted to lie down and she knew if he gathered himself to fight her, she wouldn't be able to hold him. She focused on the kitchen clock. It was five to four when she first looked, but it seemed like an hour before the big hand even reached twelve.

Robbie's breathing sounded wheezy and the back of his neck had gone an ominous purple colour. 'Let me go, Laura,' he pleaded, and his voice was squeaky. 'I'm sorry I hurt you. I shouldn't have come here, I know that now. I'll go, and never come back. I won't be able to take prison at my age.'

'No, you won't,' she agreed, struggling against a wave of dizziness. 'You'll be stuck in there with hundreds of other weasels, just like you. Only they'll be young and cocky, and they'll push you around. I almost feel sorry for you. But tell me one thing, Robbie. Why didn't Calder destroy Jackie's will?'

She could barely hold the belt now and she couldn't even see the clock hands clearly.

'He told me he had,' Robbie said, his voice growing fainter.

Laura pricked up her ears at a sound in the distance. It sounded like a police siren.

It *was* a police siren – she could hear it gradually coming closer. It wasn't a minute too soon either, she felt decidedly faint.

'Charles killed Barney,' Robbie blurted out. 'He was the hit-and-run driver. None of this would have happened but for that.'

Laura heard what he said, but the shock of it was too great to respond. There was a kind of roaring sound in her head, the room was spinning, she couldn't focus any more. Yet she could picture Charles's face at Barney's funeral so clearly, just as if he was right in front of her.

Deeply tanned, his teeth dazzling white like the shirt under his dark handmade suit, and tears trickling down his handsome face as he took her hands in his. The vicar had completed the interment, soil and flowers had been dropped on to the coffin and she could hear both Belle and Jackie sobbing.

'I am so very, very sorry, Laura,' he said. 'Belle and I will miss him so much. He was a fine boy.'

How could he have offered words of comfort when he was responsible for Barney's death?

Meggie had had a good day with Ivy, despite the heavy rain. They'd been to see an old property in Bromley High Street. It was a large shop, with two floors above, and it was perfect for renovation into two smaller shops and three, maybe four flats. It was a bargain because it was so dilapidated, and they'd put an offer in for it and had it accepted immediately.

Over a cup of tea, she and Ivy decided they would ask Laura if she would like to join them in the project, and perhaps have one of the shops. They had become really excited about it, discussing what this would mean for all of them if Laura agreed. If Ivy hadn't had a meeting at her son's school that evening, she'd have been in the car now, all fired up to talk to her sister.

Even without Ivy, Meggie's stomach was turning cartwheels as she drove home through the rain. She was convinced Laura would be as thrilled and enthusiastic as she and Ivy were. But as she turned into Bargery Road and saw two police cars and an ambulance right by her house, her blood froze.

'What's happened?' she asked as she leapt out of her car and ran towards a policeman standing outside her gate. 'This is my house. Has something happened to my sister?'

At that point the front door opened and two ambulance men brought out a stretcher with a man on it.

'It appears he called earlier and attacked your sister,' the policeman explained. 'But your neighbour Mrs Hernan will explain to you. She called us and let us in with a key she holds.'

'But Laura?'

'She's okay,' he said soothingly. 'She was very brave and fought him off. We think her attacker has had a minor stroke and they are taking him to hospital.'

Mrs Hernan came out of her house, crying and very agitated. 'Oh, Meggie,' she said, wringing her hands. 'I'm so glad you've come back. What a terrible business!'

Mrs Hernan was a widow in her sixties and she often looked after Lucy for Meggie when she had to be away from home for more than a few hours. She was a stout, kind-hearted and sensible woman, not given to hysterics, so that made Meggie even more frightened.

Her neighbour explained how she rescued Lucy from the road and then called through the letterbox when Laura didn't answer the door. 'I couldn't believe it when she called back telling me to get the police! When they got here and I let them in, I thought both Laura and the man were dead because she was slumped down on top of him on the kitchen floor. But she is all right, she'd just fainted. I suppose that was the shock. I nearly fainted myself, I'd had such a fright. Lucy's still in my house.'

Meggie wasn't one for telling anyone her business. All Mrs Hernan knew was that Laura had come to stay for a holiday. Meggie supposed she had no choice now but to tell her the truth; after all, it would be all over the papers once Laura was exonerated. 'You go indoors out of the rain and have a cup of tea,' she said. 'I'll come and get Lucy and have a chat once I've seen Laura.'

She found Laura lying on the settee in the sitting room, a tall, powerfully built sergeant with a crewcut perched on the arm talking to her. Laura looked awful; one side of her face was puffy and her eye red and swollen. There were also bruises on her neck as if her attacker had tried to strangle her.

'Don't panic,' she said, trying to smile at Meggie. 'It looks worse than it is. They've been trying to get me to go to hospital, but as far as I know they've got no miracle cure for black eyes.'

She quickly explained what had happened, making light of it. 'As for Lucy, she was as clever as Lassie, she charged out the front door and got help for me. We'd better give her something special for her tea.'

Meggie felt choked up by her sister's courage and by the

way she was trying to make her laugh even though she'd clearly had a terrifying experience.

'I've got the gist of what happened, but if it's okay with you I'll call back tomorrow and take a proper statement,' the sergeant said to Meggie. 'Are you two going to be all right here alone, or would you like us to leave someone to stay with you?'

'We'll be fine on our own,' Laura butted in. 'Just make sure you keep Robbie Fielding under lock and key. The last thing I want is him coming round here in the middle of the night and showing his face at the window like Robert De Niro in *Cape Fear*.'

That did make Meggie smile. She could remember watching the video of it with Ivy, and her sister had been too scared to drive home alone.

The police left once they'd checked the kitchen for the second man's fingerprints. Meggie got some ice cubes out of the fridge and made a pack to put on Laura's face.

'I don't know,' she said, shaking her head as she held the pack to Laura's cheek. 'Leave you alone for an afternoon and you invite a couple of men in! Sergeant Erskine was nice, did you try to chat him up too?'

'No, I don't think he realized how gorgeous I am normally,' Laura laughed. 'Anyway, I think he fancied you, I saw you whispering in the hall.'

'We were talking about you,' Meggie said defensively. 'He said how brave you were; he'd obviously done his homework and knew your case inside out. He might not have mentioned your beauty, but he did comment on your sense of humour.'

'I expect he thought it was warped!'

Meggie half smiled. Laura was right, Sergeant Erskine was nice, with soft brown eyes and a generous mouth, and he was clearly a sensitive man. '*Your sister's got a lot of guts*,' he said. '*Most people in that position freeze up. But the thing that impressed me most was her control. She used just enough force to overpower her attacker. There was no viciousness, no spite. She was even concerned when the ambulance men said he'd had a stroke. Yet that thug was trying to strangle her.'*

'No, you genuinely amused him,' Meggie said. 'But he was concerned that your cheerfulness might be just a front to cover up something which had really upset you. I said that someone trying to strangle you was fairly upsetting, but he seemed to think there was something more. Was he right?'

'He was very perceptive for a copper,' Laura admitted. 'And he was right, there was something. Robbie told me Charles was the hit-and-run driver who killed Barney.'

'Charles? Belle's husband? No, it can't have been,' Meggie exclaimed.

'I think he was telling the truth,' Laura replied. 'I never really liked Charles, you know. He was too puffed up with self-importance, liked to be seen in smart places, mixing with the right people. But whatever I felt about him, he and Belle were good with Barney – they behaved as if he was their real nephew. That makes it very hard to take.'

'Robbie Fielding sounds like a really evil man, and desperate too. I'd say it was just one last-ditch attempt to hurt you in any way he could,' Meggie said soothingly. 'Maybe he thought it would throw you enough to let him go?'

'It had the ring of truth to me,' Laura insisted. 'And it makes sense of everything. Why Belle kept me at arm's length before Barney's funeral, why Jackie put up with so much from me afterwards when I was going round the bend. And everything that happened later.'

'But surely Jackie would have turned him in?' Meggie said. 'That's what doesn't make sense to me.'

'It does to me,' Laura sighed. 'It was for Belle, and for Frank and Lena too. And she probably thought I could cope better if I thought it was a stranger. No wonder she drank too much, the pressure of it must have been awful.'

Meggie put her hand on Laura's cheek and caressed it. 'And how is it making *you* feel?' she said softly.

'Desolate,' Laura murmured and she began to cry.

Laura woke in the morning to bright sunshine slanting through a gap in the curtains. Her face, neck and ribs throbbed and she reached out for a hand mirror by the bed.

She looked a mess. Her eye was turning black, her right cheek was red and swollen, and there were fingermarks on her neck which made her shudder.

'So much for believing the new hair colour made you look ten years younger,' she muttered to herself.

The phone rang downstairs, Lucy barked, and she heard Meggie come out of the kitchen to answer it.

They had both cried a great deal the previous night and Laura had ended up telling her sister the whole story about Robbie, including the pornography and the making of the blue films. Up till now she'd only revealed an edited version of it, but she found she wanted Meggie to see the complete picture.

'I've always felt Barney's death was my punishment,' she admitted. 'But punishment means that once it's over, you should start again with a clean slate. It won't ever be like that for me.'

'Of course it will,' Meggie said firmly. 'And especially now that you've brought everything out in the open and looked at it closely.'

Laura shook her head. 'No, Meggie. That's why when you and Ivy go on about Stuart, I know it won't work out. You see, in the last ten years I've been out with dozens of men. A few of them I even liked enough to want to go to bed with. But it was a mistake, it brought it all back. I felt cheap and dirty again. I know now that I'll only ever feel okay about myself if I stay celibate.'

Meggie put her arms around her and hugged her to her chest. 'It's like that for me too,' she said softly. 'I know too much, I'm tainted. I can't even respond to men flirting with me because I'm afraid of where it will lead. The last thing I want is to end up a crabby old maid, but that's how it will be because I'm afraid of exposing myself in any way, mentally or physically.'

The last thing Laura remembered thinking before she finally dropped off to sleep was that she had been better off in prison. Everything was predictable there, from what you ate on each day of the week to who would start the next fight on the wing. On the outside nothing was predictable, not even her own feelings.

Meggie's voice wafted up to Laura from the hall below. She couldn't hear what her sister was saying, but there was a tinge of excitement in her tone that made Laura curious enough to get up and open her door.

'Bruised but not broken,' she heard Meggie say. 'The police thought she was incredibly brave and handled herself very well. But I think his visit is bound to have brought back nasty stuff from the past.'

'Who is it, Meggie?' Laura called out.

'Stuart,' Meggie shouted back. 'I thought you were asleep.'

'I always wake up when people are talking about me,' Laura said as she padded down the stairs and took the phone.

Stuart was very concerned about her and explained that Fielding had fled to London because he'd attempted to kill David Calder, the solicitor. 'It was three days ago,' he explained. 'Calder was walking from his office in Portobello to his car around seven in the evening, when a car came straight at him at speed, mounting the pavement. It knocked him flying and drove off. A witness got a partial number plate, described the driver, and apparently that description fitted Fielding. The car used had been stolen in Edinburgh earlier the same day. But by the time the police had got all this information and gone to Fielding's pub to arrest him, he'd already flown. Tipped off no doubt by someone in the force he kept in his pocket.'

'But why did he do it?' Laura asked.

'I'd make a guess that Calder was about to spill the beans about whatever it was the pair of them had been up to.'

Laura told him that she thought Fielding had discovered Belle killed Jackie and was blackmailing the couple. Stuart agreed. 'But I don't think either of them knew about the new will. I'm pretty certain Fielding forced Calder to keep quiet about that, because he knew if the Howells got nothing, neither would he.'

'Why didn't Calder just destroy it then?' Laura asked. 'Who would have known?'

'I think it must have been because his secretary witnessed it. It's one thing to pretend you've forgotten about a legal document,' Stuart said, 'quite another to destroy it. Perhaps Calder was afraid the woman would remember its existence at some time. But I think it will transpire that there was more to Calder and Fielding's relationship than just this stuff with Jackie and the Howells. I've heard a whisper about mortgage frauds and no doubt a great deal more will come out of the woodwork before long.'

'Is Calder very badly hurt?' Laura asked.

'Well, he's still in intensive care. But apparently they are hopeful he'll recover.'

Laura told Stuart then that Fielding had claimed Charles killed Barney. 'Tell me that isn't true,' she said. 'He just wanted to hurt me more, didn't he?'

Stuart's hesitation in replying was enough.

'Sorry, sweetheart,' he said very sadly. 'It is true. Charles has confessed to it. I've got to admit I suspected it some time ago but Patrick, David and I didn't tell you because we knew how upset it would make you.'

'And Jackie knew it was him?'

'Yes, I'm afraid so.'

Laura fought back tears as Stuart explained why he thought she'd done it, and how everything else that happened later was because of it.

'I don't feel angry with her,' she said. 'I'm sure she thought it would be better for me to think it was a stranger. But she obviously never realized what it would do to her. It must have been agony for her watching me crack up while Charles got away with it.'

'I think she hoped it would make Belle and Charles better people,' Stuart said. 'But look where that led!'

He suggested he came down to London to see her, but Laura put him off. She said that she'd taken up enough of his time and energy already, but the truth was she couldn't bear for him to see her looking so battered.

'I'll see you at the appeal,' she said. 'Angie has said Meggie and I can stay with her for a couple of days and maybe we can all have some sort of celebration together.'

'And afterwards?' Stuart asked. 'Have you made any plans?'

Laura told him about the property in Bromley. 'We haven't had much of a chance to discuss it properly, but Meggie and Ivy hope I'll open a dress shop there.'

'That sounds just perfect for you,' he said.

Laura had hoped she might hear disappointment in his voice, but he didn't even add a suggestion that maybe they could spend a little time together in Edinburgh before she returned to London. 'Yes, I'm sure getting stuck into another business is just what I need,' she said, forcing herself to sound excited. 'But what about you? Are you all healed up?'

'Pretty much,' he said. 'And I've had several offers of work, both here in Scotland and abroad. I think I'll stay in Scotland though, at least until this probate stuff is sorted. Jackie would have wanted me to see it all through.'

He said then that he'd have to ring off as he had a lot of things to do, but he thought Patrick Goldsmith would be in touch with her any day with the date for the appeal.

'So!' Meggie said as she came off the phone. 'Is he coming down? What are his plans?'

Laura smiled at the bright expectancy on her sister's face. 'His plans don't include me, Meggie, though I'll see him at the appeal. But after that it's goodnight and goodbye, and we both move on.'

19

'One more picture, Laura!'

'How do you feel now you are free?'

'What are your plans now, Laura? Will you stay in Scotland?'

'Do you feel angry that you were put in prison for a crime you didn't commit?'

'You'll be called as a prosecution witness when Belle Howell comes to trial. Will that be difficult for you?'

Laura fixed a smile on her face as the journalists outside the court fired questions at her. But what she really wanted to do was run away and hide, from them, the photographers and the television cameramen intent on sending her face out into every living room in the country.

She was of course ecstatically happy that finally it was publicly acknowledged that she was innocent of any crime. The judge had smiled at her and wished her well for the future, she'd been patted on the back, kissed, hugged and congratulated by a great many people. Patrick had even said she should get a hefty sum in compensation for wrongful imprisonment.

But she didn't feel any joy at the smiles of the media people here today, for almost all of them had condemned her just twenty months ago, and revelled in all the dirt they managed to dig up on her.

It was tempting to remind them of that, even to quote some of the more salacious headlines they'd used at the time and make them squirm. But if she showed spite they were likely to reciprocate, and the sooner she said a few words, the sooner she could walk away and begin her new life.

Glancing behind her at Meggie, Ivy, Angie, Stuart and Patrick, the concern etched on their faces gave her the strength she needed.

'I'm thrilled to be free, and my name cleared,' she began, looking from one face to another and trying hard not to think how good it would be to slap some of them. 'It's too soon to know where I'll live permanently. As for my wrongful imprisonment; my biggest sorrow is not that I lost my freedom for two years, awful as that was, but that people actually believed I killed my dearest friend.'

She paused for dramatic effect. 'Jackie Davies had been my lifelong friend. We had grown up together and shared so much. I loved her and I still grieve for her. My life will never be the same again because she can't be part of it.'

She was glad to see a few of them looked a little shame-faced, and that was all the revenge she needed.

'But today isn't one for blaming others, nor for anger or bitterness,' she went on. 'It is a joyful day because a wrong has been righted.'

She turned slightly, holding out one hand to indicate Stuart.

'I would like to publicly thank my old friend Stuart Macgregor. Without him I wouldn't be talking to you today. He believed in me when few others did, and dug up new evidence for my appeal. He even risked his life for me. I'd like you all to join me in applauding his courage.'

As she began to clap, the crowd joined in, many of them shouting bravo and stamping their feet in approval.

Stuart blushed like a bashful schoolboy.

'I owe Stuart more than words can ever say,' she added as the applause died down. 'He was the real hero in all this, along with his friend David Stoyle who sadly couldn't be here today. But I'd also like to thank my lawyer Patrick Goldsmith for working so tirelessly on my behalf. And for the unconditional love and support my sisters Meggie and Ivy gave me.'

There was another burst of applause but Laura made a gesture with her hands to end it.

'I would ask you now to leave me and my family in peace to get on with our lives,' she finished up. 'Thank you.'

Patrick Goldsmith took her arm and led her away from the throng. 'Well done, Laura. That was perfect,' he said. 'I doubt they'll obey your wishes, they never do. But for now a celebration drink is in order, and I've taken the liberty of hiring a private room in a restaurant down the street.'

It was four in the afternoon, chilly and spitting with rain, but for Laura Edinburgh had never looked so bright and beautiful. She and her sisters had flown up early that morning, and Meggie and Ivy would be going back the following day. Laura had not booked a return flight because she planned to stay a few days with Angie, then buy herself a car so she could go out to Fife to visit Barney's grave. After that she intended to get her belongings from Angie's mother's house and drive back to London.

Stuart fell in beside her. 'Did I tell you that you look beautiful today?' he said.

Laura smiled. She had taken great care in picking her outfit, a fitted taupe linen dress with a cream striped jacket. It wasn't just because she knew she'd be photographed, but because she wanted Stuart to see her at her best. 'You look pretty gorgeous yourself,' she retorted, noting how well the light grey pinstripe suit fitted him. 'I've never seen you in a suit before!'

She was tempted to remind him that he'd once claimed

he would never wear a suit because it was 'establishment'. But she supposed they had both grown up a lot since those days.

'Happy?' he asked as they arrived at the restaurant, giving her the kind of wide smile that brought back so many sweet memories.

'Happy doesn't even come close to covering it.' She smiled back. 'I'd like to climb right up on to the highest point of the Castle and scream out how great I feel.'

'I was glad to see your bruises have gone,' he said, reaching out and touching her cheek gently with his thumb. 'Meggie said they were bad – she was afraid they wouldn't fade in time for today.'

'I think that is down to the power of faith,' Laura giggled. 'I'm far too vain to want to look like a road accident victim, even if it would get me still more sympathy.'

Stuart laughed. 'David rang this morning to wish you luck. I'll have to phone him in a minute and tell him all about it. Next time I'm in London I could take you over to see him and meet Julia and his children, if you'd like that?'

'I would,' she said. 'But you must give me his address anyway so I can write and thank him for his help. But right now all I want is a stiff drink.'

The small private room had been decorated with yellow helium-filled balloons and yellow ribbons. Laura stood looking at it in amazement. 'I do hope no one's going to pop up and sing "Tie a yellow ribbon round the old oak tree,"' she giggled.

'I thought of it, but I've forgotten the words,' Stuart said with a grin. 'But we've got champagne and I think that says how we all feel.'

*

The champagne went straight to Laura's head as she had been too nervous to eat in the morning, and she fell silent. It was good just to be sitting around the table with everyone she loved, listening to their chatter and laughter, and marvelling that this was a dream come true.

Stuart was sitting between her and Angie, and they were having an animated discussion about the street children in South America and what Stuart thought ought to be done to help them.

Meggie and Ivy were sitting either side of Patrick and they both looked lovely. Ivy, in a pale pink suit with her flowing blonde hair, looked like a model, and Meggie, in a cream trouser suit, her dark bob shining like wet tar, was prettier than she'd ever been before. Three days earlier she'd been out on a first date with Sergeant James Erskine, the policeman who had come when Laura was attacked, and since then had looked as if she was capable of walking on water.

Laura had noticed that James was attracted to Meggie when he came round to take her statement. He made several excuses to call back, each time in the early evening when Meggie was sure to be home. There were several phone calls before Meggie finally agreed to go out to dinner with him, but even just a couple of hours before her date she was looking for excuses to let him down.

Laura bullied her into going through with it, for she felt in her very bones that James was the man Meggie needed. Aside from being a real dish, he was the same age as her and widowed. His wife had died of cancer five years ago, and his three children, who were now in their late teens to early twenties, still lived with him. He was a kind and sensitive man and Laura sensed that even if Meggie ended up telling him about her past, he'd take it in his stride.

One look at her sister's radiant face when she arrived

home that night was to know the date had been a huge success. James phoned at eight the following morning and they talked for over an hour; all day after the call Meggie was alternately giggly or dreamy, a surefire sign that she was smitten.

Part of the reason Laura intended to stay up in Scotland for a while was to give Meggie the opportunity to have her house to herself. She'd also warned Ivy not to drop in unannounced.

Patrick suddenly stood up and tapped a fork on a glass to get everyone's attention. 'I think it's about time we ordered some food. I don't know about anyone else but I'm starving.'

Everyone else agreed they were too and Patrick went off to get some menus. Stuart turned to Laura. 'What would you like?' he asked.

'It will have to be prawns,' she said.

'Any particular reason?'

'Well, when I was on remand, and still believing I would be acquitted, I used to plan the meal I'd have when I got out. I didn't think big, not even having dinner in a restaurant. I just imagined going to Marks and Spencer and buying prawns and salad, and eating it at home.'

'It so happens they do some marvellous prawns in garlic here,' he said. 'But at risk of opening up an old wound, how did you feel when they found you guilty? We've never talked about that.'

'I was completely demented,' she said ruefully. 'I couldn't believe it was happening to me. The closest thing to it is the old cliché of thinking you are stuck in a nightmare, only you don't wake up soaked in sweat and find yourself in your own bed.'

'I shouldn't have asked,' he said. 'Forgive me?'

Laura smiled. 'It's okay. But that will be the last time

I ever mention it. In fact I shall delete the word "prison" from my vocabulary, unless of course it's in connection with other people. Robbie, for instance! Have you heard anything more about him?'

'They only kept him in hospital a couple of days. The stroke turned out to be a very mild one,' Stuart replied. 'He had a court appearance and got remanded in custody in London. But Calder is still in a bad way apparently. Even if he recovers he'll never walk again.'

'Poor man,' Laura said.

'Don't waste any sympathy on him, a lawyer should be above reproach,' Stuart said. 'But I wish I knew exactly what he and Fielding were up to. I bet Patrick knows, but he's being very tight-lipped about it.'

Laura smiled at his insatiable curiosity. She couldn't care less what the two men had done. Perhaps when Belle and Charles came to trial her interest might be reawakened, but for now she wanted to forget all of them.

'So what about you?' she asked Stuart after everyone had ordered a meal. 'Are you going abroad now, or what?'

'No, I'm taking on a job near Oban.'

'Really! What on earth are you going to do there?'

'Doing up a very old place. The owners want to turn it into a hotel, so it's partly restoration and partly new build. It's a great project, the architect's drawings are marvellous, and we'll be employing local men.'

'Will you be living there then?' she asked, trying not to sound dismayed that he wasn't going to be working in London.

'I've bought a small cottage by Loch Awe,' he said nonchalantly. 'It's a bit of a mess, the old man who lived there had been on his own since his wife died, and he'd let things go. He had to go into a nursing home, so it was a quick sale.'

It stung Laura that he'd been organizing all this but hadn't mentioned any of it in his phone calls. 'That's marvellous,' she said, even though her heart was sinking. 'You always did want to live in the Highlands.'

'Yes,' he said thoughtfully. 'In those days I relished somewhere primitive, but I've had a taste of luxury over the years and I don't know that I'm going to enjoy roughing it this winter.'

'You can always come down to London for a long weekend, and we'll cosset you,' Laura suggested.

She thought that he would make a joke about her going up there to rough it with him, but he didn't.

It was well after ten when they finally left the restaurant. Patrick went on home, and though Angie asked Stuart if he'd like to come back to her flat with them, he declined.

'I'm leaving for Oban in the morning,' he said. 'I'll need to be bright-eyed and bushy-tailed. Besides, you don't want a lone male spoiling your girlie fun.'

He hailed a taxi for them, kissed them all on the cheek and said he'd keep in touch, and as the cab drew off Laura turned to watch him through the back window. He might look like a city slicker today in his smart suit, but she thought his loping walk was that of a man who would be happier in the great outdoors.

'When are you going to see him again?' Meggie asked, slurring her words because she'd had too much to drink.

'He didn't suggest anything,' Laura said sadly. 'He didn't even give me an address or a phone number.'

Laura thought she would fall asleep the moment her head touched the pillow that night, for it had been a long day, and she'd had so much to drink. But once she was tucked up in bed in Angie's tiny spare room, she found sleep eluded her.

It had been so strange seeing her old shop again, for Angie had insisted they all went to see it before going back to her flat. Very little had been changed, just a fresh coat of paint and a new carpet, but Angie was taking in more expensive designer clothes now, and a big range of costume jewellery. Ivy was thrilled to find a black leather Chanel handbag, and Meggie bought a dark red Jaeger jacket.

But while her sisters were gleefully raking though the clothes, Laura found herself looking at a chair she'd found in a junk shop and sprayed gold, and remembering how Jackie had helped her re-upholster the seat with cream velvet, and that they'd laughingly called it the 'Versailles' look.

She wondered then if she'd ever make another friend as close as Jackie had been. Some of the very sweetest moments in her life had been just sitting around chatting and laughing with her. Always so much laughter, and they had believed it would go on until they were very old ladies.

Once they had even joked about sharing a home when they got to seventy. They imagined themselves going on coach trips to Blackpool or a day out on the Yorkshire Moors, only they'd be going into pubs for brandy while all the other old ladies had cream teas.

It was only now she was free that it really hit home how empty life would be without Jackie. Meggie and Ivy were great, but on a different level. She and Jackie had always been on the same wavelength, they could pick each other's brains, tell each other off, even have a blazing row and it was forgotten in half an hour. They were in so many ways twin souls, they understood each other without lengthy explanations. How could she ever find anyone like that again?

Meggie and Ivy were sleeping on the bed-settee in the lounge, and through the open door Laura could hear Meggie snoring softly, just the way she did when she was little. Forty years had passed since the three of them slept in one bed. Laura didn't think either Meggie or Ivy remembered those days – at least, they never spoke of it. They never spoke about their father either, or Mark and Paul, but perhaps that was because they'd been so young when they were taken away by the police that they had little recollection of them.

It had been a very strange day. So much waiting around, first for the flight, then at the court for the hearing, and all the time her stomach in knots with nerves. Right up till the judge said she was free to go, she'd half expected something terrible would happen and she'd end up being taken down to the cells under the court to await the prison van.

Yet tucked away beneath the fear and trepidation there had been bubblings of excitement, and they were about Stuart, and what was going to happen next. Maybe if Meggie hadn't drip-fed the idea that he still had feelings for her, she wouldn't have allowed herself to slip into little rosy daydreams about him. She really ought to have known better: what man would want to try to relight a fire with someone who had not only hurt him badly once, but was also likely to be something of a liability?

He'd been there for her when she most needed someone, and maybe that had clouded her judgement about her feelings for him too. She would just have to keep on reminding herself how fortunate she was: she wasn't destitute, she had two loving sisters, she even had the legacy from Jackie coming to her. That was enough for anyone.

The day after the appeal hearing Angie asked Laura to go with her to a lawyer to sign a legal document transferring all the rights of the shop to her, and she paid Laura £4,000 for the lease and the fixtures and fittings. Laura felt awkward about taking the money, but both the lawyer and Angie insisted she was entitled to it, and it would also prevent her having any claim on the shop at a later date.

The money couldn't have come at a better time as Laura had only a couple of hundred pounds left in her bank account, and although Meggie had offered to lend her some more so she could buy a decent car, she'd been reluctant to do that. But now, instead of getting an old banger, she was able to buy a three-year-old red Ford Fiesta which would be far more reliable.

Once she'd got her car she went to collect her belongings from Angie's mother's house. Yet on sorting through the many stored boxes, she found that most of the pictures, china, ornaments and lamps reminded her of times and a person she'd rather forget, so she donated them to a charity shop.

All she kept was albums of photographs, most of them of Barney, books she'd loved, some bedding, a small case which she'd filled ten years ago with things of Barney's – a sweater, a pair of pyjamas, his old teddy bear and paintings he'd done at school – and a beautiful cream leather jewellery box Jackie had given her on her thirtieth birthday. It was much the same with her clothes, shoes and handbags. Most were unfashionable now, and the little reminders that came with them had nothing to do with her future. She kept the cashmere camel winter coat, boots, sweaters and trousers, and some of the best underwear. But the rest she bagged up for Angela's mother to give to a jumble sale.

Everything she wanted to keep fitted into one suitcase and two cardboard boxes. She put them in the boot of the car and drove back to the shop to say goodbye to Angie.

'You're not going already?' Angie exclaimed. 'I thought you'd at least stay till the weekend.'

Laura didn't want to admit that she felt a little uncomfortable hanging around a shop that had once been hers, and constantly running into women she knew from the past. Her face had been on the front page of all the newspapers, and though she knew that by next week those same newspapers would be wrapped round fish and chips and her story would be forgotten, she still felt exposed and vulnerable.

'I want to go out to Crail and visit Barney's grave,' she said. 'I'm less likely to run into anyone I know there during the week than at the weekend. Besides, there's nothing here for me in Edinburgh now. I'll take my time going back to London, maybe stay a couple of nights somewhere in the Borders, walk a bit and get my head together.'

Angie put her hands on her hips and studied her friend closely. 'You're disappointed about Stuart, aren't you?'

Laura shrugged. 'I don't know why everyone kept thinking we could be an item again. It wasn't as if we'd been childhood sweethearts, separated by some cruel stroke of fate. I was unfaithful to him, that's it and all about it. Some things can't be mended.'

'I don't think that's the case with you,' Angie said, shaking her head. 'No man goes to all the trouble Stuart did for you unless he's still in love.'

'You saw him after the court hearing. He hugged me once, told me I looked lovely and kissed me on the cheek when he left. Is that a man in love?'

'Maybe he was waiting for you to make the first move?'

'It's men that have to do that.'

'That, if you don't mind me saying, is a quaintly old-fashioned idea.' Angie sniffed. 'You've got bags of courage, so use some of it. Go to him.'

'I don't know where he is.'

'Well, find out. Someone's bound to know – his old landlord, Patrick. Use your imagination.'

*

It had been drizzling in Edinburgh but once Laura had driven over the Forth Bridge the sun came out, and she was acutely reminded of the last time she made this trip. It turned out to be the last time she drove anywhere of course, and it had been May then, a lovely spring day. Now it was the start of October and autumn was on its way, with the leaves beginning to turn yellow and orange on the trees.

But she was determined not to dwell on what happened that day in May. It was over now.

There wasn't much traffic and she made good time to Crail, drove past Kirkmay House, studiously not looking at it, and parked her car in Marketgate, close to St Mary's church.

She had brought some potted cyclamen and spring bulbs for Barney's grave, along with a small fork and trowel in Edinburgh, to avoid having to go into a shop here. As she entered the churchyard she filled up her water bottle from the tap at the gate and hurried over to his grave.

As always in the past, the sight of the small white marble headstone with just Barney's name, followed by 'born 1970, died 1981', brought tears to her eyes. She hadn't known what to put on the headstone, and the mason had advised her to keep it simple. But it looked so stark, with no hint of what Barney had been like, or even her feelings about him.

It was Good Friday in '93 when she had last visited the grave. He would have been twenty-three then if he'd lived, and she could remember wondering what sort of career he would have chosen. She'd planted masses of polyanthus that day and tucked some little fluffy chicks among them, because Barney had always loved it when she made chocolate nest cakes for Easter and put miniature eggs and chicks in them.

After she was arrested, she'd worried about his grave being neglected. It wasn't until Stuart turned up and came out to Crail that she heard it was very well kept. She assumed Belle had been looking after it.

As it was over a month ago that Belle was arrested, Laura had expected it to be overgrown with weeds, but to her surprise it looked lovely – weed-free and planted with red and white geraniums. She wondered who could have done it.

'I'm sorry I've been so long coming back,' she whispered, kneeling down on the grass beside the grave. 'But I've thought about you every day since the last time I came. I shall have to take these lovely geraniums away now because they'll only die when we get the first frost.'

She dug them out, placing them in a carrier bag, then forked over the whole surface and began planting the cyclamen and the bulbs. It was only as she began clearing up, brushing the soil off the marble surround, that she became aware of a man watching her from about twenty feet away. He was around sixty, of slight build, with white thinning hair and a green corduroy jacket.

She was irritated by his presence, assuming he was someone local who knew about her and hadn't the good manners to curb his curiosity.

Getting up from her knees, she picked up the bag of geranium plants and toyed with the idea of giving him a piece of her mind. But as she walked away from the grave he came towards her.

'Excuse me, but you're Laura, aren't you?' he asked.

His deep, almost growling voice struck a chord with Laura. All at once she didn't mind that he'd been watching her.

'Yes, I am. And you must be Ted?'

He nodded and looked a little bashful, but held out his hand to her. 'Yes, I'm Ted. And it is so good to meet you at last, Laura. I hope I didn't disturb you, but I was so pleased to see you there at Barney's grave I couldn't walk away.'

'Is it you that's been looking after it?' she asked.

'Yes.' He dropped his eyes from hers. 'You don't mind, do you? I met Barney many times when he was staying with Jackie and liked him a great deal. After he died Jackie came here most days, I often joined her and we'd sit on the bench and she'd pour out all her memories of him. So when you were arrested I felt I must continue to look after his grave, for both of you.'

Laura was deeply touched and her eyes prickled with tears. 'I think that is one of the kindest things anyone has ever done for me,' she said, her voice cracking with emotion. 'Especially as you must have believed I killed her.'

'I was never entirely convinced of that,' he said. 'Jackie spoke of you so often I felt I knew you. I found it comforting to have this to do, it feels like part of her is always here.'

'She should have been buried here too,' Laura said sadly. 'I don't know why she wasn't.'

'Belle's doing,' he said dourly. 'Because of the circumstances I couldn't intervene. But let's not talk about that, it's too upsetting to dwell on what she did. I was so glad to see on the television that you were exonerated. You've had a terrible time!'

'It's all over now.' Laura smiled at him. 'And I'm really glad to meet you at last. You were one secret Jackie kept from me. But let's go and sit down and have a chat.'

They sat on a bench in the sunshine and as they chatted about Stuart investigating on her behalf, Laura felt a real bond with this gentle, thoughtful man. She'd always had a problem with Roger, who'd been against her right from the start because of what she did to Steven, his old flatmate, and over the years jealousy and resentment had been added. There had been many occasions when she'd tried hard to put things right, for Jackie's benefit, but Roger wasn't the kind to forgive; he was a bombastic, stubborn man with a big ego.

Ted was so different – sensitive, unassuming – and he wanted to get to know her because they had both loved Jackie. Initially Laura couldn't see why her friend had fallen for him, for he was an almost complete opposite to her. He wasn't charismatic, sophisticated, outgoing or even sexy. Apart from his lovely duck-egg-blue eyes and his very mas- culine voice, he was ordinary, the kind of man you wouldn't even notice, let alone look at twice.

Yet as he told her about his shock at hearing Belle and Charles had been arrested, how he'd gone to see Stuart in hospital and how anxious he'd been for her, Laura saw exactly why Jackie had loved him. He was one of those rare people who cared more about others than he did about himself.

'Tell me how things are with you and your wife now. Did you tell her about Jackie?' Laura asked him after a little while.

'Yes, I did, I went home straight after seeing Stuart and told her the whole story.' He winced as if that been one of the worst moments of his life. 'Predictably Peggie was absolutely furious. She said some dreadful things and told me to get out. I couldn't of course, not when she had no one else to take care of her. It was hell for some time; the news of Belle and Charles's arrest wound her up still more. So I made plans to leave. I got a nurse lined up to come in daily.

'But when I began packing, she did a U-turn. She said she wanted me to stay.'

'Oh Ted, don't say you agreed?' Laura groaned.

Ted chuckled softly. 'I know! It makes me sound so weak. But she admitted she'd been hell to live with and she promised she'd change.'

'People rarely change, you should know that,' Laura said reprovingly.

'Maybe, but I thought I ought to give it one more shot. So far she's been much nicer, she's trying to do more for herself. Of course it's early days yet, but if she does revert back, then I will go.'

'I can't help thinking you deserve more than she can ever give you.'

'What else is there for me?' he said with a bleak look. 'Jackie was the love of my life, I know I'll never find anyone else like her. So I may as well stay in my own home looking after Peggie, which at least makes me feel useful, rather than living alone with nothing but sad memories.'

'Jackie cast a long shadow,' Laura sighed. 'I don't know how I'm going to get used to the idea she's gone for good either. But we've got to, Ted. We can feel privileged that we shared so much with her, but I don't think she'd approve of either of us moping for ever. Anyway, I ought to go now. Thank you so much for looking after Barney for me, and I'm sorry I had to dig up the geraniums.'

'I'll take them home and put them in the greenhouse for the winter. I'll keep on popping back just to keep an eye on the grave and tidy it up,' he said. 'But what are your plans now?'

She told him that she was going back to London.

'And Stuart?' he asked. 'Will he be going with you?'

Laura found herself telling him about how it was with her and Stuart and what Angie had said.

'I agree with your friend,' he said and he took her hand in his and squeezed it in understanding. 'It was patently obvious to me how he felt about you. I think the only reason he hasn't voiced his feelings is because he's afraid of rejection. We men can be far more insecure than women, you know,' he said with a little chuckle.

'The trouble is I can't be sure *how* I really feel,' she explained. 'Right now I do think we were meant for each other, but what if I'm mistaken, and it all goes wrong? I couldn't bear to hurt him again.'

'Nothing of any value in this life comes with any guarantees,' Ted said with a smile. 'You just have to have faith.'

'He told me I had to have faith in him when he first came to see me in prison,' Laura said thoughtfully. 'He didn't let me down either.'

'Go and find him, Laura. You've got nothing to lose except a bit of pride.'

He picked up the bag of geraniums and walked with her to her car. 'Will you let me know how you are from time to time?' he asked, fishing in his pocket and taking out a card. 'Jackie would've been so proud of the way you've handled this terrible business. I see no bitterness in you, and that proves what a remarkable woman you are.'

'And you, Ted, are a remarkably lovely man,' she said, putting her arms around him and hugging him. 'God bless and I hope it does work out with you and your wife. She's a very lucky woman to have you.'

Right up until she had nearly reached the Forth Bridge, Laura intended to go over it, on through Edinburgh and then take the A7 towards Carlisle, stopping off somewhere for a day or two. But when she saw the road sign for Stirling something stirred inside her. She didn't want to go to the Borders; the Highlands was where she wanted to be.

It was gone six when she reached the small town of Callander, and remembering that beyond that was open countryside where it might be hard to find a guest house with vacant rooms, she decided to stop there for the night.

She found a guest house on the main street, checked in, then went for a walk through the small town and had fish and chips in a café before returning to her room for the night.

Brae Bank was the kind of guest house Jackie had always loved to send up. Orange candlewick bedspreads, rose-strewn chintz curtains, small, thin, scratchy towels, soap in a dispenser on the bathroom wall and rather battered furniture. Laura knew without testing it that the mattress had seen better days, and the pillows would be lumpy. But it kind of pleased her, for it was good to be alone in an impersonal room. She didn't need to make chit-chat with anyone, explain herself or be grateful for anything, and she had the silence she'd craved so often in prison.

She made herself a cup of tea, smiling at the tiny packet of Highland shortbread, which was almost certainly made somewhere like Slough, and bore no resemblance to the real McCoy. She had glanced into the dining room downstairs and noted there were tartan tablecloths and a stuffed stag's head above the fireplace. She guessed there would be some haggis dished up at breakfast too.

The bed creaked ominously when she sat down on it and she smiled again, wondering how many couples had been too afraid to go into the dining room after a night of noisy passion on it. But then, the couple of other guests she'd glimpsed as she booked in looked far too old for any hanky-panky.

Taking her map out of her bag, she began to study the area around Oban, wondering where the house Stuart was working on might be. She saw that Loch Awe, just below the town, was vast, some sixteen miles long at least, so she was unlikely to find his house there just by chance.

But the road to Oban passed through a place called Taynuilt, and as it appeared to be the biggest village near the loch there was a fair chance Stuart might have been into the pub there. That was where she'd make for tomorrow.

Laura woke the following morning feeling completely rested, and to her surprise the breakfast in the guest house was superb. After buying postcards to send to her sisters and Angie, she set off again.

She had been through the Trossachs on the way to the Highlands many times before with Stuart, but twenty years on she found it even more spectacular and majestic than she remembered. Each turn of the road seemed to present an even more incredible view, and several times she had to pull over because she was overcome with emotion at the splendour. The bright blue sky was reflected in the vast expanses of shimmering water in the lochs, and the autumn colouring of the trees and the height of the hills all added up to unforgettable beauty.

She rang Patrick from a pub in Crianlarich and asked him if he had an address or phone number for Stuart, but as she expected, he hadn't. Stuart had only said he'd be in touch before long. Patrick did offer David's number, but she was loath to ring there for fear of looking needy.

She didn't actually mind the prospect of looking for a needle in a haystack. The weather was beautiful and she was happy to be alone just exploring. Even if she didn't find him, it wouldn't matter, she'd just look upon it as a holiday.

When she came to Loch Awe, she pulled over to look at it, thinking how well named it was, for it was awesome. She was at the most northerly end of it, and although it was quite narrow, perhaps not more than a mile across at the widest point, it stretched on lengthwise almost to infinity.

There was a pub in Taynuilt, and she found a place to stay for the night close by. Unlike the guest house in Callander, it was lovely, with a huge, comfortable bed and quiet, tasteful decor.

'Have you ever met a man called Stuart Macgregor?' Laura asked the young fresh-faced barmaid at the pub. As it was Friday night the public bar was crowded with men, and she couldn't bring herself to go in there alone, so she was staying in the saloon bar. 'He's mid-forties, tall, brown hair, from Edinburgh. I heard he'd come up to Oban to renovate a big house. I think he's bought a place on Loch Awe too.'

The girl shook her head, but Laura guessed she wouldn't notice any man over thirty, not even one as striking as Stuart. 'But I only work here at weekends,' she added more helpfully. 'Ask Molly, she knows everyone.' The girl pointed out an older woman pulling a pint in the public bar.

Laura didn't get a chance to question the other barmaid until some time later, when many of the customers in the public bar had gone home. By then she'd had a further two glasses of wine and a bowl of chilli. Seeing Molly come over to the saloon side of the bar, Laura jumped up and ordered another drink, then asked her question, giving a little more detail.

'I cannae think of anyone.' Molly frowned. 'You say his name is Stuart Macgregor and he stays in Edinburgh?'

'That's right,' Laura said eagerly. 'Could you ask for me in the public bar? I'm too embarrassed to go in on my own.'

Some twenty minutes passed and Laura was about to give up and go back to the guest house, when a short, wiry man of about fifty, wearing a woolly hat and working clothes, came into the saloon.

'You were asking after an Edinburgh man?' he inquired. 'I delivered some timber and roofing tiles to a man along in Kilchrenan by the loch. I dinnae ken if he was from

Edinburgh, he put me in mind of a southerner. But he did say he had work in Oban.'

Laura established that the man in question was tall, the right age, and she had no doubt that to a Highlander Stuart's accent was no longer true Scots because of the years he'd been away. But what clinched it for her was that this delivery of timber and tiles had taken place just two days earlier.

Sleep eluded Laura that night. She'd studied her map and discovered that Kilchrenan was only about five or six miles away, and the chances were that ever-practical Stuart would see mending his own roof as a priority and be working on it this weekend.

But now she was so close, she was scared. What if everyone else's opinions of his feelings for her were wrong? Patrick and David had never given her as much as a hint; all she had was Meggie's and Angie's views and they hardly knew Stuart.

Maybe he'd just been acting like a Boy Scout, wanting to help her for old times' sake and because he couldn't resist rescuing a damsel in distress. She'd said herself that he would go once his job was complete, she had really believed that. So what changed her mind?

She couldn't think of anything he'd said or done that had given her reason to think he hoped for a future with her. In fact his manner after the appeal had suggested he was coming up here to avoid any further involvement.

What could be more scary to a man than a woman he didn't want to see turning up on his doorstep?

What could she offer him anyway? She was fifty, too old to have his child. She hadn't even given herself enough time to recover from all she'd been through, much less to find out what she really wanted. She was clutching desperately to sweet memories of one summer of love, over twenty years ago. And perhaps that was evidence of how badly damaged she really was.

She woke early to see the guest-house garden sprinkled with frost and the sky an ominous grey. That seemed like an omen and made her decide it was time she grew up, packed her bag and drove back to London.

Her future was there. She could throw herself into the property in Bromley with her sisters. When probate was settled, she would sell Brodie Farm and open a dress shop. She knew fashion, she was good at selling. She'd buy a nice little house somewhere pretty like Downe, Chislehurst or Knockholt, become a good aunt to Ivy's boys, and perhaps try to make it up with her brother Freddy.

An hour later at eight, having showered, dressed in jeans and a thick sweater and eaten a small breakfast, she drove away from Taynuilt, speeding along the Pass of Brander by the River Awe towards Dalmally. She planned to take the A82 which went down past Loch Lomond and keep right on down to Glasgow and the motorway.

She had gone some twenty-five miles or more and was approaching Crianlarich where the road forked either to the A85 towards Stirling or the A82 to Glasgow, when 'Layla', by Derek and the Dominoes, came on the radio.

It was the one record which encapsulated all her and Stuart's feelings that first summer they'd spent together. It had been in the Top Ten, and every time they turned the radio on it was playing. Throughout the last twenty years it had always had the power to take her right back to Castle Douglas, and tears would spring into her eyes as she re-membered Stuart learning to play it. He would laugh and say he was no Eric Clapton, but to her he was a star in his own right. She wondered if he was listening to the radio right now, stopping to play air guitar along with it, as he had always done. Would he think of her, his Layla?

Glancing in the mirror to check the road was clear, she spun the car round in a U-turn. She had to go back and find him.

20

Back at Taynuilt, Laura took the turning off to Kilchrenan she'd spotted earlier in the morning as she left the guest house. She found it to be a narrow, winding lane, but after going through some dense woodland she came out on a hill and she could see Loch Awe below her.

The scale of her map suggested it was around five or six miles from Taynuilt, though it seemed to her that she'd already gone that far. There weren't many houses on the road, but she stopped at all of them which were in a poor state of repair, looking for anything that might suggest it could be Stuart's.

He had said it was by the loch, which to her meant right on the bank, but then she realized he might have said it had a view of the loch, and almost all of these had.

The village of Kilchrenan turned out to be tiny, just a school, a post office and a few cottages, but she couldn't see anyone to ask for directions, and she was anxious now as according to the map the road ended when it came to the loch.

Just as she reached the loch, the sun broke through. She pulled up and stared in wonder, for it was more ravishingly beautiful than any other lochs she'd seen. It wasn't very wide – she could see a lone house on the opposite side very clearly – but it was so vast lengthwise she could see no end to it. Pine and fir trees grew on the hills around it, going right down to the water's edge, but between them were other deciduous trees – elms, rowans and beech. The early frost and the brisk wind were making the leaves tumble, and the ground was a carpet of yellow, orange, russet and brown.

The road she'd come by led only to a hotel, but to her right was a single-track lane along the loch bank, so she turned that way. Some of the houses she passed were rather grand, with large, well-kept gardens and small jetties on the loch, others were tiny and looked like holiday homes, but she could see nothing as dilapidated as Stuart had said his was and she was beginning to lose hope.

Ahead was a dense copse of fir trees, the track curling around them away from the loch. But as she came to the end of the copse, there, some hundred yards ahead, she saw a traditional stone croft, and a man was up on the roof mending it.

A surge of absolute joy welled up inside her. Even though the sun was in her eyes, preventing her from seeing the man clearly, she knew it was Stuart by his shape alone. She would recognize those broad shoulders and slim hips anywhere. It was ironic that he should be on a roof as he was when she'd first met him, and her heart began to pound with a mixture of excitement and trepidation.

A dark blue estate car was parked by the croft, so she pulled over by the copse and got out.

Stuart must have heard the car engine because he turned, holding on to the chimney pot with one hand. The sunshine on his hair turned it to burnished copper, and although it was no longer the length it had been all those years ago, the image was still the same.

'Laura?' he called out tentatively.

She giggled with nervousness. 'Surprise, surprise,' she called back.

He sat down and slithered down the roof towards a ladder, and a second or two later he was on the ground and bounding towards her. There was no doubt she was welcome for he opened his arms wide and ran the last few steps to her, picking her up and swinging her round.

'I can't believe it,' he said breathlessly. 'How did you find me?'

When he put her down she was so dizzy she nearly fell over, stopped only by him catching hold of her.

'Elementary, my dear Watson,' she gasped. 'Look for the nearest pub by Loch Awe and ask if anyone had seen you.'

'In Taynuilt?'

'Yes.'

'But I haven't been in there.'

'But a man who delivered timber to you was,' she giggled.

She felt like a teenager. Although he hadn't actually said he was glad to see her, she knew he was. 'Any chance of a cup of tea?' she asked.

'Every chance, but what made you come?'

'Unfinished business?'

He cupped his two hands on either side of her face and rubbed his nose against hers. 'Does that mean what I hope it means?' he whispered.

She was tingling all over, her heart beating so fast it felt it might burst. 'You'd better tell me what you hope for,' she whispered back.

'That you want me,' he said softly.

She put her arms around him and lifted her face to be kissed.

The years fell away as she was enveloped by the sweetly familiar smell of timber on his working clothes. Then as his lips came down on hers and his arms almost crushed her, she was transported back to that first kiss in Castle Douglas, and the passion that had erupted like a volcano.

But there was timidity on her part now. Back then she'd known she was beautiful and desirable, she had no fear of rejection or of adventure. Even as his lips were devouring hers, she was aware that she was middle-aged, that her flesh was no longer as firm and supple. She wanted him, but she was also afraid.

He broke away first. 'I'd better make you a cup of tea,' he said. 'If someone comes along and sees us snogging like a pair of teenagers the news of it will spread faster than a forest fire.'

Taking her hand, he led her round the side of his cottage, stepping over pieces of timber, fragments of glass, old tree roots and broken fencing. 'Sorry it's such a mess,' he said with a faintly embarrassed chuckle. 'I had hoped to get it all straight before I came for you.'

They got to the back of the cottage, and before them was an overgrown garden which clearly had once been well tended for there were rose bushes, brick paths and the remnants of a lawn. Beyond that was the loch, just twenty or so yards from the back door.

'You were intending to come for me then?' she asked tentatively.

'Of course I was,' he said and sounded surprised she had to ask. 'I just thought you needed time to get yourself together, to find out if you had room in your new life for me.'

Laura held on to *before I came for you*, it sounded so masterful, so right. Her eyes swept around the neglected garden and she noted a wooden bench under a rowan tree, an upturned rowing boat with long grass almost hiding it, a chicken coop and a large rabbit hutch. She could almost see the old couple who had lived here, and sense the love that they'd felt for the place.

'I was intending to go back to London and start a new life with Meggie and Ivy,' she said carefully, afraid to say anything which would make her sound pushy or clingy. 'But first I went out to Barney's grave, and I ran into Ted.'

'How was he?'

'Sad, but okay. He's been looking after the grave, and that was very touching. We had a long chat, and things he said made me feel I should take the chance and come up here and see you first, before returning to London.'

'I'm very glad you did. But I intended to come down there and take you to a few swanky places,' he said.

In a flash she guessed what had been going on in his mind. Finding this croft, doing it up, living in a wild place, fishing, shooting, that was the kind of life he always wanted for himself, but he believed it would hold no attractions for her. He thought she needed city life, smart clothes, luxury, fancy restaurants and sophisticated people.

He had learned so much about her since he'd come back to help her, yet he hadn't taken on board that all those experiences had given her a different perspective.

'I'd rather walk these lanes than go to swanky places,' she said simply. 'Now, can I see inside?'

It was a hideous mess. Four dank, dark rooms with plaster falling off the walls, window frames with gaps around them, and the kitchen had nothing but an ancient sink with a rusting tap. The whole place smelled of rot and decay.

'Enough to put you off?' Stuart asked, raising one eyebrow quizzically.

'It's very Third World,' she laughed, noting he had a camp bed, a camping stove and a box of groceries. 'But it's got great potential. Look how big the rooms are! The fireplaces are lovely, the floors could be stripped and varnished, and if you extended the two back rooms, and had French windows opening out on to the garden and the view of the loch, it could be heaven on earth.'

He beamed at her enthusiasm. 'There's only an outside toilet, full of spiders, the wiring is dangerous, and if I don't finish the roof this weekend the whole place will be awash when it rains. But I just keep looking at the view and telling myself I wasn't mad to buy it.'

'Of course you weren't,' she laughed, filling up the kettle and putting it on the camping stove. 'And don't let me stop you doing the roof. I could be your labourer and pass things to you.'

He looked astounded. 'It doesn't make you want to run back to civilization then?'

'Not one bit,' she laughed again. 'But if I am in your way you can tell me to push off.'

He didn't say anything for a few minutes, just stood in the doorway watching her as she rinsed out two mugs, found the tea bags and sniffed the milk to check it hadn't gone off.

'What?' she said.

'I can't believe you are actually here, making me tea,' he said. 'Just a few hours ago I was thinking about you, wishing I hadn't been so pathetic on the day of the hearing.'

'Whatever do you mean? You weren't pathetic!'

'Well, maybe intimidated then! You see, you looked so beautiful, but so self-contained. Meggie and Ivy were wildly excited about the place in Bromley, and all their plans included you. I thought they were trying to tell me diplomatically that I was to butt out, that you had no need for me any more.'

'Oh, Stuart,' she exclaimed, 'nothing could be further from the truth. If I seemed self-contained it was only because I didn't want to look needy. And when you told us about the work you'd got up here and buying this place I was sure you felt you'd done your job getting me free, and it was time for you to move on.'

'So we were at cross-purposes?'

Laura nodded. 'But not only that, I felt I had no rights. I was the one who screwed things up all those years ago.

I became someone you wouldn't have liked, and I'm ashamed of that. All that stuff I've revealed to you weighs heavily on me. I suppose I don't think I deserve a second chance.'

'Everyone deserves that.'

'Maybe, but I'm scared, Stuart. Even now, I can't be sure my feelings for you are real, or whether they're just some fantasy brought on by gratitude and good memories.'

He looked a little disappointed at that. 'Well, I guess we'll just have to see how it goes,' he said with a shrug.

The kettle boiled and Laura made the tea and handed him his. She felt she had to explain further, but she wasn't sure she knew how to. 'This is a bit like a re-run of that first day in Castle Douglas,' she said. 'Only I'm not so reckless any more, and I don't have a blow-up bed in the boot of my car.'

He smiled, put his tea down on the floor and pulled her into his arms. 'Maybe another kiss might bring on a little more recklessness,' he said softly. 'I want you more now than I did then, but I'm more patient. I'm grubby, sweaty and unshaven and I could wait for a night in a hotel. But a kiss would tide me over while I finish the roof.'

His lips came down on hers and his arms tightened around her. Laura closed her eyes, let her anxieties go and gave herself up to the bliss of being kissed. All those long months in prison she had squashed down all thoughts of lovemaking, for even before she was arrested it had been three or four years since she'd last been with a man. She had believed she was incapable of ever wanting one again.

But as his tongue insinuated its way into her mouth, and his big hands caressed her back, she found this wasn't so. She was trembling with wanting, long-forgotten feelings rushing to the surface, pushing out all the doubts and fears.

'Well?' he said, kissing her eyes, her forehead and her cheeks. 'Any of the old magic still about?'

'I do believe there is,' she said lightly. 'But you must get back on the roof and finish it. It might rain tomorrow.'

Half an hour later, with Stuart up on the roof again, Laura had a plan. The terrible state of the toilet had given her an idea, and she called up to him to say she was going to drive back to the village shop and buy some bleach and other cleaning materials for it.

'Don't you go running out on me,' he called back. 'Another couple of hours or so and I'll be finished up here.'

It was well over an hour before Laura returned to the cottage, and she was giggling to herself because her mission had been so successful. She had the cleaning materials, bucket and rubber gloves she'd gone for, but a lot more besides. A double room was booked for the next two nights in the guest house she'd stayed at before, and she had a picnic in a box, including a bottle of wine and two glasses, candles, firelighters and a bag of logs.

She called up to Stuart and waved the bucket and bottle of bleach at him to put him off the scent. Once he was back working she quickly got the other things out of the car boot and hid them behind some bushes in the garden.

While the kettle was boiling, she went back down the garden and found a perfect spot under a tree where she gathered up heaps of dry leaves to act as a mattress, then covered them with some of the blankets from his camp bed.

There were plenty of old bricks lying around, and she made a crude sort of fireplace close to the blanket, yet hidden from Stuart's view. It was already nearly three, and the light would be fading before long. She placed the picnic box and the candles by the blanket. Collecting up twigs as kindling, she placed them over the firelighters, with the logs close by. Satisfied, she returned to the cottage to do some cleaning.

Stuart came down from the roof a couple of times while she was scrubbing out the toilet, and seemed amused by her zeal, but without any suspicion she had anything else in mind.

'I'm just putting the last tiles back now,' he yelled down a bit later. 'It'll be pitch dark soon, so we'd better find a bed and breakfast for you.'

Laura liked his assumption that she wasn't ready yet to leap into bed with him. It seemed to point out that he was thinking long term.

The toilet was finished, looking remarkably spruce and hygienic, and smelling a great deal better, so she nipped down the garden and lit the candles. They were the garden kind in pots so they wouldn't be blown out by the wind and hopefully they'd keep any stray midges at bay too.

Kneeling down, she lit the firelighters and blowing gently on the twigs as they caught fire, she soon got a blaze going.

'What are you doing?'

She jumped at Stuart's voice right behind her. She'd been so engrossed she hadn't heard him come down the garden.

'Party time,' she said. 'Come on in and sit down! I'll just put a couple of logs on the fire.'

Laughing, he bent down and crawled on to the blanket, patting it appreciatively.

Laura joined him and opened the box of goodies. 'Ta da! A bottle of wine, glasses and a corkscrew,' she said. 'You open that and I'll get out the food.'

The light was fading fast, but there was enough from the candles to see how dirty his face and hands were. She took out a packet of baby wipes and leaned forward with one to clean him up.

'Looks like you thought of everything, you scheming minx,' he said teasingly.

It was remarkably cosy as the bushes around them were keeping off the wind and the smoke from the fire was going straight up. Stuart handed her a glass of wine.

'Are we staying here all night?' he asked.

'I think we'd be frozen solid by morning.' She giggled. 'Trust me, I have a contingency plan.'

She laid out the crusty rolls, pâté, cheese, a packet of butter and a jar of olives. 'One borrowed knife,' she said, brandishing it. 'We've got to return it.'

He was just looking at her, the candle and firelight softening his features. Putting down his glass, he reached out and took her hand, rubbing her fingers with his thumb. 'This was a beautiful thought,' he said.

She just smiled. She couldn't explain that she hoped it would whisk them back to where they started, or that she wanted him to see the girl in her hadn't gone entirely. She had to trust that would be evident.

They began to talk as they drank the wine and ate the picnic. Not about the experiences of the past weeks, or the past, but about the cottage. 'I've got an architect drawing up some plans,' he said. 'I don't want to alter its character, just extend it to put a garage on the side and a bathroom behind it. But until I've got the plans approved, I can't do anything more than make it watertight.'

'You can't intend to live here all through the winter,' Laura exclaimed.

'I did intend to,' he said ruefully. 'But that was before I discovered how bad the wiring was. The last two nights were misery without lights, I couldn't see well enough by candlelight to make myself some food, let alone read. But I start the job in Oban on Monday, and they'll let me have a room out there.'

'And how long will that last?'

'Until the spring. By then I hope I'll be able to get cracking here. I thought I might get a caravan to live in while I'm doing it.'

Laura told him several ideas she'd had during the day; she was brimming over with all the possibilities.

'You could come up for the summer and help me,' he said. 'That is, if you aren't tied up with the shop in Bromley.'

'I think I need another kiss to remind me what the fringe benefits would be,' she said.

He cleared the food away into the box in a trice, put another couple of logs on the fire, and took her in his arms. All daylight was gone now, just the flickering fire and the candles creating a circle of warmth and light around them. As he began to kiss her, lowering her back on to the blanket, Laura thought there couldn't be a better place in the whole world to make love.

There was something about the groping beneath thick sweaters which added a new dimension to it, as though they were still teenagers furtively fumbling in a park. When Stuart stripped off her jeans she didn't care that it was cold, for his caressing hands were hot and tender, and she felt as if she was on fire anyway.

Everything that had gone before disappeared. The future didn't matter either; all that counted was here and now, his skin on hers, their lips searching hungrily for each other.

Stuart's body was as lean and muscular as it had been twenty years ago; hers might not be as firm as it had been then, but it still fitted into him in exactly the same way. Her fingers found the little scar on his right side, which he had told her once he'd got falling out of a tree when he was little. But when she ran her finger up the front of his shirt, she found the more recent scar, the one he'd got trying to rescue her, and tears of gratitude came into her eyes.

Maybe they weren't as frantic and energetic as they had been that first night in Castle Douglas, but for Laura at least it was far more sensual. Stuart's stubble rasped against her cheek and shoulders, and he smelled of sweat and the mildew from the cottage, but they were honest, natural smells, just like the leaf mould all around them, and the wood smoke. She loved the slow, tender way he was exploring her body, the little endearments, the moans of pleasure, and the way he seemed to know exactly what turned her on most.

She wasn't even aware of the hard ground or the cold when he entered her, all she knew was that she wanted him as badly as he wanted her.

Her orgasm took her by surprise, a fiery eruption that made her cry out. He said he loved her as he came, and suddenly she was crying and clinging to him and telling him that he was the only man in the world for her.

When she opened her eyes the moon had come out from behind a cloud, and the trees above them were bathed in a silver light. Stuart wrapped one of the blankets round her tightly and his cheek against hers was damp with tears.

'The magic is still there,' he whispered. 'You brought it back with you.'

They put their clothes back on, and wrapping the blankets round them went to sit on the bench. The moon was casting a silver path across the black water of the loch and an owl hooted somewhere nearby.

'What was your contingency plan?' he asked, as she snuggled into his shoulder.

'I've booked a room back in Taynuilt for two nights,' she said.

'How resourceful of you! And after that?'

'I'll go back to London on Monday when you go off to Oban.'

He looked down at her, and she could feel his anxiety. 'And then?' he asked.

'Whatever you want,' she said, reaching up to trace around his lips with one finger.

'I want you here, with me, for ever,' he said, taking her fingertips and kissing them.

Other men, both before she first met Stuart and after they split up, had said such things after lovemaking, but invariably she sensed they said it to all their lovers. She believed Stuart meant it, though. He never said anything he didn't mean.

'That's what I hoped you'd say,' she laughed. 'I'll give you a cooling-off period first, but if you still want me, then I'll come back. I expect we could rent a little place in Oban for the winter, couldn't we?'

'You'd better buy some warm clothes in London then,' he said, excitement in his voice. 'Next spring we'll come back here with a caravan and live like a couple of hippies while we do it up.'

Laura glanced around her, saw the bushes lit up by the candles and the fire, and she could imagine how lovely it would be in summer. She would love to learn to lay bricks, to mix concrete and study the mysteries of plumbing; it would be the greatest challenge of her life to help make their own paradise.

'I think we'd better go now, before we turn to blocks of ice,' she said. She got up and tipped the pail of water over the fire to put it out.

Stuart handed her one candle, but blew out all the others, and picking up the box of remaining food led her back to the cottage to lock it up.

She waited outside while he went in to collect a bag, and she turned to look at the loch again. The moonlight on the water brought a lump to her throat for it looked like a beautiful silver path, and it seemed to confirm that she had finally found her right road in life. The past was no importance, she could let it go and look only to the future.

Stuart had told her to have faith in him. It had wavered sometimes, but she knew now, without any doubt, that if you had enough faith, all dreams could come true.

She could hear Stuart shuffling about in the cottage and a bright beam of light came on as he found his torch. She knew with utter conviction that she loved him and belonged with him, and that she was prepared to go with him any-where he wanted to be.

It was a defining moment for her, for she'd never had that kind of certainty and faith before.

He came out of the cottage and locked the back door.

'Ready?' he said.

'For anything,' she replied.

Epilogue
1997

Laura paused as she came out through the French windows into the garden with a tray loaded with a bottle of wine, a jug of fruit squash, glasses and a platter of nibbles for her guests.

It was a glorious August morning, warm and sunny without a cloud in the sky. Jack and Harry, her two nephews, were out on the loch in the rowing boat with Stuart. The boys' shrill, excited voices carried clearly on the slight breeze as they struggled with learning to row in tandem. Stuart was seated in the stern and every now and then his much deeper voice could be heard giving instructions.

Meggie and Ivy were sitting on steamer chairs down by the small jetty, but Laura thought Ivy looked a little tense as she kept a close eye on her sons.

'They are perfectly safe,' Laura called out as she came down the garden with her tray. 'They've got life jackets on, and they can swim, but Stuart won't let them fall in, so you can relax.'

Ivy looked round, flipping her sunglasses up on to her head. 'It's the mother's curse, always thinking our kids are in permanent danger,' she said with a grin.

'That curse must have missed out on our mother then,' Meggie said drily. 'I don't remember her ever worrying about us.'

'That's because she rarely came out of the house to see what we were up to,' Ivy retorted. 'Anyway, it's one thing to learn to row on a pond in a park, quite another to be out on a vast loch. I'd just feel happier if Derek and James were here too.'

'They'll be back soon,' Laura said, putting the tray down on a small table by her sisters. 'In the meantime have a glass of wine and a little faith in Stuart. Boys need to do stuff like rowing, climbing trees and lighting fires, it's character-building.'

Her sisters, their men and the boys had arrived two days ago for a holiday. The year before, Meggie had come up with James, the policeman she'd met after Robbie Fielding attacked Laura, but the cottage wasn't finished then and they'd stayed nearby in a guest house. But all the work was completed now, and it was thrilling for Laura to be able to have her family here together. Ivy, Derek and the boys were staying in the caravan that had been Laura and Stuart's home for over a year, and Meggie and James had the spare room in the cottage.

Derek and James had gone off to buy some beer and a few groceries in the village, and they had a barbecue planned for later in the afternoon. Laura was so happy that she felt she might burst with it.

The last two years hadn't all been plain sailing for her and Stuart. The two snatched years of her life in prison had made her introspective, insecure and often irrational. She had come back from London to live with Stuart in Oban just a month after she was exonerated, because she couldn't bear to be apart from him. But though it was wonderful to be together, she hadn't taken into account the long hours of separation while he was working, the bitter winter weather, or how bored she'd become in the little seaside town without any work or even friends.

They'd had a few very heated arguments when she

accused him of caring more about his work than her. But fate stepped in just in time, when she saw an article in a magazine about a drug project in Glasgow that needed volunteers interested in helping young people.

She applied and was accepted, and after a short induction, found herself spending two days a week at a drop-in centre where addicts could go to exchange dirty needles for clean ones, receive some counselling and discuss their problems.

From her first day there, Laura sensed that she had all the right credentials to become a counsellor herself. She knew why people took the first step on the road to addiction, and the forces which kept them there. She recognized her younger self in so many of the younger addicts she met.

In February 1996 Belle stood trial. The charge had been dropped to manslaughter in the case of Jackie's death, but still held at attempted murder of Stuart. Both Laura and Stuart were witnesses for the prosecution, but once they had given their evidence they left the court, not staying to watch the rest of the trial or hear the guilty verdict.

For Laura it was a trip back to a dark place she wanted to forget she'd ever been in. She could take no pleasure in seeing Belle stripped of her former glamour, gaunt, stringy-haired and with dark-ringed eyes, knowing that even her mother and brother had abandoned her. Toby had made a statement to the police that she had taken full advantage of getting power of attorney over her mother's finances, and plundered a great deal of the money from the sale of the house in Duke's Avenue. Toby hadn't discovered this until Belle was arrested, but as soon as he found out, he came over to England and after making his statement, took Lena back to live with him, his wife and new baby in Australia.

Belle received an eighteen-year prison sentence. People remarked that they thought it was too lenient, but then they didn't know that eighteen years or life made little difference at Belle's age. She had even fewer reserves with which to cope with prison life than Laura had; she would spend each day in abject misery, and that was the real punishment.

As for Charles, he received ten years in total for concealing a crime in the case of Jackie, for aiding and abetting the attempted murder of Stuart, and for dangerous driving and failing to stop when he killed Barney.

Laura had mixed feelings about his sentence. It didn't seem much for the loss of her son, yet he had pleaded guilty to that, and showed real remorse. Stuart, who had seen him in the dock, said he looked so old and sick he doubted he'd live to finish his sentence.

In May of the previous year, Stuart had finished his work in Oban and was ready to start work on the cottage. They bought a caravan and tucked it down amongst the trees at the side of the garden, and with two local men, Stuart began to dig the foundations for the extension to the cottage.

Around that time all the legalities of Jackie's will had been finalized and Laura and her sisters put Brodie Farm and Kirkmay House in the hands of a lawyer in Fife for them to be sold.

All through that summer Laura was away in Glasgow for three days a week, staying overnight in a small guest house. Along with her volunteer work at the centre, she got herself on a counselling course and studied hard. The other four days of the week she was home with Stuart, helping to mix concrete, collecting building materials, and tending the areas of the garden that weren't part of the building site.

In October Brodie Farm was finally sold, and Laura passed her counselling course with flying colours. The cottage was coming on in leaps and bounds, and Stuart predicted they'd be able to be in there by Christmas. Laura got back from Glasgow one evening to find the plastering had been finished and the bathroom suite installed. Nothing was more exciting than their first bath, even if the floor was still rough concrete, for the shower in the caravan was tiny and the hot water erratic. They lit dozens of candles and lay either end of the bath drinking wine, and she told Stuart how clever and hard-working he'd been, and he said she was his inspiration.

It was just before Christmas in the drop-in centre, as she listened to a group of addicts talking amongst themselves, that she suddenly realized she wasn't entirely committed to the work there.

Maybe, as several friends suggested, she wanted to be at home looking at paint charts, watching Stuart painstakingly build their kitchen, or choosing curtains and furniture, but she didn't think so.

While it was true she didn't like being away from him, it was more than that. She could see so clearly that in five or ten years from now, some of the group she heard talking would be dead. The rest would have slid even further down the slope, and she doubted that any of them would have recovered and be leading useful, happy and healthy lives.

She felt ashamed that she couldn't be more optimistic, but the statistics of recovery amongst addicts from deprived backgrounds proved she was right. It struck her that she should put her energy into some project that dissuaded youngsters from taking that first step on the rocky road to addiction.

They moved into the cottage for Christmas. The newly plastered walls were all white, they had the wood floors Laura had suggested, and the kitchen and sitting room, now the cottage had been extended at the back, seemed vast because they had so little furniture. They bought a huge Christmas tree, adorned the mantelpiece of the lovely old fireplace with green garlands, and laid a big shaggy cream rug in front of it, on which they made love on Christmas Eve by the light of the tree lights. There were no curtains, but then they didn't want to shut out the view of the moonlight on the loch. And later that evening, as Laura lounged on a bean bag while Stuart played his guitar, she thought she was the luckiest woman in the world.

In the New Year they went down to Edinburgh for a few days to buy furniture and see some old friends. They took a trip out to Crail to visit Barney's grave, and while they were there they met Ted Baxter for lunch in St Andrews. It was good to find him much happier: he and Peggie were getting along much better, she was cooking again, going out with Ted in the car, and their first grandchild was expected in a few weeks' time.

They had only been back at the cottage for one night when Meggie rang to say June had been taken to hospital with a heart attack but died on the way there.

They drove down to London, and though Laura believed she would feel very little sorrow at losing her mother, once she was there with Meggie and Ivy, she found that wasn't so. All three of them went through a whole gamut of emotions – relief that they no longer had to feel guilty about the way she had lived in the last twenty years, anger at past neglect and selfishness, but love too. Stuart had people to see while they were there, and the sisters spent the days before June's funeral talking through their memories, bitter and sweet, together.

James used his police contacts to try to trace Mark and Paul, without success, but Freddy came up the night before the funeral, and Laura was able to make her peace with him at last. It was so odd to be confronted with a man of forty when all her memories were of a chubby toddler. He was tall, fit and handsome, still retaining his thick dark hair, a good family man and a well-respected naval officer, and once she'd had an opportunity to talk to him alone and say how much she regretted not keeping him in her life, he hugged her and said it didn't matter any more.

There were few mourners at the crematorium, just a few of June's neighbours and family. Freddy had put together a few well-chosen words about her, focusing on humorous anecdotes from the long distant past that touched everyone. They went back to Meggie's house afterwards and it became a real party after a few drinks had flowed. At one point Stuart had an arm-wrestling competition with Freddy in the kitchen.

'Mum would've liked this,' Ivy remarked, looking around at her boys playing Snakes and Ladders on the floor while all the adults milled around chatting nineteen to the dozen. 'She loved nothing better than dressing up and going to a party. I think we should just remember her like that, drink in one hand, fag in the other, blonde hair, high heels and a dress with a bit of glitter on it. Let's forget the rest.'

It was on the long drive back to Scotland after the funeral that Laura began reflecting on the way her, Meggie, Ivy and Freddy's lives had turned out. All four of them could easily have ended up like some of the people she'd met in the Glasgow centre, for they had all been vulnerable, exposed to crime and poverty, and without parental guidance.

She started to trace back and find reasons why they hadn't and she came to the conclusion that each of them had had a good influence during their adolescence.

Freddy had joined the Navy at a young age, Ivy had Meggie pushing her into college and lifting her horizons. Meggie had her older sister's influence, and Laura had had Lena, Frank and Jackie.

It struck her then that this was what she should be doing with the rest of her life, and the knowledge she had. To concentrate on equally vulnerable children, to give them something in their lives that would lift them up and give them a glimpse of a better way of life than they'd been born to.

She continued her work at the centre right through to May, but each time she went over to Glasgow she was putting out feelers, talking to people, thinking deeply about what could be done. Yet it was the four days a week back by the loch that gave her the idea she was now burning to start on.

For her the first summer here, waking to birdsong each morning, tramping through dew-soaked grass, revelling in the majesty of the scenery, the total lack of luxury, shops or man-made entertainment, had been a healing process. She'd learned to saw wood, to lay a few bricks, to dig, and had acquired some knowledge of plumbing. If she could give inner-city, deprived children just a little taste of that, along with the healthy fun of swimming, boating, climbing trees and campfires, maybe they wouldn't want to spend afternoons in back alleys sniffing glue and gravitate to other even more dangerous drugs, prostitution and crime.

She had the money from her inheritance from Jackie in the bank – she'd only spent a little of it on furniture and curtains – and Stuart was so proud of keeping his woman that he'd always want to be the main provider. She was also expecting to get compensation for being wrongfully imprisoned.

She could buy a piece of land somewhere beautiful and if she approached the right people she'd obtain the support and further finance to get it going and keep it going.

Jackie would have wholeheartedly loved the idea of holidays for deprived children, so it seemed a fitting thing to put her money into. The kids could camp at first while helping with the building, spending whole summers learning useful skills while they had a great time too. Students would gladly come and help out for pocket money, teaching orienteering, canoeing, climbing, and heaven knew what else.

She had half expected Stuart to scoff at her idea, or at least to say that now they had a lovely home he was hoping that they would just do nothing but enjoy themselves.

But he didn't.

His eyes lit up, and the next thing she knew he was suggesting he'd like nothing better than to spend six weeks a year playing Boy Scout leader.

'David would like it too, and maybe James and Meggie as well,' he went on. 'I could get some of the companies I've worked for to donate building materials or plant hire. They'd love it; they might even take on some of the keen kids as apprentices later on. The only real problem would be getting the council to agree to use land in an area of outstanding beauty for such a project, because you've obviously got to build some permanent structures, toilet blocks, kitchens and stuff. But they might be okay about it if it was log cabin-style and only used for part of the year.'

It occurred to Laura later that they both wanted this because they had no children of their own. Maybe she needed to lavish some love and care on neglected children as a way of proving herself to Barney. Stuart too had a surplus of love and patience that needed an outlet.

She said goodbye to the drop-in centre in the middle of May, and since then, when she wasn't working out in the garden, she had been planning her project. She had good people now lined up to help, a whole raft of ideas for fund-raising and promotion. The next step was to find some suitable land and buy it.

Later that day she and Stuart intended to tell everyone about the plan, but for now they had a barbecue to organize.

*

James and Derek arrived back from the shop with enough drink to launch the *Queen Mary* and a carrier bag full of different cheeses.

'Why so much cheese?' Laura asked James. 'Is this some sort of secret vice you want to tell me about?'

He laughed, his soft brown eyes crinkling up at the corners. Laura liked him so much — perhaps at first it was just because he had made Meggie radiant and youthful again, but now she found him a pleasure to be around. He was calm and steady, chatty enough not to be dull company, but not the pushy kind who likes to take centrestage.

He was an unlikely policeman really; he looked the part — brawny, tall and fit — but he was gentle, his voice as soft as his eyes. A deep-thinking man, kind and sensitive.

'You've got me banged to rights,' he said. 'I just love all kinds of cheese, so when I'm faced with a huge selection I have to have some of each.'

'But so much of each one?' Laura laughed. 'We'll be eating it for weeks.'

'I'm the same about beer,' Derek chimed in. 'Got to taste every single kind, and my God, there's a lot of Scottish beers to choose from.'

'Well, go easy on it today, we don't want you falling in the loch,' she said. Her brother-in-law was a party animal. Fifteen stone of noise, laughter, jokes and fun. He could be relied on to keep the party going into the early hours. Laura often thought he should have been a publican, but in fact he was a personnel officer in an insurance company. Ivy claimed he had to suppress his real personality all week and that was why he broke out at weekends and on holiday.

'Maybe I should put on a life jacket just in case,' he laughed, then, looking out at his boys in the boat, he remarked how well they were rowing now. 'Your Stuart's a good'un,' he said. 'The boys really like him.'

As Laura prepared some salads later in the kitchen she thought of that remark of Derek's. Stuart had got the boys to bring the boat in now, and he'd organized them into helping him set up a trestle table for the food, and now they were lighting the barbecue. It wasn't just children who liked Stuart, it was everyone, and that made it so easy for her. She thought he wouldn't get along with the people who worked alongside her at the drop-in centre, for they were in the main oddballs, earnest, very left wing and opinionated. But he had, even if he did laugh at some of their ideas later. He could converse just as easily with the rich barristers and Harley Street surgeons who had holiday homes around here as he could with bricklayers and plumbers at the pub.

Not a day went past without her offering up a little prayer of thanks that he came back into her life and gave her all this.

She looked around her beautiful kitchen, ran her fingers along the silky-smooth drawers and reminded herself it was all his work. Whatever she wanted, whether it was a high rail to hang pans on, a special rack for herbs and spices, wardrobes or bookshelves, he did it, with love.

It was laughable really that she'd once gauged a man's love for her by the monetary value of his gifts. Stuart didn't go in for lavish gestures like jewellery, but what he gave her was far more valuable – his time, skill and care.

Looking down the garden, she could see him now presiding over the barbecue. He'd built that too with bricks left from the house, on the same spot she'd lit the fire the first time she came here. He was wearing khaki shorts and a check shirt, and his legs, though thin and, as he always said, 'unsuitable for kilt wearing', were as brown as conkers.

They'd kept the old bench by the jetty, and they often sat out there at night watching the sun set over the loch. Somehow she knew they'd still be here together in another twenty or thirty years, just like the old couple who'd lived here before. Still in love with each other.

She had just got all the salads ready to take outside and Meggie and Ivy had been in to collect plates, cutlery and sauces, when Stuart came in, bringing her a glass of wine.

'I was just coming out,' she said, but took an appreciative gulp of it.

He came closer and hooked her hair back behind one of her ears. 'Marry me, Laura?' he said.

She giggled in surprise. 'What brought that on?'

'Because I've got everything a man could wish for, except I can't call you my wife. I'd like to, it makes a public statement about how I feel about you.'

Laura had quite often been a little embarrassed when talking to people about Stuart. Calling him her boyfriend sounded so juvenile; partner sounded so businesslike. She knew Stuart referred to her as 'my lady', which was lovely, but there was no equivalent expression to use for a man.

'Well?' he asked. 'Will you?'

She flung her arms around him. 'Yes, oh yes,' she said gleefully. 'There's nothing I'd like better.'

''That's a relief,' he said and kissed her tenderly.

'Why is it a relief?' she asked after the kiss.

'Well, I told Derek to buy some champagne when he was at the shop. He asked why and I said we might have some-thing special to celebrate later. What a chump I'd look if you'd said no.'

Laura laughed and hugged him. 'Only a complete fool would turn you down. So let's take these salads out, check the boys aren't burning the steaks, and when there's a lull in the jollity we'll tell everyone.'

'Are you absolutely sure?'

Laura looked at those kind grey eyes and smiling mouth

and saw again the hesitant, rather shy, much younger man she'd fallen in love with two decades earlier.

'Two hundred per cent sure,' she said. 'And we'll grow old and doddery here together. But right now it's party time!'

Lesley Pearse

d more
nguin.co.uk

ABOUT LESLEY

Lesley Pearse is one of the UK's best-loved novelists, with fans across the globe and book sales of over two million copies to date.

A true storyteller and a master of gripping storylines that keep the reader hooked from beginning to end, Lesley introduces readers to unforgettable characters who it is impossible not to care about. There is no easily defined genre or formula; her books, whether crime, as in *Till We Meet Again*, historical adventure like *Never Look Back*, or the passionately emotive *Trust Me*, based on the true-life scandal of British child migrants sent to Australia in the post-war period, engage the reader completely.

'Lesley's life has been as packed with drama as her books'

Truth is often stranger than fiction and Lesley's life has been as packed with drama as her books. She was three when her mother died under tragic circumstances. Her father was away at sea and it was only when a neighbour saw Lesley and her brother playing outside without coats that suspicion was aroused – their mother had been dead for some time. With her father in the Royal Marines, they spent three years in grim orphanages before her father remarried (his new wife was a veritable dragon of an ex-army nurse) and Lesley and her older brother were brought home again, to be joined by two other children who were later adopted by her father and stepmother, and a continuing stream of foster children. The impact of constant change and uncertainty in Lesley's early years is reflected in one of the recurring themes in her books: what happens to those emotionally damaged as children. Hers was an extraordinary childhood and, in all her books, Lesley has skilfully married the pain and unhappiness of her early experiences with a unique gift for story telling.

'She was three when her mother died under tragic circumstances'

Lesley's desperate need for love and affection as a young girl was almost certainly the reason she kept making bad choices in men in her youth. A party girl during the swinging sixties, Lesley did it all – from nanny to bunny girl to designing clothes. She lived in damp bedsits while burning the candle at both ends as a 'Dolly Bird' with twelve-inch mini-skirts. She was married, fleetingly, to her first husband at twenty and met her second, John Pritchard, a trumpet player in a rock band, soon after. Her debut novel, *Georgia*, was inspired by her life with John, the London clubs, crooked managers and the many musicians she met during that time, including David Bowie and Steve Marriot of the Small Faces. Lesley's first child, Lucy, was born in this period, but with John's erratic lifestyle and a small child in the house, the marriage was doomed to failure. They parted when Lucy was four.

This was a real turning point in Lesley's life – she was young and alone with a small child – but in another twist of fate, Lesley met her third husband, Nigel, while on her way to Bristol for an interview. They married a few years later and had two more daughters, Sammy and Jo. The following years were the happiest of her life – she ran a playgroup, started writing short stories and then opened a card and gift shop in Bristol's Clifton area. Writing by night, running the shop by day and fitting in all the other household chores, along with the needs of her husband and children, was tough.

'Some strange compulsion kept me writing, even when it seemed hopeless,' she says. 'I wrote three books before *Georgia*, then along came Darley Anderson, who offered to be my agent. Even so, a further six years of disappointment and massive re-writes followed before we finally found a publisher'.

There was more turmoil to follow, however, when Lesley's shop failed in the 90s recession, leaving her with a mountain of debts and bruised pride. Her eighteen-year marriage broke down, and at fifty years old she hit rock bottom. It seemed she was back where she had started in a grim flat with barely enough money for her youngest daughter's bus fares to school.

'Lesley did it all – from nanny to bunny girl to designing clothes'

'I wrote my way out of it,' she says. 'My second book, *Tara*, was shortlisted for the Romantic Novel of the Year, and I knew I was on my way.'

Lesley's own life is a rich source of material for her books; whether she is writing about the pain of first love, the experience of being an unwanted abused child, adoption, rejection, fear, poverty or revenge, she knows about it first hand. She is a fighter, and with her long fight for success has come security. She now owns a cottage in a pretty village between Bristol and Bath, which she is renovating, and a creek-side retreat in Cornwall. Her three daughters, grandson, friends, dogs and gardening have brought her great happiness. She is president of the Bath and West Wiltshire branch of the NSPCC – the charity closest to her heart.

ABOUT *FAITH*

How did you come up with the ideas for *Faith*?

I came to the plot of *Faith* through thinking how terrible it must be to be found guilty of a crime you hadn't committed. And if that crime was murder, and you were given a life sentence, how would you stay sane?

I would lie awake at night imagining myself in prison, and before long I was actually working myself up into a rage about my miscarriage of justice.

I chose to set the story in my own time scale so that I could entirely relate to the older, flawed main character as she looks back on her life, with all its wrong turnings, traumas and self-inflicted troubles.

I have always felt that each of us is dealt a hand of cards at birth – some get good ones – others get atrocious ones, but it is how we play those cards as we go through life that makes or breaks us. Also, when we are young, most of us don't fully appreciate the influence other people can have on our lives, for good or bad. I know I often feel sad that I didn't tell those who were most supportive or inspirational how much I valued them, and likewise I cringe when I think how much time and energy I wasted on others who gave me nothing but grief.

Why did you choose to set this book in Scotland?

Nostalgia mostly. Three of my oldest and best-loved friends are Scots, and their families back in Aberdeen almost became mine. Our visits there in the '60s and '70s were fun packed. I remember once arriving for New Year to find a couple of feet of snow, and being dressed for glamour rather than warmth in a sixteen-inch mini skirt with silver stars in my hair!

Yet another friend went to work at a school near Castle Douglas, and I used to hitch hike up from the south to see her. I even fell in love with a sweet romantic man from Stirling who sent me the Robbie Burns poem 'Bonny Lesley'. I wanted to move to Dumfries to be near him and went after a farm cottage offered for a low rent in return for some help. That help turned out to be milking the cows, so I beat a hasty retreat.

I like country pursuits, but I draw the line at getting up at five on a frosty morning to get up close and personal with cows!

The nostalgia made me want a good excuse to go and explore Scotland more, and in 2005 I had some lovely times doing just that with a friend from Edinburgh. I shall never forget a week spent in a dear little cottage in Cellardyke in Fife (it had just found fame with the dead 'Bird Flu' swan in the harbour). At high tide the sea came up to the garden wall and I walked miles with my dogs plotting Laura and Jackie's lives and dreaming about Stuart Macgregor and how he could manage to rescue Laura.

September in the Highlands was absolutely wonderful. Of all the places I've ever been to, the sight of Loch Awe in bright sunshine, the leaves on the trees just beginning to change colour, must be up there in the top three! It had to be the place for a happy ending for brave Laura.

And speaking of bravery ...

On 8 February this year, we held the first Women of Courage Award lunch for the five finalists at Penguin Books in the Strand. We asked people to nominate someone they believed was a true Women of Courage – ordinary women who had lived extraordinary lives.

We had hundreds of entries telling us about women who

had faced adversity, ill health, and severe problems within their families and with their children. We would never have believed that there were so many strong, brave women out there.

The award lunch for the five finalists and their families and friends was a marvellous, emotion-packed day for us all. Our winner for 2006 was Nicole Gallagher. She has two little girls, Niamh aged seven and Aisling aged five, who both have the most serious medical problems. Between them they have had to endure almost twenty operations and Nicole has borne it all with stoicism and tremendous courage, and still retained her bubbly personality and her sense of fun. She truly is a Woman of Courage.

LESLEY ON HER RESEARCH

Research for my books can take many forms – reading books on the subject required, talking to people who have specialized knowledge, newspaper archives, etc. But I find the most valuable source of inspiration to make all the facts come to life is visiting the place where my story is set.

Before and during the writing of my previous novel, *Hope*, I read dozens of books about the Crimean War, but it only really came alive for me when I went to the Crimea for a week in October.

> ## 'No one spoke English and it was a long way to the battlefields'

My heart sank when I arrived in Yalta. It reminded me of shabby seaside places built in the '50s, no one spoke English and it was a long way to the battlefields. What I really wanted to do was walk alone over these places and kind of soak up the vibes, but I couldn't do that as I had to go on an organized tour with a Russian guide, who explained all the history from the Russian point of view. What's more she rushed us along at a great pace, with no time to stand and stare, much less wander at will, and she bombarded us with information, which was mostly pretty dull.

The little harbour of Balaklava (as it is now spelt) is pretty and full of elegant yachts. The guide insisted the main building had been rebuilt in the original style, but that patently wasn't true, for I've seen old pictures of the port in the 1850s and it was very ramshackle, made a million times worse by the hordes of troops. She also showed us where Florence Nightingale had her hospital, and I was forced to point out that Florence only went to the Crimea once, fleetingly, where she became sick and went straight back to Scutari. She never nursed there at all. But despite the guide's inaccurate information, with a little imagination, old pictures and eye- witness reports, it was possible to recreate that little port as it must have been during the war.

The sheer steepness of the cliffs gives you some idea of the terrible struggle the soldiers had to get stores and equipment up to the siege. I've always been quite good at imagining unimaginable squalor and deprivation – I sometimes think I must have lived that way in a previous life!

'The Russian Navy entertained us one night with their singing'

Sevastopol (there again the spelling must have changed), is pretty impressive. It was razed to the ground during the Crimean War, rebuilt afterward, and then flattened again in the Second World War, but it did give a flavour of how it must have been. It is a jewel in Russia's crown, as the Black Sea Fleet is based there. My father, who was in the Royal Marines, would have been horrified by the rusting ships in the harbour, but then the Russian Navy entertained us one night with their singing and dancing, which was superb, so I suppose they are too busy practising to paint their ships or swab the decks!

Yet it was there that I saw the most astounding and impressive piece of art I've ever seen – a panoramic painting of the siege. You go up into a circular room and the painting wraps right around it. But it was three-dimensional, with modelled ox carts, trenches, huts and other such things in the foreground, so you felt you were stepping into the siege, not just looking at a painting.

I could have stayed and looked at it all day. Granted, it was painted from the perspective of the Russian troops – seen from inside Sevastopol – and the British and French are in the distance. But you could understand the scale and the atmosphere of the war, and get a sense of the hardships the men on both sides had to endure.

'The most stirring part of my trip was to stand where the Highlanders held their ground in the defence of Balaklava'

My trip to the battlefields gave me an important understanding of how the battles were fought. The Valley of Death isn't anything I'd envisaged. It is a plain of about three miles long and two miles wide, not some kind of ravine as I imagined when we learned Tennyson's poem at school. When you stand in different parts of it you can see why that fateful blunder, which sent so many men to their deaths, was made.

But for me the most stirring part of my trip was to stand where the Highlanders held their ground in the defence of Balaklava. Now known as the Thin Red Line, and immortalized in a painting in Edinburgh Castle, Sir Colin Campbell's instruction to his men sends shivers down my spine: 'There is no retreat from here. You must stand until you die.'

What supreme courage that must have taken! A few hundred men, facing hordes of Russian Cavalry galloping towards them. And that indomitable courage, and perhaps the Highlanders' fearsome appearance, were enough to make the Russians retreat. It's no secret I love men in uniform, but men capable of such nobility and bravery makes me weak at the knees.

The women who were at the Crimea were a tough, dogged breed too. They were few and far between, but they made their presence felt. When some of the Turkish soldiers ran away from the battle of Balaklava, one soldier's wife battered one of them around the head to try and stop him fleeing. Those soldiers' wives nursed the sick, cooked for the men, washed their clothes and carried ammunition. They lived under the most appalling conditions during the siege, and almost certainly made life just a little more bearable for their men.

'I love men in uniform, but men capable of such nobility and bravery makes me weak at the knees'

It is a terrible thing that more men died during the Crimean war from disease than were killed in battle. We have Florence Nightingale to thank for making nursing an honourable profession, and for improving the life of the ordinary soldier. But as I have pointed out in *Hope*, there were countless other unsung heroes and heroines, whose courage, determination and sheer stoicism in the face of terrible hardship should be remembered. *Hope* might be a work of fiction, but each of the characters has a counterpart in history.

'Amongst Friends'

The Lesley Pearse Newsletter

A fantastic new way to keep up-to-date with your favourite author. *Amongst Friends* is a regular email with all the latest news and views from Lesley, plus information on her forthcoming titles and the chance to win exclusive prizes.

Just go to **www.penguin.co.uk** and type your email address in the 'Join our newsletter' panel and tick the box marked 'Lesley Pearse'. Then fill in your details and you will be added to Lesley's list.

THE BOOKS

GEORGIA
Raped by her foster-father, fifteen-year-old Georgia runs away from home to the seedy back streets of Soho . . .

TARA
Anne changes her name to Tara to forget her shocking past – but can she really become someone else?

CHARITY
Charity Stratton's bleak life is changed forever when her parents die in a fire. Alone and pregnant, she runs away to London . . .

ELLIE
Eastender Ellie and spoilt Bonny set off to make a living on the stage. Can their friendship survive sacrifice and ambition?

CAMELLIA
Orphaned Camellia discovers that the past she has always been so sure of has been built on lies. Can she bear to uncover the truth about herself?

ROSIE
Rosie is a girl without a mother, with a past full of trouble. But could the man who ruined her family also save Rosie?

CHARLIE
Charlie helplessly watches her mother being senselessly attacked. What secrets have her parents kept from her?

NEVER LOOK BACK
An act of charity sends flower girl Matilda on a trip to the New World and a new life . . .

TRUST ME
Dulcie Taylor and her sister are sent to an orphanage and then to Australia. Is their love strong enough to keep them together?

FATHER UNKNOWN
Daisy Buchan is left a scrapbook with details about her real mother. But should she go and find her?

TILL WE MEET AGAIN
Susan and Beth were childhood friends. Now Susan is accused of murder, and Beth finds she must defend her.

REMEMBER ME
Mary Broad is transported to Australia as a convict and encounters both cruelty and passion. Can she make a life for herself so far from home?

SECRETS
Adele Talbot escapes a children's home to find her grandmother – but soon her unhappy mother is on her trail . . .

A LESSER EVIL
Bristol, the 1960s, and young Fif Brown defies her parents to marry a man they think is beneath her.

HOPE
Somerset, 1836, and baby Hope is cast out from a world of privilege as proof of her mother's adultery . . .

IS THERE AN AMAZING WOMAN IN YOUR LIFE?

Has someone you know done something special, either for herself or someone else? If so, we want to know about her.

The Lesley Pearse Women of Courage Award was launched by Lesley and Penguin in 2006 to celebrate the achievements of ordinary women. So, whether it's your mum, your grandma, your sister, your daughter, a friend or just an acquaintance, if they have shown courage in their life, why not nominate them for an award?

Following regional heats, five finalists and their families will be invited to a sumptuous awards lunch in February 2008. The winner will be announced and presented with her award, plus a cheque for £1000, by Lesley herself. The winner will also receive:

A FAMILY HOLIDAY ★ A DONATION FROM PENGUIN TO A CHARITY OF HER CHOICE ★ A MAKEOVER ★ A NEW WARDROBE OF CLOTHES ★ 1 YEAR'S SUBSCRIPTION TO *LOVE IT!* ★ £200 OF PENGUIN BOOKS

The other four finalists will receive a framed certificate, a 6 month subscription to *love it!* magazine and £100 of Penguin books.

To nominate your woman of courage, go to

www.womenofcourageaward.co.uk

Alternatively, you can complete the form opposite and post it to:
The Lesley Pearse Women of Courage Award,
Penguin General, 80 Strand, London, WC2R 0RL

Closing date: 30th November 2007

The
Lesley
PEARSE
Women of Courage Award

OFFICIAL ENTRY FORM

NAME OF YOUR WOMAN OF COURAGE:

HER ADDRESS:

POSTCODE:

HER CONTACT NUMBER:

YOUR RELATIONSHIP TO HER:

YOUR NAME:

YOUR ADDRESS:

POSTCODE:

YOUR DAYTIME TELEPHONE NUMBER:

YOUR EMAIL :

ON A SEPARATE SHEET, TELL US IN NO MORE THAN

250 WORDS WHY YOU THINK YOUR NOMINEE DESERVES TO WIN

THE LESLEY PEARSE WOMEN OF COURAGE AWARD

Please post your entry to:

The Lesley Pearse Women of Courage Award,

Penguin General, 80 Strand, London, WC2R 0RL

Closing date: 30th November 2007

For Terms and Conditions please visit **www.womenofcourageaward.co.uk**

By submitting your nomination you agree that *love it!* magazine may contact you or your nominee.